Nineteenth-Century Scottish Literature

The Kennedy & Boyd Anthology of Nineteenth-Century Scottish Literature

SELECTED BY AND INTRODUCED BY
Caroline McCracken-Flesher
UNIVERSITY OF WYOMING

Kennedy & Boyd
an imprint of
Zeticula
57 St Vincent Crescent
Glasgow
G3 8NQ
Scotland.

http://www.kennedyandboyd.co.uk
admin@kennedyandboyd.co.uk

First published in 2010
Reprinted 2010

Copyright © Zeticula 2010
Introduction © Caroline McCracken-Flesher 2010
Cover image © Patryk Moriak 2010
http://www.patrykmoriak.com

ISBN-13 978-1-84921-053-9 Paperback

All rights reserved. No part of this publication may be reproduced, stored in a retrieval system, or transmitted in any form or by any means, electronic, mechanical, photocopying, recording or otherwise, without the prior permission of the publishers.

Acknowledgements

An anthology depends on the vision and hard work of many people.

Gwen Enstam's enthusiasm and ability to make connections translated the vision for this book into a practical reality.

Stuart Johnston, the moving force of Kennedy and Boyd, generously invited this anthology and worked not just as publisher but as retriever of texts.

Ian Duncan, who will compile a companion volume on eighteenth-century Scottish literature, has provided much advice and moral support.

My thanks to them all.

Contents

Acknowledgements	*v*
Contents	*vii*
Introduction	*xi*
Source Texts	*xv*
Background Reading	*xv*
Glossaries	*xvi*

ROMANCES OF TIME AND PLACE

Thomas Campbell (1777-1844)	1
from Gertrude of Wyoming; or, The Pensylvanian Cottage (1809)	1
Carolina Oliphant, Lady Nairne: 1766-1845	5
Will Ye No Come Back Again?	5
The Land O' The Leal	6
Caller Herrin'	7
Elizabeth Hamilton (1756-1816)	9
from The Cottagers of Glenburnie; a Tale for the Farmer's Ingle-nook (1808)	9
Jane Porter (1776-1850)	12
from The Scottish Chiefs (1810)	12
Anne Grant (1755-1838)	22
from Essays on the Superstitions of the Highlanders (1811)	22
William Tennant (1784-1848)	24
from Anster Fair, A Poem in Six Cantos (1812)	24

ROMANCES OF GENDER AND NATION

Mary Brunton (1778-1818)	29
from Discipline: A Novel (1814)	29
Susan Ferrier (1782-1854)	39
from Marriage (1818)	39
Joanna Baillie (1762-1851)	46
Sonnet, On Leaving Greece, 1820	46

ROMANTICISM: GENRE AND THE JOURNAL

Walter Scott (1771-1832)	47
Thomas The Rhymer (1802)	47
The Twa Corbies (1802)	70
from The Fortunes of Nigel (1822)	73
The Highland Widow (1826)	85
Edinburgh Review [Henry Brougham]	131
Art. II. ***Hours of Idleness: A Series of Poems, Original and Translated.*** By George Gordon, Lord Byron, a Minor. 8vo. pp. 200. Newark. 1807. (1808)	131
Edinburgh Review [Francis Jeffrey]	135
Art. I. ***The Excursion, being a portion of the Recluse, a Poem.*** By William Wordsworth. 4to. pp.447. London, 1814. (1814)	135

George Gordon, Lord Byron (1788-1824)	**152**
Lachin y gair (1807)	152
from English Bards and Scotch Reviewers (anon, 1809)	153
from English Bards and Scotch Reviewers (1809)	155
James Hogg (1770-1835)	**157**
When The Kye Comes Hame (1822)	157
The Great Muckle Village of Balmaquhapple (1822)	159
Strange Letter Of A Lunatic (1830)	160
Blackwood's Magazine [John Wilson]	**169**
Noctes Ambrosianae: The Soup Course	169
Alexander Rodger (1784-1846)	**181**
A Bundle Of Truths: A Parody (1822)	181

THE BUSINESS OF LITERATURE: COMMERCE AND COMPLICITY

John Galt (1779-1839)	**182**
from The Provost (1822)	182
Michael Scott (1789-1835)	**185**
from Tom Cringle's Log (1831-1833)	185
Thomas Pringle (1789-1834)	**191**
The Slave Dealer (1838)	191
Thomas Babington Macaulay (1800-1859)	**193**
Minute by the Hon'ble T. B. Macaulay, dated the 2nd February 1835.	193

LITERATURE AS PROPHECY

Edward Irving (1792-1834)	**203**
from Babylon and Infidelity Foredoomed (1826)	203
Thomas Carlyle (1795-1881)	**207**
from Past and Present (1843)	207
[Robert Chambers (1802-1871)]	**212**
from Vestiges of the Natural History of Creation (1844)	212
Hugh Miller (1802-1856)	**217**
from My Schools and Schoolmasters (1854)	217

PROPHECY IN THE DAYS OF INDUSTRY

W. E. Aytoun (1813-1865)	**219**
How We Got Up The Glenmutchkin Railway, and How We Got Out Of It (1845)	219
Christian Isobel Johnstone (1781-1857)	**238**
Andrew Howie, The Hand-Loom Weaver (1846)	238
William McGonagall (1825-1902)	**249**
The Death of Lord and Lady Dalhousie (1890)	249
Attempted Assassination of the Queen (1890)	250
William Thom (1799-1848)	**252**
Whisperings For The Unwashed (1845)	252
Janet Hamilton (1795-1873)	**255**
Oor Location (1863)	255
Alexander Smith (1830-1867) 257	
Glasgow (1857) 257	

Ellen Johnston (1835-1873)	261
The Last Sark (1859)	261
David Pae (1828-1884)	262
from Lucy, The Factory Girl; Or, The Secrets Of The Tontine Close (1858)	262
Mary MacDonald (1789-1872)	272
Child in the Manger (trans. 1888 by Lachlan MacBean)	272

OTHER WORLDS AND DIFFERENT VISIONS

George MacDonald (1824-1905)	273
from Adela Cathcart (1864)	273
James Thomson "B.V." (1834-1882)	281
from The City of Dreadful Night (1874)	281
Andrew Lang (1844-1912)	291
The House of Strange Stories (1886)	291

KAILYARD DIS/COMFORTS

"Ian Maclaren"/John Watson (1850-1907)	300
from Beside The Bonnie Brier Bush (1894)	300
S. R. Crockett (1860-1914)	306
from Cleg Kelly, Arab Of The City (1896)	306
George Douglas [Brown] (1869-1902)	313
from The House With The Green Shutters (1901)	313

CRIME, DETECTION, AND LITERARY CONTROL

James McLevy (no dates)	317
from Curiosities of Crime in Edinburgh (1861)	317
Arthur Conan Doyle (1859-1930)	324
The Man with the Twisted Lip (1891)	324
Margaret Oliphant (1828-1897)	341
The Library Window (1896)	341

VIEWS OF MODERNITY

John Davidson (1857-1909)	370
Thirty Bob A Week (1894)	370
Robert Louis Stevenson (1850-1894)	373
Thrawn Janet (1881)	373
with Fanny Van de Grift Stevenson	380
from The Dynamiter: Zero's Tale Of The Explosive Bomb (1884	380
To S. C. (1889, publ. 1895)	386
"Fiona MacLeod"/William Sharp (1855-1905)	387
The Sin-Eater (1895)	387
Alice Clare MacDonell (1855-?)	406
The Weaving Of The Tartan (1896)	406

Sources	*409*
Index of Authors	*411*

Introduction

For nineteenth-century readers, the Scots and their books were everywhere, saturating British, imperial, and even American markets. Indeed, Scottish literature in Scots was widely enough read that through the period authors could sell a variety of dialects to an empire they themselves had educated. Literature of lowland and highland and all parts in between was so pervasive, the phenomenon sparked parodies like Sarah Greene's *Scotch Novel Reading* (1824), which imagines northern authors "filling their Scotch pouches, and laughing to see how easily John Bull is gulled."

This anthology invites readers to experience the liveliness of those times, with all their innovations, opportunities, and raging debates. To facilitate readers' engagement with the ideas as well as the materials of nineteenth-century Scotland in its British and international contexts, items are arranged roughly chronologically, but also thematically. General readers will be able to enjoy the sudden changes of a burgeoning literature simply by tracking this book end to end. By recognizing the light framing of this anthology, they will also be guided toward a sense of the ongoing conceptual and literary struggles in a society that is challenged yet stimulated by conflicting forces. Traffic between country, town, and city; the tension between elites founded in class, education, or gender; the idea of home, set against the industry and empire that supported it; and the new and adjusted genres allowed by manufacture (e.g. the steam press), kept Scottish authors in constant movement. This book hopes that its readers, too, will get on the move. Students can develop an interest of their own, then use the book's structural hints to track it. Instructors can use the framework to connect easily to their own pedagogical focus in Scottish and other literatures.

Such connections allow us not simply to appreciate the richness of Scottish literature, but also its reach. When literatures are arranged by language and nation, it is easy to fall into a discourse of center and periphery. This book, with its combined chronological and thematic emphases, by contrast encourages readers to appreciate Scottish literature during the nineteenth century for differences that motivated change in genre and culture far beyond Scotland.

Here, for instance, we can see how Scots, building on Macpherson's *Works of Ossian* (1760s) and Maria Edgeworth's *Castle Rackrent* (1800), energize and change the national tale. In Thomas Campbell, with his Native American Romance; Jane Porter, with her celebration of *The Scottish Chiefs*; Carolina Oliphant, with her regional and nostalgic songs; and Elizabeth Hamilton and Anne Grant, with their authorship underpinned by anthropology, we can track the way to Walter Scott's novels. From this heritage Scott reformulated the national tale for a world-wide market and (so the story goes) assisted the European "Year of Revolutions" (1848). Mark Twain mocked Scott for his imitator Fenimore Cooper, and F. R. Leavis dismissed him from *The Great Tradition* in a footnote ("Out of Scott a bad tradition came"), but readers of this book should get a sense for why the world beat a pathway to his door—William Wordsworth followed

Scott's poetry north, and later George Eliot considered the "Author of Waverley" "Dearly beloved." Tracking on through Joanna Baillie and that poet "born half a Scot, but bred a whole one," George Gordon, Lord Byron, we can appreciate that the Scots with their memory of awful events (the 1745 rebellion), conflicted identities, gothic sensibilities, and dramatic landscapes, were within and to the forefront of Romanticism. And of course, since Scotland hosted two major journals of the early nineteenth century, where ideas and their expression were hotly contested, Scots also led in Romanticism's critique. The *Edinburgh Review* attacked Byron, provoking him to his first satire: "English Bards and Scotch Reviewers"; Blackwood's routinely mocked the "Lakers" for "weeping . . . at the beauty o' the moon and stars." That this was an inward debate, as well as one in which Scots influenced thinking elsewhere, is obvious when we consider that the mocker is "The Ettrick Shepherd." The Shepherd figured James Hogg, himself an innovator in Romanticism as "King of the Mountain and Fairy School," and a (supposedly) peasant poet residing in and speaking from nature and the folk. Interestingly, that same James Hogg often fulminated against Blackwood's over the magazine's disrespect for his own work, and eventually he was defended by the editor of the *London Magazine* — with the editor dying in a duel as an indirect result. It would be hard to imagine a more trenchant cultural connection.

This volume encourages readers to identify and map out such connections for themselves. So in what follows, readers will find only a few pointers to stimulate the discussions invited by this wide range of materials. They will note the broad subject areas sketched by the anthology's divisions, but should freely overleap such divisions to follow different and perhaps newly identified themes. For instance, alongside the elite and anthropological renditions of Scottish folk that motivate tales both national and Romantic run texts by weavers, farmers, and factory girls, giving a quite other sense of demotic culture, and one worth following. Moreover, in such work, often published in popular newspapers and mass-market novels, we may find a missing link between experience and culture. Until recently, it was a critical commonplace to wonder why nineteenth-century literature did not rise to the challenge of industry. Where were the industrial novels and poems? Now, reading inclusively, we find them by the handful.

Readers will find that Scottish literature connects to and informs numerous conceptual and generic trends. Often, Scottish authors deploy expected forms, though by different routes and to unusual effects. A few patterns can communicate the possibilities. Satire asserts itself through Scottish writing, yet it is inflected by a native tradition of "flyting," with its joyous excesses of *ad hominem* abuse (see William Tennant, Susan Ferrier, Blackwood's "Noctes," Alexander Rodger, W. E. Aytoun, Janet Hamilton, James Thomson, George Douglas Brown, and John Davidson). The gothic is reworked within the calm novels of Mary Brunton, and their disturbing scenes of female confinement; it becomes an authorial attribute for Scott, the uncanny "Author of Waverley," and a test in his tales; James Thomson makes it an urban phenomenon in his nightmare city; Robert Louis Stevenson carries it to the point of parody; and it erupts at the strange conjunction between Celticism and Modernism for William Sharp (*pseud.* Fiona MacLeod). Paeans to business stand alongside more and less self-conscious discussions of slavery, the rights of man—and woman—and the oppressions of the industrial city (in Alexander Rodger, John Galt, Michael Scott, Thomas Pringle, Thomas Babington Macaulay, Christian Isobel Johnstone, William Thom, Janet Hamilton, James Thomson, Alexander Smith, and Ellen Johnston, right up to John Davidson). The disposition and discourse of prophecy resonates not just through religious texts, but also through arguments about geology, anguished considerations of the city, and reassertions of Celtic literary heritage (see Edward Irving, Thomas Carlyle, Robert Chambers, Hugh Miller, James Thomson, George MacDonald, and William Sharp). And authors insistently debated their own practices within developing theories of literature and culture (Elizabeth Hamilton, Anne Grant, Walter Scott, Thomas Carlyle, Hugh Miller, Edward Irving, James Thomson and Andrew Lang).

Of course, no outline of intellectual history or list of authors can cover all possibilities. The aim of this volume is that readers will expand its range not just by connecting to their own interests, but by recognizing links to authors outside Scotland. Here, we might note that the Kailyard (cabbage-patch) authors who sold across the empire primed the canvas for the local color so beloved of late-century America (for example. drawing on Sara Orne Jewett and influencing Willa Cather); Emerson thought Scott was "warmed with a divine ray," and sought out Thomas Carlyle; Darwin wrote in a context informed by Robert Chambers and Hugh Miller; William McGonagall's enthusiastically dreadful verse inspired Spike Milligan and Peter Sellers (pointing on to Monty Python); Kailyard writers gave plots to Hollywood; the islands of "Fiona MacLeod" lead to the *Edge of the World* (1937) and the remarkable cinematography of Michael Powell; and Sherlock Holmes has traveled far beyond Baker Street. We can look down either end of this telescope. Further, readers might catch glimpses of Scottish heritage in authors generally included in the "English" canon, but too many to address in this book. For instance, this anthology can refine our focus on John Stuart Mill, son of a Scottish philosopher; Kenneth Grahame, who, though he wrote of Ratty and Moley in a very English riverbank, was born in Edinburgh; or even Virginia Woolf, whose lighthouse (in the novel by that name), rises in the Hebrides. It should make readers seek out the whys and wherefores motivating authors like Thomas De Quincy, who moved to Edinburgh to pursue his literary career—and perhaps J. K. Rowling, today.

In thus experiencing the wide and lively range of Scottish writing in the nineteenth century, readers will not only formulate their own map of Scottish literature, but also come to appreciate how that map has been sketched over by twentieth-century criticism. During that period, Scottish literature became a victim of its own success, suffering the reactions of Modernism in a double dose. In the moment when Lytton Strachey was mocking "eminent Victorians," and Virginia Woolf describing the horrors of Victorian indoor design in Orlando, Scottish literature, as dominant during the previous century, necessarily came under attack. T. S. Eliot, remaking himself as an Englishman in ways we might now find predictable given our literary theories about self and other, set aside Scottish literature. Posing the question "Was there a Scottish Literature?" this needy American answered "No"! Scots themselves contributed to the rout as they misrecognized the meanings of provincialism while aiming at international importance. Notably, Hugh MacDiarmid denigrated his literary forebears as he strove to emerge as inter/national and modernist Scot, and the Orkney writer Edwin Muir, establishing his British credentials, declared the Scottish nineteenth-century a blank in which no worthwhile culture thrived. It has taken the rest of the twentieth century to stand back from the anxieties of canon-making, whether English or Scottish, that drove such assertions. Now, through this book, readers can work to undo them, appreciating, remaking, and making anew the map of nineteenth-century Scottish literature.

Caroline McCracken-Flesher
University of Wyoming
December, 2009

Source Texts

Source texts for this volume are in general the earliest available. Readers will find a list of sources used at the back of this volume.

Background Reading:

This is an introductory anthology, hoping to stimulate interest and exploration in nineteenth-century Scottish literature for readers of all types. Readers should be aware that, given space limitations, what they get here is a smattering of Scottish literature that constitutes an encouragement toward further literary enjoyment. Obviously, no novel is fully represented by a couple of chapters, however intriguing and well written; no author is characterized by one text. The gaps in this volume are legion. Walter Scott's *The Lay of the Last Minstrel* and any "Waverley" novel, and Robert Louis Stevenson's *Strange Case of Dr Jekyll and Mr Hyde* comprise just a sampling of the major books essential to our understanding of Scottish nineteenth-century literature, but impossible to include here. Anne Bannerman's *Tales of Superstition and Chivalry*, telling of "The Dark Ladie" well in advance of Keats's "La Belle Dame Sans Merci," is only one of the many fascinating, lesser known texts that should be better known—but again, that cannot fit in a short anthology. Furthermore, Gaelic literature hardly begins to be addressed here. This is because the volume emphasizes materials widely available and accessible to the nineteenth-century public, and lacks room for texts that need translations. So this anthology strongly encourages outside reading in all inviting directions. For a fuller sense of materials, the following companion books are an important resource:

Ian Brown et al., eds. *The Edinburgh History of Scottish Literature: Enlightenment, Britain and Empire (1707-1918)* (Edinburgh: Edinburgh University Press, 2006).

Robert Crawford, *Scotland's Books: A History of Scottish Literature* (2007; New York: Oxford University Press, 2009).

Roderick Watson, *The Literature of Scotland: The Middle Ages to the Nineteenth Century*, 2nd ed. (Houndsmills: Palgrave Macmillan, 2007).

Douglas Gifford, ed. *The History of Scottish Literature, vol. 3* (Aberdeen: Aberdeen University Press, 1989).

Glossaries:

Today's audience no longer boasts the facility with Scottish dialect that spread across the globe through the imperial markets of the nineteenth century. For us, solutions can be found in books and on websites:

The Concise Scots Dictionary (Edinburgh: Edinburgh University Press, 2000).

The Dictionary of the Scottish Language (online), which folds together the twelve volume *Dictionary of the Older Scottish Tongue* and the ten volume *Scottish National Dictionary*: http://www.dsl.ac.uk/dsl/

The Online Scots Dictionary: http://www.scots-online.org/dictionary/

The Scots Dictionary (online): http://www.britannia.org/scotland/scotsdictionary/

Thomas Campbell (1777-1844)

from Gertrude of Wyoming; or, The Pensylvanian Cottage (1809)

PART I.

I.

On Susquehana's side, fair Wyoming,
Although the wild-flower on thy ruin'd wall
And roofless homes a sad remembrance bring
Of what thy gentle people did befall,
Yet thou wert once the loveliest land of all
That see the Atlantic wave their morn restore.
Sweet land! may I thy lost delights recall,
And paint thy Gertrude in her bowers of yore,
Whose beauty was the love of Pensylvania's shore!

II.

It was beneath thy skies that, but to prune
His Autumn fruits, or skim the light canoe,
Perchance, along thy river calm at noon
The happy shepherd swain had nought to do
From morn till evening's sweeter pastime grew,
Their timbrel, in the dance of forests brown
When lovely maidens prankt in flowret new;
And aye, those sunny mountains half way down
Would echo flagelet from some romantic town.

III.

Then, where of Indian hills the daylight takes
His leave, how might you the flamingo see
Disporting like a meteor on the lakes —
And playful squirrel on his nut-grown tree:
And ev'ry sound of life was full of glee,
From merry mock-bird's song, or hum of men,
While heark'ning, fearing nought their revelry,
The wild deer arch'd his neck from glades, and then
Unhunted, sought his woods and wilderness again.

IV.

And scarce had Wyoming of war or crime
Heard but in transatlantic story rung,
For here the exile met from ev'ry clime,
And spoke in friendship ev'ry distant tongue:
Men from the blood of warring Europe sprung,
Were but divided by the running brook;
And happy where no Rhenish trumpet sung,
On plains no sieging mine's volcano shook,
The blue-ey'd German chang'd his sword to pruning-hook.

V.

Nor far some Andalusian saraband
Would sound to many a native rondelay.
But who is he that yet a dearer land
Remembers, over hills and far away?
Green Albyn! [1] what though he no more survey
Thy ships at anchor on the quiet shore,
Thy pellochs [2] rolling from the mountain bay;
Thy lone sepulchral cairn upon the moor,
And distant isles that hear the loud Corbrechtan [3] roar!

VI.

Alas! poor Caledonia's mountaineer,
That want's stern edict e'er, and feudal grief,
Had forced him from a home he loved so dear!
Yet found he here a home, and glad relief,
And plied the beverage from his own fair sheaf.
That fir'd his Highland blood with mickle glee;
And England sent her men, of men the chief,
Who taught those sires of Empire yet to be,
To plant the tree of life; to plant fair freedom's tree!

[VII to IX omitted]

X.

The rose of England bloom'd on Gertrude's cheek —
What though these shades had seen her birth, her sire
A Briton's independence taught to seek
Far western worlds; and there his household fire
The light of social love did long inspire,
And many a halcyon day he liv'd to see

Unbroken, but by one misfortune dire,
When fate had reft his mutual heart — but she
Was gone — and Gertrude climb'd a widow'd father's knee.

XI.

A lov'd bequest and I may half impart—
To them that feel the strong paternal tie,
How like a new existence to his heart
Uprose that living flow'r beneath his eye.
Dear as she was, from cherub infancy,
From hours when she would round his garden play,
To time when as the rip'ning years went by,
Her lovely mind could culture well repay,
And more engaging grew from pleasing day to day.

[XII omitted]

XIII.

And summer was the tide, and sweet the hour,
When sire and daughter saw, with fleet descent,
An Indian from his bark approach their bow'r,
Of buskin'd limb, and swarthy lineament;
The red wild feathers on his brow were blent,
And bracelets bound the arm that help'd to light
A boy, who seem'd, as he beside him went,
Of Christian vesture, and complexion bright,
Led by his dusky guide like morning brought by night.

XIV.

Yet pensive seem'd the boy for one so young,
The dimple from his polish'd cheek had fled;
When, leaning on his forest-bow unstrung,
Th' Oneyda warrior to the planter said,
And laid his hand upon the stripling's head,
'Peace be to thee! my words this belt approve;
'The paths of peace my steps have hither led:
'This little nursling, take him to thy love,
'And shield the bird unfledg'd, since gone the parent dove.

XV.

'Christian! I am the foeman of thy foe;
'Our wampum league thy brethren did embrace:

'Upon the Michagan, three moons ago,
'We launch'd our quivers for the bison chace;
'And with the Hurons planted for a space,
'With true and faithful hands, the olive-stalk;
'But snakes are in the bosoms of their race,
'And though they held with us a friendly talk,
'The hollow peace-tree fell beneath their tomohawk!

XVI.

'It was encamping on the lake's far port,
'A cry of Areouski [4] broke our sleep,
'Where storm'd an ambush'd foe thy nation's fort,
'And rapid rapid whoops came o'er the deep;
'But long thy country's war-sign on the steep
'Appear'd through ghastly intervals of light,
'And deathfully their thunders seem'd to sweep,
'Till utter darkness swallow'd up the sight,
'As if a show'r of blood had quench'd the fiery fight!

1 Scotland.
2 Pelloch is the Gaelic appellation for porpoise.
3 The great whirlpool of the Western Hebrides.
4 The Indian God of War

Carolina Oliphant, Lady Nairne: 1766-1845

Will Ye No Come Back Again?

Bonnie Charlie's now awa',
    Safely owre the friendly main;
Mony a heart will break in twa,
    Should he ne'er come back again.

        Will ye no come back again?
        Will ye no come back again?
        Better lo'ed ye canna be,
        Will ye no come back again?

Ye trusted in your Hieland men,
    They trusted you, dear Charlie;
They kent you hiding in the glen.
    Your cleadin was but barely.
        Will ye no, &c.

English bribes were a' in vain,
    An' e'en tho' puirer we may be;
Siller canna buy the heart
    That beats aye for thine and thee.
        Will ye no, &c.

We watched thee in the gloamin' hour,
    We watched thee in the mornin' grey;
Tho' thirty thousand pounds they'd gi'e,
    Oh there is nane that wad betray.
        Will ye no, &c.

Sweet's the laverock's note and lang,
    Lilting wildly up the glen;
But aye to me he sings ae sang,
    Will ye no come back again?

        Will ye no come back again?
        Will ye no come back again?
        Better lo'ed ye canna be,
        Will ye no come back again?

The Land O' The Leal.

Air — "Hey tutti taiti."

I'm wearin' awa', John,
Like snaw-wreaths in thaw, John,
I'm wearin' awa'
    To the land o' the leal.
There's nae sorrow there, John,
There's neither cauld nor care, John,
The day is aye fair
    In the land o' the leal.

Our bonnie bairn's there, John,
She was baith gude and fair, John,
And oh! we grudged her sair
    To the land o' the leal.
But sorrow's sel' wears past, John,
And joy's a-comin' fast, John,
The joy that's aye to last
    In the land o' the leal.

Sae dear's that joy was bought, John,
Sae free the battle fought, John,
That sinfu' man e'er brought
    To the land o' the leal.
Oh! dry your glist'ning e'e, John,
My saul langs to be free, John,
And angels beckon me
    To the land o' the leal.

Oh! haud ye leal and true, John,
Your day it's wearin' through, John,
And I'll welcome you
    To the land o' the leal.
Now fare ye weel, my ain John,
This warld's cares are vain, John,
We'll meet, and we'll be fain.
    In the land o' the leal.

Caller Herrin'

Air by Neil Gow.

>Wha'll buy my caller herrin'?
>They're bonnie fish and halesome farin';
>Wha'll buy my caller herrin',
>>New drawn frae the Forth?

When ye were sleepin' on your pillows,
Dream'd ye aught o' our puir fellows,
Darkling as they faced the billows,
A' to fill the woven willows?

>Buy my caller herrin',
>New drawn frae the Forth.

Wha'll buy my caller herrin'?
They're no brought here without brave daring;
Buy my caller herrin',
Haul'd through wind and rain.

>Wha'll buy my caller herrin'? &c.

Wha'll buy my caller herrin'?
Oh, ye may ca' them vulgar farin',
Wives and mithers maist despairing,
Ca' them lives o' men.

>Wha'll buy my caller herrin'? &c.

When the creel o' herrin' passes,
Ladies, clad in silks and laces,
Gather in their braw pelisses,
Cast their heads and screw their faces.

>Wha'll buy my caller herrin'? &c.

Caller herrin's no got lightlie,
Ye can trip the spring fu' tightlie,
Spite o' tauntin', flauntin,' flingin',
Gow has set you a' a-singing.'

>Wha'll buy my caller herrin'? &c

Neebour wives, now tent my tellin':
When the bonny fish ye're sellin',
At ae word be in ye're dealin' —
Truth will stand when a' thing's failin'.

    Wha'll buy my caller herrin'?
    They're bonnie fish and halesome farin'
    Wha'll buy my caller herrin',
    New drawn frae the Forth?

Elizabeth Hamilton (1756-1816)

from The Cottagers of Glenburnie; a Tale for the Farmer's Ingle-nook (1808)

Letter From The Author

TO
HECTOR MACNEILL, Esq.

Dear Sir,

INDEPENDENTLY of all considerations of esteem or friendship, I know not to whom the COTTAGERS OF GLENBURNIE could be with such propriety inscribed, as to the Author of the SKAITH OF SCOTLAND.

To the genius displayed in that admired production of the Scottish Muse, this humbler composition of dull prose has indeed no pretensions; but if it shall be admitted, that the writers have been influenced by similar motives, I shall be satisfied with the share of approbation that must inevitably follow. Had I adhered to the plan on which those sketches were originally formed, and published them as separate pieces, in form and size resembling the tracts in the "Cheap Repository," I should have had no apprehensions concerning the justice of the sentence to be passed upon them; for then they would have had little chance of falling into other hands than those of the class of persons for whose use they were intended. This exclusive perusal is, however, a happiness which no author has a right to expect; and which, to confess the truth, no author would very highly relish. For though we were to be assured, that of the number of readers in this reading age, one-half read only with the intention of gratifying their vanity, by shewing their skill in picking out the faults, yet who would not prefer going through the ordeal of this *soi-disant* criticism, to the mortification of not being read at all?

Of the mode of criticism now in vogue, I believe your opinion coincides exactly with my own. We do not consider it as originating in the pride, or spleen, or malignity of the persons by whom it has been most freely exercised, but in a mistaken notion of the species of vigour and energy attached to the censorial character, and essential to the dignity of the critic's office. It is under this misconception that persons of highly cultivated talents sometimes condescend to make use of of the contemptuous sneer, the petty cavil, the burlesque representation,— though modes of criticism in which they may easily be outdone by the vulgar and illiterate. But surely when men of genius and learning seem thus to admit, that the decisions they pronounce stand in need of other support than the justice and good sense in which they are founded, they forget the consequences that may follow. They forget, that the tone of ill nature can never be in unison with the emotions that arise from the admiration of what is beautiful; and that as far as they, by the influence of their example, contribute to give this tone to the public mind, they corrupt the public taste, and give a bias that is inimical to its progress in refinement. But however the prevalence of this style of animadversion may, in a general view, be lamented, it is not by authors of such trifling productions as the present that it ought to be condemned: for, is it not some consolation to reflect, that let the meanest performance be judged with what asperity, or spoken of with what contempt it may, it cannot be more severely judged, or more contemptuously treated, than works acknowledged to possess merit of the highest order? Let then the critics do their worst; I have found a cure for every wound they can inflict on my vanity. But there are others besides professed critics, concerning whose opinion of the propriety or tendency of this little work, I confess myself to be most anxious, — and those are the well-wishers for the improvement of their country.

A warm attachment to the country of our ancestors naturally produces a lively interest in all that concerns its happiness and prosperity; but though in this attachment few of the children of Caledonia are deficient, widely different are the views taken of the manner in which it ought to be displayed.

In the opinion of vulgar minds, it ought to produce a blind and indiscriminate partiality for national modes, manners, and customs; and a zeal that kindles into rage at whoever dares to suppose that our country has not in every instance reached perfection. Every hint at the necessity of further improvement is, by such persons, deemed a libel on all that has been already done; and the exposition of what is faulty, though with a view to its amendment, an unpardonable offence. From readers of this description, you will soon perceive, I cannot hope for quarter. Nor is it to readers of this description alone, that the intention with which my Cottage Tale is written, will appear erroneous or absurd.

The politician, who measures the interests of his country by her preponderance in the scale of empire, regards all consideration for individual happiness as a weakness; and by the man who thinks riches and happiness synonymous, all that does not directly tend to increase the influx of wealth, is held in contempt. Each of these dictates to the opinions of numbers. In the school of the former, the political value of the various classes in society is judged of by their political influence; and in that of the latter, their importance is appreciated by their power of creating wealth. It is the few by whom these privileges are possessed, that are objects of consideration in the eyes of both. The great mass of the people are, in their estimation, as so many teeth in the wheels of a piece of machinery, of no farther value than as they serve to facilitate its movements. No wonder if, in their eyes, a regard to the moral capacities and feelings of such implements should appear visionary and romantic. Not less so, perhaps, than to the war-contriving sage, at the time he coolly calculates how many of his countrymen may, without national inconvenience, be spared for slaughter!

Happily there are others, to whom the prosperity of their country is no less dear, though its interests are viewed by them through a very different medium. National happiness they consider as the aggregate of the sum of individual happiness and individual virtue. The fraternal tie, of which they feel the influence, binds them not exclusively to the poor or to the affluent — it embraces the interests of all. Every improvement in the arts, which tends to give additional grace to the elegant enjoyments of the wealthy; every discovery made by their countrymen in science; every step attained in the progress of literature or philosophy — is to them a subject of heartfelt gratulation. But while they delight in observing the effects of increasing prosperity with which they are surrounded, they forget not the claims of a class more numerous than that of the prosperous. They forget not that the pleasures of the heart, and of the understanding, as well as those of the senses, were intended by Providence to be in some degree enjoyed by all; and therefore, that in the pleasures of the heart and the understanding, all are entitled to participate. Persons of this mode of thinking do not fancy the whole duties of charity to be comprised in some efforts towards prolonging the sensitive existence of those who, without such relief, must perish; nor do they consider extreme indigence as the only object on which their benevolence ought to be exerted; nor the physical wants of the lower orders, as the only wants that ought to be supplied. Nothing by which the moral habits, or domestic comforts of their brethren of any rank, can be materially injured or promoted, can to such minds be indifferent. Precious in their eyes are the gleams of joy that illumine the poor man's cottage; sacred the peace that reigns in it; doubly sacred the virtues by which alone that peace can be established or secured. By minds such as these, my motives will not be misinterpreted. By one such mind, at least, I assure myself, they will be judged of, with the indulgence due to so many years of friendship.

May this be accepted as a testimony of the sincerity with which that friendship has ever been returned by,

Dear Sir,
Your obedient and faithful
humble servant,
THE AUTHOR.

George Street,
May 5, 1808.

Jane Porter (1776-1850)

from The Scottish Chiefs (1810)

CHAPTER I.

THE war which had desolated Scotland was now at an end. Ambition seemed satiated; and the vanquished, after passing under the yoke of their enemy, concluded they might wear their chains in peace. Such were the hopes of those Scottish noblemen who, early in the spring of 1296, signed the bond of submission to a ruthless conqueror; purchasing life at the price of all that makes life estimable — Liberty and Honour.

Prior to this act of vassalage, Edward the First of England had entered Scotland at the head of an immense army. He seized Berwick by a base stratagem; laid the country in ashes; and on the field of Dunbar forced the King and his nobles to acknowledge him their liege Lord.

While the courts of Edward, or of his representatives, were crowded by the humbled Scots, the spirit of one brave man remained unsubdued. Disgusted alike at the facility with which the sovereign of a warlike nation could resign his people and his crown into the hands of a treacherous invader, and at the pusillanimity of the nobles who could ratify such a sacrifice, William Wallace retired to the glen of Ellerslie. Withdrawn from the world, he hoped to avoid the sight of oppressions he could not redress, and the endurance of injuries beyond his power to avenge.

Checked at the opening of life in the career of glory that was his passion, secluded in the bloom of manhood from the social haunts of men, he repressed the eager aspirations of his mind; and strove to acquire that resignation to inevitable evils which could alone reconcile him to forego the promises of his youth; and enable him to view with patience that humiliation of Scotland which blighted her honor, menaced her existence, and consigned her sons to degradation or obscurity.

The latter was the choice of Wallace. Too noble to bend his spirit to the usurper, too honest to affect submission, he resigned himself to the only way left of maintaining the independence of a true Scot; and giving up the world at once, all the ambitions of youth were extinguished in his breast, since nothing was preserved in his country to sanctify his fires. Scotland seemed proud of her chains. Not to share in such debasement seemed all that was now in his power; and within the shades of Ellerslie he found a retreat and a home, whose sweets beguiled him of every care; and made him sometimes forget the wrongs of his country in the tranquil enjoyments of wedded love.

During the happy months of the preceding autumn, while Scotland was yet free, and the path of honorable distinction lay open before her young nobility, Wallace married Marion Braidfoot, the beautiful heiress of Lammington. Of the same age, and brought up from childhood together, reciprocal affection grew with their growth; and sympathy of taste, virtues and mutual tenderness, gradually mingling their spirits, made them so entirely one, that when at the age of twenty-two the enraptured lover was allowed by his grandfather to pledge that faith publicly at the altar which he had so often vowed to his Marion in secret, he clasped her heart, and softly whispered — "dearer than life! part of my being now and forever! blessed is this union that mingles thy soul with mine to all eternity!"

Edward's invasion of Scotland broke in upon their innocent joys. Wallace threw aside the wedding garment for the cuirass and the sword. But he was not permitted to use either. Scotland submitted to her enemies; and he had no alternative but to bow to her oppressors, or to become an exile from man amid the deep glens of his country.

The tower of Ellerslie was henceforth the lonely abode of himself and his bride. The neighboring nobles avoided him, because the principles he declared were a tacit reproach on their proceedings; and in the course of a short time, as he forbore to seek them, they even forgot that he was in existence. Indeed, all occasions of mixing with society were now rejected by Wallace. The hunting spear, with which he had delighted to follow the flying roe-buck from glade to glade, from mountain to mountain; the arrows with which he used to bring down the heavy termagan or the towering eagle, all were laid aside; Scottish liberty was no more; and Wallace would have blushed to have shewn himself to this free-born deer of his native hills, in communion with the spoilers of his country. Had he pursued his once favourite exercises he most have mingled with the English now garrisoned in every town; and who passed their hours of leisure in the chase.

Being resigned to bury his youth, since its strength could be no longer serviceable to his country; books, his harp, and the sweet converse of his tender Marion, were the occupations of his days. Ellerslie was his hermitage; and there closed from the world, with an angel his companion, he might have forgotten that Edward was lord in Scotland; had not what was without his little paradise, made a way to its gates, and shewed him the slavery of the nobles, and the wretchedness of the people. In these cases, his generous hand gave succour where it could not bring redress. Those whom the lawless plunderer had driven from their houses, or stripped of their covering, found shelter, clothing and food, at the house of Sir William Wallace.

Ellerslie was the refuge of the friendless and the comfort of the unhappy. Wherever Lady Wallace moved, whether looking out from her window on the accidental passenger; or taking her morning or moonlight walks through the glen leaning on the arm of her husband: she had the rapture of hearing his steps greeted and followed by the blessing of the *poor destitute*, and the prayers of them who were *ready to perish*. It was then that this happy woman would raise her husband's hand to her lips, and in silent adoration thank God for blessing her with a being made so truly in his own image.

Wallace, who read her heart in this action, would reply. — "sweetest Marion, what merit has thy Wallace in mere benevolence? contracted is now my sphere of duty, and easily fulfilled; it is only to befriend the oppressed to the utmost of my power! and while tyranny leaves me that privilege I shall not consider myself quite a slave. Were I useless to my fellow-creatures I should be miserable; for, in blessing others, I bless myself — I bless thee my Marion; and the grateful countenances of these poor people add beauty even to thine! art thou not loveliest in my eyes at this moment, thou angel of peace and love! dost thou not praise thy husband for what is common with thee?" She smiled, and a happy tear glittered in her eye. "To be lovely to thee, Wallace, is all my joy; and to see thee so worthy of all my love, fills me indeed with an angel's happiness!"

Several months of this blissful and uninterrupted solitude had elapsed, when lady Wallace saw a stranger chieftain arrive at her gate. He inquired for Sir William, requested a private conference, and retired with him into a remote room, They remained there for above an hour; when Wallace coming forth, ordered his horse and four servants to be in readiness, saying he meant to accompany his guest to Douglas castle. When he embraced his wife at parting, he told her that as it was only a few miles distant, he should be at home again before the moon rose.

She passed the tedious hours of his absence with tranquility, till after she saw the moon, the appointed signal of turn, rise behind the highest summits of the opposite mountains. So bright were its beams, that she did not need any other light to shew her the stealing sands of her hour-glass; they numbered the prolonged hours of her husband's stay. She dismissed all her servants to their rest, excepting Halbert, the gray-haired harper of Wallace; and he, like herself, was too unaccustomed to the absence of his master, to find sleep visit his eyes, whilst Ellerslie was bereft of its joy and its guard.

As the night advanced, Lady Wallace sat in the window of her bed-chamber, which looked towards the west. She watched the winding pathway that led from Lanerk down the opposite height: eager to catch a glimpse of the waving plumes of her husband, when he should emerge from behind the hill and pass through the mingling thicket which over-hung the road. How often, as a cloud obscured for an instant the moon's light, and threw a transitory shade across the path, did her heart bound with the thought that her watching was at an end. It was he whom she had seen suddenly start from some abrupt turning of the rock! They were the folds of his tartan that darkened the white cliff! But the moon again rolled through her train of clouds, and threw her light around. Where was then her Wallace? alas it was only a shadow she had seen: the hill was still lonely, and he whom she sought was yet far away! Overcome with watching, expectation, and disappointment; unable to say when arose her fears; she sat down again to look, but her eyes were blinded with tears; and in a voice interrupted by sighs, she exclaimed, "not yet, not yet! — ah, my Wallace, what evil has betided thee?"

Trembling with a nameless terror, she knew not what to dread. She believed all hostile rencontres had ceased, when Scotland no longer contended with Edward. The nobles, without remonstrance, had surrendered their castles into the hands of the usurper; and the peasantry, following the example of their lords, had allowed their homes to be ravaged without lifting an arm in their defence. Opposition being entirely over, nothing then could threaten her husband from the enemy; and was not the person who had taken him from Ellerslie, a friend!

Before Wallace's departure he had spoken to Marion alone, and told her that the stranger was Sir John Monteith, the youngest son of the brave Walter Lord Monteith,[1] who was so treacherously put to death by the

English in the early part of the last year. This young nobleman was then left by his dying father to the particular charge of his friend William Lord Douglas, at that time governor of Berwick. After the fall of that place and the captivity of its defender. Sir John Monteith had returned to Douglas castle in the vicinity of Lanerk; and was now the only master of that princely residence. Sir James Douglas, the only son of the veteran lord, was still at Paris, whither he had gone before the defeat at Dunbar, to negotiate a league between the French monarch and the then king of Scots.

Informed of the privacy in which Wallace wished to live, Monteith had never ventured to disturb it until this day; and then, knowing the steady honor of his old school-fellow, he came to entreat, by the reverence he entertained for the memory of the sacrificed Lord Monteith, by the respect he had for the brave Douglas, and by his love for his country, that he would not refuse to accompany him that day to Douglas castle.

I have a secret to disclose to you, said he, which cannot be divulged on any other spot.

Unwilling to deny so small a favor to the son of one who had so often shed his blood in his country's service, Wallace, as has been said before, consented; and was conducted by Monteith towards Douglas.

As they descended the heights which lead down to the castle, Monteith kept a profound silence; and when they crossed the draw-bridge which lay over the water at its base, he put his finger to his lips, in token to the servants for equal taciturnity: this was explained as they entered the gate and looked round, they saw it guarded by English soldiers. —Wallace started, and would have drawn back, but Monteith laid his hand on his arm and whispered, "for your country!" Upon these words, which struck like a spell upon the ear of Wallace, he proceeded; and his attendants followed him into the court-yard.

The sun was just setting as Monteith led his friend into a room which looked towards the east. The reflection of the departing orb upon the distant hills, reminded Wallace of the stretch he had to retread, to reach his home before midnight; and thinking of his anxious Marion, he proposed with impatience, to be told of the object of his journey.

Monteith closed the door, looked fearfully around for some time, and trembling at every step, approached Wallace. When drawn quite near, in a low voice, he said, "you must swear upon the cross that you will keep inviolable the secret I am now going to reveal."

Wallace put aside the hilt of the sword which Monteith presented to receive his oath; no, said he with a smile, I take no oaths. In these times I would not bind my conscience on subjects that I do not know. If you dare trust the word of a Scotsman and a friend, speak out; and if it be honest, my honor is your pledge.

And you will not swear? demanded Monteith, with a doubtful look.
"No."
Then I must not trust you.
Then our business is at an end; returned Wallace, and I may return home.

Stop! cried Monteith, forgive me, noble Wallace that I have dared to hesitate! these are indeed times of such treason to honour, that I do not wonder you should be careful how you swear. But the nature of the confidence reposed in me will, I hope, convince you that I ought not to share it rashly. Of any one but you, whose truth stands as fair as virgin purity, I would exact oaths on oaths; but your word is given, and on that I rely. Await me here.

Monteith unlocked a door which had been concealed by the tapestry of the room, and in a few minutes re-entered with a small iron box. He set it hastily on the table near his friend; then went to the great door which he had so carefully closed, tried that the bolts were secure, and returned with a still more pallid countenance towards the table. Wallace, surprised at so much precaution, and the extreme apprehension visible in these actions, awaited with wonder the promised explanation. Monteith sat down with his hand on the box, and fixing his eyes on it, began—

"I am going to mention a name which you may hear with patience, since the power by which its bearer insulted you is no more. The successful rival of Bruce, and the enemy of your family, is now a prisoner in the tower of London."

"You speak of Baliol?"

"I do," answered Monteith "and his present sufferings will perhaps soften your indignation at his too vindictive resentment of the injury he received from Sir Ronald Crawford."

"My grandfather never injured him or any man!" interrupted Wallace; "Sir Ronald Crawford was ever as incapable of injustice, as of flattering the minion of his country's enemy. But Balliol is fallen, and I forgive him."

"Did you witness his degradation," returned Monteith, "you would even pity him."

"He was always an object of my pity," continued Wallace. "I never thought him worthy of a stronger sentiment; and as you are ignorant of the cause of his enmity against Sir Ronald and myself, in justice to the character of that most venerable of men, I will explain it. I first saw Baliol four years ago, when I accompanied my grandfather to witness the arbitration of the king of England between the two contending claimants for the Scottish crown. Sir Ronald came on the part of Bruce. I was deemed too young to have a voice on the council; but I was old enough to understand what was passing; and to perceive in the crouching demeanor, with which Baliol received the crown, that it was the price for which he had sold his country. However, as Scotland acknowledged him sovereign, and as Bruce submitted, my grandfather silently acquiesced. But Baliol forgot not former opposition: his behaviour to Sir Ronald and myself at the beginning of this year, when according to the privilege of our birth, we appeared in the field against the public enemy, fully demonstrates what was the *injury* Baliol complains of; and how unjustly he drove us from the standard of Scotland. *None* said he, *shall serve under me who ever presumed to declare themselves the friends of Bruce!* Poor, weak man! the purchased vassal of England; yet enamored of his ideal kingship, he hated all who had opposed his power, even while his own treachery sapped its foundation. Edward having made use of him, all these sacrifices of honor and of conscience were insufficient to retain his favor. The treason completed, his employer detests the traitor; and Balliol is removed from his throne to a prison! can I feel one revengeful pang against a wretch so abject? No! I do pity him. And now that I have cleared my grandfather's name of his calumny, I am ready to hear you further."

Monteith, after remarking on the well known honour of Sir Ronald Crawford, resumed:

"During the massacre at the capture of Berwick, Lord Douglas, who had defended it to the last, was taken, wounded and insensible, by a trusty band of Scots, out of the citadel; and they contrived to escape with him out of the town, even through the midst of the carnage. I followed to Dunbar, where he sufficiently recovered to witness that day's dreadful loss which completed the victory of the English. When the few nobles who survived the battle, dispersed, he took the road to Forfar; hoping to meet King Baliol there, and to concert with him new plans of resistance. I accompanied him; and when we arrived, we found his majesty in close conversation with John Cummin, Earl of Athol; and this worthless Scot had thoroughly persuaded him, that by the disaster at Dunbar, all was so lost, that if he wished to save his life, he must immediately go to the King of England, at Montrose, and surrender himself to his mercy. [2]

"Our brave Douglas tried to alter Baliol's resolution but without effect. The King only wept at the picture our friend drew of the miseries to which his flight would abandon Scotland; he could not return any reasonable answers to the arguments which were offered to induce him to remain, but continued to repeat with sobs and tears, *it is my fate! it is my fate!* Athol sat knitting his black brows during this conversation; and at last, throwing out some sullen remarks to Lord Douglas on the vehemence with which he exhorted the king to defy his liege lord, he abruptly left the room.

"As soon as he was gone, Baliol rose from his seat with a very anxious countenance, and taking my patron into an adjoining room, they continued there a few minutes, and then re-entered, Douglas bearing with him this iron box. *Monteith,* said he, *I confide this to your care.* As he spoke, he put the box under my arm, and concealing it with my cloak, added, *carry it directly to my castle in Lanerkshire. I will rejoin you there in four-and-twenty hours after you arrive. Meanwhile, by your affection to me, and fidelity to your king, breathe not a word of what has passed.*

"*Look on this and be faithful,* said Baliol, putting this ruby ring on my finger. I withdrew, and as I crossed the outward hall was met by Athol. He eyed me sternly, and inquired whither I was going. I replied, to Douglas, to prepare for the coming of its lord. The hall was full of armed men in Athol's colors. Not one of the remnant who had followed Lord Douglas from the bloody field of Dunbar was visible. Athol looked round on his myrmidons: *here,* cried he, *see that you speed this fellow on his journey. His master goes with us to London.* I saw the danger that threatened Lord Douglas; but as I attempted to return to give him warning, a score of spears were presented at my breast. I was forced to desist; and to secure my charge, which farther resistance might have hazarded, I hastened into the court-yard, and being permitted to mount my horse, set off on full gallop.

"I arrived at this place on the second day; and remembering that secret closet, carefully deposited the box within it. A week passed without any tidings of Lord Douglas. However, I still flattered myself, notwithstanding the menace of Athol, that by some means he might escape the snare, and reach his castle; but the arrival of a pilgrim, on his way to the shrine of St. Ninian, in Galway, cut off all my hopes. He requested to see me alone: and fearing nothing from a man in so sacred a habit, I admitted him. He presented me with a packet, saying it had been entrusted to him by Lord Douglas, at Montrose. He proceeded to tell me that my brave friend, having been forcibly carried on board a vessel which was to convey him and the unhappy Baliol prisoners to London, (for such it seems were king Edward's orders,) he sent to the Tironensian monks, at Aberbrothick and under a pretence of making a religious confession before he sailed, begged to be visited by the subprior. *I am that prior*, continued the pilgrim, *and having been born on the Douglas lands, he well knew he had every claim to my fidelity. He gave me this packet, and conjured me to lose no time in conveying it to you. The task was difficult; and as in these calamitous times for Scotland, when every man's hand seems raised against his brother, we know not whom on earth to trust. I determined to bring it myself; and vowed to visit the holy shrine of St. Ninian, if it should please the blessed saints to carry me safely through my embassy*,

"I inquired of the reverend father whether Lord Douglas had actually sailed. *Yes*, replied he, *I stood on the beach at Montrose, till the ship disappeared!* and woeful was the sight, for it carried away the benefactor of my youth."

A half-stifled groan burst from the indignant breast of Wallace. It interrupted Monteith for an instant, but without noticing it, he proceeded, not appearing to have paused.

"Not only the brave Douglas was wrested from our country, but so was our king, and that holy pillar of Jacob[3] which prophets have declared the palladium of Scotland!"

What? inquired Wallace, with a frown, has Baliol robbed Scotland of that trophy of one of her best kings? is the sacred gift of Fergus to be made the spoil of a coward?

Baliol is not the robber, rejoined Monteith; the hallowed stone was taken from its sanctuary at Scone, by the command of the king of England, and carried on board the same vessel, with the sackings of Ikolmkill: the archives of the kingdom have also been torn from that monastery, and thrown by Edward's own hands into the fire.

Tyrant! exclaimed Wallace, thou may'st fill the cup too full!

His depredations, continued Monteith, the good monk told me, have been as wide as they were destructive. He has not left a parchment, either of public records, or of private annals, in any of the monasteries or castles around Montrose; all have been searched and plundered. And besides, Patrick Dunbar, the faithless Earl of March, and Lord Soulis, have been such parricides of their country, as to be his coadjutors, and have performed the like robberies from the eastern shores of the Highlands, to the furthest of the Western Isles. [4]

Do the traitors think, cried Wallace, that by robbing Scotland of her annals, and of that stone, that they really deprive her of her palladium? Fools! Fools! Scotland's history is the memories of her sons; her palladium is in their hearts; and Edward may one day find that she remembers the victory of Largs,[5] and needs not talismans to give her freedom.

Alas! not in our time! answered Monteith; the spear is at our breasts, and we must submit. You see this castle is full of Edward's soldiers! Every house is a garrison for England; but more of this by and by; I have yet to tell you the contents of the packet which the monk brought. As soon as he had declared to me what I have told you, I ordered proper means to forward him on his pilgrimage, and bidding him farewell, retired to open the packet It contained two, one directed to Sir James Douglas, at Paris, and the other to me; I read as follows; —

"Athol has pursuaded Baliol to his ruin, and betrayed me into the hands of Edward. I shall see Scotland no more. Send the enclosed to my son at Paris; it will inform him what is the last wish of William Douglas for his country. The iron box I confided to you, guard as your life, until you can deposit it with my son. But should he remain abroad, and you e'er be in extremity, commit the box in strict charge to the worthiest Scot you know; and tell him, *that it will be at the peril of his soul who dares to open it till Scotland be again free!* when that hour comes, then let the man by whose valor God restores her rights, receive the box *as his own,* for by him only, is it to be opened.

"Monteith, as you would not disgrace the memory of your noble father, and as you hope for honor here, or happiness hereafter, attend to these injunctions of your friend Douglas."

Monteith finished reading the letter, and remained silent. Wallace, who had listened to it with increasing indignation against the enemies of Scotland, spoke first; — "Tell me in what I can assist you? or how serve the last wishes of the brave Douglas?"

Monteith replied by reading over again this sentence: *"should my son remain abroad, and you ever be in extremity, commit the box in strict charge to the worthiest Scot you know."* I am in that extremity now. Edward had formed his plan of desolation, when he placed English governors throughout our towns: and the rapacious Heselrigge, his representative in Lanerk, is not backward to execute the despot's will. He has just issued an order for all the houses of the absent chiefs to be searched for records and secret correspondences. Two or three in the neighborhood have already gone through this ordeal; and the event has proved that it was not papers they sought, but plunder; and an excuse for dismantling the castles, or occupying them with English officers.

"A detachment of soldiers were sent hither by Heselrigge this morning by day-break, to guard the castle, until be could in person be present at the examination. This ceremony is to take place to-morrow; and as Lord Douglas is considered a traitor to Edward, I am told the place will be sacked to its bare walls. In such *an extremity,* to you, noble Wallace, as to *the worthiest Scot I know,* I fly to take charge of this box: within the remote cliffs of Ellerslie it will be safe from suspicion; and when Sir James Douglas arrives from Paris, to him you can resign the trust. Meanwhile, as I shall not resist the plunderers to-morrow, after delivering up the keys of the state apartments to Heselrigge, I will submit to necessity, and beg his permission to retire to my lodge on Ben Venu."

Wallace made no difficulty in granting this request; and desiring Monteith, when he found means to forward lord Douglas's packet to his son, to inform that young nobleman of the circumstances which deposited the box in Ellerslie, he proposed to depart immediately. There being two iron rings on each side of the casket, Wallace took the leathern belt which girded his sword, and putting it through them, swung it easily under his left arm, and covered it with his plaid.

His charge being secured, Monteith's eyes brightened, the paleness left his cheek, and with a firmer step, as if suddenly relieved of a heavy load, he called a servant to prepare Sir William Wallace's horses and attendants.

As Wallace shook hands with his friend, Monteith, in a low and solemn voice, bade him be cautious in what part of his house he kept the box; remember, said he, the penalty that hangs over him who looks into it.

Be not afraid, answered Wallace, even the outside shall never be seen by other eyes than my own, unless the same circumstance which now induces you, *mortal extremity*, should force me to confide it to safer hands.

Beware of that! exclaimied Monteith, for who is there that would adhere to the prohibition as I have done, as you will do? and, besides, as I have no doubt it contains holy relics, who knows what calamities a sacrilegious look might bring upon our already devoted country.

Relics or no relics, replied Wallace, it would be an equal sin against good faith to invade what is forbidden; but from the weight, I am rather inclined to suspect that the box contains gold; probably a treasure, with which the sordid mind of Baliol thinks to compensate the hero who may free his country, for all the miseries a traitor King, and a treacherous usurper have brought upon it.

A treasure! repeated Monteith, I never thought of that; it is indeed very heavy — As we are responsible for the contents of the box, I wish we were certain of what it contains; let us consider that!

It is no consideration of ours; returned Wallace, with what is in the box we have no concern;. all we have to do, is to preserve the contents unviolated by even our own eyes; and to that, as you have now transferred the charge to me, I pledge myself, — farewell.

But why this haste? rejoined Monteith, surely you had best stay a little, indeed I wish I had thought, — stay only a little.

I thank you, returned Wallace, proceeding to the court yard, but it is now dark, and I promised to be at home before the moon rises; I must bid you good night. If you wish me to serve you farther, I shall be happy to see you at Ellerslie to-morrow. My Marion will have pleasure in entertaining for days or weeks, the friend of her husband.

While Wallace spoke, he advanced to his horse, to which he was lighted, not only by the servants of the castle, but by several English soldiers who crowded forward out of curiosity. As he put his foot in the stirrup, he held in his hand the loosened sword which, to accommodate his charge he had unbuckled from his side. Monteith, whose dread of detection was ever awake, whispered, "a weapon in your hand will excite suspicion!" Fear incurred what it would have avoided; as he hastily pulled aside Wallace's plaid to throw it over the glittering hilt of the sword, he exposed the iron box. The light of so many torches striking upon the polished rivets, displayed it to all eyes; but no remark being made, and Wallace not observing what was done, again shook hands with Monteith, and calling his servants about him, galloped away; and being obliged to leave the northern and direct road, because the English marauders swarmed there, he was presently lost amid the thick shades of Clydesdale.

1   Walter Stewart, the father of Sir John Monteith, assumed the name and Earldom of Menteith, in right of his wife, the daughter and heiress of the preceding Earl. When his wife died he married an English woman of rank. Lord Menteith being ardently attached to the liberties of his country, his bride found means to cut him off by poison; and was rewarded by the enemies of Scotland for this treason, with the hand of an ancestor of the Dukes of Bedford.
2   This treacherous Scot who persuaded Baliol to his ruin, was John Cummins, of Strathbogie, Earl of Athol in right of his wife, the heiress of that earldom.
3   The tradition respecting this stone is as follows — Hiber or Iber, who came from the Holy Land to inhabit the coasts of Spain, brought this sacred relic along with him. From Spain he transplanted it with the colony he sent out to people the south of Ireland: and from Ireland it was brought into Scotland by the great Fergus the son of Ferchard. He placed it in Argyleshire; but MacAlpine removed it to Scone, and fixed it in the royal chair in which all succeding kings of Scotland were inaugurated. Edward the first of England caused it to be placed in Westminster Abbey, where it now stands. [In 1996, the stone was repatriated to Scotland. Publ. note.]
4   It is not necessary to remind the reader of the authorities whence these notorious facts are drawn.
5   This battle was fought by Alexander III on the first of August, 1263, against Acho, King of Norway. — That monarch invaded Scotland, with a large army, and drew his forces up before Largs, a town in Ayrshire. He here met with a great defeat, and retired, covered with disgrace to his own country.

Anne Grant (1755-1838)

from Essays on the Superstitions of the Highlanders (1811)

ESSAY VIII. [part]

Recapitulation. – Prophecy of Ercildown. – Stream of tradition continually enlarging. – Manners not to be studied in this period of Society, but general nature more obvious and distinctly seen, when advanced beyond barbarity, yet not arrived at refinement. – Love of the marvellous inherent in human nature. – Various illustrations.

> "And do they only stand by ignorance?
> "Is that their happy state;
> "The proof of their obedience and their love?" — Milt.

The reflections and observations which I have hazarded in the foregoing essays will, I am sensible, appear to many paradoxical and visionary; but the poetical records compared with existing traditions and manner, and the general habits of thought and motives of action still prevailing among the unsophisticated highlanders, form a body of evidence, which will in a great degree corroborate, if not establish the hypothesis I have ventured to advance. I have endeavoured to point out,

First, That a people accustomed to freedom, ably contending for it, and finally flying to the fastnesses of their country to secure it, must needs have carried with them high and independent feelings, such as cherish noble sentiments, and produce heroic actions: That common dangers and privations, the dread of a common foe, and sharing the common honours due to the utmost exertion of courage, patience, and fortitude, must have greatly endeared them to each other.

Second, That their conscious origin from one common stock, and that in their apprehension a noble one, must have mingled pride with that affection, which bound them to each other, and taught them to consider this common origin, and those warm affections which bound them to each other as the chief earthly good: As a dignity and privilege to be preserved at all hazards, and an abundant recompence for the severest privations.

Third, That the entire exclusion of science, and all the objects of interest and ambition, from the rocky abodes of these primitive hunters and graziers, left them free to the illusions of the imagination and the emotions of the heart. And that these circumstances, combined with the love of fame, derived from their past exploits, and only to be gratified in war or hunting, raised their minds to a highly sensitive and poetical state: That valour thus sublimed, affection thus concentrated, and imagination unchecked by sober and cultivated reason, and fed by all the peculiarities of awful and gloomy scenery, sounds of horror, and sights of wonder, furnished abundant materials for the loftiest flights of the poet, and the darkest fears of the visionary.

Hence, poetry was earlier born, and sooner matured here than in any other country; and hence, the native poetry nourished superstition by kindling enthusiasm. The native superstition, in return, enriched poetry with images of unequalled tenderness and sublimity.

Poetry conducted the warrior to the field of battle, and from thence to the grave, with all the eulogies due to pre-eminent valour, patriotism, and generosity. For superstition, it remained to give a new theme to the poet, and open new sources of sorrow and tenderness to the fair mourner, who sat in solitude by some roaring stream, deploring her lost hero.

This dreary power brought the ghost of the departed like a moon-beam, to the window of the bard's repose to challenge the permanent reward of never-dying praise. On the blast of night, it brought the whispers of an unseen form, to warn the visionary maid of her speedy re-union with the "dweller of her secret soul;" and to furnish themes for dreams of mingled hope and terror.

The unbroken lineage, the unaltered language, the unconquered country, and the ties of affinity, daily renewed, and hourly strengthened and endeared preserved, unchanged, and undiminished, every tribute paid by affection, or by genius to departed worth or valour.

Those plants of fair renown, which, in a less genial climate of the heart, are nipped by chilling indifference, or which wither, like Jonah's gourd, before the too ardent beams of public exposure, were here perennial evergreens, cherished by those who felt a dear connection with the tombs they sheltered.

The state of society was so very different from any thing we have either seen or imagined, that no conclusions could be more erroneous than those which we should draw from our own experience and observation of life, when applied to their modes of thinking and acting. I do not speak now of the views which the light of science enables us to take, but of that fluctuation in modes of apparel, habits of civility, &c. which we insensibly acquire from our association with various nations, and which as insensibly draw us away, not only from the customs, but from the opinions of our forefathers. These, in diminishing our respect for their way of thinking and acting, diminishes our reverence for their memory, and unconsciously slackens those relative ties which derive their main power from the cherished remembrance of a common ancestor.

That change is, in many respects, improvement, cannot be doubted: as little can it be denied, that at this price many of our improvements are purchased.

The case was directly contrary with our mountaineers. There came neither books nor strangers to diffuse knowledge among them. But if it was true, that nothing was acquired from extraneous sources, nothing was lost that was worth preserving, of the wisdom, the wit, or the ingenuity of their ancestors; of their poetry or their proverbs; of their history or their biography.

[Rest of essay omitted]

William Tennant (1784-1848)

from **Anster Fair, A Poem in Six Cantos (1812)**

CANTO I. [part]

I.

While some of Troy and pettish heroes sing,
    And some of Rome and chiefs of pious fame,
And some of men that thought it harmless thing
    To smite off heads in Mars's bloody game,
And some of Eden's garden gay with spring,
    And Hell's dominions terrible to name, —
I sing a theme far lovelier, happier, gladder,
I sing of ANSTER FAIR, and bonny MAGGIE LAUDER.

II.

What time from east, from west, from south, from north,
    From every hamlet, town, and smoky city,
Laird, clown, and beau, to Anster Fair came forth,
    The young, the gay, the handsome, and the witty,
To try in various sport and game their worth,
    Whilst prize before them MAGGIE sat, the pretty,
And after many a feat, and joke, and banter,
    Fair MAGGIE's hand was won by mighty ROB the RANTER.

III.

Muse, that from top of thine old Greekish hill,
    Didst the harp-fing'ring Theban younker view,
And on his lips bid bees their sweets distil,
    And gav'st the chariot that the white swans drew,
O let me scoop, from thine ethereal rill,
    Some little palmfuls of the blessed dew,
And lend the swan-drawn car, that safely I,
    Like him, may scorn the earth, and burst into the sky.

IV.

Our themes are like; for he the games extoll'd
    Held in the chariot-shaken Grecian plains,

Where the vain victor, arrogant and bold,
    A pickle parsley got for all his pains;
I sing of sports more worthy to be told,
    Where better prize the Scottish victor gains;
What were the crowns of Greece but wind and bladder,
    Compared with marriage-bed of bonnie MAGGIE LAUDER?

V.

And O that king Apollo would but grant
    A little spark of that transcendant flame,
That fir'd the Chian rhapsodist to chant
    How vied the bowmen for Ulysses' dame,
And him of Rome to sing how Atalant
    Plied, dart in hand, the suitor-slaught'ring game,
Till the bright gold, bowl'd forth along the grass,
    Betray'd her to a spouse, and stopp'd the bounding lass!

VI.

But lo! from bosom of yon southern cloud,
    I see the chariot come which Pindar bore;
I see the swans, whose white necks, arching proud,
    Glitter with golden yoke, approach my shore;
For me they come — O Phoebus, potent god!
    Spare, spare me now — Enough, good king — no more—
A little spark I ask'd in moderation.
    Why scorch me ev'n to death with fiery inspiration?

VII.

My pulse beats fire — my pericranium glows,
    Like baker's oven, with poetic heat;
A thousand bright ideas, spurning prose,
    Are in a twinkling hatch'd in Fancy's seat;
Zounds! they will fly, out at my ears and nose,
    If through my mouth they find not passage fleet;
I hear them buzzing deep within my noddle,
    Like bees that in their hives confus'dly hum and huddle.

[VIII to XXI omitted]

XXII.

Here broke the lady her soliloquy;
    For in a twink her pot of mustard, lo!
Self-moved, like Jove's wheel'd stool that rolls on high,
    'Gan caper on her table to and fro,
And hopp'd and fidgeted before her eye,
    Spontaneous, here and there, a wondrous show:
As leaps, instinct with mercury, a bladder,
    So leaps the mustard-pot of bonnie MAGGIE LAUDER.

XXIII.

Soon stopp'd its dance th'ignoble utensil,
    When from its round and small recess there came
Thin curling wreaths of paly smoke, that still,
    Fed by some magic unapparent flame,
Mount to the chamber's stucco'd roof, and fill
    Each nook with fragrance, and refresh the dame
Ne'er smelt a Phoenix-nest so sweet, I wot,
    As smelt the luscious fumes of MAGGIE'S mustard-pot.

XXIV.

It reeked censer-like; then, strange to tell!
    Forth from the smoke, that thick and thicker grows,
A fairy of the height of half an ell,
    In dwarfish pomp, majestically rose:
His feet, upon the table 'stablish'd well,
    Stood trim and splendid in their snake-skin hose;
Gleam'd topaz-like, the breeches he had on,
    Whose waistband like the bend of summer rainbow shone.

XXV.

His coat seem'd fashion'd of the threads of gold,
    That intertwine the clouds at sun-set hour,
And, certes, Iris with her shuttle bold
    Wove the rich garment in her lofty bower;
To form its buttons were the Pleiads old
    Pluck'd from their sockets, sure by genie-power.
And sew'd upon the coat's resplendent hem;
    Its neck was lovely green, each cuff a sapphire gem.

XXVI.

As when the churlish spirit of the Cape
    To Gama, voyaging to Mozambique,
Up-popp'd from sea, a tangle-tassel'd[1] shape.
    With mussels sticking inch-thick on his cheek,
And 'gan with tortoise-shell his limbs to scrape,
    And yawn'd his monstrous blobberlips to speak;
Brave Gama's hairs stood bristled at the sight,
    And on the tarry deck sunk down his men with fright.

XXVII.

So sudden (not so huge and grimly dire)
    Uprose to Maggie's stounded eyne the sprite,
As fair a fairy as you could desire,
    With ruddy cheek, and chin and temples white;
His eyes seem'd little points of sparkling fire,
    That as he look'd, charm'd with inviting light;
He was, indeed as bonny a fay and brisk,
    As e'er on long moon-beam was seen to ride and frisk.

XXVIII.

Around his bosom, by a silken zone,
    A little bagpipe gracefully was bound,
Whose pipes like hollow stalks of silver shone
    The glist'ring tiny avenues of sound;
Beneath his arm the windy bag, full-blown
    Heav'd up its purple like an orange round,
And only waited orders to discharge
    Its blasts with charming groan into the sky at large.

XXIX.

He wav'd his hand to Maggie, as she sat
    Amaz'd and startled on her carved chair;
Then took his petty feather-garnish'd hat
    In honour to the Lady, from his hair,
And made a bow so dignifiedly flat,
    That Mag was witchèd with his beauish air:
At last he spoke, with voice so soft, so kind,
    So sweet, as if his throat with fiddle-strings was lin'd—

XXX.

Lady! be not offended that I dare,
    Thus forward and impertinently rude,
Emerge, uncall'd, into the upper air,
    Intruding on a maiden's solitude;
Nay, do not be alarm'd, thou Lady fair!
    Why startle so? — I am a fairy good;
Not one of those that, envying beauteous maids,
    Speckle their skins with moles, and fill with spleens their heads.

XXXI.

For, as conceal'd in this clay-house of mine,
    I overheard thee in a lowly voice,
Weighing thy lovers' merits, with design
    Now on the worthiest lad to fix thy choice,
I have up-bolted from my paltry shrine,
    To give thee, sweet-ey'd lass, my best advice;
For by the life of Oberon my king!
    To pick good husband out is, sure, a ticklish thing.

XXXII.

And never shall good Tommy Puck permit
    Such an assemblage of unwonted charms
To cool some lecher's lewd licentious fit,
    And sleep imbounded by his boisterous arms;
What though his fields by twenty ploughs be split
    And golden wheat wave riches on his farms?
His house is shame — it cannot, shall not be;
    A greater, happier doom, O Mag, awaiteth thee.

XXXIII.

Strange are indeed the steps, by which thou must
    Thy glory's happy eminence attain;
But fate hath fix'd them, and 'tis fate's t'adjust
    The mighty links that ends to means enchain;
Nor may poor Puck his little fingers thrust
    Into the links to break Jove's steel in twain:
Then, Maggie, hear, and let my words descend
    Into thy soul, for much it boots thee to attend.

1 Tangle-tassel'd, hung round with tangle (sea-weed) as with tassels. I observe tangle in Bailey's Dict. though not in Johnson's.

Mary Brunton (1778-1818)

from Discipline: A Novel (1814)

CHAP. XXVII.

A chieftain's daughter seemed the maid.
— — — — —
And seldom o'er a breast so fair
Mantled a plaid with modest care;
And never brooch the folds confined
Above a heart more good and kind.

Walter Scott.

In the morning, when I opened my eyes, Juliet was so peacefully still, that I listened doubtfully for her breathing, and felt myself relieved by the certainty that she was alive. I was astonished to find that she was awake, though so composed; and was wondering at this unaccountable change, when she suddenly asked me whether Dr— —was reckoned a man of any skill in his profession, "for", said she, "he seemed to know nothing at all of my disorder, except what he learnt from myself; so most likely he mistakes it altogether." Shocked to see her thus obstinately cling to the broken reed, yet wanting courage to wrest it from her hold, I intreated her to consider that it would not add to the justice of Dr— —'s fears, if she should act as though they were well-founded; nor shorten her life, if she should hasten to accomplish whatever she would wish to perform ere its close. She was silent for a little; then, with a deep sigh, "You are right," said she. "Sit down and I will dictate a letter which you shall write to my brother."

I obeyed; and she began to dictate with wonderful precision a letter, in which she detailed the opinion of her counsel; named the persons who could evidence her claims; and dexterously appealed to the ruling passion of Mr Arnold, by reminding him, that if he could establish the legitimacy of his nephew, he must, in case of Lord Glendower's death, become the natural guardian of a youth possessed of five and twenty thousand pounds a year. Who could observe without a sigh, that, while with a sort of instinctive tact, she addressed herself to the faults of others, she remained in melancholy blindness to her own; and that the transient strength which the morning restored to her mind, could not reach her more than childish improvidence in regard to her most important concerns. But her powers were soon exhausted; before the letter was finished, her thoughts wandered, and she lay for some hours as if in a sort of waking dream.

How little do they know of a death-bed who have seen it only in the graceful pictures of fiction! How little do they guess the ghastly horrors of sudden dissolution, the humiliating weaknesses of slow decay! Paint them even from the life, and much remains to tell which no spectator can record, much which no language can unfold. "Oh, who that could see thee thus," thought I, as I looked upon the languid inexpressive countenance of the once playful Juliet, "who that could see thee thus, would defer to an hour like this, the hard task of learning to die with decency?"

I was sitting by the bed-side of my companion, supporting with one hand her poor deserted baby, and making with the other an awkward attempt to sketch designs for the ornaments which I had undertaken to paint, when the door was gently opened; and the lady for whom I was employed entered, followed by another, whose appearance instantly fixed my attention. Her stature was majestic,—her figure of exquisite proportion. Her complexion, though brunette, was admirably transparent; and her colour, though perhaps too florid for a sentimental eye, glowed with the finest tints of health. Her black eye-brows, straight but flexible, approached close to a pair of eyes so dark and sparkling, that their colour was undistinguishable. No simile in oriental poetry could exaggerate the regularity and whiteness of her teeth; nor painter's dream of Euphrosyne exceed the arch vivacity of her smile. Perhaps a critic might have said that her figure was too large, and too angular for feminine beauty; that it was finely, but not delicately formed. Even I could have wished the cheek-bones depressed, the contour somewhat rounded, and the lines made more soft and flowing. But Charlotte Graham had none of that ostentation of beauty which provokes the gazer to criticise.

Her face, though too handsome to be a common one, struck me at first sight as one not foreign to my acquaintance. When her companion named her, I recollected my friend Cecil; and there certainly was a family likeness between these relations, although the latter was a short square-built personage, with no great pretensions to beauty. The expressions of the two countenances were more dissimilar than the features. Cecil's was grave, penetrating, and, considering her age and sex, severe; Miss Graham's was arch, frank, and animated. Yet there was in the eye of both a keen sagacity, which seemed accustomed to look beyond the words of the speaker to his motive.

The deep mourning which Miss Graham wore, accounted to me for the cast of sorrow which often crossed a face formed by nature to far different expression. Her manners had sufficient freedom to banish restraint, and sufficient polish to make that freedom graceful; yet for me they possessed an interesting originality. They were polite, but not fashionable; they were courtly, but not artificial. They were perfectly affable, and as free from arrogance as those of a doubting lover; yet in her mien, in her gait, in every motion, in every word, Miss Graham shewed the unsubdued majesty of one who had never felt the presence of a superior; of one much accustomed to grant, but not to solicit indulgence.

Such were the impressions which I had received, almost as soon as Miss Graham's companion, with a polite apology for their intrusion, had introduced her to me by name. I was able to make the necessary compliment without any breach of sincerity, for feebler attractions would have interested me in the person with whom Cecil had already made me so well acquainted. But when Miss Graham spoke, her voice alone must have won any hearer.

"If Miss Percy excuses us," said she, in tones, which, in spite of the lively imperative accent of her country, were sweetness itself, "my conscience will be quite at rest, for I am persuaded it is with her that my business lies. No two persons could answer the description."

"You may remember," said her companion, smiling at my surprised and inquisitive look, "I yesterday mentioned a friend who was in search of a young lady of your name. We are now in hopes that her search ends in you; and this must be our apology for a great many impertinent questions."

"Oh no," said Miss Graham, "one will be sufficient. Suffer me only to ask who were your parents."

I answered the question readily and distinctly. "Then," said Miss Graham, with a smile, which at once made its passage to my heart, "I have the happiness to bring you a pleasant little surprise. My brother has been so fortunate as to recover a debt due to Mr Percy. He has transmitted it hither; and Sir William Forbes will honour your draft for L. 1500."

There are persons who will scarcely believe that I at first heard this intelligence with little joy. "Alas!" thought I, looking at poor Juliet, "it has come too late." But recollecting that I was not the less indebted to the kindness of my benefactors, I turned to Miss Graham, and offered, as I could, my warm acknowledgements. Miss Graham assured me, with looks which evinced sincerity, that she was already more than repaid for the service she had rendered me; and prevented further thanks, by proceeding in her explanation.

"My brother," said she, "traced you to the house of a Miss Mortimer, and from thence to Edinburgh; but here he lost you; and being himself at a distance, he commissioned me to search for you. I received some assistance from a very grateful protegée of yours and mine, whom I dare say you recollect by the name of Cecil Graham. She directed me to the Boswells; but they pretended to know nothing of you; so I came to town a few days ago, very much at a loss how to proceed, though determined not to see Glen Eredine again till I found you."

"And is it possible" exclaimed I, "that I have indeed excited such generous interest in strangers?"

"Call me stranger, if you will," said Miss Graham, "provided you allow that the name gives me a right to a kind reception. But do you include my brother under that title? I am sure the description he has given of you shews that he is, at least, well acquainted with your appearance."

"The dimple and the black eye-lashes, tally exactly," said her companion. "And I could swear to the smile," returned Miss Graham. "Nevertheless," said I, "it is only from the praises of his admirer, Cecil, that I know Mr Kenneth Graham, to whom I presume I am so much indebted."

The playful smile, the bright hues of health, vanished from Charlotte's face; and her eyes tilled with tears. "No," said she, "it is not to—" She paused, as if to utter the name had been an effort beyond her fortitude. "It is Mr Henry Graham," said her companion, as if to spare her the pain of explanation, "who has been so fortunate as to do you this service."

I know not exactly why, but my heart beat quicker at this intelligence. I had listened so often to Cecil's prophecies, and omens, and good wishes,

31

that I believe I felt a foolish kind of consciousness at the name of this Henry Graham, and the mention of my obligation to him.

"Have you no recollection then of ever having met with Henry?" inquired Miss Graham, recovering herself,

I rubbed my forehead and did my very utmost; but was obliged to confess that it was all in vain. The rich Miss Percy had been so accustomed to crowds of attending beaux, that my eye might have been familiar with his appearance, while his name was unknown to me.

"Well," said Miss Graham, "I can vouch for the possibility of remembering you for ever after a very transient interview; and when you know Henry better, I dare say you will not forget him."

We now talked of our mutual acquaintance, Cecil; which led Miss Graham to comment upon the peculiar manners of her countrymen, and upon the contrast which they offered to those of the lowland Scotch. Though her conversation upon this, and other subjects, betrayed no marks of extraordinary culture, it discovered a native sagacity, a quickness and accuracy of observation, which I have seldom found surpassed. Her visit was over before I guessed that it had lasted nearly two hours; and so great were her attractions, so delightful seemed the long untasted pleasures of equal and friendly converse, that I thought less of the unexpected news which she had brought me, than of the hour which she fixed for her return.

My thoughts, indeed, no sooner turned towards my newly acquired riches, than I perceived that they could not, with any shadow of justice, be called mine; and that they in truth belonged to those who had suffered by the misfortunes of my father. I therefore resolved to forget that the money was within my reach, and to labour as I should have done, had no kind friend intended my relief. Still this did not lessen my sense of obligation; and gratitude enlivened the curiosity which often turned my speculations towards Henry Graham. Once as I kept my solitary watch over Juliet's heavy unrefreshing slumbers, I thought I recollected hearing her, and some of our mutual acquaintance, descant upon the graces of an Adonis, who, for one night, had shone the meteor of the fashionable hemisphere, and then been seen no more. I had been present at his appearance, but too much occupied with Lord Frederick to observe the wonder. I afterwards endeavoured to make Juliet assist my recollection; but her memory no longer served even for much more important affairs; and all my efforts ended at last in retouching the pictures which I had accustomed myself to embody of this same Henry Graham. I imaged him with more than his sister's dignity of form and gesture, — with all her regularity of feature, and somewhat of her national squareness of contour; — with all the vivacity and intelligence of her countenance, strengthened into masculine spirit and sagacity; — with the eye which Cecil had described, as able to quell even the sallies of frenzy; — with the smile which his sister could send direct to the heart. At Charlotte's next visit, I obliged her to describe her brother; and I had guessed so well, that she only improved my picture, by adding some minuter strokes to the likeness.

At the same time she removed all my scruples in regard to appropriating the sum which he had obtained for me, by assuring me, that he had undertaken the recovery of the debt only upon this express condition, that half the amount should belong to me, and that to this condition the creditors had readily consented.

The possession of this little fortune soon became a real blessing; for Juliet's increasing helplessness loaded my time with a burden which almost precluded other labour. She was emaciated to a degree which made stillness and motion alike painful to her; a restless desire of change seemed the only human feeling which the hand of death had not already palsied; and a childish sense of her dependence upon me, was the sole wreck of human affliction which her decay had spared. Even the fear of death subsided into the listless acquiescence of necessity. Yet no nobler solicitudes seemed to replace the waning interests of this life. Feeble as it was, her mind yet retained the inexplicable power to exclude thoughts of overwhelming force. I had seen the inanity of her life; I had, alas! shared in her mad neglect of all the serious duties, of all the best hopes of man; and I did not dare to see her die in this portentous lethargy of soul. At every short revival of her strength, or transient clearness of her intellect, I spoke to her of all which I most desired to impress upon her mind. At first she answered me by tears and complainings, then by a listless silence; nor did better success attend the efforts of persons more skilled in rousing the sleeping conscience. The eloquence of friend and pastor was alike unavailing to extort one tear of genuine penitence; for the energy was wanting, without which a prophet might have smitten the rock in vain.

I must have been more or less than human, could my spirits have resisted the influence of a scene so dreary as a death-chamber without hope; yet when I saw my companion sinking to an untimely grave, closing a life without honour in a death without consolation; when I remembered that we had begun our career of folly together, — that, from equal wanderings, I had alone been restored, from equal shipwrecks I had alone escaped, — I felt that I had reason to mingle strong gratitude for what I was, with deep humiliation for what I might have been.

It was now that I became sensible of the treasure which I had found in Charlotte Graham. Taught by experience, I had at first yielded with caution to the attraction of her manners; and often (though in her absence only I must own), remembered with a sigh how many other qualities must conspire to fit the companion for the friend. But now, when she daily forsook admiration, and gaiety, and elegance, to share with me the cares of a sick-chamber, I daily felt the benefits of her piety, discretion, and sweetness of temper; and a friendship began which, I trust, will outlast our lives.

Although she had too much of the politeness of good feeling, to hint an expectation that I should forsake my unhappy charge, she constantly spoke of my visiting Castle Eredine, as of a pleasure which she could not bear to leave in uncertainty; and she detailed plans for our employments, for our studies, for our excursions among her native hills, with a minuteness which shewed how much the subject occupied her mind. I observed too, that all her plans bore a constant reference to Glen Eredine. They were incapable of completion elsewhere. My lessons on the harp were to be given under the rock of echoes, — in a certain cave she was to teach me the songs of Selma, — we were to climb Benarde together, — from Dorch'thalla we were to sketch the lake beyond, with all its mountain shadows on its breast; while the rocks, which a nameless torrent had severed from the cliff, and the roots which, with emblematic constancy, had still clung to them in their fall, were to furnish fore-grounds unequalled in the tameness of Lowland scenery. To all the objects round her native vale, Charlotte's imagination seemed to lend a kind of vitality. She loved them as I should have loved an animated being; and the more characteristic, or, as I should then have expressed it, the more savage they were, the stronger seemed their hold on her affection. I like a little innocent prejudice, so long as it does not thwart my own. I verily believe, that Charlotte would have thought Glen Eredine insulted by a comparison to the vale of Tempe. She often spoke with enthusiastic respect of her father, whom she had left at Castle Eredine; and with so much solicitude of the blank which her absence would occasion to him, that I could not help wondering why she delayed her return. She never mentioned any business that might detain her; and amusement could not be her bribe, for her time was chiefly spent in my melancholy dwelling.

Our cheerless task, however, at length was closed. By a change scarcely perceptible to us, Juliet passed from the lethargy of exhausted life, to deeper and more solemn repose. I felt the intermitting pulse, — I watched the failing breath; yet so gradual and so complete was her decay, that I knew not the moment of her departure. All suffering she was spared; for suffering would, to human apprehension, have been useless to her. I did not commit her remains to the cares of a stranger. The hand of a friend composed her for her last repose; the tears of a friend dropped upon her clay; but they were not the tears of sorrow. Poor Juliet! Less ingenuity than that which led thee through a degraded life to an unlamented grave, would have procured for thee the best which this world has to give, an unmolested passage to a better.

Two days after her death, I received from her brother a promise of protection to the heir of Lord Glendower, and permission, in case of that event, to send the boy to his uncle, together with the pledges of legitimacy, which constituted his sole hold upon the justice or compassion of Mr Arnold. Fortunately for the poor infant, the question upon which depended the tender cares of his uncle was decided in his favour. Juliet's marriage was sanctioned; and though her death left Lord Glendower at liberty to repair, in some sort, the injury which he had done to Lady Maria, the rights of his first-born son could not be transferred to the children of his more regular marriage.

When my cares were no longer necessary to my ill fated companion, I yielded to the kind persuasions of Miss Graham, and suffered her to introduce me to whatever was most worthy of observation in a city which I had as yet so imperfectly seen. Our mornings were generally spent in examining the town or its environs; our evenings, in a kind of society which I had till now known only in detached specimens; a society in which there was everything to delight, though nothing to astonish, — much good manners, and therefore little singularity, — general information, and therefore little pedantry, — much good taste, and therefore little notoriety. I could no longer complain that the ladies were inaccessible. Introduced by Miss Graham, I was everywhere received with more than courtesy; and I, who a few weeks before could scarcely obtain permission to earn a humble subsistence, was now overwhelmed with a hospitality which scarcely left me the command of an hour.

And now I was again assailed by the temptation which had formerly triumphed unresisted. There is no place on earth where beauty is more surely made dangerous to its possessor; and Charlotte and I could scarcely have attracted more attention, had we appeared mounted upon elephants. But I had lost my taste for admiration. I disliked the constant watchfulness which it imposed upon me; and its pleasures poorly compensated the pain of upbraiding myself the next moment with my folly in being so pleased. As to open compliment, it cost me an effort to answer it with good humour. "The man suspects that I am vain," thought I, as often as I was so addressed; and the suspicion was too near truth to be forgiven. The only real satisfaction which I derived from the preposterous homage paid to me, arose from the new light in which it displayed the generous nature of Charlotte Graham. Yes, trifles serve to display a great mind; and there was true generosity in the graceful willingness with which Charlotte, at a time of life when the precariousness of attentions begins to give them value, withdrew from competition with a rival inferior to her in every charm which is not affected by seven years difference of age.

Upon the whole, nothing could be more agreeably amusing, than my residence in Edinburgh; and the contrast of my late confinement heightened pleasure to delight. From the time of Lady Glendower's death, it had been settled that I was to accompany Charlotte to Glen Eredine; but I must own, that I felt no inclination to hasten our departure. Without once uttering a word which could place the delay to my account. Miss Graham deferred our departure from day to day. Yet some involuntary look or expression constantly betrayed to me, that her heart was in Glen Eredine.

"Ah that very sun is setting behind Benarde!" said she with a sigh; one evening when, from a promenade such as no other city can present, we were contemplating a gorgeous sunset.

"One would imagine by that sigh, Charlotte," said I smiling "that you and some dear friend not far from Benarde had made an appointment to watch the setting sun together."

"There's a flight!" cried she, laughing, "Now am I sure, that such a fancy would never have entered your mind, if you had not been in love. Come, look me in the face, and let me catechise you."

"Not guilty upon my honour."

"Humph! This does look very like a face of innocence, I confess. But stay till you know Henry. Let us see how you will stand examination then."

"Just as I do now, I promise you. I ought to have been in love long ago, if the thing had been possible."

"Ought? Pray what might impose the duty upon you?"

"The regard of one of the best and wisest of mankind, Charlotte. It was once my fate to draw the attention of your countryman, — the generous, the eloquent Mr Maitland."

I saw Miss Graham start; but she remained silent. "You must have heard of him?" continued I; but at that moment, casting my eyes upon Charlotte, I saw her blush painfully. "You know him then," said I.

"Yes, I – I do," answered she hesitatingly; and walked on in a profound reverie.

A long silence followed; for Charlotte's blushes and abstraction had told me a tale in which I could not be uninterested. I perceived that her acquaintance with Maitland, however slight, had been sufficient to fix her affections on a spirit so congenial to her own. "Well, well," thought I, "they will meet one day or other; and he will find out that she likes him, and the discovery will cost him trouble enough to make it worth something. She will devote herself willingly to love and solitude, which is just what he wishes, and I dare say they will be very happy. – Men can be happy with any body. And yet Maitland hates beauties; and Miss Graham certainly is a beauty." However, when I threw a glance upon Charlotte, I thought I had never seen her look so little handsome; for it must be confessed, that the lover must be more than indifferent, whom his old mistress can willingly resign to a new one.

I soon, however, began to reproach myself with the uneasiness to which I was subjecting the generous friend to whom I owed such varied forms of kindness. But the difficulty was, how I should return to the subject which we had quitted; for, in spite of the frankness of Charlotte's manners, my freedom with her had limits which were impassable. When she had once indicated the point upon which she would not be touched, I dared not even to approach it. The silence, therefore, continued till she interrupted it, by saying, "You are offended with me, Ellen; and you have reason to be so; for I put a question which no friend has a right to ask."

"Dear Charlotte," returned I, "surely you have a right to expect from me any confidence that you will accept; and I shall most readily –"

"No," interrupted Miss Graham, "such questions as mine ought neither to be asked nor answered. If an attachment is fortunate, it is to be supposed that the event will soon publish it; if not, the confession is a degradation to which no human being has a right to subject another."

"Well," thought I, "this is very intelligible, and I shall take care not to trespass. But I will not keep thy generous heart in pain. Cost what it will, thou shalt know that thou hast nothing to fear from me."

It was more easy to resolve than to execute; and I felt my cheek glow with blushes, more, I fear, of pride, than modesty, while I struggled to relieve the anxiety of my friend. "Nay Charlotte," said I, "you must listen to a confession, which is humbling enough, though not exactly of the kind you allude to. I must do Mr Maitland the justice to say, that he never put it in my power to reject him. He saw that I was no fit wife for him; and, at the very moment of confessing his weakness, he renounced it for ever. Do not look incredulous. It is not a pretty face, nor even the noble fortune I then expected, that could bribe Maitland to marry a heartless unprincipled – –. Thanks be to Heaven that I am changed – greatly changed. But I assure you, Charlotte, I have not now the slightest reason to believe myself any bar to your – to Mr Maitland's happiness with some – some – with somebody who has not my unlucky incapacity for being in love."

To this confession, Miss Graham answered only by affectionately pressing my hand, and then escaped the subject, by turning from me to speak to a passing acquaintance. From that time Charlotte, though in other points perfectly confiding, spoke no more of Maitland; and I must own, that my respect for her was increased by her reserve upon a topic prohibited alike by delicacy and discretion. We had indeed no need of boarding-school confidences to enliven our intercourse. Each eager for improvement and for information, we had been so differently educated, that each had much to communicate and to learn. Our views of common subjects were different enough to keep conversation from stagnating; while our accordance upon more important points formed a lasting bond of union. Whoever understands the delights of a kitten and a cork, may imagine that I was at times no bad companion; and Charlotte was peculiarly fitted for a friend; for she had sound principles, unconquerable sweetness of temper, sleepless discretion, and a politeness which followed her into the homeliest scenes of domestic privacy. How often, as her character unfolded itself, did I wonder what strange fatality had forbidden Maitland to return the affection of a woman so formed to satisfy his fastidious judgment. But I was forced to wonder in silence. Charlotte, open as day on every other theme, was here as impenetrable, as unapproachable, as virgin dignity could make her. Notwithstanding the recency of our friendship, it was already strong enough to render every other interest mutual; and Charlotte easily drew from me the little story of my life and sentiments, while I listened, with insatiable curiosity, to the accounts she gave me of her home, of her family, and above all, of her brother Henry.

This was a theme in which she seemed very willing to indulge me. She spoke of him frequently; and the passages which she read to me from his letters, often made me remember with a sigh that I had no brother. He seemed to address her as a friend, as an equal; and yet with the tenderness which difference of sex imposes upon a man of right feeling. She was his almoner. Through her he transmitted many a humble comfort to his native valley; and though he had been so many years an alien, he was astonishingly minute and skilful in the direction of his benevolence. He appeared to be acquainted with the character and situation of an incredible number of his clansmen; and the interest and authority with which he wrote of them seemed little less than patriarchal. Though I must own that his commands were not always consonant to English ideas of liberty, they seemed uniformly dictated by the spirit of disinterested justice and humanity; and Graham, in exercising almost the control of an absolute prince, was guided by the feelings of a father.

Though Glen Eredine seemed the passion of his soul,—though every letter was full of the concerns of his clansmen, there was nothing theatrical in his plans for their interest or improvement. They were minute and practicable, rather than magnificent. No whole communities were to be hurried into civilization, nor districts depopulated by way of improvement; but some encouragement was to be given to the schoolmaster; bibles were to be distributed to his best scholars; or Henry would account to his father for the rent of a tenant, who, with his own hands, had reclaimed a field from rock and broom; or, at his expence, the new cottages were to be plastered, and furnished with doors and sashed windows. The execution of these humble plans, was, for the present, committed to Charlotte; and the details which she gave me concerning them, described a mode of life so oddly compounded of refinement and simplicity, that curiosity somewhat balanced my regret in leaving Edinburgh.

On a fine morning in September we began our journey; and though I was accompanied by all on earth I had to love and though I was leaving what had been to me the scene of severe suffering, I could not help looking back with watery eyes upon a place which perhaps no traveller, uncertain of return, ever quitted without a sigh.

Susan Ferrier (1782-1854)

from **Marriage (1818)**

CHAPTER I.

"Love! — A word by superstition thought a God; by use turned to an humour; by self-will made a flattering madness."
Alexander and Campaspe.

"Come hither, child," said the old Earl of Courtland to his daughter, as, in obedience to his summons, she entered his study; "come hither, I say; I wish to have some serious conversation with you: so dismiss your dogs, shut the door, and sit down here."

Lady Juliana rang for the footman to take Venus; bade Pluto be quiet, like a darling, under the sofa; and, taking Cupid in her arms, assured his Lordship he need fear no disturbance from the sweet creatures, and that she would be all attention to his commands — kissing her cherished pug as she spoke.

"You are now, I think, seventeen, Juliana," said his Lordship in a solemn important tone.

"And a half, papa."

"It is therefore time you should be thinking of establishing yourself in the world. Have you ever turned your thoughts that way?"

Lady Juliana cast down her beautiful eyes, and was silent.

"As I can give you no fortune," continued the Earl, swelling with ill-suppressed importance, as he proceeded, "you have perhaps no great pretensions to a very brilliant establishment."

"Oh! none in the world, papa," eagerly interrupted Lady Juliana; "a mere competence with the man of my heart."

"The man of a fiddlestick!" exclaimed Lord Courtland in a fury; "what the devil have you to do with a heart, I should like to know? There's no talking to a young woman now about marriage, but she is all in a blaze about hearts, and darts, and — and — But hark ye, child, I'll suffer no daughter of mine to play the fool with her heart, indeed! She shall marry for the purpose for which matrimony was ordained amongst people of birth — that is, for the aggrandisement of her family, the extending of their political influence — for becoming, in short, the depository of their mutual interest. These are the only purposes for which persons of rank ever think of marriage. And pray, what has your heart to say to that?"

"Nothing, papa," replied Lady Juliana in a faint dejected tone of voice. "Have done, Cupid!" addressing her favourite, who was amusing himself in pulling and tearing the beautiful lace veil that partly shaded the head of his fair mistress.

"I thought not," resumed the Earl in a triumphant tone — "I thought not, indeed." And as this victory over his daughter put him in unusual good humour, he condescended to sport a little with her curiosity.

"And pray, can this wonderful wise heart of yours inform you who it is you are going to obtain for a husband?"

Had Lady Juliana dared to utter the wishes of that heart she would have been at no loss for a reply; but she saw the necessity of dissimulation; and after naming such of her admirers as were most indifferent to her, she declared herself quite at a loss, and begged her father to put an end to her suspense.

"Now, what would you think of the Duke of L— —?" asked the Earl in a voice of half-smothered exultation and delight.

"The Duke of L— —!" repeated Lady Juliana, with a scream of horror and surprise; "surely, papa, you cannot be serious? Why, he's red-haired and squints, and he's as old as you."

"If he were as old as the devil, and as ugly too," interrupted the enraged Earl, "he should be your husband: and may I perish if you shall have any other!"

The youthful beauty burst into tears, while her father traversed the apartment with an inflamed and wrathful visage.

"If it had been anybody but that odious Duke," sobbed the lovely Juliana.

"If it had been anybody but that odious Duke!" repeated the Earl, mimicking her, "they should not have had you. It has been my sole study, ever since I saw your brother settled, to bring about this alliance; and, when this is accomplished, my utmost ambition will be satisfied. So no more whining—the affair is settled; and all that remains for you to do is to study to make yourself agreeable to his Grace, and to sign the settlements. No such mighty sacrifice, me thinks, when repaid with a ducal coronet, the most splendid jewels, the finest equipages, and the largest jointure of any woman in England."

Lady Juliana raised her head, and wiped her eyes. Lord Courtland perceived the effect his eloquence had produced upon the childish fancy of his daughter, and continued to expatiate upon the splendid joys that awaited her in a union with a nobleman of the Duke's rank and fortune; till at length, dazzled, if not convinced, she declared herself "satisfied that it was her duty to marry whoever papa pleased; but—" and a sigh escaped her as she contrasted her noble suitor with her handsome lover: "but if I should marry him, papa, I am sure I shall never be able to love him."

The Earl smiled at her childish simplicity as he assured her that was not at all necessary; that love was now entirely confined to the *canaille*; that it was very well for ploughmen and dairymaids to marry for love; but for a young woman of rank to think of such a thing was plebeian in the extreme!

Lady Juliana did not entirely subscribe to the arguments of her father; but the gay and glorious vision that floated in her brain stifled for a while the pleadings of her heart; and with a sparkling eye and an elastic step she hastened to prepare for the reception of the Duke.

For a few weeks the delusion lasted. Lady Juliana was flattered with the homage she received as a future Duchess; she was delighted with the éclat that attended her, and charmed with the daily presents showered upon her by her noble suitor.

"Well, really, Favolle," said she to her maid, one day, as she clasped on her beautiful arm a resplendent bracelet, "it must be owned the Duke has a most exquisite taste in trinkets; don't you think so? And, do you know, I don't think him so very—very ugly. When we are married I mean to make him get a Brutus, cork his eyebrows, and have a set of teeth." But just then the smiling eyes, curling hair, and finely formed person of a certain captivating Scotsman rose to view in her mind's eye; and, with a peevish "pshaw!" she threw the bauble aside.

Educated for the sole purpose of forming a brilliant establishment, of catching the eye, and captivating the senses, the cultivation of her mind or the correction of her temper had formed no part of the system by which that aim was to be accomplished. Under the auspices of a fashionable mother and an obsequious governess the froward petulance of childhood, fostered and strengthened by indulgence and submission, had gradually ripened into that selfishness and caprice which now, in youth, formed the prominent features of her character. The Earl was too much engrossed by affairs of importance to pay much attention to anything so perfectly insignificant as the mind of his daughter. Her *person* he had predetermined should be entirely at his disposal, and therefore contemplated with delight the uncommon beauty which already distinguished it; not with the fond partiality of parental love, but with the heartless satisfaction of a crafty politician.

The mind of Lady Juliana was consequently the sport of every passion that by turns assailed it. Now swayed by ambition, and now softened by love, the struggle was violent, but it was short. A few days before the one which was to seal her fate she granted an interview to her lover, who, young, thoughtless, and enamoured as herself, easily succeeded in persuading her to elope with him to Scotland. There, at the altar of Vulcan, the beautiful daughter of the Earl of Courtland gave her hand to her handsome but penniless lover; and there vowed to immolate every ambitious desire, every sentiment of vanity and high-born pride. Yet a sigh arose as she looked on the filthy hut, sooty priest, and ragged witnesses; and thought of the special license, splendid saloon, and bridal pomp that would have attended her union with the Duke. But the rapturous expressions which burst from the impassioned Douglas made her forget the gaudy pleasures of pomp and fashion. Amid the sylvan scenes of the neighbouring lakes the lovers sought a shelter; and, mutually charmed with each other, time flew for a while on downy pinions.

At the end of two months, however, the enamoured husband began to suspect that the lips of his "angel Julia" could utter very silly things; while the fond bride, on her part, discovered that though her "adored Henry's" figure was symmetry itself, yet it certainly was deficient in a certain air—a *je ne sais quoi*—that marks the man of fashion.

"How I wish I had my pretty Cupid here," said her Ladyship, with a sigh, one day as she lolled on a sofa: "he had so many pretty tricks, he would have helped to amuse us, and make the time pass; for really this place grows very stupid and tiresome; don't you think so, love?"

"Most confoundedly so, my darling," replied her husband, yawning sympathetically as he spoke.

"Then suppose I make one more attempt to soften papa, and be received into favour again?"

"With all my heart."

"Shall I say I'm very sorry for what I have done?" asked her Ladyship, with a sigh. "You know I did not say that in my first letter."

"Ay, do; and, if it will serve any purpose, you may say that I am no less so."

In a few days the letter was returned, in a blank cover; and, by the same post, Douglas saw himself superseded in the Gazette, being absent without leave!

There now remained but one course to pursue; and that was to seek refuge at his father's, in the Highlands of Scotland. At the first mention of it Lady Juliana was transported with joy, and begged that a letter might be instantly despatched, containing the offer of a visit: she had heard the Duchess of M. declare nothing could be so delightful as the style of living in Scotland: the people were so frank and gay, and the manners so easy and engaging — oh! it was delightful! And then Lady Jane G. and Lady Mary L., and a thousand other lords and ladies she knew, were all so charmed with the country, and all so sorry to leave it. Then dear Henry's family must be so charming: an old castle, too, was her delight; she would feel quite at home while wandering through its long galleries; and she quite loved old pictures, and armour, and tapestry; and then her thoughts reverted to her father's magnificent mansion in D— —shire.

At length an answer arrived, containing a cordial invitation from the old Laird to spend the winter with them at Glenfern Castle.

All impatience to quit the scenes of their short lived felicity, they bade a hasty adieu to the now fading beauties of Windermere; and, full of hope and expectation, eagerly turned towards the bleak hills of Scotland. They stopped for a short time at Edinburgh, to provide themselves with a carriage, and some other necessaries. There, too, she fortunately met with an English Abigail and footman, who, for double wages, were prevailed upon to attend her to the Highlands; which, with the addition of two dogs, a tame squirrel, and mackaw, completed the establishment.

CHAPTER II.

"What transport to retrace our early plays,
Our easy bliss, when each thing joy supplied;
The woods, the mountains, and the warbling maze
Of the wild brooks."

Thomson

MANY were the dreary muirs and rugged mountains her Ladyship had to encounter in her progress to Glenfern Castle; and, but for the hope of the new world that awaited her beyond those formidable barriers, her delicate frame and still more sensitive feelings must have sunk beneath the horrors of such a journey. But she remembered the Duchess had said the inns and roads were execrable; and the face of the country, as well as the lower orders of people, frightful; but what signified those things? There were balls, and sailing parties, and rowing matches, and shooting parties, and fishing parties, and parties of every description; and the certainty of being recompensed by the festivities of Glenfern Castle, reconciled her to the ruggedness of the approach.

Douglas had left his paternal home and native hills when only eight years of age. A rich relation of his mother's happening to visit them at that time, took a fancy to the boy; and, under promise of making him his heir, had prevailed on his parents to part with him. At a proper age he was placed in the Guards, and had continued to maintain himself in the favor of his benefactor until his imprudent marriage, which had irritated this old bachelor so much that he instantly disinherited him, and refused to listen to any terms of reconciliation. The impressions which the scenes of his infancy had left upon the mind of the young Scotsman, it may easily be supposed, were of a pleasing description. He expatiated to his Juliana on the wild but august scenery that surrounded his father's castle, and associated with the idea the boyish exploits, which though faintly remembered, still served to endear them to his heart. He spoke of the time when he used to make one of a numerous party on the lake, and, when tired of sailing on its glassy surface to the sound of soft music, they would land at some lovely spot; and, after partaking of their banquet beneath a spreading tree, conclude the day by a dance on the grass.

Lady Juliana would exclaim, "How delightful! I doat upon picnics and dancing! — apropos, Henry, there will surely be a ball to welcome our arrival?"

The conversation was interrupted; for just at that moment they had gained the summit of a very high hill, and the post-boy, stopping to give his horses breath, turned round to the carriage, pointing at the same time, with a significant gesture, to a tall thin gray house, something resembling a tower, that stood in the vale beneath. A small sullen-looking lake was in front, on whose banks grew neither tree nor shrub. Behind rose a chain of rugged cloud-capped hills, on the declivities of which were some faint attempts at young plantations; and the only level ground consisted of a few dingy turnip fields, enclosed with stone walls, or dykes, as the post-boy called them. It was now November; the day was raw and cold; and a thick drizzling rain was beginning to fall. A dreary stillness reigned all around, broken only at intervals by the screams of the sea-fowl that hovered over the lake, on whose dark and troubled waters was dimly descried a little boat, plied by one solitary being.

"What a scene!" at length Lady Juliana exclaimed, shuddering as she spoke. "Good God, what a scene! How I pity the unhappy wretches who are doomed to dwell in such a place! and yonder hideous grim house — it makes me sick to look at it. For Heaven's sake, bid him drive on." Another significant look from the driver made the colour mount to Douglas's cheek, as he stammered out, "Surely it can't be; yet somehow I don't know. Pray, my lad," letting down one of the glasses, and addressing the post-boy, "what is the name of that house?"

"Hoose!" repeated the driver; "ca' ye thon a hoose? Thon's gude Glenfern Castle."

Lady Juliana, not understanding a word he said, sat silently wondering at her husband's curiosity respecting such a wretched-looking place.

"Impossible! you must be mistaken, my lad: why, what's become of all the fine wood that used to surround it?"

"Gin you mean a wheen auld firs, there's some of them to the fore yet," pointing to two or three tall, bare, scathed Scotch firs, that scarcely bent their stubborn heads to the wind, that now began to howl around them.

"I insist upon it that you are mistaken; you must have wandered from the right road," cried the now alarmed Douglas in a loud voice, which vainly attempted to conceal his agitation.

"We'll shune see that," replied the phlegmatic Scot, who, having rested his horses and affixed a drag to the wheel, was about to proceed, when Lady Juliana, who now began to have some vague suspicion of the truth, called to him to stop, and, almost breathless with alarm, inquired of her husband the meaning of what had passed.

He tried to force a smile, as he said, "It seems our journey is nearly ended; that fellow persists in asserting that that is Glenfern, though I can scarcely think it. If it is, it is strangely altered since I left it twelve years ago."

For a moment Lady Juliana was too much alarmed to make a reply; pale and speechless, she sank back in the carriage; but the motion of it, as it began to proceed, roused her to a sense of her situation, and she burst into tears and exclamations.

The driver, who attributed it all to fears at descending the hill, assured her she need na be the least feared, for there were na twa cannier beasts atween that and Johnny Groat's hoose; and that they wad ha'e her at the castle door in a crack, gin they were ance down the brae."

Douglas's attempts to soothe his high-born bride were not more successful than those of the driver: in vain he made use of every endearing epithet and tender expression, and recalled the time when she used to declare that she could dwell with him in a desert; her only replies were bitter reproaches and upbraidings for his treachery and deceit, mingled with floods of tears, and interrupted by hysterical sobs. Provoked at her folly, yet softened by her extreme distress, Douglas was in the utmost state of perplexity—now ready to give way to a paroxysm of rage; then yielding to the natural goodness of his heart, he sought to soothe her into composure; and, at length, with much difficulty succeeded in changing her passionate indignation into silent dejection.

That no fresh objects of horror or disgust might appear to disturb this calm, the blinds were pulled down, and in this state they reached Glenfern Castle. But there the friendly veil was necessarily with drawn, and the first object that presented itself to the highbred Englishwoman was an old man clad in a short tartan coat and striped woollen night-cap, with blear eyes and shaking hands, who vainly strove to open the carriage door.

Douglas soon extricated himself, and assisted his lady to alight; then accosting the venerable domestic as "Old Donald," asked him if he recollected him.

"Weel that, weel that, Maister Hairy, and ye're welcome hame; and ye tu, bonny sir" [1] (addressing Lady Juliana, who was calling to her footman to follow her with the mackaw); then, tottering before them, he led the way, while her Ladyship followed, leaning on her husband, her squirrel on her other arm, preceded by her dogs, barking with all their might, and attended by the mackaw, screaming with all his strength; and in this state was the Lady Juliana ushered into the drawing-room of Glenfern Castle!

1   The Highlanders use this term of respect indifferently to both sexes.

Joanna Baillie (1762-1851)

Sonnet, On Leaving Greece, 1820

HELLAS! farewell! — with anxious gaze I view,
 Lovely in tears, and injur'd as thou art,
Thy summits melting in the distant blue,
 Fade from my eyes, but linger in my heart.
Submissive, silent victim! dost thou feel
 The chains which gall thee? or has lengthen'd grief
Numb'd hate and shame alike with hope and zeal,
 And brought insensibility's relief?
Awake! adjur'd by ev'ry chief and sage
 Thou once could'st boast in many a meaner cause,
And let the tame submission of an age,
 Like Nature's hush'd and scarcely rustling pause,
Ere winds burst forth, foretell the approaching storm,
When thou shalt grasp the spear, and raise thy prostrate form.

Walter Scott (1771-1832)

Thomas The Rhymer (1802)

IN THREE PARTS.

Few personages are so renowned in tradition as THOMAS of Erceldoune, known by the appellation of *The Rhymer*. Uniting, or supposed to unite, in his person, the powers of poetical composition, and of vaticination, his memory, even after the lapse of five hundred years, is regarded with veneration by his countrymen. To give any thing like a certain history of this remarkable man, would be indeed difficult; but the curious may derive some satisfaction from the particulars here brought together.

It is agreed, on all hands, that the residence, and probably the birth place, of this ancient bard, was Erceldoune, a village situated upon the Leader, two miles above its junction with the Tweed. The ruins of an ancient tower are still pointed out as the Rhymer's castle. The uniform tradition bears, that his sirname was *Lermont*, or *Learmont*; and that the appellation of *The Rhymer* was conferred on him in consequence of his poetical compositions. There remains, nevertheless, some doubt upon this subject. In a charter, which is subjoined at length[1], the son of our poet designs himself "THOMAS of Erceldoun, son and heir of THOMAS RYMOUR of Erceldoun," which seems to imply, that the father did not bear the hereditary name of LEARMONT; or, at least, was better known and distinguished by the epithet which he had acquired by his personal accomplishments. I must however remark, that, down to a very late period, the practice of distinguishing the parties, even in formal writings, by the epithets which had been bestowed on them from personal circumstances, instead of the proper sirnames of their families, was common, and indeed necessary, among the border clans. So early as the end of the thirteenth century, when sirnames were hardly introduced in Scotland, this custom must have been universal. There is, therefore, nothing inconsistent in supposing our poet's name to have been actually *Learmont*, although, in this charter, he is distinguished by the popular appellation of *The Rhymer*.

We are better able to ascertain the period at which THOMAS of Erceldoune lived; being the latter end of the thirteenth century. I am inclined to place his death a little farther back than Mr PINKERTON, who supposes that he was alive in 1300 (*List of Scotish Poets*); which is hardly, I think, consistent with the charter already quoted, by which his son, in 1299, for himself and his heirs, conveys to the convent of the Trinity of Soltre, the tenement which he possessed by inheritance (*hereditavie*) in Ercildoun, with all claim which he, or his predecessors, could pretend thereto. From this we may infer that the Rhymer was now dead; since we find his son disposing of the family property. Still, however, the argument of the learned historian will remain unimpeached, as to the time of the poet's birth. For if, as we learn from BARBOUR, his prophecies were held in reputation[2] as early as 1306, when B*ruce* slew the *Red Cummin*, the sanctity, and (let me add to Mr PINKERTON'S words) the uncertainty, of antiquity, must have already involved his character and

47

writings. In a charter of Peter de Haga de Bemersyde, which unfortunately wants a date, the Rhymer, a near neighbour, and, if we may trust tradition, a friend of the family, appears as a witness. *Cartulary of Melrose.*

It cannot be doubted, that Thomas of Erceldoune was a remarkable and important person in his own time, since, very shortly after his death, we find him celebrated as a prophet, and as a poet. Whether he himself made any pretensions to the first of these characters, or whether it was gratuitously conferred upon him by the credulity of posterity, it seems difficult to decide. If we may believe Mackenzie, Learmont only versified the prophecies delivered by Eliza, an inspired nun, of a convent at Haddington. But of this there seems not to be the most distant proof. On the contrary, all ancient authors, who quote the Rhymer's prophecies, uniformly suppose them to have been emitted by himself. Thus, in Wintown's *Chronicle,*

> Of this fycht quilum spak Thomas
> Of Ersyldoune, that sayd in Derne,
> Thare suld meit stalwartly, starke, and sterne.
> He sayd it in his prophecy;
> But how he wyst it was ferly.

Book eight, chap. 32.

There could have been no *ferly* (marvel), in Wintown's eyes at least, how Thomas came by his knowledge of future events, had he ever heard of the inspired nun of Haddington; which, it cannot be doubted, would have been a solution of the mystery, much to the taste of the Prior of Lochlevin[3].

Whatever doubts, however, the learned might have, as to the source of the Rhymer's prophetic skill, the vulgar had no hesitation to ascribe the whole to the intercourse between the bard and the Queen of Fairy. The popular tale bears, that Thomas was carried off, at an early age, to the Fairy Land, where he acquired all the knowledge which made him afterwards so famous. After seven years residence he was permitted to return to the earth, to enlighten and astonish his countrymen by his prophetic powers; still, however, remaining bound to return to his royal mistress, when she should intimate her pleasure[4].

Accordingly, while Thomas was making merry with his friends in the tower of Erceldoune, a person came running in, and told, with marks of fear and astonishment, that a hart and hind had left the neighbouring forest, and were, composedly and slowly, parading the street of the village. The prophet instantly arose, left his habitation, and followed the wonderful animals to the forest, whence he was never seen to return. According to the popular belief, he still "drees his weird" in Fairy Land, and is one day expected to revisit earth. In the mean while, his memory is held in the most profound respect. The Eildon Tree, from beneath the shade of which he delivered his prophecies, now no longer exists; but the spot is marked by a large stone, called Eildon Tree Stone. A neighbouring rivulet takes the name of the Bogle Burn, (Goblin Brook) from the Rhymer's supernatural visitants. The veneration, paid to his dwelling place, even attached itself in some degree to a person, who, within the memory of man, chose to set up his residence in the ruins of Learmont's tower. The name of this man was

MURRAY; a kind of herbalist, who, by dint of some knowledge in simples, the possession of a musical clock, an electrical machine, and a stuffed alligator, added to a supposed communication with THOMAS the Rhymer, lived for many years in very good credit as a wizzard.

It seemed to the editor unpardonable to dismiss a person so important in border tradition as the Rhymer, without some farther notice than a simple commentary upon the following ballad. It is given from a copy obtained from a lady, residing not far from Erceldoune, corrected and enlarged by one in Mrs BROWN's MS. — The former copy, however, as might be expected, is far more minute as to local description[5]. To this old tale the editor has ventured to add a second part, consisting of a kind of Cento, from the printed prophecies vulgarly ascribed to the Rhymer; and a third part, entirely modern, founded upon the tradition of his having returned, with the hart and hind, to the Land of Faery. To make his peace with the more severe antiquaries, the editor has prefixed to the second part some remarks on LEARMONT's prophecies.

THOMAS THE RHYMER.
PART FIRST.
ANCIENT — NEVER BEFORE PUBLISHED.

True Thomas lay on Huntlie bank:
    A ferlie he spied wi' his ee;
And there he saw a lady bright,
    Come riding down by the Eildon Tree.

Her shirt was o' the grass green silk,
    Her mantle o' the velvet fyne;
At ilka tett of her horse's mane,
    Hang fifty siller bells and nine.

True Thomas, he pull'd aff his cap,
    And louted low down to his knee—
— "All hail, thou mighty Queen of Heav'n!
    For thy peer on earth I never did see." —

— "O no, O no, Thomas," she said;
    "That name does not belang to me;
I am but the Queen of fair Elfland,
    That am hither come to visit thee.

"Harp and carp, Thomas," she said;
    "Harp and carp along wi' me:
And if ye dare to kiss my lips,
    Sure of your bodie I will be." —

— "Betide me weal, betide me woe,
That weird [6] shall never danton me." —

Syne he has kissed her rosy lips,
    All underneath the Eildon Tree.

— "Now, ye maun go wi' me," she said;
    "True Thomas, ye maun go wi' me:
And ye maun serve me seven years,
    Thro' weal or woe as may chance to be." —

She mounted on her milk-white steed;
    She's ta'en true Thomas up behind;
And aye, whene'er her bridle rung,
    The steed flew swifter than the wind.

O they rade on, and further on;
    The steed gaed swifter than the wind;
Untill they reached a desert wide,
    And living land was left behind.

— "Light down, light down, now, true Thomas,
    And lean your head upon my knee:
Abide and rest a little space,
    And I will shew you ferlies three.

"O see ye not yon narrow road,
    So thick beset wi' thorns and briers?
That is the path of righteousness,
    Tho' after it but few enquires.

"And see not ye that braid braid road,
    That lies across that lily leven?
That is the path of wickedness,
    Tho' some call it the road to heaven.

"And see not ye that bonny road,
    That winds about the fernie brae?
That is the road to fair Elfland,
    Where thou and I this night maun gae.

"But, Thomas, ye maun hold your tongue,
    Whatever ye may hear or see;
For, if you speak word in Elflyn land,
    Ye'll ne'er get back to your ain countrie." —

O they rade on, and farther on,
    And they waded thro' rivers aboon the knee;
And they saw neither sun nor moon,
    But they heard the roaring of the sea.

It was mirk mirk night, and there was nae stern light,
  And they waded thro' red blude to the knee;
For a' the blude that's shed on earth,
  Rins thro' the springs o' that countrie.

Syne they came on to a garden green,
  And she pu'd an apple frae a tree [7] —
— "Take this for thy wages, true Thomas;
  It will give the tongue that can never lie." —

— "My tongue is mine ain," true Thomas said;
  "A gudely gift ye wad gie to me!
I neither dought to buy nor sell,
  At fair or tryst where I may be.

"I dought neither speak to prince or peer,
  Nor ask of grace from fair ladye." —
— "Now hold thy peace!" the lady said,
  "For, as I say, so must it be." —

He has gotten a cloth of the even cloth,
  And a pair of shoes of velvet green;
And, till seven years were gane and past,
  True Thomas on earth was never seen.

---

1 From the Chartulary of the Trinity House of Soltra, Advocates' Library, W.4.14
    ERSYLTON.
Omnibus has literas visuris vel audituris Thomas de Ercildoun filius et heres Thomæ Rymour de Ercihloun salutem in Domino. Noveritis me per fustem et baculum in pleno judicio resignasse ac per presentes quietem clamasse pro me et heredibus meis Magistro domus Sanetæ Trinitatis de Soltre et fiatribus ejusdem domus totam terram meam cum omnibus pertinentibus suis quam in tenemento de Ercildoun hereditarie tenui renunciando de toto pro me et heredibus meis omni jure et clameo que ego seu antecessores mei in eadem terra alioque tempore de perpetuo habuimus sive de futuro habere possumus. In cujus rei testimonio presentibus his sigillum meum apposui data apud Ercildoun die Martis proximo post festum Sanctorum Apostolorum Symonis et Jude Anno Domini Millessimo cc. Nonagesimo Nono.
2 The lines alluded to are these:
I hope that Tomas's prophesie,
Of Erceldoun, shall truly be,
In him, &c.
3 HENRY, the minstrel, who introduces THOMAS into the history of WALLACE, expresses the same doubt as to the source of his prophetic knowledge.
  Thomas Rhymer into the Faile was than
  With the minister, which was a worthy man.
  He used oft to that religious place;

> The people deemed of wit he meikle can,
> And so he told, though that they bless or ban,
> Which happened sooth in many divers case;
> I cannot say by wrong or righteousness.
> In rule of war whether they tint or wan:
> It may be deemed by division of grace, &c.
>
> *History of Wallace, Book second.*

4   See the dissertation on fairies, prefixed to Tamlane.
5   The editor has been since informed by a most eminent antiquary, that there is in existence a MS. copy of this ballad of very considerable antiquity, of which he hopes to avail himself on some future occasion.
6   That weird, &c. — That destiny shall never frighten me
7   She pu'd an apple frae a tree. — The traditional commentary upon this ballad informs us, that the apple was the produce of the fatal Tree of Knowledge, and that the garden was the terrestrial paradise. The repugnance of THOMAS to be debarred the use of falsehood, when he should find it convenient, has a comic effect.

THOMAS THE RHYMER.
PART SECOND.
NEVER BEFORE PUBLISHED — ALTERED FROM ANCIENT PROPHECIES.

The prophecies ascribed to THOMAS of Erceldoune have been the principal means of securing to him remembrance "amongst the sons of his people." The author of Sir TRISTREM would long ago have joined, in the vale of oblivion, "CLERK of Tranent, who wrote the adventures of SCHIR GAWAINE," if, by good hap, the same current of ideas respecting antiquity, which causes VIRGIL to be regarded as a magician by the Lazaroni of Naples, had not exalted the bard of Erceldoune to the prophetic character. Perhaps, indeed, he himself affected it during his life. We know at least for certain, that a belief in his supernatural knowledge was current soon after his death. His prophecies are alluded to by BARBOUR, by WINTOUN, and by HENRY, the minstrel; or *Blind Harry*, as he is usually termed. None of these authors, however, give the words of any of the Rhymer's vaticinations, but merely narrate historically his having predicted the events of which they speak. The earliest of the prophecies ascribed to him, which is now extant, is quoted by Mr PINKERTON from a MS. It is supposed to be a response from THOMAS of Erceldoune, to a question from the heroic Countess of MARCH, renowned for the defence of the castle of Dunbar against the English, and termed, in the familiar dialect of her time, *Black Agnes* of Dunbar. This prophecy is remarkable, in so far as it bears very little resemblance to any verses published in the printed copy of the Rhymer's supposed prophecies. The verses are as follows:

> "*La Countesse de Donbar demande a Thomas de Essedoune quant la guerre d'Escoce prendreit fyn. E yl l'a repoundy et dyt.*

"When man is mad a kyng of a capped man;
When man is levere other mones thyng than is owen;
When londe thouys forest, ant forest is felde;
When hares kendles o' the herston;
When Wyt and Wille werres togedere;
When mon makes stables of kyrkes; and steles castles with styes;
When Rokesboroughe nys no burgh ant market is at Forwyleye;
When Bambourne is donged with dede men;
When men ledes men in ropes to buyen and to sellen;
When a quarter of whaty whete is chaunged for a colt of ten markes;
When prude (pride) prikes and pees is leyd in prisoun;
When a Scot ne may hym hude ase hare in forme that the English ne shall him fynde;
When rycht ant wronge astente the togedere;
When laddes weddeth lovedies;
When Scottes flen so faste, that for faute of shep, hy drowneth hemselve;
When shal this be?
Nouther in thine tyme ne in mine;
Ah comen ant gone
Withinne twenty winter ant one."

PINKERTON'S Poems, from MAITLAND'S MS. quoting from Harl. Lib. 2253, F. 127.

As I have never seen the MS. from which Mr PINKERTON makes this extract, and as the date of it is fixed by him (certainly one of the most able antiquaries of our age), to the reign of EDWARD I. or II. it is with great diffidence that I hazard a contrary opinion. There can, however, I believe, be little doubt that these prophetic verses are a forgery, and not the production of our THOMAS the Rhymer. But I am inclined to believe them of a later date than the reign of EDWARD I. or II.

The gallant defence of the castle of Dunbar, by Black AGNES, took place in the year 1337. The Rhymer died previous to the year 1299 (see the charter by his son in the introduction to the foregoing ballad). It seems, therefore, very improbable, that the Countess of DUNBAR could ever have an opportunity of consulting THOMAS the Rhymer, since that would infer that she was married, or at least engaged in state matters, previous to 1299; whereas she is described as a young, or a middle aged, woman, at the period of her being besieged in the fortress which she so well defended. If the editor might indulge a conjecture, he would suppose, that the prophecy was contrived for the encouragement of the English invaders, during the Scotish wars; and that the names of the Countess of DUNBAR, and of THOMAS of Erceldoun, were used for the greater credit of the forgery. According to this hypothesis, it seems likely to have been composed after the siege of Dunbar, which had made the name of the Countess well known, and consequently in the reign of EDWARD III. The whole tendency of the prophecy is to aver, that there shall be no end of the Scotish war (concerning which the question was proposed) till a final conquest of the country by England, attended by all the usual severities of war. When the cultivated country shall become forest — says the prophecy; — when the wild animals shall inhabit the abode of men; — when Scots shall not be able to escape the English, should they crouch as hares in their form — all these denunciations seem to refer to the time of EDWARD III. upon whose victories the prediction was probably founded. The mention of the exchange betwixt a colt worth ten markes, and a quarter of "whaty (indifferent) wheat," seems to allude to the dreadful famine about the year 1388. The independence of Scotland was, however, as impregnable to the mines of superstition, as to the steel of our more powerful and more wealthy neighbours. The war of Scotland is, thank God, at an end; but it is ended without her people having either crouched, like hares, in their form, or being drowned in their flight, for "faute of ships" — thank God for that too. — A minute search of the records of the time would, probably, throw additional light upon the allusions contained in this ancient legend. Among various rhymes of prophetic import, which are at this day current amongst the people of Teviotdale, is one, supposed to be pronounced by THOMAS the Rhymer, presaging the destruction of his habitation and family:

> The hare sail kittle (litter) on my hearth stane,
> And there will never be a laird Learmont again.

The first of these lines is obviously borrowed from that in the MS. of the Harl. Library. "When hares kendles o' the her'stane" — an emphatic image of desolation. — It is also inaccurately quoted in the prophecy of WALDHAVE, published by ANDRO HART, 1613.

> "This is a true talking that Thomas of tells
> The hare shall hirple on the hard (hearth) stanes"

SPOTTISWOODE, an honest, but credulous historian, seems to have been a firm believer in the authenticity of the prophetic wares, vended in the name of THOMAS of Erceldoune. "The prophecies, yet extant in Scottish rhymes, whereupon he was commonly called *Thomas the Rhymer*, may justly be admired; having foretold, so many ages before, the Union of England and Scotland in the ninth degree of the BRUCE'S blood, with the succession of BRUCE himself to the crown, being yet a child, and other divers particulars which the event hath ratified and made good. BOETHIUS, in his story, relateth his prediction of King ALEXANDER'S death, and that he did foretell the same to the Earl of MARCH, the day before it fell out; saying, 'That before the next day at noon, such a tempest should blow, as Scotland had not felt for many years before.' The next morning, the day being clear, and no change appearing in the air, the nobleman did challenge THOMAS of his saying, calling him an impostor. He replied, that noon was not yet passed. About which time, a post came to advertise the Earl, of the King his sudden death. ' — Then, said THOMAS, this is the tempest I foretold; and so it shall prove to Scotland.' — Whence or how he had this knowledge, can hardly be affirmed; but sure it is that he did divine and answer truly of many things to come." — *Spottiswoode, p. 47.* Besides that notable voucher, Master HECTOR BOECE, the good archbishop might, had he been so minded, have referred to FORDUN for the prophecy of King ALEXANDER'S death. That historian calls our bard, "ruralis ille vates" FORDUN, lib. 10, c. 40.

What SPOTTISWOODE calls "the prophecies extant in Scottish rhyme," are the metrical predictions ascribed to the prophet of Erceldoune, which, with many other compositions of the same nature, bearing the names of BEDE, MERLIN, GILDAS, and other approved soothsayers, are contained in one small volume, published by ANDRO HART, at Edinburgh, 1615. The late excellent Lord HAILES made these compositions the subject of a dissertation, published in his *Remarks on the History of Scotland*. His attention is chiefly directed to the celebrated prophecy of our bard, mentioned by bishop SPOTTISWOODE, bearing, that the crowns of England and Scotland should be united in the person of a King, son of a French Queen, and related to BRUCE in the ninth degree. Lord HAILES plainly proves, that this prophecy is perverted from its original purpose, in order to apply it to the succession of James VI. The ground work of the forgery is to be found in the prophecies of BERLINGTON, contained in the same collection, and runs thus:

> Of Bruce's left side shall spring out a leafe,
> As near as the ninth degree;
> And shall be fleemit of fair Scotland,
> In France far beyond the sea.
> And then shall come again riding,
> With eyes that many men may see;
> At Aberlady he shall light,
> With hempen heltres and horse of tree.
>
> However it happen for to fall,
> The lion shal be lord of all;
> The French wife shall bear the son,
> Shall wield all Britain to the sea;
> And from the Bruce's blood shall come,
> As near as the ninth degree. —
>
> Yet shall there come a kene knight over the salt sea,
> A kene man of courage and bold man of arms;
> A duke's son doubled (*i.e.* dubbed) a born man in France,
> That shall our mirths amend, and mend all our harms,
> After the date of our Lord 1513, and thrice three thereafter;
> Which shall brook all the broad isle to himself,
> Between 13 and thrice three the threap sail be ended,
> The Saxons sall never recover thereafter.

There cannot be any doubt that this prophecy was intended to excite the confidence of the Scottish nation in the Duke of ALBANY, regent of Scotland, who arrived from France in 1515, two years after the death of JAMES IV. in the fatal battle of Flodden. The regent was descended of BRUCE by the left, *i.e.* by the female side, within the ninth degree. His mother was daughter of the Earl of BOULOGNE, his father banished from his country — "fleemit of fair Scotland." — His arrival must necessarily be by sea, and his landing was expected at Aberlady, in the Firth of Forth. He was a Duke's son, dubbed Knight; and nine years, from 1513, are allowed him by the pretended prophet, for the accomplishment of the salvation of his country, and the exaltation of Scotland over her sister and rival. All this was a pious fraud, to excite the confidence and spirit of the country.

The prophecy, put in the name of our THOMAS the Rhymer, as it stands in HART's book, refers to a later period. The narrator meets the Rhymer upon a land, beside a lee, who shews him many emblematical visions, described in no mean strain of poetry. They chiefly relate to the fields of Flodden and Pinkie, to the national distress which followed these defeats, and to future halcyon days which are promised to Scotland. One quotation or two will be sufficient to establish this fully.

> Our Scotish king sal come fill keen,
> The red lion beareth he;
> A fedder'd arrow sharp, I ween,
> Shall make him wink and warre to see.
> Out of the field he shall be led,
> When he is bloody and wo for blood;
> Yet to his men then shall he say,
> "For God's love, turn you again,
> And give yon southern folk a fray!
> Why should I lose? the right is mine:
> My date is not to die this day." —

Who can doubt for a moment that this refers to the battle of Flodden, and to the popular reports concerning the doubtful fate of JAMES IV. Allusion is immediately afterwards made to the death of GEORGE DOUGLAS, heir apparent of Angus, who fought and fell with his sovereign.

> The sternes three that day shall die
> That bears the harte in silver sheen.

The well known arms of the DOUGLAS family are the heart and three stars. In another place the battle of Pinkie is expressly mentioned by name:

> At Pinken Cleuch there shall be spilt,
> Much gentle blood that day;
> There shall the bear lose the gylte,
> And the eagle bear it away.

To the end of all this allegorical and mystical rhapsody, is interpolated, in the later edition by ANDRO HART, a new edition of BERLINGTON's verses before quoted, altered and manufactured so as to bear reference to the accession of JAMES VI. which had just then taken place. The insertion is made, with a peculiar degree of awkwardness, betwixt a question put by the narrator, concerning the name and abode of the person who shewed him these strange matters, and the answer of the prophet to that question.

> "Then to the Beirn I could say,
> Where dwellest thou, in what country?
> [Or who shall rule the isle Britain,

> From the north to the south sea?
> The French wife shall bear the son,
> Shall rule all Britain to the sea;
> Which of the Bruce's blood shall come,
> As near as the ninth degree:
> I framed fast what was his name,
> Whence that he came in what country.]
> At Erslington I dwell at hame,
> Thomas Rymer men call me."

There is surely no one who will not conclude, with Lord HAILES, that the eight lines, inclosed in brackets, are a clumsy interpolation, borrowed from BERLINGTON, with such alterations as might render the supposed prophecy applicable to the union of the crowns.

While we are on this subject, it may be proper briefly to notice the scope of some of the other predictions, in HART's collection. As the prophecy of BERLINGTON was intended to raise the spirits of the nation, during the regency of ALBANY, so those of SYBILLA and ELTRAINE refer to that of the Earl of ARRAN, afterwards Duke of CHATELHERAULT, during the minority of MARY, a period of similar calamity. This is obvious from the following verses:

> Take a thousand in calculation,
> And the longest of the lyon,
> With Saint Andrew's crosse thrice,
> Then threescore and thrice three:
> Take heid to Merling truly,
> Then shall the wars ended be,
> And never again rise.
> In that year there shall be a king,
> A duke, and no crowned king;
> Because the prince shall be young,
> And tender of years. —

The date, above hinted at, seems to be 1549, when the Scotish regent, by means of some succours derived from France, was endeavouring to repair the consequences of the fatal battle of Pinkie. Allusion is made to the supply given to the "Moldwarte (England) by the fained harte," (the Earl of ANGUS). The regent is described by his bearing the antelope; large supplies are promised from France, and compleat conquest predicted to Scotland and her allies. Thus was the same hackneyed stratagem repeated, whenever the interest of the rulers appeared to stand in need of it. The regent was not, indeed, till after this period, created Duke of CHATELHERAULT; but that honour was the object of his hopes and expectations.

The name of our renowned soothsayer is liberally used as an authority, throughout all the prophecies published by ANDRO HART. Besides those expressly put in his name, GILDAS, another assumed personage, is supposed to derive his knowledge from him; for he concludes thus:

> "True Thomas told me in a troublesome time
> In a harvest morning at Eldom (Eildon) hills."
>
> *The Prophecy of Gildas.*

In the prophecy of BERLINGTON, already quoted, we are told

> "Marvellous Merling, that many men of tells,
> And Thomas's sayings comes all at once."

While I am upon the subject of these prophecies, may I be permitted to call the attention of antiquaries to MERDYWYNN WYLLT, or *Merlin the Wild*, in whose name, and by no means in that of AMBROSE MERLIN, the friend of ARTHUR, the Scotish prophecies are issued. That this personage resided at Drummelziar, and roamed, like a second NEBUCHADNEZZAR, the woods of Tweeddale, in remorse for the death of his nephew, we learn from FORDUN. In the *Scotichronicon*, Lib. 3, cap. 31, is an account of an interview betwixt ST KENTIGERN and MERLIN, then in this distracted and miserable state. He is said to have been called *Lailoken* from his mode of life. On being commanded by the Saint to give an account of himself, he says, that the penance which he performs was imposed on him by a voice from heaven, during a bloody contest betwixt Lidel and Carwanolow, of which battle he had been the cause. According to his own prediction, he perished at once by wood, earth, and water; for, being pursued with stones by the rustics, he fell from a rock into the river Tweed, and was transfixed by a sharp stake, fixed there for the purpose of extending a fishing net.

> Sude perfossus, lapide percussus et unda
> Haec tria Merlinum fertur inire necem.

FORDUN, contrary to the Welch authorities, confounds this person with the MERLIN of ARTHUR; but concludes by informing us, that many believed him to be a different person. The grave of MERLIN is pointed out at Drummelzear, in Tweeddale, beneath an aged thorn tree. On the east side of the church-yard, the brook called Pausayl falls into the Tweed; and the following prophecy is said to have been current concerning their union:

> When Tweed and Pausayl join at Merlin's grave,
> Scotland and England shall one Monarch have.

On the day of the coronation of James VI. the Tweed accordingly overflowed, and joined the Pausayl at the prophet's grave. — PENNYCUIK'S *History of Tweeddale*, p. 26. These circumstances would seem to infer a communication betwixt the south-west of Scotland and Wales, of a nature peculiarly intimate; for I presume that MERLIN would retain sense enough to chuse for the scene of his wanderings, a country having a language and manners similar to his own.

Be this as it may, the memory of MERLIN SYLVESTER, or the Wild, was fresh among the Scots during the reign of James V. WALDHAVE[1], under whose name a set of prophecies was published, describes himself as lying upon Lomond Law; he hears a voice which bids him stand to his defence; he looks around, and beholds a flock of hares and foxes pursued over the mountain by a savage figure, to whom he can hardly give the name of man. At the sight of WALDHAVE, the apparition leaves the objects of his pursuit, and assaults him with a club.

WALDHAVE defends himself with his sword, throws the savage to the earth, and refuses to let him arise till he swear by the law and land he lives upon, "to do him no harm." This done, he permits him to arise, and marvels at his strange appearance.

> "He was formed like a freek (man) all his four quarters;
> And then his chin and his face haired so thick.
> With growing so grim hair, fearful to see."

He answers briefly to WALDHAVE's enquiry, concerning his name and nature, that he "drees his weird," i.e. does penance, in that wood; and, having hinted that questions as to his own state are offensive, he pours forth an obscure rhapsody, concerning futurity, and concludes,

> "Go musing upon Merling if thou wilt;
> For I mean no more man at this time." —

This is exactly similar to the meeting betwixt MERLIN and KENTIGERN in FORDUN. These prophecies of MERLIN seem to have been in request in the minority of James V.; for, among the amusements with which Sir DAVID LINDSAY diverted that prince during his infancy, are

> The prophecies of Rymer, Bede, and Merlin.
> *Sir D. LINDSAY's Epistle to the King.*

And we find, in WALDHAVE, at least one allusion to the very ancient prophecy addressed to the Countess of DUNBAR:

> This is a true token that Thomas of tells,
> When a ladde with a ladye shall go over the fields.

The original stands thus:

> When laddes weddeth lovedies.

Another prophecy of MERLIN, reported by WALDHAVE, seems to have been current about the time of the regent MORTON's execution. When that nobleman was committed to the charge of his accuser, Captain JAMES STEWART, newly created Earl of ARRAN, to be conducted to his trial at Edinburgh, SPOTTISWOODE says that he asked "Who was Earl of ARRAN?" and "being answered that Captain JAMES was the man; after a short pause, he said, "And is it so? I know then what I may look for!" meaning, as was thought, that the old prophecy of the 'Falling of the heart [2] by the mouth of ARRAN', should then be fulfilled. Whether this was his mind or not, it is not known; but some spared not, at the time when the HAMILTONS were banished, in which business he was held too earnest, to say, that he stood in fear of that prediction, and went that course only to disappoint it. But, if so it was, he did find himself now deluded; for he fell by the mouth of another ARRAN than he imagined." SPOTTISWOODE, 313.

Something like the fatal words alluded to, is to be found in WALDHAVE

"When the mouth of Arran the top hath overturned."

To return from these desultory remarks, into which the editor has been led by the celebrated name of MERLIN, the stile of all these prophecies, published by HART, is very much the same. The measure is alliterative, and somewhat similar to that of PIERCE PLOWMAN'S visions; a circumstance which might entitle us to ascribe to some of them an earlier date than the reign of James V. did we not know that *Sir Galoran of Galloway*, and *Gawaine and Gologras*, two romances rendered almost unintelligible by the extremity of affected alliteration, are not prior to that period. Indeed, although we may allow, that, during much earlier times, prophecies, under the names of those celebrated soothsayers, have been current in Scotland, yet those published by HARTE have obviously been so often vamped and re-vamped, to serve the political purposes of different periods, that it may be shrewdly suspected, that, as in the case of Sir JOHN CUTLER'S transmigrated stockings, very little of the original materials now remains. I cannot refrain from indulging my readers with the publisher's title to the last prophecy; as it contains certain curious information concerning the Queen of Sheba, who is identified with the Cumaean Sybil. "Here followeth a prophecie, pronounced by a noble queen and matron, called SYBILLA, Regina Austri, that came to SOLOMON. Through the which she composed four books at the instance of the said King SOLOMON and others: and the fourth book was directed to a noble king, called BALDWIN, king of the broad isle of Britain. Of the which she maketh mention of two noble princes and emperors, the which is called LIONES. Of these, two shall subdue and overcome all earthly princes to their diadem and crown, and also be glorified and crowned in heaven among saints. The first of these two is CONSTANTINUS MAGNUS; that was LEPROSUS, the son of Saint Helen, that found the crosse. The second is the sixth king of the name of the STEWART of Scotland, the which is our most noble king."

With such editors and commentators, what wonder that the text became unintelligible, even beyond the usual oracular obscurity of prediction?

If there still remain, therefore, among these predictions, any verses having a claim to real antiquity, it seems now impossible to discover them from those which are comparatively modern. Nevertheless, as there are to be found in these compositions some uncommonly wild and masculine expressions, the editor has been induced to throw a few passages together, into the sort of ballad to which this disquisition is prefixed. It would indeed have been no difficult matter for him, by a judicious selection, to have excited, in favour of THOMAS of Erceldoune, a share of the admiration bestowed by sundry wise persons upon Mass ROBERT FLEMING.

For example:

"But then the lilye shal be loused when they least think;
Then clear king's blood shal quake for fear of death;
For Churls shal chop off heads of their chief beirns,
And carfe of the crowns that Christ hath appointed.
— — — — —
Thereafter on every side sorrow shal arise;
The barges of clear barons down shal be sunken;
Seculars shal sit in spiritual seats,
Occupying offices anointed as they were."

Taking the lilye for the emblem of France, can there be a more plain prophecy of the murder of her monarch, the destruction of her nobility, and the desolation of her hierarchy?

But, without looking farther into the signs of the times, the editor, though the least of all the prophets, cannot help thinking, that every true Briton will approve of his application of the last prophecy quoted in the ballad.

HARTE'S collection of prophecies has been frequently re-printed within the century, probably to favour the pretensions of the unfortunate family of STEWART. For the prophetic renown of GILDAS and BEDE, see FORDUN, lib. 3.

Before leaving the subject of Thomas' predictions, it may be noticed, that sundry rhymes, passing for his prophetic effusions, are still current among the vulgar. — Thus, he is said to have prophecied of the very ancient family of HAIG of Bemerside,

Betide, betide, whate'er betide,
Haig shall be Haig of Bemerside.

The grandfather of the present proprietor of Bemerside had twelve daughters, before his lady brought him a male heir. The common people trembled for the credit of their favourite soothsayer. The late Mr HAIG was at length born, and their belief in the prophecy confirmed beyond a shadow of doubt.

Another memorable prophecy bore, that the Old Kirk at Kelso, constructed out of the ruins of the abbey, should fall when "at the fullest". At a very crowded sermon, about thirty years ago, a piece of lime fell from the roof of the church. The alarm, for the fulfillment of the words of the seer, became universal; and happy were they who were nearest the door of the predestined edifice. The church was in consequence deserted, and has never since had an opportunity of tumbling upon a full congregation. I hope, for the sake of a beautiful specimen of Saxo-Gothick architecture, that the accomplishment of this prophecy is far distant.

Another prediction, ascribed to the Rhymer, seems to have been founded on that sort of insight into futurity, possessed by most men of a sound and combining judgement. It runs thus:

At Eildon tree if you shall be,
A brigg ower Tweed you there may see.

The spot in question commands an extensive prospect of the course of the river; and it was easy to foresee, that, when the country should become in the least degree improved, a bridge would be somewhere thrown over the stream. In fact, you now see no less than three bridges from that elevated situation.

CORSPATRICK (Comes Patrick) Earl of MARCH, but more commonly taking his title from his castle of Dunbar, acted a noted part during the wars of Edward I. in Scotland. As THOMAS of Erceldoune is said to have delivered to him his famous prophecy of King ALEXANDER's death, the editor has chosen to introduce him into the following ballad. All the prophetic verses are selected from HARTE's publication.

1   I do not know whether the person here meant, be WALDHAVE, an abbot of Melrose, who died in the odour of sanctity, about 1160.
2   The heart was the cognisance of MORTON.

THOMAS THE RHYMER.
PART SECOND.

When seven years were come and gane,
   The sun blinked fair on pool and stream;
And Thomas lay on Huntlie bank,
   Like one awakened from a dream.

He heard the trampling of a steed;
   He saw the flash of armour flee;
And he beheld a gallant knight,
   Come riding down by the Eildon Tree.

He was a stalwart knight, and strong;
   Of giant make he 'peared to be:
He stirr'd his horse, as he were wode,
   Wi' gilded spurs of fashioun free.

Says — "Well met, well met, true Thomas!
   Some uncouth ferlies shew to me." —
Says —" Christ thee save, Corspatrick brave!
   Thrice welcome, good Dunbar, to me.

"Light down, light down, Corspatrick brave,
   And I will shew thee curses three;
Shall gar fair Scotland greet and grane,
   And change the green to the black livery.

"A storm shall roar, this very hour,
   From Rosse's Hills to Solway sea." —
— "Ye lied, ye lied, ye warlock hoar!
   For the sun shines sweet on fauld and lea." —

He put his hand on the Earlie's head;
   He shew'd him a rock, beside the sea,
Where a king lay stiff, beneath his steed [1],
   And steel-dight nobles wiped their ee.

— "The neist curse lights on Branxton hills:
   By Flodden's high and heathery side,
Shall wave a banner, red as blude,
   And chieftains throng wi' meikle pride.

"A Scotish king shall come full keen;
   The ruddy lion beareth he:
A feather'd arrow sharp, I ween,
   Shall make him wink and warre to see.

"When he is bloody, and all to bledde,
   Thus to his men he still shall say —
— "For God's sake, turn ye back again,
   And give yon southern folk a fray!
Why should I lose the right is mine?
   My doom is not to die this day [2]." —

"Yet turn ye to the eastern hand,
   And woe and wonder ye sall see;
How forty thousand spearmen stand,
   Where yon rank river meets the sea.

"There shall the lion lose the gylte,
   And the libbards bear it clean away;
At Pinkyn Cleuch there sall be spilt
   Much gentil blude that day." —

— "Enough, enough, of curse and ban;
   Some blessing shew thou now to me;
Or, by the faith o' my bodie," Corspatrick said,
   "Ye sall rue the day ye e'er saw me!" —

— "The first of blessings I sall thee shew,
   Is by a burn, that's call'd of bread [3];
Where Saxon men shall tine the bow,
   And find their arrows lack the head.

"Beside that brigg, out ower that burn,
   Where the water bickereth bright and sheen,
Shall many a falling courser spurn,
   And knights shall die in battle keen.

"Beside a headless cross of stone,
   The libbards there shall lose the gree;
The raven shall come, the erne shall go,
   And drink the Saxon blude sae free.
The cross of stone they shall not know,
   So thick the corses there shall be." —

 — "But tell me now," said brave Dunbar,
  "True Thomas, tell now unto me,
 What man shall rule the Isle Britain,
  Even from the north to the southern sea?" —

 — "A French Queen shall bear the son,
  Shall rule all Britain to the sea:
 He of the Bruce's blude shall come,
  As near as in the ninth degree.

 "The waters worship shall his race;
  Likewise the waves of the farthest sea;
 For they shall ride ower ocean wide,
  With hempen bridles, and horse of tree." —

1 King ALEXANDER; killed by a fall from his horse near Kinghorn
2 The uncertainty which long prevailed in Scotland concerning the fate of James IV. is well known.
3 One of THOMAS's rhymes, preserved by tradition, runs thus:
"The burn of breid
Sall run fow reid." —
Bannock-burn is the brook here meant. The Scots give the name of bannock to a thick round cake, of unleavened bread.

THOMAS THE RHYMER.
PART THIRD — MODERN.

THOMAS the Rhymer was renowned among his contemporaries, as the author of the celebrated romance of *Sir Tristrem*. Of this once admired poem only one copy is now known to exist, which is in the Advocates' Library. The editor has undertaken the superintendance of a very limited edition of this curious work; which, if it does not revive the reputation of the bard of Erceldoune, will be at least the earliest specimen of Scotish poetry hitherto published. Some account of this romance has already been given to the world in Mr ELLIS' *Specimens of Ancient Poetry*, VOL. I. p.165, 3d. p.410; a work, to which our predecessors and our posterity are alike obliged; the former, for the preservation of the best selected examples of their poetical taste; and the latter, for a history of the English language, which will only cease to be interesting with the existence of our mother tongue, and all that genius and learning have recorded in it. It is sufficient here to mention, that, so great was the reputation of the romance of *Sir Tristrem*, that few were thought capable of reciting it after the manner of the author, a circumstance alluded to by ROBERT DE BRUNNE, the annalist.

  I see in song, in sedgeyng tale,
  Of Erceldoun, and of Kendale.
  Now thame says as they thame wroght,
  And in thare saying it semes noght.

>   That thou may here in Sir Tristrem,
>   Over gestes it has the steme,
>   Over all that is or was;
>   If men it said as made Thomas, &c.

It appears from a very curious MS. of the 13th century, *penes* Mr DOUCE, of London, containing a French metrical romance of *Sir Tristrem*, that the work of our THOMAS the Rhymer was known, and referred to, by the minstrels of Normandy and Bretagne. Having arrived at a part of the romance, where reciters were wont to differ in the mode of telling the story, the French bard expressly cites the authority of the poet of Erceldoune.

>   Plusurs de nos granter ne volent
>   Co que del naim dire se solent
>   Ki femme Kaherdin dut aimer
>   Li naim redut Tristram narrer
>   E entusche par grant engin
>   Quant il afole Kaherdin
>   Pur cest plaie e pur cest mal
>   Enveiad Tristran Guvernal
>   En Engleterre pur Ysolt
>   THOMAS ico granter ne volt
>   Et si volt par raisun mostrer
>   Qu' ico ne put pas esteer, &c.

The tale of Sir Tristrem, as narrated in the Edinburgh MS. is totally different from the voluminous romance in French prose, compiled on the same subject by RUSTICIEN DE PUISE, and analysed by M. DE TRESSAN; but agrees in every essential particular with the metrical performance just quoted, which is a work of much higher antiquity.

The following attempt to commemorate the Rhymer's poetical fame, and the traditional account of his marvellous return to Fairy Land, being entirely modern, would have been placed with greater propriety among the class of modern ballads, had it not been for its immediate connection with the first and second parts of the same story.

THOMAS THE RHYMER.
PART THIRD.

>   When seven years more had come and gone,
>   Was war thro' Scotland spread;
>   And Ruberslaw shew'd high Dunyon, [1]
>   His beacon blazing red.
>
>
>   Then all by bonny Coldingknow, [2]
>   Pitched palliouns took their room;
>   And crested helms, and spears a rowe,
>   Glanced gaily thro' the broom.

The Leader, rolling to the Tweed,
   Resounds the ensenzie [3];
They roused the deer from Caddenhead, [4]
   To distant Torwoodlee.

The feast was spread in Erceldoune,
   In Learmont's high and ancient hall;
And there were knights of great renown,
   And ladies laced in pall.

Nor lacked they, while they sat at dine,
   The music, nor the tale;
Nor goblets of the blood-red wine,
   Nor mantling quaighs [5] of ale.

True Thomas rose, with harp in hand,
   When as the feast was done;
(In minstrel strife, in Fairy Land,
   The elfin harp he won.)

Hush'd were the throng, both limb and tongue,
   And harpers for envy pale;
And armed lords lean'd on their swords,
   And hearken'd to the tale.

In numbers high, the witching tale
   The prophet pour'd along;
No after bard might e'er avail [6]
   Those numbers to prolong.

Yet fragments of the lofty strain
   Float down the tide of years;
As, buoyant on the stormy main,
   A parted wreck appears.

He sung King Arthur's table round:
   The warrior of the lake;
How courteous Gawaine met the wound, [7]
   And bled for ladie's sake.

But chief, in gentle Tristrem's praise,
   The notes melodious swell;
Was none excell'd, in Arthur's days,
   The Knight of Lionelle.

For Marke, his cowardly uncle's right,
   A venom'd wound he bore;
When fierce Morholde he slew in fight,
   Upon the Irish shore.

No art the poison might withstand;
   No medicine could be found,
Till lovely Isolde's lilye hand
   Had probed the rankling wound.

With gentle hand and soothing tongue,
   She bore the leech's part:
And, while she o'er his sick-bed hung,
   He paid her with his heart.

O fatal was the gift, I ween!
   For, doom'd in evil tide,
The maid must be rude Cornwall's Queen,
   His cowardly uncle's bride.

Their loves, their woes, the gifted bard
   In fairy tissue wove;
Where lords, and knights, and ladies bright,
   In gay confusion strove.

The Garde Joyeuese, amid the tale,
   High rear'd its glittering head;
And Avalon's enchanted vale
   In all its wonders spread.

Brangwain was there, and Segramore,
   And fiend-born Merlin's gramarye;
Of that fam'd wizzard's mighty lore,
   O who could sing but he?

Thro' many a maze the winning song
   In changeful passion led,
Till bent at length the listening throng
   O'er Tristrem's dying bed.

His ancient wounds their scars expand;
   With agony his heart is wrung:
O where is Isolde's lilye hand,
   And where her soothing tongue?

She comes! she comes! like flash of flame
   Can lovers' footsteps fly:
She comes! she comes! — she only came
   To see her Tristrem die.

She saw him die: her latest sigh
   Joined in a kiss his parting breath:
The gentlest pair that Britain bare,
   United are in death.

There paused the harp: — its lingering sound
   Died slowly on the ear;
The silent guests still bent around,
   For still they seem'd to hear.

Then woe broke forth in murmurs weak;
   Nor ladies heaved alone the sigh;
But, half ashamed, the rugged cheek
   Did many a gauntlet dry.

On Leader's stream, and Learmont's tower,
   The mists of evening close;
In camp, in castle, or in bower,
   Each warrior sought repose.

Lord Douglas, in his lofty tent,
   Dreamed o'er the woeful tale;
When footsteps light, across the bent,
   The warrior's ears assail.

He starts, he wakes: — "What, Richard, ho!
   Arise, my page, arise!
What venturous wight, at dead of night,
   Dare step where Douglas lies!" —

Then forth they rush'd: by Leader's tide,
   A selcouth [8] sight they see —
A hart and hind pace side by side,
   As white as snow on Fairnalie.

Beneath the moon, with gesture proud,
   They stately move and slow;
Nor scare they at the gathering crowd,
   Who marvel as they go.

To Learmont's tower a message sped,
   As fast as page might run;
And Thomas started from his bed,
   And soon his cloaths did on.

First he woxe pale, and then woxe red;
   Never a word he spake but three:
— "My sand is run; my thread is spun;
   This sign regardeth me." —

The elfin harp his neck around,
   In minstrel guise he hung;
And on the wind, in doleful sound,
   Its dying accents rung.

Then forth he went; yet turned him oft
   To view his ancient hall;
On the grey tower, in lustre soft,
   The autumn moonbeams fall.

And Leader's waves, like silver sheen,
   Danced shimmering in the ray;
In deepening mass, at distance seen,
   Broad Soltra's mountains lay.

— "Farewell, my father's ancient tower!
   A long farewell," said he:
"The scene of pleasure, pomp, or power,
   Thou never more shalt be.

"To Learmont's name no foot of earth
   Shall here again belong;
And, on thy hospitable hearth,
   The hare shall leave her young.

"Adieu! Adieu!" again he cried;
   All as he turned him roun' —
— "Farewell to Leader's silver tide!
   Farewell to Erceldoune!" —

The hart and hind approached the place,
   As lingering yet he stood;
And there, before Lord Douglas' face,
   With them he cross'd the flood.

Lord Douglas leaped on his berry-brown steed,
    And spurr'd him the Leader o'er;
But, tho' he rode with lightning speed,
    He never saw them more.

Some sayd to hill, and some to glen,
    Their wond'rous course had been;
But ne'er in haunts of living men
    Again was Thomas seen.

1 Ruberslaw and Dunyon are two hills above Jedburgh.
2 An ancient tower near Erceldoune, belonging to a family of the name of HOME. One of THOMAS's prophecies is said to have run thus:
    Vengeance! vengeance! when and where?
    On the house of Coldingknow, now and ever mair.
The spot is rendered classical by its having given name to the beautiful melody, called the Broom o' the Cowdenknows.
3 Ensenzie. — War cry, or gathering word.
4 Torwoodlee and Caddenhead are places in Selkirkshire.
5 Quaighs. — Wooden cups composed of staves hooped together.
6 See introduction to this ballad.
7 See, in the Fabliaux of Monsieur LE GRAND, elegantly translated by the late GREGORY WAY, Esq. the tale of the Knight and the Sword.
8 Selcouth. — Wondrous.

The Twa Corbies (1802)

As I was walking all alane,
I heard twa corbies making a mane;
The tane unto the t'other say,
"Where sall we gang and dine to-day?"
"In behint yon auld fail [1] dyke,
"I wot there lies a new slain knight;
"And nae body kens that he lies there,
"But his hawk, his hound, and lady fair.
"His hound is to the hunting gane,
"His hawk to fetch the wild-fowl hame,
"His lady's ta'en another mate,
"So we may mak our dinner sweet.
"Ye'll sit on his white hause bane,
"And I'll pike out his bonny blue een:
"Wi' ae lock o' his gowden hair,
"We'll theek [2] our nest when it grows bare.
"Mony a one for him makes mane,
"But nane sall ken whare he is gane:
"O'er his white banes, when they are bare,
"The wind sall blaw for evermair."

1 Fail — Turf.
2 Theek — Thatch.

This poem was communicated to me by Charles Kirkpatrick Sharpe, Esq. jun. of Hoddom, as written down, from tradition, by a lady. It is a singular circumstance, that it should coincide so very nearly with the ancient dirge, called *The Three Ravens*, published by Mr Ritson, in his *Ancient Songs*; and that, at the same time, there should exist such a difference, as to make the one appear rather a counterpart than copy of the other. In order to enable the curious reader to contrast these two singular poems, and to form a judgment which may be the original, I take the liberty of copying the English ballad from Mr Ritson's Collection, omitting only the burden and repetition of the first line. The learned editor states it to be given "*From Ravencroft's Metismata. Musical phansies, fitting the cittie and country, humours to 3, 4, and 5 voyces*, London, 1611, 4to. It will be obvious (continues Mr Ritson) that this ballad is much older, not only than the date of the book, but most of the other pieces contained in it." The music is given with the words, and is adapted to four voices:

There were three rauens sat on a tre,
They were as blacke as they might be:

The one of them said to his mate,
"Where shall we our breakfast take?"

"Downe in yonder greene field,
"There lies a knight slain under his shield;

"His hounds they lie downe at his feete,
"So well they their master keepe;

"His haukes they flie so eagerly,
"There's no fowle dare come him nie.

"Down there comes a fallow doe,
"As great with yong as she might goe,

"She lift up his bloudy hed,
"And kist his wounds that were so red.

"She got him up upon her backe,
"And carried him to earthen lake.

"She buried him before the prime,
"She was dead her selfe ere euen song time.

"God send euery gentleman,
"Such haukes, such houndes, and such a leman.

Ancient Songs, 1792, p. 155.

I have seen a copy of this dirge much modernized.

THE TWA CORBIES.

As I was walking all alane,
I heard twa corbies making a mane;
The tane unto the t'other say,
"Where sall we gang and dine to-day?"

"In behint yon auld fail [1] dyke,
"I wot there lies a new slain knight;
"And nae body kens that he lies there,
"But his hawk, his hound, and lady fair.

"His hound is to the hunting gane,
"His hawk to fetch the wild-fowl hame,
"His lady's ta'en another mate,
"So we may mak our dinner sweet.

"Ye'll sit on his white hause bane,
"And I'll pike out his bonny blue een:
"Wi' ae lock o' his gowden hair,
"We'll theek [2] our nest when it grows bare.

"Mony a one for him makes mane,
"But nane sall ken whare he is gane:
"O'er his white banes, when they are bare,
"The wind sall blaw for evermair."

1 Fail—Turf.
2 Theek—Thatch.

from The Fortunes of Nigel (1822)

Introductory Epistle

CAPTAIN CLUTTERBUCK, TO THE REV. DR DRYASDUST.

Dear Sir,

I READILY accept of, and reply to the civilities with which you have been pleased to honour me in your obliging letter, and entirely agree with your quotation, of "*Quam bonum et quam jucundum.*" We may indeed esteem ourselves as come of the same family, or, according to our country proverb, as being all one man's bairns; and there needed no apology on your part, reverend and dear sir, for demanding of me any information which I may be able to supply respecting the subject of your curiosity. The interview which you allude to took place in the course of last winter, and is so deeply imprinted on my recollection, that it requires no effort to collect all its most minute details.

You are aware that the share which I had in introducing the Romance, called *The Monastery*, to public notice, has given me a sort of character in the literature of our Scottish metropolis. I no longer stand in the outer shop of our bibliopolists, bargaining for the objects of my curiosity with an unrespective shop-lad, hustled among boys who come to buy Corderies and copy-books, and servant-girls cheapening a penny-worth of paper, but am cordially welcomed by the bibliopolist himself, with, "Pray, walk into the back-shop, Captain. Boy, get a chair for Captain Clutterbuck. There is the news-paper, Captain — to-day's paper — or here is the last new work — there is a folder, make free with the leaves, or put it in your pocket and carry it home; or we will make a book-seller of you sir, you shall have it at trade price." Or, perhaps, if it is the worthy trader's own publication, his liberality may even extend itself to — "Never mind booking such a trifle to you sir, — it is an over-copy. Pray mention the work to your literary friends." I say nothing of the snug well-selected literary party arranged around a turbot, leg of five-year-old mutton, or some such gear, or of the circulation of a quiet bottle of Robert Cockburn's choicest black — or, perhaps of his best blue, to quicken our talk about old books, or our plans for new ones. All these are comforts reserved to such as are freemen of the corporation of letters, and I have the advantage of enjoying them in perfection.

But all things change under the sun; and it is with no ordinary feelings of regret, that, in my annual visits to the metropolis, I now miss the social and warm-hearted welcome of the quick-witted and kindly friend who first introduced me to the public, who had more original wit than would have set up a dozen of professed sayers of good things, and more racy humour than would have made the fortune of as many more. To this great deprivation has been added, I trust for a time only, the loss of another bibliopolical friend, whose vigorous intellect, and liberal ideas, have not only rendered his native country the mart of her own literature, but established there a Court of Letters which must command respect, even from those most inclined to dissent from many of its canons. The effect of these changes, operated in a great measure by the strong sense and sagacious calculations of an individual, who knew how to avail himself, to an unhoped-for extent, of the various kinds of talent which his country produced, will probably appear more clearly to the generation which shall follow the present.

I entered the shop at the Cross, to inquire after the health of my worthy friend, and learned with satisfaction that his residence in the south had abated the rigour of the symptoms of his disorder. Availing myself, then, of the privileges to which I have alluded, I strolled onwards in that labyrinth of small dark rooms, or *crypts*, to speak our own antiquarian language, which form the extensive back-settlements of that celebrated publishing house. Yet, as I proceeded from one obscure recess to another, filled, some of them with old volumes, some with such as, from the equality of their rank on the shelves, I suspected to be the less saleable modern books of the concern, I could not help feeling a holy horror creep upon me, when I thought of the risk of intruding on some ecstatic bard giving vent to his poetical fury; or, it might be, on the yet more formidable privacy of a band of critics, in the act of worrying the game which they had just run down. In such a supposed case, I felt by anticipation the horrors of the Highland seers, whom their gift of Deuteroscopy compels to witness things unmeet for mortal eye; and who, to use the expression of Collins,

— — "heartless, oft, like moody madness, stare,
To see the phantom train their secret work prepare."

Still, however, the irresistible impulse of an undefined curiosity drove me on through this succession of darksome chambers, till, like the jeweller of Delhi in the house of the magician Bennaskar, I at length reached a vaulted room, dedicated to secrecy and silence, and beheld, seated by a lamp, and employed in reading a blotted *revise*, the person, or perhaps I should rather say the Eidolon, or Representative Vision, of the Author of Waverley! You will not be surprised at the filial instinct which enabled me at once to acknowledge the features borne by this venerable apparition, and that I at once bended the knee, with the classical salutation of, *Salve, magne parens!* The vision, however, cut me short, by pointing to a seat, and intimating that my presence was not unexpected, and that he had something to say to me.

I sate down with humble obedience, and endeavoured to note the features of him with whom I now found myself so unexpectedly in society. But on this point I can give your reverence no satisfaction; for, besides the obscurity of the apartment, and the fluttered state of my own nerves, I seemed to myself overwhelmed by a sense of filial awe, which prevented my noting and recording what it is probable the personage before me might most desire to have concealed. Indeed, his figure was so closely veiled and wimpled, either with a mantle, morning-gown, or some such loose garb, that the verses of Spenser might well have been applied —

> "Yet, certes, by her face and physnomy,
> Whether she man or woman inly were,
> That could not any creature well descry."

I must, however, proceed as I have begun, to apply the masculine gender; for, notwithstanding very ingenious reasons, and indeed something like positive evidence, have been offered to prove the Author of Waverley to be two ladies of talent — I abide by the general opinion, that he is of the rougher sex. There are in his writings too many things

> "Quae maribus sola tribuuntur,"

to permit me to entertain any doubt on that subject. I will proceed, in the manner of dialogue, to repeat as nearly as I can what passed betwixt us, only observing, that in the course of the conversation, my timidity imperceptibly gave way under the familiarity of his address; and, latterly, I perhaps argued with fully as much confidence as was beseeming.

Author of Waverley. I was willing to see you, Captain Clutterbuck, being the person of my family whom I have most regard for, since the death of Jedediah Cleishbotham; and I am afraid I may have done you some wrong, in assigning to you the Monastery as a portion of my effects. I have some thoughts of making it up to you, by naming you godfather to this yet unborn babe — (he indicated the proof-sheet with his finger) — But first, touching The Monastery — How says the world — you are abroad, and can learn?

Captain Clutterbuck. Hem! hem! The inquiry is delicate — I have not heard any complaints from the Publishers.

Author. That is the principal matter; but yet an indifferent work is sometimes towed on by those which have left harbour before it, with the breeze in their poop. What say the Critics?

Captain. There is a general — feeling — that the White Lady is no favourite.

Author. I think she is a failure myself; but rather in execution than conception.

Could I have evoked an *esprit follet*, at the same time fantastic and interesting, capricious and kind; a sort of wildfire of the elements, bound by no fixed laws, or motives of action; faithful and fond, yet teazing and uncertain — —

Captain. If you will pardon the interruption, sir, I think you are describing a pretty woman.

Author. On my word, I believe I am. I must invest my elementary spirits with a little human flesh and blood — they are too fine-drawn for the present taste of the public.

Captain. They object too, that the object of your Nixie ought to have been more uniformly noble — her ducking the priest was no naiad-like amusement.

Author. Ah! they ought to allow for the capricios of what is after all but a better sort of goblin. The bath into which Ariel, the most delicate creation of Shakespeare's imagination, seduces our jolly friend Trinculo, was not of amber or rose-water. But no one shall find me rowing against the stream.

I care not who knows it — I write for the public amusement; and though I never will aim at popularity by what I think unworthy means, I will not, on the other hand, be pertinacious in the defence of my own errors against the voice of the public.

Captain. You abandon then, in the present work — (looking in my turn towards the proof-sheet) — the mystic, and the magical, and the whole system of signs, wonders, and omens? There are no dreams, or presages, or obscure allusions to future events?

Author. Not a Cock-lane scratch, my son — not one bounce on the drum of Tedworth — not so much as the poor tick of a solitary death-watch in the wainscoat. All is clear and above board — a Scotch metaphysician might believe every word of it.

Captain. And the story is, I hope, natural and probable; commencing strikingly, proceeding naturally, ending happily, like the course of a famed river which gushes from the mouth of some obscure and romantic grotto — then gliding on, never pausing, never precipitating, visiting, as it were by natural instinct, whatever worthy subjects of interest are presented by the country through which it passes — widening and deepening in interest as it flows on; and at length arriving at the final catastrophe as at some mighty haven, where ships of all kinds strike sail and yard.

Author. Hey! hey! what the deuce is all this? Why 'tis Ercles' vein, and it would require some one much more like Hercules than me, to produce a story which should gush, and glide, and never pause, and visit, and widen, and deepen, and all the rest on't. I should be chin-deep in the grave, man, before I was done with my task; and, in the meanwhile, all the quirks and quiddits which I might have devised for my reader's amusement, would lie rotting in my gizzard, like Sancho's suppressed witticisms when he was under his master's displeasure. There never was a novel written on this plan while the world stood.

Captain. Pardon me — Tom Jones.

Author. True, and perhaps Amelia also. Fielding had high notions of the dignity of an art which he may be considered as having founded. He challenges a comparison between the Novel and the Epic. Smollett, Le Sage, and others, emancipating themselves from the strictness of the rules he has laid down, have written rather a history of the miscellaneous adventures which befall an individual in the course of life, than the plot of a regular and connected epopeia, where every step brings us a point nearer to the final catastrophe. These great masters have been satisfied if they amused the reader upon the road, though the conclusion only arrived because the tale must have an end, just as the traveller alights at the inn because it is evening.

Captain. A very commodious mode of travelling, for the author at least. In short, sir, you are of opinion with Bayes, — "What the devil does the plot signify, except to bring in fine things?"

Author. Grant that I were so, and that I should write with sense and spirit a few scenes, unlaboured and loosely put together, but which had sufficient interest in them to amuse in one corner the pain of body; in another, to relieve anxiety of mind; in a third place, to unwrinkle a brow bent with the furrows of daily toil; in another, to fill the place of bad thoughts, or to suggest better; in yet another, to induce an idler to study the history of his country; in all, save where the perusal interrupted the discharge of serious duties, to furnish harmless amusement, — might not the author of such a work, however inartificially executed, plead for his errors and negligences the excuse of the slave who was about to be punished for having spread the false report of a victory, — "Am I to blame, O Athenians, who have given you one happy day?"

Captain. Will your goodness permit me to mention an anecdote of my excellent grandmother?

Author. I see little she can have to do with the subject, Captain Clutterbuck.

Captain. It may come into our dialogue on Bayes's plan. The sagacious old lady, rest her soul, was a good friend to the church, and could never hear a minister maligned by evil tongues, without taking his part warmly. There was one fixed point, however, at which she always abandoned the cause of her reverend *protegé* — it was so soon as she learned he had preached a regular sermon against slanderers and backbiters.

Author. And what is that to the purpose?

Captain. Only that I have heard engineers say, that one may betray the weak point to the enemy, by too much ostentation of fortifying it.

Author. And, once more I pray, what is that to the purpose?

Captain. Nay then, without farther metaphor, I am afraid this new production, in which your generosity seems willing to give me some concern, will stand much in need of apology, since you think proper to begin your defence before the case is on trial. The story is hastily huddled up, I will venture a pint of claret.

Author. A pint of port, I suppose you mean?

Captain. I say of claret — good claret of the Monastery. Ah, sir, would you but take the advice of your friends, and try to deserve at least one-half of the public favour you have met with, we might all drink Tokay!

Author. I care not what I drink, so the liquor be wholesome.

Captain. Care for your reputation then — for your fame.

Author. My fame? — I will answer you as a very ingenious, able, and experienced friend, when counsel for the notorious Jem MacCoul, replied to the opposite side of the bar, when they laid weight on his client's refusing to answer certain queries, which they said any man who had a regard for his reputation would not hesitate to reply to. "My client," said he — by the way, Jem was standing behind him at the time, and a rich scene it was — "is so unfortunate as to have no regard for his reputation; and I should deal very uncandidly with the Court, should I say he had any that was worth his attention." I am, though from very different reasons, in Jem's happy state of indifference. Let fame follow those who have a substantial shape. A shadow — and an impersonal author is nothing better — can cast no shade.

Captain. You are not now, perhaps, so impersonal as heretofore. These Letters to the Member for the University of Oxford —

Author. Shew the wit, genius, and delicacy of the author, which I heartily wish to see engaged on a subject of more importance; and shew, besides, that the preservation of my character of *incognito* has engaged early talent in the discussion of a curious question of evidence. But a cause, however ingeniously pleaded, is not therefore gained. You may remember the neatly-wrought chain of circumstantial evidence, so artificially brought forward to prove Sir Philip Francis's title to the Letters of Junius, seemed at first irrefragable; yet the influence of the reasoning has passed away, and Junius, in the general opinion, is as much unknown as ever. But on this subject I will not be soothed or provoked into saying one word more. To say who I am not, would be one step towards saying who I am; and as I desire not, any more than a certain justice of peace mentioned by Shenstone, the noise or report such things make in the world, I shall continue to be silent on a subject, which, in my opinion, is very undeserving the rout that has been made about it, and still more unworthy of the serious employment of such ingenuity as has been displayed by the young letter-writer.

Captain. But allowing, my dear sir, that you care not for your personal reputation, or for that of any literary person upon whose shoulders your faults may be visited, allow me to say, that common gratitude to the public, who have received you so kindly, and to the critics, who have treated you so leniently, ought to induce you to bestow more pains on your story.

Author. I do entreat you, my son, as Dr Johnson would have said, "free your mind from cant." For the critics, they have their business, and I mine; as the nursery proverb goes —

> "The children in Holland take pleasure in making
> What the children in England take pleasure in breaking."

I am their humble jackall, too busy in providing food for them, to have time for considering whether they swallow or reject it. — To the public, I stand pretty nearly in the relation of the postman who leaves a packet at the door of an individual. If it contains pleasing intelligence, a billet from a mistress, a letter from an absent son, a remittance from a correspondent supposed to be bankrupt, — the letter is acceptably welcome, and read and re-read, folded up, filed, and safely deposited in the bureau. If the contents are disagreeable, if it comes from a dun or from a bore, the correspondent is cursed, the letter is thrown into the fire, and the expence of postage is heartily regretted; while all the while the bearer of the dispatches is, in either case, as little thought on as the snow of last Christmas. The utmost extent of kindness between the author and the public which can really exist, is, that the world are disposed to be somewhat indulgent to the succeeding works of an original favourite, were it but on account of the habit which the public mind has acquired; while the author very naturally thinks well of *their* taste, who have so liberally applauded *his* productions. But I deny there is any call for gratitude, properly so called, either on one side or the other.

Captain. Respect to yourself, then, ought to teach caution.

Author. Ay, if caution could augment the chance of my success. But, to confess to you the truth, the works and passages in which I have succeeded, have uniformly been written with the greatest rapidity; and when I have seen some of these placed in opposition with others, and commended as more highly finished, I could appeal to pen and standish, that the parts in which I have come feebly off, were by much the more laboured. Besides, I doubt the beneficial effect of too much delay, both on account of the author and the public. A man should strike while the iron is hot, and hoist sail while the wind is fair. If a successful author keeps not the stage, another instantly takes his ground. If a writer lies by for ten years ere he produces a second work, he is superseded by others; or, if the age is so poor of genius that this does not happen, his own reputation becomes his greatest obstacle. The public will expect the new work to be ten times better than its predecessor; the author will expect it should be ten times more popular, and 'tis a hundred to ten that both are disappointed.

Captain. This may justify a certain degree of rapidity in publication, but not that which is proverbially said to be no speed. You should take time at least to arrange your story.

Author. That is a sore point with me, my son. Believe me, I have not been fool enough to neglect ordinary precautions. I have repeatedly laid down my future work to scale, divided it into volumes and chapters, and endeavoured to construct a story which I meant should evolve itself gradually and strikingly, maintain suspense, and stimulate curiosity; and which, finally, should terminate in a striking catastrophe. But I think there is a daemon who seats himself on the feather of my pen when I begin to write, and leads it astray from the purpose. Characters expand under my hand; incidents are multiplied; the story lingers, while the materials increase; my regular mansion turns out a Gothic anomaly, and the work is complete long before I have attained the point I proposed.

Captain. Resolution and determined forbearance might remedy that evil.

Author. Alas, my dear sir, you do not know the force of paternal affection. — When I light on such a character as Bailie Jarvie, or Dalgetty, my imagination brightens, and my conception becomes clearer at every step which I make in his company, although it leads me many a weary mile away from the regular road, and forces me to leap hedge and ditch to get back into the route again. If I resist the temptation, as you advise me, my thoughts become prosy, flat, and dull; I write painfully to myself, and under a consciousness of flagging which makes me flag still more; the sunshine with which fancy had invested the incidents, departs from them, and leaves every thing dull and gloomy. I am no more the same author, than the dog in a wheel, condemned to go round and round for hours, is like the same dog merrily chasing his own tail, and gambolling in all the frolic of unrestrained freedom. In short, sir, on such occasions, I think I am bewitched.

Captain. Nay, sir, if you plead sorcery, there is no more to be said — he must needs go whom the devil drives. And this, I suppose, sir, is the reason why you do not make the theatrical attempt to which you have been so often urged?

Author. It may pass for one good reason for not writing a play, that I cannot form a plot. But the truth is, that the idea adopted by too favourable judges, of my having some aptitude for that department of poetry, has been much founded on those scraps of old plays, which, being taken from a source inaccessible to collectors, they have hastily considered the offspring of my mother-wit. Now, the manner in which I became possessed of these fragments is so extraordinary, that I cannot help telling it to you.

You must know, that some twenty years since, I went down to visit an old friend in Worcestershire, who had served with me in the — — Dragoons.

Captain. Then you *have* served, sir?

Author. I have — or I have not, which signifies the same thing — Captain is a good travelling name. — I found my friend's house unexpectedly crowded with guests, and, as usual, was condemned — the mansion being an old one — to the *haunted apartment.* I have, as a great modern said, seen too many ghosts to believe in them, so betook myself seriously to my repose, lulled by the wind rustling among the lime-trees, the branches of which chequered the moonlight which fell on the floor through the diamonded casement, when, behold, a darker shadow interposed itself, and I beheld visibly on the floor of the apartment — —

Captain. The White Lady of Avenel, I suppose? — You have told the very story before.

Author. No — I beheld a female form with round mob-cap, bib, and apron, sleeves tucked up to the elbow, a dredging-box in the one hand, and in the other a sauce-ladle. I concluded, of course, that it was my friend's cook-maid walking in her sleep; and as I knew he had a value for Sally, who could toss a pancake with any girl in the county, I got up to conduct her safely to the door. But as I approached her, she said — "Hold, sir! I am not what you take me for;" — words which seemed so apposite to the circumstances, that I should not have much minded them, had it not been for the peculiarly hollow sound in which they were uttered. — "Know then," she said in the same unearthly accents, "that I am the spirit of Betty Barnes." — "Who hanged herself for love of the stage-coachman," thought I; "this is a proper spot of work." — "Of that unhappy Elizabeth or Betty Barnes, long cook-maid to Mr Warburton the painful collector, but ah! the too careless custodier of the largest collection of ancient plays ever known — of most of which the titles only are left to gladden the Prologomena of the Variorum Shakespeare. Yes, stranger, it was these ill-fated hands that consigned to grease and conflagration the scores of small quartos, which, did they now exist, would drive the whole Roxburghe Club out of their senses — it was these unhappy pickers and stealers that singed fat fowls and wiped dirty trenchers with the lost works of Beaumont and Fletcher, Massinger, Jonson, Webster — what shall I say? — even of Shakespeare himself."

Like every dramatic antiquary, my ardent curiosity, after some play named in the Book of the Master of Revels, had often been checked by finding the object of my research numbered amongst the holocaust of victims which this unhappy woman had sacrificed to the God of Good Cheer. It is no wonder then, that, like the Hermit of Parnell,

> I broke the bands of fear, and madly cried,
> 'You careless jade!' — But scarce the words began,
> When Betty brandish'd high her saucing-pan.

"Beware," she said," you do not, by your ill-timed anger, cut off the opportunity I yet have to indemnify the world for the errors of my ignorance. In yonder coal-hole, not used for many a year, repose the few greasy and blackened fragments of the elder Drama which were not totally destroyed. Do thou then" — Why, what do you stare at, Captain? By my soul, it is true; as my friend Major Longbow says, "what should I tell you a lie for?"

Captain. Lie, sir! Nay, heaven forbid I should apply the word to a person so veracious. You are only inclined to chase your tail a little this morning, that's all. Had you not better reserve this legend to form an introduction to "Three recovered Dramas," or so?

Author. You are quite right — habit's a strange thing, my son. I had forgot whom I was speaking to. Yes, Plays for the closet, not for the stage —

Captain. Right, and so you are sure to be acted; for the managers, while thousands of volunteers are desirous of serving them, are wonderfully partial to pressed men.

Author. I am a living witness, having been, like a second Laberius, made a dramatist whether I would or not. I believe my muse would be *Terry*fied into treading the stage, even if I should write a sermon.

Captain. Truly, if you did, I am afraid folks might make a farce of it; and, therefore, should you change your style, I still advise a volume of dramas like Lord Byron's.

Author. No, his lordship is a cut above me — I won't run my horse against his, if I can help myself. But there is my friend Allan has written just such a play as I might write myself, in a very sunny day, and with one of Bramah's extra patent-pens. I cannot make neat work without such appurtenances.

Captain. Do you mean Allan Ramsay?

Author. No, nor Barbara Allan either. I mean Allan Cunningham, who has just published his tragedy of Sir Marmaduke Maxwell, full of merry-making and murdering, kissing and cutting of throats, and passages which lead to nothing, and which are very pretty passages for all that. Not a glimpse of probability is there about the plot, but so much animation in particular passages, and such a vein of poetry through the whole, as I dearly wish I could infuse into my Culinary Remains, should I ever be tempted to publish them. With a popular impress, people would read and admire the beauties of Allan — as it is, they may perhaps only note his defects — or, what is worse, not note him at all. But never mind them, honest Allan; you are a credit to Caledonia for all that. — There are some lyrical effusions of his too, which you would do well to read. Captain. "It's hame, and it's hame," is equal to Burns.

Captain. I will take the hint. The club at Kennaquhair are turned fastidious since Catalani visited the Abbey. My "Poortith Cauld" has been received both poorly and coldly, and "the Banks of Bonnie Doon" have been positively coughed down — *Tempora mutantur*.

Author. They cannot stand still, they will change with all of us. What then?

"A man's a man for a' that."

But the hour of parting approaches.

Captain. You are determined to proceed then in your own system? Are you aware that an unworthy motive may be assigned for this rapid succession of publication? You will be supposed to work merely for the lucre of gain.

Author. Supposing that I did permit the great advantages which must be derived from success in literature, to join with other motives in inducing me to come more frequently before the public, — that emolument is the voluntary tax which the public pays for a certain species of literary amusement — it is extorted from no one, and paid, I presume, by those only who can afford it, and who receive gratification in proportion to the expense. If the capital sum which these volumes have put into circulation be a very large one, has it contributed to my indulgences only? or can I not say to hundreds, from honest Duncan the paper manufacturer, to the most snivelling of the printer's devils, "Didst thou not share? Hadst thou not fifteen pence?" I profess I think our modern Athens much obliged to me for having established such an extensive manufacture; and when universal suffrage comes in fashion, I intend to stand for a seat in the House on the interest of all the unwashed artificers connected with literature.

Captain. This would be called the language of a calico-manufacturer.

Author. Cant again, my dear son — there is lime in this sack too — nothing but sophistication in this world! I do say it, in spite of Adam Smith and his followers, that a successful author is a productive labourer, and that his works constitute as effectual a part of the public wealth, as that which is created by any other manufacture. If a new commodity, having an actually intrinsic and commercial value, be the result of the operation, why are the author's bales of books to be esteemed a less profitable part of the public stock than the goods of any other manufacturer? I speak with reference to the diffusion of the wealth arising to the public, and the degree of industry which even such a trifling work as the present must stimulate and reward, before the volumes leave the publisher's shop. Without me it could not exist, and to this extent I am a benefactor to the country. As for my own emolument, it is won by my toil, and I account myself answerable to Heaven only for the mode in which I expend it. The candid may hope it is not all dedicated to selfish purposes; and, without much pretensions to merit in him who expends it, a part may "wander, heaven-directed, to the poor."

Captain. Yet it is generally held base to write, from the mere motive of gain.

Author. It would be base to do so exclusively, or even to make it a principal motive of literary exertion. Nay, I will venture to say, that no work of imagination, proceeding from the mere consideration of a certain sum of copy-money, ever did, or ever will, succeed. So the lawyer who pleads, the soldier who fights, the physician who prescribes, the clergyman — if such there be — who preaches, without any zeal for their profession, or without any sense of its dignity, and merely on account of their fee, pay, or stipend, degrade themselves to the rank of sordid mechanics. Accordingly, in the case of two of the learned faculties at least, their services are considered as unappreciable, and are acknowledged not by any exact estimate of the services rendered, but by a *honorarium*, or voluntary acknowledgment. But let a client or patient make the experiment of omitting this little ceremony of the *honorarium*, which is *censé* to be a thing entirely out of consideration between them, and mark how the learned gentleman will look upon his case. Cant set apart, it is the same thing with literary emolument. No man of sense, in any rank of life, is, or ought to be, above accepting a just recompence for his time, and a reasonable share of the capital which owes its very existence to his exertions. When Czar Peter wrought in the trenches, he took the pay of a common soldier; and nobles, statesmen, and divines, the most distinguished of their time, have not scorned to square accounts with their bookseller.

Captain. (Sings.)

> O if it were a mean thing,
>   The gentles would not use it;
> And if it were ungodly,
>   The clergy would refuse it.

Author. You say well. But no man of honour, genius, or spirit, would make the mere love of gain the chief, far less the only, purpose of his labours. For myself, I am not displeased to find the game a winning one; yet while I pleased the public, I should probably continue it merely for the pleasure of playing; for I have felt as strongly as most folks that love of composition, which is perhaps the strongest of all instincts, driving the author to the pen, the painter to the pallet, often without either the chance of fame or the prospect of reward. Perhaps I have said too much of this. I might perhaps, with as much truth as most people, exculpate myself from the charge of being either of a greedy or mercenary disposition; but I am not, therefore, hypocrite enough to disclaim the ordinary motives, on account of which the whole world around me is toiling unremittingly, to the sacrifice of ease, comfort, health, and life. I do not affect the disinterestedness of that ingenious association of gentlemen mentioned by Goldsmith, who sold their magazine for sixpence a-piece, merely for their own amusement.

Captain. I have but one thing more to hint. — The world say you will run yourself out.

Author. The world say true; and what then? When they dance no longer, I will no longer pipe; and I shall not want flappers enough to remind me of the apoplexy.

Captain. And what will become of us then, your poor family? We shall fall into contempt and oblivion.

Author. Like many a poor fellow, already overwhelmed with the number of his family, I cannot help going on to increase it—"'Tis my vocation, Hal."—Such of you as deserve oblivion—perhaps the whole of you—may be consigned to it. At any rate, you have been read in your day, which is more than can be said of some of your contemporaries, of less fortune and more merit. They cannot say but what you *had* the crown. As for myself, I shall always deserve, at least, the unwilling tribute which Johnson paid to Churchill, when he said, though the fellow's genius was a tree which bore only crabs, yet it was prolific, and had plenty of fruit, such as it was. It is always something to have engaged the public attention for seven years. Had I only written Waverley, I should have long since been, according to the established phrase, "the ingenious author of a novel much admired at the time." I believe, on my soul, that the reputation of Waverley is sustained very much by the praises of those, who may be inclined to prefer that tale to its successors.

Captain. You are willing, then, to barter future reputation for present popularity?

Author. *Meliora spero.* Horace himself expected not to survive in all his works—I may hope to live in some of mine;—*non omnis moriar.* It is some consolation to reflect, that the best authors in all countries have been the most voluminous; and it has often happened, that those who have been best received in their own time, have also continued to be acceptable to posterity. I do not think so ill of the present generation, as to suppose that its present favour necessarily infers future condemnation.

Captain. Were all to act on such principles, the public would be inundated.

Author. Once more, my dear son, beware of cant. You speak as if the public were obliged to read books merely because they are printed—your friends the booksellers would thank you to make the proposition good. The most serious grievance attending such inundations as you talk of is, that they make rags dear. The multiplicity of publications does the present age no harm, and may greatly advantage that which is to succeed us.

Captain. I do not see how that is to happen.

Author. The complaints in the time of Elizabeth and James, of the alarming fertility of the press, were as loud as they are at present—yet look at the shore over which the inundation of that age flowed, and it resembles now the Rich Strand of the Faery Queen—

— — Bestrew'd all with rich array,
Of pearl and precious stones of great assay;
And all the gravel mix'd with golden ore.

Believe me, that even in the most neglected works of the present age, the next may discover treasures.

Captain. Some books will defy all alchemy.

Author. They will be but few in number; since, as for writers, who are possessed of no merit at all, unless indeed they publish their works at their own expense, like Sir Richard Blackmore, their power of annoying the public will be soon limited by the difficulty of finding undertaking booksellers.

Captain. You are incorrigible. Are there no bounds to your audacity?

Author. There are the sacred and eternal boundaries of honour and virtue. My course is like the enchanted chamber of Britomart—

Where as she look'd about, she did behold
How over that same door was likewise writ,
Be Bold—Be Bold, and every where *Be Bold.*

> Whereat she mused, and could not construe it;
> At last she spied at that room's upper end
> Another iron door, on which was writ—
> BE NOT TOO BOLD.

Captain. Well, you must take the risk of proceeding on your own principles.

Author. Do you act on yours, and take care you do not stay idling here till the dinner hour is over.—I will add this work to your patrimony, *valeat quantum.*

Here our dialogue terminated; for a little sooty-faced Apollyon from the Canongate came to demand the proof-sheet on the part of Mr M'Corkindale; and I heard Mr C. rebuking Mr F. in another compartment of the same labyrinth I have described, for suffering any one to penetrate so far into the *penetralia* of their temple.

I leave it to you to form your own opinion concerning the import of this dialogue, and I cannot but believe I shall meet the wishes of our common parent in prefixing this letter to the work which it concerns.

I am, reverend and dear Sir,
Very sincerely and affectionately
Yours, &c. &c.

CUTHBERT CLUTTERBUCK.
Kennaquhair, 1st April, 1822.

The Highland Widow (1826)

CHAPTER I.

> It wound as near as near could be,
> But what it is she cannot tell;
> On the other side it seemed to be,
> Of the huge broad-breasted old oak-tree.
>
> COLERIDGE.

MRS BETHUNE BALIOL'S memorandum begins thus:—

It is five-and-thirty, or perhaps nearer forty years ago, since, to relieve the dejection of spirits occasioned by a great family loss sustained two or three months before, I undertook what was called the short Highland tour. This had become in some degree fashionable; but though the military roads were excellent, yet the accommodation was so indifferent that it was reckoned a little adventure to accomplish it. Besides, the Highlands, though now as peaceable as any part of King George's dominions, was a sound which still carried terror, while so many survived who had witnessed the insurrection of 1745; and a vague idea of fear was impressed on many, as they looked from the towers of Stirling northward to the huge chain of mountains, which rises like a dusky rampart to conceal in its recesses a people, whose dress, manners, and language, differed still very much from those of their Lowland countrymen. For my part, I come of a race not greatly subject to apprehensions arising from imagination only. I had some Highland relatives, knew several of their families of distinction; and, though only having the company of my bower-maiden, Mrs Alice Lambskin, I went on my journey fearless.

But then I had a guide and cicerone, almost equal to Greatheart in the Pilgrim's Progress, in no less a person than Donald MacLeish, the postilion whom I hired at Stirling, with a pair of able-bodied horses, as steady as Donald himself, to drag my carriage, my duenna, and myself, wheresoever it was my pleasure to go.

Donald MacLeish was one of a race of post-boys, whom, I suppose, mail-coaches and steam-boats have put out of fashion. They were to be found chiefly at Perth, Stirling, or Glasgow, where they and their horses were usually hired by travellers, or tourists, to accomplish such journeys of business or pleasure as they might have to perform in the land of the Gael. This class of persons approached to the character of what is called abroad a *conducteur*; or might be compared to the sailing-master on board a British ship of war, who follows out after his own manner the course which the captain commands him to observe. You explained to your postilion the length of your tour, and the objects you were desirous it should embrace; and you found him perfectly competent to fix the places of rest or refreshment, with due attention that those should be chosen with reference to your convenience, and to any points of interest which you might desire to visit.

The qualifications of such a person were necessarily much superior to those of the "first ready," who gallops thrice-a-day over the same ten miles. Donald MacLeish, besides being quite alert at repairing all ordinary accidents to his horses and carriage, and in making shift to support them, where forage was scarce, with such substitutes as bannocks and cakes, was likewise a man of intellectual resources. He had acquired a general knowledge of the traditional stories of the country which he had traversed so often; and, if encouraged, (for Donald was a man of the most decorous reserve,) he would willingly point out to you the site of the principal clan-battles, and recount the most remarkable legends by which the road, and the objects which occurred in travelling it, had been distinguished. There was some originality in the man's habits of thinking and expressing himself, his turn for legendary lore strangely contrasting with a portion of the knowing shrewdness belonging to his actual occupation, which made his conversation amuse the way well enough.

Add to this, Donald knew all his peculiar duties in the country which he traversed so frequently. He could tell, to a day, when they would "be killing" lamb at Tyndrum or Glenuilt; so that the stranger would have some chance of being fed like a Christian; and knew to a mile the last village where it was possible to procure a wheaten loaf, for the guidance of those who were little familiar with the Land of Cakes. He was acquainted with the road every mile, and could tell to an inch which side of a Highland bridge was passable, which decidedly dangerous. In short, Donald MacLeish was not only our faithful attendant and steady servant, but our humble and obliging friend; and though I have known the half-classical cicerone of Italy, the talkative French valet-de-place, and even the muleteer of Spain, who piques himself on being a maize-eater, and whose honour is not to be questioned without danger, I do not think I have ever had so sensible and intelligent a guide.

Our motions were of course under Donald's direction; and it frequently happened, when the weather was serene, that we preferred halting to rest his horses even where there was no established stage, and taking our refreshment under a crag, from which leaped a waterfall, or beside the verge of a fountain, enamelled with verdant turf and wild-flowers. Donald had an eye for such spots, and though he had, I dare say, never read Gil Blas or Don Quixote, yet he chose such halting-places as Le Sage or Cervantes would have described. Very often, as he observed the pleasure I took in conversing with the country people, he would manage to fix our place of rest near a cottage where there was some old Gael, whose broadsword had blazed at Falkirk or Preston, and who seemed the frail yet faithful record of times which had passed away. Or he would contrive to quarter us, as far as a cup of tea went, upon the hospitality of some parish minister of worth and intelligence, or some country family of the better class, who mingled with the wild simplicity of their original manners, and their ready and hospitable welcome, a sort of courtesy belonging to a people, the lowest of whom are accustomed to consider themselves as being, according to the Spanish phrase, "as good gentlemen as the king, only not quite so rich."

To all such persons Donald MacLeish was well known, and his introduction passed as current as if we had brought letters from some high chief of the country.

Sometimes it happened that the Highland hospitality, which welcomed us with all the variety of mountain fare, preparations of milk and eggs, and girdle-cakes of various kinds, as well as more substantial dainties, according to the inhabitant's means of regaling the passenger, descended rather too exuberantly on Donald MacLeish in the shape of mountain dew. Poor Donald! he was on such occasions like Gideon's fleece, moist with the noble element, which, of course, fell not on us. But it was his only fault, and when pressed to drink *doch-an-dorroch* to my ladyship's good health, it would have been ill taken to have refused the pledge, nor was he willing to do such discourtesy. It was, I repeat, his only fault, nor had we any great right to complain; for if it rendered him a little more talkative, it augmented his ordinary share of punctilious civility, and he only drove slower, and talked longer and more pompously than when he had not come by a drop of usquebaugh. It was, we remarked, only on such occasions that Donald talked with an air of importance of the family of MacLeish; and we had no title to be scrupulous in censuring a foible, the consequences of which were confined within such innocent limits.

We became so much accustomed to Donald's mode of managing us, that we observed with some interest the art which he used to produce a little agreeable surprise, by concealing from us the spot where he proposed our halt to be made, when it was of an unusual and interesting character. This was so much his wont, that when he made apologies at setting off, for being obliged to stop in some strange solitary place, till the horses should eat the corn which he brought on with them for that purpose, our imagination used to be on the stretch to guess what romantic retreat he had secretly fixed upon for our noontide baiting-place.

We had spent the greater part of the morning at the delightful village of Dalmally, and had gone upon the lake under the guidance of the excellent clergyman who was then incumbent at Glenorquhy, and had heard an hundred legends of the stern chiefs of Loch Awe, Duncan with the thrum bonnet, and the other lords of the now mouldering towers of Kilchurn. Thus it was later than usual when we set out on our journey, after a hint or two from Donald concerning the length of the way to the next stage, as there was no good halting-place between Dalmally and Oban.

Having bid adieu to our venerable and kind cicerone, we proceeded on our tour, winding round the tremendous mountain called Cruachan Ben, which rushes down in all its majesty of rocks and wilderness on the lake, leaving only a pass, in which, notwithstanding its extreme strength, the warlike clan of MacDougal of Lorn were almost destroyed by the sagacious Robert Bruce. That King, the Wellington of his day, had accomplished, by a forced march, the unexpected manoeuvre of forcing a body of troops round the other side of the mountain, and thus placed them in the flank and in the rear of the men of Lorn, whom at the same time he attacked in front. The great number of cairns yet visible, as you descend the pass on the westward side, shows the extent of the vengeance which Bruce exhausted on his inveterate and personal enemies. I am, you know, the sister of soldiers, and it has since struck me forcibly that the manoeuvre which Donald described, resembled those of Wellington or of Bonaparte. He was a great man Robert Bruce, even a Baliol must admit that; although it begins now to be allowed that his title to the crown was scarce so good as that of the unfortunate family with whom he contended — But let that pass.— The slaughter had been the greater, as the deep and rapid river Awe is disgorged from the lake, just in the rear of the fugitives, and encircles the base of the tremendous mountain; so that the retreat of the unfortunate fliers was intercepted on all sides by the inaccessible character of the country, which had seemed to promise them defence and protection.

Musing, like the Irish lady in the song, "upon things which are long enough a-gone," we felt no impatience at the slow, and almost creeping pace, with which our conductor proceeded along General Wade's military road, which never or rarely condescends to turn aside from the steepest ascent, but proceeds right up and down hill, with the indifference to height and hollow, steep or level, indicated by the old Roman engineers. Still, however, the substantial excellence of these great works — for such are the military highways in the Highlands — deserved the compliment of the poet, who, whether he came from our sister kingdom, and spoke in his own dialect, or whether he supposed those whom he addressed might have some national pretension to the second sight, produced the celebrated couplet—

Had you but seen these roads *before* they were made,
You would hold up your hands, and bless General Wade.

Nothing indeed can be more wonderful than to see these wildernesses penetrated and pervious in every quarter by broad accesses of the best possible construction, and so superior to what the country could have demanded for many centuries for any pacific purpose of commercial intercourse. Thus the traces of war are sometimes happily accommodated to the purposes of peace. The victories of Bonaparte have been without results; but his road over the Simplon will long be the communication betwixt peaceful countries, who will apply to the ends of commerce and friendly intercourse that gigantic work, which was formed for the ambitious purpose of warlike invasion.

While we were thus stealing along, we gradually turned round the shoulder of Ben Cruachan, and descending the course of the foaming and rapid Awe, left behind us the expanse of the majestic lake which gives birth to that impetuous river. The rocks and precipices which stooped down perpendicularly on our path on the right hand, exhibited a few remains of the wood which once clothed them, but which had, in latter times, been felled to supply, Donald MacLeish informed us, the iron-founderies at the Bunawe. This made us fix our eyes with interest on one large oak, which grew on the left hand towards the river. It seemed a tree of extraordinary magnitude and picturesque beauty, and stood just where there appeared to be a few roods of open ground lying among huge stones, which had rolled down from the mountain. To add to the romance of the situation, the spot of clear ground extended round the foot of a proud-browed rock, from the summit of which leaped a mountain stream in a fall of sixty feet, in which it was dissolved into foam and dew. At the bottom of the fall the rivulet with difficulty collected, like a routed general, its dispersed forces, and, as if tamed by its descent, found a noiseless passage through the heath to join the Awe.

I was much struck with the tree and waterfall, and wished myself nearer them; not that I thought of sketch-book or portfolio, — for, in my younger days, Misses were not accustomed to black-lead pencils, unless they could use them to some good purpose, — but merely to indulge myself with a closer view. Donald immediately opened the chaise door, but observed it was rough walking down the brae, and that I would see the tree better by keeping the road for a hundred yards farther, when it passed closer to the spot, for which he seemed, however, to have no predilection. "He knew," he said, "a far bigger tree than that nearer Bunawe, and it was a place where there was flat ground for the carriage to stand, which it could jimply do on these braes; — but just as my leddyship liked."

My ladyship did choose rather to look at the fine tree before me, than to pass it by in hopes of a finer; so we walked beside the carriage till we should come to a point, from which, Donald assured us, we might, without scrambling, go as near the tree as we chose, "though he wadna advise us to go nearer than the high-road."

There was something grave and mysterious in Donald's sun-browned countenance when he gave us this intimation, and his manner was so different from his usual frankness, that my female curiosity was set in motion. We walked on the whilst, and I found the tree, of which we had now lost sight by the intervention of some rising ground, was really more distant than I had at first supposed.

"I could have sworn now," said I to my cicerone, "that yon tree and waterfall was the very place where you intended to make a stop to-day."

"The Lord forbid!" said Donald, hastily.

"And for what, Donald? why should you be willing to pass so pleasant a spot?" "It's ower near Dalmally, my leddy, to corn the beasts—it would bring their dinner ower near their breakfast, poor things: — an', besides, the place is not canny."

"Oh! then the mystery is out. There is a bogle or a brownie, a witch or a gyre-carlin, a bodach or a fairy, in the case?"

"The ne'er a bit, my leddy—ye are clean aff the road, as I may say. But if your leddyship will just hae patience, and wait till we are by the place and out of the glen, I'll tell ye all about it. There is no much luck in speaking of such things in the place they chanced in."

I was obliged to suspend my curiosity, observing, that if I persisted in twisting the discourse one way while Donald was twining it another, I should make his objection, like a hempen cord, just so much the tougher. At length the promised turn of the road brought us within fifty paces of the tree which I desired to admire, and I now saw to my surprise, that there was a human habitation among the cliffs which surrounded it. It was a hut of the least dimensions, and most miserable description, that I ever saw even in the Highlands. The walls of sod, or *divot*, as the Scotch call it, were not four feet high—the roof was of turf, repaired with reeds and sedges—the chimney was composed of clay, bound round by straw ropes—and the whole walls, roof and chimney, were alike covered with the vegetation of house-leek, rye-grass, and moss, common to decayed cottages formed of such materials. There was not the slightest vestige of a kale-yard, the usual accompaniment of the very worst huts; and of living things we saw nothing, save a kid which was browsing on the roof of the hut, and a goat, its mother, at some distance, feeding betwixt the oak and the river Awe.

"What man," I could not help exclaiming, "can have committed sin deep enough to deserve such a miserable dwelling!"

"Sin enough" said Donald MacLeish, with a half-suppressed groan; "and God he knoweth, misery enough too;—and it is no man's dwelling neither, but a woman's."

"A woman's!" I repeated, "and in so lonely a place—What sort of a woman can she be?"

"Come this way, my leddy, and you may judge that for yourself," said Donald. And by advancing a few steps, and making a sharp turn to the left, we gained a sight of the side of the great broad-breasted oak, in the direction opposed to that in which we had hitherto seen it.

"If she keeps her old wont, she will be there at this hour of the day," said Donald; but immediately became silent, and pointed with his finger, as one afraid of being overheard. I looked, and beheld, not without some sense of awe, a female form seated by the stem of the oak, with her head drooping, her hands clasped, and a dark-coloured mantle drawn over her head, exactly as Judah is represented in the Syrian medals as seated under her palm-tree. I was infected with the fear and reverence which my guide seemed to entertain towards this solitary being, nor did I think of advancing towards her to obtain a nearer view until I had cast an enquiring look on Donald; to which he replied in a half whisper — "She has been a fearfu' bad woman, my leddy."

"Mad woman, said you," replied I, hearing him imperfectly; "then she is perhaps dangerous?"

"No — she is not mad," replied Donald; "for then it may be she would be happier than she is; though when she thinks on what she has done, and caused to be done, rather than yield up a hairbreadth of her ain wicked will, it is not likely she can be very well settled. But she neither is mad nor mischievous; and yet, my leddy, I think you had best not go nearer to her." And then, in a few hurried words, he made me acquainted with the story which I am now to tell more in detail. I heard the narrative with a mixture of horror and sympathy, which at once impelled me to approach the sufferer, and speak to her the words of comfort, or rather of pity, and at the same time made me afraid to do so.

This indeed was the feeling with which she was regarded by the Highlanders in the neighbourhood, who looked upon Elspat MacTavish, or the Woman of the Tree, as they called her, as the Greeks considered those who were pursued by the Furies, and endured the mental torment consequent on great criminal actions. They regarded such unhappy beings as Orestes and Œdipus, as being less the voluntary perpetrators of their crimes, than as the passive instruments by which the terrible decrees of Destiny had been accomplished; and the fear with which they beheld them was not unmingled with veneration.

I also learned farther from Donald MacLeish, that there was some apprehension of ill luck attending those who had the boldness to approach too near, or disturb the awful solitude of a being so unutterably miserable; that it was supposed that whosoever approached her must experience in some respect the contagion of her wretchedness.

It was therefore with some reluctance that Donald saw me prepare to obtain a nearer view of the sufferer, and that he himself followed to assist me in the descent down a very rough path. I believe his regard for me conquered some ominous feelings in his own breast, which connected his duty on this occasion with the presaging fear of lame horses, lost linchpins, overturns, and other perilous chances of the postilion's life.

I am not sure if my own courage would have carried me so close to Elspat, had he not followed. There was in her countenance the stern abstraction of hopeless and overpowering sorrow, mixed with the contending feelings of remorse, and of the pride which struggled to conceal it. She guessed, perhaps, that it was curiosity, arising out of her uncommon story, which induced me to intrude on her solitude and she could not be pleased that a fate like hers had been the theme of a traveller's amusement. Yet the look with which she regarded me was one of scorn instead of embarrassment. The opinion of the world and all its children could not add or take an iota from her load of misery; and, save from the half smile that seemed to intimate the contempt of a being rapt by the very intensity of her affliction above the sphere of ordinary humanities, she seemed as indifferent to my gaze, as if she had been a dead corpse or a marble statue.

Elspat was above the middle stature; her hair, now grizzled, was still profuse, and it had been of the most decided black. So were her eyes, in which, contradicting the stern and rigid features of her countenance, there shone the wild and troubled light that indicates an unsettled mind. Her hair was wrapt round a silver bodkin with some attention to neatness, and her dark mantle was disposed around her with a degree of taste, though the materials were of the most ordinary sort.

After gazing on this victim of guilt and calamity till I was ashamed to remain silent, though uncertain how I ought to address her, I began to express my surprise at her choosing such a desert and deplorable dwelling. She cut short these expressions of sympathy, by answering in a stern voice, without the least change of countenance or posture — "Daughter of the stranger, he has told you my story." I was silenced at once, and felt how little all earthly accommodation must seem to the mind which had such subjects as hers for rumination. Without again attempting to open the conversation, I took a piece of gold from my purse, (for Donald had intimated she lived on alms,) expecting she would at least stretch her hand to receive it. But she neither accepted nor rejected the gift — she did not even seem to notice it, though twenty times as valuable, probably, as was usually offered. I was obliged to place it on her knee, saying involuntarily, as I did so, "May God pardon you, and relieve you!" I shall never forget the look which she cast up to Heaven, nor the tone in which she exclaimed, in the very words of my old friend, John Home —

"My beautiful, my brave!"

It was the language of nature, and arose from the heart of the deprived mother, as it did from that gifted imaginative poet, while furnishing with appropriate expressions the ideal grief of Lady Randolph.

CHAPTER II.

> O, I'm come to the Low Country,
> Och, och, ohonochie,
> Without a penny in my pouch
> To buy a meal for me.
> I was the proudest of my clan,
> Long, long may I repine;
> And Donald was the bravest man,
> And Donald he was mine.
>
> *Old Song.*

ELSPAT had enjoyed happy days, though her age had sunk into hopeless and inconsolable sorrow and distress. She was once the beautiful and happy wife of Hamish MacTavish, for whom his strength and feats of prowess had gained the title of MacTavish Mhor. His life was turbulent and dangerous, his habits being of the old Highland stamp, which esteemed it shame to want any thing that could be had for the taking. Those in the Lowland line who lay near him, and desired to enjoy their lives and property in quiet, were contented to pay him a small composition, in name of protection money, and comforted themselves with the old proverb, that it was better to "fleech the deil than fight him." Others, who accounted such composition dishonourable, were often surprised by MacTavish Mhor, and his associates and followers, who usually inflicted an adequate penalty, either in person or property, or both. The creagh is yet remembered, in which he swept one hundred and fifty cows from Monteith in one drove; and how he placed the laird of Ballybught naked in a slough, for having threatened to send for a party of the Highland Watch to protect his property.

Whatever were occasionally the triumphs of this daring cateran, they were often exchanged for reverses; and his narrow escapes, rapid flights, and the ingenious stratagems with which he extricated himself from imminent danger, were no less remembered and admired than the exploits in which he had been successful. In weal or woe, through every species of fatigue, difficulty, and danger, Elspat was his faithful companion. She enjoyed with him the fits of occasional prosperity; and when adversity pressed them hard, her strength of mind, readiness of wit, and courageous endurance of danger and toil, are said often to have stimulated the exertions of her husband.

Their morality was of the old Highland cast, faithful friends and fierce enemies: the Lowland herds and harvests they accounted their own, whenever they had the means of driving off the one, or of seizing upon the other; nor did the least scruple on the right of property interfere on such occasions. Hamish Mhor argued like the old Cretan warrior:

> My sword, my spear, my shaggy shield,
>   They make me lord of all below;
> For he who dreads the lance to wield,
>   Before my shaggy shield must bow.
> His lands, his vineyards, must resign,
>   And all that cowards have is mine.

But those days of perilous, though frequently successful depredation, began to be abridged, after the failure of the expedition of Prince Charles Edward. MacTavish Mhor had not sat still on that occasion, and he was outlawed, both as a traitor to the state, and as a robber and cateran. Garrisons were now settled in many places where a red-coat had never before been seen, and the Saxon war-drum resounded among the most hidden recesses of the Highland mountains. The fate of MacTavish became every day more inevitable; and it was the more difficult for him to make his exertions for defence or escape, that Elspat, amid his evil days, had increased his family with an infant child, which was a considerable encumbrance upon the necessary rapidity of their motions. At length the fatal day arrived. In a strong pass on the skirts of Ben Cruachan, the celebrated MacTavish Mhor was surprised by a detachment of the Sidier Roy, His wife assisted him heroically, charging his piece from time to time; and as they were in possession of a post that was nearly unassailable, he might have perhaps escaped if his ammunition had lasted. But at length his balls were expended, although it was not until he had fired off most of the silver buttons from his waistcoat, and the soldiers, no longer deterred by fear of the unerring marksman, who had slain three, and wounded more of their number, approached his stronghold, and, unable to take him alive, slew him, after a most desperate resistance.

All this Elspat witnessed and survived, for she had, in the child which relied on her for support, a motive for strength and exertion. In what manner she maintained herself it is not easy to say. Her only ostensible means of support were a flock of three or four goats, which she fed wherever she pleased on the mountain pastures, no one challenging the intrusion. In the general distress of the country, her ancient acquaintances had little to bestow; but what they could part with from their own necessities, they willingly devoted to the relief of others. From Lowlanders she sometimes demanded tribute, rather than requested alms. She had not forgotten she was the widow of MacTavish Mhor, or that the child who trotted by her knee might, such were her imaginations, emulate one day the fame of his father, and command the same influence which he had once exerted without control. She associated so little with others, went so seldom and so unwillingly from the wildest recesses of the mountains, where she usually dwelt with her goats, that she was quite unconscious of the great change which had taken place in the country around her, the substitution of civil order for military violence, and the strength gained by the law and its adherents over those who were called in Gaelic song, "the stormy sons of the sword." Her own diminished consequence and straitened circumstances she indeed felt, but for this the death of MacTavish Mhor was, in her apprehension, a sufficing reason; and she doubted not that she should rise to her former state of importance, when Hamish Bean (or Fair-haired James) should be able to wield the arms of his father. If, then, Elspat was repelled rudely when she demanded any thing necessary for her wants, or the accommodation of her little flock, by a churlish farmer, her threats of vengeance, obscurely expressed, yet terrible in their tenor, used frequently to extort, through fear of her maledictions, the relief which was denied to her necessities; and the trembling goodwife, who gave meal or money to the widow of MacTavish Mhor, wished in her heart that the stern old carlin had been burnt on the day her husband had his due.

Years thus ran on, and Hamish Bean grew up, not indeed to be of his father's size or strength, but to become an active, high-spirited, fair-haired youth, with a ruddy cheek, an eye like an eagle, and all the agility, if not all the strength, of his formidable father, upon whose history and achievements his mother dwelt, in order to form her son's mind to a similar course of adventures. But the young see the present state of this changeful world more keenly than the old. Much attached to his mother, and disposed to do all in his power for her support, Hamish yet perceived, when he mixed with the world, that the trade of the cateran was now alike dangerous and discreditable, and that if he were to emulate his father's prowess, it must be in some other line of warfare, more consonant to the opinions of the present day.

As the faculties of mind and body began to expand, he became more sensible of the precarious nature of his situation, of the erroneous views of his mother, and her ignorance respecting the changes of the society with which she mingled so little. In visiting friends and neighbours, he became aware of the extremely reduced scale to which his parent was limited, and learned that she possessed little or nothing more than the absolute necessaries of life, and that these were sometimes on the point of failing. At times his success in fishing and the chase was able to add something to her subsistence; but he saw no regular means of contributing to her support, unless by stooping to servile labour, which, if he himself could have endured it, would, he knew, have been like a death's-wound to the pride of his mother.

Elspat, meanwhile, saw with surprise, that Hamish Bean, although now tall and fit for the field, showed no disposition to enter on his father's scene of action. There was something of the mother at her heart, which prevented her from urging him in plain terms to take the field as a cateran, for the fear occurred of the perils into which the trade must conduct him; and when she would have spoken to him on the subject, it seemed to her heated imagination as if the ghost of her husband arose between them in his bloody tartans, and laying his finger on his lips, appeared to prohibit the topic. Yet she wondered at what seemed his want of spirit, sighed as she saw him from day to day lounging about in the long-skirted Lowland coat, which the legislature had imposed upon the Gael instead of their own romantic garb, and thought how much nearer he would have resembled her husband, had he been clad in the belted plaid and short hose, with his polished arms gleaming at his side.

Besides these subjects for anxiety, Elspat had others arising from the engrossing impetuosity of her temper. Her love of MacTavish Mhor had been qualified by respect and sometimes even by fear; for the cateran was not the species of man who submits to female government; but over his son she had exerted, at first during childhood, and afterwards in early youth, an imperious authority, which gave her maternal love a character of jealousy. She could not bear, when Hamish, with advancing life, made repeated steps towards independence, absented himself from her cottage at such season, and for such length of time as he chose, and seemed to consider, although maintaining towards her every possible degree of respect and kindness, that the control and responsibility of his actions rested on himself alone. This would have been of little consequence, could she have concealed her feelings within her own bosom; but the ardour and impatience of her passions made her frequently show her son that she conceived herself neglected and ill used. When he was absent for any length of time from her cottage, without giving intimation of his purpose, her resentment on his return used to be so unreasonable, that it naturally suggested to a young man fond of independence, and desirous to amend his situation in the world, to leave her, even for the very purpose of enabling him to provide for the parent whose egotistical demands on his filial attention tended to confine him to a desert, in which both were starving in hopeless and helpless indigence.

Upon one occasion, the son having been guilty of some independent excursion, by which the mother felt herself affronted and disobliged, she had been more than usually violent on his return, and awakened in Hamish a sense of displeasure, which clouded his brow and cheek. At length, as she persevered in her unreasonable resentment, his patience became exhausted, and taking his gun from the chimney corner, and muttering to himself the reply which his respect for his mother prevented him from speaking aloud, he was about to leave the hut which he had but barely entered.

"Hamish," said his mother, "are you again about to leave me?" But Hamish only replied by looking at, and rubbing the lock of his gun.

"Ay, rub the lock of your gun," said his parent, bitterly; "I am glad you have courage enough to fire it, though it be but at a roe-deer." Hamish started at this undeserved taunt and cast a look of anger at her in reply. She saw that she had found the means of giving him pain.

"Yes," she said, "look fierce as you will at an old woman, and your mother; it would be long ere you bent your brow on the angry countenance of a bearded man."

"Be silent, mother, or speak of what you understand" said Hamish, much irritated, "and that is of the distaff and the spindle."

"And was it of spindle and distaff that I was thinking when I bore you away on my back, through the fire of six of the Saxon soldiers, and you a wailing child? I tell you, Hamish, I know a hundredfold more of swords and guns than ever you will; and you will never learn so much of noble war by yourself, as you have seen when you were wrapped up in my plaid."

"You are determined at least to allow me no peace at home, mother; but this shall have an end," said Hamish, as, resuming his purpose of leaving the hut, he rose and went towards the door.

"Stay, I command you," said his mother; "stay! or may the gun you carry be the means of your ruin—may the road you are going be the track of your funeral!"

"What makes you use such words, mother? said the young man, turning a little back—"they are not good, and good cannot come of them. Farewell just now, we are too angry to speak together—farewell; it will be long ere you see me again." And he departed, his mother, in the first burst of her impatience, showering after him her maledictions, and in the next invoking them on her own head, so that they might spare her son's. She passed that day and the next in all the vehemence of impotent and yet unrestrained passion, now entreating Heaven, and such powers as were familiar to her by rude tradition, to restore her dear son, "the calf of her heart;" now in impatient resentment, meditating with what bitter terms she should rebuke his filial disobedience upon his return, and now studying the most tender language to attach him to the cottage, which, when her boy was present, she would not, in the rapture of her affection, have exchanged for the apartments of Taymouth Castle.

Two days passed, during which, neglecting even the slender means of supporting nature which her situation afforded, nothing but the strength of a frame accustomed to hardships and privations of every kind, could have kept her in existence, notwithstanding the anguish of her mind prevented her being sensible of her personal weakness. Her dwelling, at this period, was the same cottage near which I had found her, but then more habitable by the exertions of Hamish, by whom it had been in a great measure built and repaired.

It was on the third day after her son had disappeared, as she sat at the door rocking herself, after the fashion of her countrywomen when in distress, or in pain, that the then unwonted circumstance occurred of a passenger being seen on the high-road above the cottage. She cast but one glance at him—he was on horseback, so that it could not be Hamish, and Elspat cared not enough for any other being on earth, to make her turn her eyes towards him a second time. The stranger, however, paused opposite to her cottage, and dismounting from his pony, led it down the steep and broken path which conducted to her door.

"God bless you, Elspat MacTavish!"—She looked at the man as he addressed her in her native language, with the displeased air of one whose reverie is interrupted; but the traveller went on to say, "I bring you tidings of your son Hamish." At once, from being the most uninteresting object, in respect to Elspat, that could exist, the form of the stranger became awful in her eyes, as that of a messenger descended from Heaven, expressly to pronounce upon her death or life. She started from her seat, and with hands convulsively clasped together, and held up to Heaven, eyes fixed on the stranger's countenance, and person stooping forward to him, she looked those enquiries, which her faltering tongue could not articulate. "Your son sends you his dutiful remembrance and this," said the messenger, putting into Elspat's hand a small purse containing four or five dollars.

"He is gone, he is gone!" exclaimed Elspat; "he has sold himself to be the servant of the Saxons, and I shall never more behold him! Tell me, Miles MacPhadraick, for now I know you, is it the price of the son's blood that you have put into the mother's hand?"

"Now, God forbid!" answered MacPhadraick, who was a tacksman, and had possession of a considerable tract of ground under his Chief, a proprietor who lived about twenty miles off—"God forbid I should do wrong, or say wrong, to you, or to the son of MacTavish Mhor! I swear to you by the hand of my Chief, that your son is well, and will soon see you; and the rest he will tell you himself." So saying, MacPhadraick hastened back up the pathway—gained the road, mounted his pony, and rode upon his way.

CHAPTER III.

ELSPAT MACTAVISH remained gazing on the money, as if the impress of the coin could have conveyed information how it was procured.

"I love not this MacPhadraick," she said to herself; "it was his race of whom the Bard hath spoken, saying, Fear them not when their words are loud as the winter's wind, but fear them when they fall on you like the sound of the thrush's song. And yet this riddle can be read but one way: My son hath taken the sword, to win that with strength like a man, which churls would keep him from with the words that frighten children." This idea, when once it occurred to her, seemed the more reasonable, that MacPhadraick, as she well knew, himself a cautious man, had so far encouraged her husband's practices, as occasionally to buy cattle of MacTavish, although he must have well known how they were come by, taking care, however, that the transaction was so made, as to be accompanied with great profit and absolute safety. Who so likely as MacPhadraick to indicate to a young cateran the glen in which he could commence his perilous trade with most prospect of success, who so likely to convert his booty into money? The feelings which another might have experienced on believing that an only son had rushed forward on the same path in which his father had perished, were scarce known to the Highland mothers of that day. She thought of the death of MacTavish Mhor as that of a hero who had fallen in his proper trade of war, and who had not fallen unavenged. She feared less for her son's life than for his dishonour. She dreaded on his account the subjection to strangers, and the death-sleep of the soul which is brought on by what she regarded as slavery.

The moral principle which so naturally and so justly occurs to the mind of those who have been educated under a settled government of laws that protect the property of the weak against the incursions of the strong, was to poor Elspat a book sealed and a fountain closed. She had been taught to consider those whom they called Saxons, as a race with whom the Gael were constantly at war, and she regarded every settlement of theirs within the reach of Highland incursion, as affording a legitimate object of attack and plunder. Her feelings on this point had been strengthened and confirmed, not only by the desire of revenge for the death of her husband, but by the sense of general indignation entertained, not unjustly, through the Highlands of Scotland, on account of the barbarous and violent conduct of the victors after the battle of Culloden. Other Highland clans, too, she regarded as the fair objects of plunder when that was possible, upon the score of ancient enmities and deadly feuds.

The prudence that might have weighed the slender means which the times afforded for resisting the efforts of a combined government, which had, in its less compact and established authority, been unable to put down the ravages of such lawless caterans as MacTavish Mhor, was unknown to a solitary woman, whose ideas still dwelt upon her own early times. She imagined that her son had only to proclaim himself his father's successor in adventure and enterprise, and that a force of men as gallant as those who had followed his father's banner, would crowd around to support it when again displayed. To her, Hamish was the eagle who had only to soar aloft and resume his native place in the skies, without her being able to comprehend how many additional eyes would have watched his flight, how many additional bullets would have been directed at his bosom. To be brief, Elspat was one who viewed the present state of society with the same feelings with which she regarded the times that had passed away. She had been indigent, neglected, oppressed, since the days that her husband had no longer been feared and powerful, and she thought that the term of her ascendence would return when her son had determined to play the part of his father. If she permitted her eye to glance farther into futurity, it was but to anticipate that she must be for many a day cold in the grave, with the coronach of her tribe cried duly over her, before her fair-haired Hamish could, according to her calculation, die with his hand on the basket-hilt of the red claymore. His father's hair was grey, ere, after a hundred dangers, he had fallen with his arms in his hands—That she should have seen and survived the sight, was a natural consequence of the manners of that age. And better it was—such was her proud thought—that she had seen him so die, than to have witnessed his departure from life in a smoky hovel—on a bed of rotten straw, like an over-worn hound, or a bullock which died of disease. But the hour of her young, her brave Hamish, was yet far distant. He must succeed—he must conquer, like his father. And when he fell at length,—for she anticipated for him no bloodless death,—Elspat would ere then have lain long in the grave, and could neither see his death-struggle, nor mourn over his grave-sod.

With such wild notions working in her brain, the spirit of Elspat rose to its usual pitch, or rather to one which seemed higher. In the emphatic language of Scripture, which in that idiom does not greatly differ from her own, she arose, she washed and changed her apparel, and ate bread, and was refreshed.

She longed eagerly for the return of her son, but she now longed not with the bitter anxiety of doubt and apprehension. She said to herself, that much must be done ere he could in these times arise to be an eminent and dreaded leader. Yet when she saw him again, she almost expected him at the head of a daring band, with pipes playing, and banners flying, the noble tartans flattering free in the wind, in despite of the laws which had suppressed, under severe penalties, the use of the national garb, and all the appurtenances of Highland chivalry. For all this, her eager imagination was content only to allow the interval of some days.

From the moment this opinion had taken deep and serious possession of her mind, her thoughts were bent upon receiving her son at the head of his adherents in the manner in which she used to adorn her hut for the return of his father.

The substantial means of subsistence she had not the power of providing, nor did she consider that of importance. The successful caterans would bring with them herds and flocks. But the interior of her hut was arranged for their reception—the usquebaugh was brewed or distilled in a larger quantity than it could have been supposed one lone woman could have made ready. Her hut was put into such order as might, in some degree, give it the appearance of a day of rejoicing. It was swept and decorated with boughs of various kinds, like the house of a Jewess, upon what is termed the Feast of the Tabernacles. The produce of the milk of her little flock was prepared in as great variety of forms as her skill admitted, to entertain her son and his associates whom she expected to receive along with him.

But the principal decoration, which she sought with the greatest toil, was the cloud-berry, a scarlet fruit, which is only found on very high hills, and there only in small quantities. Her husband, or perhaps one of his forefathers, had chosen this as the emblem of his family, because it seemed at once to imply by its scarcity the smallness of their clan, and by the places in which it was found, the ambitious height of their pretensions.

For the time that these simple preparations of welcome endured, Elspat was in a state of troubled happiness. In fact, her only anxiety was that she might be able to complete all that she could do to welcome Hamish and the friends who she supposed must have attached themselves to his band, before they should arrive, and find her unprovided for their reception.

But when such efforts as she could make had been accomplished, she once more had nothing left to engage her save the trifling care of her goats; and when these had been attended to, she had only to review her little preparations, renew such as were of a transitory nature, replace decayed branches and fading boughs, and then to sit down at her cottage door and watch the road, as it ascended on the one side from the banks of the Awe, and on the other wound round the heights of the mountain, with such a degree of accommodation to hill and level as the plan of the military engineer permitted. While so occupied, her imagination, anticipating the future from recollections of the past, formed out of the morning mist or the evening cloud the wild forms of an advancing band, which were then called "Sidier Dhu,"—dark soldiers—dressed in their native tartan, and so named to distinguish them from the scarlet ranks of the British army. In this occupation she spent many hours of each morning and evening.

CHAPTER IV.

It was in vain that Elspat's eyes surveyed the distant path, by the earliest light of the dawn and the latest glimmer of the twilight. No rising dust awakened the expectation of nodding plumes or flashing arms—the solitary traveller trudged listlessly along in his brown lowland greatcoat, his tartans dyed black or purple, to comply with or evade the law which prohibited their being worn in their variegated hues. The spirit of the Gael, sunk and broken by the severe though perhaps necessary laws, that proscribed the dress and arms which he considered as his birthright, was intimated by his drooping head and dejected appearance. Not in such depressed wanderers did Elspat recognise the light and free step of her son, now, as she concluded, regenerated from every sign of Saxon thraldom. Night by night, as darkness came, she removed from her unclosed door to throw herself on her restless pallet, not to sleep, but to watch. The brave and the terrible, she said, walk by night—their steps are heard in darkness, when all is silent save the whirlwind and the cataract—the timid deer comes only forth when the sun is upon the mountain's peak; but the bold wolf walks in the red light of the harvest-moon. She reasoned in vain—her son's expected summons did not call her from the lowly couch, where she lay dreaming of his approach. Hamish came not.

"Hope deferred," saith the royal sage, "maketh the heart sick;" and strong as was Elspat's constitution, she began to experience that it was unequal to the toils to which her anxious and immoderate affection subjected her, when early one morning the appearance of a traveller on the lonely mountain-road, revived hopes which had begun to sink into listless despair. There was no sign of Saxon subjugation about the stranger. At a distance she could see the flutter of the belted-plaid, that drooped in graceful folds behind him, and the plume that, placed in the bonnet, showed rank and gentle birth. He carried a gun over his shoulder, the claymore was swinging by his side, with its usual appendages, the dirk, the pistol, and the *sporran mollach*. Ere yet her eye had scanned all these particulars, the light step of the traveller was hastened, his arm was waved in token of recognition—a moment more, and Elspat held in her arms her darling son, dressed in the garb of his ancestors, and looking, in her maternal eyes, the fairest among ten thousand.

The first outpouring of affection it would be impossible to describe. Blessings mingled with the most endearing epithets which her energetic language affords, in striving to express the wild rapture of Elspat's joy. Her board was heaped hastily with all she had to offer; and the mother watched the young soldier, as he partook of the refreshment, with feelings how similar to, yet how different from, those with which she had seen him draw his first sustenance from her bosom!

When the tumult of joy was appeased, Elspat became anxious to know her son's adventures since they parted, and could not help greatly censuring his rashness for traversing the hills in the Highland dress in the broad sunshine, when the penalty was so heavy, and so many red soldiers were abroad in the country.

"Fear not for me, mother," said Hamish, in a tone designed to relieve her anxiety, and yet somewhat embarrassed; "I may wear the *breacan* at the gate of Fort Augustus, if I like it."

"Oh, be not too daring, my beloved Hamish, though it be the fault which best becomes thy father's son—yet be not too daring! Alas, they fight not now as in former days, with fair weapons, and on equal terms, but take odds of numbers and of arms, so that the feeble and the strong are alike levelled by the shot of a boy. And do not think me unworthy to be called your father's widow, and your mother, because I speak thus; for God knoweth , that, man to man, I would peril thee against the best in Breadalbane, and broad Lorn besides."

"I assure you, my dearest mother" replied Hamish, "that I am in no danger. But have you seen MacPhadraick, mother, and what has he said to you on my account?" "Silver he left me in plenty, Hamish; but the best of his comfort was, that you were well, and would see me soon. But beware of MacPhadraick, my son; for when he called himself the friend of your father, he better loved the most worthless stirk in his herd, than he did the life-blood of MacTavish Mhor. Use his services, therefore, and pay him for them—for it is thus we should deal with the unworthy; but take my counsel, and trust him not."

Hamish could not suppress a sigh, which seemed to Elspat to intimate that the caution came too late. "What have you done with him?" she continued, eager and alarmed. "I had money of him, and he gives not that without value—he is none of those who exchange barley for chaff. Oh, if you repent you of your bargain, and if it be one which you may break off without disgrace to your truth or your manhood, take back his silver, and trust not to his fair words."

"It may not be, mother," said Hamish; "I do not repent my engagement, unless that it must make me leave you soon."

"Leave me! how leave me? Silly boy, think you I know not what duty belongs to the wife or mother of a daring man! Thou art but a boy yet; and when thy father had been the dread of the country for twenty years, he did not despise my company and assistance, but often said my help was worth that of two strong gillies."

"It is not on that score, mother; but since I must leave the country" —

"Leave the country!" replied his mother, interrupting him; "and think you that I am like a bush, that is rooted to the soil where it grows, and must die if carried elsewhere? I have breathed other winds than these of Ben Cruachan—I have followed your father to the wilds of Ross, and the unpenetrable deserts of Y Mac Y Mhor—Tush, man, my limbs, old as they are, will bear me as far as your young feet can trace the way."

"Alas, mother," said the young man, with a faltering accent, "but to cross the sea" —

"The sea! who am I that I should fear the sea? Have I never been in a birling in my life—never known the Sound of Mull, the Isles of Treshornish, and the rough rocks of Harris?"

"Alas, mother, I go far, far from all of these—I am enlisted in one of the new regiments, and we go against the French in America."

"Enlisted!" uttered the astonished mother—"against my will—without *my* consent—You could not—you would not,"—then rising up, and assuming a posture of almost imperial command, "Hamish, you DARED not!"

"Despair, mother, dares every thing," answered Hamish, in a tone of melancholy resolution. "What should I do here, where I can scarce get bread for myself and you, and when the times are growing daily worse? Would you but sit down and listen, I would convince you I have acted for the best."

With a bitter smile Elspat sat down, and the same severe ironical expression was on her features, as, with her lips firmly closed, she listened to his vindication.

Hamish went on, without being disconcerted by her expected displeasure. "When I left you, dearest mother, it was to go to MacPhadraick's house, for although I knew he is crafty and worldly, after the fashion of the Sassenach, yet he is wise, and I thought how he would teach me, as it would cost him nothing, in which way I could mend our estate in the world."

"Our estate in the world!" said Elspat, losing patience at the word; "and went you to a base fellow with a soul no better than that of a cowherd, to ask counsel about your conduct? Your father asked none, save of his courage and his sword."

"Dearest mother," answered Hamish, "how shall I convince you that you live in this land of our fathers, as if our fathers were yet living? You walk as it were in a dream, surrounded by the phantoms of those who have been long with the dead. When my father lived and fought, the great respected the Man of the strong right hand, and the rich feared him. He had protection from MacAllan Mhor, and from Caberfae, and tribute from meaner men. That is ended, and his son would only earn a disgraceful and unpitied death, by the practices which gave his father credit and power among those who wear the breacan. The land is conquered—its lights are quenched,—Glengary, Lochiel, Perth, Lord Lewis, all the high chiefs are dead or in exile—We may mourn for it, but we cannot help it. Bonnet, broadsword, and sporran—power, strength, and wealth, were all lost on Drummossie-muir."

"It is false!" said Elspat, fiercely; "you, and such like dastardly spirits, are quelled by your own faint hearts, not by the strength of the enemy; you are like the fearful waterfowl, to whom the least cloud in the sky seems the shadow of the eagle."

"Mother," said Hamish, proudly, "lay not faint heart to my charge. I go where men are wanted who have strong arms and bold hearts too. I leave a desert, for a land where I may gather fame."

"And you leave your mother to perish in want, age, and solitude," said Elspat, essaying successively every means of moving a resolution, which she began to see was more deeply rooted than she had at first thought.

"Not so, neither," he answered; "I leave you to comfort and certainty, which you have yet never known. Barcaldine's son is made a leader, and with him I have enrolled myself; MacPhadraick acts for him, and raises men, and finds his own in it."

"That is the truest word of the tale, were all the rest as false as hell," said the old woman, bitterly.

"But we are to find our good in it also," continued Hamish; "for Barcaldine is to give you a shieling in his wood of Letter-findreight, with grass for your goats, and a cow, when you please to have one, on the common; and my own pay, dearest mother, though I am far away, will do more than provide you with meal, and with all else you can want. Do not fear for me. I enter a private gentleman; but I will return, if hard fighting and regular duty can deserve it, an officer, and with half a dollar a-day."

"Poor child!"—replied Elspat, in a tone of pity mingled with contempt, "and you trust MacPhadraick?"

"I might, mother" said Hamish, the dark red colour of his race crossing his forehead and cheeks, "for MacPhadraick knows the blood which flows in my veins, and is aware, that should he break trust with you, he might count the days which could bring Hamish back to Breadalbane, and number those of his life within three suns more. I would kill him at his own hearth, did he break his word with me—I would, by the great Being who made us both!"

The look and attitude of the young soldier for a moment overawed Elspat; she was unused to see him express a deep and bitter mood, which reminded her so strongly of his father, but she resumed her remonstrances in the same taunting manner in which she had commenced them.

"Poor boy!" she said; "and you think that at the distance of half the world your threats will be heard or thought of! But, go—go—place your neck under him of Hanover's yoke, against whom every true Gael fought to the death—Go, disown the royal Stewart, for whom your father, and his fathers, and your mother's fathers, have crimsoned many a field with their blood.—Go, put your head under the belt of one of the race of Dermid, whose children murdered—Yes," she added, with a wild shriek, "murdered your mother's fathers in their peaceful dwellings in Glencoe!—Yes," she again exclaimed, with a wilder and shriller scream, "I was then unborn, but my mother has told me—and I attended to the voice of *my* mother—well I remember her words!—They came in peace, and were received in friendship, and blood and fire arose, and screams and murder!"

"Mother," answered Hamish, mournfully, but with a decided tone, "all that I have thought over—there is not a drop of the blood of Glencoe on the noble hand of Barcaldine—with the unhappy house of Glenlyon the curse remains, and on them God hath avenged it."

"You speak like the Saxon priest already," replied his mother; "will you not better stay, and ask a kirk from MacAllan Mhor, that you may preach forgiveness to the race of Dermid?"

"Yesterday was yesterday," answered Hamish, "and to-day is to-day. When the clans are crushed and confounded together, it is well and wise that their hatreds and their feuds should not survive their independence and their power. He that cannot execute vengeance like a man, should not harbour useless enmity like a craven. Mother, young Barcaldine is true and brave; I know that MacPhadraick counselled him, that he should not let me take leave of you, lest you dissuaded me from my purpose; but he said, 'Hamish MacTavish is the son of a brave man, and he will not break his word.' Mother, Barcaldine leads an hundred of the bravest of the sons of the Gael in their native dress, and with their fathers' arms—heart to heart—shoulder to shoulder. I have sworn to go with him—He has trusted me, and I will trust him."

At this reply, so firmly and resolvedly pronounced, Elspat remained like one thunderstruck, and sunk in despair. The arguments which she had considered so irresistibly conclusive, had recoiled like a wave from a rock. After a long pause, she filled her son's quaigh, and presented it to him with an air of dejected deference and submission.

"Drink," she said, "to thy father's roof-tree, ere you leave it for ever; and tell me,—since the chains of a new King, and of a new Chief, whom your fathers knew not save as mortal enemies, are fastened upon the limbs of your father's son,—tell me how many links you count upon them?"

Hamish took the cup, but looked at her as if uncertain of her meaning. She proceeded in a raised voice. "Tell me," she said, "for I have a right to know, for how many days the will of those you have made your masters permits me to look upon you?—In other words, how many are the days of my life—for when you leave me, the earth has nought besides worth living for!"

"Mother," replied Hamish MacTavish, "for six days I may remain with you, and if you will set out with me on the fifth, I will conduct you in safety to your new dwelling. But if you remain here, then I will depart on the seventh by daybreak—then, as at the last moment, I MUST set out for Dunbarton, for if I appear not on the eighth day, I am subject to punishment as a deserter, and am dishonoured as a soldier and a gentleman."

"Your father's foot," she answered, "was free as the wind on the heath — it were as vain to say to him where goest thou, as to ask that viewless driver of the clouds, wherefore blowest thou. Tell me under what penalty thou must — since go thou must, and go thou wilt — return to thy thraldom?"

"Call it not thraldom, mother, it is the service of an honourable soldier — the only service which is now open to the son of MacTavish Mhor."

"Yet say what is the penalty if thou shouldst not return?" replied Elspat.

"Military punishment as a deserter," answered Hamish; writhing, however, as his mother failed not to observe, under some internal feelings, which he resolved to probe to the uttermost.

"And that," she said, with assumed calmness, which her glancing eye disowned, "is the punishment of a disobedient hound, is it not?"

"Ask me no more, mother," said Hamish; "the punishment is nothing to one who will never deserve it."

"To me it is something," replied Elspat, "since I know better than thou, that where there is power to inflict, there is often the will to do so without cause. I would pray for thee, Hamish, and I must know against what evils I should beseech Him who leaves none unguarded, to protect thy youth and simplicity."

"Mother," said Hamish, "it signifies little to what a criminal may be exposed, if a man is determined not to be such. Our Highland chiefs used also to punish their vassals, and, as I have heard, severely — Was it not Lachlan MacIan, whom we remember of old, whose head was struck off by order of his chieftain for shooting at the stag before him?"

"Ay," said Elspat, "and right he had to lose it, since he dishonoured the father of the people even in the face of the assembled clan. But the chiefs were noble in their ire — they punished with the sharp blade, and not with the baton. Their punishments drew blood, but they did not infer dishonour. Canst thou say the same for the laws under whose yoke thou hast placed thy freeborn neck?"

"I cannot — mother — I cannot," said Hamish, mournfully. "I saw them punish a Sassenach for deserting, as they called it, his banner. He was scourged — I own it — scourged like a hound who has offended an imperious master. I was sick at the sight — I confess it. But the punishment of dogs is only for those worse than dogs, who know not how to keep their faith."

"To this infamy, however, thou hast subjected thyself, Hamish," replied Elspat, "if thou shouldst give, or thy officers take, measure of offence against thee. — I speak no more to thee on thy purpose. — Were the sixth day from this morning's sun my dying day, and thou wert to stay to close mine eyes, thou wouldst run the risk of being lashed like a dog at a post — yes! unless thou hadst the gallant heart to leave me to die alone, and upon my desolate hearth, the last spark of thy father's fire, and of thy forsaken mother's life, to be extinguished together!" — Hamish traversed the hut with an impatient and angry pace.

"Mother," he said at length, "concern not yourself about such things. I cannot be subjected to such infamy, for never will I deserve it; and were I threatened with it, I should know how to die before I was so far dishonoured."

"There spoke the son of the husband of my heart!" replied Elspat; and she changed the discourse, and seemed to listen in melancholy acquiescence, when her son reminded her how short the time was which they were permitted to pass in each other's society, and entreated that it might be spent without useless and unpleasant recollections respecting the circumstances under which they must soon be separated.

Elspat was now satisfied that her son, with some of his father's other properties, preserved the haughty masculine spirit which rendered it impossible to divert him from a resolution which he had deliberately adopted. She assumed, therefore, an exterior of apparent submission to their inevitable separation; and if she now and then broke out into complaints and murmurs, it was either that she could not altogether suppress the natural impetuosity of her temper, or because she had the wit to consider, that a total and unreserved acquiescence might have seemed to her son constrained and suspicious, and induced him to watch and defeat the means by which she still hoped to prevent his leaving her. Her ardent, though selfish affection for her son, incapable of being qualified by a regard for the true interests of the unfortunate object of her attachment, resembled the instinctive fondness of the animal race for their offspring; and diving little farther into futurity than one of the inferior creatures, she only felt, that to be separated from Hamish was to die.

In the brief interval permitted them, Elspat exhausted every art which affection could devise, to render agreeable to him the space which they were apparently to spend with each other. Her memory carried her far back into former days, and her stores of legendary history, which furnish at all times a principal amusement of the Highlander in his moments of repose, were augmented by an unusual acquaintance with the songs of ancient bards, and traditions of the most approved Seannachies and tellers of tales. Her officious attentions to her son's accommodation, indeed, were so unremitted as almost to give him pain; and he endeavoured quietly to prevent her from taking so much personal toil in selecting the blooming heath for his bed, or preparing the meal for his refreshment. "Let me alone, Hamish," she would reply on such occasions; "you follow your own will in departing from your mother, let your mother have hers in doing what gives her pleasure while you remain."

So much she seemed to be reconciled to the arrangements which he had made in her behalf, that she could hear him speak to her of her removing to the lands of Green Colin, as the gentleman was called, on whose estate he had provided her an asylum. In truth, however, nothing could be farther from her thoughts. From what he had said during their first violent dispute, Elspat had gathered, that if Hamish returned not by the appointed time permitted by his furlough, he would incur the hazard of corporal punishment. Were he placed within the risk of being thus dishonoured, she was well aware that he would never submit to the disgrace, by a return to the regiment where it might be inflicted. Whether she looked to any farther probable consequences of her unhappy scheme, cannot be known; but the partner of MacTavish Mhor, in all his perils and wanderings, was familiar with an hundred instances of resistance or escape, by which one brave man, amidst a land of rocks, lakes, and mountains, dangerous passes, and dark forests, might baffle the pursuit of hundreds. For the future, therefore, she feared nothing; her sole engrossing object was to prevent her son from keeping his word with his commanding officer.

With this secret purpose, she evaded the proposal which Hamish repeatedly made, that they should set out together to take possession of her new abode; and she resisted it upon grounds apparently so natural to her character, that her son was neither alarmed nor displeased. "Let me not," she said, "in the same short week, bid farewell to my only son, and to the glen in which I have so long dwelt. Let my eye, when dimmed with weeping for thee, still look around, for a while at least, upon Loch Awe and on Ben Cruachan."

Hamish yielded the more willingly to his mother's humour in this particular, that one or two persons who resided in a neighbouring glen, and had given their sons to Barcaldine's levy, were also to be provided for on the estate of the chieftain, and it was apparently settled that Elspat was to take her journey along with them when they should remove to their new residence. Thus, Hamish believed that he had at once indulged his mother's humour, and insured her safety and accommodation. But she nourished in her mind very different thoughts and projects!

The period of Hamish's leave of absence was fast approaching, and more than once he proposed to depart, in such time as to insure his gaining easily and early Dunbarton, the town where were the head-quarters of his regiment. But still his mother's entreaties, his own natural disposition to linger among scenes long dear to him, and, above all, his firm reliance in his speed and activity, induced him to protract his departure till the sixth day, being the very last which he could possibly afford to spend with his mother, if indeed he meant to comply with the conditions of his furlough.

CHAPTER V.

> But for your son, believe it — Oh, believe it —
> Most dangerously you have with him prevailed,
> If not most mortal to him. —
>
> *Coriolanus.*

ON the evening which preceded his proposed departure, Hamish walked down to the river with his fishing-rod, to practise in the Awe, for the last time, a sport in which he excelled, and to find, at the same time, the means for making one social meal with his mother on something better than their ordinary cheer. He was as successful as usual, and soon killed a fine salmon. On his return homeward an incident befell him, which he afterwards related as ominous, though probably his heated imagination, joined to the universal turn of his countrymen for the marvellous, exaggerated into superstitious importance some very ordinary and accidental circumstance.

In the path which he pursued homeward, he was surprised to observe a person, who, like himself, was dressed and armed after the old Highland fashion. The first idea that struck him was, that the passenger belonged to his own corps, who, levied by government, and bearing arms under royal authority, were not amenable for breach of the statutes against the use of the Highland garb or weapons. But he was struck on perceiving, as he mended his pace to make up to his supposed comrade, meaning to request his company for the next day's journey, that the stranger wore a white cockade, the fatal badge which was proscribed in the Highlands. The stature of the man was tall, and there was something shadowy in the outline, which added to his size; and his mode of motion, which rather resembled gliding than walking, impressed Hamish with superstitious fears concerning the character of the being which thus passed before him in the twilight. He no longer strove to make up to the stranger, but contented himself with keeping him in view, under the superstition common to the Highlanders, that you ought neither to intrude yourself on such supernatural apparitions as you may witness, nor avoid their presence, but leave it to themselves to withhold or extend their communication, as their power may permit, or the purpose of their commission require.

Upon an elevated knoll by the side of the road, just where the pathway turned down to Elspat's hut, the stranger made a pause, and seemed to await Hamish's coming up. Hamish, on his part, seeing it was necessary he should pass the object of his suspicion, mustered up his courage, and approached the spot where the stranger had placed himself; who first pointed to Elspat's hut, and made, with arm and head, a gesture prohibiting Hamish to approach it, then stretched his hand to the road which led to the southward, with a motion which seemed to enjoin his instant departure in that direction. In a moment afterwards the plaided form was gone—Hamish did not exactly say vanished, because there were rocks and stunted trees enough to have concealed him; but it was his own opinion that he had seen the spirit of MacTavish Mhor, warning him to commence his instant journey to Dunbarton, without waiting till morning, or again visiting his mother's hut.

In fact, so many accidents might arise to delay his journey, especially where there were many ferries, that it became his settled purpose, though he could not depart without bidding his mother adieu, that he neither could nor would abide longer than for that object; and that the first glimpse of next day's sun should see him many miles advanced towards Dunbarton. He descended the path, therefore, and entering the cottage, he communicated, in a hasty and troubled voice, which indicated mental agitation, his determination to take his instant departure. Somewhat to his surprise, Elspat appeared not to combat his purpose, but she urged him to take some refreshment ere he left her for ever. He did so hastily, and in silence, thinking on the approaching separation, and scarce yet believing it would take place without a final struggle with his mother's fondness. To his surprise, she filled the quaigh with liquor for his parting cup.

"Go," she said, "my son, since such is thy settled purpose; but first stand once more on thy mother's hearth, the flame on which will be extinguished long ere thy foot shall again be placed there."

"To your health, mother!" said Hamish, "and may we meet again in happiness, in spite of your ominous words."

"It were better not to part," said his mother, watching him as he quaffed the liquor, of which he would have held it ominous to have left a drop.

"And now," she said, muttering the words to herself, "go—if thou canst go." "Mother," said Hamish, as he replaced on the table the empty quaigh, "thy drink is pleasant to the taste, but it takes away the strength which it ought to give."

"Such is its first effect, my son," replied Elspat; "but lie down upon that soft heather couch, shut your eyes but for a moment, and, in the sleep of an hour, you shall have more refreshment than in the ordinary repose of three whole nights, could they be blended into one."

"Mother," said Hamish, upon whose brain the potion was now taking rapid effect, "give me my bonnet—I must kiss you and begone—yet it seems as if my feet were nailed to the floor."

"Indeed," said his mother, "you will be instantly well, if you will sit down for half an hour—but half an hour; it is eight hours to dawn, and dawn were time enough for your father's son to begin such a journey."

"I must obey you, mother—I feel I must," said Hamish, inarticulately; "but call me when the moon rises."

He sat down on the bed—reclined back, and almost instantly was fast asleep. With the throbbing glee of one who has brought to an end a difficult and troublesome enterprise, Elspat proceeded tenderly to arrange the plaid of the unconscious slumberer, to whom her extravagant affection was doomed to be so fatal, expressing, while busied in her office, her delight, in tones of mingled tenderness and triumph. "Yes," she said, "calf of my heart, the moon shall arise and set to thee, and so shall the sun; but not to light thee from the land of thy fathers, or tempt thee to serve the foreign prince or the feudal enemy! To no son of Dermid shall I be delivered, to be fed like a bondswoman; but he who is my pleasure and my pride shall be my guard and my protector. They say the Highlands are changed; but I see Ben Cruachan rear his crest as high as ever into the evening sky—no one hath yet herded his kine on the depth of Loch Awe—and yonder oak does not yet bend like a willow. The children of the mountains will be such as their fathers, until the mountains themselves shall be levelled with the strath. In these wild forests, which used to support thousands of the brave, there is still surely subsistence and refuge left for one aged woman, and one gallant youth, of the ancient race and the ancient manners."

While the misjudging mother thus exulted in the success of her stratagem, we may mention to the reader, that it was founded on the acquaintance with drugs and simples, which Elspat, accomplished in all things belonging to the wild life which she had led, possessed in an uncommon degree, and which she exercised for various purposes. With the herbs, which she knew how to select as well as how to distil, she could relieve more diseases than a regular medical person could easily believe. She applied some to dye the bright colours of the tartan, from others she compounded draughts of various powers, and unhappily possessed the secret of one which was strongly soporific. Upon the effects of this last concoction, as the reader doubtless has anticipated, she reckoned with security on delaying Hamish beyond the period for which his return was appointed; and she trusted to his horror for the apprehended punishment to which he was thus rendered liable, to prevent him from returning at all.

Sound and deep, beyond natural rest, was the sleep of Hamish MacTavish on that eventful evening, but not such the repose of his mother. Scarce did she close her eyes from time to time, but she awakened again with a start, in the terror that her son had arisen and departed; and it was only on approaching his couch, and hearing his deep-drawn and regular breathing, that she reassured herself of the security of the repose in which he was plunged.

Still, dawning, she feared, might awaken him, notwithstanding the unusual strength of the potion with which she had drugged his cup. If there remained a hope of mortal man accomplishing the journey, she was aware that Hamish would attempt it, though he were to die from fatigue upon the road. Animated by this new fear, she studied to exclude the light, by stopping all the crannies and crevices through which, rather than through any regular entrance, the morning beams might find access to her miserable dwelling; and this in order to detain amid its wants and wretchedness the being, on whom, if the world itself had been at her disposal, she would have joyfully conferred it.

Her pains were bestowed unnecessarily. The sun rose high above the heavens, and not the fleetest stag in Breadalbane, were the hounds at his heels, could have sped, to save his life, so fast as would have been necessary to keep Hamish's appointment. Her purpose was fully attained—her son's return within the period assigned was impossible. She deemed it equally impossible, that he would ever dream of returning, standing, as he must now do, in the danger of an infamous punishment. By degrees, and at different times, she had gained from him a full acquaintance with the predicament in which he would be placed by failing to appear on the day appointed, and the very small hope he could entertain of being treated with lenity.

It is well known, that the great and wise Earl of Chatham prided himself on the scheme, by which he drew together for the defence of the colonies those hardy Highlanders, who, until his time, had been the objects of doubt, fear, and suspicion, on the part of each successive administration. But some obstacles occurred, from the peculiar habits and temper of this people, to the execution of his patriotic project. By nature and habit, every Highlander was accustomed to the use of arms, but at the same time totally unaccustomed to, and impatient of, the restraints imposed by discipline upon regular troops. They were a species of militia, who had no conception of a camp as their only home. If a battle was lost, they dispersed to save themselves, and look out for the safety of their families; if won, they went back to their glens to hoard up their booty, and attend to their cattle and their farms. This privilege of going and coming at pleasure, they would not be deprived of even by their Chiefs, whose authority was in most other respects so despotic. It followed as a matter of course, that the new-levied Highland recruits could scarce be made to comprehend the nature of a military engagement, which compelled a man to serve in the army longer than he pleased; and perhaps, in many instances, sufficient care was not taken at enlisting to explain to them the permanency of the engagement which they came under, lest such a disclosure should induce them to change their mind. Desertions were therefore become numerous from the newly-raised regiment, and the veteran General who commanded at Dunbarton, saw no better way of checking them than by causing an unusually severe example to be made of a deserter from an English corps. The young Highland regiment was obliged to attend upon the punishment, which struck a people, peculiarly jealous of personal honour, with equal horror and disgust, and not unnaturally indisposed some of them to the service. The old General, however, who had been regularly bred in the German wars, stuck to his own opinion, and gave out in orders that the first Highlander who might either desert, or fail to appear at the expiry of his furlough, should be brought to the halberds, and punished like the culprit whom they had seen in that condition. No man doubted that General— — —would keep his word rigorously whenever severity was required, and Elspat, therefore, knew that her son, when he perceived that due compliance with his orders was impossible, must at the same time consider the degrading punishment denounced against his defection as inevitable, should he place himself within the General's power.[1]

When noon was well passed, new apprehensions came on the mind of the lonely woman. Her son still slept under the influence of the draught; but what if, being stronger than she had ever known it administered, his health or his reason should be affected by its potency? For the first time, likewise, notwithstanding her high ideas on the subject of parental authority, she began to dread the resentment of her son, whom her heart told her she had wronged. Of late, she had observed that his temper was less docile, and his determinations, especially upon this late occasion of his enlistment, independently formed, and then boldly carried through. She remembered the stern wilfulness of his father when he accounted himself ill-used, and began to dread that Hamish, upon finding the deceit she had put upon him, might resent it even to the extent of casting her off, and pursuing his own course through the world alone. Such were the alarming and yet the reasonable apprehensions which began to crowd upon the unfortunate woman, after the apparent success of her ill-advised stratagem.

It was near evening when Hamish first awoke, and then he was far from being in the full possession either of his mental or bodily powers. From his vague expressions and disordered pulse, Elspat at first experienced much apprehension; but she used such expedients as her medical knowledge suggested; and in the course of the night, she had the satisfaction to see him sink once more into a deep sleep, which probably carried off the greater part of the effects of the drug, for about sunrising she heard him arise, and call to her for his bonnet. This she had purposely removed, from a fear that he might awaken and depart in the night-time, without her knowledge.

"My bonnet—my bonnet," cried Hamish, "it is time to take farewell. Mother, your drink was too strong—the sun is up—but with the next morning I will still see the double summit of the ancient Dun. My bonnet—my bonnet! mother, I must be instant in my departure." These expressions made it plain that poor Hamish was unconscious that two nights and a day had passed since he had drained the fatal quaigh, and Elspat had now to venture on what she felt as the almost perilous, as well as painful task, of explaining her machinations.

"Forgive me, my son," she said, approaching Hamish, and taking him by the hand with an air of deferential awe, which perhaps she had not always used to his father, even when in his moody fits.

"Forgive you, mother—for what?" said Hamish, laughing; "for giving me a dram that was too strong, and which my head still feels this morning, or for hiding my bonnet to keep me an instant longer? Nay, do *you* forgive *me*. Give me the bonnet, and let that be done which now must be done. Give me my bonnet, or I go without it; surely I am not to be delayed by so trifling a want as that—I, who have gone for years with only a strap of deer's hide to tie back my hair. Trifle not, but give it me, or I must go bareheaded, since to stay is impossible."

"My son," said Elspat, keeping fast hold of his hand, "what is done cannot be recalled; could you borrow the wings of yonder eagle, you would arrive at the Dun too late for what you purpose,—too soon for what awaits you there. You believe you see the sun rising for the first time since you have seen him set, but yesterday beheld him climb Ben Cruachan, though your eyes were closed to his light."

Hamish cast upon his mother a wild glance of extreme terror, then instantly recovering himself, said—"I am no child to be cheated out of my purpose by such tricks as these—Farewell, mother, each moment is worth a lifetime."

"Stay," she said, "my dear—my deceived son! rush not on infamy and ruin—Yonder I see the priest upon the high-road on his white horse—ask him the day of the month and week—let him decide between us."

With the speed of an eagle, Hamish darted up the acclivity, and stood by the minister of Glenorquhy, who was pacing out thus early to administer consolation to a distressed family near Bunawe.

The good man was somewhat startled to behold an armed Highlander, then so unusual a sight, and apparently much agitated, stop his horse by the bridle, and ask him with a faltering voice the day of the week and month. "Had you been where you should have been yesterday, young man," replied the clergyman, you would have known that it was God's Sabbath; and that this is Monday, the second day of the week, and twenty-first of the month."

"And this is true?" said Hamish.

"As true," answered the surprised minister, "as that I yesterday preached the word of God to this parish.—What ails you, young man?—are you sick?—are you in your right mind?"

Hamish made no answer, only repeated to himself the first expression of the clergyman—"Had you been where you should have been yesterday;" and so saying, he let go the bridle, turned from the road, and descended the path towards the hut, with the look and pace of one who was going to execution. The minister looked after him with surprise; but although he knew the inhabitant of the hovel, the character of Elspat had not invited him to open any communication with her, because she was generally reputed a Papist, or rather one indifferent to all religion, except some superstitious observances which had been handed down from her parents. On Hamish the Reverend Mr Tyrie had bestowed instructions when he was occasionally thrown in his way, and if the seed fell among the brambles and thorns of a wild and uncultivated disposition, it had not yet been entirely checked or destroyed. There was something so ghastly in the present expression of the youth's features, that the good man was tempted to go down to the hovel, and enquire whether any distress had befallen the inhabitants, in which his presence might be consoling, and his ministry useful. Unhappily he did not persevere in this resolution, which might have saved a great misfortune, as he would have probably become a mediator for the unfortunate young man; but a recollection of the wild moods of such Highlanders as had been educated after the old fashion of the country, prevented his interesting himself in the widow and son of the far-dreaded robber MacTavish Mhor; and he thus missed an opportunity, which he afterwards sorely repented, of doing much good.

When Hamish MacTavish entered his mother's hut, it was only to throw himself on the bed he had left, and, exclaiming, "Undone, undone!" to give vent, in cries of grief and anger, to his deep sense of the deceit which had been practised on him, and of the cruel predicament to which he was reduced.

Elspat was prepared for the first explosion of her son's passion, and said to herself, "It is but the mountain torrent, swelled by the thunder shower. Let us sit and rest us by the bank; for all its present tumult, the time will soon come when we may pass it dryshod." She suffered his complaints and his reproaches, which were, even in the midst of his agony, respectful and affectionate, to die away without returning any answer; and when, at length, having exhausted all the exclamations of sorrow which his language, copious in expressing the feelings of the heart, affords to the sufferer, he sunk into a gloomy silence, she suffered the interval to continue near an hour ere she approached her son's couch.

"And now," she said at length, with a voice in which the authority of the mother was qualified by her tenderness, "have you exhausted your idle sorrows, and are you able to place what you have gained against what you have lost? Is the false son of Dermid your brother, or the father of your tribe, that you weep because you cannot bind yourself to his belt, and become one of those who must do his bidding? Could you find in yonder distant country the lakes and the mountains that you leave behind you here? Can you hunt the deer of Breadalbane in the forests of America, or will the ocean afford you the silver-scaled salmon of the Awe? Consider, then, what is your loss, and, like a wise man, set it against what you have won."

"I have lost all, mother," replied Hamish, "since I have broken my word, and lost my honour. I might tell my tale, but who, oh, who would believe me?" The unfortunate young man again clasped his hands together, and, pressing them to his forehead, hid his face upon the bed.

Elspat was now really alarmed, and perhaps wished the fatal deceit had been left unattempted. She had no hope or refuge saving in the eloquence of persuasion, of which she possessed no small share, though her total ignorance of the world as it actually existed, rendered its energy unavailing. She urged her son, by every tender epithet which a parent could bestow, to take care for his own safety.

"Leave me," she said, "to baffle your pursuers. I will save your life—I will save your honour—I will tell them that my fair-haired Hamish fell from the Corrie dhu (black precipice) into the gulf, of which human eye never beheld the bottom. I will tell them this, and I will fling your plaid on the thorns which grow on the brink of the precipice, that they may believe my words. They will believe, and they will return to the Dun of the double-crest; for though the Saxon drum can call the living to die, it cannot recall the dead to their slavish standard. Then will we travel together far northward to the salt lakes of Kintail, and place glens and mountains betwixt us and the sons of Dermid. We will visit the shores of the dark lake, and my kinsmen — (for was not my mother of the children of Kenneth, and will they not remember us with the old love?) my kinsmen will receive us with the affection of the olden time, which lives in those distant glens, where the Gael still dwell in their nobleness, unmingled with the churl Saxons, or with the base brood that are their tools and their slaves."

The energy of the language, somewhat allied to hyperbole, even in its most ordinary expressions, now seemed almost too weak to afford Elspat the means of bringing out the splendid picture which she presented to her son of the land in which she proposed to him to take refuge. Yet the colours were few with which she could paint her Highland paradise. "The hills," she said, "were higher and more magnificent than those of Breadalbane — Ben Cruachan was but a dwarf to Skooroora. The lakes were broader and larger, and abounded not only with fish, but with the enchanted and amphibious animal which gives oil to the lamp. The deer were larger and more numerous — the white-tusked boar, the chase of which the brave loved best, was yet to be roused in those western solitudes — the men were nobler, wiser, and stronger, than the degenerate brood who lived under the Saxon banner. The daughters of the land were beautiful, with blue eyes and fair hair, and bosoms of snow, and out of these she would choose a wife for Hamish, of blameless descent, spotless fame, fixed and true affection, who should be in their summer bothy as a beam of the sun, and in their winter abode as the warmth of the needful fire."

Such were the topics with which Elspat strove to soothe the despair of her son, and to determine him, if possible, to leave the fatal spot, on which he seemed resolved to linger. The style of her rhetoric was poetical, but in other respects resembled that which, like other fond mothers, she had lavished on Hamish, while a child or a boy, in order to gain his consent to do something he had no mind to; and she spoke louder, quicker, and more earnestly, in proportion as she began to despair of her words carrying conviction.

On the mind of Hamish her eloquence made no impression. He knew far better than she did the actual situation of the country, and was sensible, that, though it might be possible to hide himself as a fugitive among more distant mountains, there was now no corner in the Highlands in which his father's profession could be practised, even if he had not adopted, from the improved ideas of the time when he lived, the opinion that the trade of the cateran was no longer the road to honour and distinction. Her words were therefore poured into regardless ears, and she exhausted herself in vain in the attempt to paint the regions of her mother's kinsmen in such terms as might tempt Hamish to accompany her thither. She spoke for hours, but she spoke in vain. She could extort no answer, save groans and sighs, and ejaculations, expressing the extremity of despair.

At length, starting on her feet, and changing the monotonous tone in which she had chanted, as it were, the praises of the province of refuge, into the short, stern language of eager passion—"I am a fool," she said, "to spend my words upon an idle, poor-spirited, unintelligent boy, who crouches like a hound to the lash. Wait here, and receive your taskmasters, and abide your chastisement at their hands; but do not think your mother's eyes will behold it. I could not see it and live. My eyes have looked often upon death, but never upon dishonour. Farewell, Hamish!—We never meet again."

She dashed from the hut like a lapwing, and perhaps for the moment actually entertained the purpose which she expressed, of parting with her son for ever. A fearful sight she would have been that evening to any who might have met her wandering through the wilderness like a restless spirit, and speaking to herself in language which will endure no translation. She rambled for hours, seeking rather than shunning the most dangerous paths. The precarious track through the morass, the dizzy path along the edge of the precipice, or by the banks of the gulfing river, were the roads which, far from avoiding, she sought with eagerness, and traversed with reckless haste. But the courage arising from despair was the means of saving the life, which, (though deliberate suicide was rarely practised in the Highlands,) she was perhaps desirous of terminating. Her step on the verge of the precipice was firm as that of the wild goat. Her eye, in that state of excitation, was so keen as to discern, even amid darkness, the perils which noon would not have enabled a stranger to avoid.

Elspat's course was not directly forward, else she had soon been far from the bothy in which she had left her son. It was circuitous, for that hut was the centre to which her heartstrings were chained, and though she wandered around it, she felt it impossible to leave the vicinity. With the first beams of morning, she returned to the hut. Awhile she paused at the wattled door, as if ashamed that lingering fondness should have brought her back to the spot which she had left with the purpose of never returning; but there was yet more of fear and anxiety in her hesitation—of anxiety, lest her fair-haired son had suffered from the effects of her potion—of fear, lest his enemies had come upon him in the night. She opened the door of the hut gently, and entered with noiseless step. Exhausted with his sorrow and anxiety, and not entirely relieved perhaps from the influence of the powerful opiate, Harnish Bean again slept the stern sound sleep, by which the Indians are said to be overcome during the interval of their torments. His mother was scarcely sure that she actually discerned his form on the bed, scarce certain that her ear caught the sound of his breathing. With a throbbing heart, Elspat went to the fire-place in the centre of the hut, where slumbered, covered with a piece of turf, the glimmering embers of the fire, never extinguished on a Scottish hearth until the indwellers leave the mansion for ever.

"Feeble greishogh," she said, as she lighted, by the help of a match, a splinter of bog pine which was to serve the place of a candle; "weak greishogh, soon shalt thou be put out for ever, and may Heaven grant that the life of Elspat MacTavish have no longer duration than thine!"

While she spoke she raised the blazing light towards the bed, on which still lay the prostrate limbs of her son, in a posture that left it doubtful whether he slept or swooned. As she advanced towards him, the light flashed upon his eyes — he started up in an instant, made a stride forward with his naked dirk in his hand, like a man armed to meet a mortal enemy, and exclaimed, "Stand off! — on thy life, stand off!"

"It is the word and the action of my husband," answered Elspat; "and I know by his speech and his step the son of MacTavish Mhor."

"Mother," said Hamish, relapsing from his tone of desperate firmness into one of melancholy expostulation; "oh, dearest mother, wherefore have you returned hither?"

"Ask why the hind comes back to the fawn," said Elspat; "why the cat of the mountain returns to her lodge and her young. Know you, Hamish, that the heart of the mother only lives in the bosom of the child."

"Then will it soon cease to throb," said Hamish, "unless it can beat within a bosom that lies beneath the turf. — Mother, do not blame me; if I weep, it is not for myself but for you, for my sufferings will soon be over; but yours — O, who but Heaven shall set a boundary to them!"

Elspat shuddered and stepped backward, but almost instantly resumed her firm and upright position, and her dauntless bearing.

"I thought thou wert a man but even now," she said, "and thou art again a child. Hearken to me yet, and let us leave this place together. Have I done thee wrong or injury? if so, yet do not avenge it so cruelly — See, Elspat MacTavish, who never kneeled before even to a priest, falls prostrate before her own son, and craves his forgiveness." And at once she threw herself on her knees before the young man, seized on his hand, and kissing it an hundred times, repeated as often, in heart-breaking accents, the most earnest entreaties for forgiveness. "Pardon," she exclaimed, "pardon, for the sake of your father's ashes — pardon, for the sake of the pain with which I bore thee, the care with which I nurtured thee! — Hear it, Heaven, and behold it, Earth — the mother asks pardon of her child, and she is refused!"

It was in vain that Hamish endeavoured to stem this tide of passion, by assuring his mother, with the most solemn asseverations, that he forgave entirely the fatal deceit which she had practised upon him.

"Empty words," she said; "idle protestations, which are but used to hide the obduracy of your resentment. Would you have me believe you, then leave the hut this instant, and retire from a country which every hour renders more dangerous. — Do this, and I may think you have forgiven me — refuse it, and again I call on moon and stars, heaven and earth, to witness the unrelenting resentment with which you prosecute your mother for a fault, which, if it be one, arose out of love to you."

"Mother," said Hamish, "on this subject you move me not. I will fly before no man. If Barcaldine should send every Gael that is under his banner, here, and in this place, will I abide them; and when you bid me fly, you may as well command yonder mountain to be loosened from its foundations. Had I been sure of the road by which they are coming hither,

I had spared them the pains of seeking me; but I might go by the mountain, while they perchance came by the lake. Here I will abide my fate; nor is there in Scotland a voice of power enough to bid me stir from hence, and be obeyed."

"Here, then, I also stay," said Elspat, rising up and speaking with assumed composure. "I have seen my husband's death — my eyelids shall not grieve to look on the fall of my son. But MacTavish Mhor died as became the brave, with his good sword in his right hand; my son will perish like the bullock that is driven to the shambles by the Saxon owner who has bought him for a price."

"Mother," said the unhappy young man, "you have taken my life; to that you have a right, for you gave it; but touch not my honour! It came to me from a brave train of ancestors, and should be sullied neither by man's deed nor woman's speech. What I shall do, perhaps I myself yet know not; but tempt me no farther by reproachful words; you have already made wounds more than you can ever heal."

"It is well, my son," said Elspat, in reply. "Expect neither farther complaint nor remonstrance from me; but let us be silent, and wait the chance which Heaven shall send us."

The sun arose on the next morning, and found the bothy silent as the grave. The mother and son had arisen, and were engaged each in their separate task — Hamish in preparing and cleaning his arms with the greatest accuracy, but with an air of deep dejection. Elspat, more restless in her agony of spirit, employed herself in making ready the food which the distress of yesterday had induced them both to dispense with for an unusual number of hours. She placed it on the board before her son so soon as it was prepared, with the words of a Gaelic poet, "Without daily food, the husbandman's ploughshare stands still in the furrow; without daily food, the sword of the warrior is too heavy for his hand. Our bodies are our slaves, yet they must be fed if we would have their service. So spake in ancient days the Blind Bard to the warriors of Fion."

The young man made no reply, but he fed on what was placed before him, as if to gather strength for the scene which he was to undergo. When his mother saw that he had eaten what sufficed him, she again filled the fatal quaigh, and proffered it as the conclusion of the repast. But he started aside with a convulsive gesture, expressive at once of fear and abhorrence.

"Nay, my son," she said, "this time surely, thou hast no cause of fear."

"Urge me not, mother," answered Hamish; "or put the leprous toad into a flagon, and I will drink; but from that accursed cup, and of that mind-destroying potion, never will I taste more!"

"At your pleasure, my son," said Elspat, haughtily, and began, with much apparent assiduity, the various domestic tasks which had been interrupted during the preceding day. Whatever was at her heart, all anxiety seemed banished from her looks and demeanour. It was but from an over activity of bustling exertion that it might have been perceived, by a close observer, that her actions were spurred by some internal cause of painful excitement; and such a spectator, too, might also have observed how often she broke off the snatches of songs or tunes which she hummed, apparently without knowing what she was doing, in order to cast a hasty glance from the door of the hut. Whatever might be in the mind of Hamish, his demeanour was directly the reverse of that adopted by his mother. Having finished the task of cleaning and preparing his arms, which he arranged within the hut, he sat himself down before the door of the bothy, and watched the opposite hill, like the fixed sentinel who expects the approach of an enemy. Noon found him in the same unchanged posture, and it was an hour after that period, when his mother, standing beside him, laid her hand on his shoulder, and said, in a tone indifferent, as if she had been talking of some friendly visit, "When dost thou expect them?"

"They cannot be here till the shadows fall long to the eastward," replied Hamish; "that is, even supposing the nearest party, commanded by Sergeant Allan Breack Cameron, has been commanded hither by express from Dunbarton, as it is most likely they will."

"Then enter beneath your mother's roof once more; partake the last time of the food which she has prepared; after this, let them come, and thou shalt see if thy mother is an useless encumbrance in the day of strife. Thy hand, practised as it is, cannot fire these arms so fast as I can load them; nay, if it is necessary, I do not myself fear the flash or the report, and my aim has been held fatal."

"In the name of Heaven, mother, meddle not with this matter!" said Hamish. "Allan Breack is a wise man and a kind one, and comes of a good stem. It may be, he can promise for our officers, that they will touch me with no infamous punishment; and if they offer me confinement in the dungeon, or death by the musket, to that I may not object."

"Alas, and wilt thou trust to their word, my foolish child? Remember the race of Dermid were ever fair and false, and no sooner shall they have gyves on thy hands, than they will strip thy shoulders for the scourge,"

"Save your advice, mother," said Hamish, sternly; "for me, my mind is made up." But though he spoke thus, to escape the almost persecuting urgency of his mother, Hamish would have found it, at that moment, impossible to say upon what course of conduct he had thus fixed. On one point alone he was determined, namely, to abide his destiny, be what it might, and not to add to the breach of his word, of which he had been involuntarily rendered guilty, by attempting to escape from punishment. This act of self-devotion he conceived to be due to his own honour, and that of his countrymen. Which of his comrades would in future be trusted, if he should be considered as having broken his word, and betrayed the confidence of his officers? and whom but Hamish Bean MacTavish would the Gael accuse, for having verified and confirmed the suspicions which the Saxon General was well known to entertain against the good faith of the Highlanders? He was, therefore, bent firmly to abide his fate. But whether his intention was to yield himself peaceably into the hands of the party who should come to apprehend him, or whether he purposed, by a show of resistance, to provoke them to kill him on the spot, was a question which he could not himself have answered. His desire to see Barcaldine, and explain the cause of his absence at the appointed time, urged him to the one course; his fear of the degrading punishment, and of his mother's bitter upbraidings, strongly instigated the latter and the more dangerous purpose. He left it to chance to decide when the crisis should arrive; nor did he tarry long in expectation of the catastrophe. Evening approached, the gigantic shadows of the mountains streamed in darkness towards the east, while their western peaks were still glowing with crimson and gold. The road which winds round Ben Cruachan was fully visible from the door of the bothy, when a party of five Highland soldiers, whose arms glanced in the sun, wheeled suddenly into sight from the most distant extremity, where the highway is hidden behind the mountain. One of the party walked a little before the other four, who marched regularly and in files, according to the rules of military discipline. There was no dispute, from the firelocks which they carried, and the plaids and bonnets which they wore, that they were a party of Hamish's regiment, under a non-commissioned officer; and there could be as little doubt of the purpose of their appearance on the banks of Loch Awe.

"They come briskly forward"—said the widow of MacTavish Mhor,—"I wonder how fast or how slow some of them will return again! But they are five, and it is too much odds for a fair field. Step back within the hut, my son, and shoot from the loophole beside the door. Two you may bring down ere they quit the high-road for the footpath—there will remain but three; and your father, with my aid, has often stood against that number."

Hamish Bean took the gun which his mother offered, but did not stir from the door of the hut. He was soon visible to the party on the high-road, as was evident from their increasing their pace to a run; the files, however, still keeping together like coupled greyhounds, and advancing with great rapidity. In far less time than would have been accomplished by men less accustomed to the mountains, they had left the high-road, traversed the narrow path, and approached within pistol-shot of the bothy, at the door of which stood Hamish, fixed like a statue of stone, with his firelock in his hand, while his mother, placed behind him, and almost driven to frenzy by the violence of her passions, reproached him in the strongest terms which despair could invent, for his want of resolution and faintness of heart. Her words increased the bitter gall which was arising in the young man's own spirit, as he observed the unfriendly speed with which his late comrades were eagerly making towards him, like hounds towards the stag when he is at bay. The untamed and angry passions which he inherited from father and mother, were awakened by the supposed hostility of those who pursued him; and the restraint under which these passions had been hitherto held by his sober judgment, began gradually to give way. The sergeant now called to him, "Hamish Bean MacTavish, lay down your arms and surrender."

"Do *you* stand, Allan Breack Cameron, and command your men to stand, or it will be the worse for us all."

"Halt, men"—said the sergeant, but continuing himself to advance. "Hamish, think what you do, and give up your gun; you may spill blood, but you cannot escape punishment."

"The scourge—the scourge—my son, beware the scourge!" whispered his mother.

"Take heed, Allan Breack," said Hamish. "I would not hurt you willingly,—but I will not be taken unless you can assure me against the Saxon lash."

"Fool!" answered Cameron, "you know I cannot. Yet I will do all I can. I will say I met you on your return, and the punishment will be light—but give up your musket—Come on, men."

Instantly he rushed forward, extending his arm as if to push aside the young man's levelled firelock. Elspat exclaimed, "Now, spare not your father's blood to defend your father's hearth!" Hamish fired his piece, and Cameron dropped dead.—All these things happened, it might be said, in the same moment of time. The soldiers rushed forward and seized Hamish, who, seeming petrified with what he had done, offered not the least resistance. Not so his mother, who, seeing the men about to put handcuffs on her son, threw herself on the soldiers with such fury, that it required two of them to hold her, while the rest secured the prisoner.

"Are you not an accursed creature," said one of the men to Hamish, "to have slain your best friend, who was contriving, during the whole march, how he could find some way of getting you off without punishment for your desertion?"

"Do you hear *that*, mother?" said Hamish, turning himself as much towards her as his bonds would permit—but the mother heard nothing, and saw nothing. She had fainted on the floor of her hut. Without waiting for her recovery, the party almost immediately began their homeward march towards Dunbarton, leading along with them their prisoner. They thought it necessary, however, to stay for a little space at the village of Dalmally, from which they despatched a party of the inhabitants to bring away the body of their unfortunate leader, while they themselves repaired to a magistrate to state what had happened, and require his instructions as to the farther course to be pursued. The crime being of a military character, they were instructed to march the prisoner to Dunbarton without delay.

The swoon of the mother of Hamish lasted for a length of time; the longer perhaps that her constitution, strong as it was, must have been much exhausted by her previous agitation of three days' endurance. She was roused from her stupor at length by female voices, which cried the coronach, or lament for the dead, with clapping of hands and loud exclamations; while the melancholy note of a lament, appropriate to the clan Cameron, played on the bagpipe, was heard from time to time.

Elspat started up like one awakened from the dead, and without any accurate recollection of the scene which had passed before her eyes. There were females in the hut who were swathing the corpse in its bloody plaid before carrying it from the fatal spot. "Women," she said, starting up and interrupting their chant at once and their labour—"Tell me, women, why sing you the dirge of MacDhonuil Dhu in the house of MacTavish Mhor?"

"She-wolf, be silent with thine ill-omened yell," answered one of the females, a relation of the deceased, "and let us do our duty to our beloved kinsman! There shall never be coronach cried, or dirge played, for thee or thy bloody wolf-burd. The ravens shall eat him from the gibbet, and the foxes and wild-cats shall tear thy corpse upon the hill. Cursed be he that would sain your bones, or add a stone to your cairn!"

"Daughter of a foolish mother," answered the widow of MacTavish Mhor, "know that the gibbet with which you threaten us, is no portion of our inheritance. For thirty years the Black Tree of the Law, whose apples are dead men's bodies, hungered after the beloved husband of my heart; but he died like a brave man, with the sword in his hand, and defrauded it of its hopes and its fruit."

"So shall it not be with thy child, bloody sorceress," replied the female mourner, whose passions were as violent as those of Elspat herself. "The ravens shall tear his fair hair to line their nests, before the sun sinks beneath the Treshornish islands."

These words recalled to Elspat's mind the whole history of the last three dreadful days. At first, she stood fixed as if the extremity of distress had converted her into stone; but in a minute, the pride and violence of her temper, outbraved as she thought herself on her own threshold, enabled her to reply—"Yes, insulting hag, my fair-haired boy may die, but it will not be with a white hand—it has been dyed in the blood of his enemy, in the best blood of a Cameron—remember that; and when you lay your dead in his grave, let it be his best epitaph, that he was killed by Hamish Bean for essaying to lay hands on the son of MacTavish Mhor on his own threshold. Farewell—the shame of defeat, loss, and slaughter, remain with the clan that has endured it!"

The relative of the slaughtered Cameron raised her voice in reply; but Elspat, disdaining to continue the objurgation, or perhaps feeling her grief likely to overmaster her power of expressing her resentment, had left the hut, and was walking forth in the bright moonshine.

The females who were arranging the corpse of the slaughtered man, hurried from their melancholy labour to look after her tall figure as it glided away among the cliffs. "I am glad she is gone," said one of the younger persons who assisted. "I would as soon dress a corpse when the great Fiend himself—God sain us—stood visibly before us, as when Elspat of the Tree is amongst us.—Ay—ay, even overmuch intercourse hath she had with the Enemy in her day."

"Silly woman," answered the female who had maintained the dialogue with the departed Elspat, "thinkest thou that there is a worse fiend on earth, or beneath it, than the pride and fury of an offended woman, like yonder bloody-minded hag? Know that blood has been as familiar to her as the dew to the mountain-daisy. Many and many a brave man has she caused to breathe their last for little wrong they had done to her or theirs. But her hough-sinews are cut, now that her wolf-burd must, like a murderer as he is, make a murderer's end."

Whilst the women thus discoursed together, as they watched the corpse of Allan Breack Cameron, the unhappy cause of his death pursued her lonely way across the mountain. While she remained within sight of the bothy, she put a strong constraint on herself, that by no alteration of pace or gesture, she might afford to her enemies the triumph of calculating the excess of her mental agitation, nay, despair. She stalked, therefore, with a slow rather than a swift step, and, holding herself upright, seemed at once to endure with firmness that woe which was passed, and bid defiance to that which was about to come. But when she was beyond the sight of those who remained in the hut, she could no longer suppress the extremity of her agitation. Drawing her mantle wildly round her, she stopped at the first knoll, and climbing to its summit, extended her arms up to the bright moon, as if accusing heaven and earth for her misfortunes, and uttered scream on scream, like those of an eagle whose nest has been plundered of her brood. Awhile she vented her grief in these inarticulate cries, then rushed on her way with a hasty and unequal step, in the vain hope of overtaking the party which was conveying her son a prisoner to Dunbarton. But her strength, superhuman as it seemed, failed her in the trial, nor was it possible for her, with her utmost efforts, to accomplish her purpose.

Yet she pressed onward, with all the speed which her exhausted frame could exert. When food became indispensable, she entered the first cottage: "Give me to eat," she said; "I am the widow of MacTavish Mhor—I am the mother of Hamish MacTavish Bean,—give me to eat, that I may once more see my fair-haired son." Her demand was never refused, though granted in many cases with a kind of struggle between compassion and aversion in some of those to whom she applied, which was in others qualified by fear. The share she had had in occasioning the death of Allan Breack Cameron, which must probably involve that of her own son, was not accurately known; but, from a knowledge of her violent passions and former habits of life, no one doubted that in one way or other she had been the cause of the catastrophe; and Hamish Bean was considered, in the slaughter which he had committed, rather as the instrument than as the accomplice of his mother.

This general opinion of his countrymen was of little service to the unfortunate Hamish. As his captain, Green Colin, understood the manners and habits of his country, he had no difficulty in collecting from Hamish the particulars accompanying his supposed desertion, and the subsequent death of the non-commissioned officer. He felt the utmost compassion for a youth, who had thus fallen a victim to the extravagant and fatal fondness of a parent. But he had no excuse to plead which could rescue his unhappy recruit from the doom, which military discipline and the award of a court-martial denounced against him for the crime he had committed.

No time had been lost in their proceedings, and as little was interposed betwixt sentence and execution. General———had determined to make a severe example of the first deserter who should fall into his power, and here was one who had defended himself by main force, and slain in the affray the officer sent to take him into custody. A fitter subject for punishment could not have occurred, and Hamish was sentenced to immediate execution. All which the interference of his captain in his favour could procure, was that he should die a soldier's death; for there had been a purpose of executing him upon the gibbet.

The worthy clergyman of Glenorquhy chanced to be at Dunbarton, in attendance upon some church courts, at the time of this catastrophe. He visited his unfortunate parishioner in his dungeon, found him ignorant indeed, but not obstinate, and the answers which he received from him, when conversing on religious topics, were such as induced him doubly to regret, that a mind naturally pure and noble should have remained unhappily so wild and uncultivated.

When he ascertained the real character and disposition of the young man, the worthy pastor made deep and painful reflections on his own shyness and timidity, which, arising out of the evil fame that attached to the lineage of Hamish, had restrained him from charitably endeavouring to bring this strayed sheep within the great fold. While the good minister blamed his cowardice in times past, which had deterred him from risking his person, to save, perhaps, an immortal soul, he resolved no longer to be governed by such timid counsels, but to endeavour, by application to his officers, to obtain a reprieve, at least, if not a pardon, for the criminal, in whom he felt so unusually interested, at once from his docility of temper and his generosity of disposition.

Accordingly the divine sought out Captain Campbell at the barracks within the garrison. There was a gloomy melancholy on the brow of Green Colin, which was not lessened, but increased, when the clergyman stated his name, quality, and errand. "You cannot tell me better of the young man than I am disposed to believe," answered the Highland officer; "you cannot ask me to do more in his behalf than I am of myself inclined, and have already endeavoured to do. But it is all in vain. General – – – is half a Lowlander, half an Englishman. He has no idea of the high and enthusiastic character which in these mountains often brings exalted virtues in contact with great crimes, which, however, are less offences of the heart than errors of the understanding. I have gone so far as to tell him, that in this young man he was putting to death the best and the bravest of my company, where all, or almost all, are good and brave. I explained to him by what strange delusion the culprit's apparent desertion was occasioned, and how little his heart was accessary to the crime which his hand unhappily committed. His answer was, 'These are Highland visions, Captain Campbell, as unsatisfactory and vain as those of the second sight. An act of gross desertion may, in any case, be palliated under the plea of intoxication; the murder of an officer may be as easily coloured over with that of temporary insanity. The example must be made, and if it has fallen on a man otherwise a good recruit, it will have the greater effect.' —Such being the General's unalterable purpose," continued Captain Campbell, with a sigh, "be it your care, reverend sir, that your penitent prepare by break of day tomorrow for that great change which we shall all one day be subjected to."

"And for which," said the clergyman, "may God prepare us all, as I in my duty will not be wanting to this poor youth."

Next morning, as the very earliest beams of sunrise saluted the grey towers which crown the summit of that singular and tremendous rock, the soldiers of the new Highland regiment appeared on the parade, within the Castle of Dunbarton, and having fallen into order, began to move downward by steep staircases and narrow passages towards the external barrier-gate, which is at the very bottom of the rock. The wild wailings of the pibroch were heard at times, interchanged with the drums and fifes, which beat the Dead March.

The unhappy criminal's fate did not, at first, excite that general sympathy in the regiment which would probably have arisen had he been executed for desertion alone. The slaughter of the unfortunate Allan Breack had given a different colour to Hamish's offence; for the deceased was much beloved, and besides belonged to a numerous and powerful clan, of whom there were many in the ranks. The unfortunate criminal, on the contrary, was little known to, and scarcely connected with, any of his regimental companions. His father had been, indeed, distinguished for his strength and manhood; but he was of a broken clan, as those names were called who had no chief to lead them to battle.

It would have been almost impossible in another case, to have turned out of the ranks of the regiment the party necessary for execution of the sentence; but the six individuals selected for that purpose, were friends of the deceased, descended, like him, from the race of MacDhonuil Dhu; and while they prepared for the dismal task which their duty imposed, it was not without a stern feeling of gratified revenge. The leading company of the regiment began now to defile from the barrier-gate, and was followed by the others, each successively moving and halting according to the orders of the Adjutant, so as to form three sides of an oblong square, with the ranks faced inwards. The fourth, or blank side of the square, was closed up by the huge and lofty precipice on which the Castle rises. About the centre of the procession, bare-headed, disarmed, and with his hands bound, came the unfortunate victim of military law. He was deadly pale, but his step was firm and his eye as bright as ever. The clergyman walked by his side — the coffin, which was to receive his mortal remains, was borne before him. The looks of his comrades were still, composed, and solemn. They felt for the youth, whose handsome form, and manly yet submissive deportment had, as soon as he was distinctly visible to them, softened the hearts of many, even of some who had been actuated by vindictive feelings.

The coffin destined for the yet living body of Hamish Bean was placed at the bottom of the hollow square, about two yards distant from the foot of the precipice, which rises in that place as steep as a stone wall to the height of three or four hundred feet. Thither the prisoner was also led, the clergyman still continuing by his side, pouring forth exhortations of courage and consolation, to which the youth appeared to listen with respectful devotion. With slow, and, it seemed, almost unwilling steps, the firing party entered the square. and were drawn up facing the prisoner, about ten yards distant. The clergyman was now about to retire — "Think, my son," he said, "on what I have told you, and let your hope be rested on the anchor which I have given. You will then exchange a short and miserable existence here, for a life in which you will experience neither sorrow nor pain. — Is there aught else which you can intrust to me to execute for you?"

The youth looked at his sleeve buttons. They were of gold, booty perhaps which his father had taken from some English officer during the civil wars. The clergyman disengaged them from his sleeves.

"My mother!" he said with some effort, "give them to my poor mother! — See her, good father, and teach her what she should think of all this. Tell her Hamish Bean is more glad to die than ever he was to rest after the longest day's hunting. Farewell, sir — farewell!"

The good man could scarce retire from the fatal spot. An officer afforded him the support of his arm. At his last look towards Hamish, he beheld him alive and kneeling on the coffin; the few that were around him had all withdrawn. The fatal word was given, the rock rung sharp to the sound of the discharge, and Hamish, falling forward with a groan, died, it may be supposed, without almost a sense of the passing agony.

Ten or twelve of his own company then came forward, and laid with solemn reverence the remains of their comrade in the coffin, while the Dead March was again struck up, and the several companies, marching in single files, passed the coffin one by one, in order that all might receive from the awful spectacle the warning which it was peculiarly intended to afford. The regiment was then marched off the ground, and reascended the ancient cliff, their music, as usual on such occasions, striking lively strains, as if sorrow, or even deep thought, should as short a while as possible be the tenant of the soldier's bosom.

At the same time the small party, which we before mentioned, bore the bier of the ill-fated Hamish to his humble grave, in a corner of the churchyard of Dunbarton, usually assigned to criminals. Here, among the dust of the guilty, lies a youth, whose name, had he survived the ruin of the fatal events by which he was hurried into crime, might have adorned the annals of the brave.

The minister of Glenorquhy left Dunbarton immediately after he had witnessed the last scene of this melancholy catastrophe. His reason acquiesced in the justice of the sentence, which required blood for blood, and he acknowledged that the vindictive character of his countrymen required to be powerfully restrained by the strong curb of social law. But still he mourned over the individual victim. Who may arraign the bolt of Heaven when it bursts among the sons of the forest; yet who can refrain from mourning, when it selects for the object of its blighting aim the fair stem of a young oak, that promised to be the pride of the dell in which it flourished? Musing on these melancholy events, noon found him engaged in the mountain passes, by which he was to return to his still distant home.

Confident in his knowledge of the country, the clergyman had left the main road, to seek one of those shorter paths, which are only used by pedestrians, or by men, like the minister, mounted on the small, but surefooted, hardy, and sagacious horses of the country. The place which he now traversed, was in itself gloomy and desolate, and tradition had added to it the terror of superstition, by affirming it was haunted by an evil spirit, termed *Cloght-dearg,* that is, Redmantle, who at all times, but especially at noon and at midnight, traversed the glen, in enmity both to man and the inferior creation, did such evil as her power was permitted to extend to, and afflicted with ghastly terrors those whom she had not license otherwise to hurt.

The minister of Glenorquhy had set his face in opposition to many of these superstitions, which he justly thought were derived from the dark ages of Popery, perhaps even from those of Paganism, and unfit to be entertained or believed by the Christians of an enlightened age. Some of his more attached parishioners considered him as too rash in opposing the ancient faith of their fathers; and though they honoured the moral intrepidity of their pastor, they could not avoid entertaining and expressing fears, that he would one day fall a victim to his temerity, and be torn to pieces in the glen of the Cloght-dearg, or some of those other haunted wilds, which he appeared rather to have a pride and pleasure in traversing alone, on the days and hours when the wicked spirits were supposed to have especial power over man and beast.

These legends came across the mind of the clergyman; and, solitary as he was, a melancholy smile shaded his cheek, as he thought of the inconsistency of human nature, and reflected how many brave men, whom the yell of the pibroch would have sent headlong against fixed bayonets, as the wild bull rushes on his enemy, might have yet feared to encounter those visionary terrors, which he himself, a man of peace, and in ordinary perils no way remarkable for the firmness of his nerves, was now risking without hesitation.

As he looked around the scene of desolation, he could not but acknowledge, in his own mind, that it was not ill chosen for the haunt of those spirits, which are said to delight in solitude and desolation. The glen was so steep and narrow, that there was but just room for the meridian sun to dart a few scattered rays upon the gloomy and precarious stream which stole through its recesses, for the most part in silence, but occasionally murmuring sullenly against the rocks and large stones, which seemed determined to bar its further progress. In winter, or in the rainy season, this small stream was a foaming torrent of the most formidable magnitude, and it was at such periods that it had torn open and laid bare the broad-faced and huge fragments of rock, which, at the season of which we speak, hid its course from the eye, and seemed disposed totally to interrupt its course. "Undoubtedly," thought the clergyman, "this mountain rivulet, suddenly swelled by a water-spout, or thunder-storm, has often been the cause of those accidents, which, happening in the glen called by her name, have been ascribed to the agency of the Cloght-dearg."

Just as this idea crossed his mind, he heard a female voice exclaim, in a wild and thrilling accent, "Michael Tyrie! — Michael Tyrie!" He looked round in astonishment, and not without some fear. It seemed for an instant, as if the Evil Being, whose existence he had disowned, was about to appear for the punishment of his incredulity. This alarm did not hold him more than an instant, nor did it prevent his replying in a firm voice, "Who calls — and where are you?"

"One who journeys in wretchedness, between life and death," answered the voice; and the speaker, a tall female, appeared from among the fragments of rocks which had concealed her from view.

As she approached more closely, her mantle of bright tartan, in which the red colour much predominated, her stature, the long stride with which she advanced, and the writhen features and wild eyes which were visible from under her curch, would have made her no inadequate representative of the spirit which gave name to the valley. But Mr Tyrie instantly knew her as the Woman of the Tree, the widow of MacTavish Mhor, the now childless mother of Hamish Bean. I am not sure whether the minister would not have endured the visitation of the Cloght-dearg herself, rather than the shock of Elspat's presence, considering her crime and her misery. He drew up his horse instinctively, and stood endeavouring to collect his ideas, while a few paces brought her up to his horse's head."

"Michael Tyrie," said she, "the foolish women of the Clachan[5] hold thee as a god—be one to me, and say that my son lives. Say this, and I too will be of thy worship—I will bend my knees on the seventh day in thy house of worship and thy God shall be my God."

"Unhappy woman," replied the clergyman, "man forms not pactions with his Maker as with a creature of clay like himself. Thinkest thou to chaffer with Him, who formed the earth, and spread out the heavens, or that thou canst offer aught of homage or devotion that can be worth acceptance in his eyes? He hath asked obedience, not sacrifice; patience under the trials with which he afflicts us, instead of vain bribes, such as man offers to his changeful brother of clay, that he may be moved from his purpose."

"Be silent, priest!" answered the desperate woman; "speak not to me the words of thy white book. Elspat's kindred were of those who crossed themselves and knelt when the sacring bell was rung; and she knows that atonement can be made on the altar for deeds done in the field. Elspat had once flocks and herds, goats upon the cliffs, and cattle in the strath. She wore gold around her neck and on her hair—thick twists as those worn by the heroes of old. All these would she have resigned to the priest—all these; and if he wished for the ornaments of a gentle lady, or the sporran of a high chief, though they had been great as Macallanmore himself, MacTavish Mhor would have procured them if Elspat had promised them. Elspat is now poor, and has nothing to give. But the Black Abbot of Inchaffray would have bidden her scourge her shoulders, and macerate her feet by pilgrimage, and he would have granted his pardon to her when he saw that her blood had flowed, and that her flesh had been torn. These were the priests who had indeed power even with the most powerful—they threatened the great men of the earth with the word of their mouth, the sentence of their book, the blaze of their torch, the sound of their sacring bell. The mighty bent to their will, and unloosed at the word of the priests those whom they had bound in their wrath, and set at liberty, unharmed, him whom they had sentenced to death, and for whose blood they had thirsted. These were a powerful race, and might well ask the poor to kneel, since their power could humble the proud. But you!—against whom are ye strong, but against women who have been guilty of folly, and men who never wore sword? The priests of old were like the winter torrent which fills this hollow valley, and rolls these massive rocks against each other as easily as the boy plays with the ball which he casts before him—But you! you do but resemble the summer-stricken stream, which is turned aside by the rushes, and stemmed by a bush of sedges—Woe worth you, for there is no help in you."

The clergyman was at no loss to conceive that Elspat had lost the Roman Catholic faith without gaining any other, and that she still retained a vague and confused idea of the composition with the priesthood, by confession, alms, and penance, and of their extensive power, which, according to her notion, was adequate, if duly propitiated, even to effecting her son's safety. Compassionating her situation, and allowing for her errors and ignorance, he answered her with mildness.

"Alas, unhappy woman! Would to God I could convince thee as easily where thou oughtest to seek, and art sure to find consolation, as I can assure you with a single word, that were Rome and all her priesthood once more in the plenitude of their power, they could not, for largesse or penance, afford to thy misery an atom of aid or comfort. — Elspat MacTavish, I grieve to tell you the news."

"I know them without thy speech," said the unhappy woman — "My son is doomed to die."

"Elspat," resumed the clergyman, "he was doomed, and the sentence has been executed." The hapless mother threw her eyes up to heaven, and uttered a shriek so unlike the voice of a human being, that the eagle which soared in middle air answered it as she would have done the call of her mate.

"It is impossible!" she exclaimed, "it is impossible! Men do not condemn and kill on the same day! Thou art deceiving me. The people call thee holy — hast thou the heart to tell a mother she has murdered her only child?"

"God knows," said the priest, the tears falling fast from his eyes, "that were it in my power, I would gladly tell better tidings — But these which I bear are as certain as they are fatal — My own ears heard the death-shot, my own eyes beheld thy son's death — thy son's funeral. — My tongue bears witness to what my ears heard and my eyes saw."

The wretched female clasped her hands close together, and held them up towards heaven like a sibyl announcing war and desolation, while, in impotent yet frightful rage, she poured forth a tide of the deepest imprecations. — "Base Saxon churl!" she exclaimed, "vile hypocritical juggler! May the eyes that looked tamely on the death of my fair-haired boy be melted in their sockets with ceaseless tears, shed for those that are nearest and most dear to thee! May the ears that heard his death-knell be dead hereafter to all other sounds save the screech of the raven, and the hissing of the adder! May the tongue that tells me of his death and of my own crime, be withered in thy mouth — or better, when thou wouldst pray with thy people, may the Evil One guide it, and give voice to blasphemies instead of blessings, until men shall fly in terror from thy presence, and the thunder of heaven be launched against thy head, and stop for ever thy cursing and accursed voice! Begone, with this malison! — Elspat will never, never again bestow so many words upon living man."

She kept her word — from that day the world was to her a wilderness, in which she remained without thought, care, or interest, absorbed in her own grief, indifferent to every thing else.

With her mode of life, or rather of existence, the reader is already as far acquainted as I have the power of making him. Of her death, I can tell him nothing. It is supposed to have happened several years after she had attracted the attention of my excellent friend Mrs Bethune Baliol. Her benevolence, which was never satisfied with dropping a sentimental tear, when there was room for the operation of effective charity, induced her to make various attempts to alleviate the condition of this most wretched woman. But all her exertions could only render Elspat's means of subsistence less precarious, a circumstance which, though generally interesting even to the most wretched outcasts, seemed to her a matter of total indifference. Every attempt to place any person in her hut to take charge of her miscarried, through the extreme resentment with which she regarded all intrusion on her solitude, or by the timidity of those who had been pitched upon to be inmates with the terrible Woman of the Tree. At length, when Elspat became totally unable (in appearance at least) to turn herself on the wretched settle which served her for a couch, the humanity of Mr Tyrie's successor sent two women to attend upon the last moments of the solitary, which could not, it was judged, be far distant, and to avert the possibility that she might perish for want of assistance or food, before she sunk under the effects of extreme age, or mortal malady.

It was on a November evening, that the two women appointed for this melancholy purpose, arrived at the miserable cottage which we have already described. Its wretched inmate lay stretched upon the bed, and seemed almost already a lifeless corpse, save for the wandering of the fierce dark eyes, which rolled in their sockets in a manner terrible to look upon, and seemed to watch with surprise and indignation the motions of the strangers, as persons whose presence was alike unexpected and unwelcome. They were frightened at her looks; but, assured in each other's company, they kindled a fire, lighted a candle, prepared food, and made other arrangements for the discharge of the duty assigned them.

The assistants agreed they should watch the bedside of the sick person by turns; but, about midnight, overcome by fatigue, (for they had walked far that morning,) both of them fell fast asleep. When they awoke, which was not till after the interval of some hours, the hut was empty, and the patient gone. They rose in terror, and went to the door of the cottage, which was latched as it had been at night. They looked out into the darkness, and called upon their charge by her name. The night-raven screamed from the old oak-tree, the fox howled on the hill, the hoarse waterfall replied with its echoes, but there was no human answer. The terrified women did not dare to make further search till morning should appear; for the sudden disappearance of a creature so frail as Elspat, together with the wild tenor of her history, intimidated them from stirring from the hut. They remained, therefore, in dreadful terror, sometimes thinking they heard her voice without, and at other times, that sounds of a different description were mingled with the mournful sigh of the night-breeze, or the dash of the cascade. Sometimes, too, the latch rattled, as if some frail and impotent hand were in vain attempting to lift it, and ever and anon they expected the entrance of their terrible patient, animated by supernatural strength, and in the company, perhaps, of some being more dreadful than herself. Morning came at length. They sought brake, rock, and thicket in vain. Two hours after daylight, the minister himself appeared, and, on the report of the watchers, caused the country to be alarmed, and a general and exact search to be made through the whole neighbourhood of the cottage, and the oak-tree. But it was all in vain. Elspat MacTavish was never found, whether dead or alive; nor could there ever be traced the slightest circumstance to indicate her fate.

The neighbourhood was divided concerning the cause of her disappearance. The credulous thought that the evil spirit, under whose influence she seemed to have acted, had carried her away in the body; and there are many who are still unwilling, at untimely hours, to pass the oak-tree, beneath which, as they allege, she may still be seen seated according to her wont. Others less superstitious supposed, that had it been possible to search the gulf of the Corri Dhu, the profound deeps of the lake, or the whelming eddies of the river, the remains of Elspat MacTavish might have been discovered; as nothing was more natural, considering her state of body and mind, than that she should have fallen in by accident, or precipitated herself intentionally into one or other of those places of sure destruction. The clergyman entertained an opinion of his own. He thought that, impatient of the watch which was placed over her, this unhappy woman's instinct had taught her, as it directs various domestic animals, to withdraw herself from the sight of her own race, that the death-struggle might take place in some secret den, where, in all probability, her mortal relics would never meet the eyes of mortals. This species of instinctive feeling seemed to him of a tenor with the whole course of her unhappy life, and most likely to influence her, when it drew to a conclusion.

Edinburgh Review [Henry Brougham]

Art. II. *Hours of Idleness: A Series of Poems, Original and Translated.* By George Gordon, Lord Byron, a Minor. 8vo. pp. 200. Newark. 1807. (1808)

THE poesy of this young lord belongs to the class which neither gods nor men are said to permit. Indeed, we do not recollect to have seen a quantity of verse with so few deviations in either direction from that exact standard. His effusions are spread over a dead flat, and can no more get above or below the level, than if they were so much stagnant water. As an extenuation of this offence, the noble author is peculiarly forward in pleading minority. We have it in the title-page, and on the very back of the volume; it follows his name like a favourite part of his *style*. Much stress is laid upon it in the preface, and the poems are connected with this general statement of his case, by particular dates, substantiating the age at which each was written. Now, the law upon the point of minority, we hold to be perfectly clear. It is a plea available only to the defendant; no plaintiff can offer it as a supplementary ground of action. Thus, if any suit could be brought against Lord Byron, for the purpose of compelling him to put into court a certain quantity of poetry; and if judgement were given against him; it is highly probable that an exception would be taken, were he to deliver *for poetry*, the contents of this volume. To this he might plead *minority*; but as he now makes voluntary tender of the article, he hath no right to sue, on that ground, for the price in good current praise, should the goods be unmarketable. This is our view of the law on the point, and we dare to say, so will it be ruled. Perhaps however, in reality, all that he tells us about his youth, is rather with a view to increase our wonder, than to soften our censures. He possibly means to say, 'See how a minor can write! This poem was actually composed by a young man of eighteen, and this by one of only sixteen!' — But, alas, we all remember the poetry of Cowley at ten, and Pope at twelve; and so far from hearing, with any degree of surprise, that very poor verses were written by a youth from his leaving school to his leaving college, inclusive, we really believe this to be the most common of all occurrences; that it happens in the life of nine men in ten who are educated in England; and that the tenth man writes better verse than Lord Byron.

His other plea of privilege, our author rather brings forward in order to wave it. He certainly, however, does allude frequently to his family and ancestors — sometimes in poetry, sometimes in notes; and while giving up his claim on the score of rank, he takes care to remember us of Dr Johnson's saying, that when a nobleman appears as an author, his merit should be handsomely acknowledged. In truth, it is this consideration only, that induces us to give Lord Byron's poems a place in our review, beside our desire to counsel him, that he do forthwith abandon poetry, and turn his talents, which are considerable, and his opportunities, which are great, to better account.

With this view, we must beg leave seriously to assure him, that the mere rhyming of the final syllable, even when accompanied by the presence of a certain number of feet; nay, although (which does not always happen) those feet should scan regularly, and have been all counted accurately upon the fingers, — is not the whole art of poetry. We would entreat him to believe, that a certain portion of liveliness, somewhat of fancy, is necessary to constitute a poem; and that a poem in the present day, to be read, must contain at least one thought, either in a little degree different from the ideas of former writers, or differently expressed.' We put it to his candour, whether there is any thing so deserving the name of poetry in verses like the following, written in 1806, and whether, if a youth of eighteen could say any thing so uninteresting to his ancestors, a youth of nineteen should publish it.

'Shades of heroes, farewell! your descendant, departing
  From the seat of his ancestors, bids you, adieu!
Abroad, or at home, your remembrance imparting
  New courage, he'll think upon glory, and you.

Though a tear dim his eye, at this sad separation,
  'Tis nature, not fear, that excites his regret:
Far distant he goes, with the same emulation;
  The fame of his fathers he ne'er can forget.

That fame, and that memory, still will he cherish,
  He vows, that he ne'er will disgrace your renown;
Like you will he live, or like you will he perish;
  When decay'd, may he mingle his dust with your own.' p. 3.

Now we positively do assert, that there is nothing better than these stanzas in the whole compass of the noble minor's volume. Lord Byron should also have a care of attempting what the greatest poets have done before him, for comparisons (as he must have had occasion to see at his writing master's) are odious. — Gray's Ode on Eton College, should really have kept out the ten hobbling stanzas 'on a distant view of the village and school of Harrow.'

'Where fancy yet joys to retrace the resemblance,
  Of comrades, in friendship and mischief allied;
How welcome to me, your ne'er fading remembrance,
  Which rests in the bosom, though hope is deny'd.' — p. 4.

In like manner, the exquisite lines of Mr Rogers, '*On a Tear,*' might have warned the noble author off those premises, and spared us a whole dozen such stanzas as the following.

'Mild Charity's glow,
  To us mortals below,
Shows the soul from barbarity clear;
  Compassion will melt,
  Where this virtue is felt,
And its dew is diffus'd in a Tear.

The man doom'd to fail,
  With the blast of the gale,
Through billows Atlantic to steer,

>   As he bends o'er the wave,
>   Which may soon be his grave,
>   The green sparkles bright with a Tear.' —p. 11.

And so of instances in which former poets had failed. Thus, we do not think Lord Byron was made for translating, during his non-age, Adrian's Address to his Soul, when Pope succeeded so indifferently in the attempt. If our readers, however, are of another opinion, they may look at it.

>   'Ah! gentle, fleeting, wav'ring sprite,
>   Friend and associate of this clay!
>   To what unknown region borne,
>   Wilt thou, now, wing thy distant flight?
>   No more, with wonted humour gay,
>   But pallid, cheerless, and forlorn.' —page 72.

However, be this as it may, we fear his translations and imitations are great favourites with Lord Byron. We have them of all kinds, from Anacreon to Ossian; and, viewing them as school exercises, they may pass. Only, why print them after they have had their day and served their turn? And why call the thing in p. 79. a translation, where *two* words (θελω λεγειν) of the original are expanded into four lines, and the other thing in p. 81, where μερουχζιοις ποι' ὁ ξαιζ, is rendered by means of six hobbling verses? — As to his Ossianic poesy, we are not very good judges, being, in truth, so moderately skilled in that species of composition, that we should, in all probability, be criticizing some bit of the genuine Macpherson itself, were we to express our opinion of Lord Byron's raphsodies. *If,* then, the following beginning of a 'Song of bards,' is by his Lordship, we venture to object to it, as far as we can comprehend it. 'What form rises on the roar of clouds, whose dark ghost gleams on the red stream of tempests? His voice rolls on the thunder;'tis Orla, the brown chief of Otihona. He was, '&c. After detaining this 'brown chief some time, the bards conclude by giving him their advice to 'raise his fair locks;' then to 'spread them on the arch of the rainbow;' and 'to smile through the tears of the storm'. Of this kind of thing there are no less than nine pages; and we can so far venture an opinion in their favour, that they look very like Macpherson; and we are positive they are pretty nearly as stupid and tiresome.

It is a sort of privilege of poets to be egotists; but they should 'use it as not abusing it;' and particularly one who piques himself (though indeed at the ripe age of nineteen), of being 'an infant bard,' — ('The artless Helicon I boast is youth;') —should either not know, or should seem not to know, so much about his own ancestry. Besides a poem above cited on the family seat of the Byrons, we have another of eleven pages, on the self-same subject, introduced with an apology, 'he certainly had no intention of inserting it'; but really, 'the particular request of some friends,' &c. &c. It concludes with five stanzas on himself, 'the last and youngest of a noble line.' There is a good deal also about his maternal ancestors, in a poem on Lachin-y-gair, a mountain where he spent part of his youth, and might have learnt that *pibroch* is not a bagpipe, any more than duet means a fiddle.

As the author has dedicated so large a part of his volume to immortalize his employments at school and college, we cannot possibly dismiss it without presenting the reader with a specimen of these ingenious effusions. In an ode with a Greek motto, called Granta, we have the following magnificent stanzas.

  'There, in apartments small and damp,
   The candidate for college prize?,
  Sits poring by the midnight lamp,
   Goes late to bed, yet early rise?

  Who reads false quantities in Sele,
   Or puzzles o'er the deep triangle;
  Depriv'd of many a wholesome meal,
   In barbarous Latin, doom'd to wrangle.

  Renouncing every pleasing page,
   From authors of historic use;
  Preferring to the lettered sage,
   The square of the hypothenuse.

  Still harmless are these occupations,
   That hurt none but the hapless student,
  Compar'd with other recreations,
   Which bring together the imprudent.
             p. 123, 124, 125.

We are sorry to hear so bad an account of the college psalmody as is contained in the following Attic stanzas.

  'Our choir would scarcely be excus'd,
   Even as a band of raw beginners;
  All mercy, now, must be refus'd
   To such a set of croaking sinners.

  If David, when his toils were ended,
   Had heard these blockheads sing before him,
  To us, his psalms had ne'er descended;
   In furious mood, he would have tore 'em.' — p. 126, 127.

But whatever judgment may be passed on the poems of this noble minor, it seems we must take them as we find them, and be content; for they are the last we shall ever have from him. He is at best, he says, but an intruder into the groves of Parnassus; he never lived in a garret, like thorough-bred poets; and 'though he once roved a careless mountaineer in the Highlands of Scotland,' he has not of late enjoyed this advantage. Moreover, he expects no profit from his publication; and whether it succeeds or not, 'it is highly improbable from his situation and pursuits hereafter,' that he should again condescend to become an author. Therefore, let us take what we get and be thankful. What right have we poor devils to be nice? We are well off to have got so much from a man of this Lord's station, who does not live in a garret, but 'has the sway' of Newstead Abbey. Again, we say, let us be thankful; and, with honest Sancho, bid God bless the giver, nor look the gift horse in the mouth.

Edinburgh Review [Francis Jeffrey]

Art. I. *The Excursion, being a portion of the Recluse, a Poem.* By William Wordsworth. 4to. pp.447. London, 1814. (1814)

This will never do. It bears no doubt the stamp of the author's heart and fancy; but unfortunately not half so visibly as that of his peculiar system. His former poems were intended to recommend that system, and to bespeak favour for it by their individual merit; — but this, we suspect, must be recommended by the system — and can only expect to succeed where it has been previously established. It is longer, weaker, and tamer, than any of Mr Wordsworth's other productions; with less boldness of originality, and less even of that extreme simplicity and lowliness of tone which wavered so prettily, in the Lyrical Ballads, between silliness and pathos. We have imitations of Cowper, and even of Milton here, engrafted on the natural drawl of the Lakers — and all diluted into harmony by that profuse and irrepressible wordiness which deluges all the blank verse of this school of poetry, and lubricates and weakens the whole structure of their style.

Though it fairly fills four hundred and twenty good quarto pages without note, vignette, or any sort of extraneous assistance, it is stated in the title — with something of an imprudent candour — 'to be but a portion' of a larger work; and in the preface, where an attempt is rather unsuccessfully made to explain the whole design, it is still more rashly disclosed, that it is but 'a part of the second part of a *long* and laborious work' — which is to consist of three parts.

What Mr Wordsworth's ideas of length are we have no means of accurately judging; but we cannot help suspecting that they are liberal, to a degree that will alarm the weakness of most modern readers. As far as we can gather from the preface, the entire poem — or one of them, for we really are not sure whether there is to be one or two — is of a biographical nature; and is to contain the history of the author's mind, and of the origin and progress of his poetical powers, up to the period when they were sufficiently matured to qualify him for the great work on which he has been so long employed. Now, the quarto before us contains 'an account of one of his youthful rambles in the vales of Cumberland, and occupies precisely the period of three days; so that, by the use of a very powerful calculus, some estimate may be formed of the probable extent of the entire biography.

This small specimen, however, and the statements with which it is prefaced, have been sufficient to set our minds at rest in one particular. The case of Mr Wordsworth, we perceive, is now manifestly hopeless; and we give him up as altogether incurable, and beyond the power of criticism. We cannot indeed altogether omit taking precautions now and then against the spreading of the malady; — but for himself, though we shall watch the progress of his symptoms as a matter of professional curiosity and instruction, we really think it right not to harass him any longer with nauseous remedies, — but rather to throw in cordials and lenitives, and wait in patience for the natural termination of the disorder. In order to justify this desertion of our patient, however, it is proper to state why we despair of the success of a more active practice.

A man who has been for twenty years at work on such matter as is now before us, and who comes complacently forward with a whole quarto of it after all the admonitions he has received, cannot reasonably be expected to 'change his hand, or check his pride,' upon the suggestion of far weightier monitors than we can pretend to be. Inveterate habit must now have given a kind of sanctity to the errors of early taste; and the very powers of which we lament the perversion, have probably become incapable of any other application. The very quantity, too, that he has written, and is at this moment working up for publication upon the old pattern, makes it almost hopeless to look for any change of it. All this is so much capital already sunk in the concern; which must be sacrificed if it be abandoned: and no man likes to give up for lost the time and talent and labour which he has embodied in any permanent production. We were not previously aware of these obstacles to Mr Wordsworth's conversion; and, considering the peculiarities of his former writings merely as the result of certain wanton and capricious experiments on public taste and indulgence, conceived it to be our duty to discourage their repetition by all the means in our power. We now see clearly, however, how the case stands; — and, making up our minds, though with the most sincere pain and reluctance, to consider him as finally lost to the good cause of poetry, shall endeavour to be thankful for the occasional gleams of tenderness and beauty which the natural force of his imagination and affections must still shed over all his productions, — and to which we shall ever turn with delight, in spite of the affectation and mysticism and prolixity, with which they are so abundantly contrasted.

Long habits of seclusion, and an excessive ambition of originality, can alone account for the disproportion which seems to exist between this author's taste and his genius; or for the devotion with which he has sacrificed so many precious gifts at the shrine of those paltry idols which he has set up for himself among his lakes and his mountains. Solitary musings, amidst such scenes, might no doubt be expected to nurse up the mind to the majesty of poetical conception, — (though it is remarkable, that all the greater poets lived, or had lived, in the full current of society): — But the collision of equal minds, — the admonition of prevailing impressions — seems necessary to reduce its redundancies, and repress that tendency to extravagance or puerility, into which the self-indulgence and self admiration of genius is so apt to be betrayed, when it is allowed to wanton, without awe or restraint, in the triumph and delight of its own intoxication. That its flights should be graceful and glorious in the eyes of men, it seems almost to be necessary that they should be made in the consciousness that mens' eyes are to behold them, — and that the inward transport and vigour by which they are inspired should be tempered by an occassional reference to what will be thought of them by those ultimate dispensers of glory. An habitual and general knowledge of the few settled and permanent maxims, which form the canon of general taste in all large and polished societies — a certain tact, which informs us at once that many things, which we still love and are moved by in secret, must necessarily be despised as childish, or derided as absurd, in all such societies—though it will not stand in the place of genius, seems necessary to the success of its exertions; and though it will never enable any one to produce the higher beauties of art, can alone secure the talent which does produce them, from errors that must render it useless. Those who have most of the talent, however, commonly acquire this knowledge with the greatest facility;—and if Mr Wordsworth, instead of confining himself almost entirely to the society of the dalesmen and cottagers, and little children, who form the subjects of his book, had condescended to mingle a little more with the people that were to read and judge of it, we cannot help thinking, that its texture would have been considerably improved: At least it appears to us to be absolutely impossible, that any one who had lived or mixed familiarly with men of literature and ordinary judgment in poetry, (of course we exclude the coadjutors and disciples of his own school), could ever have fallen into such gross faults, or so long mistaken them for beauties. His first essays we looked upon in a good degree as poetical paradoxes,—maintained experimentally, in order to display talent, and court notoriety;—and so maintained, with no more serious belief in their truth, than is usually generated by an ingenious and animated defence of other paradoxes. But when we find, that he has been for twenty years exclusively employed upon articles of this very fabric, and that he has still enough of raw material on hand to keep him so employed for twenty years to come, we cannot refuse him the justice of believing that he is a sincere convert to his own system, and must ascribe the peculiarities of his composition, not to any transient affectation, or accidental caprice of imagination, but to a settled perversity of taste or understanding, which has been fostered, if not altogether created, by the circumstances to which we have already alluded.

The volume before us, if we were to describe it very shortly, we should characterize as a tissue of moral and devotional ravings, in which innumerable changes are rung upon a few very simple and familiar ideas:—but with such an accompaniment of long words, long sentences, and unwieldy phrases—and such a hub-bub of strained raptures and fantastical sublimities, that it is often extremely difficult for the most skilful and attentive student to obtain a glimpse of the author's meaning—and altogether impossible for an ordinary reader to conjecture what he is about. Moral and religious enthusiasm, though undoubtedly poetical emotions, are at the same time but dangerous inspirers of poetry; nothing being so apt to run into interminable dulness or mellifluous extravagance, without giving the unfortunate author the slightest intimation of his danger. His laudable zeal for the efficacy of his preachments, he very naturally mistakes for the ardour of poetical inspiration—and, while dealing out the high words and glowing phrases which are so readily supplied by themes of this description, can scarcely avoid believing that he is eminently original and impressive:— All sorts of commonplace notions and expressions are sanctified in his eyes, by the sublime ends for which they are employed; and the mystical verbiage of the methodist pulpit is repeated, till the speaker entertains no doubt that he is the elected organ of divine truth and persuasion. But if such be the common hazards of seeking inspiration from those potent fountains, it may easily be conceived what chance Mr Wordsworth had of escaping their enchantment,—with his natural propensities to wordiness, and his unlucky habit of debasing pathos with vulgarity. The fact accordingly is, that in this production he is more obscure than a Pindaric poet of the seventeenth century; and more verbose 'than even himself of yore;' while the wilfulness with which he persists in choosing his examples of intellectual dignity and tenderness exclusively from the lowest ranks of society, will be sufficiently apparent, from the circumstance of his having thought fit to make his chief prolocutor in this poetical dialogue, and chief advocate of Providence and Virtue, an old Scotch Pedlar—retired indeed from business—but still rambling about in his former haunts, and gossiping among his old customers, without his pack on his shoulders. The other persons of the drama are, a retired military chaplain, who has grown half an atheist and half a misanthrope—the wife of an unprosperous weaver—a servant girl with her infant—a parish pauper, and one or two other personages of equal rank and dignity.

The character of the work is decidedly didactic; and more than nine tenths of it are occupied with a species of dialogue, or rather a series of long sermons or harangues which pass between the pedlar, the author, the old chaplain, and a worthy vicar, who entertains the whole party at dinner on the last day of their excursion. The incidents which occur in the course of it are as few and trifling as can be imagined;—and those which the different speakers narrate in the course of their discourses, are introduced rather to illustrate their arguments or opinions, than for any interest they are supposed to possess of their own.—The doctrine which the work is intended to enforce, we are by no means certain that we have discovered. In so far as we can collect, however, it seems to be neither more nor less than the old familiar one, that a firm belief in the providence of a wise and beneficent Being must be our great stay and support under all afflictions and perplexities upon earth—and that, there are indications of his power and goodness in all the aspects of the visible universe, whether living or inanimate—every part of which should therefore be regarded with love and reverence, as exponents of those great attributes. We can testify, at least, that these salutary and important truths are inculcated at far greater length, and with more repetitions, than in any ten volumes of sermons that are ever perused. It is also maintained, with equal conciseness and originality, that there is frequently much good sense, as well as much enjoyment, in the humbler conditions of life; and that, in spite of great vices and abuses, there is a reasonable allowance both of happiness and goodness in society at large. If there be any deeper or more recondite doctrines in Mr Wordsworth's book, we must confess that they have escaped us;—and, convinced as we are of the truth and soundness of those to which we have alluded, we cannot help thinking that they might have been better enforced with less parade and prolixity. His effusions on what may be called the physiognomy of external nature, or its moral and theological expression, are eminently fantastic, obscure, and affected.—It is quite time, however, that we should give the reader a more particular account of this singular performance.

It opens with a picture of the author toiling across a bare common in a hot summer day, and reaching at last a ruined hut surrounded with tall trees, where he meets by appointment with a hale old man, with an iron-pointed staff lying beside him. Then follows a retrospective account of their first acquaintance—formed, it seems, when the author was at a village school; and his aged friend occupied 'one room,—the fifth part of a house' in the neighbourhood. After this, we have the history of this reverend person at no small length. He was born, we are happy to find, in Scotland—among the hills of Athol; and his mother, after his father's death, married the parish schoolmaster—so that he was taught his letters betimes: But then, as it is here set forth with much solemnity,

'From his sixth year, the boy, of whom I speak,
In summer, tended cattle on the hills.'

And again, a few pages after, that there may be no risk of mistake as to a point of such essential importance -

From early childhood, even, as hath been said,
From his *sixth year*, he had been sent abroad,
In *summer*, to tend herds: Such was his task!'

In the course of this occupation, it is next recorded, that he acquired such a taste for rural scenery and open air, that when he was sent to teach a school in a neighbouring village, he found it a misery to him; 'and determined to embrace the more romantic occupation of a Pedlar' or, as Mr Wordsworth more musically expresses it,

'A vagrant merchant bent beneath his load;'

—and in the course of his peregrinations had acquired a very large acquaintance, which, after he had given up dealing, he frequently took a summer ramble to visit.

The author, on coming up to this interesting personage, finds him sitting with his eyes half shut;—and, not being quite sure whether he is asleep or awake, stands 'some minutes space' in silence beside him. 'At length,' says he, with his own delightful simplicity—

'At length I hailed him—*seeing that his hat*
Was moist with water-drops, as if the brim
Had newly scooped a running stream!—
————'"Tis, "said I," a burning day;
My lips are parched with thirst;—but you, I guess,
Have somewhere found relief." '

Upon this, the benevolent old man points him out a well in a corner, to which the author repairs; and, after minutely describing its situation, beyond a broken wall, and between two alders that 'grew in a cold damp nook,' he thus faithfully chronicles the process of his return.

'My thirst I slaked—and from the cheerless spot
Withdrawing, straightway to the shade returned,
Where sate the old man on the cottage bench.'

The Pedlar then gives an account of the last inhabitants of the deserted cottage beside them. These were, a good industrious weaver and his wife and children. They were very happy for a while; till sickness and want of work came upon them; and then the father enlisted as a soldier, and the wife pined in the lonely cottage—growing every year more careless and desponding, as her anxiety and fears for her absent husband, of whom no tidings ever reached her, accumulated. Her children died, and left her cheerless and alone; and at last she died also; and the cottage fell to decay. We must say, that there is very considerable pathos in the telling of this simple story; and that they who can get over the repugnance excited by the triteness of its incidents, and the lowness of its objects, will not fail to be struck with the author's knowledge of the human heart, and the power he possesses of stirring up its deepest and gentlest sympathies. His prolixity, indeed, it is not so easy to get over. This little story fills about twenty-five quarto pages; and abounds, of course, with mawkish sentiment, and details of preposterous minuteness. When the tale is told, the travellers take their staffs, and end their first day's journey, without further adventure, at a little inn.

The Second book sets them forward betimes in the morning. They pass by a Village Wake; and as they approach a more solitary part of the mountains, the old man tells the author that he is taking him to see an old friend of his, who had formerly been chaplain to a Highland regiment—had lost a beloved wife—been roused from his dejection by the first enthusiasm of the French Revolution—had emigrated on its miscarriage to America—and returned disgusted to hide himself in the retreat to which they were now ascending. That retreat is then most tediously described—a smooth green valley in the heart of the mountain, without trees, and with only one dwelling. Just as they get sight of it from the ridge above, they see a funeral train proceeding from the solitary abode, and hurry on with some apprehension for the fate of the misanthrope—whom they find, however, in very tolerable condition at the door, and learn that the funeral was that of an aged pauper who had been boarded out by the parish in that cheap farmhouse, and had died in consequence of long exposure to heavy rain. The old chaplain, or, as Mr Wordsworth is pleased to call him, the Solitary, tells this dull story at prodigious length; and after giving an inflated description of an effect of mountain-mists in the evening sun, treats his visitors with a rustic dinner—and they walk out to the fields at the close of the second book.

The Third makes no progress in the excursion. It is entirely filled with moral and religious conversation and debate, and with a more ample detail of the Solitary's past life, than had been given in the sketch of his friend. The conversation is exceedingly dull and mystical; and the Solitary's confessions insufferably diffuse. Yet there is very considerable force of writing and tenderness of sentiment in this part of the work.

The Fourth book is also filled with dialogues ethical and theologial; and, with the exception of some brilliant and forcible expressions here and there, consists of an exposition of truisms, more cloudy, wordy, and inconceivably prolix, than any thing we ever met with.

In the beginning of the Fifth book, they leave the solitary valley, taking its pensive inhabitant along with them, and stray on to where the landscape sinks down into milder features, till they arrive at a church, which stands on a moderate elevation in the centre of a wide and fertile vale. Here they meditate for a while among the monuments, till the vicar comes out and joins them;—and recognizing the pedlar for an old acquaintance, mixes graciously in the conversation, which proceeds in a very edifying manner till the close of the book.

The Sixth contains a choice obituary, or characteristic account of several of the persons who lie buried before this groupe of moralizers; — an unsuccessful lover, who finds consolation in natural history — a miner, who worked on for twenty years, in despite of universal ridicule, and at last found the vein he had expected — two political enemies reconciled in old age to each other — an old female miser — a seduced damsel — and two widowers, one who devoted himself to the education of his daughters, and one who married a prudent middle-aged woman to take care of them.

In the beginning of the Eighth Book, the worthy vicar expresses, in the words of Mr Wordsworth's own epitome, 'his apprehensions that he had detained his auditors too long—invites them to his house—Solitary, disinclined to comply, rallies the Wanderer, and somewhat playfully draws a comparison between his itinerant profession and that of a knight-errant—which leads to the Wanderer giving an account of changes in the country, from the manufacturing spirit—Its favourable effects—The other side of the picture,' &c. &c. After these very poetical themes are exhausted, they all go into the house, where they are introduced to the Vicar's wife and daughter; and while they sit chatting in the parlour over a family dinner, his son and one of his companions come in with a fine dish of trouts piled on a blue slate; and, after being caressed by the company, are sent to dinner in the nursery.—This ends the eighth book.

The Ninth and last is chiefly occupied with the mystical discourses of the Pedlar; who maintains, that the whole universe is animated by an active principle, the noblest seat of which is in the human soul; and moreover, that the final end of old age is to train and enable us

'To hear the mighty stream of *Tendency*
Uttering, for elevation of our thought,
A clear sonorous voice, inaudible
To the vast multitude whose doom it is
To run the giddy round of vain delight —'

with other matters as luminous and emphatic. The hostess at length breaks off the harangue, by proposing that they should all make a little excursion on the lake,—and they embark accordingly; and, after navigating for some time along its shores, and drinking tea on a little island, land at last on a remote promontory, from which they see the sun go down,—and listen to a solemn and pious, but rather long prayer from the Vicar. They then walk back to the parsonage door, where the author and his friend propose to spend the evening;—but the Solitary prefers walking back in the moonshine to his own valley, after promising to take another ramble with them—

'If time, with free consent, be yours to give.
And season favours.'

—And here the publication somewhat abruptly closes.

Our abstract of the story has been so extremely concise, that it is more than usually necessary for us to lay some specimens of the work itself before our readers. Its grand staple, as we have already said, consists of a kind of mystical morality: and the chief characteristics of the style are, that it is prolix and very frequently unintelligible: and though we are very sensible that no great gratification is to be expected from the exhibition of those qualities, yet it is necessary to give our readers a taste of them, both to justify the sentence we have passed, and to satisfy them that it was really beyond our power to present them with any abstract or intelligible account of those long conversations which we have had so much occasion to notice in our brief sketch of its contents. We need give ourselves no trouble however to select passages for this purpose. Here is the first that presents itself to us on opening the volume; and if our readers can form the slightest guess at its meaning, we must give them credit for a sagacity to which we have no pretension.

> 'But, by the storms of *circumstance* unshaken.
> And subject neither to eclipse or wane.
> Duty exists;—"immutably survive,
> For our support, the measures and the forms,
> Which an abstract Intelligence supplies;
> Whose kingdom is, where Time and Space are not:
> Of other converse, which mind, soul, and heart,
> Do, with united urgency, require,
> What more, that may not perish? Thou, dread Source,
> Prime, self-existing Cause and End of all,
> That, in the scale of Being, fill their place.
> Above our human region, or below,
> Set and sustained;—" Thou—who didst wrap the cloud
> Of Infancy around us, that Thyself,
> Therein, with our simplicity awhile
> Might'st hold, on earth, communion undisturbed—
> For adoration thou endurest; endure
> For consciousness the motions of thy will;
> For apprehension those transcendent truths
> Of the pure Intellect, that stand as laws,
> (Submission constituting strength and power)
> Even to thy Being's infinite majesty!'
> 'Tis, by comparison, an easy task
> Earth to despise; but to converse with Heaven,
> This is not easy:—to relinquish all
> We have, or hope, of happiness and joy,—
> And stand in freedom loosened from this world;
> I deem not arduous:—but must needs confess
> That 'tis a thing impossible to frame
> Conceptions equal to the Soul's desires.' p. 144-147.

This is a fair sample of that rapturous mysticism which eludes all comprehension, and fills the despairing reader with painful giddiness and terror. The following, which we meet with on the very next page, is in the same general strain:—though the first part of it affords a good specimen of the author's talent for enveloping a plain and trite observation in all the mock majesty of solemn verbosity. A reader of plain understanding, we suspect, could hardly recognize the familiar remark, that excessive grief for our departed friends is not very consistent with a firm belief in their immortal felicity, in the first twenty lines of the following passage:—In the sequel we do not ourselves pretend to recognize any thing.

'From this infirmity of mortal kind
Sorrow proceeds, which else were not; — at least.
[Text omitted]
I cannot doubt that They whom you deplore
Are glorified.' p. 118, 149.

If any farther specimen be wanted of the learned author's propensity to deal out the most familiar truths as the oracles of his own inspired understanding, the following wordy paraphrase of the ordinary remark, that the best consolation in distress is to be found in the exercises of piety, and the testimony of a good conscience, may be found on turning the leaf.

'What then remains? — To seek
Those helps, for his occasions ever near,
[Text omitted]
As God's most intimate Presence in the soul,
And his most perfect Image in the world.' p. 151.

We have kept the book too long open, however, at one place, and shall now take a dip in it nearer the beginning. The following account of the pedlar's early training, and lonely meditations among the mountains, is a good example of the forced and affected ecstasies in which this author abounds.

' — — — Nor did he fail,
While yet a Child, with a Child's eagerness
[Text omitted]
And vainly by all other means, he strove
To mitigate the fever of his heart.' p. 16-18.

The whole book, indeed, is full of such stuff. The following is the author's own sublime aspiration after the delight of becoming a *Motion* or a *Presence*, or an *Energy* among multitudinous Streams.

'Oh! what a Joy it were, in vigorous health,
To have a Body (this our Vital Frame
[Text omitted]
Be this continued so from day to day,
Nor let it have an end from month to month!" p. 164, 165

We suppose the reader is now satisfied with Mr Wordsworth's sublimities which occupy rather more than half the volume: — Of his tamer and more creeping prolixity, we have not the heart to load him with many specimens. The following amplification of the vulgar comparison of human life to a stream, has the merit of adding much obscurity to wordiness; at least, we have not ingenuity enough to refer the conglobated bubbles and murmurs, and floating islands to their vital prototypes. — -

' — — — The tenor
Which my life holds, he readily may conceive
Whoe'er hath stood to watch a mountain Brook
[Text omitted]
.... Such a stream
Is human Life.' p. 139, 140.

The following, however, is a better example of the useless and most tedious minuteness with which the author so frequently details circumstances of no interest in themselves, — of no importance to the story, — and possessing no graphical merit whatsoever as pieces of description. On their approach to the old chaplain's cottage, the author gets before his companion,

     '— — —when behold
     An object that enticed my steps aside!
     It was an Entry, narrow as a door;
     A passage whose brief windings opened out
     Into a platform; that lay, *sheepfold-wise*,
     Enclosed between a single mass of rock
     And one old moss-grown wall;—a cool Recess,
     And fanciful! For, where the rock and wall
     Met in an angle, hung a tiny roof,
     Or penthouse, which most quaintly had been framed,
     By thrusting two rude sticks into the wall
     And overlaying them with mountain sods;
     To weather-fend a little turf-built seat
     Whereon a full-grown man might rest, nor dread
     The burning sunshine, or a transient shower;
     But the whole plainly wrought by Children's hands!
     Whose simple skill had thronged the grassy floor
     With work of frame less solid, a proud show
     Of baby-houses, curiously arranged;
     Nor wanting ornament of walks between,
     With mimic trees inserted in the turf,
     And gardens interposed. Pleased with the sight,
     I could not choose but beckon to my Guide,
     Who, having entered, carelessly looked round,
     And now would have passed on; when I exclaimed,
     "Lo! what is here?" and, stooping down, drew forth
     A Book,' &c. p. 71, 72.

And this book, which he

     '— — — —found to be a work
     In the French Tongue, a Novel of Voltaire,'

leads to no incident or remark of any value or importance, to apologize for this long story of its finding. There is no beauty, we think, it must be admitted, in such passages; and so little either of interest or curiosity in the incidents they disclose, that we can scarcely conceive that any man to whom they had actually occurred, should take the trouble to recount them to his wife and children by his idle fireside:—but, that man or child should think them worth writing down in blank verse, and printing in magnificent quarto, we should certainly have supposed altogether impossible, had it not been for the ample proofs which Mr Wordsworth has afforded to the contrary.

    Sometimes their silliness is enhanced by a paltry attempt at effect and emphasis:—as in the following account of that very touching and extraordinary occurrence of a lamb bleating among the mountains. The poet would actually persuade us that he thought the mountains themselves were bleating;—and that nothing could be so grand or impressive. 'List!' cries the old Pedlar, suddenly breaking off in the middle of one of his daintiest ravings—

     — — — —"List!— I heard,

>   From yon huge breast of rock, a solemn bleat;
>   Sent forth as if it were the Mountain's voice!
>   As if the visible Mountain made the cry!
>   Again!" — The effect upon the soul was such
>   As he expressed; for, from the Mountain's heart
>   The solemn bleat appeared to come; there was
>   No other — and the region all around
>   Stood silent, empty of all shape of life.
>   — It was a Lamb — left somewhere to itself!' p. 159.

What we have now quoted will give the reader a notion of the taste and spirit in which this volume is composed; and yet, if it had not contained something a good deal better, we do not know how we should have been justified in troubling him with any account of it. But the truth is, that Mr Wordsworth, with all his perversities, is a person of great powers; and has frequently a force in his moral declamations, and a tenderness in his pathetic narratives, which neither his prolixity nor his affectation can altogether deprive of their effect. We shall venture to give some extracts from the simple tale of the weaver's solitary cottage. Its heroine is the deserted wife; and its chief interest consists in the picture of her despairing despondence and anxiety after his disappearance. The Pedlar, recurring to the well to which he had directed his companion, observes,

>   — — — As I stooped to drink,
>   Upon the slimy foot-stone I espied
>   [Text omitted]
>   In sickness she remained; and here she died.
>   Last human Tenant of these ruined Walls.' p. 46.

The story of the old chaplain, though a little less lowly, is of the same mournful cast, and almost equally destitute of incidents; — for Mr Wordsworth delineates only feelings — and all his adventures are of the heart. The narrative which is given by the sufferer himself, is, in our opinion, the most spirited and interesting part of the poem. He begins thus, and addressing himself, after a long pause, to his ancient countryman and friend the Pedlar —

>   'You never saw, your eyes did never look
>   On the bright Form of Her whom once I loved. -
>   Her silver voice was heard upon the earth,
>   A sound unknown to you; else, honored Friend,
>   Your heart had borne a pitiable share
>   Of what I suffered, when I wept that loss,
>   And suffer now, not seldom, from the thought
>   That I remember, and can weep no more.' p. 117.

The following account of his marriage and early felicity is written with great sweetness — a sweetness like that of Massinger, in his softer and more mellifluous passages.

>   — — — This fair Bride—
>   In the devotedness of youthful Love
>   [Text omitted]
>   With hearts at ease, and knowledge in our hearts
>   "That all the grove and all the day was ours."'p. 118-120.

There, seven years of unmolested happiness were blessed with two lovely children.

'And on these pillars rested, as on air,
Our solitude.'

Suddenly a contagious malady swept off both the infants.

'Calm as a frozen Lake when ruthless Winds
[Text omitted]
And, so consumed, She melted from my arms;
And left me, on this earth, disconsolate.' p. 125, 126.

The agony of mind into which the survivor was thrown, is described with a powerful eloquence; as well as the doubts and distracting fears which the sceptical speculations of his careless days had raised in his spirit. There is something peculiarly grand and terrible to our feelings in the imagery of these three lines —

'By pain of heart, now checked, and now impelled,
The Intellectual Power, through words and things,
Went sounding on, a dim and perilous way!'

At last he is roused from this dejected mood, by the glorious promises which seemed held out to human nature at the first dawn of the French Revolution; — and it indicates a fine perception of the secret springs of character and emotion, to choose a being so circumstanced as the most ardent votary of that far-spread enthusiasm.

'Thus was I reconverted to the world;
Society became my glittering Bride,
[Text omitted]
The Wife and Mother, pitifully fixing
Tender reproaches, insupportable!' p. 133, 134.

His disappointment, and ultimate seclusion in England, have been already sufficiently detailed.

We must trespass upon our readers with the fragments of yet another story. It is that of a simple, seduced and deserted girl, told with great sweetness, pathos and indulgence by the Vicar of the parish, by the side of her untimely grave. Looking down on the turf, he says —

'As, on a sunny bank, a tender Lamb,
Lurks in safe shelter, from the winds of March
Screened by its Parent, so that little mound
Lies guarded by its neighbour; the small heap
Speaks for itself; — an Infant there doth rest,
The sheltering Hillock is the Mother's grave. —
There, by her innocent Baby's precious grave.
Yea, doubtless, on the turf that roofs her own,
The Mother oft was seen to stand, or kneel
In the broad day, a weeping Magdalene.
Now she is not; the swelling turf reports
Of the fresh shower, but of poor Ellen's tears
Is silent; nor is any vestige left
Upon the pathway, of her mournful tread;
Nor of that pace with which she once had moved
In virgin fearlessness — a step that seemed
Caught from the pressure of elastic turf
Upon the mountains wet with morning dew,
In the prime hour of sweetest scents and airs.' p. 285-287.
[Text omitted]

These passages, we think, are among the most touching with which the volume presents us; though there are many in a more lofty and impassioned style. The following commemoration of a beautiful and glorious youth, the love and the pride of the valley, is full of warmth and poetry.

> – – – 'The mountain Ash,
> Decked with autumnal berries that outshine
> Spring's richest blossoms, yields a splendid show,
> Amid the leafy woods; and ye have seen,
> By a brook side or solitary tarn,
> How she her station doth adorn, – the pool
> Glows at her feet, and all the gloomy rocks
> Are brightened round her. In his native Vale
> Such and so glorious did this Youth appear;
> A sight that kindled pleasure in all hearts
> By his ingenuous beauty, by the gleam
> Of his fair eyes, by his capacious brow,
> By all the graces with which nature's hand
> Had bounteously arrayed him. As old Bards
> Tell in their idle songs of wandering Gods,
> Pan or Apollo, veiled in human form;
> Yet, like the sweet-breathed violet of the shade,
> Discovered in their own despite to sense
> Of Mortals, (if such fables without blame
> May find chance-mention on this sacred ground),
> So, through a simple rustic garb's disguise,
> In him revealed a Scholar's genius shone;
> And so, not wholly hidden from men's sight,
> In him the spirit of a Hero walked
> Our unpretending valley.' p. 342, 343.

This is lofty and energetic; – but Mr Wordsworth descends, we cannot think very gracefully, when he proceeds to describe how the quoit *whizzed* when his arm launched it – and how the football mounted as high as a lark, at the touch of his toe; – neither is it a suitable catastrophe, for one so nobly endowed, to catch cold by standing too long in the river washing sheep, and die of spasms in consequence. The general reflections on the indiscriminating rapacity of death, though by no means original in themselves, and expressed with too bold a rivalry of the seven ages of Shakespeare, have yet a character of vigour and truth about them that entitles them to notice.

> 'This file of Infants; some that never breathed,
> And the besprinkled Nursling, unrequired
> [Text omitted]
> Society were touched with kind concern,
> And gentle "Nature grieved that One should die." '
>
> p. 214, 245.

There is a lively and impressive appeal on the injury done to the health, happiness, and morality of the lower orders, by the unceasing and premature labours of our crowded manufactories. The description of night-working is picturesque. In lonely and romantic regions, he says, when silence and darkness incline all to repose –

> ———An unnatural light,
> Prepared for never-resting Labour's eyes,
> *[Text omitted]*
> To Gain—the Master Idol of the Realm,
> Perpetual sacrifice.' p. 367.

The effects on the ordinary life of the poor are delineated in graver colours.

> ———'Domestic bliss,
> (Or call it comfort, by a humbler name,)
> *[Text omitted]*
> Till their short holiday of childhood ceased,
> Ne'er to return! That birth-right now is lost.' 371, 372.

The dissertation is closed with an ardent hope, that the farther improvement and the universal diffusion of these arts may take away the temptation for us to embark so largely in their cultivation; and that we may once more hold out inducements for the return of old manners and domestic charities,

> 'Learning, though late, that all true glory rests,
> All praise, all safety, and all happiness,
> Upon the Moral law. Egyptian Thebes;
> Tyre by the margin of the sounding waves;
> Palmyra, central in the Desart, fell;
> And the Arts died by which they had been raised,
> —Call Archimedes from his buried Tomb
> Upon the plain of vanished Syracuse,
> And feelingly the Sage shall make report
> How insecure, how baseless in itself,
> Is that Philosophy, whose sway is framed
> For mere material instruments:—How weak
> Those Arts, and high Inventions, if unpropped
> By Virtue.' p. 369.

There is also a very animated exhortation to the more general diffusion of education among the lower orders; and a glowing and eloquent assertion of their capacity for all virtues and all enjoyments.

> ———'Believe it not:
> The primal duties shine aloft—like stars;
> The charities that soothe, and heal, and bless,
> Are scattered at the feet of Man—like flowers.
> The generous inclination, the just rule,
> Kind wishes, and good actions, and pure thoughts—.
> No mystery is here; no special boon
> For high and not for low, for proudly graced
> And not for meek of heart. The smoke ascends
> To heaven as lightly from the Cottage hearth
> As from the haughty palace.' p. 398.
> *[Text omitted]*

There is a good deal of fine description in the course of this work; but we have left ourselves no room for any specimen. The following few lines, however, are a fine epitome of a lake voyage,

> ———'Right across the Lake

>   Our pinnace moves: then, coasting creek and bay,
>   Glades we behold—and into thickets peep—
>   Where couch the spotted deer; or raise our eyes
>   To shaggy steeps on which the careless goat
>   Browzed by the side of dashing waterfalls.' p. 412.

We add also the following more elaborate and fantastic picture—which, however, is not without its beauty.

>   'Then having reached a bridge, that overarched
>   The hasty rivulet where it lay becalmed
>   In a deep pool, by happy chance we saw
>   A two-fold Image; on a grassy bank
>   A snow-white Ram, and in the crystal flood
>   Another and the same! Most beautiful,
>   On the green turf, with his imperial front
>   Shaggy and bold, and wreathed horns superb,
>   The breathing Creature stood! as beautiful,
>   Beneath him, showed his shadowy Counterpart.
>   Each had his glowing mountains, each his sky,
>   And each seemed centre of his own fair world;
>   Antipodes unconscious of each other,
>   Yet, in partition, with their several spheres,
>   Blended in perfect stillness, to our sight!' p. 407.

Besides those more extended passages of interest or beauty, which we have quoted, and omitted to quote, there are scattered up and down the book, and in the midst of its most repulsive portions, a very great number of single lines and images, that sparkle like gems in the desert, and startle us with an intimation of the great poetic powers that lie buried in the rubbish that has been heaped around them. It is difficult to pick up these, after we have once passed them by; but we shall endeavour to light upon one or two. The beneficial effect of intervals of relaxation and pastime on youthful minds, is finely expressed, we think, in a single line, when it is said to be—

>   'Like vernal ground to Sabbath sunshine left.'

The following image of the bursting forth of a mountain-spring, seems to us also to be conceived with great elegance and beauty.

>   'And a few steps may bring us to the spot,
>   Where haply crown'd with flowrets and green herbs;
>   The Mountain Infant to the Sun comes forth
>   Like human life from darkness.'—

The ameliorating effects of song and music on the minds which most delight in them, are likewise very poetically expressed.

>   — — —'And when the stream
>   Which overflowed the soul was passed away,
>   A consciousness remained that it had left,
>   Deposited upon the silent shore
>   Of Memory, images and precious thoughts,
>   That shall not die, and cannot be destroyed.'

Nor is any thing more elegant than the representation of the graceful tranquillity occasionally put on by one of the author's favourites; who, though gay and airy, in general—

'Was graceful, when it pleased him, smooth and still
As the mute Swan that floats adown the stream,
Or on the waters of th' unruffled lake
Anchored her placid beauty. Not a leaf
That flutters on the bough more light than he,
And not a flower that droops in the green shade,
More winningly reserved.' —

Nor are there wanting morsels of a sterner and more majestic beauty; as when, assuming the weightier diction of Cowper, he says, in language which the hearts of all readers of modern history must have responded —

— — — 'Earth is sick,
And Heaven is weary of the hollow words
Which States and Kingdoms utter when they speak
Of Truth and Justice.'

These examples, we perceive, are not very well chosen — but we have not leisure to improve the selection; and, such as they are, they may serve to give the reader a notion of the sort of merit which we meant to illustrate by their citation. — When we look back to them, indeed, and to the other passages which we have now extracted, we feel half inclined to rescind the severe sentence which we passed on the work at the beginning: — But when we look into the work itself, we perceive that it cannot be rescinded. Nobody can be more disposed to do justice to the great powers of Mr Wordsworth than we are; and, from the first time that he came before us, down to the present moment, we have uniformly testified in their favour, and assigned indeed our high sense of their value as the chief ground of the bitterness with which we resented their perversion. That perversion, however, is now far more visible than their original dignity; and while we collect the fragments, it is impossible not to lament the ruins from which we are condemned to pick them. If any one should doubt of the existence of such a perversion, or be disposed to dispute about the instances we have hastily brought forward, we would just beg leave to refer him to the general plan and the characters of the poem now before us. — Why should Mr Wordsworth have made his hero a superannuated Pedlar? What but the most wretched and provoking perversity of taste and judgment, could induce any one to place his chosen advocate of wisdom and virtue in so absurd and fantastic a condition? Did Mr Wordsworth really imagine, that his favourite doctrines were likely to gain any thing in point of effect or authority by being put into the mouth of a person accustomed to higgle about tape, or brass sleeve-buttons? Or is it not plain that, independent of the ridicule and disgust which such a personification must give to many of his readers, its adoption exposes his work throughout to the charge of revolting incongruity, and utter disregard of probability or nature? For, after he has thus wilfully debased his moral teacher by a low occupation, is there one word that he puts into his mouth, or one sentiment of which he makes him the organ, that has the most remote reference to that occupation? Is there any thing in his learned, abstracted, and logical harangues, that savours of the calling that is ascribed to him? Are any of their materials such as a pedlar could possibly have dealt in? Are the manners, the diction, the sentiments, in any, the very smallest degree, accommodated to a person in that condition? or are they not eminently and conspicuously such as could not by possibility belong to it? A man who went about selling flannel and pocket-handkerchiefs in this lofty diction, would soon frighten away all his customers; and would infallibly pass either for a madman, or for some learned and affected gentleman, who, in a frolic, had taken up a character which he was peculiarly ill qualified for supporting.

The absurdity in this case, we think, is palpable and glaring; but it is exactly of the same nature with that which infects the whole substance of the work—a puerile ambition of singularity engrafted on an unlucky predilection for truisms; and an affected passion for simplicity and humble life, most awkwardly combined with a taste for mystical refinements, and all the gorgeousness of obscure phraseology. His taste for simplicity is evinced, by sprinkling up and down his interminable declamations, a few descriptions of baby-houses, and of old hats with wee brims; and his amiable partiality for humble life, by assuring us, that a wordy rhetorician, who talks about Thebes, and allegorizes all the heathen mythology, was once a pedlar—and making him break in upon his magnificent orations with two or three awkward notices of something that he had seen when selling winter raiment about the country—or of the changes in the state of society, which had almost annihilated his former calling.

George Gordon, Lord Byron (1788-1824)
Lachin y gair (1807)

LACHIN Y GAIR, or as it is pronounced in the Erse, LOCH NA GARR, towers pre-eminent in the Northern Highlands, near Invercauld. One of our modern Tourists mentions it as the highest mountain perhaps in GREAT BRITAIN; be this as it may, it is certainly one of the most sublime, and picturesque, amongst our "Caledonian Alps." Its appearance is of a dusky hue, but the summit is the seat of eternal snows; near Lachin y Gair, I spent some of the early part of my life, the recollections of which has given birth to the following stanzas – –

1.

Away, ye gay landscapes, ye garden of roses!
   In you let the minions of luxury rove;
Restore me the rocks, where the snow-flake reposes,
   Though still they are sacred to freedom and love:
Yet, Caledonia! Belov'd are thy mountains,
   Round their white summits though elements war;
Though cataracts foam, 'stead of smooth-flowing fountains,
   I sigh, for the valley of dark Loch na Garr.

2.

Ah! there my young footsteps, in infancy, wander'd;
   My cap was the bonnet, my cloak was the plaid; [1]
On chieftains, long perish'd, my memory ponder'd,
   As daily I strode through the pine-cover'd glade;
I sought not my home, till the day's dying glory
   Gave place to the rays of the bright polar star;
For fancy was cheer'd, by traditional story,
   Disclos'd by the natives of dark Loch na Garr.

3.

"Shades of the dead! have I not heard your voices
   Rise on the night-rolling breath of the gale?"
Surely the soul of the hero rejoices,
   And rides on the wind, o'er his own Highland vale.
Round Loch na Garr, while the stormy mist gathers,
   Winter presides in his cold icy car:
Clouds, there, encircle the forms of my fathers;
   They dwell in the tempests of dark Loch na Garr.

4.

"Ill-starred,[2] though brave, did no visions foreboding
  Tell you that Fate had forsaken your cause?"
Ah! were you destin'd to die at Culloden, [3]
  Victory crown'd not your fall with applause:
Still were you happy, in death's earthy slumber,
  You rest with your clan, in the caves of Braemar; [4]
The pibroch [5] resounds, to the piper's loud number,
  Your deeds, on the echoes of dark Loch na Garr.

5.

Years have roll'd on, Loch na Garr, since I left you,
  Years must elapse, e'er I tread you again:
Nature of verdure and flowers has bereft you,
  Yet still are you dearer than Albion's plain.
England! thy beauties are tame and domestic,
  To one who has rov'd on the mountains afar:
Oh! for the crags that are wild and majestic,
  The steep, frowning glories of dark Loch na Garr.

1. This word is erroneously pronounce plad, the proper pronounciation (according to the Scotch) is shewn by the Orthography.
2. I allude here to my maternal ancestors, the "Gordons," many of whom fought for the unfortunate Prince Charles, better known by the name of the Pretender. This branch was nearly allied by blood, as well as attachment, to the Stewarts. George, the 2d. Earl of Huntley, married the Princess Annabella Stewart, daughter of James 1st of Scotland, by her he left four sons; the 3d. Sir William Gordon, I have the honour to claim as one of my progenitors.
3. Whether any perished in the Battle of Culloden, I am not certain; but as many fell in the insurrection, I have used the name of the principal action, "pars pro toto."
4. A Tract of the Highlands so called; there is also a Castle of Braemar.
5. The Bagpipe.

from English Bards and Scotch Reviewers (anon,1809)[1]

Lines 27 to 72

Behold! in various throngs the scribbling crew,
For notice eager, pass in long review:
Each spurs his jaded Pegasus apace,
And Rhyme and Blank maintain an equal race;
Sonnets on sonnets crowd, and ode on ode;
And Tales of Terror jostle on the road;

Immeasurable measures move along,
For simpering Folly loves a varied song,
To strange mysterious Dullness still the friend,
Admires the strain she cannot comprehend.
Thus Lays of Minstrels[2] — may they be the last! —
On half-strung harps whine mournful to the blast,
While mountain spirits prate to river sprites,
That dames may listen to the sound at nights;
And goblin-brats of Gilpin Horner's brood
Decoy young Border-nobles through the wood.
And skip at every step. Lord knows how high.
And frighten foolish babes, the Lord knows why,
While high-born ladies, in their magic cell,
Forbidding Knights to read who cannot spell,
Dispatch a courier to a wizard's grave,
And fight with honest men to shield a knave.

Next view in state, proud prancing on his roan.
The golden-crested haughty Marmion,
Now forging scrolls, now foremost in the fight,
Not quite a Felon, yet but half a Knight,
The gibbet or the field prepar'd to grace;
A mighty mixture of the great and base.
And think'st thou, SCOTT! by vain conceit perchance,
On public taste to foist thy stale romance,
Though MURRAY with his MILLER may combine
To yield thy muse just half-a-crown per line?
No I when the sons of song descend to trade,
Their bays are sear, their former laurels fade.
Let such forego the poet's sacred name,
Who rack their brains for lucre, not for fame:
Low may they sink to merited contempt,
And scorn remunerate the mean attempt!
Such be their meed, such still the just reward
Of prostituted Muse and hireling bard!
For this we spurn Apollo's venal son,
And bid a long, "good night to Marmion."[3]
These are the themes, that claim our plaudits now;
These are the Bards to whom the Muse must bow:
While MILTON, DRYDEN, POPE, alike forgot.
Resign their hallow'd Bays to WALTER SCOTT.

1 Byron published the first version of this poem anonymously, in 1809. His second, now signed edition (1809) expanded considerably. We lead with a piece from the first version, then follow with an expansion from the second version. In the second edition, the expansion comes before our 1809 example — hence the oddity of the Kennedy and Boyd line numbers.

2   See the "Lay of the Last Minstrel," passim. Never was any plan so incongruous and absurd as the ground-work of this production. The entrance of Thunder and Lightning prologuising to Bayes' Tragedy, unfortunately takes away the merit of originality from the dialogue between Messieurs the Spirits of Flood and Fell in the first canto. Then we have the amiable William of Deloraine, "a stark moss-trooper," videlicet, a happy compound of poacher, sheep-stealer, and highwayman. The propriety of his magical lady's injunction not to read can only be equalled by his candid acknowledgment of his independence of the trammels of spelling, although, to use his own elegant phrase, "'twas his neck-verse at hairibee," i.e. the gallows.
The biography of Gilpin Horner, and the marvellous pedestrian page, who travelled twice as fast as his master's horse, without the aid of seven leagued boots, are chef-d'oeuvres in the improvement of taste. For incident we have the invisible, but by no means sparing, box on the ear bestowed on the page, and the entrance of a Knight and Charger into the castle, under the very natural disguise of a wain of hay. Marmion, the hero of the latter romance, is exactly what William of Deloraine would have been, had he been able to read and write. The Poem was manufactured for Messrs. CONSTABLE, MURRAY, and MILLER, worshipful booksellers, in consideration of the receipt of a sum of money, and truly, considering the inspiration, it is a very creditable production. If Mr. SCOTT will write for hire, let him do his best for his paymasters, but not disgrace his genius, which is undoubtedly great, by a repetition of Black letter Ballad imitations.

3 "Good night to Marmion" — the pathetic and also prophetic exclamation of HENRY BLOUNT, Esquire, on the death of honest Marmion.

from English Bards and Scotch Reviewers (1809)

LINES 63 TO 88

A man must serve his time to ev'ry trade
Save Censure, Critics all are ready-made.
Take hackneyed jokes from MILLER, got by rote,
With just enough of learning to misquote;
A mind well skilled to find or forge a fault,
A turn for punning, call it Attic salt;
To JEFFREY go, be silent and discreet,
His pay is just ten sterling pounds per sheet:
Fear not to lie, 'twill seem a lucky hit,
Shrink not from blasphemy, 'twill pass for wit;
Care not for feeling — pass your proper jest,
And stand a Critic hated yet caressed.

And shall we own such judgment? no — as soon
Seek roses in December — ice in June;
Hope constancy in wind, or corn in chaff,
Believe a woman, or an epitaph,

Or any other thing that's false before
You trust in Critics who themselves are sore;
Or yield one single thought to be misled
By JEFFREY's heart or LAMB's Boeotian head [1].

To these young tyrants[2], by themselves misplaced
Combined usurpers on the Throne of Taste:
To these when Authors bend in humble awe
And hail their voice as Truth, their word as Law;
While these are Censors, 'twould be sin to spare;
While such are Critics, why should I forbear?
But yet so near all modern worthies run,
"Tis doubtful whom to seek, or whom to shun;
Nor know we when to spare, or where to strike
Our Bards and Censors are so much alike.

1   Messrs. JEFFREY and LAMB are the Alpha and Omega, the first and last of the Edinburgh Review; the others are mentioned hereafter.
2   "Stulta est Clementia, cum tot ubique
    " – – occurras periturae parcere chartae.
                                        Juvenal, Sat. 1.

James Hogg (1770-1835)

When The Kye Comes Hame (1822)

In the title and chorus of this favourite pastoral song, I choose rather to violate a rule in grammar, than a Scottish phrase so common, that when it is altered into the proper way, every shepherd and shepherd's sweetheart account it nonsense. I was once singing it at a wedding with great glee the latter way, ("when the kye come hame,") when a tailor, scratching his head, said, "It was a terrible affectit way that!" I stood corrected, and have never sung it so again. It is to the old air of "Shame fa' the gear and the blathrie o't," with an additional chorus. It is set to music in the Noctes, at which it was first sung, and in no other place that I am aware of.

Come all ye jolly shepherds
  That whistle through the glen,
I'll tell ye of a secret
  That courtiers dinna ken:
What is the greatest bliss
  That the tongue o' man can name?
'Tis to woo a bonny lassie
  When the kye comes hame.

    When the kye comes hame,
    When the kye comes hame,
'Tween the gloaming and the mirk.
    When the kye comes hame.

'Tis not beneath the coronet,
  Nor canopy of state,
'Tis not on couch of velvet,
  Nor arbour of the great—
'Tis beneath the spreading birk,
  In the glen without the name,
Wi' a bonny, bonny lassie,
  When the kye comes hame.
    When the kye comes hame, &c.

There the blackbird bigs his nest
  For the mate he loes to see,
And on the topmost bough,
  O, a happy bird is he;
Where he pours his melting ditty,
  And love is a' the theme,
And he'll woo his bonny lassie,
  When the kye comes hame.
    When the kye comes hame, &c.

When the blewart bears a pearl,
   And the daisy turns a pea,
And the bonny lucken gowan
   Has fauldit up her ee,
Then the laverock frae the blue lift
   Drops down, an' thinks nae shame
To woo his bonny lassie
   When the kye comes hame.
         When the kye comes hame, &c.

See yonder pawkie shepherd,
   That lingers on the hill,
His ewes are in the fauld,
   An' his lambs are lying still;
Yet he downa gang to bed,
   For his heart is in a flame,
To meet his bonny lassie
   When the kye comes hame.
         When the kye comes hame, &c.

When the little wee bit heart
   Rises high in the breast,
An' the little wee bit starn
   Rises red in the east,
O there's a joy sae dear,
   That the heart can hardly frame,
Wi' a bonny, bonny lassie,
   When the kye comes hame!
         When the kye comes hame, &c.

Then since all nature joins
   In this love without alloy,
O, wha wad prove a traitor
   To Nature's dearest joy?
Or wha wad choose a crown,
   Wi' its perils and its fame,
And *miss* his bonny lassie
   When the kye comes hame?
         When the kye comes hame.
         When the kye comes hame,
   'Tween the gloaming and the mirk,
         When the kye comes hame!

   I composed the foregoing song I neither know how nor when; for when the "Three Perils of Man" came first to my hand, and I saw this song put into the mouth of a drunken poet, and mangled in the singing, I had no recollection of it whatever. I had written it off hand along with the prose, and quite forgot it. But I liked it, altered it, and it has been my favourite pastoral for singing ever since. It is too long to be sung from beginning to end; but only the second and antepenult verses can possibly be dispensed with, and these not very well neither.

The Great Muckle Village of Balmaquhapple (1822)

D'YE ken the big village of Balmaquhapple,
The great muckle village of Balmaquhapple?
'Tis steep'd in iniquity up to the thrapple,
An' what's to become o' poor Balmaquhapple?
Fling a' aff your bannets, an' kneel for your life, fo'ks,
And pray to St Andrew, the god o' the Fife fo'ks;
Gar a' the hills yout wi' sheer vociferation,
And thus you may cry on sic needfu' occasion:

"O, blessed St Andrew, if e'er ye could pity fo'k,
Men fo'k or women fo'k, country or city fo'k,
Come for this aince wi' the auld thief to grapple,
An' save the great village of Balmaquhapple
Frae drinking an' leeing, an' flyting an' swearing.
An' sins that ye wad be affrontit at hearing.
An' cheating an' stealing; O, grant them redemption,
All save an' except the few after to mention:

"There's Johnny the elder, wha hopes ne'er to need ye,
Sae pawkie, sae holy, sae gruff, an' sae greedy;
Wha prays every hour as the wayfarer passes,
But aye at a hole where he watches the lasses;
He's cheated a thousand, an' e'en to this day yet,
Can cheat a young lass, or they're leears that say it
Then gie him his gate; he's sae slee an' sae civil,
Perhaps in the end he may wheedle the devil.

"There's Cappie the cobbler, an' Tammie the tinman,
An' Dickie the brewer, an' Peter the skinman,
An' Geordie our deacon, for want of a better,
An' Bess, wha delights in the sins that beset her.
O, worthy St Andrew, we canna compel ye,
But ye ken as weel as a body can tell ye,
If these gang to heaven, we'll a' be sae shockit,
Your garret o' blue will but thinly be stockit.

"But for a' the rest, for the women's sake, save them,
Their bodies at least, an' their sauls, if they have them;
But it puzzles Jock Lesly, an' sma' it avails,
If they dwell in their stamocks, their heads, or their tails.
An' save, without word of confession auricular,
The clerk's bonny daughters, an' Bell in particular;
For ye ken that their beauty's the pride an' the staple
Of the great wicked village of Balmaquhapple!"

Strange Letter Of A Lunatic (1830)

To Mr. James Hogg, of Mount Benger.

Sir; — As you seem to have been born for the purpose of collecting all the whimsical and romantic stories of this country, I have taken the fancy of sending you an account of a most painful and unaccountable one that happened to myself, and at the same time leave you at liberty to make what use of it you please. An explanation of the circumstances from you would give me great satisfaction.

Last summer in June, I happened to be in Edinburgh, and walking very early on the Castle Hill one morning, I perceived a strange looking figure of an old man watching all my motions, as if anxious to introduce himself to me, yet still kept at the same distance. I beckoned him, on which he came waddling briskly up, and taking an elegant gold snuff-box, set with jewels, from his pocket, he offered me a pinch. I accepted of it most readily, and then without speaking a word, he took his box again, thrust it into his pocket, and went away chuckling and laughing in perfect ecstasy. He was even so overjoyed, that, in hobbling down the platform, he would leap from the ground, clap his hands on his loins, and laugh immoderately.

"The devil I am sure is in that body," said I to myself, "What does he mean? Let me see. I wish I may be well enough! I feel very queer since I took that snuff of his." I stood there I do not know how long, like one who had been knocked on the head, until I thought I saw the body peering at me from a shady place in the rock. I hasted to him; but on going up, I found myself standing there. Yes, sir, myself. My own likeness in every respect. I was turned to a rigid statue at once, but the unaccountable being went down the hill convulsed with laughter.

I felt very uncomfortable all that day, and at night having adjourned from the theatre with a party to a celebrated tavern well known to you, judge of my astonishment when I saw another me sitting at the other end of the table. I was struck speechless, and began to watch this unaccountable fellow's motions, and perceived that he was doing the same with regard to me. A gentleman on his left hand, asked his name, that he might drink to their better acquaintance. " Beatman, sir," said the other: "James Beatman, younger, of Drumloning, at your service; one who will never fail a friend at a cheerful glass."

"I deny the premises, principle and proposition," cried I, springing up and smiting the table with my closed hand. "James Beatman, younger, of

Drumloning, you cannot be. I am he. I am the right James Beatman, and I appeal to the parish registers, to witnesses innumerable, to —

"Stop, stop, my dear fellow," cried he, "this is no place to settle a matter of such moment as that. I suppose all present are quite satisfied with regard to the premises; let us therefore drop the subject, if you please."

" O yes, yes, drop the dispute!" resounded from every part of the table. No more was said about this strange coincidence; but I remarked, that no one present knew the gentleman, excepting those who took him for me. I heard them addressing him often regarding my family and affairs, and I really thought the fellow answered as sensibly and as much to the point as I could have done for my life, and began seriously to doubt which of us was the *right* James Beatman.

We drank long and deep, for the song and the glass went round, and the greatest hilarity prevailed; but at length the gentleman at the head of the table proposed calling the bill, at the same time remarking, that we should find it a swinging one. "George, bring the bill, that we may see what is to pay."

"All's paid, sir."

"All paid? You are dreaming, George, or drunk. There has not a farthing been paid by any of us here."

"I assure you all's paid, however, sir. And there's six of claret to come in, and three Glen-Livat."

"Come, George, let us understand one another. Do you persist in asserting that our bill is positively paid?"

"Yes, certainly, sir."

"By whom then?"

"By this good gentleman here, tapping me on the shoulder."

"Oh, Mr. Beatman, that's unfair! That's unfair! You have taken us at a disadvantage. But it is so like yourself!"

"Is it, gentlemen? Is it indeed so like myself? I'm sorry for it then; I'll take a bet yon rascal is the *right* James Beatman after all. For, upon the word and honour of a gentleman, I *did not* pay the bill. No, not a farthing of it."

"Gie ower, lad, an' haud the daft tongue o' thee," cried a countryman from the other end of the table. "Ye hae muckle to flee intil a rage about. I think the best thing ye can do to oblige us a', will be to pouch the affront; or I sal take it aff thee head for half a mutchkin; for I ken thou wast out twice, and stayed a gay bitty while baith times. Thou'rt fou. Count the siller, lad."

This speech set them in a roar of laughter, and, convinced that the countryman was right, and that I, their liberal entertainer, was quite drunk, they all rose simultaneously, and wishing me a good night, left me haranguing them on the falsity of the waiter's statement.

The next morning I intended to have gone with the Stirling morning coach, but arriving a few minutes too late, I went into the office, and began abusing the book-keeper for letting the coach go off too soon. "No, no, sir, you wrong me," said he; "the coach started at the very minute. But as you had not arrived, another took your place, and here is your money again."

" The devil it is," said I; "why, sir, I gave you no money, therefore mine it cannot possibly be."

"Is not your name Mr. James Beatman?"

"Yes, to he sure it is. But how came you to know my name?"

"Because I have it in the coachbook here. See! —Mr. James Beatman, paid 17s.6d.; so here it is."

I took the money, fully convinced that I was under the power of some strange enchantment. And ever on these occasions, my mind reverted to the little crooked gentleman, and the gold snuff-box.

From the coach-office I hasted to Newhaven, to catch one of the steamboats going up the Frith; and on the quay whom should I meet face to face but my whimsical namesake and second self, Mr. James Beatman. I had almost fainted, and could only falter out, "How is this? You here again?"

"Yes, here I am," said he, with perfect frankness; "I lost my seat in the Stirling coach by sleeping a few minutes too long; but the lad gave me my money again, though I had quite forgot having paid it. And as I must be at Stirling to-day to meet Mr. Walker, I have taken my passage in the Morning Star of Alloa, and from thence I must post it to Stirling."

I was stupified, bamboozled, dumbfounded! And could do nothing but stand and gape, for I had lost my place in the coach, got my money again, which I never paid—had taken my passage in the Morning Star of Alloa, and proposed posting it to Stirling to meet Mr. Walker. It must have been the devil, thought I, from whom I took the pinch on the Castle Hill, for I am either become two people, else I am not the right James Beatman.

I took my seat on one of the sofas in the elegant cabin of the Morning Star—Mr. Beatman *secundus* placed himself right over against me. I looked at him—he at me. I grinned —he did the same; but I thought there was a sly leer in his eye which I could not attain, though I was conscious of having been master of it once; and just as I was considering who of us could be the *right* James Beatman, he accosted me as follows:—

"Yon was truly a clever trick you played us last night, though rather an expensive one to yourself. However, as it made me come off with flying colours, I shall take care to requite it in some way, and with interest too?"

"Do you say so:" said I; "you are a strange wag, and I wish I could comprehend you! I suppose you will be talking of requiting me for the Stirling coach hire next."

"Very well remembered," cried he; "I could not recollect of having paid that money, but I now see the trick. You are a strange wag; but here is the sum for you in full."

"Thank you, kindly, sir! very much obliged to you indeed! Five and thirty shillings into pocket! Good! Ha! ha! ha!"

"Ha! ha! ha!" echoed he; " and now, sir, if you will be so friendly and affable as to accept the one half of last night's bill from me, just the half, I will take it kind, and shall regard that business as settled."

"With all my heart, sir! with all my heart, sir!" said I, " only tell me this simple question. Do you suppose that I *am not* the right James Beatman, younger, of Drumloning? For I tell you, sir, and tremble while I do so, that *I am* the right James Beatman;" and saying so, I gave a tremendous tramp on the floor, on which the captain seized me by the shoulder behind, saying,

"Who doubts it, sir? No one I am sure can be mistaken in that. Come into the starboard chamber here, and let us have something to drink."

I went with all my heart; but at that moment I felt my mind running on the old warlock on the Castle Hill; and I had no sooner taken my seat, than, on lifting my eyes, there was my companion sitting opposite to me, with the same confounded leer on his face as before. However, we began our potations in great good humour. Ginger beer and brandy mixed was the delicious beverage, and we swigged at it till I felt the far-famed Morning Star begin to twirl round with me like a te-totum. Thinking we were going to sink, I clambered above. All was going on well, but with a strong head-wind, and the ladies mortal sick. I felt quite dizzy, and the roll of the boat rendered it terribly difficult for me to keep my feet. The ladies began to titter and laugh at me. They were all sitting on two forms, the one row close behind the other, and looking miserably bad; and as one freedom courts another, I put my hands in the pockets of my trousers, and steadying myself right in front of them, began an address, condoling with them on their deplorable and melancholy faces, and advising them to go down below, and drink ginger beer mixed with a *leetle* brandy, and there was no fear; when, unluckily, at this point of my harangue, a great roll of the vessel ruining my equipoise, threw me right across four of the ladies, who screamed horribly; and my hands being entangled in my pockets, my head top heavy, and my ears stunned with female shrieks, all that I could do I could not get up: but my efforts made matters still worse. The ladies at length, by a joint effort, tumbled me over, but it was only to throw me upon other four on the next bench, and these I fairly overset. Then there was laughing, screaming, clapping of hands, and loud hurras, all mixed together, for every person on board was above by this time. I never was so much ashamed in my life, and had no other resource, but to haste down once more to the brandy and ginger beer.

We drank on and sung until we came near the quay at Alloa. There were five of us; but I had not seen my namesake from the time we first entered, for he never molested me, unless when I was quite sober. But on calling the steward, and enquiring what was to pay, he told us all was paid for our party. The party stared at one another, and I at the steward; till a Mr. Anderson asked, who had the kindness, or rather the insolence to do such a thing. The man said it was I; but I being conscious of having done no such thing, denied it with many oaths. Each of the party, however, flung down his share, which the steward obliged me to pocket. I felt myself in a strange state indeed, and quite uncertain whether I was the *right* James Beatman or not.

On going up to the Tontine, I found dinner and a chaise for Stirling ordered in my name; and, though feeling quite as if in a dream, I sat down with the rest of our boat party. But scarcely had I taken my seat, ere I was desired to speak with one in another room. There I found the captain, who received me with a grave face, and said, "This is a very disagreeable business, Mr. Beatman."

"What is it, sir?"

"About this young lady who was on board. Her brother wants to challenge you; but I told him that you were a little intoxicated, else you were quite incapable of such a thing, and I was sure you would make any apology."

"I will, indeed, sir. I will make any apology that shall be required; for, in truth, it was a mere accident, which I could not help, and I am truly sorry for it. I will make any apology."

He then took me away to a genteel house out of the town, and introduced me to a most beautiful and elegant young lady, still in teens, who eyed me with a most ungracious look, and then said, "Sir, had it not been for the dread of peril, I would have scorned an apology from such a person; but as matters stand at present, I am content to accept of one. But I must tell you, that if you had not been a coward and a poltroon, you never would have presumed to look me again in the face."

"My dear madam," said I, "there is some confounded mistake here; for, on the word of a gentleman, I declare, and by the honour of manhood, I swear that I never till this moment beheld that lovely face of yours."

The whole party uttered exclamations of astonishment and abhorrence on hearing these words, and the captain said, " Good G—, Mr. Beatman, did you not confess it to me, saying you were sorry for it, and that you were willing to make any apology?"

"Because I thought this had been one of the ladies whom I overthrew on deck," said I, " when yon unmannerly wave made me lose my equilibrium; but on honour and conscience, this divine creature I never saw before. And if I had, sooner than have offered her any insult, I would have cut off my right hand."

The lady declared I was the person. Other two gentlemen did the same, and the irritated brother had me committed for a criminal assault, and carried to prison, which I liked very ill. But on being conducted off, I said, "Gentlemen, I cannot explain this matter to you, though I understand well enough who is the aggressor. I have for the last twenty-four hours been struggling with an inextricable phenomenon—plague on the old fellow with the gold snuffbox! But I have *now* the satisfaction of knowing that *I am* the right James Beatman after all!"

There was I given over to the constables, and put under confinement till I could find bail, which detained me in Alloa till next day at noon; and ere I reached Stirling, Mr. Walker had gone off to the Highlands without me, at which I was greatly vexed, as he was to have taken me with him in his gig to the braes of Glen-Orchy, where we were to have shot together. I asked the landlord when Mr. Walker went away, and the former told me he only went off that day, for that he had waited four and twenty hours on a companion of his, a strange fish, who had got into a scrape with a pretty girl about Alloa, but that he came at last, and Walker and he went off together: this was a clinker. Who was I to think was the *right* James Beatman now?

I could get no conveyance for two days, and at length I reached Inverauran, where the only person I found was my namesake, who once more placed himself over against me, and still with the same malicious leer on his face. I accused him at once of the insult to the young lady, which was like to cost me so dear. He shook his head with a leering smile, and said, "I well knew it was not he who was guilty, but myself; for saving that he was pitched headlong right upon a whole covey of ladies, when he was tipsy with ginger beer and brandy, he had never so much as seen a lady during the passage."

"You sir," said I. "Do you presume to say that you were tipsy with ginger beer and brandy, and that you were pitched upon the two tiers of ladies? Then, sir, let me tell you that you are one of the most notorious impostors that ever lived. A most unaccountable and impalpable being, who has taken a fancy to personate me, and to cross and confound me in every relation of life. I will submit to this no longer, and therefore pray favour me with your proper address." He gave me my own, on which I got into such a rage at him, that I believe I would have pistoled him on the spot, had not Mr. Fletcher, the landlord, at that moment, tapped me on the shoulder, and told me that Mr. Watten and Mr. Walker wanted me in the next room. I followed him; but in such bad humour that my chagrin would not hide, and forthwith accused Mr. Walker of leaving me behind, and bringing an impostor with him. He blamed me for such an unaccountable joke, a mistake it could not be, for I surely never would pretend to say that I did not come along with him. Mr. Watten, an English gentleman, then asked me if I would likewise deny having won a bet from him at angling of five pounds. I begged his pardon, and said, I recollected of no such thing. "Well then, to assist your memory, here is your money," said he. I said, "I would not take it, but run double or quits with him for the greatest number of birds bagged on the following day; for the real fact was, that neither trout nor bait had I taken since I left Edinburgh. Walker and he stared at one another, and began a reasoning with me, but I lost all manner of temper at their absurdity, and went away to my bed.

Never was there a human creature in such a dilemma as I now found myself. I was conscious of possessing the same body and spirit that I ever did, without any dereliction of my mental faculties. But here was another being endowed with the same personal qualifications, who looked as I looked, thought as I thought, and expressed what I would have said; and more than all seemed to be engaged in every transaction along with me, or did what I should have done and left me out. What was I next to do, for in this state I could not live? I had become, as it were, two bodies, with only one soul between them, and felt that some decisive measures behoved to be resorted to immediately, for I would much rather be out of the world than remain in it on such terms.

Overpowered by these bewildering thoughts, I fell asleep, and the whole night over dreamed about the old man and the gold snuff-box, who told me that I was now himself, and that he had transformed his own nature and spirit into my shape and form; and so strong was the impression, that when I awoke, I was quite stupid. On going out early for a mouthful of fresh air, my second was immediately by my side. I was just going to break out in a rage at this endless counterfeiting of my person, when he prevented me, by beginning first.

"I am sorry to see you looking so disturbed this morning," said he, "and must really entreat of you to give up this foolery. The joke is worn quite stale, I assure you. For the first day or so it did very well, and was rather puzzling; but now I cannot help pitying you, and beg that you will forthwith appear in your own character, and drop mine."

"Sir, I have no other character to appear in," said I. "I was born, christened, and educated as James Beatman, younger, of Drumloning; and that designation I will maintain against all the counterfeits on earth."

"Well, your perversity confounds me," replied he; "for you must be perfectly sensible that you are acting a part that is not your own. That you are either a rank counterfeit, or, what I rather begin to suspect, the devil in my likeness."

These words overpowered me so much, that I fell a trembling, for I thought of the vision of last night, and what the old man had told me; and the thoughts of having become the devil in my own likeness, was more than my heart could brook, and I dare say I looked fearfully ill.

"O ho! old Cloots, are you caught?" cried he, jeeringly; "well, your sublime majesty will choose to keep your distance in future, as I would rather dispense with your society."

"Sir, I'll let you know that I am *not* the devil," cried I, in great wrath, "and if you dare, sir, it shall be tried this moment, and on this spot, who is the counterfeit, and who is the *right* James Beatman, you or I."

"To-night at the sun going down, that shall be tried here, if you change not your purpose before that time," said he. "In the meanwhile let us hie to the moors, for our companions are out, and I have a bet of ten guineas with that Englishman." And forthwith he hasted after the other two, and left me in dreadful perplexity, whether I was the devil or James Beatman. I followed to the moors—those dark and interminable moors of Buravurich—but not one bird could I get. They would scarcely let me come in view of them; and, moreover, my dog seemed to be in a dream as well as myself. He would do nothing but stare about him like a crazed beast, as if constantly in a state of terror. At the croak of the raven he turned up his nose, as if making a dead point at heaven, and at the yell of the eagle he took his tail between his legs and ran. I lost heart and gave up the sport, convinced that all was not right with me. How could a person shoot game while in a state of uncertainty whether he was the devil or not?

I returned to Inverouran, and at night-fall Mr. Watten came in, but no more. He was no sooner seated than he began to congratulate me on my success, acknowledging that he was again fairly beat.

"And pray how do you know that I have beat you?" said I.

"Why, what means this perversity?" said he; "did we not meet at six o'clock as agreed, and count our birds, and found that you had a brace more? You cannot have forgot that."

"Very well, my dear sir," said I, "as I do not choose to give a gentleman the lie, against my own interest, I'll thank you for my money, and then I'll tell you what I suppose to be the truth." He paid it. "And now," continued I, " the d—l a bird did I count with you or any other person to-day, for the best of reasons, I had not one to count."

At the setting of the sun I loaded my pistols and attended at the appointed place, which was in a little concealed dell near the corner of the lake. My enemy met me. We fired at six paces distance, and I fell. Rather a sure sign that I *was* the right James Beatman, but which of the I's it was that fell I never knew till this day, nor ever can.

These, sir, are all the incidents that I recollect relating to this strange adventure. When I next came a little to myself, I found myself in this lunatic asylum, with my head shaven, and my wounds dressed, and waited upon by a great burly vulgar fellow, who refuses to open his mouth in answer to any question of mine. I have been frequently visited by my father, and by several surgeons; but they, too, preserve toward me looks of the most superb mystery, and often lay their fingers on their lips. One day I teazed my keeper so much, that he lost patience, and said, " Whoy, sur, un you wooll knaw the treuth, you have droonken away your seven senses. That's all, so never mind."

Now, sir, this vile hint has cut me to the heart. It is manifest that I have been in a state of derangement; but instead of having been driven to it by drinking, it has been solely caused by my wound, and by having been turned into two men, acting on various and distinct principles, yet still conscious of an idiosyncracy.— These circumstances, as they affected me, were enough to overset the mind of any one, and though to myself quite unintelligible, I send them to you, in hopes that, by publishing them, you may induce an inquiry, which may tend to the solution of this mystery that hangs over my fate. I remain, sir, your perplexed, but very humble servant,

JAMES BEATMAN.

This letter puzzled me exceedingly, and certainly I would have regarded it altogether as the dream of a lunatic, had it not been for two circumstances. These were his being left behind at Stirling, and posting the rest of the road himself; and the duel, and wound at the last. These I could not identify with the visions of a disordered imagination, if there were any proofs abiding. And having once met with Mr. Walker, of Crowell, at the house of my friend Mr. Stein, the distiller, I wrote to him, requesting an explanation of these circumstances, and all others relating to the unfortunate catastrophe, which came under his observation. His answer was as follows:—

"Sir;—I feel that I cannot explain the circumstances relating to my young friend's misfortune to your satisfaction, and for the sake of his family who are my near relatives, I dare not tell you what I think, because these thoughts will not conform to human reason. This thing is certain, that neither Mr. Watten nor I ever saw more than one person. I took him from Stirling to Inverouran on the Black Mount with me in my own gig; yet strange to say, a chaise arrived at the inn the night but one after our arrival with the same gentleman, as we supposed, who blamed me bitterly for leaving him behind. The chaise came after dark. Mr. Beatman had been with us on the previous evening, and we had not seen him subsequently till he stepped out of the carriage. These are the facts, reconcile them if you can. Mr. Beatman's hallucinations were first manifested that night. The landlord came into us, and said, 'I wat pe te mhotter with te prave shentleman in te oter rhoom? Hu she pe cot into creat pig tarnnation twarvel with her own self. She pe eiter trunk or horn mat."

"I sent for him and he came on the instant but looked much disturbed. On the 12th he shot as well as I ever saw him do, and was excellent company; but that night he was shot, as he affirms in a duel, and carried in dangerously wounded, in a state of utter insensibility, in which he continued for six weeks.

"This duel, is of all things I ever heard of, the most mysterious. He was seen go by himself into the little dell at the head of the loch. I myself heard the two shots, yet there was no other man there that any person knew of, and still it was quite impossible that the pistol could have been fired by his own hand. The ball had struck him on the right side of the head, leaving a considerable fracture, cut the top of his right ear, and lodged in his shoulder; so that it must either have been fired at him while in a stooping posture, or from the air straight above him. Both the pistols were found discharged, and lying very near one another. This is all that I or any mortal man know of the matter, save himself; and though he is now nearly well and quite collected, he is still perfectly incoherent about that,

"I remain,sir, yours truly,
" ALEXANDER WALKER.
" Crowell, Nov. 6, 1827."

Blackwood's Magazine XXIII (April 1830.)

from Noctes Ambrosianae

THE SOUP COURSE

ΧΡΗ ΔΕΝ ΣΥΜΠΟΣΙΩ ΚΥΛΙΚΩΝ ΠΕΡΙΝΙΣΣΟΜΕΝΑΩΝ
ΗΔΕΑ ΚΩΤΙΛΛΟΝΤΑ ΚΑΘΗΜΕΝΟΝ ΟΙΝΟΠΟΤΑΖΕΙΝ

Σ.
PHOC. *Ap Ath.*

[*This is a distich by wise old Phocylides,*
An ancient who wrote crabbed Greek in no silly days;
Meaning, "'TIS RIGHT FOR GOOD WINEBIBBING PEOPLE,
NOT TO LET THE JUG PACE ROUND THE BOARD LIKE A CRIPPLE;
BUT GAILY TO CHAT WHILE DISCUSSING THEIR TIPPLE."
An excellent rule of the hearty old cock 'tis –
And a very fit motto to put to our Noctes.]

C.N. ap. Ambr.

SCENE, – *The Saloon, illuminated by the grand Gas Orrery.* TIME, – *First of April – Six o'clock.* PRESENT, – NORTH, *the* ENGLISH OPIUM-EATER, SHEPHERD, TICKLER, *in Court Dresses. – The three celebrated young Scottish* LEANDERS, *with their horns, in the hanging gallery.* AIR, *"Brose and Brochan and a'."*

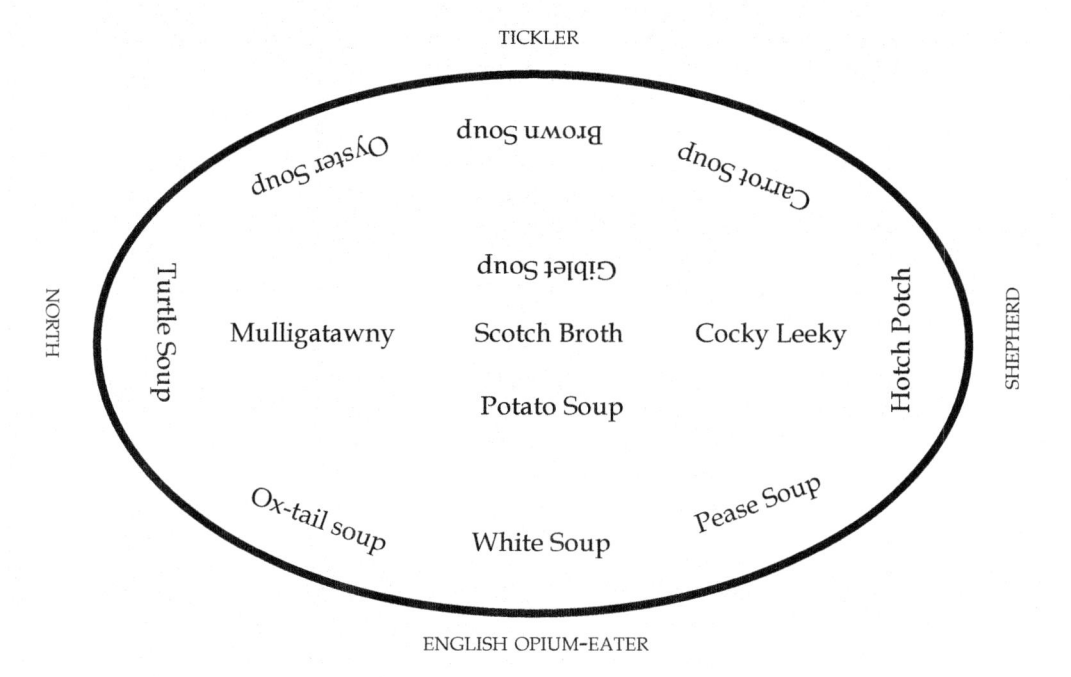

TICKLER

	Brown Soup	
Oyster Soup		Carrot Soup
	Giblet Soup	
Turtle Soup	Mulligatawny Scotch Broth Cocky Leeky	Hotch Potch
	Potato Soup	
Ox-tail soup		Pease Soup
	White Soup	

NORTH (left)   SHEPHERD (right)

ENGLISH OPIUM-EATER

169

SHEPHERD.

An' that's an Orrery! The infinitude o' the starry heavens reduced sae as to suit the ceilin o' the Saloon! — Whare's Virgo?

TICKLER.

Yonder she is, James — smiling in the shade of —

SHEPHERD.

I see her — just aboon the cocky-leeky. Weel, sic anither contrivance! Some o' the stars and planets — moons and suns lichter than ithers, I jalouse, by lettin in upon them a greater power o' coal-gas; and ithers again, just by moderatin the pipe-conductors, faint and far awa' in the system, sae that ye scarcely ken whether they are lichted wi' the gawseous vapour ava', or only a sort o' fine, tender, delicate porcelain, radiant in its ain transparent nature, and though thin, yet stronger than the storms.

NORTH.

The first astronomers were shepherds —

SHEPHERD.

Ay, Chaldean shepherds like mysel — but no a mother's son o' them could hae written the Manuscripp. Ha, ha, ha!

TICKLER.

What a misty evening!

SHEPHERD.

Nae wonder — wi' thirteen soups a' steamin up to the skies! O! but the Orrery is sublime the noo, in its shroud! Naethin like hotch-potch for gien a dim grandeur to the stars. See, yonder Venus — peerless planet — shining like the face o' a virgin bride through her white nuptial veil! He's a grim chiel yon Saturn. Nae wonder he devourit his weans — he has the coontenance o' a cannibal. Thank you, Mr Awmrose, for opening the door — for this current o' air has swept awa the mists frae heaven, and gien us back the beauty o' the celestial spheres.

NORTH (*aside to the* ENGLISH OPIUM-EATER).

You hear, Mr De Quincey, how he begins to blaze even before broth.

ENGLISH OPIUM-EATER (*aside to* NORTH).

I have always placed Mr Hogg, *in genius*, far above Burns. He is indeed "of imagination all compact." Burns had strong sense — and strong sinews — and brandished a pen pretty much after the same fashion as he brandished a flail. You never lose sight of the thresher —

SHEPHERD.

Dinna abuse Burns, Mr De Quinshy. Neither you nor ony ither Englishman can thoroughly understaun' three sentences o' his poems —

ENGLISH OPIUM-EATER (*with much animation*).

I have for some years past longed for an opportunity to tear into pieces that gross national delusion, born of prejudice, ignorance, and bigotry, in which, from highest to lowest, all literary classes of Scotchmen are as it were incarnated — to wit, a belief, strong as superstition, that all their various dialects must be as unintelligible, as I grant that most of them are uncouth and barbarous, to English ears — even to those of the most accomplished and consummate scholars. Whereas, to a Danish, Norwegian, Swedish,

Saxon, German, French, Italian, Spanish—and let me add, Latin and Greek scholar, there is not even a monosyllable that—

SHEPHERD.

What's *a gowpen o' glaur*?

ENGLISH OPIUM-EATER.

Mr Hogg—Sir, I will not be interrupted—

SHEPHERD.

You cannot tell. It's just *twa neif-fu's o' clarts*.

NORTH.

James—James—James!

SHEPHERD.

Kit—Kit—Kit. But beg your pardon, Mr De Quinshy—afore dinner I'm aye unco snappish. I admit you're a great grammarian. But kennin' something o' a language by bringin to bear upon't a' the united efforts o' knowledge and understaunin'—baith first-rate—is ae thing, and feelin' every breath and every shadow that keeps playin' ower a' its syllables, as if by a natural and born instinct, is anither; the first you may aiblins hae—naebody likelier,—but to the second, nae man may pretend that hasna had the happiness and the honour o' havin been born and bred in bonny Scotland. What can ye ken o' Kilmeny?

ENGLISH OPIUM-EATER (*smiling graciously*).

'Tis a ballad breathing the sweetest, simplest, wildest spirit of Scottish traditionary song—music, as of some antique instrument long-lost, but found at last in the Forest among the decayed roots of trees, and touched, indeed, as by an instinct, by the only man who could reawaken its sleeping chords—the Ettrick Shepherd.

SHEPHERD.

Na—if you say that sincerely—and I never saw a broo smoother wi' truth than your ain—I maun qualify my former apophthegm, and alloo you to be an exception frae the general rule. I wish, sir, you wou'd write a Glossary o' the Scottish Language. I ken naebody fitter.

NORTH.

Our distinguished guest is aware that this is "All Fool's Day,"—and must, on that score, pardon these court-dresses. We consider them, my dear sir, appropriate to this Anniversary.

SHEPHERD.

Mine wasna originally a coort-dress. It's the uniform o' the Border Club. But nane o' the ither members wou'd wear them, except me and the late Dyuk o' Buccleuch. So when the King came to Scotland, and expeckit to be introduced to me at Holyrood-house, I got the tiler at Yarrow-Ford to cut it doun after a patron frae Embro'—

ENGLISH OPIUM-EATER.

Green and gold—to my eyes the most beautiful of colours—the one characteristic of earth, the other of heaven—and, therefore, the two united, emblematic of genius.

SHEPHERD.

Oh! Mr De Quinshy—sir, but you're a pleasant cretur—and were I ask't to gie a notion o' your mainners to them that had never seen you, I should just use twa words, Urbanity and Amenity—meanin', by the first, that saft bricht polish that a man gets by leevin' amang gentlemen scholars in towns and cities, burnished on the solid metal o' a happy natur' hardened by the rural atmosphere o' the pure kintra air, in which I ken you hae ever delighted; and, by the ither, a peculiar sweetness, amaist like that o' a woman's, yet sae far frae bein' feminine, as masculine as that o' Allan Ramsay's ain Gentle Shepherd—and breathin o' a harmonious union between the heart, the intelleck, and the imagination, a' the three keepin' their ain places, and thus makin the vice, speech, gesture, and motion o' a man as composed as a figur' on a pictur' by some painter that was a master in his art, and produced his effects easily—and ane kens nae hoo—by his lichts and shadows. Mr North, am na I richt in the thocht, if no in the expression?

NORTH.

You have always known my sentiments, James —

SHEPHERD.

I'm thinkin we had better lay aside our swurds. They're kittle dealin', when a body's stannin' or walkin'; but the very deevil's in them when ane claps his doup on a chair, for here's the hilt o' mine interferin' wi' my ladle-hand.

TICKLER.

Why, James, you have buckled it on the wrong side.

SHEPHERD.

What? Is the richt the wrang?

NORTH.

Let us all untackle. Mr Ambrose, hang up each man's sword on his own hat-peg.—There.

SHEPHERD.

Mr de Quinshy! but you look weel in a single-breisted snuff-olive, wi' cut-steel buttons, figured waistcoat, and—

ENGLISH OPIUM-EATER.

There is a beautiful propriety, Mr Hogg, in a court-dress, distinguished as it is, both by material and form, from the apparel suitable to the highest occasions immediately below the presence of royalty, just as that other apparel is distinguished from the costume worn on the less ceremonious—

SHEPHERD.

Eh?

ENGLISH OPIUM-EATER.

Occasions of civilised life,—and *that* again in due degree from *that* sanctioned by custom, in what I may call, to use the language of Shakespeare, and others of our elder dramatists, the "worky-day" world,—whether it be in those professions peculiar, or nearly so, to towns and cities, or belonging more appropriately—though the distinction, perhaps, is popular rather than philosophical—to rural districts on either side of your beautiful river the Tweed.

SHEPHERD.

O, sir! but I'm unco fond o' the English accent. It's like an instrument wi' a' the strings o' silver,—and though I canna help thinkin' that you speak rather a wee ower slow, yet there's sic music in your vice, that I'm just perfectly enchanted wi' the soun', while a sense o' truth prevents me frae sayin that I aye a'thegither comprehend the meaning,—for that's aye, written or oral alike, sae desperate metapheesical.—But what soup will you tak, sir. Let me recommend the hotch-potch.

ENGLISH OPIUM-EATER.

I prefer vermicelli.

SHEPHERD.

What? Worms! They gar me scunner,—the verra look o' them. Sae, you're a worm-eater, sir, as weel's an Opium-eater?

ENGLISH OPIUM-EATER.

Mr Wordsworth, sir, I think it is, who says, speaking of the human being under the thraldom of the senses,—

"He is a slave, the meanest we can meet."

SHEPHERD.

I beseech ye, my dear sir, no to be angry sae sune on in the afternoon. There's your worms—and I wuss you muckle gude o' them—only compare them—Thank you, Mr Tickler—wi' this bowl-deep trencher o' hotch-potch—an emblem o' the haill vegetable and animal creation.

TICKLER.

Why, James, though now invisible to the naked eye, boiled down as they are in baser matter, that tureen on which your face has for some minutes been fixed as gloatingly as that of a Satyr on a sleeping Wood-nymph, or of Pan himself on Matron Cybele, contains, as every naturalist knows, some scores of snails, a gowpenful of gnats, countless caterpillars, of our smaller British insects numbers without number numberless as the sea-shore sands—

SHEPHERD.

No at this time o' the year, you gowk. You're thinking o' simmer colleyfloor—

TICKLER.

But their larvae, James—

SHEPHERD.

Confound their larvae! Awmrose! the pepper. *(Dashes in the pepper along with the silver top of the cruet.)* Pity me! whare's the cruet? It has sunk doun intill the hotch-potch, like a mailed horse and his rider intill a swamp. I maun tak tent no to swallow the bog-trotter. What the deevil, Awmrose, you've gien me the Cayawne!!

MR AMBROSE, (tremens.)

My dear sir, it was Tappytoorie.

SHEPHERD (to Tappy).

You wee sinner, did ye tak me for Mosshy Shawbert?

ENGLISH OPIUM-EATER.

I have not seen it recorded, Mr Hogg, in any of the Public Journals, at least it was not so in the Standard,—in fact the only newspaper I now read, and

an admirable evening paper it is, unceasingly conducted with consummate ability,—that that French charlatan had hitherto essayed Cayenne pepper; and indeed such an exhibition would be preposterous, seeing that the lesser is contained within the greater, and consequently all the hot varieties of that plant—all the possibilities of the pepper-pod—are included within Phosphorus and Prussic acid. Meanly as I think of the logic —
SHEPHERD.
O ma mouth! ma mouth!—Logic indeed! I didna think there had been sic a power o' pepper about a' the premises.
ENGLISH OPIUM-EATER.
The only conclusion that can be legitimately drawn—
SHEPHERD.
Whisht wi' your College clavers—and, Awmrose, gie me a caulker o' Glenlivet to cool the roof o' my pallet. Ma tongue's like red-het airn—and blisters ma verra lips. Na! it'll melt the siller-spoon—
NORTH.
I pledge you, my dear James—
ENGLISH OPIUM-EATER.
Vermicelli soup, originally Italian, has been so long naturalized in this island, that it may now almost be said, by those not ambitious of extremest accuracy of thought and expression, to be indigenous in Britain — and as it sips somewhat insipid, may I use the freedom, Mr Tickler — scarcely pardonable, perhaps, from our short acquaintance — to request you to join me in a glass of the same truly Scottish liquor?
TICKLER.
Most happy indeed to cultivate the friendship of Mr De Quincey.
[The Four turn up their little fingers.
SHEPHERD.
Mirawcolous! My tongue's a' at aince as cauld 's the rim o' a cart-wheel on a winter's nicht! My pallet cool as the lift o' a spring-mornin'! And the inside o' my mouth just like a wee mountain-well afore sunrise, when the bit moorland birdies are hoppin' on its margin, about to wat their whustles in the blessed beverage, after their love-dreams amang the dewy heather!
ENGLISH OPIUM-EATER.
I would earnestly recommend it to you, Mr Hogg, to abstain—
SHEPHERD.
Thank you, sir, for your timeous warnin'—for, without thinkin' what I was about, I was just on the verra eve o' fa'in' to again till the self-same fiery trencher. It's no everybody that has your philosophical composure. But it sits weel on you, sir—and I like baith to look and listen to you; for, in spite o' your classical learning, and a' your outlandish logic, you're at a' times—and I'm nae bad judge—shepherd as I am—*intus et in cute*—that is, tooth and nail—naething else but a perfeck gentleman. But oh, you're a lazy cretur, man, or you would hae putten out a dizzen vollumms sin' the Confessions.
ENGLISH OPIUM-EATER.
I am at present, my dear friend—allow me to call myself so—in treaty with Mr Blackwood for a novel

SHEPHERD.

In ae volumm—in ae volumm, I hope—and that'ill tie you doun to whare your strength lies, condensation at ance vigorous and exquisite—like a man succinct for hap-step-and-loup on the greensward—each spang langer than anither—till he clears a peat hand-barrow at the end like a catastrophe.—Hae I eaten anither dish o' hotch-potch, think ye, sirs, without bein' aware o't?

TICKLER.

No, James—North changed the fare upon you, and you have devoured, in a fit of absence, about half-a-bushel of peas.

SHEPHERD.

I'm glad it wasna carrots—for they aye gie me a sair belly.—But hae ye been at the Exhibition o' Pictures by leevin' artists at the Scottish Academy, Mr North,—and what think ye o't?

NORTH.

I look in occasionally, James, of a morning, before the bustle begins, for a crowd is not for a crutch.

SHEPHERD.

But ma faith, a crutch is for a crood, as is weel kent o' yours, by a' the blockheads in Britain.—Is't gude the year?

NORTH.

Good, bad, and indifferent, like all other mortal exhibitions. In landscape, we sorely miss Mr Thomson of Duddingstone.

SHEPHERD.

What can be the maitter wi' the minister?—He's no deid?

NORTH.

God forbid! But Williams is gone—dear delightful Williams—with his aerial distances into which the imagination sailed as on wings, like a dove gliding through sunshine into gentle gloom—with his shady foregrounds, where Love and Leisure reposed—and his middle regions, with towering cities grove-embowered, solemn with the spirit of the olden time—and all, all embalmed in the beauty of those deep Grecian skies!

SHEPHERD.

He's deid. What matters it? In his virtues he was happy, and in his genius he is immortal. Hoots, man! If tears are to drap for ilka freen "who is not," our een wad be seldom dry.—Tak some mair turtle.

NORTH.

Mr Thomson of Duddingstone is now our greatest landscape painter. In what sullen skies he sometimes shrouds the solitary moors!

SHEPHERD.

And wi' what blinks o' beauty he aften brings out frae beneath the clouds the spire o' some pastoral parish kirk, till you feel it is the Sabbath!

NORTH.

Time and decay crumbling his castles seem to be warring against the very living rock—and we feel their endurance in their desolation.

SHEPHERD.

I never look at his roarin rivers, wi' a' their precipices, without thinkin, some hoo or ither, o' Sir William Wallace! They seem to belang to an unconquerable country.

NORTH.

Yes, James! he is a patriotic painter. Moor, mountain and glen — castle, hall, and hut — all breathe sternly or sweetly o' auld Scotland. So do his seas and his friths — roll, roar, blacken and whiten with Caledonia — from the Mull of Galloway to Cape Wrath. Or when summer stillness is upon them, are not all the soft shadowy pastoral hills Scottish, that in their still deep transparency, invert their summits in the transfiguring magic of the far-sleeping main?

TICKLER.

William Simpson, now gone to live in London, is in genius no whit inferior to Mr Thomson, and superior in mastery over the execution of the Art.

NORTH.

A first-rater. Ewbank's moonlights this season are meritorious; but 'tis difficult to paint Luna, though she is a still sitter in the shy. Be she veiled nun — white-robed vestal — blue-cinctured huntress — full-orbed in Christian meekness — or, bright misbeliever! brow-rayed with the Turkish crescent — still meetest is she, spiritual creature, for the Poet's love!

SHEPHERD.

They tell me that a lad o' the name o' Fleming, frae the west kintra, has shown some bonny landscapes.

NORTH.

His pictures are rather deficient in depth, James — his scenes are scarcely sufficiently like portions of the solid globe — but he has a sense of beauty — and with that a painter may do almost anything — without it, nothing. For of the painter as of the poet, we may employ the exquisite image of Wordsworth, that beauty

"Pitches her tents before him."

For example, there is Gibb, who can make a small sweet pastoral world, out of a bank and a brae, a pond and a couple of cows, with a simple lassie sitting in her plaid upon the stump of an old tree. Or, if a morning rainbow spans the moor, he shows you brother and sister — it may be — or perhaps childish lovers — facing the showery wind — in the folds of the same plaid — straining merrily, with their colley before them, towards the hut whose smoke is shivered as soon as it reaches the tops of the sheltering grove. Gibb is full of feeling and genius.

SHEPHERD.

But is na his colourin' ower blue?

NORTH.

No, — James. Show me anything bluer than the sky — at its bluest. — Not even *her* eye —

SHEPHERD.

What! Mrs Gentle's? Her een aye seemed to me to be greenish.

NORTH.

Hush, blasphemer! Their zones are like the sky-light of the longest night in the year — when all the earth lies half asleep and half awake in the beauty of happy dreams.

SHEPHERD.

Hech! hech!

"O love! love! love!
Love's like a dizziness,
It wunna let a puir bodie
Gang about his bizziness!"

ENGLISH OPIUM-EATER.

I have often admired the prodigious power of perspective displayed in the large landscapes of Nasmyth. He gives you at one *coup-d'oeil* a metropolitan city—with its river, bridges, towers, and temples—engirdled with groves, and far-retiring all around the garden-fields, tree-dropped, or sylvan-shaded, of merry England. I allude now to a noble picture of London.

NORTH.

And all his family are geniuses like himself. In the minutiæ of nature, Peter is perfect—it would not be easy to say which of his unmarried daughters excels her sisters in truth of touch—though I believe the best judges are disposed to give Mrs Terry the palm—who now—since the death of her lamented husband—teaches painting in London with eminent success.

TICKLER.

Colvin Smith has caught Jeffrey's countenance at last—and a fine countenance it is—alive with intellect—armed at all points—acute without a quibble—clothed all over with cloudless perspicacity—and eloquent on the silent canvass, as if all the air within the frame were murmuring with winged words.

NORTH.

Not murmuring—his voice tinkles like a silver bell.

SHEPHERD.

But wha can tell that frae the canvass?

NORTH.

James, on looking at a portrait, you carry along with you all the characteristic individualities of the original—his voice—his gesture—his action—his motion—his manner—and thus the likeness is made up "of what you half-create and half-perceive,"—else dead—thus only spiritualised into perfect similitude.

SHEPHERD.

Mr De Quinshy should hae said that!

ENGLISH OPIUM-EATER.

Pardon me, Mr Hogg, I could not have said it nearly so well—and in this case, I doubt not, most truly—as Mr North.

NORTH.

No one feature, perhaps, of Mr Jeffrey's face is very fine, except, indeed, his mouth, which is the firmest, and, at the same time, the mildest—the most resolute, and yet, at the same time, the sweetest, I ever saw—inferior in such mingled expression only to Canning's, which was perfect; but look on them all together, and they all act together in irresistible union; forehead, eyes, cheeks, mouth, and chin, all declaring, as Burns said of Matthew Henderson, that "Francis is a bright man,"—ever in full command of all his great and various talents, with just enough of genius to preserve them all in due order and subordination—for, with either more or less genius, we may not believe that his endowments could have been so finely, yet so firmly balanced, so powerful both in speculative and practical skill, making him at once, perhaps, on the whole, the most philosophic critic of his age, and, beyond all comparison, the most eloquent orator of his country.

ENGLISH OPIUM-EATER.

To much of that eulogium, Mr North, great as my admiration is of Mr Jeffrey's abilities, I must demur.

SHEPHERD.

And me too.

TICKLER.

And I also.

NORTH.

Well, gentlemen, demur away; but such for many years has been my opinion, and 'tis the opinion of all Scotland.

ENGLISH OPIUM-EATER.

Since you speak of Mr Jeffrey, and of his achievements in law, literature, and philosophy, in Scotland, and without meaning to include the Southern Intellectual Empire of Britain, why, then, with one exception, *(bowing to Mr North)*, I do most cordially agree with you, though of his law I know nothing, and nothing of his oral eloquence, but judge of him solely from the Edinburgh Review, which, *(bowing again to Mr North)*, with the same conspicuous exception—maugre all its manifold and miserable mistakes—unquestionably stands—or did stand—for I have not seen a number of it since the April number of 1826—at the head of the Periodical Literature of the Age — and that the Periodical Literature of the Age is infinitely superior to all its other philosophical criticism—for example, the charlatanerie of the Schlegels, *et id genus omne*, is as certain—Mr Hogg, pardon me for imitating your illustrative imagery, or attempting to imitate what all the world allows to be inimitable—as that the hotch-potch which you are now swallowing, in spite of heat that seems breathed from the torrid zone—

SHEPHERD.

It's no hotch-potch—this platefu's cocky-leeky.

ENGLISH OPIUM-EATER.

As that cocky-leeky which, though hot as purgatory (the company will pardon me for yielding to the influence of the *genius loci*), your mouth is, and for a quarter of an hour has been, vortex-like engulfing, transcends, in all that is best in animal and vegetable matter — worthy indeed of Scotland's manly Shepherd—the *soup maigre*, that, attenuated almost to invisibility, drenches the odiously-guttural gullet of some monkey Frenchman of the old school, by the incomprehensible interposition of Providence saved at the era of the Revolution from the guillotine.

OMNES!

Bravo! bravo! bravo! — Encore — encore — encore!

SHEPHERD.

That's capital—it's just me; gin ye were aye to speak that gate, man, folk would understaun' you. Let's hae a caulker thegither—There's a gurgle—

your health, sir—no forgettin the wife and the weans. It's a pity you're no a Scotchman.

NORTH.

John Watson's "Lord Dalhousie" is a noble picture. But John's always great—his works win upon you the longer you study them—and that, after all, is at once the test and the triumph of the art. On some portraits you at once exhaust your admiration; and are then ashamed of yourself for having mistaken the vulgar pleasure, so cheaply inspired, of a staring likeness, for that high emotion breathed from the mastery of the painter's skill—and blush to have doated on a daub.

TICKLER.

Duncan's "Braw Wooer," from Burns's
"Yestreen a braw wooer cam down the lang glen,
 And sair wi' his love he did deave me;
 I said there was naething I hated like men,—
 The deuce gang wi' him to believe me,"
is a masterpiece. What a fellow, James! Not unlike yourself in your younger days, perhaps—but without a particle of the light of genius that ever ennobles your rusticity, and makes the plaid on our incomparable Shepherd's shoulders graceful as the poet's mantle—But rather like some son of yours, James, of whom you had not chanced to think it worth your while to take any very particular notice, yet who, by hereditary talents, had made his way in the world up to head-shepherd on a four-thousand-acre hill-farm,—his face glowing with love and health like a peony over which a milk-pail had happened to be upset—bonnet cocked as crousely on his hard brow as the comb upon the tappin' o' chanticleer when sidling up, with dropped wing, to a favourite pullet—buckskin breeches, such as Burns used to wear himself, brown and burnished to a most perilous polish—and top-boots, the images of your own, my beloved boy—on which the journey down the lang glen has brought the summer-dust to blend with the well-greased blacking—broad chest, gorgeously apparelled in a flapped waistcoat, manifestly made for him by his great grandmother, out of the damask-hangings of a bed that once must have stood firm in a Ha' on four posts, though now haply in a hut but a trembling truckle—strong harn shirt, clean as a lily, bleached in the showery sunshine on a brent gowany brae, nor untinged with a faint scent of thyme that, in oaken drawer, will lie odorous for years upon years,—and cravat with a knot like a love-posy, and two pointed depending stalks, tied in the gleam of a water-pail, or haply in the mirror of the pool in which that Apollo had just been floundering like a porpoise, and in which, when drought had dried the shallows, he had leistered many a fish impatient of the sea;—there, James, he sits on a bank, leaning and leering, a lost and love-sick man, yet not forgetful nor unconscious of the charms so prodigally lavished upon him both by nature and art, the BRAW WOOER, who may not fail in his suit, till blood be wersh as water, and flesh indeed fushionless as grass growing in a sandy desert.

SHEPHERD.

Remember, Mr Tickler, what a lee-way you hae to mak up, on the sea o' soup, and be na sae descriptive, for we've a' gotten to windward; you seem to hae drapt anchor, and baith mainsail and foresail are flappin' to the extremity o' their sheets.

TICKLER.

And is not she, indeed, James, a queenlike quean? What scorn and skaith in the large full orbs of her imperial eyes! How she tosses back her head in triumph, till the yellow lustre of her locks seems about to escape from the bondage of that ribbon, the hope-gift of another suitor who wooed her under happier auspices, among last-year's "rigs o' barley," at winter's moonless midnight, beneath the barn-balk where roosts the owl,—by spring's dewy eve on the dim primrose bank, while the lark sought his nest among the green braird, descending from his sunset-song!

SHEPHERD.

Confound me—if this be no just perfectly intolerable—Mr North, Mr De Quinshy, Mr Tickler, and a', men, women, and children, imitatin' ma style o' colloquial oratory, till a' that's specific and original about me's lost in universal plagiarism.

TICKLER.

Why, James, your genius is as contagious—as infectious as the plague,—if, indeed, it be not epidemical—like a fever in the air.

SHEPHERD.

You're a' glad to sook up the miasmata. But, mercy on us! a' the tureens seem to me amaist dried up—as laigh's wells in midsummer drought. The vermicelli, especially, is drained to its last worms. Mr De Quinshy, you've an awfu' appeteet!

ENGLISH OPIUM-EATER.

I shall dine to-day entirely on soup,—for your Edinburgh beef and mutton, however long kept, are difficult of mastication,—the sinews seeming to me all to go transversely, thus,—and not longitudinally,—so—

NORTH.

Hark! my gold repeater is smiting seven. We allow an hour, Mr De Quincey, to each course—and then—

[*The Leanders play "The Boatie Bows," — the door flies open, — enter Picardy and his clan.*

Alexander Rodger (1784-1846)

A Bundle Of Truths: A Parody (1822)

Written about the time of Hone's Trial

George, the Regent, 's chaste and wise,
Castlereagh's an honest man,
Southey tells no fulsome lies,
England's free—likewise Japan:
Sidmouth's acts are all upright,
Canning's modest as a maid;
Darkness can he proven light,
So can Britain's debt be paid.
     Hey triangle, derry down,
     Doctor, old bags, wig and gown,
     O how grave a judge can tell,
     'Truth's a libel'—'false as hell.'

Johnny Bull is plump and stout,
All his sons are fat and fair;
Spies are worthy men—no doubt;
Taxes are as light as air.
Ellenborough's mild and just;
Ministers no rights invade;
Prison keys are brown with rust,
Jailors starve for lack of trade.
     Hey triangle, &c.

Parsons are a liberal race,
Noble paupers waste no cash;
Everything now thrives apace—
Paper's sterling, gold is trash.
Parliament is pure as snow—
Vile corruption hides her head:
Every body now must know,
Dearest grain makes cheapest bread.
     Hey triangle, &c.

Trying times are fairly past;
Want no more dare show his face;
Treason is pent up at last,
Close within a *thimble's space.*
Wealth has banished discontent,
Press and people both are free,
Doctor Sadmouth—pious saint—
Grunts 'Amen: so let it be.'
     Hey triangle, &c.

John Galt (1779-1839)

from **The Provost (1822)**

CHAP. I.

THE FORECAST.

It must be allowed in the world, that a man who has thrice reached the highest station of life, in his line, has a good right to set forth the particulars of the discretion and prudence by which he lifted himself so far above the ordinaries of his day and generation; indeed, the generality of mankind may claim this as a duty; for the conduct of public men, as it has been often wisely said, is a species of public property, and their rules and observances have in all ages been considered things of a national concernment. I have therefore well weighed the importance it may be of to posterity, to know by what means I have thrice been made an instrument to represent the supreme power and authority of Majesty, in the royal borough of Gudetown, and how I deported myself in that honour and dignity, so much to the satisfaction of my superiors in the state and commonwealth of the land, to say little of the great respect in which I was held by the townsfolk, and far less of the terror that I was to evildoers. But not to be over circumstantial, I propose to confine this history of my life to the public portion thereof, on the which account I will take up the beginning at the crisis when I first entered into business, after having served more than a year above my time, with the late Mr. Thomas Remnant, than whom there was not a more creditable man in the borough; and he died in the possession of the functionaries and faculties of town Treasurer, much respected by all acquainted with his orderly and discreet qualities.

Mr. Remnant was, in his younger years, when the growth of luxury and prosperity had not come to such a head as it has done since, a taylor that went out to the houses of the adjacent lairds and country gentry, whereby he got an inkling of the policy of the world, that could not have been gathered in any other way by a man of his station and degree of life. In process of time he came to be in a settled way, and when I was bound 'prentice to him, he had three regular journeymen, and a cloth shop. It was therefore not so much for learning the tayloring, as to get an insight into the conformity between the traffic of the shop and the board that I was bound to him, being destined by my parents for the profession appertaining to the former, and to conjoin thereto something of the mercery and haberdashery; my uncle, that had been a sutler in the army along with General Wolfe, who made a conquest of Quebec, having left me a legacy of three hundred pounds, because I was called after him, the which legacy was a consideration for to set me up in due season in some genteel business.

Accordingly, as I have narrated, when I had passed a year over my 'prenticeship with Mr. Remnant, I took up the corner shop at the Cross, facing the Tolbooth, and having had it adorned in a befitting manner, about a month before the summer fair thereafter, I opened it on that day with an excellent assortment of goods, the best, both for taste and variety, that had ever been seen in the borough of Gudetown; and the winter following, finding by my books that I was in a way to do so, I married my wife: she was daughter to Mrs. Broderip, who kept the head inn in Irville, and by whose death, in the fall of the next year, we got a nest egg that, without a vain pretension, I may say we have not failed to lay upon, and clok to some purpose.

Being thus settled in a shop and in life, I soon found that I had a part to perform in the public world but I looked warily about me before casting my nets, and therefore I laid myself out, rather to be entreated than to ask; for I had often heard Mr. Remnant observe, that the nature of man could not abide to see a neighbour taking place and preferment of his own accord. I therefore assumed a coothy and obliging demeanour towards my customers and the community in general; and sometimes even with the very beggars I found a jocose saying as well received as a bawbee, although naturally I dinna think I was ever what could be called a funny man, but only just as ye would say a thought ajee in that way. Howsever, I soon became, both by habit and repute, a man of popularity in the town, in so much, that it was a shrewd saying of old James Alpha, the bookseller, that mair gude jokes were cracked ilka day in James Pawkie's shop, than in Thomas Curl, the barber's, on a Saturday night."

CHAP. II.

A KITHING.

I could plainly discern that the prudent conduct which I had adopted towards the public was gradually growing into effect. Disputative neighbours made me their referee, and I became, as it were, an oracle that was better than the law, in so much that I settled their controversies without the expence that attends the same. But what convinced me more than any other thing that the line I pursued was verging towards a satisfactory result, was, that the elderly folk that came into the shop to talk over the news of the day, and to rehearse the diverse uncos, both of a national and a domestic nature, used to call me bailie, and my lord; the which jocular derision was as a symptom and foretaste within their spirits of what I was ordained to be. Thus was I encouraged, by little and little, together with a sharp remarking of the inclination and bent of men's minds, to entertain the hope and assurance of rising to the top of all the town, as this book maketh manifest, and the incidents thereof will certificate.

Nothing particular, however, came, to pass till my wife lay in of her second bairn, our daughter Sarah; at the christening of whom, among divers friends and relations, forbye the minister, we had my father's cousin, Mr. Alexander Clues, that was then deacon Covener, and a man of great potency in his way, and possessed of an influence in the town council, of which he was well worthy, being a person of good discernment, and well versed in matters appertaining to the guildry. Mr. Clues, as we were mellowing over the toddy bowl, said, that by and by the council would be looking to me to fill up the first gap that might happen therein; and Doctor

Swapkirk, the then minister, who had officiated on the occasion, observed, that it was a thing, that in the course of nature, could not miss to be, for I had all the douce demeanour and sagacity which it behoved a magistrate to possess. But I cannily replied, though I was right contented to hear this, that I had no time for governing, and it would be more for the advantage of the commonwealth to look for the counselling of an older head than mine, happen when a vacancy might in the town council.

In this conjuncture of our discoursing, Mrs. Pawkie, my wife, who was sitting by the fire-side in her easy chair, with a cod at her head, for she had what was called a sore time o't, said,

"Na, na, gudeman, ye need ne be sae mim; every body kens, and I ken too, that ye're ettling at the magistracy. Its as plain as a pike staff, gudeman, and I'll no let ye rest if ye dinna mak me a bailie's wife or a' be done—"

I was not ill pleased to hear Mrs. Pawkie so spiritful; but I replied, "Dinna try to stretch your arm, gudewife, farther than your sleeve will let you; we maun ca' canny mony a day yet, before we think of dignities."

The which speech, in a way of implication, made deacon Clues to understand that I would not absolutely refuse an honour thrust upon me, while it maintained an outward show of humility and moderation.

There was, however, a gleg old carlin among the gossips then present, one Mrs. Sprowl, the widow of a deceased magistrate, and she cried out aloud,

"Deacon Clues, deacon Clues, I redde you no to believe a word that Mr. Pawkie's saying, for that was the very way my friend that's no more laid himself out to be fleeched to tak what he was greenan for; so get him intill the council when ye can; we a' ken he'll be credit to the place," and "so here's to the health of Bailie Pawkie, that is to be," cried Mrs. Sprowl. All present pledged her in the toast, by which we had a wonderful share of diversion. Nothing, however, immediately rose out of this, but it set men's minds a barming and working, so that before there was any vacancy in the council, I was considered in a manner as the natural successor to the first of the counsellors that might happen to depart this life.

Michael Scott (1789-1835)

from Tom Cringle's Log (1831-1833)

from CHAPTER XVIII - THE CRUISE OF THE WAVE (1833)

"I am distressed beyond measure at having led you and your excellent friends, Wagtail and Gelid, into this danger; but I could not help it, and I have satisfied my conscience on that point; so I have only to entreat that you will stay below, and not unnecessarily expose yourselves. And if I should fall—may I take this liberty, my dear sir," and I involuntarily took his hand,—"if I should fall, and *I doubt if I shall ever see the sun set again*, as we are fearfully overmatched" —

Bang struck in.—

"Why, if our friend be too big—why not be off then? Pull foot, man, eh?—Havannah under your lee?"

"A thousand reasons against it, my dear sir. I am a young man and a young officer, my character is to make in the service—No, no, it is impossible—an older and more tried hand might have bore up, but I must fight it out. If any stray shot carries me off, my dear sir, will you take" — Mary, I would have said, but I could not pronounce her name for the soul of me—"will you take charge of *her* miniature, and say I died as I have" — A choking lump rose in my throat, and I could not proceed for a second; "and will you send my writing desk to my poor mother, there are letters in" — The lump grew bigger, the hot tears streamed from my eyes in torrents. I trembled like an aspen leaf, and grasping my excellent friend's hand more firmly, I sunk down on my knees in a passion of tears, and wept like a woman, and fervently prayed to that great God, in whose almighty hand I stood, that I might that day do my duty as an English seaman. Bang knelt by me, and wept also. Presently the passion was quelled. I rose, and so did he.

"Before you, my dear sir, I am not ashamed to have" -

"Don't mention it—my good boy—don't mention it; neither of us, as the old general said, will fight a bit the worse."

I looked at him. "Do you then mean to fight?" said I.

"To be sure I do—why not? I have no wife. Fight? To be sure I do."

"Another gun, sir," said Tailtackle, through the open skylight. Now all was bustle, and we hastened on deck. Our antagonist was a large brig, three hundred tons at the least, a long low vessel, painted black, out and in, and her sides round as an apple, with immensely square yards. She was apparently full of men. The sun was getting high, and she was coming down fast on us, on the verge of the dark blue water of the sea breeze. I could make out ten ports and nine guns of a side. I inwardly prayed they might not be long ones, but I was not a little startled to see through the glass that there were crowds of naked negroes at quarters, and on the forecastle and poop. That she was a contraband Guineaman, I had already made up my mind to believe; and that she had some fifty hands of a crew,

I also considered likely; but that her captain should have resorted to such a perilous measure, perilous to themselves as well as to us, as arming the captive slaves, was quite unexpected, and not a little alarming, as it evinced his determination to make the most desperate resistance.

Tailtackle was standing beside me at this time, with his jacket off, his cutlass girded on his thigh, and the belt drawn very tight. All the rest of the crew were armed in a similar fashion; the small-arm-men with muskets in their hands, and the rest at quarters at the guns; while the pikes were cast loose from the spars round which they had been stopped, with tubs of wadding, and boxes of grape, all ready ranged, and every thing clear for action.

"Mr Tailtackle," said I, "you are gunner here, and should be in the magazine. Cast off that cutlass; it is not your province to lead the boarders." The poor fellow blushed, having, in the excitement of the moment, forgotten that he was any thing more than captain of the Firebrand's maintop.

"Mr Timotheus," said Bang, "have you one of these bodkins to spare?"

Timothy laughed. "Certainly, sir; but you don't mean to head the boarders, sir—do you?"

"Who knows, now since I have learned to walk on this dancing cork of a craft?" rejoined Aaron, with a grim smile, while he pulled off his coat, braced on his cutlass, and tied a large red cotton shawl round his head. He then took off his neckerchief and fastened it round his waist, as tight as he could draw.

"Strange that all men in peril—on the uneasiness, like," said he, "should always gird themselves as tightly as they can." The slaver was now within musket-shot, when he put his helm to port, with the view of passing under our stern. To prevent being raked, we had to luff up sharp in the wind, and fire a broadside. I noticed the white splinters glance from his black wales; and once more the same sharp yell rung in our ears, followed by the long melancholy howl, already described.

"We have pinned some of the poor blacks again," said Tailtackle, who still lingered on the deck; small space for remark, for the slaver again fired his broadside at us, with the same cool precision as before.

"Down with the helm, and let her come round," said I; "that will do master, run across his stern—out sweeps forward, and keep her there—get the other carronade over to leeward—that is it—now, blaze away while he is becalmed—fire, small-arm-men, and take good aim."

We were now right across his stern, with his spanker boom within ten yards of us; and although he worked his two stem chasers with great determination, and poured whole showers of musketry from his rigging, and poop, and cabin-windows, yet, from the cleverness with which our sweeps were pulled, and the accuracy with which we were kept in our position, right athwart his stern, our fire, both from the cannon and musketry, the former loaded with round and grape, was telling, I could see, with fearful effect.

Crash—"There, my lads, down goes his maintopmast—pepper him well, while they are blinded and confused among the wreck. Fire away—there goes the peak, shot away cleverly, close by the throat. Don't cease firing, although his flag be down—it was none of his doing. There, my lads, there he has it again; you have shot away the weather foretopsail sheet, and he cannot get from under you."

Two men at this moment lay out on his larboard foreyard-arm, apparently with the intention of splicing the sheet, and getting the clew of the foretopsail once more down to the yard; if they had succeeded in this, the vessel would again have fetched way, and drawn out from under our fire. Mr Bang and Paul Gelid had all this time been firing with murderous precision, from where they had ensconced themselves under the shelter of the larboard bulwark, close to the taffril, with their three black servants in the cabin, loading the six muskets, and little Wagtail, who was no great shot, sitting on the deck, handing them up and down.

"Now, Mr Bang," cried I, "for the love of Heaven"—and may Heaven forgive me for the ill-placed exclamation—"mark these two men—down with them!"

Bang turned towards me with all the coolness in the world "What, those chaps on the end of the long stick?"

"Yes—yes," (I here spoke of the larboard foreyardarm,) "yes, down with them."

He lifted his piece as steadily as if he had really been duck shooting.

"I say, Gelid, my lad, take you the innermost."

"Ah!" quoth Paul. They fired—and down dropped both men, and squattered for a moment in the water, like wounded waterfowl, and then sank for ever, leaving two small puddles of blood on the surface.

"Now, master," shouted I, "put the helm up and lay him alongside—there—stand by with the grapnels—one round the backstay—the other through the chainplate there—so,—you have it." As we ranged under his counter—"Mainchains are your chance, men—boarders, follow me." And in the enthusiasm of the moment I jumped into the slaver's main channel, followed by twenty-eight men. We were in the act of getting over the netting when the enemy rallied, and fired a volley of small arms, which sent four out of the twenty-eight to their account, and wounded three more. We gained the quarterdeck, where the Spanish captain, and about forty of his crew, shewed a determined front, cutlass and pistol in hand—we charged them—they stood their ground. Tailtackle (who, the moment he heard the boarders called, had jumped out of the magazine, and followed me) at a blow cut the Spanish captain down to the chine; the lieutenant, or second in command, was my bird, and I had disabled him by a sabre-cut on the sword-arm, when he drew his pistol, and shot me through the left shoulder. I felt no pain, but a sharp pinch, and then a cold sensation, as if water had been poured down my neck.

Jigmaree was close by me with a boarding-pike, and our fellows were fighting with all the gallantry inherent in British sailors. For a moment the battle was poised in equal scales. At length our antagonists gave way, when about fifteen of the slaves, naked barbarians, who had been ranged with muskets in their hands on the forecastle, suddenly jumped down into the waist with a yell, and came to the rescue of the Spanish part of the crew.

I thought we were lost. Our people, all but Tailtackle and Jigmaree, held back. The Spaniards rallied, and fought with renewed courage, and it was now, not for glory, but for dear life, as all retreat was cut off by the parting of the grapnels and warps, that had lashed the schooner alongside of the slaver, for the Wave had by this time forged ahead, and lay across the brig's bows, in place of being on her quarter, with her foremast jammed against the slaver's bowsprit, whose spritsail-yard crossed our deck between the masts. We could not therefore retreat to our own vessel if we had wished it, as the Spaniards had possession of the waist and forecastle; all at once, however, a discharge of round and grape crashed through the bowsprit of the brig, and swept off three of the black auxiliaries before mentioned, and wounded as many more, and the next moment an unexpected ally appeared on the field. When we boarded, the Wave had been left with only Peter Mangrove; the five dockyard negroes; Pearl, one of the Captain's gigs, the handsome black already introduced on the scene; poor little Reefpoint, who, as already stated, was badly hurt; Aaron Bang, Paul Gelid, and Wagtail. But this Pearl without price, at the very moment of time when I thought the game was up, jumped on deck through the bowport, cutlass in hand, followed by the five black carpenters and Peter Mangrove, after whom appeared no less a personage than Aaron Bang himself and the three blackamoor valets, armed with boarding-pikes. Bang flourished his cutlass for an instant.

"Now, Pearl, my darling, shout to them in Coromantee—shout;" and forthwith the black quartermaster sung out, "Coromantee Sheik Cocoloo, kockernony populorum fiz;" which, as I afterwards learned, being interpreted, is, "Behold the Sultan Cocoloo, the great ostrich, with a feather in his tail like a palm branch; fight for him, you sons of female dogs." In an instant the black Spanish auxiliaries sided with Pearl, and Bang, and the negroes, and joined in charging the white Spaniards, who were speedily driven down the main hatchway, leaving one half of their number dead, or badly wounded, on the blood-slippery deck. But they still made a desperate defence, by firing up the hatchway. I hailed them to surrender.

"Zounds," cried Jigmaree, "there's the clink of hammers; they are knocking off the fetters of the slaves."

"If you let the blacks loose," I sung out in Spanish, "by the Heaven above us, I will blow you up, although I should go with you! Hold your hands, Spaniards! Mind what you do, madmen!"

"On with the hatches, men," shouted Tailtackle. They had been thrown overboard, or put out of the way, they could nowhere be seen. The firing from below continued.

"Cast loose that carronade there; clap in a canister of grape—so—now—run it forward, and fire down the hatchway." It was done, and taking effect amongst the pent-up slaves, such a yell arose—oh God! oh God!—I never can forget it. Still the maniacs continued firing up the hatchway.

"Load and fire again." My people were now furious, and fought more like incarnate fiends broke loose from hell than human beings.

"Run the gun up to the hatchway once more." They ran the carronade so furiously forward, that the coaming or ledge was split off, and down went the gun, carriage and all, with a crash, into the hold. Presently smoke appeared rising up the fore-hatchway.

"They have set fire to the brig; overboard! — regain the schooner, or we shall all be blown into the air like peels of onions!" sung out little Jigmaree. But where was the Wave? She had broke away, and was now a cable's length ahead, apparently fast leaving us, with Paul Gelid and Wagtail, and poor little Reefpoint, who, badly wounded as he was, had left his hammock, and come on deck in the emergency, making signs of their inability to cut away the halyards; and the tiller being shot away, the schooner was utterly unmanageable.

"Up, and let fall the foresail, men — down with the foretack — cheerily now — get way on the brig, and overhaul the Wave promptly, or we are lost," cried I. It was done with all the coolness of desperate men. I took the helm, and presently we were once more alongside of our own vessel. Time we were so, for about one hundred and fifty of the slaves, whose shackles had been knocked off, now scrambled up the fore hatchway, and we had only time to jump overboard, when they made a rush aft; and no doubt, exhausted as we were, they would have massacred us on the spot, frantic and furious as they evidently were from the murderous fire of grape that had been directed down the hatchway.

But the fire was as quick as they were. The cloud of smouldering smoke that was rising like a pillar of cloud from the fore-hatchway, was now streaked with tongues of red flame, which, licking the masts and spars, ran up and caught the sails and rigging. In an instant, the flames spread to every part of the gear aloft, while the other element, the sea, was also striving for the mastery in the destruction of the doomed vessel; for our shot, or the fall of the carronade into the hold, had started some of the bottom planks, and she was fast settling down by the head. We could hear the water rushing in like a mill stream. The fire increased — her guns went off as they became heated — she gave a sudden heel — and while five hundred human beings, pent up in her noisome hold, split the heavens with their piercing death-yells, down she went with a heavy lurch, head foremost, right in the wake of the setting sun, whose level rays made the thick dun wreaths that burst from her as she disappeared, glow with the hue of the amethyst; and while the whirling clouds, gilded by his dying radiance, curled up into the blue sky, in rolling masses, growing thinner and thinner, until they vanished away, even like the wreck whereout they arose, — and the circling eddies, created by her sinking, no longer sparkled and flashed in the red light — and the stilled waters where she had gone down, as if oil had been cast on them, were spread out like polished silver, shining like a mirror, while all around was dark blue ripple, — a puff of fat black smoke, denser than any we had yet seen, suddenly emerged with a loud gurgling noise, from out the deep bosom of the calmed sea, and rose like a balloon, rolling slowly upwards, until it reached a little way above our mast-heads, where it melted and spread out into a dark pall, that overhung the scene of death, as if the incense of such a horrible and polluted sacrifice could not ascend into the pure heaven, but had been again crushed back upon our devoted heads, as a palpable manifestation of the wrath of *Him* who hath said — "Thou shalt not kill."

For a few moments all was silent as the grave, and I felt as if the air had become too thick for breathing, while I looked up like another Cain.

Presently, about one hundred and fifty of the slaves, *men, women,* and *children*, who had been drawn down by the vortex, rose amidst numberless pieces of smoking wreck, to the surface of the sea; the strongest yelling like fiends in their despair, while the weaker, the women, and the helpless gasping little ones, were choking, and gurgling, and sinking all around. Yea, the small thin expiring cry of the innocent sucking infant torn from its sinking mother's breast, as she held it for a brief moment above the waters, which had already for ever closed over herself, was there. —But we could not perceive one single individual of her white crew; like desperate men, they had all gone down with the brig. We picked up about one half of the miserable Africans, and—my pen trembles as I write it—fell necessity compelled us to fire on the remainder, as it was utterly impossible for us to take them on board. Oh that I could erase such a scene for ever from my memory! One incident I cannot help relating. We had saved a woman, a handsome clear skinned girl, of about sixteen years of age. She was very faint when we got her in, and was lying with her head over a port-sill, when a strong athletic young negro swam to the part of the schooner where she was. She held down her hand to him; he was in the act of grasping it, when he was shot through the heart from above. She instantly jumped overboard, and, clasping him in her arms, they sank, and disappeared together. "Oh, woman, whatever may be the colour of your skin, your heart is of one only!" said Aaron.

Soon all was quiet; a wounded black here and there was shrieking in his great agony, and struggling for a moment before he sank into his watery grave for ever; a few pieces of wreck were floating and sparkling on the surface of the deep in the blood-red sunbeams, which streamed in a flood of glorious light on the bloody deck, and shattered hull, and torn rigging of the Wave, and on the dead bodies and mangled limbs of those who had fallen; while some heavy scattering drops of rain fell sparkling from a passing cloud, as if Nature had wept in pity over the dismal scene; or as if they had been blessed tears, shed by an angel, in his heavenward course, as he hovered for a moment, and looked down in pity on the fantastic tricks played by the worm of a day—by weak man, in his little moment of power and ferocity. I said something—ill and hastily. Aaron was close beside me, sitting on a carronade slide, while the surgeon was dressing the pike wound in his neck. He looked up solemnly in my face, and then pointed to the blessed luminary, that was now sinking in the sea, and blazing up into the resplendent heavens—"Cringle, for shame—for shame—your impatience is blasphemous. Remember this morning—and thank *Him*"—here he looked up and crossed himself—"thank Him who has mercifully brought us to the end of this fearful day;—oh, thank Him, Tom, *that you have seen the sun set once more!*"

Thomas Pringle (1789-1834)

The Slave Dealer (1838)

From ocean's wave a Wanderer came,
   With visage tanned and dun:
His Mother, when he told his name,
   Scarce knew her long-lost son;
So altered was his face and frame
   By the ill course he had run.

There was hot fever in his blood,
   And dark thoughts in his brain;
And oh! to turn his heart to good
   That Mother strove in vain,
For fierce and fearful was his mood,
   Racked by remorse and pain.

And if, at times, a gleam more mild
   Would o'er his features stray,
When knelt the Widow near her Child,
   And he tried with her to pray,
It lasted not—for visions wild
   Still scared good thoughts away.

"There's blood upon my hands!" he said,
   "Which water cannot wash;
It was not shed where warriors bled—
   It dropped from the gory lash,
As I whirled it o'er and o'er my head,
   And with each stroke left a gash.

"With every stroke I left a gash,
   While Negro blood sprang high;
And now all ocean cannot wash
   My soul from murder's dye;
Nor e'en thy prayer, dear Mother, quash
   That Woman's wild death-cry!

"Her cry is ever in my ear,
   And it will not let me pray;
Her look I see—her voice I hear—
   As when in death she lay,
And said, 'With me thou must appear
   On God's great Judgment-day!'"

"Now, Christ from frenzy keep my son!"
   The woeful Widow cried;
"Such murder foul thou ne'er hast done —
   Some fiend thy soul belied!" —
" — Nay, Mother! the Avenging One
   Was witness when she died!

"The writhing wretch with furious heel
   I crushed — no mortal nigh;
But that same hour her dread appeal
   Was registered on high;
And now with God I have to deal,
   And dare not meet His eye!"

Thomas Babington Macaulay (1800-1859)

Minute by the Hon'ble T. B. Macaulay, dated the 2nd February 1835.

As it seems to be the opinion of some of the gentlemen who compose the Committee of Public Instruction, that the course which they have hitherto pursued was strictly prescribed by the British Parliament in 1813, and as, if that opinion be correct, a legislative act will be necessary to warrant a change, I have thought it right to refrain from taking any part in the preparation of the adverse statements which are now before us, and to reserve what I had to say on the subject till it should come before me as a Member of the Council of India.

It does not appear to me that the Act of Parliament can, by any art of construction, be made to bear the meaning which has been assigned to it. It contains nothing about the particular languages or sciences which are to be studied. A sum is set apart 'for the revival and promotion of literature, and the encouragement of the learned natives of India, and for the introduction and promotion of a knowledge of the sciences among the inhabitants of the British territories.' It is argued, or rather taken for granted, that by literature the Parliament can have meant only Arabic and Sanscrit literature, that they never would have given the honourable appellation of 'a learned native' to a native who was familiar with the poetry of Milton, the metaphysics of Locke, and the physics of Newton; but that they meant to designate by that name only such persons as might have studied in the sacred books of the Hindoos all the uses of cusa-grass, and all the mysteries of absorption into the Deity. This does not appear to be a very satisfactory interpretation. To take a parallel case; suppose that the Pacha of Egypt, a country once superior in knowledge to the nations of Europe, but now sunk far below them, were to appropriate a sum for the purpose 'of reviving and promoting literature, and encouraging learned natives of Egypt,' would any body infer that he meant the youth of his pachalic to give years to the study of hieroglyphics, to search into all the doctrines disguised under the fable of Osiris, and to ascertain with all possible accuracy the ritual with which cats and onions were anciently adored? Would he be justly charged with inconsistency if, instead of employing his young subjects in deciphering obelisks, he were to order them to be instructed in the English and French languages, and in all the sciences to which those languages are the chief keys?

The words on which the supporters of the old system rely do not bear them out, and other words follow which seem to be quite decisive on the other side. This lac of rupees is set apart not only for 'reviving literature in India,' the phrase on which their whole interpretation is founded, but also 'for the introduction and promotion of a knowledge of the sciences among the inhabitants of the British territories' — words which are alone sufficient to authorize all the changes for which I contend.

If the Council agree in my construction no legislative act will be necessary. If they differ from me, I will propose a short act rescinding that clause of the Charter of 1813 from which the difficulty arises.

The argument which I have been considering affects only the form of proceeding. But the admirers of the oriental system of education have used another argument, which, if we admit it to be valid, is decisive against all change. They conceive that the public faith is pledged to the present system, and that to alter the appropriation of any of the funds which have hitherto been spent in encouraging the study of Arabic and Sanscrit would be downright spoliation. It is not easy to understand by what process of reasoning they can have arrived at this conclusion. The grants which are made from the public purse for the encouragement of literature differ in no respect from the grants which are made from the same purse for other objects of real or supposed utility. We found a sanatarium on a spot which we suppose to be healthy. Do we thereby pledge ourselves to keep a sanatarium there if the result should not answer our expectations? We commence the erection of a pier. Is it a violation of the public faith to stop the works, if we afterwards see reason to believe that the building will be useless? The rights of property are undoubtedly sacred. But nothing endangers those rights so much as the practice, now unhappily too common, of attributing them to things to which they do not belong. Those who would impart to abuses the sanctity of property are in truth imparting to the institution of property the unpopularity and the fragility of abuses. If the Government has given to any person a formal assurance; nay, if the Government has excited in any person's mind a reasonable expectation that he shall receive a certain income as a teacher or a learner of Sanscrit or Arabic, I would respect that person's pecuniary interests — I would rather err on the side of liberality to individuals than suffer the public faith to be called in question. But to talk of a Government pledging itself to teach certain languages and certain sciences, though those languages may become useless, though those sciences may be exploded, seems to me quite unmeaning. There is not a single word in any public instructions from which it can be inferred that the Indian Government ever intended to give any pledge on this subject, or ever considered the destination of these funds as unalterably fixed. But, had it been otherwise, I should have denied the competence of our predecessors to bind us by any pledge on such a subject. Suppose that a Government had in the last century enacted in the most solemn manner that all its subjects should, to the end of time, be inoculated for the small-pox, would that Government be bound to persist in the practice after Jenner's discovery? These promises, of which nobody claims the performance, and from which nobody can grant a release; these vested rights which vest in nobody; this property without proprietors; this robbery, which makes nobody poorer, may be comprehended by persons of higher faculties than mine — I consider this plea merely as a set form of words, regularly used both in England and in India, in defence of every abuse for which no other plea can be set up.

I hold this lac of rupees to be quite at the disposal of the Governor-General in Council, for the purpose of promoting learning in India, in any way which may be thought most advisable. I hold his Lordship to be quite as free to direct that it shall no longer be employed in encouraging Arabic and Sanscrit, as he is to direct that the reward for killing tigers in Mysore shall be diminished, or that no more public money shall be expended on the chaunting at the cathedral.

We now come to the gist of the matter. We have a fund to be employed as Government shall direct for the intellectual improvement of the people of this country. The simple question is, what is the most useful way of employing it?

All parties seem to be agreed on one point, that the dialects commonly spoken among the natives of this part of India contain neither literary nor scientific information, and are moreover so poor and rude that, until they are enriched from some other quarter, it will not be easy to translate any valuable work into them. It seems to be admitted on all sides, that the intellectual improvement of those classes of the people who have the means of pursuing higher studies can at present be affected only by means of some language not vernacular amongst them.

What then shall that language be? One-half of the committee maintain that it should be the English. The other half strongly recommend the Arabic and Sanscrit. The whole question seems to me to be, which language is the best worth knowing?

I have no knowledge of either Sanscrit or Arabic. — But I have done what I could to form a correct estimate of their value. I have read translations of the most celebrated Arabic and Sanscrit works. I have conversed, both here and at home, with men distinguished by their proficiency in the Eastern tongues. I am quite ready to take the Oriental learning at the valuation of the Orientalists themselves. I have never found one among them who could deny that a single shelf of a good European library was worth the whole native literature of India and Arabia. The intrinsic superiority of the Western literature is, indeed, fully admitted by those members of the committee who support the Oriental plan of education.

It will hardly be disputed, I suppose, that the department of literature in which the Eastern writers stand highest is poetry. And I certainly never met with any Orientalist who ventured to maintain that the Arabic and Sanscrit poetry could be compared to that of the great European nations. But when we pass from works of imagination to works in which facts are recorded and general principles investigated, the superiority of the Europeans becomes absolutely immeasurable. It is, I believe, no exaggeration to say that all the historical information which has been collected from all the books written in the Sanscrit language is less valuable than what may be found in the most paltry abridgments used at preparatory schools in England. In every branch of physical or moral philosophy, the relative position of the two nations is nearly the same.

How then stands the case? We have to educate a people who cannot at present be educated by means of their mother-tongue. We must teach them some foreign language. The claims of our own language it is hardly necessary to recapitulate. It stands pre-eminent even among the languages of the West. It abounds with works of imagination not inferior to the noblest which Greece has bequeathed to us; with models of every species of eloquence, — with historical composition, which, considered merely as narratives, have seldom been surpassed, and which, considered as vehicles of ethical and political instruction, have never been equalled; with just and lively representations of human life and human nature; with the most profound speculations on metaphysics, morals, government, jurisprudence, and trade; with full and correct information respecting every experimental science which tends to preserve the health, to increase the comfort, or to expand the intellect of man. Whoever knows that language, has ready access to all the vast intellectual wealth which all the wisest nations of the earth have created and hoarded in the course of ninety generations. It may safely be said that the literature now extant in that language is of greater value than all the literature which three hundred years ago was extant in all the languages of the world together. Nor is this all. In India, English is the language spoken by the ruling class. It is spoken by the higher class of natives at the seats of Government. It is likely to become the language of commerce throughout the seas of the East. It is the language of two great European communities which are rising, the one in the south of Africa, the other in Australia; communities which are every year becoming more important and more closely connected with our Indian empire. Whether we look at the intrinsic value of our literature, or at the particular situation of this country, we shall see the strongest reason to think that, of all foreign tongues, the English tongue is that which would be the most useful to our native subjects.

The question now before us is simply whether, when it is in our power to teach this language, we shall teach languages in which, by universal confession, there are no books on any subject which deserve to be compared to our own; whether, when we can teach European science, we shall teach systems which, by universal confession, wherever they differ from those of Europe, differ for the worse, and whether, when we can patronize sound Philosophy and true History, we shall countenance, at the public expense, medical doctrines which would disgrace an English Farrier — Astronomy, which would move laughter in girls at an English boarding school — History, abounding with kings thirty feet high and reigns thirty thousand years long — and Geography made of seas of treacle and seas of butter.

We are not without experience to guide us. History furnishes several analogous cases, and they all teach the same lesson. There are, in modern times, to go no further, two memorable instances of a great impulse given to the mind of a whole society — of prejudices overthrown — of knowledge diffused — of taste purified — of arts and sciences planted in countries which had recently been ignorant and barbarous.

The first instance to which I refer is the great revival of letters among the Western nations at the close of the fifteenth and the beginning of the sixteenth century. At that time almost everything that was worth reading was contained in the writings of the ancient Greeks and Romans. Had our ancestors acted as the Committee of Public Instruction has hitherto acted; had they neglected the language of Cicero and Tacitus; had they confined their attention to the old dialects of our own island; had they printed nothing and taught nothing at the universities but Chronicles in Anglo-Saxon and Romances in Norman French, would England ever have been what she now is? What the Greek and Latin were to the contemporaries of More and Ascham, our tongue is to the people of India. The literature of England is now more valuable than that of classical antiquity. I doubt whether the Sanscrit literature be as valuable as that of our Saxon and Norman progenitors. In some departments — in History, for example — I am certain that it is much less so.

Another instance may be said to be still before our eyes. Within the last hundred and twenty years, a nation which had previously been in a state as barbarous as that in which our ancestors were before the Crusades has gradually emerged from the ignorance in which it was sunk, and has taken its place among civilized communities — I speak of Russia. There is now in that country a large educated class abounding with persons fit to serve the State in the highest functions, and in nowise inferior to the most accomplished men who adorn the best circles of Paris and London. There is reason to hope that this vast empire which, in the time of our grandfathers, was probably behind the Punjab, may in the time of our grandchildren, be pressing close on France and Britain in the career of improvement. And how was this change effected? Not by flattering national prejudices; not by feeding the mind of the young Muscovite with the old woman's stories which his rude fathers had believed: not by filling his head with lying legends about St. Nicholas: not by encouraging him to study the great question, whether the world was or not created on the 13th of September: not by calling him 'a learned native' when he had mastered all these points of knowledge: but by teaching him those foreign languages in which the greatest mass of information had been laid up, and thus putting all that information within his reach. The languages of western Europe civilised Russia. I cannot doubt that they will do for the Hindoo what they have done for the Tartar.

And what are the arguments against that course which seems to be alike recommended by theory and by experience? It is said that we ought to secure the co-operation of the native public, and that we can do this only by teaching Sanscrit and Arabic.

I can by no means admit that, when a nation of high intellectual attainments undertakes to superintend the education of a nation comparatively ignorant, the learners are absolutely to prescribe the course which is to be taken by the teachers. It is not necessary however to say anything on this subject. For it is proved by unanswerable evidence that we are not at present securing the co-operation of the natives. It would be bad enough to consult their intellectual taste at the expense of their intellectual health. But we are consulting neither — we are withholding from them the learning which they are craving; we are forcing on them the mock-learning which they nauseate.

This is proved by the fact that we are forced to pay our Arabic and Sanscrit students, while those who learn English are willing to pay us. All the declamations in the world about the love and reverence of the natives for their sacred dialects will never, in the mind of any impartial person, outweigh the undisputed fact, that we cannot find, in all our vast empire, a single student who will let us teach him those dialects unless we will pay him.

I have now before me the accounts of the Mudrassa for one month — the month of December, 1833. The Arabic students appear to have been seventy-seven in number. All receive stipends from the public. The whole amount paid to them is above 500 rupees a month. On the other side of the account stands the following item: Deduct amount realized from the out-students of English for the months of May, June, and July last — 103 rupees.

I have been told that it is merely from want of local experience that I am surprised at these phenomena, and that it is not the fashion for students in India to study at their own charges. This only confirms me in my opinions. Nothing is more certain than that it never can in any part of the world be necessary to pay men for doing what they think pleasant or profitable. India is no exception to this rule. The people of India do not require to be paid for eating rice when they are hungry, or for wearing woollen cloth in the cold season. To come nearer to the case before us, the children who learn their letters and a little elementary arithmetic from the village schoolmaster are not paid by him. He is paid for teaching them. Why, then, is it necessary to pay people to learn Sanscrit and Arabic? Evidently because it is universally felt that the Sanscrit and Arabic are languages the knowledge of which does not compensate for the trouble of acquiring them. On all such subjects the state of the market is the decisive test.

Other evidence is not wanting, if other evidence were required. A petition was presented last year to the committee by several ex-students of the Sanscrit College. The petitioners stated that they had studied in the college ten or twelve years; that they had made themselves acquainted with Hindoo literature and science; that they had received certificates of proficiency. And what is the fruit of all this? 'Notwithstanding such testimonials,' they say, 'we have but little prospect of bettering our condition without the kind assistance of your Honourable Committee, the indifference with which we are generally looked upon by our countrymen leaving no hope of encouragement and assistance from them.' They therefore beg that they may be recommended to the Governor-General for places under the Government — not places of high dignity or emolument, but such as may just enable them to exist. 'We want means,' they say, 'for a decent living, and for our progressive improvement, which, however, we cannot obtain without the assistance of Government, by whom we have been educated and maintained from childhood.' They conclude by representing, very pathetically, that they are sure that it was never the intention of Government, after behaving so liberally to them during their education, to abandon them to destitution and neglect.

I have been used to see petitions to Government for compensation. All those petitions, even the most unreasonable of them, proceeded on the supposition that some loss had been sustained — that some wrong had been inflicted. These are surely the first petitioners who ever demanded compensation for having been educated gratis — for having been supported by the public during twelve years, and then sent forth into the world well furnished with literature and science. They represent their education as an injury which gives them a claim on the Government for redress, as an injury, for which the stipends paid to them during the infliction were a very inadequate compensation. And I doubt not that they are in the right. They have wasted the best years of life in learning what procures for them neither bread nor respect. Surely we might, with advantage, have saved the cost of making these persons useless and miserable; surely, men may be brought up to be burdens to the public and objects of contempt to their neighbours at a somewhat smaller charge to the State. But such is our policy. We do not even stand neuter in the contest between truth and falsehood. We are not content to leave the natives to the influence of their own hereditary prejudices. To the natural difficulties which obstruct the progress of sound science in the East, we add great difficulties of our own making. Bounties and premiums, such as ought not to be given even for the propagation of truth, we lavish on false taste and false philosophy.

By acting thus we create the very evil which we fear. We are making that opposition which we do not find. What we spend on the Arabic and Sanscrit Colleges is not merely a dead loss to the cause of truth. It is bounty-money paid to raise up champions of error. It goes to form a nest, not merely of helpless place-hunters but of bigots prompted alike by passion and by interest to raise a cry against every useful scheme of education. If there should be any opposition among the natives to the change which I recommend, that opposition will be the effect of our own system. It will be headed by persons supported by our stipends and trained in our colleges. The longer we persevere in our present course, the more formidable will that opposition be. It will be every year reinforced by recruits whom we are paying.

From the native society, left to itself, we have no difficulties to apprehend; all the murmuring will come from that oriental interest which we have, by artificial means, called into being and nursed into strength.

There is yet another fact, which is alone sufficient to prove that the feeling of the native public, when left to itself, is not such as the supporters of the old system represent it to be. The committee have thought fit to lay out above a lac of rupees in printing Arabic and Sanscrit books. These books find no purchasers. It is very rarely that a single copy is disposed of. Twenty-three thousand volumes, most of them folios and quartos, fill the libraries or rather the lumber-rooms of this body. The committee contrive to get rid of some portion of their vast stock of oriental literature by giving books away. But they cannot give so fast as they print. About twenty thousand rupees a year are spent in adding fresh masses of waste paper to a hoard which, one should think, is already sufficiently ample. During the last three years, about sixty thousand rupees have been expended in this manner. The sale of Arabic and Sanscrit books, during those three years, has not yielded quite one thousand rupees. In the meantime, the Schoolbook Society is selling seven or eight thousand English volumes every year, and not only pays the expenses of printing, but realizes a profit of 20 per cent. on its outlay.

The fact that the Hindoo law is to be learned chiefly from Sanscrit books, and the Mahomedan law from Arabic books, has been much insisted on, but seems not to bear at all on the question. We are commanded by Parliament to ascertain and digest the laws of India. The assistance of a law commission has been given to us for that purpose. As soon as the code is promulgated, the Shasters and the Hedaya will be useless to a Moonsiff or a Sudder Ameen. I hope and trust that, before the boys who are now entering at the Madrassa and the Sanscrit College have completed their studies, this great work will be finished. It would be manifestly absurd to educate the rising generation with a view to a state of things which we mean to alter before they reach manhood.

But there is yet another argument which seems even more untenable. It is said that the Sanscrit and the Arabic are the languages in which the sacred books of a hundred millions of people are written, and that they are on that account entitled to peculiar encouragement. Assuredly it is the duty of the British Government in India to be not only tolerant, but neutral on all religious questions. But to encourage the study of a literature, admitted to be of small intrinsic value, only because that literature inculcates the most serious errors on the most important subjects, is a course hardly reconcilable with reason, with morality, or even with that very neutrality which ought, as we all agree, to be sacredly preserved. It is confessed that a language is barren of useful knowledge. We are told to teach it because it is fruitful of monstrous superstitions. We are to teach false history, false astronomy, false medicine, because we find them in company with a false religion. We abstain, and I trust shall always abstain, from giving any public encouragement to those who are engaged in the work of converting the natives to Christianity. And while we act thus, can we reasonably or decently bribe men, out of the revenues of the State, to waste their youth in learning how they are to purify themselves after touching an ass, or what texts of the Vedas they are to repeat to expiate the crime of killing a goat?

It is taken for granted by the advocates of Oriental learning that no native of this country can possibly attain more than a mere smattering of English. They do not attempt to prove this. But they perpetually insinuate it. They designate the education which their opponents recommend as a mere spelling-book education. They assume it as undeniable, that the question is between a profound knowledge of Hindoo and Arabian literature and science on the one side, and a superficial knowledge of the rudiments of English on the other. This is not merely an assumption, but an assumption contrary to all reason and experience. We know that foreigners of all nations do learn our language sufficiently to have access to all the most abstruse knowledge which it contains, sufficiently to relish even the more delicate graces of our most idiomatic writers. There are in this very town natives who are quite competent to discuss political or scientific questions with fluency and precision in the English language. I have heard the very question on which I am now writing discussed by native gentlemen with a liberality and an intelligence which would do credit to any member of the Committee of Public Instruction. Indeed, it is unusual to find, even in the literary circles of the continent, any foreigner who can express himself in English with so much facility and correctness as we find in many Hindoos. Nobody, I suppose, will contend that English is so difficult to a Hindoo as Greek to an Englishman. Yet an intelligent English youth, in a much smaller number of years than our unfortunate pupils pass at the Sanscrit College, becomes able to read, to enjoy, and even to imitate, not unhappily, the compositions of the best Greek authors. Less than half the time which enables an English youth to read Herodotus and Sophocles ought to enable a Hindoo to read Hume and Milton.

To sum up what I have said: I think it clear that we are not fettered by the Act of Parliament of 1813; that we are not fettered by any pledge expressed or implied; that we are free to employ our funds as we choose; that we ought to employ them in teaching what is best worth knowing; that English is better worth knowing than Sanscrit or Arabic; that the natives are desirous to be taught English, and are not desirous to be taught Sanscrit or Arabic; that neither as the languages of law, nor as the languages of religion, have the Sanscrit and Arabic any peculiar claim to our encouragement; that it is possible to make natives of this country thoroughly good English scholars, and that to this end our efforts ought to be directed.

In one point I fully agree with the gentlemen to whose general views I am opposed. I feel, with them, that it is impossible for us, with our limited means, to attempt to educate the body of the people. We must at present do our best to form a class who may be interpreters between us and the millions whom we govern; a class of persons Indian in blood and colour, but English in tastes, in opinions, in morals and in intellect. To that class we may leave it to refine the vernacular dialects of the country, to enrich those dialects with terms of science borrowed from the Western nomenclature, and to render them by degrees fit vehicles for conveying knowledge to the great mass of the population.

I would strictly respect all existing interests. I would deal even generously with all individuals who have had fair reason to expect a pecuniary provision. But I would strike at the root of the bad system which has hitherto been fostered by us. I would at once stop the printing of Arabic and Sanscrit books. I would abolish the Madrassa and the Sanscrit College at Calcutta. Benares is the great seat of Brahmanical learning; Delhi, of Arabic learning. If we retain the Sanscrit College at Benares and the Mahomedan college at Delhi we do enough, and much more than enough in my opinion, for the Eastern languages. If the Benares and Delhi Colleges should be retained, I would at least recommend that no stipends shall be given to any students who may hereafter repair thither, but that the people shall be left to make their own choice between the rival systems of education without being bribed by us to learn what they have no desire to know. The funds which would thus be placed at our disposal would enable us to give larger encouragement to the Hindoo college at Calcutta, and establish in the principal cities throughout the Presidencies of Fort William and Agra schools in which the English language might be well and thoroughly taught.

If the decision of His Lordship in Council should be such as I anticipate, I shall enter on the performance of my duties with the greatest zeal and alacrity. If, on the other hand, it be the opinion of the Government that the present system ought to remain unchanged, I beg that I may be permitted to retire from the chair of the Committee. I feel that I could not be of the smallest use there — I feel, also, that I should be lending my countenance to what I firmly believe to be a mere delusion. I believe that the present system tends, not to accelerate the progress of truth, but to delay the natural death of expiring errors. I conceive that we have at present no right to the respectable name of a Board of Public Instruction. We are a Board for wasting the public money, for printing books which are of less value than the paper on which they are printed was while it was blank; for giving artificial encouragement to absurd history, absurd metaphysics, absurd physics, absurd theology; for raising up a breed of scholars who find their scholarship an encumbrance and a blemish, who live on the public while they are receiving their education, and whose education is so utterly useless to them that, when they have received it, they must either starve or live on the public all the rest of their lives. Entertaining these opinions, I am naturally desirous to decline all share in the responsibility of a body which, unless it alters its whole mode of proceedings, I must consider, not merely as useless, but as positively noxious.

T. B. MACAULAY
2nd February 1835.

I give my entire concurrence to the sentiments expressed in this Minute.
W. C. BENTINCK.

Edward Irving (1792-1834)

from Babylon and Infidelity Foredoomed (1826)

DEDICATION.

TO MY BELOVED FRIEND, AND BROTHER IN CHRIST,
HATLEY FRERE, ESQ.

When I first met you, worthy Sir, in a company of friends, and, moved I know not by what, asked you to walk forth into the fields, that we might commune together, while the rest enjoyed their social converse, you seemed to me as one who dreamed, while you opened in my ear your views of the present times, as foretold in the book of Daniel and the Apocalypse. But being ashamed of my own ignorance, and having been blessed from my youth with the desire of instruction, I dared not to scoff at what I heard, but resolved to consider the matter. More than a year passed before it pleased Providence to bring us together again, at the house of the same dear friend and brother in the Lord, when you answered so sweetly and temperately the objections made to your views, that I was more and more struck with the outward tokens of a calm and sincere believer in truth. And I was again ashamed at my own ignorance, and again resolved to consider the matter. After which I had no rest in my spirit, until I waited upon you and offered myself as your pupil, to be instructed in prophecy according to your ideas, thereof. And for the ready good-will with which you undertook, and the patience with which you performed this kind office, I am for ever beholden .to you, most kind and worthy friend!

As becometh one that is ignorant towards his teacher, I received without cavilling, and endeavoured to comprehend the whole scheme and substance of your interpretations, both of Daniel and the Apocalypse; and then withdrew to consider and try the matter by the two great criterions, — the structure of the books themselves, and the correspondence with the events which had been fulfilled; adding a careful consideration of the Discursive Prophecies also, which cast many cross-lights upon the subject. Now I am not ashamed to confess, that, at first, my mind fell away from the system of interpretation, which, with Mede and Moore, and other exact interpreters, you have followed, and inclined to the simple idea, that the Apocalypse is a narrative of events running on in regular historical order. Nor was it till after your system of interpretation had decomposed itself in my mind, that it gradually recomposed itself, under a more patient and assiduous consideration of the subject. Which I mention, because I believe it to be the true way, in which this or any other subject ought to. be studied, and in which I wish this discourse to be read; with the humility of one who desireth to comprehend the whole matter, then to be weighed apart from the authority of a teacher, and the forms of his arguments, and so expect the approval or disapproval of the conscience, expected and waited for. I mention it, moreover, in order publicly to declare my acknowledgments to you, most kind and generous friend! For I am not willing that any one should account of me, as if I were worthy to have had revealed to me the important truths contained in this discourse, which may all be found written in your Treatise on the Prophecies of Daniel: only the Lord accounted me worthy to receive the faith of those things, which he had first made known to you, his more worthy servant. And if he make me the instrument of conveying that faith to any of his Church, that they may make themselves ready for his coming, or to any of the world, that they may take refuge in the ark of his salvation from the deluge of wrath which abideth the impenitent, to his name shall all the praise and glory be ascribed by me, his unworthy servant, who, through mercy, dareth to subscribe himself,

Your brother in the bond of the Spirit, and. the desire of the Lord's coming,

EDWARD IRVING.

PREFACE.

This Discourse, which is now published to the Church and to the world, was composed for the special instruction of the members of a society, called, the Continental society, established in London some years ago, for the purpose of seeking the Lord, exercising carefulness, and labouring by all means for the spiritual condition of the Continent of Europe; distressed at present on the one hand, by the superstition of the Papists, and, on the other, by the Infidelity of those calling themselves Reformed. To the right discharge of which duty, it seemed to me fit and necessary, as a minister of the word, to examine what the word said, concerning that same Papal Superstition, and Protestant Infidelity, against which they had undertaken the spiritual warfare; and the substance of this discourse was the fruit of the inquiry, in which I was mainly helped and directed, by the dear friend and fellow-servant in Christ, to whom, as is most due, I have dedicated these fruits of our mutual-study!

After having been preached, it was destined to the quiet shelf, as having done the office to which it was devoted; but, unfortunately, it was attended with the effect of disturbing and disquieting those for whose edification it was written, of whom, some in authority, as I have understood, had not the Christian decorum to hear it to an end. Which effect foreseeing, (for I am not ignorant of the hay and stubble, which now, as in Paul's time, is builded with gold, and silver, and precious stones, into the temple of the visible Church,) I had, beforehand, besought of the Continental Society, either to be exonerated from this burden, or to be permitted to discharge it as a minister of Christ, not as an advocate of theirs. It was the weakness and ignorance of those who took offence, to suppose that, from the vantage ground of the pulpit, I was contending with the political advocates of the Catholic claims, from which, and every other question of politics, except that fundamental question of obedience, to the magistrate, I do, by God's grace continually refrain myself both in preaching and in prayer. Now, it so happened, on the other hand, as was most natural, that the opposers of the Catholic claims, very awkwardly, I perceived, set me down as a fighter on their side of the question, which was equally far from my thoughts; for

Jesus hath said to his disciples "Follow me, and let the dead bury their dead." There was, besides, a goodly number of those, who, in this city, are waiting for the kingdom of Christ, who besought me very earnestly, that, by publishing this discourse, I would do my part with other faithful ministers of the Church, who have lately bestirred themselves to the work of making ready a people prepared for the Lord. And thus it hath come to pass, that to clear myself from being a political partizan in a ministerial garb, and to gratify the desires of these faithful servants of Christ, I set forth this publication, on which I pray the blessing of God to rest.

I had a desire to separate the doom of Infidelity from the doom of Babylon; fear lest upon a subject so unpalatable as prophecy, both taken together might form too large a Discourse. But they can ill be separated: Infidelity being as the sword of Cyrus, in delivering the Church from the stronghold of Babylon, and afterwards, for lifting the sword against Christ and his witnesses, sharing the fate of Amalek and the nations of Canaan, in order that the Church may enter into her rest. Thirty-three years ago, Infidelity struck the first-blow of Babylon's fall, since which time the hopes of the Church have been revived. Infidelity hath to strike another, and, lo! the Church is free. For Infidelity hath no time, but goeth into perdition, with all other Antichristian spirits, in the approaching battle of Armageddon, which is to the Gentile dispensation, what the destruction of Jerusalem was to the dispensation of the Jews:—of that generation, being required the blood of all the martyrs which they have shed, from the crucifixion of the Son of God, down to that time. Now as I judge, and have maintained, in this Discourse, that this is that generation, and this is that time, every day must quicken the pulse of anxiety in men and make them patient of more instruction when the time will come, to address the Church concerning many other things connected with the second coming of the Lord, of which she is utterly oblivious; and concerning the false and fond expectations with which she is deluding herself, instead of that blessed promise. But if these interpretations and calculations be not true, and the present expectation of many be disappointed, then enough, and more than enough, has been written and published in this Discourse.

Furthermore, believing as I do, all the things which are written; in this Discourse, I cannot conclude the Preface, without entreating my brethren in the ministry of the Church of Christ, to take into their most serious and solemn consideration, whether these things are so; for the agreement on these matters, among the interpreters of prophecy, is now sufficient to have made-out a case to the most sceptical; and if the approach of our Lord be so near at hand; if, of his kingdom, the first thirty-three years have already been running their unobserved course, and preparing the way for the great event of his appearing; holding out to us all the signs of his coming; what manner of servants are we? what manner of stewards of his house, if we be found careless ourselves, and careless in admonishing his flock? The years of omen are nearly at an end, and the day of His coming approacheth: blessed is he that watcheth. This brotherly exhortation, I tender especially to my fathers and brethren of the Church of Scotland, which, heretofore suffered so much for Christ's kingly office; but now that he is ready to be revealed as King upon the earth, are grown, methinks, indifferent, at least, I can discover no symptoms of wakeful expectation, nor hear any ministrations of warning even of such a kind as are to be found in the writings and discourses of the brethren of the sister Church. Far removed from your counsel and fellowship, and labouring what I can to maintain the sound doctrine and wholesome discipline for which the founders of our Church offered up their precious lives, I commend these thoughts especially to your considerations, with the respect of a son to his fathers, and with the love of a brother to his brethren.

    I could have wished to appear before my fathers and brethren of the Church of Scotland in a style more worthy of their acknowledgment; with a matter more worthy of their grave consideration I could not appear. But the short recess which I permit myself from ministerial and pastoral duties, and which I had devoted to the perfecting of this Discourse, was much broken by domestic anxiety and sorrow; since which time it hath pleased the Lord to try me with infirmity of health, of which I can perceive many traces in looking over the pages of this Discourse. The more do I pray, that into this unworthy and infirm vessel, the excellency of His Spirit may be poured of God, that to Him may be reckoned all the glory. And the desire that the momentous matters herein set forth, might be first offered to the Church of Scotland, moved me to publish it at a distance from my residence, which hindered that careful revisal of the press which I desired to give. May the Lord, who looketh chiefly upon the heart, while yet he expecteth the obedience of every member, be pleased to bless these pages to the stirring up of many, and especially of his own people, to the solemn examination and meditation of the things which are herein set forth out of the desire of his glory, and for the good of his Church.

                                                  Caledonian Church, London,
10th March, 1826.

Thomas Carlyle (1795-1881)

from Past and Present (1843)

CHAPTER IV.

CAPTAINS OF INDUSTRY.

If I believed that Mammonism with its adjuncts was to continue henceforth the one serious principle of our existence, I should reckon it idle to solicit remedial measures from any Government, the disease being insusceptible of remedy. Government can do much, but it can in no wise do all. Government, as the most conspicuous object in Society, is called upon to give signal of what shall be done; and, in many ways, to preside over, further, and command the doing of it. But the Government cannot do, by all its signaling and commanding, what the Society is radically indisposed to do. In the long-run every Government is the exact symbol of its People, with their wisdom and unwisdom; we have to say, Like People like Government. — The main substance of this immense Problem of Organising Labour, and first of all of Managing the Working Classes, will, it is very clear, have to be solved by those who stand practically in the middle of it; by those who themselves work and preside over work. Of all that can be enacted by any Parliament in regard to it, the germs must already lie potentially extant in those two Classes, who are to obey such enactment. A Human Chaos *in* which there is no light, you vainly attempt to irradiate by light shed *on* it: order never can arise there.

But it is my firm conviction that the 'Hell of England' will *cease* to be that of 'not making money;' that we shall get a nobler Hell and a nobler Heaven! I anticipate light *in* the Human Chaos, glimmering, shining more and more; under manifold true signals from without That light shall shine. Our deity no longer being Mammon, — O Heavens, each man will then say to himself: "Why such deadly haste to make money? I shall not go to Hell, even if I do not make money! There is another Hell, I am told!" Competition, at railway-speed, in all branches of commerce and work will then abate: — good felt-hats for the head, in every sense, instead of seven-feet lath-and-plaster hats on wheels, will then be discoverable! Bubble-periods, with their panics and commercial crises, will again become infrequent; steady modest industry will take the place of gambling speculation. To be a noble Master, among noble Workers, will again be the first ambition with some few; to be a rich Master only the second. How the Inventive Genius of England, with the whirr of its bobbins and billy-rollers shoved somewhat into the backgrounds of the brain, will contrive and devise, not cheaper produce exclusively, but fairer distribution of the produce at its present cheapness! By degrees, we shall again have a Society with something of Heroism in it, something of Heaven's Blessing on it; we shall again have, as my German friend asserts, 'instead of Mammon-Feudalism with unsold cotton-shirts and Preservation of the Game, noble just Industrialism and Government by the Wisest!'

It is with the hope of awakening here and there a British man to know himself for a man and divine soul, that a few words of parting admonition, to all persons to whom the Heavenly Powers have lent power of any kind in this land, may now be addressed. And first to those same Master-Workers, Leaders of Industry; who stand nearest and in fact powerfulest, though not most prominent, being as yet in too many senses a Virtuality rather than an Actuality.

The Leaders of Industry, if Industry is ever to be led, are virtually the Captains of the World, if there be no nobleness in them, there will never be an Aristocracy more. But let the Captains of Industry consider; once again, are they born of other clay than the old Captains of Slaughter; doomed forever to be no Chivalry, but a mere gold-plated *Doggery*—what the French well name *Canaille*, 'Doggery' with more or less gold carrion at its disposal? Captains of Industry are the true Fighters, henceforth recognisable as the only true ones: Fighters against Chaos, Necessity and the Devils and Jötuns; and lead on Mankind in that great, and alone true, and universal warfare; the stars in their courses fighting for them, and all Heaven and all Earth saying audibly, Well done! Let the Captains of Industry retire into their own hearts, and ask solemnly. If there is nothing but vulturous hunger, for fine wines, valet reputation and gilt carriages, discoverable there? Of hearts made by the Almighty God I will not believe such a thing. Deep-hidden under wretchedest god-forgetting Cants, Epicurisms, Dead-Sea Apisms; forgotten as under foulest fat Lethe mud and weeds, there is yet, in all hearts born into this God's World, a spark of the Godlike slumbering. Awake, O nightmare sleepers; awake, arise, or be forever fallen! This is not playhouse poetry; it is sober fact. Our England, our world cannot live as it is. It will connect itself with a God again, or go down with nameless throes and fire-consummation to the Devils. Thou who feelest aught of such a Godlike stirring in thee, any faintest intimation of it as through heavy-laden dreams, follow *it*, I conjure thee. Arise, save thyself, be one of those that save thy country.

Bucaniers, Chactaw Indians, whose supreme aim in fighting is that they may get the scalps, the money, that they may amass scalps and money: out of such came no Chivalry, and never will! Out of such came only gore and wreck, infernal rage and misery; desperation quenched in annihilation. Behold it, I bid thee, behold there, and consider! What is it that thou have a hundred thousand-pound bills laid-up in thy strong-room, a hundred scalps hung-up in thy wigwam? I value not them or thee. Thy scalps and thy thousand-pound bills are as yet nothing, if no nobleness from within irradiate them; if no Chivalry, in action, or in embryo ever struggling towards birth and action, be there.

Love of men cannot be bought by cash-payment; and without love men cannot endure to be together. You cannot lead a Fighting World without having it regimented, chivalried: the thing, in a day, becomes impossible; all men in it, the highest at first, the very lowest at last, discern consciously, or by a noble instinct, this necessity. And can you any more continue to lead a Working World unregimented, anarchic? I answer, and the Heavens and Earth are now answering, No! The thing becomes not 'in a day' impossible; but in some two generations it does. Yes, when fathers and mothers, in Stockport hunger-cellars, begin to eat their children, and Irish widows have to prove their relationship by dying of typhus-fever; and amid Governing 'Corporations of the Best and Bravest' busy to preserve their game by 'bushing,' dark millions of God's human creatures start up in mad Chartisms, impracticable Sacred-Months, and Manchester Insurrections;—and there is a virtual Industrial Aristocracy as yet only half-alive, spell-bound amid money-bags and ledgers; and an actual Idle Aristocracy seemingly near dead in somnolent delusions, in trespasses and double-barrels; 'sliding,' as on inclined-planes, which every new year they soap with new Hansard's-jargon under God's sky, and so are 'sliding,' ever faster, towards a 'scale' and balance scale whereon is written *Thou art found Wanting:*—in such days, after a generation or two, I say, it does become, even to the low and simple, very palpably impossible! No Working World, any more than a Fighting World, can be led on without a noble Chivalry of Work, and laws and fixed rules which follow out of that,—far nobler than any Chivalry of Fighting was. As an anarchic multitude on mere Supply-and-demand, it is becoming inevitable that we dwindle in horrid suicidal convulsion and self-abrasion, frightful to the imagination, into Chactaw Workers. With wigwams and scalps,—with palaces and thousand-pound bills; with savagery, depopulation, chaotic desolation! Good Heavens, will not one French Revolution and Reign of Terror suffice us, but must there be two? There will be two if needed; there will be twenty if needed; there will be precisely as many as are needed. The Laws of Nature will have themselves fulfilled. That is a thing certain to me.

Your gallant battle-hosts and work-hosts, as the others did, will need to be made loyally yours; they must and will be regulated, methodically secured in their just share of conquest under you;—joined with you in veritable brotherhood, son-hood, by quite other and deeper ties than those of temporary day's wages! How would mere red-coated regiments, to say nothing of chivalries, fight for you, if you could discharge them on the evening of the battle, on payment of the stipulated shillings,—and they discharge you on the morning of it! Chelsea Hospitals, pensions, promotions, rigorous lasting covenant on the one side and on the other, are indispensable even for a hired fighter. The Feudal Baron, much more,—how could he subsist with mere temporary mercenaries round him, at sixpence a day; ready to go over to the other side, if sevenpence were offered? He could not have subsisted;—and his noble instinct saved him from the necessity of even trying! The Feudal Baron had a Man's Soul in him; to which anarchy, mutiny, and the other fruits of temporary mercenaries, were intolerable: he had never been a Baron otherwise, but had continued a Chactaw and Bucanier. He felt it precious, and at last it became habitual, and his fruitful enlarged existence included it as a necessity, to have men round him who in heart loved him; whose life he watched over with rigour yet with love; who were prepared to give their life for him, if need came. It was beautiful; it was human! Man lives not otherwise, nor can live contented, anywhere or any when. Isolation is the sum total of wretchedness to man. To be cut off, to be left solitary: to have a world alien, not your world; all a hostile camp for you; not a home at all, of hearts and faces who are yours, whose you are! It is the frightfulest enchantment; too truly a work of the Evil One. To have neither superior, nor inferior, nor equal, united manlike to you. Without father, without child, without brother. Man knows no sadder destiny. 'How is each of us,' exclaims Jean Paul, 'so lonely in the wide bosom of the All!' Encased each as in his transparent 'ice-palace;' our brother visible in his, making signals and gesticulations to us; — visible, but forever unattainable: on his bosom we shall never rest, nor he on ours. It was not a God that did this; no!

Awake, ye noble Workers, warriors. In the one true war: all this must be remedied. It is you who are already half-alive, whom I will welcome into life; whom I will conjure, in God's name, to shake off your enchanted sleep, and live wholly! Cease to count scalps, gold-purses; not in these lies your or our salvation. Even these, if you count only these, will not long be left. Let bucaniering be put far from you; alter, speedily abrogate all laws of the bucaniers, if you would gain any victory that shall endure. Let God's justice, let pity, nobleness and manly valour, with more gold-purses or with fewer, testify themselves in this your brief Life-transit to all the Eternities, the Gods and Silences. It is to you I call; for ye are not dead, ye are already half-alive: there is in you a sleepless dauntless energy, the prime-matter of all nobleness in man. Honour to you in your kind. It is to you I call: ye know at least this. That the mandate of God to His creature man is: Work! The future Epic of the World rests not with those that are near dead, but with those that are alive, and those that are coming into life.

Look around you. Your world-hosts are all in mutiny, in confusion, destitution; on the eve of fiery wreck and madness! They will not march farther for you, on the sixpence a day and supply-and-demand principle: they will not; nor ought they, nor can they. Ye shall reduce them to order, begin reducing them. To order, to just subordination; noble loyalty in return for noble guidance. Their souls are driven nigh mad; let yours be sane and ever saner. Not as a bewildered bewildering mob; but as a firm regimented mass, with real captains over them, will these men march any more. All human interests, combined human endeavours, and social growths in this world, have, at a certain stage of their development, required organising: and Work, the grandest of human interests does now require it.

God knows, the task will be hard: but no noble task was ever easy. This task will wear away your lives, and the lives of your sons and grandsons: but for what purpose, if not for tasks like this, were lives given to men? Ye shall cease to count your thousand-pound scalps, the noble of you shall cease! Nay the very scalps, as I say, will not long be left if you count only these. Ye shall cease wholly to be barbarous vulturous Chactaws, and become noble European Nineteenth-Century Men. Ye shall know that Mammon, in never such gigs and flunky 'respectabilities,' is not the alone God; that of himself he is but a Devil, and even a Brute-god.

Difficult? Yes, it will be difficult. The short-fibre cotton; that too was difficult. The waste cotton-shrub, long useless, disobedient, as the thistle by the wayside, — have ye not conquered it; made it into beautiful bandana webs; white woven shirts for men; bright-tinted air-garments wherein flit goddesses? Ye have shivered mountains asunder, made the hard iron pliant to you as soft putty: the Forest-giants, Marsh-jötuns bear sheaves of golden-grain; Ægir the Sea-demon himself stretches his back for a sleek highway to you, and on Firehorses and Windhorses ye career. Ye are most strong, Thor red-bearded, with his blue sun-eyes, with his cheery heart and strong thunder-hammer, he and you have prevailed. Ye are most strong, ye Sons of the icy North, of the far East,—far marching from your rugged Eastern Wildernesses, hitherward from the gray Dawn of Time! Ye are Sons of the *Jötun*-land; the land of Difficulties Conquered. Difficult? You must try this thing. Once try it with the understanding that it will and shall have to be done. Try it as ye try the paltrier thing, making of money! I will bet on you once more, against all Jötuns, Tailor-gods, Double-barrelled Law-wards, and Denizens of Chaos whatsoever!

[Robert Chambers (1802-1871)]

from Vestiges of the Natural History of Creation (1844)

Chapter 12 [part]

A candid consideration of all these circumstances can scarcely fail to introduce into our minds a somewhat different idea of organic creation from what has hitherto been generally entertained. That God created animated beings, as well as the terraqueous theatre of their being, is a fact so powerfully evidenced, and so universally received, that I at once take it for granted. But in the particulars of this so highly supported idea, we surely here see cause for some re-consideration. It may now be inquired,— In what way was the creation of animated beings effected? The ordinary notion may, I thinks be not unjustly described as this—that the Almighty author produced the progenitors of all existing species by some sort of personal or immediate exertion. But how does this notion comport with what we have seen of the gradual advance of species, from the humblest to the highest? How can we suppose an immediate exertion of this creative power at one time to produce zoophytes, another time to add a few marine mollusks, another to bring in one or two conchifers, again to produce crustaceous fishes, again perfect fishes, and so on to the end? This would surely be to take a very mean view of the Creative Power—to, in short, anthropomorphize it, or reduce it to some such character as that borne by the ordinary proceedings of mankind. And yet this would be unavoidable; for that the organic creation was thus progressive through a long space of time, rests on evidence which nothing can over turn or gainsay. Some other idea must then be come to with regard to *the mode* in which the Divine Author proceeded in the organic creation. Let us seek in the history of the earth's formation for a new suggestion on this point. We have seen powerful evidence, that the construction of this globe and its associates, and inferentially that of all the other globes of space, was the result, not of any immediate or personal exertion on the part of the Deity, but of natural laws which are expressions of his will. What is to hinder our supposing that the organic creation is also a result of natural laws, which are in like manner an expression of his will? More than this, the fact of the cosmical arrangements being an effect of natural law, is a powerful argument for the organic arrangements being so likewise, for how can we suppose that the august Being who brought all these countless worlds into form by the simple establishment of a natural principle flowing from his mind, was to interfere personally and specially on every occasion when a new shell-fish or reptile was to be ushered into existence on *one* of these worlds? Surely this idea is too ridiculous to be for a moment entertained.

It will be objected that the ordinary conceptions of Christian nations on this subject are directly derived from Scripture, or, at least, are in conformity with it. If they were clearly and unequivocally supported by Scripture, it may readily be allowed that there would be a strong objection to the reception of any opposite hypothesis. But the fact is, however startling the present announcement of it may be, that the first chapter of the Mosaic record is not only not in harmony with the ordinary ideas of mankind respecting cosmical and organic creation, but is opposed to them, and only in accordance with the views here taken. When we carefully peruse it with awakened minds, we find that all the procedure is represented primarily and pre-eminently as flowing from *commands and expressions of will, not from direct acts.* Let there be light—let there be a firmament—let the dry land appear—let the earth bring forth grass, the herb, the tree—let the waters bring forth the moving creature that hath life—let the earth bring forth the living creature after his kind—these are the terms in which the principal acts are described. The additional expressions,—God made the firmament—God made the beast of the earth, &c., occur subordinately, and only in a few instances; they do not necessarily convey a different idea of the mode of creation, and indeed only appear as alternative phrases, in the usual duplicative manner of Eastern narrative. Keeping this in view, the words used in a subsequent place, "God *formed* man in his own image," cannot well be understood as implying any more than what was implied before,—namely, that man was produced in consequence of an expression of the Divine will to that effect. Thus, the scriptural objection quickly vanishes, and the prevalent ideas about the organic creation appear only as a mistaken inference from the text, formed at a time when man's ignorance prevented him from drawing therefrom a just conclusion. At the same time, I freely own that I do not think it right to adduce the Mosaic record, either in objection to, or support of any natural hypothesis, and this for many reasons, but particularly for this, that there is not the least appearance of an intention in that book to give philosophically exact views of nature.

To a reasonable mind the Divine attributes must appear, not diminished or reduced in any way, by supposing a creation by law, but infinitely exalted. It is the narrowest of all views of the Deity, and characteristic of a humble class of intellects, to suppose him acting constantly in particular ways for particular occasions. It, for one thing, greatly detracts from his foresight, the most undeniable of all the attributes of Omnipotence. It lowers him towards the level of our own humble intellects. Much more worthy of him it surely is, to suppose that all things have been commissioned by him from the first, though neither is he absent from a particle of the current of natural affairs in one sense, seeing that the whole system is continually supported by his providence. Even in human affairs, if I may be allowed to adopt a familiar illustration, there is a constant progress from specific action for particular occasions, to arrangements which, once established, shall continue to answer for a great multitude of occasions. Such plans the enlightened readily form for themselves, and conceive as being adopted by all who have to attend to a multitude of affairs, while the ignorant suppose every act of the greatest public functionary to be the result of some special consideration and care on his part alone. Are we to suppose the Deity adopting plans which harmonize only with the modes of procedure of the less enlightened of our race? Those who would object to the hypothesis of a creation by the intervention of law, do not perhaps consider how powerful an argument in favour of the existence of God is lost by rejecting this doctrine. When all is seen to be the result of law, the idea of an Almighty Author becomes irresistible, for the creation of a law for an endless series of phenomena—an act of intelligence above all else that we can conceive—could have no other imaginable source, and tells, moreover, as powerfully for a sustaining as for an originating power. On this point a remark of Dr. Buckland seems applicable: "If the properties adopted by the elements at the moment of their creation adapted them beforehand to the infinity of complicated useful purposes which they have already answered, and may have still farther to answer, under many dispensations of the material world, such an aboriginal constitution, so far from superseding an intelligent agent, would only exalt our conceptions of the consummate skill and power that could comprehend such an infinity of future uses under future systems, in the original groundwork of his creation."

A late writer, in a work embracing a vast amount of miscellaneous knowledge, but written in a dogmatic style, argues at great length for the doctrine of more immediate exertions on the part of the Deity in the works of his creation. One of the most striking of his illustrations is as follows:— The coral polypi, united by a common animal bond, construct a defined form in stone; many kinds construct many forms. An allotted instinct may permit each polypus to construct its own cell, but there is no superintending one to direct the pattern, nor can the workers unite by consultation for such an end. There is no recipient for an instinct by which the pattern might be constructed. It is God alone, therefore, who is the architect; and for this end, consequently, he must dispose of every new polypus required to continue the pattern, in a new and peculiar position, which the animal could not have discovered by itself. Yet more, millions of these blind workers unite their works to form an island, which is also wrought out according to a constant general pattern, and of a very peculiar nature, though the separate coral works are numerously diverse. Still less, then, here is an instinct possible. The Great Architect himself must execute what he planned, in each case equally. He uses these little and senseless animals as hands; but they are hands which himself must direct. He must direct each one everywhere, and therefore he is ever acting."[1] This is a most notable example of a dangerous kind of reasoning. It is now believed that corals have a general life and sensation throughout the whole mass, residing in the nervous tissue which envelops them; consequently, there is nothing more wonderful in their determinate general forms than in those of other animals.

It may here be remarked that there is in our doctrine that harmony in all the associated phenomena which generally marks great truths. First, it agrees, as we have seen, with the idea of planet creation by natural law. Secondly, upon this supposition, all that geology tells us of the succession of species appears natural and intelligible. Organic life presses in, as has been remarked, wherever there was room and encouragement for it, the forms being always such as suited the circumstances, and in a certain relation to them, as, for example, where the limestone-forming seas produced an abundance of corals, crinoidea, and shell fish. Admitting for a moment a re-origination of species after a cataclysm, as has been surmised by some geologists, though the hypothesis is always becoming less and less tenable, it harmonizes with nothing so well as the idea of a creation by law. The more solitary commencements of species, which would have been the most inconceivably paltry exercise for an immediately creative power, are sufficiently worthy of one operating by laws.

It is also to be observed, that the thing to be accounted for is not merely the origination of organic being upon this little planet, third of a series which is but one of hundreds of thousands of series, the whole of which again form but one portion of an apparently infinite globe-peopled space, where all seems analogous. We have to suppose, that every one of these numberless globes is either a theatre of organic being, or in the way of becoming so. This is a conclusion which every addition to our knowledge makes only the more irresistible. Is it conceivable, as a fitting mode of exercise for creative intelligence, that it should be constantly moving from one sphere to another, to form and plant the various species which may be required in each situation at particular times? Is such an idea accordant with our general conception of the dignity, not to speak of the power, of the Great Author? Yet such is the notion which we must form, if we adhere to the doctrine of special exercise. Let us see, on the other hand, how the doctrine of a creation by law agrees with this expanded view of the organic world.

Unprepared as most men may be for such an announcement, there can be no doubt that we are able, in this limited sphere, to form some satisfactory conclusions as to the plants and animals of those other spheres which move at such immense distances from us. Suppose that the first persons of an early nation who made a ship and ventured to sea in it, observed, as they sailed along, a set of objects which they had never before seen—namely, a fleet of other ships—would they not have been justified in supposing that those ships were occupied, like their own, by human beings possessing hands to row and steer, eyes to watch the signs of the weather, intelligence to guide them from one place to another—in short, beings in all respects like themselves, or only shewing such differences as they knew to be producible by difference of climate and habits of life. Precisely in this manner we can speculate on the inhabitants of remote spheres. We see that matter has originally been diffused in one mass, of which the spheres are portions. Consequently, inorganic matter must be presumed to be everywhere the same, although probably with differences in the proportions of ingredients in different globes, and also some difference of conditions. Out of a certain number of the elements of inorganic matter are composed organic bodies, both vegetable and animal; such must be the rule in Jupiter and in Sirius, as it is here. We, therefore, are all but certain that herbaceous and ligneous fibre, that flesh and blood, are the constituents of the organic beings of all those spheres which are as yet seats of life. Gravitation we see to be an all-pervading principle: therefore there must be a relation between the spheres and their respective organic occupants, by virtue of which they are fixed, as far as necessary, on the surface. Such a relation, of course, involves details as to the density and elasticity of structure, as well as size, of the organic tenants, in proportion to the gravity of the respective planets—peculiarities, however, which may quite well consist with the idea of a universality of general types, to which we are about to come. Electricity we also see to be universal; if, therefore, it be a principle concerned in life and in mental action, as science strongly suggests, life and mental action must everywhere be of one general character. We come to comparatively a matter of detail, when we advert to heat and light; yet it is important to consider that these are universal agents, and that, as they bear marked relations to organic life and structure on earth, they may be presumed to do so in other spheres also. The considerations as to light are particularly interesting, for, on our globe, the structure of one important organ, almost universally distributed in the animal kingdom, is in direct and precise relation to it. Where there is light there will be eyes, and these, in other spheres, will be the same in all respects as the eyes of tellurian animals, with only such differences as may be necessary to accord with minor peculiarities of condition and of situation. It is but a small stretch of the argument to suppose that, one conspicuous organ of a large portion of our animal kingdom being thus universal, a parity in all the other organs—species for species, class for class, kingdom for kingdom—is highly likely, and that thus the inhabitants of all the other globes of space bear not only a general, but a particular resemblance to those of our own.

Assuming that organic beings are thus spread over all space, the idea of their having all come into existence by the operation of laws everywhere applicable, is only conformable to that principle, acknowledged to be so generally visible in the affairs of Providence, to have all done by the employment of the smallest possible amount of means. Thus, as one set of laws produced all orbs and their motions and geognostic arrangements, so one set of laws overspread them all with life. The whole productive or creative arrangements are therefore in perfect unity.

1   Macculloch on the Attributes of the Deity, iii 569.

Hugh Miller (1802-1856)

from My Schools and Schoolmasters (1854)

CHAPTER XVII [part]

The opinions formed at this time on this matter of prime importance I found no after occasion to alter or modify. On the contrary, in passing from the subjective to the objective view, I have seen the doctrine of the union of the two natures greatly confirmed. The truths of geology appear destined to exercise in the future no inconsiderable influence on natural theology; and with this especial doctrine they seem very much in accordance. Of that long and stately march of creation with which the records of the stony science bring us acquainted, the distinguishing characteristic is progress. There appears to have been a time when there existed on our planet only dead matter unconnected with vitality; and then a time in which plants and animals of a low order began to be, but in which even fishes, the humblest of the vertebrata, were so rare and exceptionable, that they occupied a scarce appreciable place in Nature. Then came an age of fishes huge of size, and that to the peculiar ichthyic organization added certain well-marked characteristics of the reptilian class immediately above them. And then, after a time, during which the reptile had occupied a place as inconspicuous as that occupied by the fish in the earlier periods of animal life, an age of reptiles of vast bulk and high standing was ushered in. And when, in the lapse of untold ages, *it* also had passed away, there succeeded an age of great mammals. Molluscs, fishes, reptiles, mammals, had each in succession their periods of vast extent; and then there came a period that differed even more, in the character of its master-existence, from any of these creations, than they, with their many vitalities, had differed from the previous inorganic period in which life had not yet begun to be. The human period began — the period of a fellow-worker with God, created in God's own image. The animal existences of the previous ages formed, if I may so express myself, mere figures in the landscapes of the great garden which they inhabited. Man, on the other hand, was placed in it to "keep and to dress it;" and such has been the effect of his labours, that they have altered and improved the face of whole continents. Our globe, even as it might be seen from the moon, testifies, over its surface, to that unique nature of man, unshared in by any of the inferior animals, which renders him, in things physical and natural, a fellow-worker with the Creator who first produced it. And of the identity of at least his intellect with that of his Maker, and, of consequence, of the integrity of the revelation which declares that he was created in God's own image, we have direct evidence in his ability of not only conceiving of God's contrivances, but even of reproducing them; and this, not as a mere imitator, but as an original thinker. He may occasionally borrow the principles of his contrivances from the works of the Original Designer, but much more frequently, in studying the works of the Original Designer does he discover in them the principles of his own contrivances.

He has not been an imitator: he has merely been exercising, with resembling results. the resembling mind, i.e., the mind made in the Divine image. But the existing scene of things is not destined to be the last. High as it is, it is too low and too imperfect to be regarded as God's finished work: it is merely one of the *progressive* dynasties; and Revelation and the implanted instincts of our nature alike teach us to anticipate a glorious *terminal* dynasty. In the first dawn of being, simple vitality was united to matter: the vitality thus united became, in each succeeding period, of a higher and yet higher order; it was in succession the vitality of the mollusc, of the fish, of the reptile, of the sagacious mammal, and, finally, of responsible, immortal man, created in the image of God. What is to be the next advance? Is there to be merely a repetition of the past an introduction a second time of "man made in the image of God"? No! The geologist, in the tables of stone which form his records, finds no example of dynasties once passed away again returning. There has been no repetition of the dynasty of the fish—of the reptile—of the mammal. The dynasty of the future is to have glorified man for its inhabitant; but it is to be the dynasty—the *"kingdom"*—not of glorified man made in the image of God, but of God himself in the form of man. In the doctrine of the two natures, and in the further doctrine that the terminal dynasty is to be peculiarly the dynasty of Him in whom the natures are united, we find that required progression beyond which progress cannot go. Creation and the Creator meet at one point, and in one person. The long ascending line from dead matter to man has been a progress Godwards—not an asymptotical progress, but destined from the beginning to furnish a point of union; and, occupying that point as true God and true man, as Creator and created, we recognise the adorable Monarch of all the Future. It is, as urged by the Apostle, the especial glory of our race, that it should have furnished that point of contact at which Godhead has united Himself, not to man only, but also, through man, to His own Universe to the Universe of Matter and of Mind.

W. E. Aytoun (1813-1865)

How We Got Up The Glenmutchkin Railway, and How We Got Out Of It (1845)

I WAS confoundedly hard up. My patrimony, never of the largest, had been for the last year on the decrease — a herald would have emblazoned it, "ARGENT, a moneybag improper, in detriment" — and though the attenuating process was not excessively rapid, it was, nevertheless, proceeding at a steady ratio. As for the ordinary means and appliances by which men contrive to recruit their exhausted exchequers, I knew none of them. Work I abhorred with a detestation worthy of a scion of nobility; and, I believe, you could just as soon have persuaded the lineal representative of the Howards or Percys to exhibit himself in the character of a mountebank, as have got me to trust my person on the pinnacle of a three-legged stool. The rule of three is all very well for base mechanical souls; but I flatter myself I have an intellect too large to be limited to a ledger. "Augustus," said my poor mother to me, while stroking my hyacinthine tresses, one fine morning, in the very dawn and budding-time of my existence — "Augustus, my dear boy, whatever you do, never forget that you are a gentleman." The maternal maxim sunk deeply into my heart, and I never for a moment have forgotten it.

Notwithstanding this aristocratical resolution, the great practical question "How am I to live!" began to thrust itself unpleasantly before me. I am one of that unfortunate class who have neither uncles nor aunts. For me, no yellow liverless individuals, with characteristic bamboo and pigtail — emblems of half-a-million — returned to his native shores from Ceylon or remote Penang. For me, no venerable spinster hoarded in the Trongate, permitting herself few luxuries during a long-protracted life, save a lass and a lanthorn, a parrot, and the invariable baudrons of antiquity. No such luck was mine. Had all Glasgow perished by some vast epidemic, I should not have found myself one farthing the richer. There would have been no golden balsam for me in the accumulated woes of Tradestown, Shettleston, and Camlachie. The time has been when — according to Washington Irving and other veracious historians — a young man had no sooner got into difficulties than a guardian angel appeared to him in a dream, with the information that at such and such a bridge, or under such and such a tree, he might find, at a slight expenditure of labour, a gallipot secured with bladder, and filled with glittering tomauns; or in the extremity of despair, the youth had only to append himself to a cord, and straightaway the other end thereof, forsaking its staple in the roof, would disclose amidst the fractured ceiling the glories of a profitable pose. These blessed days have long since gone by — at any rate, no such luck was mine. My guardian angel was either woefully ignorant of metallurgy or the stores had been surreptitiously ransacked; and as to the other expedient, I frankly confess I should have liked some better security for its result, than the precedent of the 'Heir of Lynn.'

It is a great consolation amidst all the evils of life, to know that, however bad your circumstances may be, there is always somebody else in nearly the same predicament. My chosen friend and ally, Bob M'Corkindale, was equally hard up with myself, and, if possible, more averse to exertion. Bob was essentially a speculative man — that is, in a philosophical sense. He had once got hold of a stray volume of Adam Smith, and muddled his brains for a whole week over the intricacies of the *Wealth of Nations*. The result was a crude farrago of notions regarding the true nature of money, the soundness of currency, and relative value of capital, with which he nightly favoured an admiring audience at 'The Crow'; for Bob was by no means — in the literal acceptation of the word — a dry philosopher. On the contrary, he perfectly appreciated the merits of each distinct distillery; and was understood to be the compiler of a statistical work entitled, *A Tour through the Alcoholic Districts of Scotland*. It had very early occurred to me, who knew as much of political economy as of the bagpipes, that a gentleman so well versed in the art of accumulating national wealth, must have some remote ideas of applying his principles profitably on a smaller scale. Accordingly, I gave M'Corkindale an unlimited invitation to my lodgings; and, like a good hearty fellow as he was, he availed himself every evening of the license; for I had laid in a fourteen-gallon cask of Oban whisky, and the quality of the malt was undeniable.

These were the first glorious days of general speculation. Railroads were emerging from the hands of the greater into the fingers of the lesser capitalists. Two successful harvests had given a fearful stimulus to the national energy; and it appeared perfectly certain that all the populous towns would be united, and the rich agricultural districts intersected, by the magical bands of iron. The columns of the newspapers teemed every week with the parturition of novel schemes; and the shares were no sooner announced than they were rapidly subscribed for. But what is the use of my saying anything more about the history of last year? Every one of us remembers it perfectly well. It was a capital year on the whole, and put money into many a pocket. About that time, Bob and I commenced operations. Our available capital, or negotiable bullion, in the language of my friend, amounted to about three hundred pounds, which we set aside as a joint fund for speculation. Bob, in a series of learned discourses, had convinced me that it was not only folly, but a positive sin, to leave this sum lying in the bank at a pitiful rate of interest, and otherwise unemployed, whilst every one else in the kingdom was having a pluck at the public pigeon. Somehow or other, we were unlucky in our first attempts. Speculators are like wasps; for when they have once got hold of a ripening and peach-like project, they keep it rigidly for their own swarm, and repel the approach of interlopers. Notwithstanding all our efforts, and very ingenious ones they were, we never, in a single instance, succeeded in procuring an allocation of original shares; and though we did now and then make a hit by purchase, we more frequently bought at a premium, and parted with our scrip at a discount. At the end of six months, we were not twenty pounds richer than before.

"This will never do," said Bob, as he sat one evening in my rooms compounding his second tumbler. "I thought we were living in an enlightened age; but I find I was mistaken. That brutal spirit of monopoly is still abroad and uncurbed. The principles of free-trade are utterly forgotten, or misunderstood. Else how comes it that David Spreul received but yesterday an allocation of two hundred shares in the Westermidden junction; whilst your application and mine, for a thousand each, were overlooked? Is this a state of things to be tolerated? Why should he, with his fifty thousand pounds, receive a slapping premium, whilst our three hundred of available capital remains unrepresented? The fact is monstrous, and demands the immediate and serious interference of the legislature."

"It is a bloody shame," I said, fully alive to the manifold advantages of a premium.

"I'll tell you what, Dunshunner," rejoined M'Corkindale. "It's no use going on in this way. We haven't shown half pluck enough. These fellows consider us as snobs, because we don't take the bull by the horns. Now's the time for a bold stroke. The public are quite ready to subscribe for anything — and we'll start a railway for ourselves."

"Start a railway with three hundred pounds of capital?"

"Pshaw, man! you don't know what you're talking about — we've a great deal more capital than that. Have not I told you seventy times over, that everything a man has — his coat, his hat, the tumblers he drinks from, nay, his very corporeal existence — is absolute marketable capital? What do you call that fourteen-gallon cask, I should like to know?"

"A compound of hoops and staves, containing about a quart and a half of spirits — you have effectually accounted for the rest."

"Then it has gone to the fund of profit and loss, that's all. Never let me hear you sport those old theories again. Capital is indestructible, as I am ready to prove to you any day, in half an hour. But let us sit down seriously to business. We are rich enough to pay for the advertisements, and that is all we need care for in the mean time. The public is sure to step in, and bear us out handsomely with the rest."

"But where in the face of the habitable globe shall the railway be? England is out of the question, and I hardly know of a spot in the Lowlands that is not occupied already."

"What do you say to a Spanish scheme — the Alcantara Union? Hang me if I know whether Alcantara is in Spain or Portugal; but nobody else does, and the one is quite as good as the other. Or what would you think of the Palermo Railway, with a branch to the sulphur mines? — that would be popular in the North — or the Pyrenees Direct? They would all go to a premium."

"I must confess I should prefer a line at home."

"Well, then, why not try the Highlands? There must be lots of traffic there in the shape of sheep, grouse, and Cockney tourists, not to mention salmon and other et ceteras. Couldn't we tip them a railway somewhere in the west?"

"There's Glenmutchkin, for instance — "

"Capital, my dear fellow! Glorious? By Jove, first-rate!" shouted Bob in an ecstasy of delight. "There's a distillery there, you know, and a fishing-village at the foot — at least there used to be six years ago, when I was living with the exciseman. There may be some bother about the population, though. The last laird shipped every mother's son of the aboriginal Celts to America; but, after all, that's not of much consequence. I see the whole thing! Unrivalled scenery — stupendous waterfalls — herds of black cattle — spot where Prince Charles Edward met Macgrugar of Glengrugar and his clan! We could not possibly have lighted on a more promising place. Hand us over that sheet of paper, like a good fellow, and a pen. There is no time to be lost, and the sooner we get out the prospectus the better."

"But, heaven bless you, Bob, there's a great deal to be thought of first. Who are we to get for a provisional committee?"

"That's very true," said Bob, musingly. "We *must* treat them to some respectable names, that is, good sounding ones. I'm afraid there is little chance of our producing a Peer to begin with?"

"None whatever — unless we could invent one, and that's hardly safe — *Burke's Peerage* has gone through too many editions. Couldn't we try the Dormants?"

"That would be rather dangerous in the teeth of the standing orders. But what do you say to a baronet? There's Sir Polloxfen Tremens. He got himself served the other day to a Nova Scotia baronetcy, with just as much title as you or I have; and he has sported the riband, and dined out on the strength of it ever since. He'll join us at once, for he has not a sixpence to lose."

"Down with him, then," and we headed the Provisional list with the pseudo Orange-tawny.

"Now," said Bob, "it's quite indispensable, as this is a Highland line, that we should put forward a Chief or two. That has always a great effect upon the English, whose feudal notions are rather of the mistiest, and principally derived from Waverley."

"Why not write yourself down as the Laird of M'Corkindale?" said I. "I daresay you would not be negatived by a counterclaim."

"That would hardly do," replied Bob, "as I intend to be Secretary. After all, what's the use of thinking about it? Here goes for an extempore Chief; and the villain wrote down the name of Tavish M'Tavish of Invertavish.

"I say, though," said I, "we must have a real Highlander on the list. If we go on this way, it will become a Justiciary matter."

"You're devilish scrupulous, Gus," said Bob, who, if left to himself, would have stuck in the names of the heathen gods and goddesses, or borrowed his directors from the Ossianic chronicles, rather than have delayed the prospectus. "Where the mischief are we to find the men? I can think of no others likely to go the whole hog, can you?"

"I don't know a single Celt in Glasgow except old M'Closkie, the drunken porter at the corner of Jamaica Street."

"He's the very man! I suppose, after the manner of his tribe, he will do anything for a pint of whisky. But what shall we call him? Jamaica Street, I fear, will hardly do for a designation."

"Call him THE M'CLOSKIE. It will be sonorous in the ears of the Saxon!"

"Bravo!" and another Chief was added to the roll of the clans.

"Now," said Bob, "we must put you down. Recollect, all the management — that is, the allocation — will be intrusted to you. Augustus —

you haven't a middle name I think? — well, then, suppose we interpolate 'Reginald', it has a smack of the Crusades. Augustus Reginald Dunshunner, Esq. of — where, in the name of Munchausen?"

"I'm sure I don't know. I never had any land beyond the contents of a flower-pot. Stay — I rather think I have a superiority somewhere about Paisley."

"Just the thing," cried Bob. "It's heritable property, and therefore titular. What's the denomination?"

"St. Mirrens."

"Beautiful! Dunshunner of St. Mirrens, I give you joy! Had you discovered that a little sooner — and I wonder you did not think of it — we might both of us have had lots of allocations. These are not the times to conceal hereditary distinctions. But now comes the serious work. We must have one or two men of known wealth upon the list. The chaff is nothing without a decoy-bird. Now, can't you help me with a name?"

"In that case," said I, "the game is up, and the whole scheme exploded. I would as soon undertake to evoke the ghost of Crœsus."

"Dunshunner," said Bob very seriously, "to be a man of information, you are possessed of marvellous few resources. I am quite ashamed of you. Now listen to me. I have thought deeply upon this subject, and am quite convinced that, with some little trouble, we may secure the co-operation of a most wealthy and influential body — one, too, that is generally supposed to have stood aloof from all speculation of the kind, and whose name would be a tower of strength in the moneyed quarters. I allude," continued Bob, reaching across for the kettle, "to the great Dissenting Interest."

"The what?" cried I, aghast.

"The great Dissenting Interest. You can't have failed to observe the row they have lately been making about Sunday travelling and education. Old Sam Sawley, the coffin-maker, is their principal spokesman here; and wherever he goes the rest will follow, like a flock of sheep bounding after a patriarchal ram. I propose, therefore, to wait upon him to-morrow, and request his co-operation in a scheme which is not only to prove profitable, but to make head against the lax principles of the present age. Leave me alone to tickle him. I consider his name, and those of one or two others belonging to the same meeting-house-fellows with bank-stock and all sorts of tin, as perfectly secure. These dissenters smell a premium from an almost incredible distance. We can fill up the rest of the committee with ciphers, and the whole thing is done."

"But the engineer — we must announce such an officer as a matter of course."

"I never thought of that," said Bob. "Couldn't we hire a fellow from one of the steamboats?"

"I fear that might get us into trouble. You know there are such things as gradients and sections to be prepared. But there's Watty Solder, the gas-fitter, who failed the other day. He's a sort of civil engineer by trade, and will jump at the proposal like a trout at the tail of a May fly."

"Agreed. Now, then, let's fix the number of shares. This is our first experiment, and I thing we ought to be moderate. No sound political economist is avaricious. Let us say twelve thousand, at twenty pounds a-piece."

"So be it."

"Well, then, that's arranged. I'll see Sawley and the rest to-morrow; settle with Solder, and then write out the prospectus. You look in upon me in the evening, and we'll revise it together. Now, by your leave, let's have in the Welsh rabbit and another tumbler to drink success and prosperity to the Glenmutchkin Railway."

I confess that, when I rose on the morrow, with a slight headache and a tongue indifferently parched, I recalled to memory, not without perturbation of conscience, and some internal qualms, the conversation of the previous evening. I felt relieved, however, after two spoonfuls of carbonate of soda, and a glance at the newspaper, wherein I perceived the announcement of no less than four other schemes equally preposterous with our own. But, after all, what right had I to assume that the Glenmutchkin project would prove an ultimate failure? I had not a scrap of statistical information that might entitle me to form such an opinion. At any rate, Parliament, by substituting the Board of Trade as an initiating body of inquiry, had created a responsible tribunal, and freed us from the chance of obloquy. I saw before me a vision of six months' steady gambling, at manifest advantage, in the shares, before a report could possibly be pronounced, or our proceedings be in any way overhauled. Of course I attended that evening punctually at my friend M'Corkindale's. Bob was in high feather; for Sawley no sooner heard of the principles upon which the railway was to be conducted, and his own nomination as a director, than he gave in his adhesion, and promised his unflinching support to the uttermost. The Prospectus ran as follows:

"DIRECT GLENMUTCHKIN RAILWAY
In 12,000 Shares of L. 20 each. Deposit L.1 per Share.
Provisional Committee

SIR POLLOXFEN TREMENS, Bart. of Toddymains.
TAVISH M'TAVISH of Invertavish.
THE M'CLOSKIE.
AUGUSTUS REGINALD DUNSHUNNER, Esq., of St. Mirrens.
SAMUEL SAWLEY, Esq., Merchant.
MHIC-MHAC-VICH-INDUIBH.
PHELIM O'FINLAN, Esq., of Castle-rook, Ireland.
THE CAPTAIN of M'Alcohol.
FACTOR for GLENTUMBLERS.
JOHN JOB JOBSON, Esq., Manufacturer.
EVAN M'CLAW of Glenscart and Inveryewky.
JOSEPH HECKLES, Esq.
HABBAKUK GRABBIE, Portioner in Ramoth-Drumclog.
Engineer — WALTER SOLDER, Esq.
Interim Secretary — ROBERT M'CORKINDALE, Esq.

"The necessity of a direct line of Railway communication through the fertile and populous district known as the Valley of Glenmutchkin, has been long felt and universally acknowledged. Independently of the surpassing grandeur of its mountain scenery, which shall immediately be referred to, and other considerations of even greater importance, GLENMUTCHKIN is known to the capitalist as the most important BREEDING STATION in the Highlands of Scotland, and indeed as the great emporium from which the southern markets are supplied. It has been calculated by a most eminent authority, that every acre in the strath is capable of rearing twenty head of cattle; and, as has been ascertained after a careful admeasurement, that there are not less than TWO HUNDRED THOUSAND improvable acres immediately contiguous to the proposed line of Railway, it may confidently be assumed that the number of cattle to be conveyed along the line will amount to FOUR MILLIONS annually, which, at the lowest estimate, would yield a revenue larger, in proportion to the capital subscribed, than that of any Railway as yet completed within the United Kingdom. From this estimate the traffic in Sheep and Goats, with which the mountains are literally covered, has been carefully excluded, it having been found quite impossible (from its extent) to compute the actual revenue to be drawn from that most important branch. It may, however, be roughly assumed as from seventeen to nineteen *per cent* upon the whole, after deduction of the working expenses.

"The population of Glenmutchkin is extremely dense. Its situation on the west coast has afforded it the means of direct communication with America, of which for many years the inhabitants have actively availed themselves. Indeed, the amount of exportation of live stock, from this part of the Highlands to the Western continent, has more than once attracted the attention of Parliament. The Manufacturers are large and comprehensive, and include the most famous distilleries in the world. The Minerals are most abundant, and amongst these may be reckoned quartz, porphyry, felspar, malachite, manganese, and basalt.

"At the foot of the valley, and close to the sea, lies the important village known as the CLACHAN OF INVERSTARVE. It is supposed by various eminent antiquaries to have been the capital of the Picts, and, amongst the busy inroads of commercial prosperity, it still retains some interesting traces of its former grandeur. There is a large fishing station here, to which vessels from every nation resort, and the demand for foreign produce is daily and steadily increasing.

"As a sporting country Glenmutchkin is unrivalled; but it is by the tourists that its beauties will most greedily be sought. These consist of every combination which plastic nature can afford—cliffs of unusual magnitude and grandeur—waterfalls only second to the sublime cascades of Norway—woods, of which the bark is a remarkably valuable commodity. It need scarcely be added, to rouse the enthusiasm inseparable from this glorious glen, that here, in 1745, Prince Charles Edward Stuart, then in the zenith of his hopes, was joined by the brave Sir Grugar M'Grugar at the head of his devoted clan.

"The Railway will be twelve miles long, and can be completed within six months after the Act of Parliament is obtained. The gradients are easy, and the curves obtuse. There are no viaducts of any importance, and only four tunnels along the whole length of the line. The shortest of these does not exceed a mile and a half.

"In conclusion, the projectors of this Railway beg to state that they have determined, as a principle, to set their face AGAINST ALL SUNDAY TRAVELLING

WHATSOEVER, and to oppose EVERY BILL which may hereafter be brought into Parliament, unless it shall contain a clause to that effect. It is also their intention to take up the cause of the poor and neglected STOKER, for whose accommodation, and social, moral, religious, and intellectual improvement, a large stock of evangelical tracts will speedily be required. Tenders of these, in quantities of not less than 12,000 may be sent in to the Interim Secretary. Shares must be applied for within ten days from the present date."

By order of the Provisional Committee.

ROBT. M'CORKINDALE, *Secretary.*

"There!" said Bob, slapping down the prospectus on the table, with the jauntiness of a Cockney vouchsafing a Pint of Hermitage to his guests— "What do you think of that? If it doesn't do the business effectually, I shall submit to be caned a Dutchman. That last touch about the stoker will bring us in the subscriptions of the old ladies by the score."

"Very masterly, indeed?" said I. "But who the deuce is Mhic-Mhac-vich-Induibh?"

"A *bona-fide* chief, I assure you, though a little reduced: I picked him up upon the Broomielaw. His grandfather had an island somewhere to the west of the Hebrides; but it is not laid down in the maps."

"And the Captain of M'Alcohol?"

"A crack distiller."

"And the Factor for Glentumblers?"

"His principal customer. But, bless you, my dear St. Mirrens! don't bother yourself any more about the committee. They are as respectable a set—on paper at least—as you would wish to see of a summer's morning, and the beauty of it is that they will give us no manner of trouble. Now about the allocation. You and I must restrict ourselves to a couple of thousand shares a-piece. That's only a third of the whole, but it won't do to be greedy."

"But, Bob, consider! Where on earth are we to find the money to pay up the deposits?"

"Can you, the principal director of the Glemmutchkin Railway, ask me, the secretary, such a question? Don't you know that any of the banks will give us tick to the amount 'of half the deposits.' All that is settled already, and you can get your two thousand pounds whenever you please merely for the signing of a bill. Sawley must get a thousand according to stipulation— Jobson, Heckles, and Grabbie, at least five hundred a-piece, and another five hundred, I should think, will exhaust the remaining means of the committee. So that, out of our whole stock, there remain just five thousand shares to be allocated to the speculative and evangelical public. My eyes! won't there be a scramble for them!"

Next day our prospectus appeared in the newspapers. It was read, canvassed, and generally approved of. During the afternoon, I took an opportunity of looking into the Tontine, and whilst under shelter of the *Glasgow Herald*, my ears were solaced with such ejaculations as the following:—

"I say, Jimsy, hae ye seen this grand new prospectus for a railway tae Glenmutchkin?"

"Ay—it looks no that ill. The Hieland lairds are pitting their best fit foremost. Will ye apply for shares?"

"I think I'll tak' twa hundred. Wha's Sir Polloxfen Tremens?"

"He'll be yin o' the Ayrshire folk. He used to rin horses at the Paisley races."

("The devil he did!" thought I.)

"D'ye ken ony o' the directors, Jimsy?"

"I ken Sawley fine. Ye may depend on't, it's a gude thing if he's in't, for he's a howkin' body."

"Then it's sure to gae up. What prem. d'ye think it will bring?"

"Twa pund a share, and maybe mair."

"'Od, I'll apply for three hundred!"

"Heaven bless you, my dear countrymen!" thought I as I sallied forth to refresh myself with a basin of soup, "do but maintain this liberal and patriotic feeling — this thirst for national improvement, internal communication, and premiums — a short while longer, and I know whose fortune will be made."

On the following morning my breakfast-table was covered with shoals of letters, from fellows whom I scarcely ever had spoken to — or who, to use a franker phraseology, had scarcely ever condescended to speak to me — entreating my influence as a director to obtain them shares in the new undertaking. I never bore malice in my life, so I chalked them down, without favouritism, for a certain proportion. Whilst engaged in this charitable work, the door flew open, and M'Corkindale, looking utterly haggard with excitement, rushed in.

"You may buy an estate whenever you please, Dunshunner," cried he, "the world's gone perfectly mad! I have been to Blazes the broker, and he tells me that the whole amount of the stock has been subscribed for four times over already, and he has not yet got in the returns from Edinburgh and Liverpool!"

"Are they good names though, Bob — sure cards — none of your M'Closkies, and M'Alcohols?"

"The first names in the city, I assure you, and most of them holders for investment. I wouldn't take ten millions for their capita."

"Then the sooner we close the list the better."

"I think so too. I suspect a rival company will be out before long. Blazes says the shares are selling already conditionally on allotment, at seven-and-sixpence premium."

"The deuce they are! I say, Bob, since we have the cards in our hands, would it not be wise to favour them with a few hundred at that rate? A bird in the hand, you know, is worth two in the bush, eh?"

"I know no such maxim in political economy," replied the secretary. "Are you mad, Dunshunner? How are the shares ever to go up, if it gets wind that the directors are selling already? Our business just now, is to *bull* the line, not to *bear* it; and if you will trust me, I shall show them such an operation on the ascending scale, as the Stock Exchange has not witnessed for this long and many a day. Then, to-morrow, I shall advertise in the papers that the committee, having received applications for ten times the amount of stock, have been compelled, unwillingly, to close the lists. That will be a slap in the face to the dilatory gentlemen, and send up the shares like wildfire."

Bob was right. No sooner did the advertisement appear, than a simultaneous groan was uttered by some hundreds of disappointed speculators, who with unwonted and unnecessary caution had been anxious to see their way a little before committing themselves to our splendid enterprise. In consequence, they rushed into the market, with intense anxiety to make what terms they could at the earliest stage, and the seven-and-sixpence of premium was doubled in the course of a forenoon.

The allocation passed over very peaceably. Sawley, Heckles, Jobson, Grabbie, and the Captain of M'Alcohol, besides myself, attended, and took part in the business. We were also threatened with the presence of the M'Closkie and Vich-Induibh; but M'Corkindale, entertaining some reasonable doubts as the effect which their corporeal appearance might have upon the representatives of the dissenting interest, had taken the precaution to get them snugly housed in a tavern, where an unbounded supply of gratuitous Ferintosh deprived us of the benefit of their experience. We, how ever, allotted them twenty shares a-piece. Sir Polloxfen Tremens sent a handsome, though rather illegible letter of apology, dated from an island in Lochlomond, where he was said to be detained on particular business.

Mr. Sawley, who officiated as our chairman, was kind enough, before parting, to pass a very flattering eulogium upon the excellence and candour of all the preliminary arrangements. It would now, he said, go forth to the public that this line was not, like some others he could mention, a mere bubble, emanating from the stank of private interest, but a solid, lasting superstructure, based upon the principles of sound return for capital, and serious evangelical truth (hear, hear). The time was fast approaching, when the gravestone, with the words 'Hic Obiit' chiselled upon it, would be placed at the head of all the other lines which rejected the grand opportunity of conveying education to the stoker. The stoker, in his (Mr. Sawley's) opinion, had a right to ask the all important question, "Am I not a man and a brother?" (Cheers). Much had been said and written lately about a work called *Tracts for the Times*. With the opinions contained in that publication he was not conversant, as it was conducted by persons of another community from that to which he (Mr. Sawley) had the privilege to belong. But he hoped very soon, under the auspices of the Glenmutchkin Railway Company, to see a new periodical established, under the title of *Tracts for the Trains*. He never for a moment would relax his efforts to knock a nail into the coffin, which, he might say, was already made, and measured, and cloth-covered for the reception of all establishments; and with these sentiments, and the conviction that the shares must rise, could it be doubted that he would remain a fast friend to the interests of this Company for ever? (Much cheering).

After having delivered this address, Mr. Sawley affectionately squeezed the hands of his brother directors, leaving several of us much overcome. As, however, M'Corkindale had told me that every one of Sawley's shares had been disposed of in the market the day before, I felt less compunction at having refused to allow that excellent man an extra thousand beyond the amount he had applied for, not withstanding of his broadest hints, and even private entreaties.

"Confound the greedy hypocrite!" said Bob; "does he think we shall let him Burke the line for nothing? No-no! let him go to the brokers and buy his shares back, if he thinks they are likely to rise. I'll be bound he has made a cool five hundred out of them already."

On the day which succeeded the allocation, the following entry appeared in the Glasgow share-lists. 'Direct Glenmutchkin Railway 15s. 15s. 6d. 15s. 6d. 16s. 15s. 6d. 16s. 16s. 6d. 16s. 6d. 16s. 17s. 18s. 18s. 19s. 6d. 21s. 21s. 22s. 6d. 24s. 25s. 6d. 27s. 29s. 29s. 6d. 30s. 31s. p^m.'

"They might go higher, and they ought to go higher," said Bob musingly; "but there's not much more stock to come and go upon, and these two share-sharks, Jobson and Grabbie, I know, will be in the market to-morrow. We must not let them have the whiphand of us. I think upon the whole, Dunshunner, though it's letting them go dog cheap, that we ought to sell half our shares at the present premium, whilst there is a certainty of getting it."

"Why not sell the whole? I'm sure I have no objections to part with every stiver of the scrip on such terms."

"Perhaps," said Bob, "upon general principles you might be right; but then remember that we have a vested interest in the line.

"Vested interest be hanged!"

"That's very well—at the same time it is no use to kill your salmon in a hurry. The bulls have done their work pretty well for us, and we ought to keep something on hand for the bears; they are snuffing at it already. I could almost swear that some of those fellows who have sold to-day are working for a time-bargain."

We accordingly got rid of a couple of thousand shares, the proceeds of which not only enabled us to discharge the deposit loan, but left us a material surplus. Under these circumstances, a two-hand banquet was proposed and unanimously carried, the commencement of which I distinctly remember, but am rather dubious as to the end. So many stories have lately been circulated to the prejudice of railway directors, that I think it my duty to state that this entertainment was scrupulously defrayed by ourselves, and not carried to account, either of the preliminary survey, or the expense of the provisional committee.

Nothing effects so great a metamorphosis in the bearing of the outer man as a sudden change of fortune. The anemone of the garden differs scarcely more from its unpretending prototype of the Woods, than Robert M'Corkindale, Esq., Secretary and Projector of the Glenmutchkin Railway, differed from Bob M'Corkindale, the seedy frequenter of 'The Crow'. In the days of yore, men eyed the surtout—napless at the velvet collar, and preternaturally white at the seams—which Bob vouchsafed to wear, with looks of dim suspicion, as if some faint reminiscence, similar to that which is said to recall the memory of a former state of existence, suggested to them a notion that the garment had once been their own. Indeed, his whole appearance was then wonderfully second-hand. Now he had cast his slough. A most undeniable Taglioni, with trimmings just bordering upon frogs, gave dignity to his demeanour and twofold amplitude to his chest. The horn eyeglass was exchanged for one of purest gold, the dingy high-lows for well-waxed Wellingtons, the Paisley fogle for the fabric of the

China loom. Moreover, he walked with a swagger, and affected in common conversation a peculiar dialect which he opined to be the purest English, but which no one — except a bagman — could be reasonably expected to understand. His pockets were invariably crammed with share-lists; and he quoted, if he did not comprehend, the money article from the *Times*. This sort of assumption, though very ludicrous in itself, goes down wonderfully. Bob gradually became a sort of authority, and his opinions got quoted on 'Change. He was no ass, notwithstanding his peculiarities, and made good use of his opportunity.

For myself, I bore my new dignities with an air of modest meekness. A certain degree of starchness is indispensable for a railway director, if he means to go forward in his high calling and prosper; he must abandon all juvenile eccentricities, and aim at the appearance of a decided enemy to free trade in the article of Wild Oats. Accordingly, as the first step towards respectability, I eschewed coloured waistcoats, and gave out that I was a marrying man. No man under forty, unless he is a positive idiot, will stand forth as a theoretical bachelor. It is all nonsense to say that there is anything unpleasant in being courted. Attention, whether from male or female, tickles the vanity; and although I have a reasonable, and I hope, not unwholesome regard for the gratification of my other appetites, I confess that this same vanity is by far the most poignant of the whole. I therefore surrendered myself freely to the soft allurements thrown in my way by such matronly denizens of Glasgow as were possessed of stock in the shape of marriageable daughters; and walked the more readily into their toils, because every party, though nominally for the purposes of tea, wound up with a hot supper, and something hotter still by way of assisting the digestion.

I don't know whether it was my determined conduct at the allocation, my territorial title, or a most exaggerated idea of my circumstances, that worked upon the mind of Mr. Sawley. Possibly it was a combination of the three; but sure enough few days had elapsed before I received a formal card of invitation to a tea and serious conversation. Now serious conversation is a sort of thing that I never shone in, possibly because my early studies were framed in a different direction; but as I really was unwilling to offend the respectable coffin-maker, and as I found that the Captain of M'Alcohol — a decided trump in his way — had also received a summons, I notified my acceptance.

M'Alcohol and I went together. The Captain, an enormous browny Celt, with superhuman whiskers, and a shock of the fieriest hair, had figged himself out, *more majorum*, in the full Highland costume. I never saw Rob Roy on the stage look half so dignified or ferocious. He glittered from head to foot, with dirk, pistol, and skean-dhu, and at least a hundredweight of cairngorms cast a prismatic glory around his person. I felt quite abashed beside him.

We were ushered into Mr. Sawley's drawing-room. Round the walls, and at considerable distances from each other, were seated about a dozen characters, male and female, all of them dressed in sable, and wearing countenances of woe. Sawley advanced, and wrung me by the hand with so piteous an expression of visage, that I could not help thinking some awful catastrophe had just befallen his family.

"You are welcome, Mr. Dunshunner—welcome to my humble tabernacle. Let me present you to Mrs. Sawley"—and a lady, who seemed to have bathed in the Yellow Sea, rose from her seat, and favoured me with a profound curtsy.

"My daughter—Miss Selina Sawley."

I felt in my brain the scorching glance of the two darkest eyes it ever was my fortune to behold, as the beauteous Selina looked up from the perusal of her handkerchief hem. It was a pity that the other features were not corresponding; for the nose was flat, and the mouth of such dimensions, that Harlequin might have jumped down it with impunity—but the eyes *were* splendid.

In obedience to a sign from the hostess, I sank into a chair beside Selina; and not knowing exactly what to say, hazarded some observation about the weather.

"Yes, it is indeed a suggestive season. How deeply, Mr. Dunshunner, we ought to feel the pensive progress of autumn towards a soft and premature decay! I always think, about this time of the year, that nature is falling into a consumption!"

"To be sure, ma'am," said I, rather taken aback by this style of colloquy, "the trees are looking devilishly hectic."

"Ah, you have remarked that too! Strange! it was but yesterday that I was wandering through Kelvin Grove, and as the phantom breeze brought down the withered foliage from the spray, I thought how probable it was that they might ere long rustle over young and glowing hearts deposited prematurely in the tomb!"

This, which struck me as a very passable imitation of Dickens's pathetic writings, was a poser. In default of language, I looked Miss Sawley straight in the face, and attempted a substitute for a sigh. I was rewarded with a tender glance.

"Ah!" said she, "I see you are a congenial spirit. How delightful, and yet how rare it is to meet with any one who thinks in unison with yourself! Do you ever walk in the Necropolis, Mr. Dunshunner? It is my favourite haunt of a morning. There we can wean ourselves, as it were, from life, and, beneath the melancholy yew and cypress, anticipate the setting star. How often there have I seen the procession—the funeral of some very, *very* little child"—

"Selina, my love," said Mrs. Sawley, "have the kindness to ring for the cookies."

I, as in duty bound, started up to save the fair enthusiast the trouble, and was not sorry to observe my seat immediately occupied by a very cadaverous gentleman, who was evidently jealous of the progress I was rapidly making. Sawley, with an air of great mystery, informed me that this was a Mr. Dalgleish of Raxmathrapple, the representative of an ancient Scottish family who claimed an important heritable office. The name, I thought, was familiar to me, but there was something in the appearance of Mr. Dalgleish which, notwithstanding the smiles of Miss Selina, rendered a rivalship in that quarter utterly out of the question.

I hate injustice, so let me do due honour in description to the Sawley banquet. The tea-urn most literally corresponded to its name. The table was decked out with divers platters, containing seed-cakes cut into rhomboids, almond biscuits, and ratafia drops. Also, on the sideboard, there were two salvers, each of which contained a congregation of glasses, filled with port and sherry. The former fluid, as I afterwards ascertained, was of the kind advertised as 'curious,' and proffered for sale at the reasonable rate of sixteen shillings per dozen. The banquet, on the whole, was rather peculiar than enticing; and, for the life of me, I could not divest myself of the idea that the selfsame viands had figured, not long before, as funeral refreshments at a dirgie. No such suspicion seemed to cross the mind of M'Alcohol, who hitherto had remained uneasily surveying his nails in a corner, but at the first symptom of food started forwards, and was in the act of making a clean sweep of the china, when Sawley proposed the singular preliminary of a hymn.

The hymn was accordingly sung. I am thankful to say it was such a one as I never heard before, or expect to hear again; and unless it was composed by the Reverend Saunders Peden in an hour of paroxysm on the moors, I cannot conjecture the author. After this original symphony, tea was discussed, and after tea, to my amazement, more hot brandy-and-water than I ever remember to have seen circulated at the most convivial party. Of course this effected a radical change in the spirits and coversation of the circle. It was again my lot to be placed by the side of the fascinating Selina, whose sentimentality gradually thawed away beneath the influence of sundry sips, which she accepted with a delicate reluctance. This time Dalgleish of Raxmathrapple had not the remotest chance. M'Alcohol got furious, sang Gaelic songs, and even delivered a sermon in genuine Erse, without incurring a rebuke; whilst, for my own part, I must needs confess that I waxed unnecessarily amorous, and the last thing I recollect was the pressure of Mr. Sawley's hand at the door, as he denominated me his dear boy, and hoped I would soon come back and visit Mrs. Sawley and Selina. The recollection of these passages next morning was the surest antidote to my return.

Three weeks had elapsed, and still the Glenmutchkin Railway shares were at a premium, though rather lower than when we sold. Our engineer, Watty Solder, returned from his first survey of the line, along with an assistant who really appeared to have some remote glimmerings of the science and practice of mensuration. It seemed, from a verbal report, that the line was actually practicable; and the survey would have been completed in a very short time—"If," according to the account of Solder, "there had been ae hoos in the glen. But ever sin' the distillery stoppit—and that was twa year last Martinmas—there wasna a hole whaur a Christian could lay his head, muckle less get white sugar to his toddy, forbye the change-house at the clachan; and the auld luckie that keepit it was sair forfochten wi' the palsy, and maist in the dead-thraws. There was naebody else living within twal miles o' the line, barring a tacksman, a lamiter, and a bauldie."

We had some difficulty in preventing Mr. Solder from making this report open and patent to the public, which premature disclosure might have interfered materially with the preparation of our traffic tables, not to mention the marketable value of the shares. We therefore kept him steadily at work out of Glasgow, upon a very liberal allowance, to which, apparently, he did not object.

"Dunshunner," said M'Corkindale to me one day, "I suspect that there is something going on about our railway more than we are aware of. Have you observed that the shares are preternaturally high just now?"

"So much the better. Let's sell."

"I did this morning—both yours and mine, at two pounds ten shillings premium."

"The deuce you did! Then we're out of the whole concern."

"Not quite. If my suspicions are correct, there's a good deal more money yet to be got from the speculation. Somebody has been bulling the stock without orders; and, as they can have no information which we are not perfectly up to, depend upon it, it is done for a purpose. I suspect Sawley and his friends. They have never been quite happy since the allocation; and I caught him yesterday pumping our broker in the back shop. We'll see in a day or two. If they are beginning a bearing operation, I know how to catch them."

And, in effect, the bearing operation commenced. Next day, heavy sales were affected for delivery in three weeks; and the stock, as if waterlogged, began to sink. The same thing continued for the following two days, until the premium became nearly nominal. In the mean time, Bob and I, in conjunction with two leading capitalists whom we let into the secret, bought up steadily every share that was offered; and at the end of a fortnight we found that we had purchased rather more than double the amount of the whole original stock. Sawley and his disciples, who, as M'Corkindale suspected, were at the bottom of the whole transaction, having beared to their heart's content, now came into the market to purchase, in order to redeem their engagements. The following extracts from the weekly share-lists will show the results of their endeavours to regain their lost position:—

	Sat.	Mon	Tues.	Wed	Thurs.	Frid	Sat.
GLENMUTCHKIN RAIL., L.1 paid	$1^2/_8$	$2¼$	$4⅜$	$7½$	$10¾$	$15⅜$	17,

and Monday was the day of delivery.

I have no means of knowing in what frame of mind Mr. Sawley spent the Sunday, or whether he had recourse for mental consolation to Peden; but on Monday morning he presented himself at my door in full funeral costume, with about a quarter of a mile of crape swathed round his hat, black gloves, and a countenance infinitely more doleful than if he had been attending the internment of his beloved wife.

"Walk in, Mr. Sawley," said I cheerfully. "What a long time it is since I have had the pleasure of seeing you—too long indeed for brother directors. How are Mrs. Sawley and Miss Selina—won't you take a cup of coffee?"

"Grass, sir, grass!" said Mr. Sawley, with a sigh like the groan of a furnace-bellows. "We are all flowers of the oven—weak, erring creatures, every one of us. Ah! Mr. Dunshunner! you have been a great stranger at Lykewake Terrace!"

"Take a muffin, Mr. Sawley. Anything new in the railway world?"

"Ah, my dear sir—my good Mr. Augustus Reginald—I wanted to have some serious conversation with you on that very point. I am afraid there is something far wrong indeed in the present state of our stock."

"Why, to be sure it is high; but that, you know, is a token of the public confidence in the line. After all, the rise is nothing compared to that of several English railways; and individually, I suppose, neither of us have any reason to complain."

"I don't like it," said Sawley, watching me over the margin of his coffee-cup. "I don't like it. It savours too much of gambling for a man of my habits. Selina, who is a sensible girl, has serious qualms on the subject."

"Then why not get out of it? I have no objection to run the risk, and if you like to transact with me, I will pay you ready money for every share you have at the present market price."

Sawley writhed uneasily in his chair.

"Will you sell me five hundred, Mr. Sawley? Say the word and it is a bargain."

"A time bargain?" quavered the coffin-maker.

"No. Money down, and scrip handed over."

"I—I can't. The fact is, my dear friend, I have sold all my stock already!"

"Then permit me to ask, Mr. Sawley, what possible objection you can have to the present aspect of affairs? You do not surely suppose that we are going to issue new shares and bring down the market, simply because you have realised at a handsome premium?"

"A handsome premium! O Lord!" moaned Sawley.

"Why, what did you get for them?"

"Four, three, and two and a half."

"A very considerable profit indeed," said I; "and you ought to be abundantly thankful. We shall talk this matter over at another time, Mr. Sawley, but just now I must beg you to excuse me. I have a particular engagement this morning with my broker—rather a heavy transaction to settle—and so—"

"It's no use beating about the bush, any longer," said Mr. Sawley in an excited tone, at the same time dashing down his crape-covered castor on the floor. "Did you ever see a ruined man with a large family? Look at me, Mr. Dunshunner—I'm one, and you've done it!"

"Mr. Sawley! are you in your senses?"

"That depends on circumstances. Haven't you been buying stock lately?"

"I am glad to say I have—two thousand Glenmutchkins, I think, and this is the day of delivery."

"Well, then—can't you see how the matter stands? It was I who sold them!"

"Well!"

"Mother of Moses, sir! don't you see I'm ruined?"

"By no means—but you must not swear. I pay over the money for your scrip, and you pocket a premium. It seems to me a very simple transaction."

"But I tell you I haven't got the scrip!" cried Sawley, gnashing his teeth, whilst the cold beads of perspiration gathered largely on his brow.

"This is very unfortunate! Have you lost it?"

"No!—the devil tempted me, and I oversold!"

There was a very long pause, during which I assumed an aspect of serious and dignified rebuke.

"Is it possible?" said I in a low tone, after the manner of Kean's offended fathers. "What! you, Mr. Sawley—the stoker's friend—the enemy of gambling—the father of Selina—condescend to so equivocal a transaction?

You amaze me! But I never was the man to press heavily on a friend"—here Sawley brightened up—"your secret is safe with me, and it shall be your own fault if it reaches the ears of the Session. Pay me over the difference at the present market price, and I release you of your obligation."

"Then I'm in the Gazette, that's all," said Sawley doggedly, "and a wife and nine beautiful babes upon the parish! I had hoped other things from you, Mr. Dunshunner—I thought you and Selina—"

"Nonsense, man! Nobody goes into the Gazette just now—it will be time enough when the general crash comes. Out with your cheque-book, and write me an order for four-and-twenty thousand. Confound fractions! in these days one can afford to be liberal."

"I haven't got it," said Sawley. "You have no idea how bad our trade has been of late, for nobody seems to think of dying. I have not sold a gross of coffins this fortnight. But I'll tell you what—I'll give you five thousand down in cash, and ten thousand in shares—further I can't go."

"Now, Mr. Sawley," said I, "I may be blamed by worldly-minded persons for what I am going to do; but I am a man of principle, and feel deeply for the situation of your amiable wife and family. I bear no malice, though it is quite clear that you intended to make me the sufferer. Pay me fifteen thousand over the counter, and we cry quits for ever."

"Won't you take Camlachie Cemetery shares? They are sure to go up."

"No!"

"Twelve Hundred Cowcaddens' Water, with an issue of new stock next week?"

"Not if they disseminated the Ganges!"

"A thousand Ramshorn Gas—four per cent guaranteed until the act?"

"Not if they promised twenty, and melted down the sun in their retort!"

"Blawweary Iron? Best spec. going."

"No, I tell you once for all! If you don't like my offer—and it is an uncommonly liberal one—say so, and I'll expose you this afternoon upon 'Change."

"Well, then—there's a cheque. But may the—"

"Stop, sir! Any such profane expressions, and I shall insist upon the original bargain. So, then—now we're quits. I wish you a very good-morning, Mr. Sawley, and better luck next time. Pray remember me to your amiable family."

The door had hardly closed upon the discomfited coffin-maker, and I was still in the preliminary steps of an extempore *pas seul*, intended as the outward demonstration of exceedingly inward joy, when Bob M'Corkindale entered. I told him the result of the morning's conference.

"You have let him off too easily," said the Political Economist. "Had I been his creditor, I certainly should have sacked the shares into the bargain. There is nothing like rigid dealing between man and man."

"I am contented with moderate profits," said I; "besides, the image of Selina overcame me. How goes it with Jobson and Grabbie?"

"Jobson has paid, and Grabbie compounded. Heckles—may he die an evil death!—has repudiated, become a lame duck, and waddled; but no doubt his estate will pay a dividend."

"So, then, we are clear of the whole Glenmutchkin business, and at a handsome profit."

"A fair interest for the outlay of capital—nothing more. But I'm not quite done with the concern yet."

"How so? not another bearing operation?"

"No; that cock would hardly fight. But you forget that I am secretary of the company, and have a small account against them for services already rendered. I must do what I can to carry the bill through Parliament; and, as you have now sold your whole shares, I advise you to resign from the direction, go down straight to Glenmutchkin, and qualify yourself for a witness. We shall give you five guineas a day, and pay all your expenses."

"Not a bad notion. But what has become of M'Closkie, and the other fellow with the jaw-breaking name?"

"Vich-Induibh? I have looked after their interests, and in duty bound, sold their shares at a large premium, and despatched them to their native hills on annuities."

"And Sir Polloxfen?"

"Died yesterday of spontaneous combustion."

As the company seemed breaking up, I thought I could not do better than take M'Corkindale's hint, and accordingly betook myself to Glenmutchkin, along with the Captain of M'Alcohol, and we quartered ourselves upon the Factor for Glentumblers. We found Watty Solder very shaky, and his assistant also lapsing into habits of painful inebriety. We saw little of them except of an evening, for we shot and fished the whole day, and made ourselves remarkably comfortable. By singular good-luck, the plans and sections were lodged in time, and the Board of Trade very handsomely reported in our favour, with a recommendation of what they were pleased to call 'the Glenmutchkin system,' and a hope that it might generally be carried out. What this system was, I never clearly understood; but, of course, none of us had any objections. This circumstance gave an additional impetus to the shares, and they once more went up. I was, however too cautious to plunge a second time into Charybdis, but M'Corkindale did, and again emerged with plunder.

When the time came for the parliamentary contest, we all emigrated to London. I still recollect, with lively satisfaction, the many pleasant days we spent in the metropolis at the company's expense. There were just a neat fifty of us, and we occupied the whole of an hotel. The discussion before the committee was long and formidable. We were opposed by four other companies who patronised lines, of which the nearest was at least a hundred miles distant from Glenmutchkin; but as they founded their opposition upon dissent from 'the Glenmutchkin system' generally, the committee allowed them to be heard. We fought for three weeks a most desperate battle, and might in the end have been victorious, had not our last antagonist, at the very close of his case, pointed out no less than seventy-three fatal errors in the parliamentary plan deposited by the unfortunate Solder. Why this was not done earlier, I never exactly understood; it may be, that our opponents, with gentlemanly consideration, were unwilling to curtail our sojourn in London—and their own. The drama was now finally closed, and after all preliminary expenses were paid, sixpence per share was returned to the holders upon surrender of their scrip. Such is an accurate history of the Origin, Rise, Progress and Fall of the Direct Glenmutchkin Railway. It contains a deep moral, if anybody has sense enough to see it; if not, I have a new project in my eye for next session, of which timely notice shall be given.

Christian Isobel Johnstone (1781-1857)

Andrew Howie, The Hand-Loom Weaver (1846)

It was a day of public rejoicing in Glasgow; and Mr. Mathewson, one of the most respectable, if not the largest of the manufacturers of the town, had taken charge of his own warehouse, that his son and two young clerks, with sundry inferior assistants, who usually officiated there, might have an opportunity of witnessing and sharing in the gaieties of the holiday. Already had Mr. Mathewson himself, by what was thought an extraordinary degree of condescension, viewed, examined, and paid for several pieces of cloth, brought in by hand-loom workers. He was going through the same process with an exhausted, broken-down workman, yet one who in years seemed scarce in the prime of life, when an elderly, small, thin man, of poor but decent appearance, entered on the same errand, was saluted with more than ordinary attention, and desired to sit down on the bench. The old man nodded, and obeyed; wiped the perspiration from his thin temples and bald forehead, and then fixed a keen, hollow, gray eye on the speakers before him. He who stood in the place of workman was making a low, but earnest expostulation, to which the master answered at first calmly; and then, with a show of impatience, he whipped up a bundle of cotton yarn, saying aloud, "Do ye think we would wrong ye, Robert? If ye are not pleased with what we can give, ye are welcome to take your change. This is a land of liberty;—we can find weavers, and ye are just as free to look out for another warehouse." The poor man laid his emaciated, eager fingers upon the bundle: "Say no more about it, sir. Weel do ye ken I *must* take it."

This poor man had brought in the fruits of his own and his neighbour's fortnight's labour from his cottage, five miles off in the country, that he might have a stolen sight of the grand procession. With thanks he had accepted wages reduced a full half below the prices of former years. These diminutions he had met by gradually retrenching and, in many instances, entirely surrendering the little comforts of his home, and at the same time eking out his hours of labour: but to hear of farther reduction, which lowered the price of his labour to three-eighths of what had been given for the same kind and quantity of work twenty years before, and to be told that in this sort of barter between *capital* and *labour*, the manufacturer and the workman meet on equal terms, wrung forth a hasty expression of impatience which he afterwards regretted.

"Ay ay, Mr. William," said the old man, as the poor weaver sung dumb, "so he is, quite free to seek another warehouse; only where will the poor fellow find it, when every master has a third mair hands hanging on, than he can fully employ. So he is free to jump o'er the brig as he gangs hame; and maybe, in a sense, that would be the best thing he could do, only he would rin a chance o' drownin', and o' leavin' an orphan family to whole starve, instead o' half starving; and also o' committin' a deadly sin. Had a war been going on, and the king needed soldiers, he might have left his family and ta'en the bounty. This is all the *real* choice he has between working for what ye think best; or starving, and seeing them suffer who can worse bear hardship. Ye ken, sir, better than I can tell ye, it's little a weaver can turn his hand to. But I am far from blaming you, sir. When I see your full shelves, I ken weel ye are mair to be pitied than blamed. —But oh, there's something sair wrang among us."

After this lecture the weaver, having now carefully knotted up the yarn in his ragged *Monteith handkerchief*, left the warehouse.

"An' how is a' wi' you, Andrew?" said Mr. Mathewson to the old man, when they were left alone. "A man o' sense, like you, is no doubt surprised to hear half their unreasonable nonsense. Ye may all know that in the present state of the market, our house, and too many others in this same town, are stuffing our warehouses with goods, for which there is neither demand nor likelihood of demand; and dipping rashly into our capitals, rather than throw our hands all at once idle. Prices, such as we once got, need never be looked for again; and how, then, can men be so unjust as to expect the same wages?"

"It may be sae, sir," said the old man." And it might be better for us all if there were less *labour*, and less *stuffing* up of the white goods: but oh, Mr. William, dinna go to aggravate and exasperate a poor worn-out, half-starved workman, by telling him he is as free to refuse work as ye are to refuse him employment. I canna thole to hear that even from you, sir.—So were ye, when a bairn boarded wi' the gudewife—and a dour loonie ye were—to tarry[1] at your porridge; but ye ken weel that in an hour or twa afterwards ye were fain to draw to your bicker."

Mr. Mathewson smiled: "And how, Andrew, is my kind old nurse? You should remember (for the sake of poor weavers) that if I *persevered* in not eating, she would at last give the porridge a tempting dash of cream, and coax me to eat."

"It will be lang ere you masters pour cream on our cogs, or cox huz to eat, Mr. William," said the old man, smiling grimly. "Where saw ye ever, for twenty years bygane, in town or country, in this land, masters in any calling that could not find hands,—ay, and double, and triple hands. In the Back Woods of America there may sometimes be lack of labourers, but seldom at our door-cheek,—and in our trade never; and never again will be, I jalouse. It will be fine times for the workman when he is able, for any length of time, to refuse an ill-paid job, Mr. William."

Andrew's business was now despatched, and the conversation became more general. Mr. Mathewson inquired about lodgings, which he wished to procure in his native air, and in Andrew's neighbourhood. Something had disgusted him with his handsome villa on the Ayrshire coast, which he was trying to sell; and his health required change of air.

"Ye are looking, like myself, thin, auld-like, and yellow enough, sir," said Andrew, with compassionate interest.

"It's but a thin, yellow, hungry trade grown, this of ours, Andrew, compared with what we have both seen it," replied the manufacturer, smiling at Andrew's homely compliment to his complexion. "There is a change of times since I wont to come out on the top of the yarn in my uncle's caravan on a Saturday afternoon, to get an afternoon's fishing with

239

your laddies, and a capital *four-hours* of tea and bacon, or burn trouts, from my old nurse; while the overseer went about pressing webs on you. Those were happy days."

"Ye let us come to you now, sir. Ay, a weaver's wife could gie a bairn a piece, or a friend a *four-hours* then. Weel weel!"—The old man's sigh filled up the sentence. "But I am wae to hear ye need country quarters for health, sir; and there is ane at hame will be much concerned. What is like the matter?"

"No great matter, Andrew; something and nothing. The doctor says air, the pony, and ease of mind, will soon make all right; but the last is a commodity become right scarce among us."

"With a' those shelfs, and bales, and muckle count-books, sir, and so many poor folk about ye, I can weel understand that," replied Andrew, glancing over the array of desks, and on through the long perspective of the deep and well-stored warehouse, room after room retiring from view. Mr. Mathewson's complaint was that of hundreds of commercial men in these times. He was nervous, he was dyspeptic, his sleep was broken, his appetite uncertain. Then he became almost quite well again, or much better, or nothing particular; and again there was a sense of languor, oppression, and exhaustion, or irritation; and the physician saw something was going wrong, but could neither tell exactly what, nor yet confess ignorance. His most distinct fear was for water on the chest; and "the pony, and ease of mind," were his universal prescription for all men in business. "If it's to be got ony where, it will be found about—side, by me, Andrew; so make the gudewife look for some bit room—no fine place—and I'll try to get out on Saturday; and now for your news."

"Yours it maun be, sir; The BILL is to do us a' a power of good, nae doubt? But what's come ower the Factory Bill?—the wives will a' be at me for news about that. Whatever comes of us auld, doited, weaver bodies, it would be heartsome to see the bits o' bairns, poor, dowie, spiritless, dwining, decrepit things, eased of their lang hours. I wonder what the manufacturing tribe will crine and dwindle into, sir, in a generation or twa."

"If the wives would take care of their bairns themselves, Andrew, that would be better than ten bills. There has been a deal of senseless clamour about this same story. The Government have more wit than interfere with the entire freedom of all contracts between capitalists and labourers. The Factory Bill will get the go-bye, ye'll see."

"Entire freedom!—how can *ye* ca' it sae, sir? It's a' delusion and mockery to tell even huz, that's grown men, that we have entire freedom of working at ony price. But freedom of contract for children! Na, na. Can they manage for themselves? Are they free? Alack, alack!"

"They have their parents, and friends, Andrew, to take charge of their engagements. May they not be safely left to them?"

"No, sir, they cannot—ye see they *cannot*. In a cot-house on a moor, with a kail-yard and potatoes enow, I would leave, cheerfully, a bairn to its ain mother; but in this weary town of yours, wi' a man thrown clean out of work, or brought down to the starving point in wages, hunger and cauld pinching, and a mill open for bairns, be the hours short, or those of black niggers, be the place healthy or murderous, we are come to that state, that fathers and mothers *maun* sell their bairns' labour. Necessity has no law; the poor thing of eight maun slave for the sister of two or three. Ye have read in our auld Josephus o' mothers so bested as to eat the very fruit of their bodies."

"And now we may hear of them *drinking* it, Andrew," said the manufacturer, sharply.

"I'm no denying *our* faults, sir; would we were in a way to mend them, or had encouragement thereto. But it's plain to be seen that we are far, far departed frae the healthy state, in whilk things might be left to themselves, and *ourselves* to *ourselves*. But think ye it is right to meddle or make only to scathe us? If you protect your corn, and your whisky, and your what not, by laws and statutes, and fines and felonies, why no protect ours and our bairns' wearied limbs and exhausted bodies, as well as at our cost the bread which should nourish us?"

"I have nothing to say for the Corn laws, Andrew; yet I cannot see that one bad law should be an apology for another useless one.

These are difficult complicated questions, and we have scarce leisure for them; but you will surely own, the world is much more prosperous than when you first saw it, sixty years back?"

"Indeed, and I'll no be rash there," cried Andrew, briskly; "but I freely own it's a *brawer* warld; and plenty changes in it, too, whilk young folk say are lightsome. Changes especially in our *line*; and, as far as machinery goes, changes for the better, I'll not dispute, — sair as machines have borne on me in my ain peculiar. — But oh, we have surely made an ill use o' these marvellous inventions Providence has enabled us to make. They have no been blessed to us, sir, in the use. We are making man's master o' the dumb creations of iron and timber that should be man's servants."

"A little of the old leaven still, Andrew," said Mr. Mathewson, smiling, "But hark, the music of our lads, and the procession."

"Then I must be off to get a sight of their daft doings. It's aye some good THE BILL has done, when it gives them a play-day or two, and causes a brushing up among lads and lasses for a walk in the free air. But I would like to argue out the point with you, too, sir; for I'm almost sure I could convince ye."

The honest weaver showed such divided inclination between witnessing the Reform Procession and expounding his opinions, that his old foster-child, or boarder, compassionately suggested the adjournment of the question, to be resumed on — — — banks, or in Andrew's garden seat, under the bourtrees. The old man's eye brightened. As he took a glass of medicated port, kept in the warehouse, because prescribed for the manufacturer at his noon-day hour, he pledged to his better health, and shook his head with earnest gesticulation, saying, "'Od, but Mr. William, this o' ours should be a better warld if we kenned but right how to manage't. I'm not just sure if the birkies up-bye yonder," — and he pointed over his shoulder towards London, — "ken a' the rights and wrangs o't, or the real outs and ins; but howsomever, I hope they're honest men this new Whig set; and, wi' the aid of Divine wisdom" — ["And our good advising," interrupted the smiling manufacturer,] — "they may make some small beginning to set us in the right way. I could leave the warld in peace, if I but saw it aince in the right way."

"In which for forty years ye have been showing it how to walk." — —

"I'll no deny — it would be fause shame, — that since Mr. Muir's[2] day, I may have been ettling at that," replied the philosopher of Spindleton; "It's a man's duty, sir, — and though but a poor man and a weaver, I would be loath to forget, 'A man's a man for a' that.'" "But here the musical instruments attending an Irish detachment of the procession, now just at hand, poured forth "*St. Patrick's Day*" so loudly, that it was only by signs the friends took leave; and thus ended the first *idle*, leisurely talk that had taken place in that busy warehouse for months or probably years, at least when the master was present.

By Saturday evening Mr. Mathewson and his youngest daughter were settled in the small rural lodging near Spindleton, which Mrs. Howie had engaged for them in a gardener's house. His lady and elder daughters were reported to be prodigiously fine people, but in manners and simplicity of character, though his habits had become more luxurious, Mathewson himself was the same man as when an under clerk in the establishment to which he had succeeded, and which he had so much extended. Yet he had in many things gone with the stream which he now fancied it his duty to oppose, at least, in the instance of his own thoughtless family. He deferred his visit to his foster-mother till Monday; but saw, with satisfaction, the decent, quiet couple in their old back pew in the parish church, from which Andrew's gray eye ever and anon shot a challenge to renewal of their argument.

Andrew Howie, for a hand-loom weaver of 1832, might be considered a comfortable man. His good fortune, like that of most other men and weavers, was the fruit of his own good conduct. His cottage, the looms in one end, the dwelling in the other, with chambers above, was, together with the garden, his own property, on paying twenty-five shillings a-year of feu. His substantial long-used furniture was still in sufficient quantity, and well-kept. Fuel was cheap here. He had long since put "a little to the fore." It was, indeed, very little, but still something; and for the sake of a kind and dutiful daughter, Andrew would have suffered any hardship, save the humiliation of receiving parish aid, before he had touched it. This fund, of £23. 17s. was deposited in a Glasgow bank, for Andrew's prudent wife would not trust this treasure even to her fosterchild. "There were so many ups and downs," she said wisely, "amang the great masters." Two benefit societies to which he sometimes grudged having paid for forty years, without being above three times sick, placed Andrew above the dread of destitution in illness, or of wanting decent and Christian burial, which always supposes expense; and the membership of a book-club which he had mainly established, and of a newspaper-club which originally took in "The Gazetteer!" supported his social importance in the neighbourhood. He kept his seat in the church, though that too was felt a heavy cess in bad times, and having surmounted the evil political fame of his youth, he was now on the new Minister's leet for an elder. It was indeed suspected that Mr. Draunt the clergyman, had done this as a stroke of policy, at a time when a rumour of building a

Seceder Meeting-house arose in the village. Andrew had at one time kept a couple of apprentices; but this source of profit was stopt; he however let his loom stances, and was often not paid the rent. His own gains were little indeed; not above 4s. 6d. a week on the average; but somehow he contrived to maintain his place as patriarch of the village. The only aid he received was from his daughter, who kept him clear of arrears with his societies; and who once, when in a desperate fit of necessary economy he gave up both his clubs, which cost a shilling a quarter each, entered him anew. Deprived of the distinction of having the newspaper directed, as for forty years, to "Mr. Andrew Howie, Manufacturer, Spindleton," the old man had become spiritless and insignificant in his own esteem. What is life deprived of life's enjoyments! Restored to his club, Andrew read, expounded, and rehearsed with greater zest than before; and was again the village oracle.

Andrew Howie, though not an idler, was on principle not keenly industrious. "Constant *slavery* at the loom," as he called the modern long hours, was against his creed and also his habits; and though the old man toiled only ten hours a-day, where his poor neighbours worked fourteen, and sixteen, he never ceased to maintain, that his own hours were much too long, and the necessity for such continued labour owing to a bad constitution of society. Man was intended, Andrew loftily affirmed, for something better than perpetual, monotonous drudgery.

Long before Mr. Owen, or Spence, or any of those apostles, or their new systems, were heard of, Andrew's benevolent speculations had wandered into forms, to which some of his neighbours looked with interest, and others with amusement. His visionary Cooperative Societies, and manufacturing villages, were to be centres of domestic comfort, leisure, instruction, health, happiness for all,

For the young who labour, and the old who rest.

He, however, differed entirely from Mr. Owen in one essential particular. Every household in Andrew's town, was to have its own sacred fireside. If more extravagant in politics, Andrew Howie was more strictly religious than many of his younger neighbours. The spirit of Christianity entered fully into his weaving Utopia, and mingled with all his visions of the social Millennium of Spindleton.

When the old couple returned from afternoon service, on the Sunday after Mr. Mathewson's arrival, the conversation naturally turned on their former boarder, and as naturally reverted to their own changed condition. Sunday was now the only day of the week, in which they indulged in the extravagance of that thin *blue* dilution, which they, perhaps from habit, named tea; and which a weekly slice of wheaten bread, and a sprinkling of treacle, which Andrew thought good for his elocution, accompanied. Yet it ill becomes me to speak thus slightingly of the beverage which the philosophic weaver sucked up like a leviathan, even to the sixth or seventh maceration of the bitter many-coloured leaves.

Though curtailed at his board, Andrew enjoyed many little comforts and great blessings unknown to his brethren in "yon weary Glasgow." He retained, after all his losses, the blessings — how great! — of fresh air, a roomy lodging, his garden, his good bed and useful furniture, the *leisure* which he took, preferring it, in a balance of comfort, to what others might have reckoned necessaries; though he thus forfeited the trifle of more wages, at which men with families greedily grasped, at the expense of weary limbs, exhausted spirits, and finally of ruined health. He also enjoyed, to the full, his own importance in his ancient neighbourhood, and the superiority he ever maintained in argument and conversation. Though his wages were scarcely a third of what he had once earned, his kitchen in a cold night was almost as snug as ever, his bed as warm, his church seat as sacred. How few old hand-loom weavers could boast of as much!

"That's a dish of prime tea, gudewife," said Andrew, breathing hard, from gulping down the fifth filling, the last three without sugar; "Whate'er Mr. Cobbett may say, and he is a wonderful man, I wadna' care, in my auld days now, to take as much every night; he's a strong stamacket man o' his nature, I reckon, Mr. Cobbett, and doesna ken the wants o' sedentary callings."

"And sair do I wish, Andrew, joe, I could gie ye a dish ilka evening, after toiling at that weary loom for six lang hours frae dinner to supper, upon may-be potatoes and salt."

"And under a good dispensation o' civil government, I ken not, Tibby, what should forbid. I told you how kindly Mr. William bore in mind the hearty Saturday *four-hours* ye wont to give him and the laddies langsyne."

"We durst na bid him to a dish o' tea now; and it's the less matter, as we have it not to offer. Then I had baith a bit sweet butter and loaf sugar for a stranger. But oh! he looks wan, and defaite, poor man; muckle worse than ye let on to me. That extravagant family is breaking his heart. They say, Andrew, his wife and tawpie daughters ne'er entered the kirk door six times in the same gown. They say Dr. Chalmers gledged off the book, and glowered braid at them ae day they rustled in, in their silks and satins."

"Hout lass, ye ken little about it; it's no a woman's gown or fifty o' them — gude kens they're ower cheap — could have played *phew!* on a trade like his. It's the trade itsel, Tibby, that's ruined. The losses in South America, and the crosses in North America, and Botany, and Van Diemen's. Shops fu' o' finished goods rotting in the faulds of the hydraulic press, or roupit abroad for far below the first cost."

"Poor man! I wot nae, Andrew, but auld Geordie Mathewson's trade, though sma', was, when a' comes to a', a surer calling than this high-flying o' Mr. William's: wi' a' their new-fangled tackle, throwing greedy grips to the ends of the earth, and spreading out gauze duds to bring hame midges."

"Partly right, but far mair wrang, Tibby, as the women-folk generally are," said Tibby's apostle. "Mr. William and his neighbours have done good and ill baith to themselves and to huz weavers. But this jabbering about temporalities, is scarce Sabbath-e'ening discourse; so ye'll rinse up your tea-tackle, as Mr. Cobbett ca's it, and let's get in the Books, my woman."

Mr. Mathewson on this Sabbath-night, was also at *his Books*, brought out on the previous day in his gig-box; and as a first draught of the prescribed ease of mind, in his rural abode, he dwelt upon them, comparing the fair and glittering array of figures in the ledger, showing what ought to be the profits of the year, with what he feared they might eventually turn out, till Andrew Howie was awakened after his tea-supper, out of his long refreshing first sleep, by the twittering of the swallows in the eaves of his cottage.

All next day Andrew hung over his loom, full-primed, and at half-cock, prepared for a vigorous discharge of argument and eloquence upon the manufacturer. It was evening before Mr. Mathewson paid his visit; and then he appeared fonder of a fireside chat with Tibby, than political discussion. But ben came Andrew, his Kilmarnock nightcap in one hand, a bunch of well-thumbed pamphlets in the other, consisting of a few select numbers of *Cobbett's Register*, a stray *Carpenter's Political Magazine*, some old *Examiners*, and the last *Trades' Advocate*. Without loss of time or ceremony he opened his broadside.

"Think ye still, sir," said Andrew, following the eye of his visiter round the apartment, which, as contrasted with the memory of former years, showed few tokens of increasing national prosperity; "Think ye still this a better world than that of the last generation? Have we mair meat, mair leisure to make ourselves wiser and better men, fitter for another warld; mair peace of mind, mair comfort at the fireside, and in our families, than the auld folk ye remember here?

"There's more, and merrier of you, any way," said the manufacturer smiling, as a squad of ragged children scoured yelling past the door.

"Granted, sir, and mair work too, — far mair production; and if we could warm ourselves with brass and metal trinkums, and eat crockery ware and our ain saft goods, it would be a brave world this coming up among us: the lady has her two silken gowns, and the lass her three printed ones, *o' Peel's rotten cottons*, as Mr. Cobbett ca's them, for one langsyne; but does that, sir, make up to you and me for our long, weary work hours, our anxious minds, and outlay of siller. — If four gowns, and a dozen needles, or candlesticks, bring huz labourers no more bread than the half o' them did long ago, it will be ill to make me believe our world is the gainer by our reduced wage and lengthened hours. A' thing has thriven among us but the meat and the mense,[3] Mr. William."

"The mouths have thriven pretty well, too, Andrew. Do ye reckon for nothing the immense increase of the manufacturing population? enough of itself to account for the reduction of wages."

"Scarce enough, sir, when we have fifty times more production. But something I own: — the wives had a saying in my young day, 'God never sends the mouth, but He sends the meat with it.' But we must give up that, and adopt the new and unhappily ower true doctrine, that with the numerous mouths come the famine and the pestilence."

"Well, well, Andrew, when the *bill* gets us down the meal and the bread, this will be half-mended — for I fear it will be but half even then. If we could only get these Chinese and Hindoo creatures, to make or grow some useful product, to send us in return for the goods we can furnish them, we could then pay ye, and content ye better."

"I own that, sir, — and Tibby there for one, would be glad to get a reasonable hold of a little more of their tea and sugar, among other good things. 'But ye are not altogether right about the number of mouths producing so great a glut of labour; for, compared with our young days, every single hand-loom hand is now equal to a man and a-fifth."

"A man and a-fifth, what do ye mean by that?"

"Our Andrew has sic droll similitudes," said the admiring Tibby; and Andrew, with a suppressed exulting chuckle, of which vanity he was ashamed in an affair so serious, replied, "The long hours—the long, exhausting, weary hours of toil, make every man's labour now-a-days equal to that of a man and a-fifth of former times. And if frail nature would sustain eighteen hours' work out of the twenty-four, we would soon see such hours; and if the cold form of religion subsisting among us, permitted Sabbath- work, we would have that too, and the poor folks in three months no a bawbee the better for it."

"Operatives are quite as free to restrict their hours of work, as to make their own wages."

"Now, sir, that's no like you," cried Andrew hastily. "Dinna provoke a starving man, by telling him he may eat if he likes, and showing him bread and meat locked-up in an iron cage far beyond his grip. But you masters, I grant, are not without your ain share in the miseries of these times. And for what is't a'? That the lady may have two shawls, and the laird two coats, where their father and mother had but one—that the mistress may have three sets of china tea-tackle, where one served her good mother: this three to be bought with a prodigiously increased quantity of our labour."

"Of my capital, or profits, Andrew?"

"We shall not dispute about words, sir; yours and ours together, and what ought to be your profits. You great folks, the Cotton Lords as Mr. Cobbett ca's ye, are far from free of troubles and anxieties. And what for incurred? Twa or three gold seals with coats o' arms dangling at the gold watch, give unco little comfort, aboon the auld clumsey clicking turnip, if the chief business is to remind the owner that the fatal hour is drawing nigh, and little to meet Johnnie Carrick's[4] peremptor demand." Mr. Mathewson gave a half-smile, which Andrew construed into assent, or perhaps approbation.

"I may be speaking ower long, sir; but looking on this nation as one great family and fellowship, and B, the cotton spinner or weaver, as equally the child of the commonwealth with C, ye observe, the landed man, or *great* farmer,—the question with our rulers, or stewards rather—for the people maun rule themselves,—stewards I say, who fear the Lord, and understand their duty, is this—if what C suffers or sacrifices shall not be met by more than an equivalent, in what B gains—"

But here, when Andrew had almost foundered at any rate, Tibby, with woman's tact perceiving symptoms of weariness in her visiter broke in with, "Sic a man!—bothering Mr. William wi' his B's and C's—when Andrew gets to the B's and C's, he is as wud as ever was Johnnie Waldie, reading the 10th of Nehemiah. Ye mind auld John Waldie, sir? He died only last Michaelmas."

Andrew turned eyes of stern reproof upon his helpmate, who, however, bore his rebuke with great *sang froid*. "It is not for the mere conveniences of life I speak," he said, "but something far mair lasting and precious, lost sight of, made shipwreck of altogether. By-and-by we must alter our Single Book, and make the answer to the question 'What's the chief end of man?' — at least of manufacturing man, to be — To work fourteen or fifteen hours out of the twenty-four, fabricating, half the time, trash worth no rational body's buying; and half-starving while he is about it."

"There is much truth and much error in what you say, Andrew," replied Mr. Mathewson. "But how do you system-mongers, and state-tinkers propose mending your condition — would ye advise a Strike."

"Na, sir; I'm for nae Strike, unless it were better managed than ever I saw a strike yet. If the yearthen vesshel smite itself against the vesshel of iron, where will lie the potsherds? But if you would give up underselling each other, sir. —"

"And I may retort, if ye would give up your under-working, Andrew — and overworking, and long hours, and diminish your numbers."

"I showed you how it could not be, sir, — situate as *we* are; entangled every limb and power o' us, in that weary loom."

"And how do you know that we are not equally entangled — Reckon ye for nought all our mills, machinery, goods, debts; binding us hand and foot as firmly as the necessity of daily supplying the daily meal does you to your loom — character, capital, and credit, are with us all at stake; — ye should be considerate in your judgments of us, Andrew."

"Ay that they should; and that's what I aye tell them," put in Tibby. "It would be wiser like, Andrew Howie, if you, that's a man of knowledge and experience, gave Mr. William a gude advice." Tibby had unlimited faith in the wisdom of her head.

"Then I would caution you masters, sir, how ye build mair mills, and machinery; though we had a spurt of better trade lately."

"And try ye, Andrew, and advise your neighbours to make at least three out of every five of their boys, some other trade than weavers, though brisk times should come."

"We must have down the peck too, sir — and that shortly; but how are we to keep it down if ye go on at tills same rate. Ye may cover all the prairies in America with Paisley shawls, and the plains of India with ginghams and mull muslins, and hang yarns on ilka buss o' the wilderness; but what the better would we be? Cheap bread itself, the blessing we are all craving, will last but for a short time, if we manage no a' the better. If by underselling, and over-producing, we learn the agriculturist, by small degrees, to get six ells for his bushel instead o' three, what the richer, better fed I mean, will us poor operatives be, in the long run? Till we can make the field yield its increase as rapidly as the machine does its products, or limit those products, it makes little odds whether the loaf is nominally a sixpence or a shilling. It will still be aboon our hand."

"Na, Andrew Howie, ye are surely gaen clean daft now!" cried Tibby. "My certes! a sixpence or a shilling for a loaf! There's an unco odds."

Andrew looked from his half-closed eyelids with a sort of pitying contempt of the weaker vessel, which was irresistible to Mr. Mathewson, low as his spirits were. Laughing heartily, he declared that Tibby had the best of it.

Her delight was complete, and Andrew himself was much gratified when, rising, the manufacturer requested his old fosterer to cook for him the well remembered supper of his simple childhood, the only dish he could now fancy for his early rural supper.

"Sowens! sowens!" cried Tibby, with glowing eyes, "eh, sir! and do ye think ye could sup sowens yet! atweel ye'se no want them." Mr. Mathewson believed he was thus undegenerate,—Master Manufacturer, and great Cotton Lord, as he had so long been.

Andrew, putting on his night-cap to ward off the night air, and still carrying his printed documents, convoyed the visiter to the end of the village, adding "line upon line."

"That's Mathewson the great manufacturer," was whispered among the lounging groups in the village street. "He's had great losses lately they say, and is come out here to seek his health.—I'll wager Andrew Howie has been gi'en him a hecklin. I see it in Andrew's eyne."

Nor could Andrew, beset by friends on his return, deny the honourable impeachment.

"It will be twa days, lads, ere Mr. William say again, man and *master* meet on equal terms, at this time, in this country." But we leave Andrew to the glory of fighting his battle over again, till Tibby had three times summoned him to his water-gruel supper.

If any courteous reader shall imagine that in ANDREW HOWIE, he recognises an old acquaintance, we trust that he will like our hero none the worse for such recollection of another honest man.

1   Take the pet at—refuse.— See Jamieson.
2   Thomas Muir, Advocate, one of the Political Martyrs of 1798.
3   Mense,—manners, and something more: mensefu' includes discretion, sod propriety of conduct.
4   A celebrated Glasgow banker.

William McGonagall (1825-1902)

The Death of Lord and Lady Dalhousie (1890)

ALAS! Lord and Lady Dalhousie are dead, and buried at last,
Which causes many people to feel a little downcast;
And both lie side by side in one grave,
But I hope God in His goodness their souls will save.

And may He protect their children that are left behind,
And may they always food and raiment find;
And from the paths of virtue may they ne'er be led,
And may they always find a house wherein to lay their head.

Lord Dalhousie was a man worthy of all praise,
And to his memory I hope a monument the people will raise,
That will stand for many ages to come
To commemorate the good deeds he has done.

He was beloved by men of high and low degree,
Especially in Forfarshire by his tenantry:
And by many of the inhabitants in and around Dundee,
Because he was affable in temper, and void of all vanity.

He had great affection for his children, also his wife,
'Tis said he loved her as dear as his life;
And I trust they are now in heaven above,
Where all is joy, peace, and love.

At the age of fourteen he resolved to go to sea,
So he entered the training ship Britannia belonging the navy,
And entered as a midshipman as he considered most fit
Then passed through the course of training with the greatest credit.

In a short time he obtained the rank of lieutenant,
Then to her Majesty's ship Galatea he was sent;
Which was under the command of the Duke of Edinburgh,
And during his service there he felt but little sorrow.

And from that he was promoted to be commander of the Britannia,
And was well liked by the men, for what he said was law;
And by him Prince Albert Victor and Prince George received a naval education,
Which met with the Prince of Wales' most hearty approbation.

'Twas in the year 1877 he married the Lady Ada Louisa Bennett,
And by marrying that noble lady he ne'er did regret;
And he was ever ready to give his service in any way,
Most willingly and cheerfully by night or by day.

'Twas in the year of 1887, and on Thursday the 1st of December,
Which his relatives and friends will long remember
That were present at the funeral in Cockpen, churchyard,
Because they had for the noble Lord a great regard.

About eleven o'clock the remains reached Dalhousie,
And were met by a body of the tenantry.
They conveyed them inside the building all seemingly woe begone
And among those that sent wreaths was Lord Claude Hamilton.

Those that sent wreaths were but very few,
But one in particular was the Duke of Buccleuch;
Besides Dr. Herbert Spencer, and Countess Rosebery, and Lady Bennett,
Which no doubt were sent by them with heartfelt regret.

Besides those that sent wreaths in addition were the Earl and
    Countess of Aberdeen,
Especially the Prince of Wales' was most lovely to be seen,
And the Earl of Dalkeith's wreath was very pretty too,
With a mixture of green and white flowers, beautiful to view.

Amongst those present at the interment were Mr Marjoribanks, M.P.,
Also ex-Provost Ballingall from Bonnie Dundee;
Besides the Honourable W. G. Colville, representing the Duke and
    Duchess of Edinburgh,
While in every one's face standing at the grave was depicted sorrow.

The funeral service was conducted in the Church of Cockpen
By the Rev. J. Crabb, of St. Andrew's Episcopal Church, town of Brechin;
And as the two coffins were lowered into their last resting place,
Then the people retired with sad hearts at a quick pace.

Attempted Assassination of the Queen (1890)

God prosper long our noble Queen,
    And long may she reign!
Maclean he tried to shoot her,
    But it was all in vain.

For God He turned the ball aside
    Maclean aimed at her head;
And he felt very angry
    Because he didn't shoot her dead.

There's a divinity that hedges a king,
    And so it does seem,

And my opinion is, it has hedged
    Our most gracious Queen.

Maclean must be a madman,
    Which is obvious to be seen,
Or else he wouldn't have tried to shoot
    Our most beloved Queen.

Victoria is a good Queen,
    Which all her subjects know,
And for that God has protected her
    From all her deadly foes.

She is noble and generous,
    Her subjects must confess;
There hasn't been her equal
    Since the days of good Queen Bess.

Long may she be spared to roam
    Among the bonnie Highland floral,
And spend many a happy day
    In the palace of Balmoral.

Because she is very kind
    To the old women there,
And allows them bread, tea, and sugar,
    And each one get a share.

And when they know of her coming,
    Their hearts feel overjoy'd,
Because, in general, she finds work
    For men that's unemploy'd.

And she also gives the gipsies money
    While at Balmoral, I've been told,
And, mind ye, seldom silver,
    But very often gold.

I hope God will protect her
    By night and by day,
At home and abroad,
    When she's far away.

May He be as a hedge around her,
    As he's been all along,
And let her live and die in peace
    Is the end of my song.

William Thom (1799-1848)

Whisperings For The Unwashed (1845)

"Tyrants make not slaves — slaves make tyrants."

SCENE – *A Town in the North.* TIME – *Six o'clock morning.*
Enter TOWN DRUMMER. [1]

RUBADUB, rubadub, row-dow-dow!
The sun is glinting on hill and knowe,
An' saft the pillow to the fat man's pow —
Sae fleecy an' warm the guid *"hame-made,"*
An' cozie the happin o' the farmer's bed.
The feast o' yestreen how it oozes through,
In bell an' blab on his burly brow.
Nought recks he o' drum an' bell,
The girnal's fou an' sure the "sale;"
The laird an' he can crap an keep[2] — "
Weel, weel may he laugh in his gowden sleep.
His dream abounds in stots, or full
Of cow an' corn, calf an' bull;
Of cattle shows, of dinner speaks —
Toom, torn, and patch'd like weavers' breeks;
An' sic like meaning hae, I trow,
As rubadub, rubadub, row-dow-dow.

Rubadub, rubadub, row-dow-dow!
Hark, how he waukens the Weavers now!
Wha lie belair'd in a dreamy steep —
A mental swither 'tween death an' sleep —
Wi' hungry wame and hopeless breast,
Their food no feeding, their sleep no rest.
Arouse ye, ye sunken, unravel your rags.
No coin in your coffers, no meal in your bags;
Yet cart, barge, and waggon, with load after load,
Creak mockfully, passing your breadless abode.
The stately stalk of Ceres bears,
But not for you, the bursting ears;
In vain to you the lark's lov'd note,
For you no summer breezes float,
Grim winter through your hovel pours —
Dull, din, and healthless vapour yours.

The nobler Spider[3] weaves alone,
And feels the little web his *own*,
His hame, his fortress, foul or fair,

Nor factory whipper swaggers there.
Should ruffian wasp, or flaunting fly
Touch his lov'd lair, 'T IS TOUCH AND DIE!
Supreme in rags, ye weave, in tears,
The shining robe your murderer wears;
Till worn, at last, to very "*waste*,'
A hole to die in, at the best;
And, dead, the session saints begrudge ye
The twa-three deals in death to lodge ye;
They grudge the grave wherein to drap ye,
An' grudge the very *muck* to hap ye.
* * * *
Rubadub, rubadub, row-dow-dow!
The drunkard clasps his aching brow;
And there be they, in their squalor laid,
The supperless brood on loathsome bed;
Where the pallid mother croons to rest,
The withering babe at her milkless breast.
She, wakeful, views the risen day
Break gladless o'er her home's decay,
And God's blest light a ghastly glare
Of grey and deathy dimness there.
In all things near, or sight or sounds,
Sepulchral rottenness abounds;
Yet he, the sovereign filth, will prate,
In stilted terms, of Church and State,
As things that *he* would mould anew —
Could all but his brute self subdue.
Ye vilest of the crawling things,
Lo! how well the fetter clings
To recreant collar! Oh, may all
The self-twined lash unbroken fall.
Nor hold until our land is free'd
Of craven, crouching slugs, that breed
In fetid holes, and, day by day,
Yawn their unliving life away!
But die they will not, cannot — why?
They live not — therefore, cannot die.
In soul's dark deadness dead are they,
Entomb'd in thick corkswollen clay.
What tho' they yield their fulsome breath,
The change but mocks the name of death!
Existence, skulking from the sun,
In misery many, in meanness one.
When brave hearts would the fight renew,
Hope, weeping, withering points to you!

Arouse ye, but neither with bludgeon nor blow.

Let *mind* be your armour, *darkness* your foe;
'T is not in the ramping of demagogue rage,
Nor yet in the mountebank patriot's page,
In sounding palaver, nor pageant, I ween,
In blasting of trumpet, nor vile tambourine;
For these are but mockful and treacherous things —
The thorns that "crackle" to sharpen their stings.
When fair Science gleams over city and plain,
When Truth walks abroad all unfetter'd again,
When the breast glows to Love and the brow beams in Light —
Oh! hasten it Heaven! M<small>AN LONGS FOR HIS RIGHT</small>.

1 In most of the small boroughs of the north of Scotland there is a town drummer, who parades at five in the summer and six o'clock in the winter. In Nairn a man blows a cow-horn.
2 Had Heaven intended corn to be the property of *one* class only, corn would grow in *one land* only, and only on one stem. But corn is the child of every soil; its grains and its stems are numberless as the tears of the hungry. The wide spread bounty of God was never willed to be a wide spread sorrow to man.
3 It was at Inverury, after losing seven battles against the English, that Robert Bruce, lying ill in his bed, marked a spider, which was endeavouring to mount to the ceiling, fall down seven times, but on the eighth attempt succeed. The Scotch and English army were just preparing for battle, when Bruce, inspired by this omen, rose, and heading his dispirited troops, after a desperate struggle succeeded in routing the enemy, and laid the foundation of a series of successes against the usurping invader, which secured the glory and independence of the kingdom of Scotland. The welcome he received at Inverury, in his dark hour of distress, induced him to bestow on it the privileges of a royal burgh.
Nor is this the only time that the spider has influenced the destiny of kingdoms. In our own times the careful investigation of their habits in different weather, by a prisoner in his dungeon, afforded the indices upon which Dumourier invaded and overrun Holland in 1797.

Belair'd, *stuck*; Bell an' blab, *sweat drop*; Brood, *family*;
Corkswollen, *beery*; Crap, *crop*; Croons, *groans*;
Deals, *boards for a coffin*; Din, *noise*; Fou, *full*
Girnal, *meal bin*; Glinting, *beaming*; Hae, *have*
Hame-made, *blanket*; Hap, *cover*; Happin, *covering*
Knowe, *knoll*; Laird, *landlord*; Muck, *dirt*
Pow, *head*; Session saints, *elders*; Sovereign filth, *drunkard*
Stots, *young cattle*; Swither, *hesitation*; Toom, *shallow*
Wame, *belly*; Waste, in weavers' language *broken threads*
Yestreen, *last night*.

Janet Hamilton (1795-1873)

Oor Location (1863)

A HUNNER funnels bleezin', reekin',
Coal an' ironstane charrin', smeekin';
Navvies, miners, keepers, fillers,
Puddlers, rollers, iron millers;
Reestit, reekit, raggit laddies,
Firemen, enginemen, an' paddies;
Boatmen, banksmen, rough an' rattlin',
'Bout the wecht wi' colliers battlin',
Sweatin', swearin', fechtin', drinkin';
Change-house bells an' gill-stoups clinkin';
Police—ready men and willin'—
Aye at han' whan stoups are fillin';
Clerks an' counter-loupers plenty,
Wi' trim moustache and whiskers dainty—
Chaps that winna staun at trifles!
Min' ye, they can han'le rifles!
   'Bout the wives in oor location—
An' the lassies' botheration—
Some are decent, some are dandies,
An' a gey wheen drucken randies;
Aye to neebors houses sailin',
Greetin' bairns ahint them trailing',
Gaun for nouther bread nor butter,
Juist to drink an' rin the cutter!
O the dreadfu' curse o' drinkin'!—
Men are ill, but, to my thinkin',
Leukin' through the drucken fock,
There's a Jenny for ilk Jock.
Oh the dool an' desolation,
An' the havock in the nation
Wrocht by dirty, drucken wives!
Oh hoo many bairnies lives
Lost ilk year through their neglec'
Like a millstane roun' the neck
O' the strugglin', toilin' masses
Hing drucken wives an' wanton lassies.
To see sae mony unwed mithers
Is sure a shame that taps a' ithers.
   An' noo I'm fairly set a-gaun;
On baith the whisky-shop and pawn
I'll speak my min'—and what for no?

Frae whence cums misery, want, an' wo,
The ruin, crime, disgrace, an' shame
That quenches a' the lichts o' hame?
Ye needna speer, the feck ot's drawn
Oot o' the change-hoose an' the pawn.
   Sin an' Death, as poets tell,
On ilk side the doors o' hell
Wait to ha'rl mortals in —
Death gets a' that's catcht by sin:
There are doors where Death an' Sin
Draw their tens o' thoosan's in;
Thick an' thrang we see them gaun,
First the dram-shop, then the pawn;
Owre a' kin's o' ruination,
Drink's the King in oor location!

Alexander Smith (1830-1867)

Glasgow (1857)

Sing, Poet, 'tis a merry world;
That cottage smoke is rolled and curled
      In sport, that every moss
Is happy, every inch of soil; —
Before *me* runs a road of toil
      With my grave cut across.
Sing, trailing showers and breezy downs —
      I know the tragic hearts of towns.

City! I am true son of thine;
Ne'er dwelt I where great mornings shine
      Around the bleating pens;
Ne'er by the rivulets I strayed,
And ne'er upon my childhood weighed
      The silence of the glens.
Instead of shores where ocean beats,
I hear the ebb and flow of streets.

Black Labour draws his weary waves,
Into their secret-moaning caves;
      But with the morning light,
That sea again will overflow
With a long weary sound of woe,
      Again to faint in night.
Wave am I in that sea of woes,
Which, night and morning, ebbs and flows.

I dwelt within a gloomy court,
Wherein did never sunbeam sport;
      Yet there my heart was stirr'd —
My very blood did dance and thrill,
When on my narrow window sill,
      Spring lighted like a bird.
Poor flowers — I watched them pine for weeks,
With leaves as pale as human cheeks.

Afar, one summer, I was borne;
Through golden vapours of the morn,
      I heard the hills of sheep:
I trod with a wild ecstasy
The bright fringe of the living sea:
      And on a ruined keep
I sat, and watched an endless plain
Blacken beneath the gloom of rain.

O fair the lightly sprinkled waste,
O'er which a laughing shower has raced !
    O fair the April shoots !
O fair the woods on summer days,
While a blue hyacinthine haze
    Is dreaming round the roots!
In thee, O City ! I discern
Another beauty, sad and stern.

Draw thy fierce streams of blinding ore,
Smite on a thousand anvils, roar
    Down to the harbour-bars;
Smoulder in smoky sunsets, flare
On rainy nights, with street and square
    Lie empty to the stars.
From terrace proud to alley base
I know thee as my mother's face.

When sunset bathes thee in his gold,
In wreaths of bronze thy sides are rolled,
    Thy smoke is dusky fire;
And, from the glory round thee poured,
A sunbeam like an angel's sword
    Shivers upon a spire.
Thus have I watched thee. Terror ! Dream !
    While the blue Night crept up the stream.

The wild Train plunges in the hills,
He shrieks across the midnight rills;
    Streams through the shifting glare,
The roar and flap of foundry fires,
That shake with light the sleeping shires;
    And on the moorlands bare,
He sees afar a crown of light
Hang o'er thee in the hollow night.

At midnight, when thy suburbs lie
As silent as a noonday sky,
    When larks with heat are mute,
I love to linger on thy bridge,
All lonely as a mountain ridge,
    Disturbed but by my foot:
While the black lazy stream beneath,
Steals from its far-off wilds of heath.

And through thy heart, as through a dream,
Flows on that black disdainful stream;
    All scornfully it flows.

Between the huddled gloom of masts,
Silent as pines unvexed by blasts —
    'Tween lamps in streaming rows,
O wondrous sight ! O stream of dread !
    O long dark river of the dead !

Afar, the banner of the year
Unfurls: but dimly prisoned here,
    'Tis only when I greet
A dropt rose lying in my way,
A butterfly that flutters gay
    Athwart the noisy street,
I know the happy Summer smiles
Around thy suburbs, miles on miles.

'T were neither pæan now, nor dirge,
The flash and thunder of the surge
    On flat sands wide and bare;
No haunting joy or anguish dwells
In the green light of sunny dells,
    Or in the starry air.
Alike to me the desert flower,
The rainbow laughing o'er the shower.

While o'er thy walls the darkness sails,
I lean against the churchyard rails;
    Up in the midnight towers
The belfried spire, the street is dead,
I hear in silence over head
    The clang of iron hours:
It moves me not — I know her tomb
Is yonder in the shapeless gloom.

All raptures of this mortal breath,
Solemnities of life and death,
    Dwell in thy noise alone:
Of me thou hast become a part —
Some kindred with my human heart
    Lives in thy streets of stone;
For we have been familiar more
Than galley-slave and weary oar.

The beech is dipped in wine; the shower
Is burnished; on the swinging flower
    The latest bee doth sit.
The low sun stares through dust of gold,
And o'er the darkening heath and wold
    The large ghost-moth doth flit.

In every orchard Autumn stands,
With apples in his golden hands.

But all these sights and sounds are strange;
Then wherefore from thee should I range?
    Thou hast my kith and kin:
My childhood, youth, and manhood brave;
Thou hast that unforgotten grave
    Within thy central din.
A sacredness of love and death
Dwells in thy noise and smoky breath.

Ellen Johnston (1835-1873)

The Last Sark (1859)

Gude guide me, are you hame again, an' ha'e ye got nae wark?
We've naething noo tae put awa' unless yer auld blue sark;
My head is rinnin' roon about far lichter than a flee —
What care some gentry if they're weel though a' the puir wad dee!

Our merchants an' mill masters they wad never want a meal
Though a' the banks in Scotland wad for a twelvemonth fail;
For some o' them have far mair goud than ony ane can see —
What care some gentry if they're weel though a' the puir wad dee!

This is a funny warld, John, for it's no divided fair,
And whiles I think some o' the rich have got the puir folk's share,
Tae see us starving here the nicht wi' no ae bless'd bawbee —
What care some gentry if they're weel though a' the puir wad dee!

Oor hoose ance bean an' cosey, John; oor beds ance snug an warm
Feels unco cauld an' dismal noo, an' empty as a barn;
The weans sit greeting in oor face, and we ha'e noucht to gie —
What care some gentry if they're weel though a' the puir wad dee!

It is the puir man's hard-won toil that fills the rich man's purse;
I'm sure his gouden coffers they are het wi' mony a curse;
Were it no for the working men what wad the rich men be?
What care some gentry if they're weel though a' the puir wad dee!

My head is licht, my heart is weak, my een are growing blin';
The bairn is fa'en aff my knee — oh! John, catch hand o' him,
You ken I hinna tasted meat for days far mair than three;
Were it no for my helpless bairns I wadna care to dee.

David Pae (1828-1884)

from Lucy, The Factory Girl; Or, The Secrets Of The Tontine Close (serialised 1858-59 in *The North Briton*)

CHAPTER I

IN WHICH THE READER MAKES THE ACQUAINTANCE OF TWO PERSONAGES, NOT WARRANTED RESPECTABLE, YET NECESSARY TO BE KNOWN IF OUR STORY IS TO BE WRITTEN AND READ.

On a dim November day, a middle-aged man sat in a room in St. Vincent Street reading letters. Though it was only a little after mid-day, the light which penetrated into the apartment was of a faint, sickly, dubious character, and hardly served to show him the words and sentences of his various correspondents. This darkness and dimness was caused by a dense fog which hung over the city, turning the atmosphere into a dirty yellow hue, and hiding every object a few yards distant. Dismal and dreary it was to look out upon the shrouded streets, and see passengers and vehicles emerge from the haze, and after becoming faintly visible for a moment, plunge into it again, and become lost to view; to see the houses rise up on the opposite side like huge spectres, their chimney-stalks and gables being scarcely discernible, and a dim, oppressive immensity hanging above them.

But the middle aged man in the room in St. Vincent Street was not gazing out at the window upon the fog and the jostling pedestrians—he was busy opening and perusing the batch of letters which the postman had just handed in, and while he so reads, let us take the opportunity to note his appearance.

We have twice remarked that he was middle-aged. By that we mean that he was somewhere between forty and fifty—probably nearer the former than the latter. Judged by the laws of physiognomy, he was anything but prepossessing. A thin, sharp countenance, heavy eyebrows, and, of course, sunken eyes, a small hard-drawn mouth, a tapering chin, and a severe cast of features, gave indication of much that was repulsive. The forehead was not ill-developed; but, from the top of what phrenologists call the intellectual region, it sloped back, and the slope did not redeem itself till it came to the ridge of the crown, at which point the head towered with a marked prominence. There was not a want of brain in that head; but you could see at a glance, without being at all versed in the "bumps," that the development was not in the best direction. The slope of it was such as to tell you intuitively that it indicated a character you could not admire. You could not probably explain why it led you to take up such an opinion; but there is something in every one which impels them to judge of a man by the appearance of his head and face, and the judgments founded on such an index are seldom wrong.

You already don't like this middle-aged man, then? Though he has not spoken or acted, but only sat while we have hastily sketched his portrait, you are convinced that he is not one of the best of men; nay, you are prepared to find him, on a closer acquaintance, heartless, unscrupulous, selfish, cruel, and backed up in these qualities by a firmness which makes him at once determined and relentless? Well, it is a thousand chances to one that you are right; however, we shall not at present go on to describe his positive character, but let that be revealed in part by his own words and actions. We have now introduced him, and shall finish the introduction by telling his name and profession. He was known to his acquaintances as Daniel Dexter, the commission-agent.

Sitting in the dingy room, he opened letter after letter, read their contents, wrote a few words on each, and laid them on one side—doing all with a passionless and unmoved countenance. At length, however, he opened one whose first few lines produced a marked change in his countenance; and, as he proceeded, the expression of interest deepened, quick changes passed over his face, as many strong thoughts rushed to and fro within.

His sunken eyes actually gleamed in the dull light, and his compressed lips twitched, as the vision of his gathering purpose grew more distinct, and emerged from the desirable into the possible, and from the possible into the likely. But we shall get a better understanding of the mood into which he was thrown by reading the letter for ourselves. And here it is:—

"Belfast, Nov. 16, 18—.

"Sir,—I have already informed you of the death of Mr George Livingstone, which event took place some months ago. On opening his will, which was in my possession, I found that his estate of forty thousand pounds is equally divided between his two children—George and Lucy—who are, as you doubtless know, of the respective ages of eight and six years. He directs that the boy, with his share of the property, be sent to the care of an uncle abroad, and that the girl be entrusted to your care to be brought up and educated. The will has now been proved and the estate realised, and if you go, on receipt, to Messrs Wilson and Baird, bankers, Queen Street, you will receive a letter of credit for the amount of Lucy's fortune—twenty thousand pounds—which you will, of course, invest in a way at once sure and advantageous for the benefit of your ward, over whom you will have perfect control until she comes of age, when she will have power to assume the direction of her own affairs, and demand an account of your intromissions. The girl herself will be despatched on Wednesday by steamer, in care of the captain, from whose hands you will receive her when the vessel reaches Glasgow.—I am, Sir,

Your obedient servant,
Patrick O'Kelly.

"Twenty thousand pounds!" mused Mr Dexter. "That sum would enable me to reach the object of my ambition. It would start me comfortably—would lay the foundation of a magnificent fortune! By all that is lucky, my life-dream is to be realised yet! I have waited long and schemed incessantly. All my scheming came to nought; but here, in a moment, and without ever thinking of it, the way is opened for me. Ha! it is glorious!

Twenty thousand pounds! But then the girl? Pshaw! I must get rid of her. It would be dangerous to bring her up: for she might, by some foul chance, get to know about the money and try to wrench it from me. No - no—such a peradventure must be made impossible. But how—how shall I get rid of her? It must be decided on, quickly. She must not even come to the house; for if my wife comes to know anything, it will spoil all. Mary is so horribly troubled with the thing called conscience, that were she to suspect how matters stand with the twenty thousand pounds, I would never have peace in its use. What a plague it is to be concerned with these squeamish, silly people, who are constantly frightened themselves, and who try to frighten others, about justice, generosity, and such like things. Bah! what have we got to do in the world but make the most of it, and by whatever means we can? Priests would tell us about a world after this. Well, perhaps there is; but we have got nothing to do with it yet, and it is soon enough to think of it when we are put into it. It is the present world we have got to live in now, and it is utter folly to he squeamish about making one's self right here, for fear of what is to come in the next. Well, now, let me see. About this girl. How am I to be quit of her? Must I—No, faith, I durst not do that—my theory won't carry me through there. No—I won't—at least not with my own hands. Is there nobody I could employ? I can think of none. Let me see. What age is she? Six years. Pshaw! it surely cannot be difficult to deal with a child so young? She can tell nothing. I can lose her. I can—Oh, I must think of some plan. Meanwhile, I'll to the bank and get the bill placed to my account."

Musing thus diabolically, Dexter folded the paper carefully up, when a thought struck him. "Shall I burn it?" he mentally asked himself. "It is the safer plan, and then all traces will be lost; all, yet stay, it may be necessary to show it to the bankers; I'll keep it till I have seen them, and get the cash entered in my own name."

Having come to this resolution, he put the letter into his pocket, and, locking the door of his office, went out into the fog, to go along to Queen Street.

The moment Mr Baird, the banker, saw Dexter enter, he came out of his private room and approached with an obsequious bow.

"Ha! the remittance has come," thought Dexter to himself.

"Good day, Mr Dexter," said the banker, with one of his blandest smiles. "Hope I see you well, sir. Dreadfully foggy."

"Very thick indeed, Mr Baird; I was afraid I was too late."

"Not at all, sir—not at all. It wants several minutes to our shutting hour; but even though it had been past it, you should have been attended to."

"Thank you. By a letter from Ireland to-day I am advised that a letter of credit for twenty thousand pounds has been forwarded to you."

"Just received it, sir. Beg to congratulate you, Mr Dexter. A wealthy relation deceased, I suppose?"

"Yes! It was rather unexpected though; I confess I had little or no expectation from that quarter. Pray, Mr Baird, will you be good enough to place the sum to my account—my credit, I should say?"

"Surely, sir, surely; and I trust, Mr Dexter, you will continue to favour us with your confidence?"

"Certainly, Mr Baird, such is my intention. Now that I am in a position to do so, I think of attempting to realise a long-cherished ambition of mine — the establishment of a cotton-mill."

"Capital idea, sir; hope the speculation will realise a princely fortune. But it cannot fail, sir — it cannot fail. Planned and guided by a gentleman of your business talents and sound judgment, it will be certain to succeed."

"Why, yes; I flatter myself I could build up such a concern, and by-and-by my son will be old enough to come under training, so that when I get too advanced in life for business, he'll be ready to carry it on — that is what I look to."

"A prospect most soberly and substantially based, sir," rejoined the banker. "Then, Mr Dexter," he immediately added, "may we cancel the letter of credit and make the transference?"

"If you please, Mr Baird."

It was done; and the credit column of Mr Daniel Dexter's account, with Messrs Wilson and Baird, showed an increase of twenty thousand pounds.

The commission agent left the Bank and proceeded eastward to his own residence. On nearing the top of the High Street, it struck him that he had forgot to burn the lawyer's letter.

"I'll do it now," he said, as he looked up and saw a flaming torch suspended over an apple-stall, kept by a lame man.

He crossed over, took the letter from his pocket, and after satisfying himself that it was it and no other, he was about to thrust it forward into the flame, when his eye fell on a wild, haggard figure, standing over against him.

It was a female. A cloak of faded tartan enveloped her body, and a scarlet handkerchief covered her head, and was fastened under the chin, but from beneath the handkerchief strayed a few locks of her coal-black hair, which fell down her cheeks and were cast over her shoulders. Her countenance was at the moment lighted up with a strange angry wildness as she gazed steadfastly at Dexter, with two large eyes as black as her hair, which pierced and flashed with very brilliance. Her face was oval, and had once been beautiful; but now, marks of coarseness, of passion, and reckless boldness, telling of a present and past lawless life, were stamped upon it.

Dexter paused when he saw this weird figure, and encountered her penetrating eyes; and, half starting back, be hastily returned the letter to his bosom and walked on.

When passing by the end of the Cathedral, and within its shadow, a hand was laid on his arm, and a hollow voice uttered his name. He turned round. It was the same figure he had seen in the High Street.

"Daniel Dexter!" she repeated in a tone that unaccountably impressed him.

"What know you of me? or what would you with me?" he asked.

"So, you do not know me? — you have forgotten me?" she said, while a momentary scorn flashed from her face.

"Forgotten you!" he echoed; "I never knew you — never saw you before."

"That is false!" returned the woman. "Once you knew me, and, alas for me, too well. Hast no remembrance of Sarah Gordon?"

"Sarah Gordon!" he repeated, starting violently. "Are you Sarah Gordon?"

"I am," she rejoined. "I am she; who, before she listened to your false promises, was innocent and pure. Now, you see what I have become — what you, by injury and wrong, made me to become."

"It is a long time since we met," he said in a tone of growing coolness.

"It is indeed, she returned. "Not since — since I knew it was vain to trust you longer, or hope anything at your hand — not, Daniel Dexter, since the day you wronged me for ever by marrying Mary Fulton. From the hour when you cast off, cruelly and without a word, her whom you had betrayed, I have never sought you."

"And why seek me now?" he asked coldly.

"I sought you not," she rejoined. "It was by accident I saw you, and I address you now only by an impulse born of that accident. But when I saw, in my degradation and blighted misery, him who had tarnished and trampled me under foot, I could not refrain from accosting him to tell him that I yet lived — lived to curse him, to cherish towards him an implacable hatred! Dost wonder that I have addressed you, Daniel Dexter? Do you not know how fearfully you wronged me, how remorselessly you left me, unarmed and all exposed, to the mercy and charity of a merciless and uncharitable world? Helpless, friendless, you turned from me, and went to the arms of another. It was then I learned how utterly base and selfish was the man I had trusted — the man I had loved."

"Pshaw, Sarah! you know I could not do otherwise. It would have been madness to have married you. I would thereby have lost my worldly position for ever. You don't think I was such a fool as do that?"

"No; you chose rather to be a knave than a fool," rejoined the woman bitterly. "But in looking to what you considered your own interests, you had no thought for me. Having served your base uses, I was turned adrift to beg or steal, or sin with others as I had done with you, or die. I have done the three first, and no doubt I shall die one day. But you, Daniel Dexter, think ye a day of reckoning will never come for you? Are my heavy wrongs not to be visited on your head? Am I to be the only sufferer? Was it I alone who sinned? Think of it, Daniel Dexter — think of it and tremble!"

"Bah I don't attempt to frighten me," said the agent. "I am not one of those silly people who are to be terrified by such words. We must all play the game of life as skilfully as we can, and if others suffer by our moves, that is their misfortune, not our blame. As I have already said, I would have been ruined for life if I had married you."

"Then, why did you betray — why did you wrong me?" asked the woman with a burst of scorn.

"Ah, well," replied the villain carelessly, "I suppose we must place that to the account of — of youth, and passion, and — and that sort of thing. But you wrong me by saying that I never thought of you. I did think of you very often, and wondered what had become of you; and if I have done nothing for you, it was because I could discover no traces of you."

"Did you search?" she asked, bending her piercing eyes upon him incredulously.

"How could I search when I had no clue?" he answered. "But now that we have met, we may be mutually benefited. Our meeting is, indeed, fortunate, for at the present time I want a piece of service done me; you can do it, and I will pay you well for it."

"A service!" she slowly repeated, and gazed as if she would look into his soul and read his heart.

"Ay, a service. Wilt do it? Wilt earn a handsome reward?"

"Name the service," said the other, never taking her eyes from Dexter's face.

"Well, it is a very simple one. Merely to rid me of a child — a girl whose presence will prove troublesome to me. Do you understand?"

"A child! Is it your own?"

And her eyes gleamed with a double flashing light as she put the question.

"No, it is not mine," he replied. "But ask no more questions. All I want you to do is to relieve me of her. Do with her as you will, only make it impossible for her ever to trouble me. Dost consent? I will reward you handsomely."

The woman stood silent for some time, evidently revolving some thoughts in her mind. At length she spoke—

"This matter requires consideration," she said. "Let us, if you will, adjourn to yonder public-house. I know the back entrance to it, and we can get in without being observed. I will there think of your proposal, and tell you if I can agree to it."

"Lead the way, then, for this is not business for the street," he muttered; and she took him across to a low house at the entrance to a lane. The front door was open, and one or two half-clad forms were drinking at the counter; but instead of entering there, she passed towards the end, and dived beneath a doorway which led to the back of the premises. At the end of a dark and narrow passage they came to a closed door, but on the woman giving three peculiar knocks, it was opened by a man with a dark scowling visage, who bestowed a keen glance on Dexter as he passed into the interior, behind his companion.

No sooner were they admitted than the gruff, savage-looking porter closed the heavy door and pushed in the iron bolts. The woman seemed familiar with the locality, for she walked unhesitatingly along the dark passage, and into a room towards the right. The gas was burning low, but a man who glided in behind them put it up, and the apartment was revealed — a small dingy room with a fixed table in the centre, and two or three deal forms standing along the sides of the walls.

"What will yon have, sir?" asked the man, after directing a momentary glance towards the female, and receiving from her a secret sign.

"Ah! well, I don't know; suppose we have a glass of ale the piece, Sarah?" said Dexter.

Sarah nodded, and Dexter in his turn nodded to the waiter, who instantly vanished to execute the order.

The agent sat down at one side of the table, and the woman seated herself at the other, exactly opposite — the flaming gas above shining full on both their features, and showing them plainly to each other.

They sat in silence for some minutes — Sarah gazing with a steadfast intensity into Dexter's face, till the latter grew uneasy under the dark piercing eyes.

"Why are you staring at me so?" he at length asked with a frown.

"I was thinking of the time when last we met," she replied, as a flash leapt out from the penetrating orbs.

"Ah, things have changed much since then. You are so altered, Sarah, that I would not have known you."

"Can you wonder that it is so? Have I not been made to suffer that which takes all gentleness from the heart, and all softness from the countenance? When last you saw me I had fallen no doubt, but still I trusted. I then doubted nothing—suspected nothing. Since then I have learned to doubt all, to suspect everybody, to fight for a place among the rough and the lawless. Is that not enough to change my countenance? For years I have lived in scenes of debauchery, of crime, of—no matter. I was driven to it: you drove me, Daniel, and yet you wonder to find me altered."

"Pshaw! we did not come here to speak of the past, but the present. About that child. Do you consent to take her off my hand?"

"Where is she?"

"I tell you, you must ask no questions. If you agree, meet me at Nelson's Monument to-morrow night at midnight, and receive her from me."

"And what is the sum?"

"Fifty pounds."

"Fifty pounds for bringing up a girl?" said the woman with a sneer.

"Why, if you *do* mean to bring her up she'll not cost you much, and in a year or two she'll be able to earn something. But she *may* be no burden to you at all. There are many chances of her — *dying*! and in that case you have the fifty pounds for -"

"For risking my neck," interrupted the woman fiercely." I see what you are pointing at. You would have me murder the girl."

"Nay, I advise nothing, Sarah. You can do with her as you choose, and I shall ask no questions."

Before the other had time to reply, the man returned with two glasses of ale, one of which he set down before Sarah and the other before Dexter, while another meaning look, altogether unnoticed by the agent, passed between him and the former.

There was evidently an understanding betwixt the two, which Dexter never suspected—never dreamt of.

"Leave us, and be sure that we are not interrupted," said Dexter, pointing to the door.

With a bow the waiter retired.

"Now, Sarah, drink, and say that it is a bargain."

Without speaking, she raised the glass to her lips and drank. The agent did the same. She eagerly watched him as he drained his glass, and when its bottom was nearly parallel with the ceiling, a gleam of triumph danced in her eyes, and a grim smile played round her lips.

"You receive the girl, then?" he said, as he placed his empty glass upon the table.

"Not for the sum you named," she answered.

"What will content ye?"

"The double. Give me a hundred, and I'll do it."

"The sum is a large one," said Dexter after a pause.

"So is the service," rejoined the woman promptly, and with a nod of decision.

"Well, I agree. Do you promise to meet me at the Monument to-morrow night at twelve to receive the girl and the hundred pounds?"

"I do."

"Enough. I shall—shall—sh—. Why, how drowsy I feel."

"So do I—that ale must be strong!"

"It is most unaccountable," said the agent, struggling in vain against the sleep that was coming over him. He made one or two attempts to rise, but failed; stronger and stronger became the potent spell, and in two minutes he lay with his head upon the table in a deep sleep.

The woman, who had appeared indifferent, yet was all the time watching him like a hunter, who has a lion in the toils, no sooner heard him begin to breathe heavily, than she rose hastily from her seat, and passed round to where he sat.

"That letter," she muttered, "I must see that letter. I am certain it will give me some explanation of this business. It was into this pocket he put it."

She thrust her hand into his breast and pulled out the letter he was about to burn on the street: hastily she unfolded it and read. What joy, what triumph, was on her countenance as she made herself mistress of the contents.

"I see it all," she muttered with wild delight. "He wants to get rid of the girl, and take the twenty thousand pounds to himself! Oh, the villain, the dark ruthless villain! But, I'll baulk him! I'll be revenged at last! I have waited long, but the chance has come now, and a glorious chance it is! Now, Daniel Dexter, you shall know what it is to have incurred a woman's revenge!"

She paused a moment, and mused. "Yes!" she exclaimed eagerly; Shuffle shall copy it, and I'll put the copy into Daniel's pocket, and keep the original! Oh, I shall triumph over him some day!"

She flew from the room, closing the door behind her. In the passage she met the man who had brought in the ale.

"Ha! Sall, what's your game to-night?" he hurriedly asked. "Do you want the help of the Swaggerer, or the Captain himself?"

"No, I want nobody! And you must say nothing about this to any of them! Don't go near him! Stay, I'll lock him in, and take the key with me!"

She stept back as she spoke, and locking the room in which Dexter was, extracted the key.

"But what's your game?" persisted the man.

"Never mind, but be you secret; remember, if you blab one word, I shall ruin you—you know my power?"

"Yes, yes—well, I won't!"

"Right. In an hour I shall be back."

She hurried along, and the savage porter let her out by the same door at which they had entered. She glided along from street to street, till she entered one composed of good-looking houses, and paused at an archway leading to a court. On both sides of the archway were painted the names and professions of the occupants, and about the centre, within a deep yellow line, on a Prussian-blue ground, and in very white letters, appeared the words "SHUFFLE & SLEEK, *Writers.*"

She appeared to know the place quite well; for though she paused, it was only to see that no one was observing her. Satisfied on this point, she passed quickly beneath the arch, and up the court, turning into a door to the right. Within the door was a staircase. This she ascended without once looking at the painted hand, with one finger out, which surmounted the words "To Messrs Shuffle & Sleek's chambers."

Upon a door on the second landing the name of this honourable firm appeared again. Through it the woman disappeared and entered a lobby surrounded by other doors leading to apartments whose designation and uses were printed upon them. One only bore no inscription, and this she opened, proceeding along a passage, at the far end of which was another door. Opening it likewise, she glided into the small room to which it led, where sat an elderly man at a desk, writing very busily.

He looked up on hearing the noise made by the opening of the door, and started when he beheld his visiter.

"Ah! Sall, you here at this time?" he said. "What's in the wind to-night? None of them in trouble — none of them caught? Eh?"

"No, no; my business is entirely private. No one knows it, and I want no one to know of it. Here is a letter; I want it copied immediately, and in a hand as similar as you can assume."

"A letter! what is it about?"

"Now, ask nothing; for I'll not tell. Just do as I say, and quickly."

"Oh, well, give it me, and I'll do my best."

He took it, glanced it over, and looked at Sall inquiringly; but she put her finger to her lip, and motioned him to proceed to copy it.

He obeyed; and while he is writing, we shall say, in two or three sentences, what sort of a man he looked like.

He was short and stout, was bald on the crown, though elsewhere a good crop of black hair covered his head. He had a round face, and a most inquisitive eye; was somewhat restless in his motions, and had a curious way of regarding people with a side look. Thus, while he sat copying the letter and seemed to be intently regarding the paper, he was constantly casting furtive glances at Sall, as if trying to read her, and understand from her face what she refused to tell him with her tongue. To read Sall by her face, however, was a feat which even he could not accomplish, and he was forced to confess to himself, when he had done copying the letter, that he was quite baffled.

"Is it done?" she asked, seeing him pause.

"It is."

"Then let me have it. I have not a moment to lose, Have you made a good imitation?"

"Very. You can hardly know it from the original."

"Good!"

She caught up the original and the copy and glided to the door. Before finally making her exit she looked back towards Mr Shuffle, who was sitting looking at her, and, holding up her finger, admonishingly said —"

"Remember, not a word to any one."

"I understand."

The next moment she was gone.

"Very strange," muttered Shuffle. "Curious business; but I must know more about it. Let me see, the vessel from Belfast arrives to-morrow night. I'll be on the watch."

Making this resolve, he returned again to his work.

Meanwhile Sall was on her way back to the public house where she had left Dexter, and entered it a few minutes before the time she said.

The agent had not stirred. Noiselessly she put the key into the lock, pushed open the door, and looked within. Dexter still lay with his head on the table breathing heavily.

She slipped up to him and put the copy of the letter, into the pocket from whence she had abstracted the original. Then lingering till she had bestowed on him a look of mingled scorn, hate and triumph, she retired.

Not long after, he began to stir, stretched his arms, yawned, and opened his eyes.

"Confound it!" he muttered. "What has made me so drowsv? I have almost been asleep. Where is Sall? Gone! Ha! the letter! I hope it is safe?"

He darted his hand into his pocket, and the expression of anxiety vanished when he grasped the paper. He took it out, looked at it with his drowsy eyes, and was satisfied.

"It's all right!" he murmured. "I'll make sure work of it now, however."

And, as he spoke, he put it to the flame of the gas, and held in his hand till it was reduced to ashes.

"There, I am safe now—quite safe," he said with a sigh of satisfaction. "What a lucky day this has been to me. There was Sarah just turned up when I wanted her, and by means of her I shall get rid of the girl. Nothing could be better. How very drowsy I am!"

He rung the bell—the waiter appeared.

"What sort of ale did you give us?" he asked.

"Very good, sir—strong and heady."

"Faith, it is strong enough," said Dexter. "It has put me nearly asleep."

"Perhaps you have not got dinner, sir?" suggested the man.

"No, I have not."

"Ah! that accounts for it. Ale like that on an empty stomach is sure to produce sleep. The lady is gone, sir; she said she could not stay any longer, but will be sure to meet you at the hour and place agreed on."

"That's all right," said Dexter rising; just show me the way out."

"This way, sir."

He led him out by the front, and Mr Daniel Dexter took this way through the fog to his own residence.

Mary MacDonald (1789-1872)

Child in the Manger (trans. 1888 by Lachlan MacBean)

Child in the manger!
Infant of Mary;
Outcast and Stranger,
    Lord of us all!
Child who inherits
All our transgressions,
All our demerits
    On Him fall.

Monarchs have tender
Delicate children,
Nourished in splendour,
    Proud and gay;
Death soon shall banish
Honour and beauty,
Pleasure shall vanish,
    Forms decay.

But the most holy
Child of salvation
Gently and lowly
    Lived below;
Now as our glorious
Mighty Redeemer,
See Him victorious
    O'er each foe.

Prophets foretold Him —
Infant of wonder;
Angels behold Him
    On His throne.
Worthy our Saviour
Of all our praises;
Happy forever
    Are His own.

George MacDonald (1824-1905)

from Adela Cathcart (1864)

THE SCHOOLMASTER'S STORY

Volume 1 Chapter 7 [part]
"BIRTH, DREAMING, AND DEATH."

"In a little room, scantily furnished, lighted, not from the window, for it was dark without, and the shutters were closed, but from the peaked flame of a small, clear-burning lamp, sat a young man, with his back to the lamp and his face to the fire. No book or paper on the table indicated labour just forsaken; nor could one tell from his eyes, in which the light had all retreated inwards, whether his consciousness was absorbed in thought, or reverie only. The window curtains, which scarcely concealed the shutters, were of coarse texture, but of brilliant scarlet—for he loved bright colours; and the faint reflection they threw on his pale, thin face, made it look more delicate than it would have seemed in pure daylight. Two or three bookshelves, suspended by cords from a nail in the wall, contained a collection of books, poverty-stricken as to numbers, with but few to fill up the chronological gap between the Greek New Testament and stray volumes of the poets of the present century. But his love for the souls of his individual books was the stronger that there was no possibility of its degenerating into avarice for the bodies or outsides whose aggregate constitutes the piece of house-furniture called a library.

"Some years before, the young man (my story is so short, and calls in so few personages, that I need not give him a name) had aspired, under the influence of religious and sympathetic feeling, to be a clergyman; but Providence, either in the form of poverty, or of theological difficulty, had prevented his prosecuting his studies to that end. And now he was only a village schoolmaster, nor likely to advance further. I have said *only* a village schoolmaster; but is it not better to be a teacher *of* babes than a preacher *to* men, at any time; not to speak of those troublous times of transition, wherein a difference of degree must so often assume the appearance of a difference of kind? That man is more happy—I will not say more blessed—who, loving boys and girls, is loved and revered by them, than he who, ministering unto men and women, is compelled to pour his words into the filter of religious suspicion, whence the water is allowed to pass away unheeded, and only the residuum is retained for the analysis of ignorant party-spirit.

"He had married a simple village girl, in whose eyes he was nobler than the noblest—to whom he was the mirror, in which the real forms of all things around were reflected. Who dares pity my poor village schoolmaster? I fling his pity away. Had he not found in her love the verdict of God, that he was worth loving? Did he not in her possess the eternal and unchangeable? Were not her eyes openings through which he looked into the great depths that could not be measured or represented? She was his public, his society, his critic. He found in her the heaven of his rest. God gave unto him immortality, and he was glad. For his ambition, it had died of its own mortality. He read the words of Jesus, and the words of great prophets whom he has sent; and learned that the wind-tossed anemone is a word of God as real and true as the unbending oak beneath which it grows — that reality is an absolute existence precluding degrees. If his mind was, as his room, scantily furnished, it was yet lofty; if his light was small, it was brilliant. God lived, and he lived. Perhaps the highest moral height which a man can reach, and at the same time the most difficult of attainment, is the willingness to be *nothing* relatively, so that he attain that positive excellence which the original conditions of his being render not merely possible, but imperative. It is nothing to a man to be greater or less than another — to be esteemed or otherwise by the public or private world in which he moves. Does he, or does he not, behold and love and live the unchangeable, the essential, the divine? This he can only do according as God has made him. He can behold and understand God in the least degree, as well as in the greatest, only by the godlike within him; and he that loves thus the good and great has no room, no thought, no necessity for comparison and difference. The truth satisfies him. He lives in its absoluteness. God makes the glow-worm as well as the star; the light in both is divine. If mine be an earth-star to gladden the wayside, I must cultivate humbly and rejoicingly its green earth-glow, and not seek to blanch it to the whiteness of the stars that lie in the fields of blue. For to deny God in my own being is to cease to behold him in any. God and man can meet only by the man's becoming that which God meant him to be. Then he enters into the house of life, which is greater than the house of fame. It is better to be a child in a green field, than a knight of many orders in a state ceremonial.

"All night long he had sat there, and morning was drawing nigh. He has not heard the busy wind all night, heaping up snow against the house, which will make him start at the ghostly face of the world when at length he opens the shutters, and it stares upon him so white. For up in a little room above, white-curtained, like the great earth without, there has been a storm, too, half the night — moanings and prayers — and some forbidden tears; but now, at length, it is over; and through the portals of two mouths instead of one, flows and ebbs the tide of the great air-sea which feeds the life of man. With the sorrow of the mother, the new life is purchased for the child; our very being is redeemed from nothingness with the pains of a death of which we know nothing.

"An hour has gone by since the watcher below has been delivered from the fear and doubt that held him. He has seen the mother and the child — the first she has given to life and him — and has returned to his lonely room, quiet and glad.

"But not long did he sit thus before thoughts of doubt awoke in his mind. He remembered his scanty income, and the somewhat feeble health of his wife. One or two small debts he had contracted, seemed absolutely to press on his bosom; and the newborn child — 'oh! how doubly welcome,' he thought, 'if I were but half as rich again as I am!' — brought with it, as its own love, so its own care. The dogs of need, that so often hunt us up to heaven, seemed hard upon his heels; and he prayed to God with fervour; and as he prayed he fell asleep in his chair, and as he slept he dreamed. The fire and the lamp burned on as before, but threw no rays into his soul; yet now, for the first time, he seemed to become aware of the storm without; for his dream was as follows: —

"He lay in his bed, and listened to the howling of the wintry wind. He trembled at the thought of the pitiless cold, and turned to sleep again, when he thought he heard a feeble knocking at the door. He rose in haste, and went down with a light. As he opened the door, the wind, entering with a gust of frosty particles, blew out his candle; but he found it unnecessary, for the grey dawn had come. Looking out, he saw nothing at first; but a second look, turned downwards, showed him a little half-frozen child, who looked quietly, but beseechingly, in his face. His hair was filled with drifted snow, and his little hands and cheeks were blue with cold. The heart of the schoolmaster swelled to bursting with the spring-flood of love and pity that rose up within it. He lifted the child to his bosom, and carried him into the house; where, in the dream's incongruity, he found a fire blazing in the room in which he now slept. The child said never a word. He set him by the fire, and made haste to get hot water, and put him in a warm bath. He never doubted that this was a stray orphan who had wandered to him for protection, and he felt that he could not part with him again; even though the train of his previous troubles and doubts once more passed through the mind of the dreamer, and there seemed no answer to his perplexities for the lack of that cheap thing, gold — yea, silver. But when he had undressed and bathed the little orphan, and having dried him on his knees, set him down to reach something warm to wrap him in, the boy suddenly looked up in his face, as if revived, and said with a heavenly smile, 'I am the child Jesus.' 'The child Jesus!' said the dreamer, astonished. 'Thou art like any other child.' 'No, do not say so,' returned the boy; 'but say, *Any other child is like me.*' And the child and the dream slowly faded away; and he awoke with these words sounding in his heart — 'Whosoever shall receive one of such children in my name, receiveth me; and whosoever shall receive me, receiveth not me, but him that sent me.' It was the voice of God saying to him: 'Thou wouldst receive the child whom I sent thee out of the cold, stormy night; receive the new child out of the cold waste into the warm human house, as the door by which it can enter God's house, its home. If better could be done for it, or for thee, would I have sent it hither? Through thy love, my little one must learn my love and be blessed. And thou shall not keep it without thy reward. For thy necessities — in thy little house, is there not yet room? in thy barrel, is there not yet meal? and thy purse is not empty quite. Thou canst not eat more than a mouthful at once. I have made thee so. Is it any trouble to me to take care of thee? Only I prefer to feed thee from my own hand, and not from thy store.' And the schoolmaster sprang up in joy, ran upstairs, kissed his wife, and clasped the baby in his arms in the name of the child Jesus. And in that embrace, he knew that he received God to his heart. Soon, with a tender, beaming face, he was wading through the snow to the school-house, where he spent a happy day amidst the rosy faces and bright eyes of his boys and girls. These, likewise, he loved the more dearly and joyfully for that dream, and those words in his heart; so that, amidst their true child-faces, (all going well with them, as not unfrequently happened in his schoolroom), he felt as if all the elements of Paradise were gathered around him, and knew that he was God's child, doing God's work.

"But while that dream was passing through the soul of the husband, another visited the wife, as she lay in the faintness and trembling joy of the new motherhood. For although she that has been mother before, is not the less a new mother to the new child, her former relation not covering with its wings the fresh bird in the nest of her bosom, yet there must be a peculiar delight in the thoughts and feelings that come with the first-born. — As she lay half in a sleep, half in a faint, with the vapours of a gentle delirium floating through her brain, without losing the sense of existence she lost the consciousness of its form, and thought she lay, not a young mother in her bed, but a nosegay of wild flowers in a basket, crushed, flattened and half-withered. With her in the basket lay other bunches of flowers, whose odours, some rare as well as rich, revealed to her the sad contrast in which she was placed. Beside her lay a cluster of delicately curved, faintly tinged, tea-scented roses; while she was only blue hyacinth bells, pale primroses, amethyst anemones, closed blood-coloured daisies, purple violets, and one sweet-scented, pure white orchis. The basket lay on the counter of a well-known little shop in the village, waiting for purchasers. By and by her own husband entered the shop, and approached the basket to choose a nosegay. 'Ah!' thought she, 'will he choose me? How dreadful if he should not, and I should be left lying here, while he takes another! But how should he choose me? They are all so beautiful; and even my scent is nearly gone. And he cannot know that it is I lying here. Alas! alas!' But as she thought thus, she felt his hand clasp her, heard the ransom-money fall, and felt that she was pressed to his face and lips, as he passed from the shop. He *had* chosen her; he *had* known her. She opened her eyes: her husband's kiss had awakened her. She did not speak, but looked up thankfully in his eyes, as if he had, in fact, like one of the old knights, delivered her from the transformation of some evil magic, by the counter-enchantment of a kiss, and restored her from a half-withered nosegay to be a woman, a wife, a mother. The dream comforted her much, for she had often feared that she, the simple, so-called uneducated girl, could not be enough for the great schoolmaster. But soon her thoughts flowed into another channel; the tears rose in her dark eyes, shining clear from beneath a stream that was not of sorrow; and it was only weakness that kept her from uttering audible words like these: — 'Father in heaven, shall I trust my husband's love, and doubt thine? Wilt thou meet less richly the fearing hope of thy child's heart, than he in my dream met the longing of his wife's? He was perfected in my eyes by the love he bore me — shall I find thee less complete? Here I lie on thy world, faint, and crushed, and withered; and my soul often seems as if it had lost all the odours that should float up in the sweet-smelling savour of thankfulness and love to thee. But thou hast only to take me, only to choose me, only to clasp me to thy bosom, and I shall be a beautiful singing angel, singing to God, and comforting my husband while I sing. Father, take me, possess me, fill me!'

"So she lay patiently waiting for the summer-time of restored strength that drew slowly nigh. With her husband and her child near her, in her soul, and God everywhere, there was for her no death, and no hurt. When she said to herself, 'How rich I am!' it was with the riches that pass not away — the riches of the Son of man; for in her treasures, the human and the divine were blended — were one.

"But there was a hard trial in store for them. They had learned to receive what the Father sent: they had now to learn that what he gave he gave eternally, after his own being — his own glory. For ere the mother awoke from her first sleep, the baby, like a frolicsome child-angel, that but tapped at his mother's window and fled — the baby died; died while the mother slept away the pangs of its birth, died while the father was teaching other babes out of the joy of his new fatherhood.

"When the mother woke, she lay still in her joy — the joy of a doubled life; and knew not that death had been there, and had left behind only the little human coffin.

"'Nurse, bring me the baby,' she said at last. 'I want to see it.'

"But the nurse pretended not to hear.

"'I want to nurse it. Bring it.'

"She had not yet learned to say *him*; for it was her first baby.

"But the nurse went out of the room, and remained some minutes away. When she returned, the mother spoke more absolutely, and the nurse was compelled to reply — at last.

"'Nurse, do bring me the baby; I am quite able to nurse it now.'

"'Not yet, if you please, ma'am. Really you must rest a while first. Do try to go to sleep.'

"The nurse spoke steadily, and looked her too straight in the face; and there was a constraint in her voice, a determination to be calm, that at once roused the suspicion of the mother; for though her first-born was dead, and she had given birth to what was now, as far as the eye could reach, the waxen image of a son, a child had come from God, and had departed to him again; and she was his mother.

"And the fear fell upon her heart that it might be as it was; and, looking at her attendant with a face blanched yet more with fear than with suffering, she said,

"'Nurse, is the baby — ?'

"She could not say *dead*; for to utter the word would be at once to make it possible that the only fruit of her labour had been pain and sorrow.

"But the nurse saw that further concealment was impossible; and, without another word, went and fetched the husband, who, with face pale as the mother's, brought the baby, dressed in its white clothes, and laid it by its mother's side, where it lay too still.

"'Oh, ma'am, do not take on so,' said the nurse, as she saw the face of the mother grow like the face of the child, as if she were about to rush after him into the dark.

"But she was not 'taking on' at all. She only felt that pain at her heart, which is the farewell kiss of a long-cherished joy. Though cast out of paradise into a world that looked very dull and weary, yet, used to suffering, and always claiming from God the consolation it needed, and satisfied with that, she was able, presently, to look up in her husband's face, and try to reassure him of her well-being by a dreary smile.

"'Leave the baby,' she said; and they left it where it was. Long and earnestly she gazed on the perfect tiny features of the little alabaster countenance, and tried to feel that this was the child she had been so long waiting for. As she looked, she fancied she heard it breathe, and she thought—'What if it should be only asleep!' but, alas! the eyes would not open, and when she drew it close to her, she shivered to feel it so cold. At length, as her eyes wandered over and over the little face, a look of her husband dawned unexpectedly upon it; and, as if the wife's heart awoke the mother's she cried out, 'Baby! baby!' and burst into tears, during which weeping she fell asleep.

"When she awoke, she found the babe had been removed while she slept. But the unsatisfied heart of the mother longed to look again on the form of the child; and again, though with remonstrance from the nurse, it was laid beside her. All day and all night long, it remained by her side, like a little frozen thing that had wandered from its home, and now lay dead by the door.

"Next morning the nurse protested that she must part with it, for it made her fret; but she knew it quieted her, and she would rather keep her little lifeless babe. At length the nurse appealed to the father; and the mother feared he would think it necessary to remove it; but to her joy and gratitude he said, 'No, no; let her keep it as long as she likes.' And she loved her husband the more for that; for he understood her.

"Then she had the cradle brought near the bed, all ready as it was for a live child that had open eyes, and therefore needed sleep—needed the lids of the brain to close, when it was filled full of the strange colours and forms of the new world. But this one needed no cradle, for it slept on. It needed, instead of the little curtains to darken it to sleep, a great sunlight to wake it up from the darkness, and the ever-satisfied rest. Yet she laid it in the cradle, which she had set near her, where she could see it, with the little hand and arm laid out on the white coverlet. If she could only keep it so! Could not something be done, if not to awake it, yet to turn it to stone, and let it remain so for ever? No; the body must go back to its mother, the earth, and the *form* which is immortal, being the thought of God, must go back to its Father—the Maker. And as it lay in the white cradle, a white coffin was being made for it. And the mother thought: 'I wonder which trees are growing coffins for my husband and me.'

"But ere the child, that had the prayer of Job in his grief, and had died from its mother's womb, was carried away to be buried, the mother prayed over it this prayer:—'O God, if thou wilt not let me be a mother, I have one refuge: I will go back and be a child: I will be thy child more than ever. My mother-heart will find relief in childhood towards its Father. For is it not the same nature that makes the true mother and the true child? Is it not the same thought blossoming upward and blossoming downward? So there is God the Father and God the Son. Thou wilt keep my little son for me. He has gone home to be nursed for me. And when I grow well, I will be more simple, and truthful, and joyful in thy sight. And now thou art taking away my child, my plaything, from me. But I think how pleased I should be, if I had a daughter, and she loved me so well that she only smiled when I took her plaything from her. Oh! I will not disappoint thee—thou shall have thy joy. Here I am, do with me what thou wilt; I will only smile.'

"And how fared the heart of the father? At first, in the bitterness of his grief, he called the loss of his child a punishment for his doubt and unbelief; and the feeling of punishment made the stroke more keen, and the heart less willing to endure it. But better thoughts woke within him ere long.

"The old woman who swept out his schoolroom, came in the evening to inquire after the mistress, and to offer her condolences on the loss of the baby. She came likewise to tell the news, that a certain old man of little respectability had departed at last, unregretted by a single soul in the village but herself, who had been his nurse through the last tedious illness.

"The schoolmaster thought with himself:

"'Can that soiled and withered leaf of a man, and my little snow-flake of a baby, have gone the same road? Will they meet by the way? Can they talk about the same thing—anything? They must part on the borders of the shining land, and they could hardly speak by the way.'

"'He will live four-and-twenty hours, nurse,' the doctor had said.

"'No, doctor; he will die to-night,' the nurse had replied; during which whispered dialogue, the patient had lain breathing quietly, for the last of suffering was nearly over.

He was at the close of an ill-spent life, not so much selfishly towards others as indulgently towards himself. He had failed of true joy by trying often and perseveringly to create a false one; and now, about to knock at the gate of the other world, he bore with him no burden of the good things of this; and one might be tempted to say of him, that it were better he had not been born. The great majestic mystery lay before him—but when would he see its majesty?

"He was dying thus, because he had tried to live as Nature said he should not live; and he had taken his own wages—for the law of the Maker is the necessity of his creature. His own children had forsaken him, for they were not perfect as their Father in heaven, who maketh his sun to shine on the evil and on the good. Instead of doubling their care as his need doubled, they had thought of the disgrace he brought on them, and not of the duty they owed him; and now, left to die alone for them, he was waited on by this hired nurse, who, familiar with death-beds, knew better than the doctor—knew that he could live only a few hours.

"Stooping to his ear, she had told him, as gently as she could—for she thought she ought not to conceal it—that he must die that night. He had lain silent for a few moments; then had called her, and, with broken and failing voice, had said, 'Nurse, you are the only friend I have: give me one kiss before I die.' And the woman-heart had answered the prayer.

"'And,' said the old woman, 'he put his arms round my neck, and gave me a long kiss, such a long kiss! and then he turned his face away, and never spoke again.'

"So, with the last unction of a woman's kiss, with this baptism for the dead, he had departed.

"'Poor old man! he had not quite destroyed his heart yet,' thought the schoolmaster. 'Surely it was the child-nature that woke in him at the last, when the only thing left for his soul to desire, the only thing he could think of as a preparation for the dread something, was a kiss. Strange conjunction, yet simple and natural! Eternity—a kiss. Kiss me; for I am going to the Unknown!—Poor old man!' the schoolmaster went on in his thoughts, 'I hope my baby has met him, and put his tiny hand in the poor old shaking hand, and so led him across the borders into the shining land, and up to where Jesus sits, and said to the Lord: "Lord, forgive this old man, for he knew not what he did." And I trust the Lord has forgiven him.'

"And then the bereaved father fell on his knees, and cried out:

"'Lord, thou hast not punished me. Thou wouldst not punish for a passing thought of troubled unbelief, with which I strove. Lord, take my child and his mother and me, and do what thou wilt with us. I know thou givest not, to take again.'

"And ere the schoolmaster could call his protestantism to his aid, he had ended his prayer with the cry:

"'And O God! have mercy upon the poor old man, and lay not his sins to his charge.'

"For, though a woman's kiss may comfort a man to eternity, it is not all he needs. And the thought of his lost child had made the soul of the father compassionate."

He ceased, and we sat silent.

James Thomson "B.V." (1834-1882)

from The City of Dreadful Night (1874)

"Per me si va nella citta dolente."

— *Dante*

"Poi di tanto adoprar, di tanti moti
D'ogni celeste, ogni terrena cosa,
Girando senza posa,
Per tornar sempre la donde son mosse;
Uso alcuno, alcun frutto
Indovinar non so."

"Sola nel mondo eterna, a cui si volve
Ogni creata cosa,
In te, morte, si posa
Nostra ignuda natura;
Lieta no, ma sicura
Dell' antico dolor . . .
Pero ch' esser beato
Nega ai mortali e nega a' morti il fato."

— *Leopardi*

PROEM

Lo, thus, as prostrate, "In the dust I write
    My heart's deep languor and my soul's sad tears."
Yet why evoke the spectres of black night
    To blot the sunshine of exultant years?
Why disinter dead faith from mouldering hidden?
Why break the seals of mute despair unbidden,
    And wail life's discords into careless ears?

Because a cold rage seizes one at whiles
    To show the bitter old and wrinkled truth
Stripped naked of all vesture that beguiles,
    False dreams, false hopes, false masks and modes of youth;
Because it gives some sense of power and passion
In helpless innocence to try to fashion
    Our woe in living words howe'er uncouth.

Surely I write not for the hopeful young,
    Or those who deem their happiness of worth,
Or such as pasture and grow fat among
    The shows of life and feel nor doubt nor dearth,
Or pious spirits with a God above them
To sanctify and glorify and love them,
    Or sages who foresee a heaven on earth.

For none of these I write, and none of these
        Could read the writing if they deigned to try;
So may they flourish in their due degrees,
        On our sweet earth and in their unplaced sky.
If any cares for the weak words here written,
It must be some one desolate, Fate-smitten,
        Whose faith and hopes are dead, and who would die.

Yes, here and there some weary wanderer
        In that same city of tremendous night,
Will understand the speech and feel a stir
        Of fellowship in all-disastrous fight;
"I suffer mute and lonely, yet another
Uplifts his voice to let me know a brother
        Travels the same wild paths though out of sight."

O sad Fraternity, do I unfold
        Your dolorous mysteries shrouded from of yore?
Nay, be assured; no secret can be told
        To any who divined it not before:
None uninitiate by many a presage
Will comprehend the language of the message,
        Although proclaimed aloud for evermore.

I

The City is of Night; perchance of Death
        But certainly of Night; for never there
Can come the lucid morning's fragrant breath
        After the dewy dawning's cold grey air:
The moon and stars may shine with scorn or pity
The sun has never visited that city,
        For it dissolveth in the daylight fair.

Dissolveth like a dream of night away;
        Though present in distempered gloom of thought
And deadly weariness of heart all day.
        But when a dream night after night is brought
Throughout a week, and such weeks few or many
Recur each year for several years, can any
        Discern that dream from real life in aught?

For life is but a dream whose shapes return,
        Some frequently, some seldom, some by night
And some by day, some night and day: we learn,
        The while all change and many vanish quite,
In their recurrence with recurrent changes
A certain seeming order; where this ranges
        We count things real; such is memory's might.

A river girds the city west and south,
    The main north channel of a broad lagoon,
Regurging with the salt tides from the mouth;
    Waste marshes shine and glister to the moon
For leagues, then moorland black, then stony ridges;
Great piers and causeways, many noble bridges,
    Connect the town and islet suburbs strewn.

Upon an easy slope it lies at large
    And scarcely overlaps the long curved crest
Which swells out two leagues from the river marge.
    A trackless wilderness rolls north and west,
Savannahs, savage woods, enormous mountains,
Bleak uplands, black ravines with torrent fountains;
    And eastward rolls the shipless sea's unrest.

The city is not ruinous, although
    Great ruins of an unremembered past,
With others of a few short years ago
    More sad, are found within its precincts vast.
The street-lamps always burn; but scarce a casement
In house or palace front from roof to basement
    Doth glow or gleam athwart the mirk air cast.

The street-lamps burn amid the baleful glooms,
    Amidst the soundless solitudes immense
Of ranged mansions dark and still as tombs.
    The silence which benumbs or strains the sense
Fulfils with awe the soul's despair unweeping:
Myriads of habitants are ever sleeping,
    Or dead, or fled from nameless pestilence!

Yet as in some necropolis you find
    Perchance one mourner to a thousand dead,
So there: worn faces that look deaf and blind
    Like tragic masks of stone. With weary tread,
Each wrapt in his own doom, they wander, wander,
Or sit foredone and desolately ponder
    Through sleepless hours with heavy drooping head.

Mature men chiefly, few in age or youth,
    A woman rarely, now and then a child:
A child! If here the heart turns sick with ruth
    To see a little one from birth defiled,
Or lame or blind, as preordained to languish
Through youthless life, think how it bleeds with anguish
    To meet one erring in that homeless wild.

They often murmur to themselves, they speak
    To one another seldom, for their woe
Broods maddening inwardly and scorns to wreak
    Itself abroad; and if at whiles it grow
To frenzy which must rave, none heeds the clamour,
Unless there waits some victim of like glamour,
    To rave in turn, who lends attentive show.

The City is of Night, but not of Sleep;
    There sweet sleep is not for the weary brain;
The pitiless hours like years and ages creep,
    A night seems termless hell. This dreadful strain
Of thought and consciousness which never ceases,
Or which some moments' stupor but increases,
    This, worse than woe, makes wretches there insane.

They leave all hope behind who enter there:
    One certitude while sane they cannot leave,
One anodyne for torture and despair;
    The certitude of Death, which no reprieve
Can put off long; and which, divinely tender,
But waits the outstretched hand to promptly render
    That draught whose slumber nothing can bereave. [1]

1 Though the Garden of thy Life be wholly waste, the sweet flowers withered, the fruit-trees barren, over its wall hang ever the rich dark clusters of the Vine of Death, within easy reach of thy hand, which may pluck of them when it will.

[II and III omitted]

IV

He stood alone within the spacious square
    Declaiming from the central grassy mound,
With head uncovered and with streaming hair,
    As if large multitudes were gathered round:
A stalwart shape, the gestures full of might,
The glances burning with unnatural light: —

As I came through the desert thus it was,
As I came through the desert: All was black,
In heaven no single star, on earth no track;
A brooding hush without a stir or note,
The air so thick it clotted in my throat;
And thus for hours; then some enormous things
Swooped past with savage cries and clanking wings:
    But I strode on austere;
    No hope could have no fear.

As I came through the desert thus it was,
As I came through the desert: Eyes of fire
Glared at me throbbing with a starved desire;
The hoarse and heavy and carnivorous breath
Was hot upon me from deep jaws of death;
Sharp claws, swift talons, fleshless fingers cold
Plucked at me from the bushes, tried to hold:
        But I strode on austere;
        No hope could have no fear.

As I came through the desert thus it was,
As I came through the desert: Lo you, there,
That hillock burning with a brazen glare;
Those myriad dusky flames with points a-glow
Which writhed and hissed and darted to and fro;
A Sabbath of the Serpents, heaped pell-mell
For Devil's roll-call and some *fête* of Hell:
        Yet I strode on austere;
        No hope could have no fear.

As I came through the desert thus it was,
As I came through the desert: Meteors ran
And crossed their javelins on the black sky-span;
The zenith opened to a gulf of flame,
The dreadful thunderbolts jarred earth's fixed frame;
The ground all heaved in waves of fire that surged
And weltered round me sole there unsubmerged:
        Yet I strode on austere;
        No hope could have no fear.

As I came through the desert thus it was,
As I came through the desert: Air once more,
And I was close upon a wild sea-shore;
Enormous cliffs arose on either hand,
The deep tide thundered up a league-broad strand;
White foambelts seethed there, wan spray swept and flew;
The sky broke, moon and stars and clouds and blue:
        And I strode on austere;
        No hope could have no fear.

As I came through the desert thus it was,
As I came through the desert: On the left
The sun arose and crowned a broad crag-cleft;
There stopped and burned out black, except a rim,
A bleeding eyeless socket, red and dim;
Whereon the moon fell suddenly south-west,
And stood above the right-hand cliffs at rest:
        Still I strode on austere;
        No hope could have no fear.

As I came through the desert thus it was,
As I came through the desert: From the right
A shape came slowly with a ruddy light;
A woman with a red lamp in her hand,
Bareheaded and barefooted on that strand;
O desolation moving with such grace!
O anguish with such beauty in thy face!
        I fell as on my bier,
        Hope travailed with such fear.

As I came through the desert thus it was,
As I came through the desert: I was twain,
Two selves distinct that cannot join again;
One stood apart and knew but could not stir,
And watched the other stark in swoon and her;
And she came on, and never turned aside,
Between such sun and moon and roaring tide:
        And as she came more near
        My soul grew mad with fear.

As I came through the desert thus it was,
As I came through the desert: Hell is mild
And piteous matched with that accursed wild;
A large black sign was on her breast that bowed,
A broad black band ran down her snow-white shroud;
That lamp she held was her own burning heart,
Whose blood-drops trickled step by step apart:
        The mystery was clear;
        Mad rage had swallowed fear.

As I came through the desert thus it was,
As I came through the desert: By the sea
She knelt and bent above that senseless me;
Those lamp-drops fell upon my white brow there,
She tried to cleanse them with her tears and hair;
She murmured words of pity, love, and woe,
She heeded not the level rushing flow:
        And mad with rage and fear,
        I stood stonebound so near.

As I came through the desert thus it was,
As I came through the desert: When the tide
Swept up to her there kneeling by my side,
She clasped that corpse-like me, and they were borne
Away, and this vile me was left forlorn;
I know the whole sea cannot quench that heart,
Or cleanse that brow, or wash those two apart:
        They love; their doom is drear,
        Yet they nor hope nor fear;
        But I, what do I here?

[V to XIX omitted]

XX

I sat me weary on a pillar's base,
  And leaned against the shaft; for broad moonlight
O'erflowed the peacefulness of cloistered space,
  A shore of shadow slanting from the right:
The great cathedral's western front stood there,
A wave-worn rock in that calm sea of air.

Before it, opposite my place of rest,
  Two figures faced each other, large, austere;
A couchant sphinx in shadow to the breast,
  An angel standing in the moonlight clear;
So mighty by magnificence of form,
They were not dwarfed beneath that mass enorm.

Upon the cross-hilt of the naked sword
  The angel's hands, as prompt to smite, were held;
His vigilant intense regard was poured
  Upon the creature placidly unquelled,
Whose front was set at level gaze which took
No heed of aught, a solemn trance-like look.

And as I pondered these opposed shapes
  My eyelids sank in stupor, that dull swoon
Which drugs and with a leaden mantle drapes
  The outworn to worse weariness. But soon
A sharp and clashing noise the stillness broke,
And from the evil lethargy I woke.

The angel's wings had fallen, stone on stone,
  And lay there shattered; hence the sudden sound:
A warrior leaning on his sword alone
  Now watched the sphinx with that regard profound;
The sphinx unchanged looked forthright, as aware
Of nothing in the vast abyss of air.

Again I sank in that repose unsweet,
  Again a clashing noise my slumber rent;
The warrior's sword lay broken at his feet:
  An unarmed man with raised hands impotent
Now stood before the sphinx, which ever kept
Such mien as if open eyes it slept.

My eyelids sank in spite of wonder grown;
  A louder crash upstartled me in dread:
The man had fallen forward, stone on stone,
  And lay there shattered, with his trunkless head
Between the monster's large quiescent paws,
Beneath its grand front changeless as life's laws.

The moon had circled westward full and bright,
  And made the temple-front a mystic dream,
And bathed the whole enclosure with its light,
  The sworded angel's wrecks, the sphinx supreme:
I pondered long that cold majestic face
Whose vision seemed of infinite void space.

XXI

Anear the centre of that northern crest
  Stands out a level upland bleak and bare,
From which the city east and south and west
  Sinks gently in long waves; and throned there
An Image sits, stupendous, superhuman,
The bronze colossus of a winged Woman,
  Upon a graded granite base foursquare.

Low-seated she leans forward massively,
  With cheek on clenched left hand, the forearm's might
Erect, its elbow on her rounded knee;
  Across a clasped book in her lap the right
Upholds a pair of compasses; she gazes
With full set eyes, but wandering in thick mazes
  Of sombre thought beholds no outward sight.

Words cannot picture her; but all men know
  That solemn sketch the pure sad artist wrought
Three centuries and threescore years ago,
  With phantasies of his peculiar thought:
The instruments of carpentry and science
Scattered about her feet, in strange alliance
  With the keen wolf-hound sleeping undistraught;

Scales, hour-glass, bell, and magic-square above;
  The grave and solid infant perched beside,
With open winglets that might bear a dove,
  Intent upon its tablets, heavy-eyed;
Her folded wings as of a mighty eagle,
But all too impotent to lift the regal
  Robustness of her earth-born strength and pride;

And with those wings, and that light wreath which seems
   To mock her grand head and the knotted frown
Of forehead charged with baleful thoughts and dreams,
   The household bunch of keys, the housewife's gown
Voluminous, indented, and yet rigid
As if a shell of burnished metal frigid,
   The feet thick-shod to tread all weakness down;

The comet hanging o'er the waste dark seas,
   The massy rainbow curved in front of it
Beyond the village with the masts and trees;
   The snaky imp, dog-headed, from the Pit,
Bearing upon its batlike leathern pinions
Her name unfolded in the sun's dominions,
   The "MELENCOLIA" that transcends all wit.

Thus has the artist copied her, and thus
   Surrounded to expound her form sublime,
Her fate heroic and calamitous;
   Fronting the dreadful mysteries of Time,
Unvanquished in defeat and desolation,
Undaunted in the hopeless conflagration
   Of the day setting on her baffled prime.

Baffled and beaten back she works on still,
   Weary and sick of soul she works the more,
Sustained by her indomitable will:
   The hands shall fashion and the brain shall pore,
And all her sorrow shall be turned to labour,
Till Death the friend-foe piercing with his sabre
   That mighty heart of hearts ends bitter war.

But as if blacker night could dawn on night,
   With tenfold gloom on moonless night unstarred,
A sense more tragic than defeat and blight,
   More desperate than strife with hope debarred,
More fatal than the adamantine Never
Encompassing her passionate endeavour,
   Dawns glooming in her tenebrous regard:

To sense that every struggle brings defeat
   Because Fate holds no prize to crown success;
That all the oracles are dumb or cheat
   Because they have no secret to express;
That none can pierce the vast black veil uncertain
Because there is no light beyond the curtain;
   That all is vanity and nothingness.

Titanic from her high throne in the north,
　That City's sombre Patroness and Queen,
In bronze sublimity she gazes forth
　Over her Capital of teen and threne,
Over the river with its isles and bridges,
The marsh and moorland, to the stern rock-bridges,
　Confronting them with a coeval mien.

The moving moon and stars from east to west
　Circle before her in the sea of air;
Shadows and gleams glide round her solemn rest.
　Her subjects often gaze up to her there:
The strong to drink new strength of iron endurance,
The weak new terrors; all, renewed assurance
　And confirmation of the old despair.

Andrew Lang (1844-1912)

The House of Strange Stories (1886)

The House of Strange Stories, as I prefer to call it (though it is not known by that name in the county), seems the very place for a ghost. Yet, though so many peoples have dwelt upon its site and in its chambers, though the ancient Elizabethan oak, and all the queer tables and chairs that a dozen generations have bequeathed, might well be tenanted by ancestral spirits, and disturbed by rappings, it is a curious fact that there is *not* a ghost in the House of Strange Stories. On my earliest visit to this mansion, I was disturbed, I own, by a not unpleasing expectancy. There *must*, one argued, be a shadowy lady in green in the bedroom, or, just as one was falling asleep, the spectre of a Jesuit would creep out of the priest's hole, where he was starved to death in the "spacious times of great Elizabeth," and would search for a morsel of bread. The priest was usually starved out, sentinels being placed in all the rooms and passages, till at last hunger and want of air would drive the wretched man to give himself up, for the sake of change of wretchedness. Then perhaps he was hanged, or he "died in our hands," as one of Elizabeth's officers euphemistically put it, when the Jesuit was tortured to death in the Tower. No "House of Seven Gables" across the Atlantic can have quite such memories as these, yet, oddly enough, I do not know of more than one ghost of a Jesuit in all England. *He* appeared to a learned doctor in a library, and the learned doctor described the phantom, not long ago, in the *Athenaeum*.

"Does the priest of your 'priest-hole' walk?" I asked the squire one winter evening in the House of Strange Stories.

Darkness had come to the rescue of the pheasants about four in the afternoon, and all of us, men and women, were sitting at afternoon tea in the firelit study, drowsily watching the flicker of the flame on the black panelling. The characters will introduce themselves, as they take part in the conversation.

"No," said the squire, "even the priest does not walk. Somehow very few of the Jesuits have left ghosts in country houses. They are just the customers you would expect to 'walk,' but they don't."

There is, to be sure, one priestly ghost-story, which you may or may not know, and I tell it here, though I don't believe it, just as I heard it from the Bishop of Dunchester himself. According to this most affable and distinguished prelate, now no more, he once arrived in a large country house shortly before dinner-time; he was led to his chamber, he dressed, and went downstairs. Not knowing the plan of the house, he found his way into the library, a chamber lined with the books of many studious generations. Here the learned bishop remained for a few minutes, when the gong sounded for dinner, and a domestic, entering the apartment showed the prelate the way to the drawing-room, where the other guests were now assembled. The bishop, when the company appeared complete, and was beginning to manoeuvre towards the dining-room, addressed his host (whom we shall call Lord Birkenhead), and observed that the ecclesiastic had not yet appeared.

"What ecclesiastic?" asked his lordship.

"The priest," replied the bishop, "whom I met in the library."

Upon this Lord Birkenhead's countenance changed somewhat, and, with a casual remark, he put the question by. After dinner, when the ladies had left the men to their wine, Lord Birkenhead showed some curiosity as to "the ecclesiastic," and learned that he had seemed somewhat shy and stiff, yet had the air of a man just about to enter into conversation.

"At that moment," said the bishop, "I was summoned to the drawing-room, and did not at first notice that my friend the priest had not followed me. He had an interesting and careworn face," added the bishop.

"You have certainly seen the family ghost," said Lord Birkenhead; "he only haunts the library, where, as you may imagine, his retirement is but seldom disturbed." And, indeed, the habits of the great, in England, are not studious, as a rule. "Then I must return, Lord Birkenhead, to your library," said the bishop, "and that without delay, for this appears to be a matter in which the services of one of the higher clergy, however unworthy, may prove of incalculable benefit."

"If I could only hope," answered Lord Birkenhead (who was a Catholic) with a deep sigh, "that his reverence would recognize Anglican orders!"

The bishop was now, as may be fancied, on his mettle, and without further parley, retired to the library. The rest of the men awaited his return, and beguiled the moments of expectation with princely havannas.

In about half an hour the bishop reappeared, and a close observer might have detected a shade of paleness on his apostolic features, yet his face was radiant like that of a good man who has performed a good action. Being implored to relieve the anxiety of the company, the worthy prelate spoke as follows:

"On entering the library, which was illuminated by a single lamp, I found myself alone. I drew a chair to the fire, and, taking up a volume of M. Renan's which chanced to be lying on the table, I composed myself to detect the sophistries of this brilliant but unprincipled writer. Thus, by an effort of will, I distracted myself from that state of 'expectant attention' to which modern science attributes such phantoms and spectral appearances as can neither be explained away by a morbid condition of the liver, nor as caused by the common rat (*Mus rattus*). I should observe by the way," said the learned bishop, interrupting his own narrative, "that scepticism will in vain attempt to account, by the latter cause, namely rats, for the spectres, *Lemures, simulacra,* and haunted houses of the ancient Greeks and Romans. With these supernatural phenomena, as they prevailed in Athens and Rome, we are well acquainted, not only from the *Mostellaria* of Plautus, but from the numerous ghost-stories of Pliny, Plutarch, the *Philopseudes* of Lucian, and similar sources. But it will at once be perceived, and admitted even by candid men of science, that these spiritual phenomena of the classical period cannot plausibly, nor even possibly, be attributed to the agency of rats, when we recall the fact that the rat was an animal unknown to the ancients. As the learned M. Sélys Longch observes in his *Études de*

Micromammalogie (Paris,1839, p. 59), 'the origin of the rat is obscure, the one thing certain is that the vermin was unknown to the ancients, and that it arrived in Europe, introduced, perhaps, by the Crusaders, after the Middle Ages.' I think," added the prelate, looking round, not without satisfaction, "that I have completely disposed of the rat hypothesis, as far, at least, as the ghosts of classical tradition are concerned."

"Your reasoning, bishop," replied Lord Birkenhead, "is worthy of your reputation; but pray pardon the curiosity which entreats you to return from the *simulacra* of the past to the ghost of the present."

"I had not long been occupied with M. Renan," said the bishop, thus adjured, "when I became aware of the presence of another person in the room. I think my eyes had strayed from the volume, as I turned a page, to the table, on which I perceived the brown strong hand of a young man. Looking up, I beheld my friend the priest, who was indeed a man of some twenty-seven years of age, with a frank and open, though somewhat careworn, aspect. I at once rose, and asked if I could be of service to him in anything, and I trust I did not betray any wounding suspicion that he was other than a man of flesh and blood.

"'You can, indeed, my lord, relieve me of a great burden,' said the young man, and it was apparent enough that he *did* acknowledge the validity of Anglican orders. 'Will you kindly take from the shelf that volume of Cicero "De Officiis," he said, pointing to a copy of an Elzevir *variorum* edition,— not the small duodecimo Elzevir,—' remove the paper you will find there, and burn it in the fire on the hearth.'

"' Certainly I will do as you say, but will you reward me by explaining the reason of your request? '

"' In me,' said the appearance, 'you behold Francis Wilton, priest. I was born in 1657, and, after adventures and an education with which I need not trouble you, found myself here as chaplain to the family of the Lord Birkenhead of the period. It chanced one day that I heard in confession, from the lips of Lady Birkenhead, a tale so strange, moving, and, but for the sacred circumstances of the revelation, so incredible, that my soul had no rest for thinking thereon. At last, neglecting my vow, and fearful that I might become forgetful of any portion of so marvellous a narrative, I took up my pen and committed the confession to the security of manuscript. *Litera scripta manet.* Scarcely had I finished my unholy task when the sound of a distant horn told me that the hunt (to which pleasure I was passionately given) approached the demesne. I thrust the written confession into that volume of Cicero, hurried to the stable, saddled my horse with my own hands, and rode in the direction whence I heard the music of the hounds. On my way a locked gate barred my progress. I put Rupert at it, he took off badly, fell, and my spirit passed away in the fall. But not to the place of repose did my sinful spirit wing its flight. I found myself here in the library, where, naturally, scarcely any one ever comes except the maids. When I would implore them to destroy the unholy document that binds me to earth, they merely scream; nor have I found any scion of the house, nor any guest, except your lordship, of more intrepid resolution or more charitable mood. And now, I trust, you will release me.'

"I rose (for I had seated myself during his narrative), my heart was stirred with pity; I took down the Cicero, and lit on a sheet of yellow paper covered with faded manuscript, which, of course, I did not read, I turned to the hearth, tossed on the fire the sere old paper, which blazed at once, and then, hearing the words *pax vobiscum*, I looked round. But I was alone. After a few minutes, devoted to private ejaculations, I returned to the dining-room; and that is all my story. Your maids need no longer dread the ghost of the library. He is released."

"Will any one take any more wine?" asked Lord Birkenhead, in tones of deep emotion. "No? Then suppose we join the ladies."

"Well," said one of the ladies, the Girton girl, when the squire had finished the prelate's narrative, "*I* don't call that much of a story. What was Lady Birkenhead's confession about? That's what one really wants to know."

"The bishop could not possibly have read the paper," said the Bachelor of Arts, one of the guests; "not as a gentleman, nor a bishop."

"I wish *I* had had the chance," said the Girton girl. "Perhaps the confession was in Latin," said the Bachelor of Arts.

The Girton girl disdained to reply to this unworthy sneer.

"I have often observed," she said in a reflective voice, "that the most authentic and best attested bogies don't come to very much. They appear in a desultory manner, without any context, so to speak, and, like other difficulties, require a context to clear up their meaning."

These efforts of the Girton girl to apply the methods of philology to spectres, were received in silence. The women did not understand them, though they had a strong personal opinion about their learned author.

"The only ghost *I* ever came across, or, rather, came within measurable distance of, never appeared at all so far as one knew."

"Miss Lebas has a story," said the squire. "Won't she tell us her story?"

The ladies murmured, "Do, please."

"It really cannot be called a ghost-story," remarked Miss Lebas, "it was only an uncomfortable kind of coincidence, and I never think of it without a shudder. But I know there is not any reason at all why it should make any of *you* shudder; so don't be disappointed.

"It was the Long Vacation before last," said the Girton girl, "and I went on a reading-party to Bantry Bay, with Wyndham and Toole of Somerville, and Clare of Lady Margaret's. Leighton coached us."

"Dear me! With all these young men, my dear?" asked the maiden aunt.

"They were all women of my year, except Miss Leighton of Newnham, who was our coach," answered the Girton girl composedly.

"Dear me! I beg your pardon for interrupting you," said the maiden aunt.

"Well, term-time was drawing near, and Bantry Bay was getting pretty cold, when I received an invitation from Lady Garryowen to stay with them at Dundellan on my way south. They were two very dear, old, hospitable Irish ladies, the last of their race, Lady Garryowen and her sister, Miss Patty. They were *so* hospitable that, though I did not know it, Dundellan was quite full when I reached it, overflowing with young people. The house has nothing very remarkable about it: a grey, plain building, with remains of the chateau about it, and a high park wall. In the garden wall there is a small round tower, just like those in the precinct wall at St. Andrews. The ground floor is not used. On the first floor there is a furnished chamber with a deep round niche, almost a separate room, like that in Queen Mary's apartments in Holy Rood. The first floor has long been fitted up as a bedroom and dressing-room, but it had not been occupied, and a curious old spinning-wheel in the corner (which has nothing to do with my story, if you can call it a story), must have been unused since '98, at least. I reached Dublin late—our train should have arrived at half-past six—it was ten before we toiled into the station. The Dundellan carriage was waiting for me, and, after an hour's drive, I reached the house. The dear old ladies had sat up for me, and I went to bed as soon as possible, in a very comfortable room. I fell asleep at once, and did not waken till broad daylight, between seven and eight, When, as my eyes wandered about, I saw, by the pictures on the wall, and the names on the books beside my bed, that Miss Patty must have given up her own room to me. I was quite sorry and, as I dressed, determined to get her to let me change into any den rather than accept this sacrifice. I went downstairs, and found breakfast ready, but neither Lady Garryowen nor Miss Patty. Looking out of the window into the garden, I heard, for the only time in my life, the wild Irish *keen* over the dead, and saw the old nurse wailing and wringing her hands and hurrying to the house. As soon as she entered she told me, with a burst of grief, and in language I shall not try to imitate, that Miss Patty was dead.

"When I arrived the house was so full that there was literally no room for me. But 'Dundellan was never beaten yet,' the old ladies had said. There was still the room in the tower. But this room had such an evil reputation for being 'haunted 'that the servants could hardly be got to go near it, at least after dark, and the dear old ladies never dreamed of sending any of their guests to pass a bad night in a place with a bad name. Miss Patty, who had the courage of a Bayard, did not think twice. She went herself to sleep in the haunted tower, and left her room to me. And when the old nurse went to call her in the morning, she could not waken Miss Patty. She was dead. Heart-disease, they called it. Of course," added the Girton girl, "as I said, it was only a coincidence. But the Irish servants could not be persuaded that Miss Patty had not seen whatever the thing was that they believed to be in the garden tower. I don't know what it was. You see the context was dreadfully vague, a mere fragment."

There was a little silence after the Girton girl's story.

"I never heard before in my life," said the maiden aunt, at last, "of any host or hostess who took the haunted room themselves, when the house happened to be full. They always send the stranger within their gates to it, and then pretend to be vastly surprised when he does not have a good night. I had several bad nights myself once. In Ireland too."

"Tell us all about it, Judy," said her brother, the squire.

"No," murmured the maiden aunt. "You would only laugh at me. There was no ghost. I didn't hear anything. I didn't see anything. I didn't even *smell* anything, as they do in that horrid book, 'The Haunted Hotel.'"

"Then why had you such bad nights?"

"Oh, I *felt*," said the maiden aunt, with a little shudder.

"What did you *feel*, Aunt Judy?"

"I *know* you will laugh," said the maiden aunt, abruptly entering on her nervous narrative." I felt all the time *as if somebody was looking through the window*. Now, you know, there *couldn't* be anybody. It was in an Irish country house where I had just arrived, and my room was on the second floor. The window was old-fashioned and narrow, with a deep recess. As soon as I went to bed, my dears, I *felt* that some one was looking through the window, and meant to come in. I got up, and bolted the window, though I knew it was impossible for anybody to climb up there, and I drew the curtains, but I could not fall asleep. If ever I began to dose, I would waken with a start, and turn and look in the direction of the window. I did not sleep all night, and next night, though I was dreadfully tired, it was just the same thing. So I had to take my hostess into my confidence, though it was extremely disagreeable, my dears, to seem so foolish. I only told her that I thought the air, or something. must disagree with me, for I could not sleep. Then, as some one was leaving the house that day, she implored me to try another room, where I slept beautifully, and afterwards had a very pleasant visit. But, the day I went away, my hostess asked me if I had been kept awake by anything in particular, for instance, by a feeling that some one was trying to come in at the window. Well, I admitted that I *had* a nervous feeling of that sort, and she said that she was very sorry, and that every one who lay in the room had exactly the same sensation. She supposed they must all have heard the history of the room, in childhood, and forgotten that they had heard it, and then been consciously reminded of it by reflex action. It seems, my dears, that that is the new scientific way of explaining all these things, presentiments and dreams and wraiths, and all that sort of thing. We have seen them before, and remember them without being aware of it. So I said I'd never heard the history of the room; but she said I *must* have, and so must all the people who felt as if some one was coming in by the window. And I said that it was rather a curious thing they should *all* forget they knew it, and *all* be reminded of it without being aware of it, and that, if she did not mind, I'd like to be reminded of it again. So she said that these objections had all been replied to (just as clergymen always say in sermons), and then she told me the history of the room. It only came to this, that, three generations before, the family butler (whom every one had always thought a most steady, respectable man), dressed himself up like a ghost, or like his notion of a ghost, and got a ladder, and came in by the window to steal the diamonds of the lady of the house, and he frightened her to death, poor woman! That was all. But, ever since, people who sleep in the room don't sleep, so to speak, and keep thinking that some one is coming in by the casement. That's all; and I told you it was not an interesting story, but perhaps you will find more interest in the scientific explanation of all these things."

The story of the maiden aunt, so far as it recounted her own experience, did not contain anything to which the judicial faculties of the mind refused assent. Probably the Bachelor of Arts felt that something a good deal more unusual was wanted, for he instantly started without being asked, on the following narrative:—

"I also was staying," said the Bachelor of Arts, "at the home of my friends, the aristocracy in Scotland. The name of the house, and the precise rank in the peerage of my illustrious host, it is not necessary for me to give. All, however, who know those more than feudal and baronial halls, are aware that the front of the castle looks forth on a somewhat narrow drive, bordered by black and funereal pines. On the night of my arrival at the castle, although I went late to bed, I did not feel at all sleepy. Something, perhaps, in the mountain air, or in the vicissitudes of *baccarat*, may have banished slumber. I had been in luck, and a pile of sovereigns and notes lay, in agreeable confusion, on my dressing-table. My feverish blood declined to be tranquillized, and at last I drew up the blind, threw open the latticed window, and looked out on the drive and the pine-wood. The faint and silvery blue of dawn was just wakening in the sky, and a setting moon hung, with a peculiarly ominous and wasted appearance, above the crests of the forest. But conceive my astonishment when I beheld, on the drive, and right under my window, a large and well-appointed hearse, with two white horses, with plumes complete, and attended by mutes, whose black staffs were tipped with silver that glittered pallid in the dawn.

I exhausted my ingenuity in conjectures as to the presence of this remarkable vehicle with the white horses, so unusual, though, when one thinks of it, so appropriate to the chariot of Death. Could some belated visitor have arrived in a hearse, like the lady in Miss Ferrier's novel? Could one of the domestics have expired, and was it the intention of my host to have the body thus honourably removed without casting a gloom over his guests?

Wild as these hypotheses appeared, I could think of nothing better, and was just about to leave the window, and retire to bed, when the driver of the strange carriage, who had hitherto sat motionless, turned, and looked me full in the face. Never shall I forget the appearance of this man, whose sallow countenance, close-shaven dark chin, and small, black moustache, combined with I know not what of martial in his air, struck into me a certain indefinable alarm. No sooner had he caught my eye, than he gathered up his reins, just raised his whip, and started the mortuary vehicle at a walk down the road. I followed it with my eyes till a bend in the avenue hid it from my sight. So wrapt up was my spirit in the exercise of the single sense of vision that it was not till the hearse became lost to view that I noticed the entire absence of sound which accompanied its departure. Neither had the bridles and trappings of the white horses jingled as the animals shook their heads, nor had the wheels of the hearse crashed upon the gravel of the avenue. I was compelled by all these circumstances to believe that what I had looked upon was not of this world, and, with a beating heart, I sought refuge in sleep.

"Next morning, feeling far from refreshed, I arrived among the latest at a breakfast which was a desultory and movable feast. Almost all the men had gone forth to hill, forest, or river, in pursuit of the furred, finned, or feathered denizens of the wilds — —"

"You speak," interrupted the schoolboy, "like a printed book! I like to hear you speak like that. Drive on, old man! Drive on your hearse!"

The Bachelor of Arts "drove on," without noticing this interruption. "I tried to 'lead up' to the hearse," he said, "in conversation with the young ladies of the castle. I endeavoured to assume the languid and preoccupied air of the guest who, in ghost-stories, has had a bad night with the family spectre. I drew the conversation to the topic of apparitions, and even to warnings of death. I knew that every family worthy of the name has its omen: the Oxenhams a white bird, another house a brass band, whose airy music is poured forth by invisible performers, and so on. Of course I expected some one to cry, 'Oh, *we've* got a hearse with white horses,' for that is the kind of heirloom an ancient house regards with complacent pride. But nobody offered any remarks on the local omen, and even when I drew near the topic of hearses, one of the girls, my cousin, merely quoted, 'Speak not like a death's-head, good Doll '(my name is Adolphus), and asked me to play at lawn-tennis.

In the evening, in the smoking-room, it was no better, nobody had ever heard of an omen in this particular castle. Nay, when I told my story, for it came to that at last, they only laughed at me, and said I must have dreamed it. Of course I expected to be wakened in the night by some awful apparition, but nothing disturbed me. I never slept better, and hearses were the last things I thought of during the remainder of my visit. Months passed, and I had almost forgotten the vision, or dream, for I began to feel apprehensive that, after all, it was a dream. So costly and elaborate an apparition as a hearse with white horses and plumes complete, could never have been got up, regardless of expense, for one occasion only, and to frighten one undergraduate, yet it was certain that the hearse was not 'the old family coach.' My entertainers had undeniably never heard of it in their lives before. Even tradition at the castle said nothing of a spectral hearse, though the house was credited with a white lady deprived of her hands, and a luminous boy."

Here the Bachelor of Arts paused, and a shower of chaff began.

"Is that really all?" asked the Girton girl. "Why, this is the third ghost-story to-night without any ghost in it!"

"I don't remember saying that it was a ghost-story," replied the Bachelor of Arts; "but I thought a little anecdote of a mere 'warning' might not be unwelcome."

"But where does the warning come in?" asked the schoolboy.

"That's just what I was arriving at," replied the narrator, "when I was interrupted with as little ceremony as if I had been Mr. Gladstone in the middle of a most important speech. I was going to say that, in the Easter Vacation after my visit to the castle, I went over to Paris with a friend, a fellow of my college. We drove to the *Hôtel d'Alsace* (I believe there is no hotel of that name; if there is, I beg the spirited proprietor's pardon, and assure him that nothing personal is intended). We marched upstairs with our bags and baggage, and jolly high stairs they were. When we had removed the soil of travel from our persons, my friend called out to me, 'I say, Jones, why shouldn't we go down by the lift' [1] 'All right,' said I, and my friend walked to the door of the mechanical apparatus, opened it, and got in. I followed him, when the porter whose business it is to 'personally conduct' the inmates of the hotel, entered also, and was closing the door.

"His eyes met mine, and I knew him in a moment. I had seen him once before. His sallow face, black, closely shaven chin, furtive glance, and military bearing, were the face and the glance and bearing of the driver of that awful hearse!

"In a moment—more swiftly than I can tell you—I pushed past the man, threw open the door, and just managed, by a violent effort, to drag my friend on to the landing. Then the lift rose with a sudden impulse, fell again, and rushed, with frightful velocity, to the basement of the hotel, whence we heard an appalling crash, followed by groans. We rushed downstairs, and the horrible spectacle of destruction that met our eyes I shall never forget. The unhappy porter was expiring in agony; but the warning had saved my life and my friend's."

"*I was that friend*," said I—the collector of these anecdotes; "and so far I can testify to the truth of Jones's story."

At this moment, however, the gong for dressing sounded, and we went to our several apartments, after this emotional specimen of "Evenings at Home."

1   "Lift" is English for "elevator," or "elevator" is American for "lift."

"Ian Maclaren"/John Watson (1850-1907)

from **Beside The Bonnie Brier Bush (1894)**

DOMSIE
I.
A LAD O' PAIRTS

The Revolution reached our parish years ago, and Drumtochty has a School Board, with a chairman and a clerk, besides a treasurer and an officer. Young Hillocks, who had two years in a lawyer's office, is clerk, and summons meetings by post, although he sees every member at the market or the kirk. Minutes are read with much solemnity, and motions to expend ten shillings upon a coal-cellar door passed, on the motion of Hillocks, seconded by Drumsheugh, who are both severely prompted for the occasion, and move uneasily before speaking.

Drumsheugh was at first greatly exalted by his poll, and referred freely on market days to his "plumpers," but as time went on the irony of the situation laid hold upon him.

"Think o' you and me, Hillocks, veesitin' the schule and sittin' wi' bukes in oor hands watchin' the Inspector. Keep's a', its eneuch to mak' the auld Dominie turn in his grave. Twa meenisters cam' in his time, and Domsie put Geordie Hoo or some ither gleg laddie, that was makin' for college, thro' his facin's, and maybe some bit lassie brocht her copy-buke. Syne they had their dinner, and Domsie tae, wi' the Doctor. Man, a've often thocht it was the prospeck o' the Schule Board and its weary bit rules that feenished Domsie. He wasna maybe sae shairp at the elements as this pirjinct body we hae noo, but a'body kent he was a terrible scholar and a credit tae the parish. Drumtochty was a name in thae days wi' the lads he sent tae college. It was maybe juist as weel he slippit awa' when he did, for he wud hae taen ill with thae new fikes, and nae college lad to warm his hert."

The present school-house stands in an open place beside the main road to Muirtown, treeless and comfortless, built of red, staring stone, with a playground for the boys and another for the girls, and a trim, smug-looking teacher's house, all very neat and symmetrical, and well regulated. The local paper had a paragraph headed "Drumtochty," written by the Muirtown architect, describing the whole premises in technical language that seemed to compensate the ratepayers for the cost, mentioning the contractor's name, and concluding that "this handsome building of the Scoto-Grecian style was one of the finest works that had ever come from the accomplished architect's hands." It has pitch-pine benches and map-cases, and a thermometer to be kept at not less than 58° and not more than 62°, and ventilators which the Inspector is careful to examine. When I stumbled in last week the teacher was drilling the children in Tonic Sol-fa with a little harmonium, and I left on tiptoe.

It is difficult to live up to this kind of thing, and my thoughts drift to the auld schule-house and Domsie. Some one with the love of God in his heart had built it long ago, and chose a site for the bairns in the sweet pine-woods at the foot of the cart road to Whinnie Knowe and the upland farms. It stood in a clearing with the tall Scotch firs round three sides, and on the fourth a brake of gorse and bramble bushes, through which there was an opening to the road. The clearing was the playground, and in summer the bairns annexed as much wood as they liked, playing tig among the trees, or sitting down at dinner-time on the soft, dry spines that made an elastic carpet everywhere. Domsie used to say there were two pleasant sights for his old eyes every day. One was to stand in the open at dinner-time and see the flitting forms of the healthy, rosy sonsie bairns in the wood, and from the door in the afternoon to watch the schule skail, till each group was lost in the kindly shadow, and the merry shouts died away in this quiet place. Then the Dominie took a pinch of snuff and locked the door, and went to his house beside the school. One evening I came on him listening bare-headed to the voices, and he showed so kindly that I shall take him as he stands. A man of middle height, but stooping below it, with sandy hair turning to grey, and bushy eye-brow covering keen, shrewd grey eyes. You will notice that his linen is coarse but spotless, and that, though his clothes are worn almost threadbare, they are well brushed and orderly. But you will be chiefly arrested by the Dominie's coat, for the like of it was not in the parish. It was a black dress coat, and no man knew when it had begun its history; in its origin and its continuance it resembled Melchisedek. Many were the myths that gathered round that coat, but on this all were agreed, that without it we could not have realised the Dominie and it became to us the sign and trappings of learning. He had taken a high place at the University, and won a good degree, and I've heard the Doctor say that he had a career before him. But something happened in his life, and Domsie buried himself among the woods with the bairns of Drumtochty. No one knew the story, but after he died I found a locket on his breast, with a proud, beautiful face within, and I have fancied it was a tragedy. It may have been in substitution that he gave all his love to the children, and nearly all his money too, helping lads to college, and affording an inexhaustible store of peppermints for the little ones.

Perhaps one ought to have been ashamed of that school-house, but yet it had its own distinction, for scholars were born there, and now and then to this day some famous man will come and stand in the deserted playground for a space. The door was at one end, and stood open in summer, so that the boys saw the rabbits come out from their holes on the edge of the wood, and birds sometimes flew in unheeded. The fireplace was at the other end, and was fed in winter with the sticks and peats brought by the scholars. On one side Domsie sat with the half-dozen lads he hoped to send to college, to whom he grudged no labour, and on the other gathered the very little ones, who used to warm their bare feet at the fire, while down the sides of the room the other scholars sat at their rough old desks, working sums and copying. Now and then a class came up and did some task, and at times a boy got the tawse for his negligence, but never a girl. He kept the girls in as their punishment, with a brother to take them home, and both had tea in Domsie's house, with a bit of his best honey, departing much torn between an honest wish to please Domsie and a pardonable longing for another tea.

"Domsie," as we called the schoolmaster, behind his back in Drumtochty, because we loved him, was true to the tradition of his kind, and had an unerring scent for "pairts" in his laddies. He could detect a scholar in the egg, and prophesied Latinity from a boy that seemed fit only to be a cowherd. It was believed that he had never made a mistake in judgment, and it was not his blame if the embryo scholar did not come to birth. "Five and thirty years have I been minister at Drumtochty," the Doctor used to say at school examinations, "and we have never wanted a student at the University, and while Dominie Jamieson lives we never shall." Whereupon Domsie took snuff, and assigned his share of credit to the Doctor, "who gave the finish in Greek to every lad of them, without money and without price, to make no mention of the higher mathematics." Seven ministers, four schoolmasters, four doctors, one professor, and three civil service men had been sent out by the auld schule in Domsie's time, besides many that "had given themselves to mercantile pursuits."

He had a leaning to classics and the professions, but Domsie was catholic in his recognition of "pairts," and when the son of Hillocks' foreman made a collection of the insects of Drumtochty, there was a council at the manse. "Bumbee Willie," as he had been pleasantly called by his companions, was rescued from ridicule and encouraged to fulfil his bent. Once a year a long letter came to Mr. Patrick Jamieson, M.A., Schoolmaster, Drumtochty, N.B., and the address within was the British Museum. When Domsie read this letter to the school, he was always careful to explain that "Dr. Graham is the greatest living authority on beetles," and, generally speaking, if any clever lad did not care for Latin, he had the alternative of beetles.

But it was Latin Domsie hunted for as for fine gold, and when he found the smack of it in a lad he rejoiced openly. He counted it a day in his life when he knew certainly that he had hit on another scholar, and the whole school saw the identification of George Howe. For a winter Domsie had been "at point," racing George through Caesar, stalking him behind irregular verbs, baiting traps with tit-bits of Virgil. During these exercises Domsie surveyed George from above his spectacles with a hope that grew every day in assurance, and came to its height over a bit of Latin prose. Domsie tasted it visibly, and read it again in the shadow of the firs at mealtime, slapping his leg twice.

"He'll dae! he'll dae!" cried Domsie aloud, ladling in the snuff. "George, ma mannie, tell yir father that I am comin' up to Whinnie Knowe the nicht on a bit o' business."

Then the "schule" knew that Geordie Hoo was marked for college, and pelted him with fir cones in great gladness of heart.

"Whinnie" was full of curiosity over the Dominie's visit, and vexed Marget sorely, to whom Geordie had told wondrous things in the milkhouse. "It canna be coals 'at he's wantin' frae the station, for there's a fell puckle left."

"And it'll no be seed taties," she said, pursuing the principle of exhaustion, "for he hes some Perthshire reds himsel'. I doot it's somethin' wrang with Geordie," and Whinnie started on a new track.

"He's been playin' truant maybe. A' mind gettin' ma paiks for birdnestin' masel. I'll wager that's the verra thing."

"Weel, yir wrang, Weelum," broke in Marget, Whinnie's wife, a tall, silent woman, with a speaking face; "its naither the ae thing nor the ither, but something I've been prayin' for since Geordie was a wee bairn. Clean yirsel and meet Domsie on the road, for nae man deserves more honour in Drumtochty, naither laird nor farmer."

Conversation with us was a leisurely game, with slow movements and many pauses, and it was our custom to handle all the pawns before we brought the queen into action.

Domsie and Whinnie discussed the weather with much detail before they came in sight of George, but it was clear that Domsie was charged with something weighty, and even Whinnie felt that his own treatment of the turnip crop was wanting in repose.

At last Domsie cleared his throat and looked at Marget, who had been in and out, but ever within hearing.

"George is a fine laddie, Mrs. Howe."

An ordinary Drumtochty mother, although bursting with pride, would have responded, "He's weel eneuch, if he hed grace in his heart," in a tone that implied it was extremely unlikely, and that her laddie led the reprobates of the parish. As it was, Marget's face lightened, and she waited.

"What do you think of making him?" and the Dominie dropped the words slowly, for this was a moment in Drumtochty.

There was just a single ambition in those humble homes, to have one of its members at college, and if Domsie approved a lad, then his brothers and sisters would give their wages, and the family would live on skim milk and oat cake, to let him have his chance.

Whinnie glanced at his wife and turned to Domsie.

"Marget's set on seein' Geordie a minister, Dominie."

"If he's worthy o't, no otherwise. We haena the means though; the farm is highly rented, and there's barely a penny over at the end o' the year."

"But you are willing George should go and see what he can do. If he disappoint you, then I dinna know a lad o' pairts when I see him, and the Doctor is with me."

"Maister Jamieson," said Marget, with great solemnity, "ma hert's desire is to see George a minister, and if the Almichty spared me to hear ma only bairn open his mouth in the Evangel, I wud hae naething mair to ask . . . but I doot sair it canna be managed."

Domsie had got all he asked, and he rose in his strength.

"If George Howe disna get to college, then he's the first scholar I've lost in Drumtochty . . . ye 'ill manage his keep and sic like?"

"Nae fear o' that," for Whinnie was warming, 'tho' I haena a steek (stitch) o' new claithes for four years. But what about his fees and ither outgaeins?"

"There's ae man in the parish can pay George's fees without missing a penny, and I'll warrant he 'ill dae it."

"Are ye meanin' Drumsheugh?" said Whinnie, "for ye 'ill never get a penny piece oot o' him. Did ye no hear hoo the Frees wiled him intae their kirk, Sabbath past a week, when Netherton's sister's son frae Edinburgh wes preaching the missionary sermon, expectin' a note, and if he didna change a shillin' at the public-hoose and pit in a penny. Sall, he's a lad Drumsheugh; a'm thinking ye may save yir journey, Dominie."

But Marget looked away from her into the past, and her eyes had a tender light. "He hed the best hert in the pairish aince."

Domsie found Drumsheugh inclined for company, and assisted at an exhaustive and caustic treatment of local affairs. When the conduct of Piggie Walker, who bought Drumsheugh's potatoes and went into bankruptcy without paying for a single tuber, had been characterized in language that left nothing to be desired, Drumsheugh began to soften and show signs of reciprocity.

"Hoo's yir laddies, Dominie?" whom the farmers regarded as a risky turnip crop in a stiff clay that Domsie had 'to fecht awa in.' "Are ony o' them shaping weel?"

Drumsheugh had given himself away, and Domsie laid his first parallel with a glowing account of George Howe's Latinity, which was well received.

"Weel, I'm gled tae hear sic accoonts o' Marget Hoo's son; there's naething in Whinnie but what the spune puts in."

But at the next move Drumsheugh scented danger and stood at guard. "Na, na, Dominie, I see what yir aifter fine; ye mind hoo ye got three notes oot o' me at Perth market Martinmas a year past for ane o' yir college laddies. Five punds for four years; my word, yir no blate. And what for sud I educat Marget Hoo's bairn? If ye kent a' ye wudna ask me; it's no reasonable, Dominie. So there's an end o't."

Domsie was only a pedantic old parish schoolmaster, and he knew little beyond his craft, but the spirit of the Humanists awoke within him, and he smote with all his might, bidding goodbye to his English as one flings away the scabbard of a sword.

"Ye think that a'm asking a great thing when I plead for a pickle notes to give a puir laddie a college education. I tell ye, man, a'm honourin' ye and givin' ye the fairest chance ye'll ever hae o' winning wealth. Gin ye store the money ye hae scrapit by mony a hard bargain, some heir ye never saw 'ill gar it flee in chambering and wantonness. Gin ye bed the heart to spend it on a lad o' pairts like Geordie Hoo, ye wud hae twa rewards nae man could tak frae ye. Ane wud be the honest gratitude o' a laddie whose desire for knowledge ye hed sateesfied, and the second wud be this — anither scholar in the land; and a'm thinking with auld John Knox that ilka scholar is something added to the riches of the commonwealth. And what 'ill it cost ye? Little mair than the price o' a cattle beast. Man, Drumsheugh, ye poverty-stricken cratur, I've naethin' in this world but a handfu' o' books and a ten-pund note for my funeral, and yet, if it wasna I have all my brither's bairns tae keep, I wud pay every penny mysel'. But I'll no see Geordie sent to the plough, tho' I gang frae door to door. Na, na, the grass 'ill no grow on the road atween the college and the schule-hoose o' Drumtochty till they lay me in the auld kirkyard."

"Sall, Domsie was roosed," Drumsheugh explained in the Muirtown inn next market. "'Miserly wratch' was the ceevilest word on his tongue. He wud naither sit nor taste, and was half way doon the yaird afore I cud quiet him. An' a'm no sayin' he hed na reason if I'd been meanin' a' I said. It wud be a scan'al to the pairish if a likely lad cudna win tae college for the want o' siller. Na, na, neeburs, we hae oor faults, but we're no sae dune mean as that in Drumtochty."

As it was, when Domsie did depart he could only grip Drumsheugh's hand, and say Maecenas, and was so intoxicated, but not with strong drink, that he explained to Hillocks on the way home that Drumsheugh would be a credit to Drumtochty, and that his Latin style reminded him of Cicero. He added as an afterthought that Whinnie Knowe had promised to pay Drumsheugh's fees for four years at the University of Edinburgh.

S. R. Crockett (1860-1914)

from Cleg Kelly, Arab Of The City (1896)

ADVENTURE I
THE OUTCASTING OF CLEG KELLY

'It's all a dumb lie! — God's dead!'

Such a silence had never fallen upon the Sunday-school, since the fatal day when the grate was blown into the middle of the floor by Mickey McGranaghan, a recent convert (and a temporary one) to the peculiar orthodoxy of Hunker Court. But the new explosion far outstripped the old in its effects. For it contained a denial of all the principles upon which the school was founded, and especially it confounded and blasphemed the cheerful optimism of Mr. James Lugton, its superintendent, otherwise and more intimately known as 'Pund o' Cannles.'

The statement which contained so emphatic a denial of the eternity of the Trinity was made by Cleg Kelly, a bare-legged loon of twelve, who stood lone and unfriended on the floor before the superintendent's desk in the gloomy cellar known as Hunker Court Mission School. Cleg Kelly had at last been reported by his teacher for incorrigible persistence in misconduct. He had introduced pins point upwards through the cracks in the forms. He had been caught with an instrument of wire cunningly plaited about his fingers, by means of which he could nip unsuspecting boys sitting as many as three or four from him — which is a great advantage to a boy in a Sunday-school. Lastly, he had fallen backwards over a seat when asked a question. He had stood upon his hands and head while answering it, resuming his first position as if nothing had happened so soon as the examination passed on to the next boy. In fact, he had filled the cup of his iniquities to the brim.

His teacher did not so much object to the pranks of Cleg Kelly himself. He objected mainly because, being ragged, barelegged, with garments picturesquely ventilated, and a hat without a crown, he was as irresistible in charm and fascination to all the other members of his class as if he had been arrayed in silver armour starry clear. For though Hunker Court was a mission school, it was quite a superior mission. And (with the exception of one division, which was much looked down upon) the lowest class of children were not encouraged to attend. Now Cleg Kelly, by parentage and character, was almost, if not quite, as the mothers of the next social grade said, 'the lowest of the low.'

So when Cleg's teacher, a respectable young journeyman plumber, could stand no more pranks and had grown tired of cuffing and pulling, he led Cleg up to the awful desk of the superintendent from which the rebukes and prizes were delivered.

Thereupon 'Pund o' Cannles,' excellent but close-fisted tallow chandler and general dealer, proceeded to rebuke Cleg. Now the rebukes of 'Pund o' Cannles' smelt of the counter, and were delivered in the tone in which he addressed his apprentice boys when there were no customers in the shop—a tone which was entirely different from the bland suavity he used when he joined his hands and asked, 'And what is the next article, madam?'

'Do you know, boy,' said the superintendent, 'that by such sinful conduct you are wilfully going on the downward road? You are a wicked boy, and instead of becoming better under your kind teacher, and taking advantage of the many advantages of this institution devoted to religious instruction, you stick pins—brass pins—into better conducted boys than yourself. And so, if you do not repent, God will 'take you in your iniquity and cast you into hell. For, remember, God sees everything and punishes the bad people and rewards the good.'

The superintendent uttered, though he knew it not, the most ancient of heresies—that which Job refuted.

It was at this point in the oration of 'Pund o' Cannles' that Cleg Kelly's startling interruption occurred. The culprit suddenly stopped making O's on the dusty floor with his toe, amongst the moist paper pellets which were the favourite distraction of the inattentive at Hunker Court; and, in a clear voice, which thrilled through the heart of every teacher and scholar within hearing, he uttered his denial of the eternity of the Trinity.

'It's all a dumb lie—God's dead!' he said.

There was a long moment's silence, and small wonder, as the school waited for the shivering trump of doom to split the firmament. The patient and self-sacrificing teachers who gave their unthanked care to the youth of the court every Sunday, felt their breaths come quick and short, and experienced a feeling as if they were falling over a precipice in a dream. At last Mr. James Lugton found his voice.

'Young and wicked blasphemer!' he said sternly, 'your presence must no longer, like that of the serpent in Paradise, poison the instruction given at this Sabbath school—I shall expel you from our midst —'

Here Cleg's teacher interposed. He was far from disliking his scholar, and had anticipated no such result arising from his most unfortunate reference of his difficulty to the superintendent. For he liked Cleg's ready tongue, and was amused by the mongrel dialect of Scots and Irish into which, in moments of excitement, he lapsed.

'I beg pardon, sir,' he said, 'but I am quite willing to give Kelly another chance—he is not such a bad boy as you might think.'

The superintendent waved his hand in a dignified way. He rather fancied himself in such scenes, and considered that his manner was quite as distinguished as that of his minister, when the latter was preaching his last memorable course of sermons upon the imprecatory psalms, and making solemn applications of them to the fate of members of a sister denomination which worshipped just over the way.

'The boy is a bold blasphemer and atheist!' he said; 'he shall be cast out from among our innocent lambs. Charles Kelly, I solemnly expel you upon this Christian Sabbath day, as a wicked and incorrigible boy, and a disgrace to any respectable mission school.'

The attitude of the superintendent was considered especially fine at this point. And he went home personally convinced that the excellent and fitting manner in which he vindicated the good name of Hunker Court upon this occasion, was quite sufficient to balance an extensive practice of the use of light weights in the chandler's shop at the comer of Hunker's Row. He further entirely believed that judicious severity of this kind was acceptable in the highest quarters.

So as the resisting felon is taken to prison, Cleg Kelly, heathen of twelve years, was haled to the outer door and cast forth of Hunker Court. But as the culprit went he explained his position.

'It's all gammon, that about prayin',' he cried; 'I've tried it heaps of times—never fetched it once! An' look at my mother. She just prays lashings, and all the time. An' me father, he's never a bit the better—no, nor her neither. For he thrashes us black and blue when he comes hame just the same. Ye canna gammon me, Pund o' Cannles, with your lang pray-prayin' and your short weight. I tell you God's dead, and it's all a dumb lie! '

The last accents of the terrible renunciation lingered upon the tainted air even after the door had closed, and Cleg Kelly was an outcast. But the awed silence was sharply broken by a whiz and jingle which occurred close to the superintendent's ear, as Cleg Kelly, Iconoclast, punctuated his thesis of defiance by sending a rock of offence clear through the fanlight over the door of Hunker Court Mission School.

ADVENTURE II

THE BURNING OF THE WHINNY KNOWES

Cleg Kelly was now outcast and alien from the commonwealth. He had denied the faith, cast aside every known creed, and defied the Deity Himself. Soon he would defy the policeman and break the laws of man—which is the natural course of such progression in iniquity, as every one knows.

So leaving Hunker Court he struck across the most unfrequented streets, where only an occasional stray urchin (probably a benighted Episcopalian) was spending the Sabbath chivying cats, to the mountainous regions of Craigside, where the tall 'lands' of St. Leonards look out upon the quarried craigs and steep hill ridges of Arthur's Seat. For Cleg was fortunate enough to be a town boy who had the country at his command just over the wall— and a wall, too, which he could climb at as many as twenty points. Only bare stubby feet, however, could overpass these perilous clefts. Cleg's great toes, horny as if shod with iron, fitted exactly into the stone crevices from which the mortar had been loosened. His grimy little fingers found a purchase in the slightest nicks. And once on the other side, there was no policeman, park-keeper, or other person in authority, who could make the pace with Cleg's bare brown legs, at least up the loose clatter of the shingle between the lower greensward and the Radical Road.

So, after being expelled from Hunker Court, Cleg made straight for a nook of his own among the crags. Here, like a prudent outlaw, he took account of his possessions with a view to arranging his future career of crime. He turned out his pockets into his hat. This was, indeed, a curious thing to do. For the article which he wore upon his shaggy locks was now little more than the rim of what had once been a covering for the head, proof against wind and water. But though Cleg's treasures rested upon the ground, the fact that they were within his hat-rim focussed them, as it were, and their relative worth was the more easily determined.

The first article which Cleg deposited upon the ground inside his hat was a box of matches, which had been given him to light the gas with in the outlying comers of Hunker Court School, for that dank cellar was gloomy enough even on a summer's afternoon. Then came some string, the aforesaid long-pronged nipping-wires which he had taken from his father's stores, a pair of pincers, a knife with one whole and one broken blade, a pipe, some brown-paper tobacco of a good brand, a half-written exercise-book from the day-school at which Cleg occasionally looked in, five marbles of the variety known as 'commonies,' one noble knuckler of alabaster which Cleg would not have parted with for his life, a piece of dry bread, and, lastly, half an apple with encroaching bays and projecting promontories, indicating in every case but one, the gap in Cleg's dental formation on the left side of his upper jaw, which dated from his great fight with Hole in the Wa' in the police yard. The exception was a clean, crisp semicircle, bitten right in to the apple-core. This was the tidemark of a friendly bite Cleg had given to a friend, in whose shining double row were no gaps. The perfect crescent had been made by the teeth of a lassie—one Vara Kavannah.

The box of matches was to its owner the most attractive article in all this array of wealth. Cleg looked into his hat-rim with manifest pleasure. He slapped his knee. He felt that he was indeed well equipped for the profession of outlaw. If he had to be a Cain, he could at least make it exceedingly lively in the Land of Nod.

It was a chilly day on the craigs, the wind blowing bask from the East, and everything underfoot as dry as tinder. The wild thought of a yet untried ploy surged up in Cleg's mind. He grasped the matchbox quickly, with thoughts of arson crystallising in his mind. He almost wished that he had set Hunker Court itself on fire. Just in time he remembered Vara Kavannah and her little brother Hugh.

'I'll get them to gang to anither school first,' he said.

But in the meantime, with the thought of setting fire to something in his heart and the matchbox in his hand, it was necessary to find the materials for a blaze. He had no powder with him or he would have made a 'peeoye'—the simple and inexpensive firework of metropolitan youth.

He glanced up at the heather and whin which covered the Nether Hill. His heart bounded within him at the thought. He looked again at his matchbox, which was one of the old oval shape, containing matches so exceedingly and gratuitously sulphurous, that the very smell of one of them was well worth the halfpenny charged for the lot. So, without any further pause for reflection, Cleg stowed away all the possessions, inventoried with such accuracy above, into various outlying nooks and crevices among the seams and pockets of his flapping attire.

Having collected the last one of these, Cleg climbed up a crumbling cliff at the eastern end of the craigs, where the fallen stones lie about in slats. Upon each of them, for all the world like green post-office wax dripped upon grey paper, was to be found some curious mineral — which Cleg, in his hours of decent citizenship, collected and sold at easy rates to the boys of the Pleasance as a charm. This mysterious green stuff had even been made a seal of initiation into one of the most select, aristocratic, and bloody secret societies of which Cleg was a member. Indeed, if the truth must be told. Cleg had formed the association chiefly that he might be able profitably to supply these badges of membership, for he had a corner in green mineral wax — at least so long as the mine at the east angle of the craigs remained undiscovered by the other adventurous loons of the south side.

Cleg soon reached the tawny, thin-pastured, thick-furzed slopes which constitute the haunch of Arthur's lion hill. In the days of Cleg's youth these were still clad thick with whins and broom, among which the birds built in the spring, and where in the evenings lovers sat in long converse on little swarded oases.

'I'll juist set fire to this wee bit knowe,' said Cleg, his heart beating within him at the enormity of the offence. 'There's no a "keelie" in the toon that wad dare to do as muckle!'

For the ranger of that particular part of the hill was an old soldier of great size and surprising swiftness in a race. And many had been the Arthur Street urchins who had suffered a sore skin and a night in the cells after being taken in dire offence. So 'the Warrior' they called him, for an all-sufficient name.

In a sheltered spot, and with the wind behind him, Cleg opened his matchbox. He struck a match upon the rough oval bottom. It spurted faintly blue, burned briskly, and then flickered out within Cleg's hollowed hands. Cleg grunted.

'A fizz an' a stink,' said he, summing up the case in a popular phrase.

The next went somewhat better. The flame reached the wood, dipped as if to expire, took hold again, and finally burned up in a broad-based yellow triangle. Cleg let it drop among the crisp, dry, rustling grasses at the roots of the whin bushes. Instantly a little black line ran forward and crossways, with hardly any flame showing. Cleg was interested, and laid the palm of his hand upon the ground. He lifted it instantly with a cry of pain. What had seemed a black line with an edge of flickering blue was really a considerable fire, which, springing from the dry couch grass and bent, was briskly licking up the tindery prickles of the gorse.

The next moment, with an upward bound and a noise like the flapping of a banner, the flame sprang clear of the whin bushes, and the blue smoke streamed heavenwards. Cleg watched the progress, chained to the spot. He well knew that it was time for him to be off. But with the unhallowed fascination of the murderer for the scene of his crime, he watched bush after bush being swallowed up, and shouted and leaped with glee. But the progress of the flame was further and swifter than he had intended. One little knoll would have satisfied him. But in a minute, driven forward by a level-blowing, following wind, the flame overleaped the little strait of short turf, and grasped at the next and far larger continent of whin.

Cleg, surprised, began to shrink from the consequences of his act. He had looked to revenge himself upon society for his expulsion from

Hunker Court by making a little private fire, and lo! he had started a world conflagration. He ran round to the edge of the gorse covert. Two hedge-sparrows were fluttering and dashing hither and thither, peeping and crying beseechingly. Cleg looked for the objective point of their anxiety, and there, between two whin branches, was the edge of a nest, and a little compact yellow bundle of three gaping mouths, without the vestige of a body to be seen.

'Guid life,' cried Cleg, who kept kindness to birds and beasts as the softest spot of his outlaw heart, 'guid life, I never thocht the birds wad be biggin' already!'

And with that he took off his coat, and seizing it in both hands he charged boldly into the front of the flame, disdainful of prickles and scorchings. He dashed the coat down upon a bush which was just beginning to crackle underneath; and by dint of hard fighting and reckless bravery he succeeded in keeping the fire from the little island, in the central bush of which was situated the hedge-sparrows' nest. Here he stood, with his coat threshing every way, keeping the pass with his life—brave as Horatius at the bridge (or any other man)—while the flames crackled and roared past him.

Suddenly there burst forth a great fizzing and spitting from the ragged coat which Cleg wielded as a quenching weapon. The fatal matchbox, cause of all the turmoil, had exploded. The fumes were stifling, but the flames still threatened to spread, and Cleg laid about him manfully. The tails of the coat disappeared. There was soon little left but the collar. Cleg stood like a warrior whose sword has broken in his hand in the face of the triumphant enemy. But the boy had a resource which is not usually open to the soldier. He cast the useless coat-collar from him, stripped a sleeved waistcoat, which had been given him by the wife of a mason's labourer, and, taking the garment by the two arms, he made an exceedingly efficient beater of the moleskin, which had the dried lime yet crumbly upon it at the cuffs.

When at last 'the Warrior' came speeding up the hill, warned out of his Sabbath afternoon's sleep by the cry that the whins were on fire, he was in no pleasant temper. He found, however, that the fire had been warded from the greater expanses by a black imp of a boy, burned and smutted, who held the remains of a mole-skin garment clasped in a pair of badly singed hands.

When the inevitable crowd of wanderers had gathered from all parts of the hill, and the fire had been completely trampled out, the ranger began his inquiries. Cleg was the chief suspect, because no one had seen any other person near the fire except himself. On the other hand no one had seen him light the whins, while all had seen him single-handed fighting the flames.

'It's Tim Kelly's loon, the housebreaker, him that leeves in the Sooth Back!' said the usual officious stranger with the gratuitous local knowledge. At his father's ill-omened name there was an obvious hardening in the faces of the men who stood about.

'At ony rate, the loon is better in the lock-up,' said the ranger sententiously.

At this Cleg's heart beat faster than ever. Many had been his perilous ploys, but never yet had he seen the inside of the prison. He acknowledged that he deserved it, but it was hard thus to begin his prison experience after having stayed to fight the fire, when he could so easily have run away. There was unfairness somewhere. Cleg felt.

So, with the burnt relics of his sleeved waistcoat still in his hands. Cleg was dragged along down the edge of the Hunter's Bog. The ranger grasped him roughly by a handful of dirty shirt collar, and his strides were so long that Cleg's short legs were not more than half the time upon the ground.

But at a certain spring of clear, crystal water, which gushes out of the hillside from beneath a large round stone, the ranger paused.

He too had fought the flames, and he had cause to thirst. For it was Sunday afternoon, and he had arisen from his usual lethargic after-dinner sleep upon the settle opposite the kitchen fire.

So at the well he stooped to drink, one hand still on Cleg's collar, and the palm of the other set flat on the side of the boulder. It was Cleg's opportunity. He twisted himself suddenly round, just after the ranger's lips had touched the water. The rotten cloth of his shirt tore, and Cleg sprang free. The ranger, jerked from the support of the stone, and at the same moment detached from his prisoner, fell forward with his head in the spring, while Cleg sped downhill like the wind. He was ready stripped for the race. So, leaving the panting chase far behind, he made for a portion of the encompassing wall, which none but he had ever scaled. Having clambered upon the top, he crossed his legs and calmly awaited the approach of the ranger.

'It's a warm day, Warrior,' said Cleg; 'ye seem to be sweatin'!'

'Ye limb o' Sawtan,' panted the ranger, 'gin ever I get ye this side o' the dyke, I'll break every bane in your body.'

'Faith,' answered Cleg, 'ye should be braw an' thankfu', Warrior, for ye hae gotten what ye haena had for years, and had muckle need o'! '

'And what was that, ye de'il's buckie? 'cried the angry ranger.

'A wash!' said Cleg Kelly, as he dropped down the city side of the wall, and sped home to his fortress.

George Douglas [Brown] (1869-1902)

from The House With The Green Shutters (1901)

Chapter 1

The frowsy chamber-maid of the "Red Lion" had just finished washing the front door steps. She rose from her stooping posture, and, being of slovenly habit, flung the water from her pail, straight out, without moving from where she stood. The smooth round arch of the falling water glistened for a moment in mid-air. John Gourlay, standing in front of his new house at the head of the brae, could hear the swash of it when it fell. The morning was of perfect stillness.

The hands of the clock across "the Square "were pointing to the hour of eight. They were yellow in the sun.

Blowsalinda, of the Red Lion, picked up the big bass that usually lay within the porch and, carrying it clumsily against her breast, moved off round the corner of the public house, her petticoat gaping behind. Halfway she met the ostler with whom she stopped in amorous dalliance. He said something to her, and she laughed loudly and vacantly. The silly tee-hee echoed up the street.

A moment later a cloud of dust drifting round the corner, and floating white in the still air, shewed that she was pounding the bass against the end of the house.

All over the little town the women of Barbie were equally busy with their steps and door-mats. There was scarce a man to be seen either in the Square, at the top of which Gourlay stood, or in the long street descending from its near corner. The men were at work; the children had not yet appeared; the women were busy with their household cares.

The freshness of the air, the smoke rising thin and far above the red chimneys, the sunshine glistering on the roofs and gables, the rosy clearness of everything beneath the dawn, above all the quietness and peace, made Barbie, usually so poor to see, a very pleasant place to look down at on a summer morning. At this hour there was an unfamiliar delicacy in the familiar scene, a freshness and purity of aspect—almost an unearthliness—as though you viewed it through a crystal dream. But it was not the beauty of the hour that kept Gourlay musing at his gate. He was dead to the fairness of the scene, even while the fact of its presence there before him wove most subtly with his mood. He smoked in silent enjoyment because on a morning such as this, everything he saw was a delicate flattery to his pride. At the beginning of a new day to look down on the petty burgh in which he was the greatest man, filled all his being with a consciousness of importance. His sense of prosperity was soothing and pervasive; he felt it all round him like the pleasant air, as real as that and as subtle; bathing him, caressing. It was the most secret and intimate joy of his life to go out and smoke on summer mornings by his big gate, musing over Barbie ere he possessed it with his merchandise.

He had growled at the quarry carters for being late in setting on this morning (for like most resolute dullards he was sternly methodical), but in his heart he was secretly pleased. The needs of his business were so various that his men could rarely start at the same hour, and in the same direction. To-day, however, because of the delay, all his carts would go streaming through the town together, and that brave pomp would be a slap in the face to his enemies. "I'll shew them," he thought, proudly. "Them" was the town-folk, and what he would shew them was what a big man he was. For, like most scorners of the world's opinion, Gourlay was its slave, and shewed his subjection to the popular estimate by his anxiety to flout it. He was not great enough for the carelessness of perfect scorn.

Through the big green gate behind him came the sound of carts being loaded for the day. A horse, weary of standing idle between the shafts, kicked ceaselessly and steadily against the ground with one impatient hinder foot, clink, clink, clink upon the paved yard. "Easy, damn ye; ye'll smash the bricks!" came a voice. Then there was the smart slap of an open hand on a sleek neck, a quick start, and the rattle of chains as the horse quivered to the blow.

"Run a white tarpaulin across the cheese, Jock, to keep them frae melting in the heat," came another voice. "And canny on the top there wi' thae big feet o' yours; d'ye think a cheese was made for you to dance on wi' your mighty brogues?" Then the voice sank to the hoarse warning whisper of impatience; loudish in anxiety, yet throaty from fear of being heard. "Hurry up, man—hurry up, or he'll be down on us like bleezes for being so late in getting off!"

Gourlay smiled, grimly, and a black gleam shot from his eye as he glanced round to the gate and caught the words. His men did not know he could hear them.

The clock across the Square struck the hour, eight soft slow strokes, that melted away in the beauty of the morning. Five minutes passed. Gourlay turned his head to listen, but no further sound came from the yard. He walked to the green gate, his slippers making no noise.

"Are ye sleeping, my pretty men?" he said, softly. . . . "Eih?"

The "Eih" leapt like a sword, with a slicing sharpness in its tone, that made it a sinister contrast to the first sweet question to his "pretty men." "Eih?" he said again, and stared with open mouth and fierce dark eyes.

"Hurry up, Peter," whispered the gaffer, "hurry up, for Godsake. He has the black glower in his e'en."

"Ready, sir; ready now!" cried Peter Riney, running out to open the other half of the gate. Peter was a wizened little man, with a sandy fringe of beard beneath his chin, a wart on the end of his long, slanting-out nose, light blue eyes, and bushy eyebrows of a reddish gray. The bearded red brows, close above the pale blueness of his eyes, made them more vivid by contrast; they were like pools of blue light amid the brownness of his face. Peter always ran about his work with eager alacrity. A simple and willing old man, he affected the quick readiness of youth to atone for his insignificance.

"Hup horse; hup then!" cried courageous Peter, walking backwards with curved body through the gate, and tugging at the reins of a horse the feet of which struck sparks from the paved ground as they stressed painfully on edge to get weigh on the great waggon behind. The cart rolled through, then another, and another, till twelve of them had passed. Gourlay stood aside to watch them. All the horses were brown; "he makes a point of that," the neighbours would have told you. As each horse passed the gate the driver left its head, and took his place by the wheel, cracking his whip, with many a "hup horse; yean horse; woa lad; steady!"

In a dull little country town the passing of a single cart is an event, and a gig is followed with the eye till it disappears. Anything is welcome that breaks the long monotony of the hours, and suggests a topic for the evening's talk. "Any news?" a body will gravely enquire; "Ou aye," another will answer with equal gravity, "I saw Kennedy's gig going past in the forenoon." "Aye, man, where would he be off till? He's owre often in his gig, I'm thinking—" and then Kennedy and his affairs will last them till bedtime.

Thus the appearance of Gourlay's carts woke Barbie from its morning lethargy. The smith came out in his leather apron, shoving back, as he gazed, the grimy cap from his white-sweating brow; bowed old men stood in front of their doorways, leaning with one hand on short trembling staffs, while the slaver slid unheeded along the cutties which the left hand held to their toothless mouths; white-mutched grannies were keeking past the jambs; an early urchin, standing wide-legged to stare, waved his cap and shouted, "Hooray!" —and all because John Gourlay's carts were setting off upon their morning rounds, a brave procession for a single town! Gourlay, standing great-shouldered in the middle of the road, took in every detail, devoured it grimly as a homage to his pride. "Ha! ha! ye dogs," said the soul within him. Past the pillar of the Red Lion door he could see a white peep of the landlord's waistcoat—though the rest of the mountainous man was hidden deep within his porch. (On summer mornings the vast totality of the landlord was always inferential to the town from the tiny white peep of him revealed.) Even fat Simpson had waddled to the door to see the carts going past. It was fat Simpson—might the Universe blast his adipose—who had once tried to infringe Gourlay's monopoly as the sole carrier in Barbie. There had been a rush to him at first, but Gourlay set his teeth and drove him off the road, carrying stuff for nothing till Simpson had nothing to carry, so that the local wit suggested "a wee parcel in a big cart" as a new sign for his hotel. The twelve browns prancing past would be a pill to Simpson! There was no smile about Gourlay's mouth—a fiercer glower was the only sign of his pride—but it put a bloom on his morning, he felt, to see the suggestive round of Simpson's waistcoat, down yonder at the porch. Simpson, the swine! He had made short work o' him!

Ere the last of the carts had issued from the yard at the House with the Green Shutters the foremost was already near the Red Lion. Gourlay swore beneath his breath when Miss Toddle—described in the local records as "a spinster of independent means"—came fluttering out with a silly little parcel to accost one of the carriers. Did the auld fool mean to stop Andy Gow about her petty affairs—and thus break the line of carts on the only morning they had ever been able to go down the brae together? But no. Andy tossed her parcel carelessly up among his other packages, and left her bawling instructions from the gutter, with a portentous shaking of her corkscrew curls. Gourlay's men took their cue from their master, and were contemptuous of Barbie, most unchivalrous scorners of its old maids.

Gourlay was pleased with Andy for snubbing Sandy Toddle's sister. When he and Elshie Hogg reached the Cross they would have to break off from the rest to complete their loads, but they had been down Main Street over night as usual picking up their commissions, and until they reached the Bend o' the Brae it was unlikely that any business should arrest them now. Gourlay hoped that it might be so, and he had his desire, for, with the exception of Miss Toddle, no customer appeared. The teams went slowly down the steep side of the Square in an unbroken line, and slowly down the street leading from its near corner. On the slope the horses were unable to go fast—being forced to stell themselves back against the heavy propulsion of the carts behind; and thus the procession endured for a length of time worthy its surpassing greatness. When it disappeared round the Bend o' the Brae the watching bodies disappeared too; the event of the day had passed and vacancy resumed her reign. The street and the Square lay empty to the morning sun. Gourlay alone stood idly at his gate, lapped in his own satisfaction.

It had been a big morning, he felt. It was the first time for many a year that all his men, quarry-men and carriers, carters of cheese and carters of grain, had led their teams down the brae together in the full view of his rivals. "I hope they liked it!" he thought, and he nodded several times at the town beneath his feet, with a slow up and down motion of the head, like a man nodding grimly to his beaten enemy. It was as if he said, "See what I have done to ye!"

James McLevy (no dates)

from Curiosities of Crime in Edinburgh

The Dead Child's Leg (1861)

Some years ago, the scavenger whose district lies about the Royal Exchange, came to the office in a state of great excitement.—He had a parcel in his hand, and, laying it on the table, said, "I've found something this morning you won't guess."

"A bag of gold, perhaps?" said I.

"I wish it had been," said the man, looking at the parcel, a dirty rolled-up napkin, with increased fear; "it's a bairn's leg."

"A bairn's leg!" said I, taking up the parcel, and undoing it with something like a tremor in my own hand, which had never shaken when holding by the throat such men as Adam M'Donald.

And there, to be sure, was a child's leg, severed about the middle of the thigh. On examining it, it was not difficult to see that it was a part of a new-born infant, and a natural curiosity suggested a special look to the severed end, to know what means had been taken to cut it from the body. The result was peculiar. It appeared as if a hatchet had been applied to cut the bone, and that the operator had finished the work by dragging he member from the body,—a part of the muscle and integuments looking lacerated and torn. The leg was bleached, as if it had lain in water for a time, and it was altogether a ghastly spectacle.

"Where did you find it?" I asked.

"Why," replied the man, "I was sweeping about in Writers' Court at gray dawn, and, with a turn of my broom, I threw out of a sewer something white; then it was so dark I was obliged to stoop down to get a better look, and the five little toes appeared so strange that I staggered back, knowing very well now what it was. But I have always been afraid of dead bodies. Then I tied it up in my handkerchief, more to conceal it from my own sight than for any other reason."

"And you can't tell where it came from?" said I.

"Not certainly," answered he; "but I have a guess."

And the man, an Irishman, looked very wise, as if his guess was a very dark ascertained reality, something terribly mysterious.

"Out with your guess, man," said I; "it looks like a case of murder, and we must get at the root of it."

"And I will be brought into trouble," answered he; "faith, I'll say no more, I've given you the leg, and that's pretty well, anyhow. It's not every day you get the like o' that brought to ye, all for nothing; and ye're not content."

"You know more than you have told us," said I; "and how are we to be sure that you did not put the leg there yourself 1"

"Put the leg there myself, and then bring it to you!" said he; "first kill the bairn, and then come to be hanged! Not just what an Irishman would do. We're not so fond of trouble as all that."

"Trouble or no trouble, you must tell us where you think it came from, otherwise we will detain you as a suspected murderer."

"Mercy save us! me a suspected murderer!" cried he, getting alarmed; "well now, to be plain, you see, the leg was lying just at the bottom of the main soil-pipe that comes from the whole of the houses on the east side of the court, and it must be somebody in some family in some flat in some house in some part of the row that's the mother,—that's pretty certain; and I think I have told you enough, to get at the thief of a mother."

The man, no doubt, pointed at the proper source, however vaguely; so taking him along with me I walked over to Writers' Court, and, after examining the place where the leg was found, I was in some degree satisfied the man was right. It was exceedingly unlikely that the member would be thrown down there by any one entering the court, or by any one from a window, for this would just have been to exhibit a piece of evidence that a murder, or at least a concealed birth, had taken place somewhere in the neighbourhood, and to send the officers of the law upon inquiry. Besides, the leg was found in the gutter leading from the main pipe of the tenements, and, though there was no water flowing at the time, there had been a sufficiency either on the previous night or early morning to wash it to where it had lain.

But after coming to this conclusion, the difficulty took another shape not less unpromising. The pipe, as the man truly said, was a main pipe, into which all the pipes of the different houses led. One of these houses was Mr W—te's inn, which contained several females, and the other divisions of flats had each its servant; but, in addition to all this, there were females of a higher grade throughout the lands, and I shrunk from an investigation so general, and carrying an imputation so terrible. My inquiry was not to be among people of degraded character, where a search or a charge was only a thing of course,—doing no harm where they could not be more suspected than they deserved,—but among respectable families, some with females of tender feelings, regardful of a reputation which, to be suspected, was to be lost for ever; and I required to be on my guard against precipitation and imprudence.

Yet my course so far was clear enough. I could commit no imprudence, while I might expect help, in confining my first inquiries to the heads of the families; and this I had resolved upon while yet standing in the court in the hazy morning. The man and I were silent —he sweeping, and I meditating— when, in the stillness which yet prevailed, I heard a window drawn up in that stealthy way I am accustomed to hear when crime is on the outlook. It was clear that the greatest care had been taken to avoid noise; but ten times the care, and a bottle of oil to boot, would not have enabled this morning watcher to escape my ear. On the instant I slipt into an entry, the scavenger still sweeping away, and, notwithstanding of his shrewdness, not alive to an important part of the play. I could see without being seen; and looking up, I saw a white cap with a young and pale face under it, peering down upon the court. I had so good a look of the object, that I could have picked out that face, so peculiar was it, from among a thousand. I could even notice the eye, nervous and snatchy, and the secret-like movement of withdrawing the head as she saw the man, and then protruding it a little again as she observed him busy. Then there was a careful survey, not to ascertain the kind of morning, or to converse with a neighbouring protruded head, but to watch, and see, and hear what was going on below, where probably she had heard the voices of me and the man. Nay, I could have sworn that she directed her eye to the conduit—a suspicion on my part which afterwards appeared to me to be absurd, as in the event of her being the criminal, and knowing the direction of the pipes, she never would have trusted her life to such an open mode of concealment as sending the mutilated body down through the inside pipes, to be there exposed.

After looking anxiously and timidly for some time, and affording me, as I have, said, sufficient opportunity to scan and treasure up her features, she quietly drew in her pale, and, as I thought, beautiful face, let down the sash, almost with a long whisper of the wood, and all was still. I now came out of my hiding-place, and telling the man not to say a word to any one of what had been seen or done, I went round to the Exchange, and satisfied myself of the house thus signalised by the head of the pale watcher of the morning.

I need not say I had my own thoughts of this transaction, but still I saw that to have gone and directly impeached this poor, timid looker-out upon the dawn for scarcely any other reason than that she did then and there look out, and that she had a delicate appearance, would have been unauthorised, and perhaps fraught with painful consequences. What if I had failed in bringing home to her a tittle of evidence, and left her with a ruined reputation for life? The thought alarmed me, and I behoved to be careful, however strict, in the execution of my duty; so I betook myself during the forenoon to my first resolution of having conferences with the heads of the houses.

I took the affair systematically, beginning at one end and going through the families. No master or mistress could I find who could say they had observed any signs in any of their female domestics. The last house was a reservation—that house from which my watcher of the morning had been intent upon the doings in the court. It was the inn occupied, as I have said, by Mr W—te. Strangely enough, the door was opened by that same pale-faced creature. I threw my eye over her,—the same countenance, delicate and interesting,—the same nervous eye, and look of shrinking fear,—but now a smart cap on her head, which was like a mockery of her sadness and melancholy. She eyed me curiously and fearfully as I asked for Mr W—te, and ran with an irregular and irresolute motion to shew me in, I made no inquiry of her further, nor did I look at her intently to rouse her suspicion, for I had got all I wanted, even that which a glance carried to me. But if she shewed me quickly in, I could see that she had no disposition to run away when the door of the room opened. No doubt she was about the outside of it. I took care she could learn nothing there, but few will ever know what she had suffered there.

I questioned Mr W—te confidentially; told him all the circumstances; and ended by inquiring whether any of his female domestics had shewn any signs for a time bypast.

"No," said he; "such a thing could hardly have escaped me; and if I had suspected, I would have made instant inquiry, for the credit of my house,"

"What is the name of the young girl who opened the door to me?"

"Mary B— —n, but I cannot allow myself to suspect her; she is a simple-hearted, innocent creature, and is totally incapable of such a thing."

"But is she not pale and sickly-looking, as if some such event as that I allude to might have taken place in her case?"

"Why, yes; I admit," said be, "that she is paler than she used to be, but she has been often so while with me; and then her conduct is so circumspect, I can not listen to the suspicion,"

"Might I see the others?" said I.

"Certainly;" replied he, "I can bring them here upon pretences,"

"You may, except Mary B— —n," said I; "I have seen enough of her,"

And Mr W—te brought up several females on various pretences, all of whom I surveyed with an eye not more versed in these indications than what a very general knowledge of human nature might have enabled one to be. Each of them bore my scrutiny well and successfully — all healthy, blithe queans, with neither blush nor paleness to shew anything wrong about the heart or conscience.

"All these are free," said I, "but I must take the liberty to ask you to shew me the openings to the soil-pipe belonging to the tenement, but in such a way as not to produce suspicion; for I think you will find Mary about the door of the room,"

And so it turned out, for no sooner had we come forth than we could see the poor girl escaping by the turn of the lobby.

"That is my lass," said I to myself.

The investigation of the pipes shewed me nothing. There was not in any of the closets a drop of blood, nor sign of any kind of violence to a child, nor in any bed-room a trace of a birth, and far less a murder; but I could not be driven from my theory. My watcher of the morning of day was she who had taken the light of the morning of life from the new-born babe.

I next consulted with Dr Littlejohn, and he saw at once the difficulties of the case. The few facts, curious and adventitious as they were, which had come under my own eye, were almost for myself alone; no other would have been moved by them, because they might have been supposed to be coloured by my own fancy. Yet I felt I had a case to make out in some way, however much the reputation of a poor young girl should be implicated, and not less my own character and feelings. As yet, proof there was none. To have taken up a girl merely because she had a pale face — the only indication I could point to that others could judge of — was not according to my usual tactics; but I could serve my purpose without injuring the character of the girl were she innocent, and yet convict her if guilty. So I thought; and my plan, which was my own, was, as a mere tentative one, free from the objections of hardship or cruelty to the young woman.

About twelve o'clock I rolled up the leg of the child in a neat paper parcel, and writing an address upon it to Mary B— —n, at Mr W—te's, I repaired to the inn. Mary, who was not exclusively "the maid of the inn," did not this time open the door; it was done by one whose ruddy cheeks would have freed her from the glance of the keenest detective. "Is Mary B— —n in?" asked I.

"Yes," she replied somewhat carelessly; for I need not say there was not a suspicion in the house, except in the breast of Mr W—te, who was too discreet and prudent to have said a word.

"Tell her I have a parcel from the country to her," said I, walking in, and finding my way into a room.

The girl went for Mary, and I waited a considerable time; but then, probably, she might have been busy making the beds, perhaps her own, in a careful way, though she scarcely needed, after my eye had surveyed the sheets and blankets, as well as everything else. At length I heard some one at the door,—the hand not yet on the catch—a shuffling, a sighing, a flustering—the hand then applied and withdrawn—a sighing again— at length a firmer touch,—the door opened, and Mary stood before me. She was not pale now; a sickly flush overspread the lily—the lip quivered— the body swerved; she would have fallen had not she called up a little resolution not to betray herself.

"What—what—you have a parcel for me, sir?" she stuttered out.

"Yes, Mary," said I, as I still watched her looks, now changed again to pure pallor.

"Where is it from?" said she again, with still increased emotion.

"I do not know," said I, "but here it is," handing it to her.

The moment her hand touched it, she shrunk from the soft feel as one would do from that of a cold snake, or why should I not say the dead body of a child? It fell at her feet, and she stood motionless, as one transfixed, and unable to more even a muscle of the face.

"That is not the way to treat a gift," said I. "I insist upon you taking it up."

"O God, I cannot!" she cried.

"Well, I must do so for you," said I, taking up the parcel. "Is that the way you treat the presents of your friends; come," laying it on the table, "come, open it; I wish to see what is in it,"

"I cannot,—oh, sir, have mercy on me,—I cannot."

"Then do you wish me to do it for you?"

"Oh, no, no,—I would rather you took it away," she said, with a spasm.

"But why so? what do you think is in it?" said I, getting more certain every moment of my woman.

"Oh, I do not know," she cried again; "but I cannot open that dreadful thing."

And as she uttered the words, she burst into tears, with a suppressed scream, which I was afraid would reach the lobby, I then went to the door, and snibbed it. The movement was still more terrifying to her, for she followed me, and grasped me convulsively by the arm. On returning to the table, I again pointed to the parcel

"You must open that," said I, "or I will call in your master to do it for you."

"Oh,—for God's sake, no," she ejaculated; "I will,— oh, yes, sir, be patient,—I will, I will" But she didn't—she couldn't. Her whole frame shook, so that her hands seemed palsied, and I am sure she-could not have held the end of the string.

"Well," said I, drawing in a chair, and seating myself, "I shall wait till you are able,"

The sight of the poor creature was now painful to me, but I had my duty to do, and I knew how much depended on her applying her own hand to this strange work. I sat peaceably and silently, my eye still fixed, upon her.

She got into a meditation—looked piteously at me, then fearfully at the parcel—approached it—touched it—recoiled from it—touched it again and again—recoiled;—but I would wait.

"Why, what is all this about?" said I calmly, and I suspect even with a smile on my face, for I wanted to impart to her at least so much confidence as might enable her to do this one act, which I deemed necessary to my object. "What is all this about? I only bear this parcel to you, and for aught I know, there may be nothing in it to authorise all this terror. If you are innocent of crime, Mary, nothing should move you. Come, undo the string."

And now, having watched my face, and seen the good-humour on it, she began to draw up a little, and then picked irresolutely at the string.

"See," said I, taking out a knife, "this will help you."

But whether it was that she had been busy with a knife, that morning for another purpose than cutting the bread for her breakfast, I know not; she shrunk from the instrument, and, rather than touch it, took to undoing the string with a little more resolution. And here I could not help noticing a change that came over her almost of a sudden. I have noticed the same thing in cases where necessity seemed to be the mother of energy. She began to gather resolution from some thought; and, as it appeared, the firmness was something like a new-born energy to overcome the slight lacing of the parcel. That it was an effort bordering on despair, I doubt not, but it was not the less an effort. Nay, she became almost calm, drew the ends, laid the string upon the table, unfolded the paper, laid the object bare, and —the effort was gone—fell senseless at my feet.

I was not exactly prepared for this. I rose, and seeing some spirits in a press, poured out a little, wet her lips, dropped some upon her brow, and waited for her return to consciousness; and I waited longer than I expected,—indeed, I was beginning to fear I had carried my experiment too far. I thought the poor creature was dead, and for a time I took on her own excitement and fear, though from a cause so very different. I bent over her, watching her breath, and holding her wrist; at last a long sigh,—oh, how deep! — then a staring of the eyes, and a rolling of the pupils, then a looking to the table, then a ragging at me as if she thought I had her fate in my hands.

"Oh, where is it?" she cried. "Take it away; but you will not hang me, will you? Say you will not, and I will tell you all." I got her lifted up, and put upon a chair. She could now sit, but such was the horror she felt at the grim leg, torn as it was at the one end, and blue and hideous, that she turned her eyes to the wall, and I believe her smart cap actually moved by the rising of the black hair beneath it,

"Mary B— —n," said I, calmly, and in a subdued voice, "you have seen what is in the parcel?"

"Oh, yes, sir; oh, yes," she muttered.

"Do you know what it is?"

"Oh, too well, sir; too well."

"Then tell me," said I.

"Oh, sir," she cried, as she threw herself upon the floor on her knees, and grasped and clutched me round my legs, and held up her face,—her eyes now streaming with tears, her cap off, her hair let loose,—"if I do, will you take pity on me, and not hang me?"

"I can say, at least, Mary," I replied, "that it will be better for you if you make a clean breast, and tell the truth. I can offer no promises. I am merely an officer of the law; but, as I have said, I know it will be better for you to speak the truth."

"Well, then, sir," she cried, while the sobbing interrupted every other word; "well, then, before God, whom I have offended, but who may yet have mercy upon a poor sinner left to herself,—and, oh, sir, seduced by a wicked man,—I confess that I bore that child—but, sir, it was dead when it came into the world; and, stung by shame, and wild with pain, I cut it into pieces, and put it down into the soil-pipe; and may the Lord Jesus look down upon me in pity!"

"Well, Mary," said I, as I lifted her up,—feeling the weight of a body almost dead,—and placed her again upon the chair; "you must calm yourself, and then go and get your shawl and bonnet, for you must——"

"Go with you to prison," she cried, "and be hanged. Oh, did you not lead me to believe you would save me?"

"No," said I; "but I can safely tell you that, if what you have told me is true, that the child was still-born, you will not be hanged, you will only be confined for a little. Come," I continued, letting my voice down, "come, rise, and get your shawl and bonnet. Say nothing to any one, but come back to me."

But I had not an easy task here. She got wild again at the thought of prison, crying—

"I am ruined. Oh, my poor mother! I can never look her in the face again; no, nor hold up my head among decent people."

"Softly, softly," said I. "You must be calm, and obey; or see," holding up a pair of handcuffs, "I will put these upon your wrists."

Again necessity came to my help. She rose deliberately—stood for a moment firm—looked into my face wistfully, yet mildly—then turned up her eyes, ejaculating, "Thy will, O Lord, be done,"—and went out.

I was afraid, notwithstanding, she might try to escape, for she seemed changeful; and a turn might come of frantic fear, which would carry her off, not knowing herself whither she went. I, therefore, watched in the lobby, to intercept her in case of such an emergency; but the poor girl was true to her purpose. I tied up the fatal parcel which had so well served my object, put it under my arm, and quietly led her over to the office.

Her confession was subsequently taken by the Crown officers, and she never swerved from it. I believe if I had not fallen upon this mode of extorting an admission, the proof would have failed, for every vestige of mark had been carefully removed; while the deception she had practised on the people of the inn had been so adroit, that no one had the slightest suspicion of her. The other parts of the child were not, I think, got; indeed it was scarcely necessary to search for them, confined as they were, probably, in the pipes. She was tried before the High Court; and, in the absence of any evidence to shew that the child had ever breathed, —which could only have been ascertained by examining some parts of the chest,—she was condemned upon the charge of concealment, and sentenced to nine months' imprisonment.

Arthur Conan Doyle (1859-1930)

The Man with the Twisted Lip (1891)

Isa Whitney, brother of the late Elias Whitney, D.D., Principal of the Theological College of St. George's, was much addicted to opium. The habit grew upon him, as I understand, from some foolish freak when he was at college; for having read De Quincey's description of his dreams and sensations, he had drenched his tobacco with laudanum in an attempt to produce the same effects. He found, as so many more have done, that the practice is easier to attain than to get rid of, and for many years he continued to be a slave to the drug, an object of mingled horror and pity to his friends and relatives. I can see him now, with yellow, pasty face, drooping lids, and pin-point pupils, all huddled in a chair, the wreck and ruin of a noble man.

One night—it was in June, '89—there came a ring to my bell, about the hour when a man gives his first yawn, and glances at the clock. I sat up in my chair, and my wife laid her needlework down in her lap and made a little face of disappointment.

"A patient!" said she. "You'll have to go out."

I groaned, for I was newly come back from a weary day.

We heard the door open, a few hurried words, and then quick steps upon the linoleum. Our own door flew open, and a lady, clad in some dark-coloured stuff, with a black veil, entered the room.

"You will excuse my calling so late," she began, and then, suddenly losing her self-control, she ran forward, threw her arms about my wife's neck, and sobbed upon her shoulder. "Oh, I'm in such trouble!" she cried; "I do so want a little help."

"Why," said my wife, pulling up her veil, "it is Kate Whitney. How you startled me, Kate! I had not an idea who you were when you came in."

"I didn't know what to do, so I came straight to you." That was always the way. Folk who were in grief came to my wife like birds to a light-house.

"It was very sweet of you to come. Now, you must have some wine and water, and sit here comfortably and tell us all about it. Or should you rather that I sent James off to bed?"

"Oh, no, no! I want the doctor's advice and help, too. It's about Isa. He has not been home for two days. I am so frightened about him!"

It was not the first time that she had spoken to us of her husband's trouble, to me as a doctor, to my wife as an old friend and school companion. We soothed and comforted her by such words as we could find. Did she know where her husband was? Was it possible that we could bring him back to her?

It seems that it was. She had the surest information that of late he had, when the fit was on him, made use of an opium den in the furthest east of the City. Hitherto his orgies had always been confined to one day, and he had come back, twitching and shattered, in the evening. But now the spell had been upon him eight-and-forty hours, and he lay there, doubtless among the dregs of the docks, breathing in the poison or sleeping off the effects. There he was to be found, she was sure of it, at the "Bar of Gold", in Upper Swandam-lane. But what was she to do? How could she, a young and timid woman, make her way into such a place, and pluck her husband out from among the ruffians who surrounded him?

There was the case, and of course there was but one way out of it. Might I not escort her to this place? And then, as a second thought, why should she come at all? I was Isa Whitney's medical adviser, and as such I had influence over him. I could manage it better if I were alone. I promised her on my word that I would send him home in a cab within two hours if he were indeed at the address which she had given me. And so in ten minutes I had left my arm-chair and cheery sitting-room behind me, and was speeding eastward in a hansom on a strange errand, as it seemed to me at the time, though the future only could show how strange it was to be.

But there was no great difficulty in the first stage of my adventure. Upper Swandam-lane is a vile alley lurking behind the high wharves which line the north side of the river to the east of London Bridge. Between a slop shop and a gin shop, approached by a steep flight of steps leading down to a black gap like the mouth of a cave, I found the den of which I was in search. Ordering my cab to wait, I passed down the steps, worn hollow in the centre by the ceaseless tread of drunken feet, and by the light of a flickering oil-lamp above the door I found the latch and made my way into a long, low room, thick and heavy with the brown opium smoke, and terraced with wooden berths, like the forecastle of an emigrant ship.

Through the gloom one could dimly catch a glimpse of bodies lying in strange fantastic poses, bowed shoulders, bent knees, heads thrown back and chins pointing upward, with here and there a dark, lack-lustre eye turned upon the newcomer. Out of the black shadows there glimmered little red circles of light, now bright, now faint, as the burning poison waxed or waned in the bowls of the metal pipes. The most lay silent, but some muttered to themselves, and others talked together in a strange, low, monotonous voice, their conversation coming in gushes, and then suddenly tailing off into silence, each mumbling out his own thoughts, and paying little heed to the words of his neighbour. At the further end was a small brazier of burning charcoal, beside which on a three-legged wooden stool there sat a tall, thin old man, with his jaw resting upon his two fists, and his elbows upon his knees, staring into the fire.

As I entered, a sallow Malay attendant had hurried up with a pipe for me and a supply of the drug, beckoning me to an empty berth.

"Thank you. I have not come to stay," said I. "There is a friend of mine here, Mr. Isa Whitney, and I wish to speak with him."

There was a movement and an exclamation from my right, and peering through the gloom I saw Whitney, pale, haggard, and unkempt, staring out at me.

"My God! It's Watson," said he. He was in a pitiable state of reaction, with every nerve in a twitter. "I say, Watson, what o'clock is it?"

"Nearly eleven."

"Of what day?"

"Of Friday, June 19th."

"Good heavens! I thought it was Wednesday. It *is* Wednesday. What d'you want to frighten the chap for?" He sank his face onto his arms and began to sob in a high treble key.

"I tell you that it is Friday, man. Your wife has been waiting this two days for you. You should be ashamed of yourself!"

"So I am. But you've got mixed, Watson, for I have only been here a few hours, three pipes, four pipes—I forget how many. But I'll go home with you. I wouldn't frighten Kate—poor little Kate. Give me your hand! Have you a cab?"

"Yes, I have one waiting."

"Then I shall go in it. But I must owe something. Find what I owe, Watson. I am all off colour. I can do nothing for myself."

I walked down the narrow passage between the double row of sleepers, holding my breath to keep out the vile, stupefying fumes of the drug, and looking about for the manager. As I passed the tall man who sat by the brazier I felt a sudden pluck at my skirt, and a low voice whispered, "Walk past me, and then look back at me." The words fell quite distinctly upon my ear. I glanced down. They could only have come from the old man at my side, and yet he sat now as absorbed as ever, very thin, very wrinkled, bent with age, an opium pipe dangling down from between his knees, as though it had dropped in sheer lassitude from his fingers. I took two steps forward and looked back. It took all my self-control to prevent me from breaking out into a cry of astonishment. He had turned his back so that none could see him but I. His form had filled out, his wrinkles were gone, the dull eyes had regained their fire, and there, sitting by the fire and grinning at my surprise, was none other than Sherlock Holmes. He made a slight motion to me to approach him, and instantly, as he turned his face half round to the company once more, subsided into a doddering, loose-lipped senility.

"Holmes!" I whispered, "what on earth are you doing in this den?"

"As low as you can," he answered; "I have excellent ears. If you would have the great kindness to get rid of that sottish friend of yours I should be exceedingly glad to have a little talk with you."

"I have a cab outside."

"Then pray send him home in it. You may safely trust him, for he appears to be too limp to get into any mischief. I should recommend you also to send a note by the cabman to your wife to say that you have thrown in your lot with me. If you will wait outside, I shall be with you in five minutes."

It was difficult to refuse any of Sherlock Holmes's requests, for they were always so exceedingly definite, and put forward with such a quiet air of mastery. I felt, however, that when Whitney was once confined in the cab my mission was practically accomplished; and for the rest, I could not wish anything better than to be associated with my friend in one of those singular adventures which were the normal condition of his existence. In a few minutes I had written my note, paid Whitney's bill, led him out to the cab, and seen him driven through the darkness. In a very short time a decrepit figure had emerged from the opium den, and I was walking down the street with Sherlock Holmes. For two streets he shuffled along with a bent back and an uncertain foot. Then, glancing quickly round, he straightened himself out and burst into a hearty fit of laughter.

"I suppose, Watson," said he, "that you imagine that I have added opium-smoking to cucaine injections, and all the other little weaknesses on which you have favored me with your medical views."

"I was certainly surprised to find you there."

"But not more so than I to find you."

"I came to find a friend."

"And I to find an enemy."

"An enemy?"

"Yes; one of my natural enemies, or, shall I say, my natural prey. Briefly, Watson, I am in the midst of a very remarkable inquiry, and I have hoped to find a clew in the incoherent ramblings of these sots, as I have done before now. Had I been recognized in that den my life would not have been worth an hour's purchase; for I have used it before now for my own purposes, and the rascally Lascar who runs it has sworn to have vengeance upon me. There is a trap-door at the back of that building, near the corner of Paul's Wharf, which could tell some strange tales of what has passed through it upon the moonless nights."

"What! You do not mean bodies?"

"Ay, bodies, Watson. We should be rich men if we had 1000 pounds for every poor devil who has been done to death in that den. It is the vilest murder-trap on the whole riverside, and I fear that Neville St. Clair has entered it never to leave it more. But our trap should be here." He put his two forefingers between his teeth and whistled shrilly—a signal which was answered by a similar whistle from the distance, followed shortly by the rattle of wheels and the clink of horses' hoofs.

"Now, Watson," said Holmes, as a tall dog-cart dashed up through the gloom, throwing out two golden tunnels of yellow light from its side lanterns. "You'll come with me, won't you?

"If I can be of use."

"Oh, a trusty comrade is always of use; and a chronicler still more so. My room at 'The Cedars' is a double-bedded one."

" 'The Cedars'?"

"Yes; that is Mr. St. Clair's house. I am staying there while I conduct the inquiry."

"Where is it, then?"

"Near Lee, in Kent. We have a seven-mile drive before us."

"But I am all in the dark."

"Of course you are. You'll know all about it presently. Jump up here. All right, John; we shall not need you. Here's half a crown. Look out for me to-morrow, about eleven. Give her her head. So long, then!"

He flicked the horse with his whip, and we dashed away through the endless succession of sombre and deserted streets, which widened gradually, until we were flying across a broad balustraded bridge, with the murky river flowing sluggishly beneath us. Beyond lay another dull wilderness of bricks and mortar, its silence broken only by the heavy, regular footfall of the policeman, or the songs and shouts of some belated party of revellers. A dull wrack was drifting slowly across the sky, and a star or two twinkled dimly here and there through the rifts of the clouds. Holmes drove in silence, with his head sunk upon his breast, and the air of a man who is lost in thought, while I sat beside him, curious to learn what this new quest might be which seemed to tax his powers so sorely, and yet afraid to break in upon the current of his thoughts. We had driven several miles, and were beginning to get to the fringe of the belt of suburban villas, when he shook himself, shrugged his shoulders, and lit up his pipe with the air of a man who has satisfied himself that he is acting for the best.

"You have a grand gift of silence, Watson," said he. "It makes you quite invaluable as a companion. 'Pon my word, it is a great thing for me to have someone to talk to, for my own thoughts are not over-pleasant. I was wondering what I should say to this dear little woman to-night when she meets me at the door."

"You forget that I know nothing about it."

"I shall just have time to tell you the facts of the case before we get to Lee. It seems absurdly simple, and yet, somehow I can get nothing to go upon. There's plenty of thread, no doubt, but I can't get the end of it into my hand. Now, I'll state the case clearly and concisely to you, Watson, and maybe you can see a spark where all is dark to me."

"Proceed then."

"Some years ago—to be definite, in May, 1884—there came to Lee a gentleman, Neville St. Clair by name, who appeared to have plenty of money. He took a large villa, laid out the grounds very nicely, and lived generally in good style. By degrees he made friends in the neighborhood, and in 1887 he married the daughter of a local brewer, by whom he now has two children. He had no occupation, but was interested in several companies and went into town as a rule in the morning, returning by the 5.14 from Cannon-street every night. Mr. St. Clair is now thirty-seven years of age, is a man of temperate habits, a good husband, a very affectionate father, and a man who is popular with all who know him. I may add that his whole debts at the present moment, as far as we have been able to ascertain amount to £88 10s., while he has £220 standing to his credit in the Capital and Counties Bank. There is no reason, therefore, to think that money troubles have been weighing upon his mind.

"Last Monday, Mr. Neville St. Clair went into town rather earlier than usual, remarking before he started that he had two important commissions to perform, and that he would bring his little boy home a box of bricks. Now, by the merest chance, his wife received a telegram upon this same Monday, very shortly after his departure, to the effect that a small parcel of considerable value which she had been expecting was waiting for her at the offices of the Aberdeen Shipping Company. Now, if you are well up in your London, you will know that the office of the company is in Fresno-street, which branches out of Upper Swandam-lane, where you found me to-night. Mrs. St. Clair had her lunch, started for the City, did some shopping, proceeded to the company's office, got her packet, and found herself at exactly 4.35 walking through Swandam-lane on her way back to the station. Have you followed me so far?"

"It is very clear."

"If you remember, Monday was an exceedingly hot day, and Mrs. St. Clair walked slowly, glancing about in the hope of seeing a cab, as she did not like the neighbourhood in which she found herself. While she was walking in this way down Swandam-lane, she suddenly heard an ejaculation or cry, and was struck cold to see her husband looking down at her, and, as it seemed to her, beckoning to her from a second-floor window. The window was open, and she distinctly saw his face, which she describes as being terribly agitated. He waved his hands frantically to her, and then vanished from the window so suddenly that it seemed to her that he had been plucked back by some irresistible force from behind. One singular point which struck her quick feminine eye was that although he wore some dark coat, such as he had started to town in, he had on neither collar nor necktie.

"Convinced that something was amiss with him, she rushed down the steps — for the house was none other than the opium den in which you found me to-night — and running through the front room she attempted to ascend the stairs which led to the first floor. At the foot of the stairs, however, she met this Lascar scoundrel of whom I have spoken, who thrust her back and, aided by a Dane, who acts as assistant there, pushed her out into the street. Filled with the most maddening doubts and fears, she rushed down the lane and, by rare good-fortune, met in Fresno-street a number of constables with an inspector, all on their way to their beat. The inspector and two men accompanied her back, and in spite of the continued resistance of the proprietor, they made their way to the room in which Mr. St. Clair had last been seen. There was no sign of him there. In fact, in the whole of that floor there was no one to be found save a crippled wretch of hideous aspect, who, it seems, made his home there. Both he and the Lascar stoutly swore that no one else had been in the front room during the afternoon. So determined was their denial that the inspector was staggered, and had almost come to believe that Mrs. St. Clair had been deluded when, with a cry, she sprang at a small deal box which lay upon the table and tore the lid from it. Out there fell a cascade of children's bricks. It was the toy which he had promised to bring home.

"This discovery, and the evident confusion which the cripple showed, made the inspector realize that the matter was serious. The rooms were carefully examined, and results all pointed to an abominable crime. The front room was plainly furnished as a sitting-room and led into a small bed-room, which looked out upon the back of one of the wharves. Between the wharf and the bedroom window is a narrow strip, which is dry at low tide but is covered at high tide with at least four and a half feet of water. The bed-room window was a broad one and opened from below. On examination traces of blood were to be seen upon the window sill, and several scattered drops were visible upon the wooden floor of the bedroom. Thrust away behind a curtain in the front room were all the clothes of Mr. Neville St. Clair, with the exception of his coat. His boots, his socks, his hat, and his watch — all were there. There were no signs of violence upon any of these garments, and there were no other traces of Mr. Neville St.

Clair. Out of the window he must apparently have gone, for no other exit could be discovered, and the ominous bloodstains upon the sill gave little promise that he could save himself by swimming, for the tide was at its very highest at the moment of the tragedy.

"And now as to the villains who seemed to be immedlately implicated in the matter. The Lascar was known to be a man of the vilest antecedents, but as, by Mrs. St. Clair's story, he was known to have been at the foot of the stair within a very few seconds of her husband's appearance at the window, he could hardly have been more than an accessory to the crime. His defence was one of absolute ignorance, and he protested that he had no knowledge as to the doings of Hugh Boone, his lodger, and that he could not account in any way for the presence of the missing gentleman's clothes.

"So much for the Lascar manager. Now for the sinister cripple who lives upon the second floor of the opium den, and who was certainly the last human being whose eyes rested upon Neville St. Clair. His name is Hugh Boone, and his hideous face is one which is familiar to every man who goes much to the City. He is a professional beggar, though in order to avoid the police regulations he pretends to a small trade in wax vestas. Some little distance down Threadneedle-street, upon the left hand side, there is, as you may have remarked, a small angle in the wall. Here it is that this creature takes his daily seat, cross-legged, with his tiny stock of matches on his lap, and as he is a piteous spectacle a small rain of charity descends into the greasy leather cap which lies upon the pavement beside him. I have watched the fellow more than once before ever I thought of making his professional acquaintance, and I have been surprised at the harvest which he has reaped in a short time. His appearance, you see, is so remarkable that no one can pass him without observing him. A shock of orange hair, a pale face disfigured by a horrible scar, which, by its contraction, has turned up the outer edge of his upper lip, a bulldog chin, and a pair of very penetrating dark eyes, which present a singular contrast to the color of his hair, all mark him out from amid the common crowd of mendicants, and so, too, does his wit, for he is ever ready with a reply to any piece of chaff which may be thrown at him by the passers-by. This is the man whom we now learn to have been the lodger at the opium den, and to have been the last man to see the gentleman of whom we are in quest."

"But a cripple!" said I. "What could he have done single-handed against a man in the prime of life?"

"He is a cripple in the sense that he walks with a limp; but in other respects he appears to be a powerful and well-nurtured man. Surely your medical experience would tell you, Watson, that weakness in one limb is often compensated for by exceptional strength in the others."

"Pray continue your narrative."

"Mrs. St. Clair had fainted at the sight of the blood upon the window, and she was escorted home in a cab by the police, as her presence could be of no help to them in their investigations. Inspector Barton, who had charge of the case, made a very careful examination of the premises, but without finding anything which threw any light upon the matter. One mistake had been made in not arresting Boone instantly, as he was allowed some few minutes during which he might have communicated with his friend the Lascar, but this fault was soon remedied, and he was seized and searched, without anything being found which could incriminate him. There were, it is true, some blood-stains upon his right shirt-sleeve, but he pointed to his ring-finger, which had been cut near the nail, and explained that the bleeding came from there, adding that he had been to the window not long before, and that the stains which had been observed there came doubtless from the same source. He denied strenuously having ever seen Mr. Neville St. Clair and swore that the presence of the clothes in his room was as much a mystery to him as to the police. As to Mrs. St. Clair's assertion that she had actually seen her husband at the window, he declared that she must have been either mad or dreaming. He was removed, loudly protesting, to the police station, while the inspector remained upon the premises in the hope that the ebbing tide might afford some fresh clue.

"And it did, though they hardly found upon the mudbank what they had feared to find. It was Neville St. Clair's coat, and not Neville St. Clair, which lay uncovered as the tide receded. And what do you think they found in the pockets?"

"I cannot imagine."

"No, I don't think you would guess. Every pocket stuffed with pennies and half-pennies — 421 pennies and 270 half-pennies. It was no wonder that it had not been swept away by the tide. But a human body is a different matter. There is a fierce eddy between the wharf and the house. It seemed likely enough that the weighted coat had remained when the stripped body had been sucked away into the river."

"But I understand that all the other clothes were found in the room. Would the body be dressed in a coat alone?"

"No, sir, but the facts might be met speciously enough. Suppose that this man Boone had thrust Neville St. Clair through the window, there is no human eye which could have seen the deed. What would he do then? It would of course instantly strike him that he must get rid of the tell-tale garments. He would seize the coat then, and be in the act of throwing it out, when it would occur to him that it would swim and not sink. He has little time, for he has heard the scuffle downstairs when the wife tried to force her way up, and perhaps he has already heard from his Lascar confederate that the police are hurrying up the street. There is not an instant to be lost. He rushes to some secret hoard, where he has accumulated the fruits of his beggary, and he stuffs all the coins upon which he can lay his hands into the pockets to make sure of the coat's sinking. He throws it out, and would have done the same with the other garments had not he heard the rush of steps below, and only just had time to close the window when the police appeared."

"It certainly sounds feasible."

"Well, we will take it as a working hypothesis for want of a better. Boone, as I have told you, was arrested and taken to the station, but it could not be shown that there had ever before been anything against him. He had for years been known as a professional beggar, but his life appeared to have been a very quiet and innocent one. There the matter stands at present, and the questions which have to be solved, what Neville St. Clair was doing in the opium den, what happened to him when there, where is he now, and what Hugh Boone had to do with his disappearance, are all as far from a solution as ever. I confess that I cannot recall any case within my experience which looked at the first glance so simple, and yet which presented such difficulties."

While Sherlock Holmes had been detailing this singular series of events, we had been whirling through the outskirts of the great town until the last straggling houses had been left behind, and we rattled along with a country hedge upon either side of us. Just as he finished, however, we drove through two scattered villages, where a few lights still glimmered in the windows.

"We are on the outskirts of Lee," said my companion. "We have touched on three English counties in our short drive, starting in Middlesex, passing over an angle of Surrey, and ending in Kent. See that light among the trees? That is The Cedars, and beside that lamp sits a woman whose anxious ears have already, I have little doubt, caught the clink of our horse's feet."

"But why are you not conducting the case from Baker-street?" I asked.

"Because there are many inquiries which must be made out here. Mrs. St. Clair has most kindly put two rooms at my disposal, and you may rest assured that she will have nothing but a welcome for my friend and colleague. I hate to meet her, Watson, when I have no news of her husband. Here we are. Whoa, there, whoa!"

We had pulled up in front of a large villa which stood within its own grounds. A stable-boy had run out to the horse's head, and, springing down, I followed Holmes up the small, winding gravel drive which led to the house. As we approached, the door flew open, and a little blonde woman stood in the opening, clad in some sort of light mousseline de soie, with a touch of fluffy pink chiffon at her neck and wrists. She stood with her figure outlined against the flood of light, one hand upon the door, one half raised in her eagerness, her body slightly bent, her head and face protruded, with eager eyes and parted lips, a standing question.

"Well?" she cried, "well?" And then, seeing that there were two of us, she gave a cry of hope which sank into a groan as she saw that my companion shook his head and shrugged his shoulders.

"No good news?"

"None."

"No bad?"

"No."

"Thank God for that. But come in. You must be weary, for you have had a long day."

"This is my friend, Dr. Watson. He has been of most vital use to me in several of my cases, and a lucky chance has made it possible for me to bring him out and associate him with this investigation."

"I am delighted to see you," said she, pressing my hand warmly. "You will, I am sure, forgive anything that may be wanting in our arrangements, when you consider the blow which has come so suddenly upon us."

"My dear madam," said I, "I am an old campaigner, and if I were not, I can very well see that no apology is needed. If I can be of any assistance, either to you or to my friend here, I shall be indeed happy."

"Now, Mr. Sherlock Holmes," said the lady as we entered a well-lit dining-room, upon the table of which a cold supper had been laid out, "I should very much like to ask you one or two plain questions, to which I beg that you will give a plain answer."

"Certainly, madam."

"Do not trouble about my feelings. I am not hysterical, nor given to fainting. I simply wish to hear your real, real opinion."

"Upon what point?"

"In your heart of hearts, do you think that Neville is alive?"

Sherlock Holmes seemed to be embarrassed by the question. "Frankly, now!" she repeated, standing upon the rug and looking keenly down at him as he leaned back in a basket-chair.

"Frankly, then, madam, I do not."

"You think that he is dead?"

"I do."

"Murdered?"

"I don't say that. Perhaps."

"And on what day did he meet his death?"

"On Monday."

"Then perhaps, Mr. Holmes, you will be good enough to explain how it is that I have received a letter from him to-day."

Sherlock Holmes sprang out of his chair as if he had been galvanized.

"What!" he roared.

"Yes, to-day." She stood smiling, holding up a little slip of paper in the air.

"May I see it?"

"Certainly."

He snatched it from her in his eagerness, and smoothing it out upon the table he drew over the lamp and examined it intently. I had left my chair and was gazing at it over his shoulder. The envelope was a very coarse one and was stamped with the Gravesend post-mark and with the date of that very day, or rather of the day before, for it was considerably after midnight.

"Coarse writing," murmured Holmes. "Surely this is not your husband's writing, madam."

"No, but the enclosure is."

"I perceive also that whoever addressed the envelope had to go and inquire as to the address."

"How can you tell that?"

"The name, you see, is in perfectly black ink, which has dried itself. The rest is of the grayish color, which shows that blotting-paper has been used. If it had been written straight off, and then blotted, none would be of a deep black shade. This man has written the name, and there has then been a pause before he wrote the address, which can only mean that he was not familiar with it. It is, of course, a trifle, but there is nothing so important as trifles. Let us now see the letter. Ha! there has been an enclosure here!"

"Yes, there was a ring. His signet-ring."

"And you are sure that this is your husband's hand?"

"One of his hands."

"One?"

"His hand when he wrote hurriedly. It is very unlike his usual writing, and yet I know it well."

"'Dearest do not be frightened. All will come well. There is a huge error which it may take some little time to rectify. Wait in patience.—Neville.' Written in pencil upon the fly-leaf of a book, octavo size, no water-mark. Hum! Posted to-day in Gravesend by a man with a dirty thumb. Ha! And the flap has been gummed, if I am not very much in error, by a person who had been chewing tobacco. And you have no doubt that it is your husband's hand, madam?"

"None. Neville wrote those words."

"And they were posted to-day at Gravesend. Well, Mrs. St. Clair, the clouds lighten, though I should not venture to say that the danger is over."

"But he must be alive, Mr. Holmes."

"Unless this is a clever forgery to put us on the wrong scent. The ring, after all, proves nothing. It may have been taken from him."

"No, no; it is, it is, it is his very own writing!"

"Very well. It may, however, have been written on Monday and only posted to-day."

"That is possible."

"If so, much may have happened between."

"Oh, you must not discourage me, Mr. Holmes. I know that all is well with him. There is so keen a sympathy between us that I should know if evil came upon him. On the very day that I saw him last he cut himself in the bedroom, and yet I in the dining-room rushed upstairs instantly with the utmost certainty that something had happened. Do you think that I would respond to such a trifle and yet be ignorant of his death?"

"I have seen too much not to know that the impression of a woman may be more valuable than the conclusion of an analytical reasoner. And in this letter you certainly have a very strong piece of evidence to corroborate your view. But if your husband is alive and able to write letters, why should he remain away from you?"

"I cannot imagine. It is unthinkable."

"And on Monday he made no remarks before leaving you?"

"No."

"And you were surprised to see him in Swandam-lane?"

"Very much so."

"Was the window open?"

"Yes."

"Then he might have called to you?"

"He might."

"He only, as I understand, gave an inarticulate cry?"

"Yes."

"A call for help, you thought?"

"Yes. He waved his hands."

"But it might have been a cry of surprise. Astonishment at the unexpected sight of you might cause him to throw up his hands?"

"It is possible."

"And you thought he was pulled back?"

"He disappeared so suddenly."

"He might have leaped back. You did not see anyone else in the room?"

"No, but this horrible man confessed to having been there, and the Lascar was at the foot of the stairs."

"Quite so. Your husband, as far as you could see, had his ordinary clothes on?"

"But without his collar or tie. I distinctly saw his bare throat."

"Had he ever spoken of Swandam-lane?"

"Never."

"Had he ever showed any signs of having taken opium?"

"Never."

"Thank you, Mrs. St. Clair. Those are the principal points about which I wished to be absolutely clear. We shall now have a little supper and then retire, for we may have a very busy day to-morrow."

A large and comfortable double-bedded room had been placed at our disposal, and I was quickly between the sheets, for I was weary after my night of adventure. Sherlock Holmes was a man, however, who, when he had an unsolved problem upon his mind, would go for days, and even for a week, without rest, turning it over, rearranging his facts, looking at it from every point of view until he had either fathomed it or convinced himself that his data were insufficient. It was soon evident to me that he was now preparing for an all-night sitting. He took off his coat and waistcoat, put on a large blue dressing-gown, and then wandered about the room collecting pillows from his bed and cushions from the sofa and armchairs. With these he constructed a sort of Eastern divan, upon which he perched himself cross-legged, with an ounce of shag tobacco and a box of matches laid out in front of him. In the dim light of the lamp I saw him sitting there, an old brier pipe between his lips, his eyes fixed vacantly upon the corner of the ceiling, the blue smoke curling up from him, silent, motionless, with the light shining upon his strong set aquiline features. So he sat as I dropped off to sleep, and so he sat when a sudden ejaculation caused me to wake up, and I found the summer sun shining into the apartment. The pipe was still between his lips, the smoke still curled upward, and the room was full of a dense tobacco haze, but nothing remained of the heap of shag which I had seen upon the previous night.

"Awake, Watson?" he asked.

"Yes."

"Game for a morning drive?"

"Certainly."

"Then dress. No one is stirring yet, but I know where the stable boy sleeps, and we shall soon have the trap out." He chuckled to himself as he spoke, his eyes twinkled, and he seemed a different man to the sombre thinker of the previous night.

As I dressed I glanced at my watch. It was no wonder that no one was stirring. It was twenty-five minutes past four. I had hardly finished when Holmes returned with the news that the boy was putting in the horse.

"I want to test a little theory of mine," said he, pulling on his boots. "I think, Watson, that you are now standing in the presence of one of the most absolute fools in Europe. I deserve to be kicked from here to Charing Cross. But I think I have the key of the affair now."

"And where is it?" I asked, smiling.

"In the bath-room," he answered. "Oh, yes, I am not joking," he continued, seeing my look of incredulity. "I have just been there, and I have taken it out, and I have got it in this Gladstone bag. Come on, my boy, and we shall see whether it will not fit the lock."

We made our way downstairs as quietly as possible, and out into the bright morning sunshine. In the road stood our horse and trap, with the half-clad stable boy waiting at the head. We both sprang in, and away we dashed down the London-road. A few country carts were stirring, bearing in vegetables to the metropolis, but the lines of villas on either side were as silent and lifeless as some city in a dream.

It has been in some points a singular case," said Holmes, flicking the horse on into a gallop. "I confess that I have been as blind as a mole, but it is better to learn wisdom late than never to learn it at all."

In town the earliest risers were just beginning to look sleepily from their windows as we drove through the streets of the Surrey side. Passing down the Waterloo Bridge-road we crossed over the river, and dashing up Wellington-street wheeled sharply to the right and found ourselves in Bow-street. Sherlock Holmes was well known to the force, and the two constables at the door saluted him. One of them held the horse's head while the other led us in.

"Who is on duty?" asked Holmes.

"Inspector Bradstreet, sir."

"Ah, Bradstreet, how are you?" A tall, stout official had come down the stone-flagged passage, in a peaked cap and frogged jacket. "I wish to have a quiet word with you, Bradstreet."

"Certainly, Mr. Holmes. Step into my room here."

It was a small, office-like room, with a huge ledger upon the table, and a telephone projecting from the wall. The inspector sat down at his desk.

"What can I do for you, Mr. Holmes?"

"I called about that beggarman, Boone—the one who was charged with being concerned in the disappearance of Mr. Neville St. Clair, of Lee."

"Yes. He was brought up and remanded for further inquiries."

"So I heard. You have him here?"

"In the cells."

"Is he quiet?"

"Oh, he gives no trouble. But he is a dirty scoundrel."

"Dirty?"

"Yes, it is all we can do to make him wash his hands, and his face is as black as a tinker's. Well, when once his case has been settled, he will have a regular prison bath; and I think, if you saw him, you would agree with me that he needed it."

"I should like to see him very much."

"Would you? That is easily done. Come this way. You can leave your bag."

"No, I think that I'll take it."

"Very good. Come this way, if you please." He led us down a passage, opened a barred door, passed down a winding stair, and brought us to a whitewashed corridor with a line of doors on each side.

"The third on the right is his," said the inspector. "Here it is!" He quietly shot back a panel in the upper part of the door and glanced through.

"He is asleep," said he. "You can see him very well."

We both put our eyes to the grating. The prisoner lay with his face towards us, in a very deep sleep, breathing slowly and heavily. He was a middle-sized man, coarsely clad as became his calling, with a coloured shirt protruding through the rent in his tattered coat. He was, as the inspector had said, extremely dirty, but the grime which covered his face could not conceal its repulsive ugliness. A broad wheal from an old scar ran right across it from eye to chin, and by its contraction had turned up one side of the upper lip, so that three teeth were exposed in a perpetual snarl. A shock of very bright red hair grew low over his eyes and forehead.

"He's a beauty, isn't he?" said the inspector.

"He certainly needs a wash," remarked Holmes. "I had an idea that he might, and I took the liberty of bringing the tools with me." He opened the Gladstone bag as he spoke, and took out, to my astonishment, a very large bath sponge.

"He! he! You are a funny one," chuckled the inspector.

"Now, if you will have the great goodness to open that door very quietly, we will soon make him cut a much more respectable figure."

"Well, I don't know why not," said the inspector. "He doesn't look a credit to the Bow Street cells, does he?" He slipped his key into the lock, and we all very quietly entered the cell. The sleeper half turned, and then settled down once more into a deep slumber. Holmes stooped to the waterjug, moistened his sponge, and then rubbed it twice vigorously across and down the prisoner's face.

"Let me introduce you," he shouted, "to Mr. Neville St. Clair, of Lee, in the county of Kent."

Never in my life have I seen such a sight. The man's face peeled off under the sponge like the bark from a tree. Gone was the coarse brown tint! Gone, too, was the horrid scar which had seamed it across, and the twisted lip which had given the repulsive sneer to the face! A twitch brought away the tangled red hair, and there, sitting up in his bed, was a pale, sad-faced, refined-looking man, black-haired and smooth-skinned, rubbing his eyes and staring about him with sleepy bewilderment. Then suddenly realizing the exposure, he broke into a scream and threw himself down with his face to the pillow.

"Great heavens!" cried the inspector, "it is, indeed, the missing man. I know him from the photograph."

The prisoner turned with the reckless air of a man who abandons himself to his destiny. "Be it so," said he. "And pray what am I charged with?"

"With making away with Mr. Neville St. — — Oh, come, you can't be charged with that unless they make a case of attempted suicide of it," said the inspector with a grin. "Well, I have been twenty-seven years in the force, but this really takes the cake."

"If I am Mr. Neville St. Clair, then it is obvious that no crime has been committed, and that, therefore, I am illegally detained."

"No crime, but a very great error has been committed," said Holmes. "You would have done better to have trusted your wife."

"It was not the wife; it was the children," groaned the prisoner. "God help me, I would not have them ashamed of their father. My God! What an exposure! What can I do?"

Sherlock Holmes sat down beside him on the couch, and patted him kindly on the shoulder.

"If you leave it to a court of law to clear the matter up," said he, "of course you can hardly avoid publicity. On the other hand, if you convince the police authorities that there is no possible case against you, I do not know that there is any reason that the details should find their way into the papers. Inspector Bradstreet would, I am sure, make notes upon anything which you might tell us and submit it to the proper authorities. The case would then never go into court at all."

"God bless you!" cried the prisoner passionately. "I would have endured imprisonment, aye, even execution, rather than have left my miserable secret as a family blot to my children."

"You are the first who have ever heard my story. My father was a schoolmaster in Chesterfield, where I received an excellent education. I travelled in my youth, took to the stage, and finally became a reporter on an evening paper in London. One day my editor wished to have a series of articles upon begging in the metropolis, and I volunteered to supply them. There was the point from which all my adventures started.

It was only by trying begging as an amateur that I could get the facts upon which to base my articles. When an actor I had, of course, learned all the secrets of making up, and had been famous in the green-room for my skill. I took advantage now of my attainments. I painted my face, and to make myself as pitiable as possible I made a good scar and fixed one side of my lip in a twist by the aid of a small slip of flesh-colored plaster. Then with a red head of hair, and an appropriate dress, I took my station in the business part of the city, ostensibly as a match-seller but really as a beggar. For seven hours I plied my trade, and when I returned home in the evening I found to my surprise that I had received no less than twenty-six shillings and fourpence.

"I wrote my articles and thought little more of the matter until, some time later, I backed a bill for a friend and had a writ served upon me for £25. I was at my wit's end where to get the money, but a sudden idea came to me. I begged a fortnight's grace from the creditor, asked for a holiday from my employers, and spent the time in begging in the City under my disguise. In ten days I had the money and had paid the debt.

"Well, you can imagine how hard it was to settle down to arduous work at £2 a week when I knew that I could earn as much in a day by smearing my face with a little paint, laying my cap on the ground, and sitting still. It was a long fight between my pride and the money, but the dollars won at last, and I threw up reporting and sat day after day in the corner which I had first chosen, inspiring pity by my ghastly face and filling my pockets with coppers. Only one man knew my secret. He was the keeper of a low den in which I used to lodge in Swandam-lane, where I could every morning emerge as a squalid beggar and in the evenings transform myself into a well-dressed man about town. This fellow, a Lascar, was well paid by me for his rooms, so that I knew that my secret was safe in his possession.

"Well, very soon I found that I was saving considerable sums of money. I do not mean that any beggar in the streets of London could earn seven hundred pounds a year — which is less than my average takings — but I had exceptional advantages in my power of making up, and also in a facility of repartee, which improved by practice and made me quite a recognized character in the City. All day a stream of pennies, varied by silver, poured in upon me, and it was a very bad day in which I failed to take two pounds.

"As I grew richer I grew more ambitious, took a house in the country, and eventually married, without anyone having a suspicion as to my real occupation. My dear wife knew that I had business in the City. She little knew what.

"Last Monday I had finished for the day, and was dressing in my room above the opium den, when I looked out of my window and saw, to my horror and astonishment, that my wife was standing in the street, with her eyes fixed full upon me. I gave a cry of surprise, threw up my arms to cover my face, and, rushing to my confidant, the Lascar, entreated him to prevent anyone from coming up to me. I heard her voice downstairs, but I knew that she could not ascend. Swiftly I threw off my clothes, pulled on those of a beggar, and put on my pigments and wig. Even a wife's eyes could not pierce so complete a disguise. But then it occurred to me that there might be a search in the room, and that the clothes might betray me. I threw open the window, re-opening by my violence a small cut which I had inflicted upon myself in the bedroom that morning. Then I seized my coat, which was weighted by the coppers which I had just transferred to it from the leather bag in which I carried my takings. I hurled it out of the window, and it disappeared into the Thames. The other clothes would have followed, but at that moment there was a rush of constables up the stair, and a few minutes after I found, rather, I confess, to my relief, that instead of being identified as Mr. Neville St. Clair, I was arrested as his murderer.

"I do not know that there is anything else for me to explain. I was determined to preserve my disguise as long as possible, and hence my preference for a dirty face. Knowing that my wife would be terribly anxious, I slipped off my ring and confided it to the Lascar at a moment when no constable was watching me, together with a hurried scrawl, telling her that she had no cause to fear."

"That note only reached her yesterday," said Holmes.

"Good God! What a week she must have spent!"

"The police have watched this Lascar," said Inspector Bradstreet, "and I can quite understand that he might find it difficult to post a letter unobserved. Probably he handed it to some sailor customer of his, who forgot all about it for some days."

"That was it," said Holmes, nodding approvingly; "I have no doubt of it. But have you never been prosecuted for begging?"

"Many times; but what was a fine to me?"

"It must stop here, however," said Bradstreet. "If the police are to hush this thing up, there must be no more of Hugh Boone."

"I have sworn it by the most solemn oaths which a man can take."

"In that case I think that it is probable that no further steps may be taken. But if you are found again, then all must come out. I am sure, Mr. Holmes, that we are very much indebted to you for having cleared the matter up. I wish I knew how you reach your results."

"I reached this one," said my friend, "by sitting upon five pillows and consuming an ounce of shag. I think, Watson, that if we drive to Baker-street we shall just be in time for breakfast."

Margaret Oliphant (1828-1897)

The Library Window (1896)

A STORY OF THE SEEN AND THE UNSEEN.

I WAS not aware at first of the many discussions which had gone on about that window. It was almost opposite one of the windows of the large old-fashioned drawing-room of the house in which I spent that summer, which was of so much importance in my life. Our house and the library were on opposite sides of the broad High Street of St Rule's, which is a fine street, wide and ample, and very quiet, as strangers think who come from noisier places; but in a summer evening there is much coming and going, and the stillness is full of sound the sound of foot-steps and pleasant voices, softened by the summer air. There are even exceptional moments when it is noisy: the time of the fair, and on Saturday nights sometimes, and when there are excursion trains. Then even the softest sunny air of the evening will not smooth the harsh tones and the stumbling steps; but at these unlovely moments we shut the windows, and even I, who am so fond of that deep recess where I can take refuge from all that is going on inside, and make myself a spectator of all the varied story out of doors, withdraw from my watch-tower. To tell the truth, there never was very much going on inside. The house belonged to my aunt, to whom (she says, Thank God!) nothing ever happens. I believe that many things have happened to her in her time; but that was all over at the period of which I am speaking, and she was old, and very quiet. Her life went on in a routine never broken. She got up at the same hour every day, and did the same things in the same rotation, day by day the same. She said that this was the greatest support in the world, and that routine is a kind of salvation. It may be so; but it is a very dull salvation, and I used to feel that I would rather have incident, what-ever kind of incident it might be. But then at that time I was not old, which makes all the difference.

At the time of which I speak the deep recess of the drawing-room window was a great comfort to me. Though she was an old lady (perhaps because she was so old) she was very tolerant, and had a kind of feeling for me. She never said a word, but often gave me a smile when she saw how I had built myself up, with my books and my basket of work. I did very little work, I fear — now and then a few stitches when the spirit moved me, or when I had got well afloat in a dream, and was more tempted to follow it out than to read my book, as sometimes happened. At other times, and if the book were interesting, I used to get through volume after volume sitting there, paying no attention to anybody. And yet I did pay a kind of attention. Aunt Mary's old ladies came in to call, and I heard them talk, though I very seldom listened; but for all that, if they had anything to say that was interesting, it is curious how I found it in my mind afterwards, as if the air had blown it to me. They came and went, and I had the sensation of their old bonnets gliding out and in, and their dresses rustling; and now and then had to jump up and shake hands with some one who knew me,

341

and asked after my papa and mamma. Then Aunt Mary would give me a little smile again, and I slipped back to my window. She never seemed to mind. My mother would not have let me do it, I know. She would have remembered dozens of things there were to do. She would have sent me up-stairs to fetch something which I was quite sure she did not want, or down-stairs to carry some quite unnecessary message to the housemaid. She liked to keep me running about. Perhaps that was one reason why I was so fond of Aunt Mary's drawing-room, and the deep recess of the window, and the curtain that fell half over it, and the broad window-seat, where one could collect so many things without being found fault with for untidiness. Whenever we had anything the matter with us in these days, we were sent to St Rule's to get up our strength. And this was my case at the time of which I am going to speak.

Everybody had said, since ever I learned to speak, that I was fantastic and fanciful and dreamy, and all the other words with which a girl who may happen to like poetry, and to be fond of thinking, is so often made uncomfortable. People don't know what they mean when they say fantastic. It sounds like Madge Wildfire or something of that sort. My mother thought I should always be busy, to keep nonsense out of my head. But really I was not at all fond of nonsense. I was rather serious than otherwise. I would have been no trouble to anybody if I had been left to myself. It was only that I had a sort of second-sight, and was conscious of things to which I paid no attention. Even when reading the most interesting book, the things that were being talked about blew in to me; and I heard what the people were saying in the streets as they passed under the window. Aunt Mary always said I could do two or indeed three things at once — both read and listen, and see. I am sure that I did not listen much, and seldom looked out, of set purpose— as some people do who notice what bonnets the ladies in the street have on; but I did hear what I couldn't help hearing, even when I was reading my book, and I did see all sorts of things, though often for a whole half-hour I might never lift my eyes.

This does not explain what I said at the beginning, that there were many discussions about that window. It was, and still is, the last window in the row, of the College Library, which is opposite my aunt's house in the High Street. Yet it is not exactly opposite, but a little to the west, so that I could see it best from the left side of my recess. I took it calmly for granted that it was a window like any other till I first heard the talk about it which was going on in the drawing-room. "Have you never made up your mind, Mrs Balcarres," said old Mr Pitmilly, "whether that window opposite is a window or no?" He said Mistress Balcarres — and he was always called Mr Pitmilly, Morton: which was the name of his place.

"I am never sure of it, to tell the truth," said Aunt Mary, "all these years."

"Bless me!" said one of the old ladies, "and what window may that be?"

Mr Pitmilly had a way of laughing as he spoke, which did not please me; but it was true that he was not perhaps desirous of pleasing me. He said, "Oh, just the window opposite," with his laugh running through his words; "our friend can never make up her mind about it, though she has been living opposite it since —"

"You need never mind the date," said another; "the Leebrary window! Dear me, what should it be but a window up at that height it could not be a door."

"The question is," said my aunt, "if it is a real window with glass in it, or if it is merely painted, or if it once was a window, and has been built up. And the oftener people look at it, the less they are able to say."

"Let me see this window," said old Lady Carnbee, who was very active and strong minded; and then they all came crowding upon me — three or four old ladies, very eager, and Mr Pitmilly's white hair appearing over their heads, and my aunt sitting quiet and smiling behind.

"I mind the window very well," said Lady Carnbee; "ay: and so do more than me. But in its present appearance it is just like any other window; but has not been cleaned, I should say, in the memory of man."

"I see what ye mean," said one of the others. "It is just a very dead thing without any reflection in it; but I've seen as bad before."

"Ay, it's dead enough," said another, "but that's no rule; for these hizzies of women-servants in this ill age —"

"Nay, the women are well enough," said the softest voice of all, which was Aunt Mary's. "I will never let them risk their lives cleaning the outside of mine. And there are no women servants in the Old Library: there is maybe something more in it than that."

They were all pressing into my recess, pressing upon me, a row of old faces, peering into something they could not understand. I had a sense in my mind how curious it was, the wall of old ladies in their old satin gowns all glazed with age, Lady Carnbee with her lace about her head. Nobody was looking at me or thinking of me; but I felt unconsciously the contrast of my youngness to their oldness, and stared at them as they stared over my head at the Library window. I had given it no attention up to this time. I was more taken up with the old ladies than with the thing they were looking at.

"The framework is all right at least, I can see that, and pented black —"

"And the panes are pented black too. It's no window, Mrs Balcarres. It has been filled in, in the days of the window duties: you will mind, Leddy Carnbee."

"Mind!" said that oldest lady. "I mind when your mother was marriet, Jeanie: and that's neither the day nor yesterday. But as for the window, it's just a delusion: and that is my opinion of the matter, if you ask me."

"There's a great want of light in that muckle room at the college," said another. "If it was a window, the Leebrary would have more light."

"One thing is clear," said one of the younger ones, "it cannot be a window to see through. It may be filled in or it may be built up, but it is not a window to give light."

"And who ever heard of a window that was no to see through?" Lady Carnbee said. I was fascinated by the look on her face, which was a curious scornful look as of one who knew more than she chose to say: and then my wandering fancy was caught by her hand as she held it up, throwing back the lace that drooped over it. Lady Carnbee's lace was the chief thing about her — heavy black Spanish lace with large flowers. Everything she wore was trimmed with it. A large veil of it hung over her old bonnet. But her hand coming out of this heavy lace was a curious thing to see. She had very long fingers, very taper, which had been much admired in her youth; and her hand was very white, or rather more than white, pale, bleached, and bloodless, with large blue veins standing up upon the back; and she wore some fine rings, among others a big diamond in an ugly old claw setting. They were too big for her, and were wound round and round with yellow silk to make them keep on: and this little cushion of silk, turned brown with long wearing, had twisted round so that it was more conspicuous than the jewels; while the big diamond blazed underneath in the hollow of her hand, like some dangerous thing hiding and sending out darts of light. The hand, which seemed to come almost to a point, with this strange ornament underneath, clutched at my half-terrified imagination. It too seemed to mean far more than was said. I felt as if it might clutch me with sharp claws, and the lurking, dazzling creature bite — with a sting that would go to the heart.

Presently, however, the circle of the old faces broke up, the old ladies returned to their seats, and Mr Pitmilly, small but very erect, stood up in the midst of them, talking with mild authority like a little oracle among the ladies. Only Lady Carnbee always contradicted the neat, little, old gentleman. She gesticulated, when she talked, like a Frenchwoman, and darted forth that hand of hers with the lace hanging over it, so that I always caught a glimpse of the lurking diamond. I thought she looked like a witch among the comfortable little group which gave such attention to everything Mr Pitmilly said.

"For my part, it is my opinion there is no window there at all," he said. "It's very like the thing that's called in scienteefic language an optical illusion. It arises generally, if I may use such a word in the presence of ladies, from a liver that is not just in the perfitt order and balance that organ demands — and then you will see things — a blue dog, I remember, was the thing in one case, and in another —"

"The man has gane gyte," said Lady Carnbee; "I mind the windows in the Auld Leebrary as long as I mind anything. Is the Leebrary itself an optical illusion too?"

"Na, na," and "No, no," said the old ladies; "a blue dogue would be a strange vagary: but the Library we have all kent from our youth," said one. "And I mind when the Assemblies were held there one year when the Town Hall was building," another said.

"It is just a great divert to me," said Aunt Mary: but what was strange was that she paused there, and said in a low tone, "now": and then went on again, "for whoever comes to my house, there are aye discussions about that window. I have never just made up my mind about it myself. Sometimes I think it's a case of these wicked window duties, as you said, Miss Jeanie, when half the windows in our houses were blocked up to save the tax. And then, I think, it may be due to that blank kind of building like the great new buildings on the Earthen Mound in Edinburgh, where the windows are just ornaments. And then whiles I am sure I can see the glass shining when the sun catches it in the afternoon."

"You could so easily satisfy yourself, Mrs Balcarres, if you were to —"

"Give a laddie a penny to cast a stone, and see what happens," said Lady Carnbee.

"But I am not sure that I have any desire to satisfy myself," Aunt Mary said. And then there was a stir in the room, and I had to come out from my recess and open the door for the old ladies and see them down-stairs, as they all went away following one another. Mr Pitmilly gave his arm to Lady Carnbee, though she was always contradicting him; and so the tea-party dispersed. Aunt Mary came to the head of the stairs with her guests in an old-fashioned gracious way, while I went down with them to see that the maid was ready at the door. When I came back Aunt Mary was still standing in the recess looking out. Returning to my seat she said, with a kind of wistful look, "Well, honey: and what is your opinion?"

"I have no opinion. I was reading my book all the time," I said.

"And so you were, honey, and no' very civil; but all the same I ken well you heard every word we said."

II

It was a night in June; dinner was long over, and had it been winter the maids would have been shutting up the house, and my Aunt Mary preparing to go upstairs to her room. But it was still clear daylight, that daylight out of which the sun has been long gone, and which has no longer any rose reflections, but all has sunk into a pearly neutral tint—a light which is daylight yet is not day.

We had taken a turn in the garden after dinner, and now we had returned to what we called our usual occupations. My aunt was reading. The English post had come in, and she had got her 'Times,' which was her great diversion. The 'Scotsman' was her morning reading, but she liked her 'Times' at night.

As for me, I too was at my usual occupation, which at that time was doing nothing. I had a book as usual, and was absorbed in it: but I was conscious of all that was going on all the same. The people strolled along the broad pavement, making remarks as they passed under the open window which came up into my story or my dream, and sometimes made me laugh. The tone and the faint sing-song, or rather chant, of the accent, which was "a wee Fifish," was novel to me, and associated with holiday, and pleasant; and sometimes they said to each other something that was amusing, and often something that suggested a whole story; but presently they began to drop off, the footsteps slackened, the voices died away. It was getting late, though the clear soft daylight went on and on. All through the lingering evening, which seemed to consist of interminable hours, long but not weary, drawn out as if the spell of the light and the outdoor life might never end, I had now and then, quite unawares, cast a glance at the mysterious window which my aunt and her friends had discussed, as I felt, though I dared not say it even to myself, rather foolishly. It caught my eye without any intention on my part, as I paused, as it were, to take breath, in the flowing and current of undistinguishable thoughts and things from without and within which carried me along. First it occurred to me, with a little sensation of discovery, how absurd to say it was not a window, a living window, one to see through! Why, then, had they never *seen* it, these old folk? I saw as I looked up suddenly the faint greyness as of visible space within—a room behind, certainly—dim, as it was natural a room should be on the other side of the street—quite indefinite: yet so clear that if some one were to come to the window there would be nothing surprising in it. For certainly there was a feeling of space behind the panes which these old half-blind ladies had disputed about whether they were glass or only fictitious panes marked on the wall. How silly! when eyes that could see could make it out in a minute. It was only a greyness at present, but it was unmistakable, a space that went back into gloom, as every room does when you look into it across a street. There were no curtains to show whether it was inhabited or not; but a room—oh, as distinctly as ever room was! I was pleased with myself, but said nothing, while Aunt Mary rustled her paper, waiting for a favourable moment to announce a discovery which settled her problem at once. Then I was carried away upon the stream again, and forgot the window, till somebody threw unawares a word from the outer world, "I'm goin' hame; it'll soon be dark." Dark! what was the fool thinking of? it never would be dark if one waited out, wandering in the soft air for hours longer; and then my eyes, acquiring easily that new habit, looked across the way again.

Ah, now! nobody indeed had come to the window; and no light had been lighted, seeing it was still beautiful to read by—a still, clear, colourless light; but the room inside had certainly widened.

I could see the grey space and air a little deeper, and a sort of vision, very dim, of a wall, and something against it; something dark, with the blackness that a solid article, however indistinctly seen, takes in the lighter darkness that is only space—a large, black, dark thing coming out into the grey. I looked more intently, and made sure it was a piece of furniture, either a writing-table or perhaps a large bookcase. No doubt it must be the last, since this was part of the old library. I never visited the old College Library, but I had seen such places before, and I could well imagine it to myself. How curious that for all the time these old people had looked at it, they had never seen this before!

It was more silent now, and my eyes, I suppose, had grown dim with gazing, doing my best to make it out, when suddenly Aunt Mary said, "Will you ring the bell, my dear? I must have my lamp."

"Your lamp?" I cried, "when it is still daylight." But then I gave another look at my window, and perceived with a start that the light had indeed changed: for now I saw nothing. It was still light, but there was so much change in the light that my room, with the grey space and the large shadowy bookcase, had gone out, and I saw them no more: for even a Scotch night in June, though it looks as if it would never end, does darken at the last. I had almost cried out, but checked myself, and rang the bell for Aunt Mary, and made up my mind I would say nothing till next morning, when to be sure naturally it would be more clear.

Next morning I rather think I forgot all about it—or was busy: or was more idle than usual: the two things meant nearly the same. At all events

I thought no more of the window, though I still sat in my own, opposite to it, but occupied with some other fancy. Aunt Mary's visitors came as usual in the afternoon; but their talk was of other things, and for a day or two nothing at all happened to bring back my thoughts into this channel. It might be nearly a week before the subject came back, and once more it was old Lady Carnbee who set me thinking; not that she said anything upon that particular theme. But she was the last of my aunt's afternoon guests to go away, and when she rose to leave she threw up her hands, with those lively gesticulations which so many old Scotch ladies have. "My faith!" said she, "there is that bairn there still like a dream. Is the creature bewitched, Mary Balcarres? and is she bound to sit there by night and by day for the rest of her days? You should mind that there's things about, uncanny for women of our blood."

I was too much startled at first to recognise that it was of me she was speaking. She was like a figure in a picture, with her pale face the colour of ashes, and the big pattern of the Spanish lace hanging half over it, and her hand held up, with the big diamond blazing at me from the inside of her uplifted palm. It was held up in surprise, but it looked as if it were raised in malediction; and the diamond threw out darts of light and glared and twinkled at me. If it had been in its right place it would not have mattered; but there, in the open of the hand! I started up, half in terror, half in wrath. And then the old lady laughed, and her hand dropped. "I've wakened you to life, and broke the spell," she said, nodding her old head at me while the large black silk flowers of the lace waved and threatened. And she took my arm to go downstairs, laughing and bidding me be steady, and no' tremble and shake like a broken reed. "You should be as steady as a rock at your age. I was like a young tree," she said, leaning so heavily that my willowy girlish frame quivered—"I was a support to virtue, like Pamela, in my time."

"Aunt Mary, Lady Carnbee is a witch!" I cried, when I came back.

"Is that what you think, honey? well: maybe she once was," said Aunt Mary, whom nothing surprised.

And it was that night once more after dinner, and after the post came in, and the 'Times,' that I suddenly saw the Library window again. I had seen it every day—and noticed nothing; but to-night, still in a little tumult of mind over Lady Carnbee and her wicked diamond which wished me harm, and her lace which waved threats and warnings at me, I looked across the street, and there I saw quite plainly the room opposite, far more clear than before. I saw dimly that it must be a large room, and that the big piece of furniture against the wall was a writing-desk. That in a moment, when first my eyes rested upon it, was quite clear: a large old-fashioned escritoire, standing out into the room: and I knew by the shape of it that it had a great many pigeon-holes and little drawers in the back, and a large table for writing. There was one just like it in my father's library at home. It was such a surprise to see it all so clearly that I closed my eyes, for the moment almost giddy, wondering how papa's desk could have come here—and then when I reminded myself that this was nonsense, and that there were many such writing-tables besides papa's, and looked again—lo! it had all become quite vague and indistinct as it was at first; and I saw nothing but the blank window, of which the old ladies could never be certain whether it was filled up to avoid the window-tax, or whether it had ever been a window at all.

This occupied my mind very much, and yet I did not say anything to Aunt Mary. For one thing, I rarely saw anything at all in the early part of the day; but then that is natural: you can never see into a place from outside, whether it is an empty room or a looking-glass, or people's eyes, or anything else that is mysterious, in the day. It has, I suppose, something to do with the light. But in the evening in June in Scotland — then is the time to see. For it is daylight, yet it is not day, and there is a quality in it which I cannot describe, it is so clear, as if every object was a reflection of itself.

I used to see more and more of the room as the days went on. The large escritoire stood out more and more into the space: with sometimes white glimmering things, which looked like papers, lying on it: and once or twice I was sure I saw a pile of books on the floor close to the writing-table, as if they had gilding upon them in broken specks, like old books. It was always about the time when the lads in the street began to call to each other that they were going home, and sometimes a shriller voice would come from one of the doors, bidding somebody to "cry upon the laddies" to come back to their suppers. That was always the time I saw best, though it was close upon the moment when the veil seemed to fall and the clear radiance became less living, and all the sounds died out of the street, and Aunt Mary said in her soft voice, "Honey! will you ring for the lamp?" She said honey as people say darling: and I think it is a prettier word.

Then finally, while I sat one evening with my book in my hand, looking straight across the street, not distracted by anything, I saw a little movement within. It was not any one visible — but everybody must know what it is to see the stir in the air, the little disturbance — you cannot tell what it is, but that it indicates some one there, even though you can see no one. Perhaps it is a shadow making just one flicker in the still place. You may look at an empty room and the furniture in it for hours, and then suddenly there will be the flicker, and you know that something has come into it. It might only be a dog or a cat; it might be, if that were possible, a bird flying across; but it is some one, something living, which is so different, so completely different, in a moment from the things that are not living. It seemed to strike quite through me, and I gave a little cry. Then Aunt Mary stirred a little, and put down the huge newspaper that almost covered her from sight, and said, "What is it, honey?" I cried "Nothing," with a little gasp, quickly, for I did not want to be disturbed just at this moment when somebody was coming! But I suppose she was not satisfied, for she got up and stood behind to see what it was, putting her hand on my shoulder. It was the softest touch in the world, but I could have flung it off angrily: for that moment everything was still again, and the place grew grey and I saw no more.

"Nothing," I repeated, but I was so vexed I could have cried. "I told you it was nothing, Aunt Mary. Don't you believe me, that you come to look — and spoil it all!"

I did not mean of course to say these last words; they were forced out of me. I was so much annoyed to see it all melt away like a dream: for it was no dream, but as real as — as real as — myself or anything I ever saw.

She gave my shoulder a little pat with her hand. "Honey," she said, "were you looking at something? Is't that? is't that?" "Is it what?" I wanted to say, shaking off her hand, but something in me stopped me: for I said nothing at all, and she went quietly back to her place. I suppose she must have rung the bell herself, for immediately I felt the soft flood of the light behind me, and the evening outside dimmed down, as it did every night, and I saw nothing more.

It was next day, I think, in the afternoon that I spoke. It was brought on by something she said about her fine work. "I get a mist before my eyes," she said; "you will have to learn my old lace stitches, honey—for I soon will not see to draw the threads."

"Oh, I hope you will keep your sight," I cried, without thinking what I was saying. I was then young and very matter-of-fact. I had not found out that one may mean something, yet not half or a hundredth part of what one seems to mean: and even then probably hoping to be contradicted if it is anyhow against one's self.

"My sight!" she said, looking up at me with a look that was almost angry; "there is no question of losing my sight—on the contrary, my eyes are very strong. I may not see to draw fine threads, but I see at a distance as well as ever I did—as well as you do."

"I did not mean any harm, Aunt Mary," I said. "I thought you said—But how can your sight be as good as ever when you are in doubt about that window? I can see into the room as clear as—" My voice wavered, for I had just looked up and across the street, and I could have sworn that there was no window at all, but only a false image of one painted on the wall.

"Ah!" she said, with a little tone of keenness and of surprise: and she half rose up, throwing down her work hastily, as if she meant to come to me: then, perhaps seeing the bewildered look on my face, she paused and hesitated—"Ay, honey!" she said, "have you got so far ben as that?"

What did she mean? Of course I knew all the old Scotch phrases as well as I knew myself; but it is a comfort to take refuge in a little ignorance, and I know I pretended not to understand whenever I was put out. "I don't know what you mean by 'far ben,'" I cried out, very impatient. I don't know what might have followed, but some one just then came to call, and she could only give me a look before she went forward, putting out her hand to her visitor. It was a very soft look, but anxious, and as if she did not know what to do: and she shook her head a very little, and I thought, though there was a smile on her face, there was something wet about her eyes. I retired into my recess, and nothing more was said.

But it was very tantalising that it should fluctuate so; for sometimes I saw that room quite plain and clear—quite as clear as I could see papa's library, for example, when I shut my eyes. I compared it naturally to my father's study, because of the shape of the writing-table, which, as I tell you, was the same as his. At times I saw the papers on the table quite plain, just as I had seen his papers many a day. And the little pile of books on the floor at the foot—not ranged regularly in order, but put down one above the other, with all their angles going different ways, and a speck of the old gilding shining here and there. And then again at other times I saw nothing, absolutely nothing, and was no better than the old ladies who had peered over my head, drawing their eyelids together, and arguing that the window had been shut up because of the old long-abolished window tax, or else that it had never been a window at all. It annoyed me very much at those dull moments to feel that I too puckered up my eyelids and saw no better than they.

Aunt Mary's old ladies came and went day after day while June went on. I was to go back in July, and I felt that I should be very unwilling indeed to leave until I had quite cleared up — as I was indeed in the way of doing — the mystery of that window which changed so strangely and appeared quite a different thing, not only to different people, but to the same eyes at different times. Of course I said to myself it must simply be an effect of the light. And yet I did not quite like that explanation either, but would have been better pleased to make out to myself that it was some superiority in me which made it so clear to me, if it were only the great superiority of young eyes over old — though that was not quite enough to satisfy me, seeing it was a superiority which I shared with every little lass and lad in the street. I rather wanted, I believe, to think that there was some particular insight in me which gave clearness to my sight — which was a most impertinent assumption, but really did not mean half the harm it seems to mean when it is put down here in black and white. I had several times again, however, seen the room quite plain, and made out that it was a large room, with a great picture in a dim gilded frame hanging on the farther wall, and many other pieces of solid furniture making a blackness here and there, besides the great escritoire against the wall, which had evidently been placed near the window for the sake of the light.

One thing became visible to me after another, till I almost thought I should end by being able to read the old lettering on one of the big volumes which projected from the others and caught the light; but this was all preliminary to the great event which happened about Midsummer Day — the day of St John, which was once so much thought of as a festival, but now means nothing at all in Scotland any more than any other of the saints' days: which I shall always think a great pity and loss to Scotland, whatever Aunt Mary may say.

III

It was about midsummer, I cannot say exactly to a day when, but near that time, when the great event happened. I had grown very well acquainted by this time with that large dim room. Not only the escritoire, which was very plain to me now, with the papers upon it, and the books at its foot, but the great picture that hung against the farther wall, and various other shadowy pieces of furniture, especially a chair which one evening I saw had been moved into the space before the escritoire, — a little change which made my heart beat, for it spoke so distinctly of some one who must have been there, the some one who had already made me start, two or three times before, by some vague shadow of him or thrill of him which made a sort of movement in the silent space: a movement which made me sure that next minute I must see something or hear something which would explain the whole—if it were not that something always happened outside to stop it, at the very moment of its accomplishment. I had no warning this time of movement or shadow. I had been looking into the room very attentively a little while before, and had made out everything almost clearer than ever; and then had bent my attention again on my book, and read a chapter or two at a most exciting period of the story: and consequently had quite left St Rule's, and the High Street, and the College Library, and was really in a South American forest, almost throttled by the flowery creepers, and treading softly lest I should put my foot on a scorpion or a dangerous snake. At this moment something suddenly calling my attention to the outside, I looked across, and then, with a start, sprang up, for I could not contain myself. I don't know what I said, but enough to startle the people in the room, one of whom was old Mr Pitmilly. They all looked round upon me to ask what was the matter. And when I gave my usual answer of "Nothing," sitting down again shamefaced but very much excited, Mr Pitmilly got up and came forward, and looked out, apparently to see what was the cause. He saw nothing, for he went back again, and I could hear him telling Aunt Mary not to be alarmed, for Missy had fallen into a doze with the heat, and had startled herself waking up, at which they all laughed: another time I could have killed him for his impertinence, but my mind was too much taken up now to pay any attention. My head was throbbing and my heart beating. I was in such high excitement, however, that to restrain myself completely, to be perfectly silent, was more easy to me then than at any other time of my life. I waited until the old gentleman had taken his seat again, and then I looked back. Yes, there he was! I had not been deceived. I knew then, when I looked across, that this was what I had been looking for all the time—that I had known he was there, and had been waiting for him, every time there was that flicker of movement in the room—him and no one else. And there at last, just as I had expected, he was. I don't know that in reality I ever had expected him, or any one: but this was what I felt when, suddenly looking into that curious dim room, I saw him there.

He was sitting in the chair, which he must have placed for himself, or which some one else in the dead of night when nobody was looking must have set for him, in front of the escritoire—with the back of his head towards me, writing. The light fell upon him from the left hand, and therefore upon his shoulders and the side of his head, which, however, was too much turned away to show anything of his face. Oh, how strange that there should be some one staring at him as I was doing, and he never to turn his head, to make a movement! If any one stood and looked at me, were I in the soundest sleep that ever was, I would wake, I would jump up, I would feel it through everything. But there he sat and never moved. You are not to suppose, though I said the light fell upon him from the left hand, that there was very much light. There never is in a room you are looking into like that across the street; but there was enough to see him by—the outline of his figure dark and solid, seated in the chair, and the fairness of his head visible faintly, a clear spot against the dimness. I saw this outline against the dim gilding of the frame of the large picture which hung on the farther wall.

I sat all the time the visitors were there, in a sort of rapture, gazing at this figure. I knew no reason why I should be so much moved. In an ordinary way, to see a student at an opposite window quietly doing his work might have interested me a little, but certainly it would not have moved me in any such way. It is always interesting to have a glimpse like this of an unknown life—to see so much and yet know so little, and to wonder, perhaps, what the man is doing, and why he never turns his head. One would go to the window—but not too close, lest he should see you and think you were spying upon him—and one would ask, Is he still there? is he writing, writing always? I wonder what he is writing! And it would be a great amusement: but no more. This was not my feeling at all in the present case. It was a sort of breathless watch, an absorption. I did not feel that I had eyes for anything else, or any room in my mind for another thought. I no longer heard, as I generally did, the stories and the wise remarks (or foolish) of Aunt Mary's old ladies or Mr Pitmilly. I heard only a murmur behind me, the interchange of voices, one softer, one sharper; but it was not as in the time when I sat reading and heard every word, till the story in my book, and the stories they were telling (what they said almost always shaped into stories), were all mingled into each other, and the hero in the novel became somehow the hero (or more likely heroine) of them all. But I took no notice of what they were saying now. And it was not that there was anything very interesting to look at, except the fact that he was there. He did nothing to keep up the absorption of my thoughts. He moved just so much as a man will do when he is very busily writing, thinking of nothing else. There was a faint turn of his head as he went from one side to another of the page he was writing; but it appeared to be a long long page which never wanted turning. Just a little inclination when he was at the end of the line, outward, and then a little inclination inward when he began the next. That was little enough to keep one gazing. But I suppose it was the gradual course of events leading up to this, the finding out of one thing after another as the eyes got accustomed to the vague light: first the room itself, and then the writing-table, and then the other furniture, and last of all the human inhabitant who gave it all meaning. This was all so interesting that it was like a country which one had discovered. And then the extraordinary blindness of the other people who disputed among themselves whether it was a window at all! I did not, I am sure, wish to be disrespectful, and I was very fond of my Aunt Mary, and I liked Mr Pitmilly well enough, and I was afraid of Lady Carnbee. But yet to think of the—I know I ought not to say stupidity—the blindness of them, the foolishness, the insensibility! discussing it as if a thing that your eyes could see was a thing to discuss! It would have been unkind to think it was because they were old and their faculties dimmed. It is so sad to think that the faculties grow dim, that such a woman as my Aunt Mary should fail in seeing, or hearing, or feeling, that I would not have dwelt on it for a moment, it would have seemed so cruel! And then such a clever old lady as Lady Carnbee, who could see through a millstone, people said—and Mr Pitmilly, such an old man of the world. It did indeed bring tears to my eyes to think that all those clever people, solely by reason of being no longer young as I was, should have the simplest things shut out from them; and for all their wisdom and their knowledge be unable to see what a girl like me could see so easily. I was too much grieved for them to dwell upon that thought, and half ashamed, though perhaps half proud too, to be so much better off than they.

All those thoughts flitted through my mind as I sat and gazed across the street. And I felt there was so much going on in that room across the street! He was so absorbed in his writing, never looked up, never paused for a word, never turned round in his chair, or got up and walked about the room as my father did. Papa is a great writer, everybody says: but he would have come to the window and looked out, he would have drummed with his fingers on the pane, he would have watched a fly and helped it over a difficulty, and played with the fringe of the curtain, and done a dozen other nice, pleasant, foolish things, till the next sentence took shape. "My dear, I am waiting for a word," he would say to my mother when she looked at him, with a question why he was so idle, in her eyes; and then he would laugh, and go back again to his writing-table. But He over there never stopped at all. It was like a fascination. I could not take my eyes from him and that little scarcely perceptible movement he made, turning his head. I trembled with impatience to see him turn the page, or perhaps throw down his finished sheet on the floor, as somebody looking into a window like me once saw Sir Walter do, sheet after sheet. I should have cried out if this Unknown had done that. I should not have been able to help myself, whoever had been present; and gradually I got into such a state of suspense waiting for it to be done that my head grew hot and my hands cold. And then, just when there was a little movement of his elbow, as if he were about to do this, to be called away by Aunt Mary to see Lady Carnbee to the door! I believe I did not hear her till she had called me three times, and then I stumbled up, all flushed and hot, and nearly crying. When I came out from the recess to give the old lady my arm (Mr Pitmilly had gone away some time before), she put up her hand and stroked my cheek. "What ails the bairn?" she said; "she's fevered. You must not let her sit her lane in the window, Mary Balcarres. You and me know what comes of that." Her old fingers had a strange touch, cold like something not living, and I felt that dreadful diamond sting me on the cheek.

I do not say that this was not just a part of my excitement and suspense; and I know it is enough to make any one laugh when the excitement was all about an unknown man writing in a room on the other side of the way, and my impatience because he never came to an end of the page. If you think I was not quite as well aware of this as any one could be! but the worst was that this dreadful old lady felt my heart beating against her arm that was within mine. "You are just in a dream," she said to me, with her old voice close at my ear as we went down-stairs. "I don't know who it is about, but it's bound to be some man that is not worth it. If you were wise you would think of him no more."

"I am thinking of no man!" I said, half crying. "It is very unkind and dreadful of you to say so, Lady Carnbee. I never thought of—any man, in all my life!" I cried in a passion of indignation. The old lady clung tighter to my arm, and pressed it to her, not unkindly.

"Poor little bird," she said, "how it's strugglin' and flutterin'! I'm not saying but what it's more dangerous when it's all for a dream."

She was not at all unkind; but I was very angry and excited, and would scarcely shake that old pale hand which she put out to me from her carriage window when I had helped her in. I was angry with her, and I was afraid of the diamond, which looked up from under her finger as if it saw through and through me; and whether you believe me or not, I am certain that it stung me again—a sharp malignant prick, oh full of meaning! She never wore gloves, but only black lace mittens, through which that horrible diamond gleamed.

I ran up-stairs—she had been the last to go—and Aunt Mary too had gone to get ready for dinner, for it was late. I hurried to my place, and looked across, with my heart beating more than ever. I made quite sure I should see the finished sheet lying white upon the floor. But what I gazed at was only the dim blank of that window which they said was no window. The light had changed in some wonderful way during that five minutes I had been gone, and there was nothing, nothing, not a reflection, not a glimmer. It looked exactly as they all said, the blank form of a window painted on the wall. It was too much: I sat down in my excitement and cried as if my heart would break. I felt that they had done something to it, that it was not natural, that I could not bear their unkindness—even Aunt Mary. They thought it not good for me! not good for me! and they had done something—even Aunt Mary herself—and that wicked diamond that hid itself in Lady Carnbee's hand. Of course I knew all this was ridiculous as well as you could tell me; but I was exasperated by the disappointment and the sudden stop to all my excited feelings, and I could not bear it. It was more strong than I.

I was late for dinner, and naturally there were some traces in my eyes that I had been crying when I came into the full light in the dining-room, where Aunt Mary could look at me at her pleasure, and I could not run away. She said, "Honey, you have been shedding tears. I'm loth, loth that a bairn of your mother's should be made to shed tears in my house."

"I have not been made to shed tears," cried I; and then, to save myself another fit of crying, I burst out laughing and said, "I am afraid of that dreadful diamond on old Lady Carnbee's hand. It bites—I am sure it bites! Aunt Mary, look here."

"You foolish lassie," Aunt Mary said; but she looked at my cheek under the light of the lamp, and then she gave it a little pat with her soft hand. "Go away with you, you silly bairn. There is no bite; but a flushed cheek, my honey, and a wet eye. You must just read out my paper to me after dinner when the post is in: and we'll have no more thinking and no more dreaming for tonight."

"Yes, Aunt Mary," said I. But I knew what would happen; for when she opens up her 'Times', all full of the news of the world, and the speeches and things which she takes an interest in, though I cannot tell why—she forgets. And as I kept very quiet and made not a sound, she forgot to-night what she had said, and the curtain hung a little more over me than usual, and I sat down in my recess as if I had been a hundred miles away. And my heart gave a great jump, as if it would have come out of my breast; for he was there. But not as he had been in the morning—I suppose the light, perhaps, was not good enough to go on with his work without a lamp or candles—for he had turned away from the table and was fronting the window, sitting leaning back in his chair, and turning his head to me. Not to me—he knew nothing about me. I thought he was not looking at anything; but with his face turned my way. My heart was in my mouth: it was so unexpected, so strange! though why it should have seemed strange I know not, for there was no communication between him and me that it should have moved me; and what could be more natural than that a man, wearied of his work, and feeling the want perhaps of more light, and yet that it was not dark enough to light a lamp, should turn round in his own chair, and rest a little, and think—perhaps of nothing at all? Papa always says he is thinking of nothing at all. He says things blow through his mind as if the doors were open, and he has no responsibility. What sort of things were blowing through this man's mind?? or was he thinking, still thinking, of what he had been writing and going on with it still? The thing that troubled me most was that I could not make out his face. It is very difficult to do so when you see a person only through two windows, your own and his. I wanted very much to recognise him afterwards if I should chance to meet him in the street. If he had only stood up and moved about the room, I should have made out the rest of his figure, and then I should have known him again; or if he had only come to the window (as papa always did), then I should have seen his face clearly enough to have recognised him. But, to be sure, he did not see any need to do anything in order that I might recognise him, for he did not know I existed; and probably if he had known I was watching him, he would have been annoyed and gone away.

But he was as immovable there facing the window as he had been seated at the desk. Sometimes he made a little faint stir with a hand or a foot, and I held my breath, hoping he was about to rise from his chair—but he never did it. And with all the efforts I made I could not be sure of his face. I puckered my eyelids together as old Miss Jeanie did who was shortsighted, and I put my hands on each side of my face to concentrate the light on him: but it was all in vain. Either the face changed as I sat staring, or else it was the light that was not good enough, or I don't know what it was. His hair seemed to me light—certainly there was no dark line about his head, as there would have been had it been very dark—and I saw, where it came across the old gilt frame on the wall behind, that it must be fair: and I am almost sure he had no beard. Indeed I am sure that he had no beard, for the outline of his face was distinct enough; and the daylight was still quite clear out of doors, so that I recognised perfectly a baker's boy who was on the pavement opposite, and whom I should have known again whenever I had met him: as if it was of the least importance to recognise a baker's boy! There was one thing, however, rather curious about this boy. He had been throwing stones at something or somebody. In St Rule's they have a great way of throwing stones at each other, and I suppose there had been a battle. I suppose also that he had one stone in his hand left over from the battle, and his roving eye took in all the incidents of the street to judge where he could throw it with most effect and mischief. But apparently he found nothing worthy of it in the street, for he suddenly turned round with a flick under his leg to show his cleverness, and aimed it straight at the window. I remarked without remarking that it struck with a hard sound and without any breaking of glass, and fell straight down on the pavement. But I took no notice of this even in my mind, so intently was I watching the figure within, which moved not nor took the slightest notice, and remained just as dimly clear, as perfectly seen, yet as indistinguishable, as before. And then the light began to fail a little, not diminishing the prospect within, but making it still less distinct than it had been. Then I jumped up, feeling Aunt Mary's hand upon my shoulder. "Honey," she said, "I asked you twice to ring the bell; but you did not hear me."

"Oh, Aunt Mary!" I cried in great penitence, but turning again to the window in spite of myself.

"You must come away from there: you must come away from there," she said, almost as if she were angry: and then her soft voice grew softer, and she gave me a kiss: "never mind about the lamp, honey; I have rung myself, and it is coming; but, silly bairn, you must not aye be dreaming — your little head will turn."

All the answer I made, for I could scarcely speak, was to give a little wave with my hand to the window on the other side of the street.

She stood there patting me softly on the shoulder for a whole minute or more, murmuring something that sounded like, "She must go away, she must go away." Then she said, always with her hand soft on my shoulder, "Like a dream when one awaketh." And when I looked again, I saw the blank of an opaque surface and nothing more.

Aunt Mary asked me no more questions. She made me come into the room and sit in the light and read something to her. But I did not know what I was reading, for there suddenly came into my mind and took possession of it, the thud of the stone upon the window, and its descent straight down, as if from some hard substance that threw it off: though I had myself seen it strike upon the glass of the panes across the way.

IV

I am afraid I continued in a state of great exaltation and commotion of mind for some time. I used to hurry through the day till the evening came, when I could watch my neighbour through the window opposite. I did not talk much to any one, and I never said a word about my own questions and wonderings. I wondered who he was, what he was doing, and why he never came till the evening (or very rarely); and I also wondered much to what house the room belonged in which he sat. It seemed to form a portion of the old College Library, as I have often said. The window was one of the line of windows which I understood lighted the large hall; but whether this room belonged to the library itself, or how its occupant gained access to it, I could not tell. I made up my mind that it must open out of the hall, and that the gentleman must be the Librarian or one of his assistants, perhaps kept busy all the day in his official duties, and only able to get to his desk and do his own private work in the evening. One has heard of so many things like that—a man who had to take up some other kind of work for his living, and then when his leisure-time came, gave it all up to something he really loved—some study or some book he was writing. My father himself at one time had been like that. He had been in the Treasury all day, and then in the evening wrote his books, which made him famous. His daughter, however little she might know of other things, could not but know that! But it discouraged me very much when somebody pointed out to me one day in the street an old gentleman who wore a wig and took a great deal of snuff, and said, That's the Librarian of the old College. It gave me a great shock for a moment; but then I remembered that an old gentleman has generally assistants, and that it must be one of them.

Gradually I became quite sure of this. There was another small window above, which twinkled very much when the sun shone, and looked a very kindly bright little window, above that dulness of the other which hid so much. I made up my mind this was the window of his other room, and that these two chambers at the end of the beautiful hall were really beautiful for him to live in, so near all the books, and so retired and quiet, that nobody knew of them. What a fine thing for him! and you could see what use he made of his good fortune as he sat there, so constant at his writing for hours together. Was it a book he was writing, or could it be perhaps Poems? This was a thought which made my heart beat; but I concluded with much regret that it could not be Poems, because no one could possibly write Poems like that, straight off, without pausing for a word or a rhyme. Had they been Poems he must have risen up, he must have paced about the room or come to the window as papa did—not that papa wrote Poems: he always said, "I am not worthy even to speak of such prevailing mysteries," shaking his head—which gave me a wonderful admiration and almost awe of a Poet, who was thus much greater even than papa. But I could not believe that a poet could have kept still for hours and hours like that. What could it be then? perhaps it was history; that is a great thing to work at, but you would not perhaps need to move nor to stride up and down, or look out upon the sky and the wonderful light.

He did move now and then, however, though he never came to the window. Sometimes, as I have said, he would turn round in his chair and turn his face towards it, and sit there for a long time musing when the light had begun to fail, and the world was full of that strange day which was night, that light without colour, in which everything was so clearly visible, and there were no shadows. "It was between the night and the day, when the fairy folk have power." This was the after-light of the wonderful, long, long summer evening, the light without shadows. It had a spell in it, and sometimes it made me afraid: and all manner of strange thoughts seemed to come in, and I always felt that if only we had a little more vision in our eyes we might see beautiful folk walking about in it, who were not of our world. I thought most likely he saw them, from the way he sat there looking out: and this made my heart expand with the most curious sensation, as if of pride that, though I could not see, he did, and did not even require to come to the window, as I did, sitting close in the depth of the recess, with my eyes upon him, and almost seeing things through his eyes.

I was so much absorbed in these thoughts and in watching him every evening—for now he never missed an evening, but was always there—that people began to remark that I was looking pale and that I could not be well, for I paid no attention when they talked to me, and did not care to go out, nor to join the other girls for their tennis, nor to do anything that others did; and some said to Aunt Mary that I was quickly losing all the ground I had gained, and that she could never send me back to my mother with a white face like that. Aunt Mary had begun to look at me anxiously for some time before that, and, I am sure, held secret consultations over me, sometimes with the doctor, and sometimes with her old ladies, who thought they knew more about young girls than even the doctors. And I could hear them saying to her that I wanted diversion, that I must be diverted, and that she must take me out more, and give a party, and that when the summer visitors began to come there would perhaps be a ball or two, or Lady Carnbee would get up a picnic. "And there's my young lord coming home," said the old lady whom they called Miss Jeanie, "and I never knew the young lassie yet that would not cock up her bonnet at the sight of a young lord."

But Aunt Mary shook her head. "I would not lippen much to the young lord," she said. "His mother is sore set upon siller for him; and my poor bit honey has no fortune to speak of. No, we must not fly so high as the young lord; but I will gladly take her about the country to see the old castles and towers. It will perhaps rouse her up a little."

"And if that does not answer we must think of something else," the old lady said.

I heard them perhaps that day because they were talking of me, which is always so effective a way of making you hear—for latterly I had not been paying any attention to what they were saying; and I thought to myself how little they knew, and how little I cared about even the old castles and curious houses, having something else in my mind. But just about that time Mr Pitmilly came in, who was always a friend to me, and, when he heard them talking, he managed to stop them and turn the conversation into another channel. And after a while, when the ladies were gone away, he came up to my recess, and gave a glance right over my head. And then he asked my Aunt Mary if ever she had settled her question about the window opposite, "that you thought was a window sometimes, and then not a window, and many curious things," the old gentleman said.

My Aunt Mary gave me another very wistful look; and then she said, "Indeed, Mr Pitmilly, we are just where we were, and I am quite as unsettled as ever; and I think my niece she has taken up my views, for I see her many a time looking across and wondering, and I am not clear now what her opinion is."

"My opinion!" I said, "Aunt Mary." I could not help being a little scornful, as one is when one is very young. "I have no opinion. There is not only a window but there is a room, and I could show you—" I was going to say, "show you the gentleman who sits and writes in it," but I stopped, not knowing what they might say, and looked from one to another. "I could tell you—all the furniture that is in it," I said. And then I felt something like a flame that went over my face, and that all at once my cheeks were burning. I thought they gave a little glance at each other, but that may have been folly. "There is a great picture, in a big dim frame," I said, feeling a little breathless, "on the wall opposite the window—"

"Is there so?" said Mr Pitmilly, with a little laugh. And he said, "Now I will tell you what we'll do. You know that there is a conversation party, or whatever they call it, in the big room tonight, and it will be all open and lighted up. And it is a handsome room, and two-three things well worth looking at. I will just step along after we have all got our dinner, and take you over to the pairty, madam—Missy and you—"

"Dear me!" said Aunt Mary. "I have not gone to a pairty for more years than I would like to say—and never once to the Library Hall." Then she gave a little shiver, and said quite low, "I could not go there."

"Then you will just begin again to-night, madam," said Mr Pitmilly, taking no notice of this, "and a proud man will I be leading in Mistress Balcarres that was once the pride of the ball."

"Ah, once!" said Aunt Mary, with a low little laugh and then a sigh. "And we'll not say how long ago;" and after that she made a pause, looking always at me: and then she said, "I accept your offer, and we'll put on our braws; and I hope you will have no occasion to think shame of us. But why not take your dinner here?"

That was how it was settled, and the old gentleman went away to dress, looking quite pleased. But I came to Aunt Mary as soon as he was gone, and besought her not to make me go. "I like the long bonnie night and the light that lasts so long. And I cannot bear to dress up and go out, wasting it all in a stupid party. I hate parties, Aunt Mary!" I cried, "and I would far rather stay here."

"My honey," she said, taking both my hands, "I know it will maybe be a blow to you,—but it's better so."

"How could it be a blow to me?" I cried; "but I would far rather not go."

"You'll just go with me, honey, just this once: it is not often I go out. You will go with me this one night, just this one night, my honey sweet."

I am sure there were tears in Aunt Mary's eyes, and she kissed me between the words. There was nothing more that I could say; but how I grudged the evening! A mere party, a conversazione (when all the College was away, too, and nobody to make conversation!), instead of my enchanted hour at my window and the soft strange light, and the dim face looking out, which kept me wondering and wondering what was he thinking of, what was he looking for, who was he? all one wonder and mystery and question, through the long, long, slowly fading night!

It occurred to me, however, when I was dressing—though I was so sure that he would prefer his solitude to everything—that he might perhaps, it was just possible, be there. And when I thought of that, I took out my white frock—though Janet had laid out my blue one—and my little pearl necklace which I had thought was too good to wear. They were not very large pearls, but they were real pearls, and very even and lustrous though they were small; and though I did not think much of my appearance then, there must have been something about me—pale as I was but apt to colour in a moment, with my dress so white, and my pearls so white, and my hair all shadowy—perhaps, that was pleasant to look at: for even old Mr Pitmilly had a strange look in his eyes, as if he was not only pleased but sorry too, perhaps thinking me a creature that would have troubles in this life, though I was so young and knew them not. And when Aunt Mary looked at me, there was a little quiver about her mouth. She herself had on her pretty lace and her white hair very nicely done, and looking her best. As for Mr Pitmilly, he had a beautiful fine French cambric frill to his shirt, plaited in the most minute plaits, and with a diamond pin in it which sparkled as much as Lady Carnbee's ring; but this was a fine frank kindly stone, that looked you straight in the face and sparkled, with the light dancing in it as if it were pleased to see you, and to be shining on that old gentleman's honest and faithful breast: for he had been one of Aunt Mary's lovers in their early days, and still thought there was nobody like her in the world.

I had got into quite a happy commotion of mind by the time we set out across the street in the soft light of the evening to the Library Hall. Perhaps, after all, I should see him, and see the room which I was so well acquainted with, and find out why he sat there so constantly and never was seen abroad. I thought I might even hear what he was working at, which would be such a pleasant thing to tell papa when I went home. A friend of mine at St Rule's—oh, far, far more busy than you ever were, papa!—and then my father would laugh as he always did, and say he was but an idler and never busy at all.

The room was all light and bright, flowers wherever flowers could be, and the long lines of the books that went along the walls on each side, lighting up wherever there was a line of gilding or an ornament, with a little response. It dazzled me at first all that light: but I was very eager, though I kept very quiet, looking round to see if perhaps in any corner, in the middle of any group, he would be there. I did not expect to see him among the ladies. He would not be with them, he was too studious, too silent: but perhaps among that circle of grey heads at the upper end of the room—perhaps—

No: I am not sure that it was not half a pleasure to me to make quite sure that there was not one whom I could take for him, who was at all like my vague image of him. No: it was absurd to think that he would be here, amid all that sound of voices, under the glare of that light. I felt a little proud to think that he was in his room as usual, doing his work, or thinking so deeply over it, as when he turned round in his chair with his face to the light.

I was thus getting a little composed and quiet in my mind, for now that the expectation of seeing him was over, though it was a disappointment, it was a satisfaction too—when Mr Pitmilly came up to me, holding out his arm. "Now," he said, "I am going to take you to see the curiosities." I thought to myself that after I had seen them and spoken to everybody I knew, Aunt Mary would let me go home, so I went very willingly, though I did not care for the curiosities. Something, however, struck me strangely as we walked up the room. It was the air, rather fresh and strong, from an open window at the east end of the hall. How should there be a window there? I hardly saw what it meant for the first moment, but it blew in my face as if there was some meaning in it, and I felt very uneasy without seeing why.

Then there was another thing that startled me. On that side of the wall which was to the street there seemed no windows at all. A long line of bookcases filled it from end to end. I could not see what that meant either, but it confused me. I was altogether confused. I felt as if I was in a strange country, not knowing where I was going, not knowing what I might find out next. If there were no windows on the wall to the street, where was my window? My heart, which had been jumping up and calming down again all the time, gave a great leap at this, as if it would have come out of me — but I did not know what it could mean.

Then we stopped before a glass case, and Mr Pitmilly showed me some things in it. I could not pay much attention to them. My head was going round and round. I heard his voice going on, and then myself speaking with a queer sound that was hollow in my ears; but I did not know what I was saying or what he was saying. Then he took me to the very end of the room, the east end, saying something that I caught — that I was pale, that the air would do me good. The air was blowing full on me, lifting the lace of my dress, lifting my hair, almost chilly. The window opened into the pale daylight, into the little lane that ran by the end of the building. Mr Pitmilly went on talking, but I could not make out a word he said. Then I heard my own voice speaking through it, though I did not seem to be aware that I was speaking. "Where is my window? — where, then, is my window?" I seemed to be saying, and I turned right round, dragging him with me, still holding his arm. As I did this my eye fell upon something at last which I knew. It was a large picture in a broad frame, hanging against the farther wall.

What did it mean? Oh, what did it mean? I turned round again to the open window at the east end, and to the daylight, the strange light without any shadow, that was all round about this lighted hall, holding it like a bubble that would burst, like something that was not real. The real place was the room I knew, in which that picture was hanging, where the writing-table was, and where he sat with his face to the light. But where was the light and the window through which it came? I think my senses must have left me. I went up to the picture which I knew, and then I walked straight across the room, always dragging Mr Pitmilly, whose face was pale, but who did not struggle but allowed me to lead him, straight across to where the window was — where the window was not; — where there was no sign of it. "Where is my window? — where is my window?" I said. And all the time I was sure that I was in a dream, and these lights were all some theatrical illusion, and the people talking; and nothing real but the pale, pale, watching, lingering day standing by to wait until that foolish bubble should burst.

"My dear," said Mr Pitmilly, "my dear! Mind that you are in public. Mind where you are. You must not make an outcry and frighten your Aunt Mary. Come away with me. Come away, my dear young lady! and you'll take a seat for a minute or two and compose yourself; and I'll get you an ice or a little wine." He kept patting my hand, which was on his arm, and looking at me very anxiously. "Bless me! bless me! I never thought it would have this effect," he said.

But I would not allow him to take me away in that direction. I went to the picture again and looked at it without seeing it: and then I went across the room again, with some kind of wild thought that if I insisted I should find it. "My window — my window!" I said.

There was one of the professors standing there, and he heard me. "The window!" said he. "Ah, you've been taken in with what appears outside. It was put there to be in uniformity with the window on the stair. But it never was a real window. It is just behind that bookcase. Many people are taken in by it," he said. His voice seemed to sound from somewhere far away, and as if it would go on for ever; and the hall swam in a dazzle of shining and of noises round me; and the daylight through the open window grew greyer, waiting till it should be over, and the bubble burst.

V

It was Mr Pitmilly who took me home; or rather it was I who took him, pushing him on a little in front of me, holding fast by his arm, not waiting for Aunt Mary or any one. We came out into the daylight again outside, I, without even a cloak or a shawl, with my bare arms, and uncovered head, and the pearls round my neck. There was a rush of the people about, and a baker's boy, that baker's boy, stood right in my way and cried, "Here's a braw ane!" shouting to the others: the words struck me somehow, as his stone had struck the window, without any reason. But I did not mind the people staring, and hurried across the street, with Mr Pitmilly half a step in advance. The door was open, and Janet standing at it, looking out to see what she could see of the ladies in their grand dresses. She gave a shriek when she saw me hurrying across the street; but I brushed past her, and pushed Mr Pitmilly up the stairs, and took him breathless to the recess, where I threw myself down on the seat, feeling as if I could not have gone another step farther, and waved my hand across to the window. "There! there!" I cried. Ah! there it was — not that senseless mob not the theatre and the gas, and the people all in a murmur and clang of talking. Never in all these days had I seen that room so clearly. There was a faint tone of light behind, as if it might have been a reflection from some of those vulgar lights in the hall, and he sat against it, calm, wrapped in his thoughts, with his face turned to the window. Nobody but must have seen him. Janet could have seen him had I called her up-stairs. It was like a picture, all the things I knew, and the same attitude, and the atmosphere, full of quietness, not disturbed by anything. I pulled Mr Pitmilly's arm before I let him go, — "You see, you see!" I cried. He gave me the most bewildered look, as if he would have liked to cry. He saw nothing! I was sure of that from his eyes. He was an old man, and there was no vision in him. If I had called up Janet, she would have seen it all. "My dear!" he said. "My dear!" waving his hands in a helpless way.

"He has been there all these nights," I cried, "and I thought you could tell me who he was and what he was doing; and that he might have taken me in to that room, and showed me, that I might tell papa. Papa would understand, he would like to hear. Oh, can't you tell me what work he is doing, Mr Pitmilly?

He never lifts his head as long as the light throws a shadow, and then when it is like this he turns round and thinks, and takes a rest!"

Mr Pitmilly was trembling, whether it was with cold or I know not what. He said, with a shake in his voice, "My dear young lady — my dear — " and then stopped and looked at me as if he were going to cry. "It's peetiful, it's peetiful," he said; and then in another voice, "I am going across there again to bring your Aunt Mary home; do you understand, my poor little thing, my — I am going to bring her home — you will be better when she is here." I was glad when he went away, as he could not see anything: and I sat alone in the dark which was not dark, but quite clear light — a light like nothing I ever saw. How clear it was in that room! not glaring like the gas and the voices, but so quiet, everything so visible, as if it were in another world. I heard a little rustle behind me, and there was Janet, standing staring at me with two big eyes wide open. She was only a little older than I was. I called to her, "Janet, come here, come here, and you will see him, — come here and see him!" impatient that she should be so shy and keep behind. "Oh, my bonnie young leddy!" she said, and burst out crying. I stamped my foot at her, in my indignation that she would not come, and she fled before me with a rustle and swing of haste, as if she were afraid. None of them, none of them! not even a girl like myself, with the sight in her eyes, would understand. I turned back again, and held out my hands to him sitting there, who was the only one that knew. "Oh," I said, "say something to me! I don't know who you are, or what you are: but you're lonely and so am I; and I only — feel for you. Say something to me!" I neither hoped that he would hear, nor expected any answer. How could he hear, with the street between us, and his window shut, and all the murmuring of the voices and the people standing about? But for one moment it seemed to me that there was only him and me in the whole world.

But I gasped with my breath, that had almost gone from me, when I saw him move in his chair! He had heard me, though I knew not how. He rose up, and I rose too, speechless, incapable of anything but this mechanical movement. He seemed to draw me as if I were a puppet moved by his will. He came forward to the window, and stood looking across at me. I was sure that he looked at me. At last he had seen me: at last he had found out that somebody, though only a girl, was watching him, looking for him, believing in him. I was in such trouble and commotion of mind and trembling, that I could not keep on my feet, but dropped kneeling on the window-seat, supporting myself against the window, feeling as if my heart were being drawn out of me. I cannot describe his face. It was all dim, yet there was a light on it: I think it must have been a smile; and as closely as I looked at him he looked at me. His hair was fair, and there was a little quiver about his lips. Then he put his hands upon the window to open it. It was stiff and hard to move; but at last he forced it open with a sound that echoed all along the street. I saw that the people heard it, and several looked up. As for me, I put my hands together, leaning with my face against the glass, drawn to him as if I could have gone out of myself, my heart out of my bosom, my eyes out of my head. He opened the window with a noise that was heard from the West Port to the Abbey. Could any one doubt that?

And then he leaned forward out of the window, looking out. There was not one in the street but must have seen him. He looked at me first, with a little wave of his hand, as if it were a salutation—not exactly that either, for I thought he waved me away; and then he looked up and down in the dim shining of the ending day, first to the east, to the old Abbey towers, and then to the west, along the broad line of the street where so many people were coming and going, but so little noise, all like enchanted folk in an enchanted place. I watched him with such a melting heart, with such a deep satisfaction as words could not say; for nobody could tell me now that he was not there,—nobody could say I was dreaming any more. I watched him as if I could not breathe—heart in my throat, my eyes upon him. He looked up and down, and then he looked back to me. I was the first, and I was the last, though it was not for long: he did know, he did see, who it was that had recognised him and sympathised with him all the time. I was in a kind of rapture, yet stupor too; my look went with his look, following it as if I were his shadow; and then suddenly he was gone, and I saw him no more.

I dropped back again upon my seat, seeking something to support me, something to lean upon. He had lifted his hand and waved it once again to me. How he went I cannot tell, nor where he went I cannot tell; but in a moment he was away, and the window standing open, and the room fading into stillness and dimness, yet so clear, with all its space, and the great picture in its gilded frame upon the wall. It gave me no pain to see him go away. My heart was so content, and I was so worn out and satisfied—what doubt or question could there be about him now? As I was lying back as weak as water, Aunt Mary came in behind me, and flew to me with a little rustle as if she had come on wings, and put her arms round me, and drew my head on to her breast. I had begun to cry a little, with sobs like a child. "You saw him, you saw him!" I said. To lean upon her, and feel her so soft, so kind, gave me a pleasure I cannot describe, and her arms round me, and her voice saying "Honey, my honey!" —if she were nearly crying too. Lying there I came back to myself, quite sweetly, glad of everything. But I wanted some assurance from them that they had seen him too. I waved my hand to the window that was still standing open, and the room that was stealing away into the faint dark. "This time you saw it all?" I said, getting more eager. "My honey!" said Aunt Mary, giving me a kiss: and Mr Pitmilly began to walk about the room with short little steps behind, as if he were out of patience. I sat straight up and put away Aunt Mary's arms. You cannot be so blind, so blind!" I cried. "Oh, not to-night, at least not to-night!" But neither the one nor the other made any reply. I shook myself quite free, and raised myself up. And there, in the middle of the street, stood the baker's boy like a statue, staring up at the open window, with his mouth open and his face full of wonder—breathless, as if he could not believe what he saw. I darted forward, calling to him, and beckoned him to come to me. "Oh, bring him up! bring him, bring him to me!" I cried.

Mr Pitmilly went out directly, and got the boy by the shoulder. He did not want to come. It was strange to see the little old gentleman, with his beautiful frill and his diamond pin, standing out in the street, with his hand upon the boy's shoulder, and the other boys round, all in a little crowd.

And presently they came towards the house, the others all following, gaping and wondering. He came in unwilling, almost resisting, looking as if we meant him some harm. "Come away, my laddie, come and speak to the young lady," Mr Pitmilly was saying. And Aunt Mary took my hands to keep me back. But I would not be kept back.

"Boy," I cried, "you saw it too: you saw it: tell them you saw it! It is that I want, and no more."

He looked at me as they all did, as if he thought I was mad. "What's she wantin' wi' me?" he said; and then, "I did nae harm, even if I did throw a bit stane at it and it's nae sin to throw a stane."

"You rascal!" said Mr Pitmilly, giving him a shake; "have you been throwing stones? You'll kill somebody some of these days with your stones." The old gentleman was confused and troubled, for he did not understand what I wanted, nor anything that had happened. And then Aunt Mary, holding my hands and drawing me close to her, spoke. "Laddie," she said, "answer the young lady, like a good lad. There's no intention of finding fault with you. Answer her, my man, and then Janet will give ye your supper before you go."

"Oh speak, speak!" I cried; "answer them and tell them! you saw that window opened, and the gentleman look out and wave his hand?"

"I saw nae gentleman," he said, with his head down, "except this wee gentleman here."

"Listen, laddie," said Aunt Mary. "I saw ye standing in the middle of the street staring. What were ye looking at?"

"It was naething to make a wark about. It was just yon windy yonder in the library that is nae windy. And it was open — sure's death. You may laugh if you like. Is that a' she's wantin' wi' me?"

"You are telling a pack of lies, laddie," Mr Pitmilly said.

"I'm tellin' nae lees — was standin' open just like ony ither windy. It's as sure's death. I couldna believe it mysel'; but it's true."

"And there it is," I cried, turning round and pointing it out to them with great triumph in my heart. But the light was all grey, it had faded, it had changed. The window was just as it had always been, a sombre break upon the wall.

I was treated like an invalid all that evening, and taken up-stairs to bed, and Aunt Mary sat up in my room the whole night through. Whenever I opened my eyes she was always sitting there close to me, watching. And there never was in all my life so strange a night. When I would talk in my excitement, she kissed me and hushed me like a child. "Oh, honey, you are not the only one!" she said. "Oh whisht, whisht, bairn! I should never have let you be there!"

"Aunt Mary, Aunt Mary, you have seen him too?"

"Oh whisht, whisht, honey!" Aunt Mary said: her eyes were shining — there were tears in them. "Oh whisht, whisht! Put it out of your mind, and try to sleep. I will not speak another word," she cried.

But I had my arms round her, and my mouth at her ear. "Who is he there? — tell me that and I will ask no more —"

"Oh honey, rest, and try to sleep! It is just — how can I tell you? — a dream, a dream! Did you not hear what Lady Carnbee said? the women of our blood—"

"What? what? Aunt Mary, oh Aunt Mary—"

"I canna tell you," she cried in her agitation, "I canna tell you! How can I tell you, when I know just what you know and no more? It is a longing all your life after—it is a looking—for what never comes."

"He will come," I cried. "I shall see him to-morrow—that I know, I know!"

She kissed me and cried over me, her cheek hot and wet like mine. "My honey, try if you can sleep—if you can sleep: and we'll wait to see what to-morrow brings."

"I have no fear," said I; and then I suppose, though it is strange to think of, I must have fallen asleep—as so worn-out, and young, and not used to lying in my bed awake. From time to time I opened my eyes, and sometimes jumped up remembering everything: but Aunt Mary was always there to soothe me, and I lay down again in her shelter like a bird in its nest.

But I would not let them keep me in bed next day. I was in a kind of fever, not knowing what I did. The window was quite opaque, without the least glimmer in it, flat and blank like a piece of wood. Never from the first day had I seen it so little like a window. "It cannot be wondered at," I said to myself, "that seeing it like that, and with eyes that are old, not so clear as mine, they should think what they do." And then I smiled to myself to think of the evening and the long light, and whether he would look out again, or only give me a signal with his hand. I decided I would like that best: not that he should take the trouble to come forward and open it again, but just a turn of his head and a wave of his hand. It would be more friendly and show more confidence,—not as if I wanted that kind of demonstration every night.

I did not come down in the afternoon, but kept at my own window upstairs alone, till the tea-party should be over. I could hear them making a great talk; and I was sure they were all in the recess staring at the window, and laughing at the silly lassie. Let them laugh! I felt above all that now. At dinner I was very restless, hurrying to get it over; and I think Aunt Mary was restless too. I doubt whether she read her 'Times' when it came; she opened it up so as to shield her, and watched from a corner. And I settled myself in the recess, with my heart full of expectation. I wanted nothing more than to see him writing at his table, and to turn his head and give me a little wave of his hand, just to show that he knew I was there. I sat from half-past seven o'clock to ten o'clock: and the daylight grew softer and softer, till at last it was as if it was shining through a pearl, and not a shadow to be seen. But the window all the time was as black as night, and there was nothing, nothing there.

Well: but other nights it had been like that; he would not be there every night only to please me. There are other things in a man's life, a great learned man like that. I said to myself I was not disappointed. Why should I be disappointed? There had been other nights when he was not there. Aunt Mary watched me, every movement I made, her eyes shining, often wet, with a pity in them that almost made me cry: but I felt as if I were more sorry for her than for myself. And then I flung myself upon her, and asked her, again and again, what it was, and who it was, imploring her to tell me if she knew? and when she had seen him, and what had happened? and what it meant about the women of our blood? She told me that how it was she could not tell, nor when: it was just at the time it had to be; and that we all saw him in our time—"that is," she said, "the ones that are like you and me." What was it that made her and me different from the rest? but she only shook her head and would not tell me. "They say," she said, and then stopped short. "Oh, honey, try and forget all about it—if I had but known you were of that kind! They say—that once there was one that was a Scholar, and liked his books more than any lady's love. Honey, do not look at me like that. To think I should have brought all this on you!"

"He was a Scholar?" I cried.

"And one of us, that must have been a light woman, not like you and me — But maybe it was just in innocence; for who can tell? She waved to him and waved to him to come over: and yon ring was the token: but he would not come. But still she sat at her window and waved and waved—till at last her brothers heard of it, that were stirring men; and then—oh, my honey, let us speak of it no more!"

"They killed him!" I cried, carried away. And then I grasped her with my hands, and gave her a shake, and flung away from her. "You tell me that to throw dust in my eyes—when I saw him only last night: and he as living as I am, and as young!"

"My honey, my honey!" Aunt Mary said.

After that I would not speak to her for a long time; but she kept close to me, never leaving me when she could help it, and always with that pity in her eyes. For the next night it was the same; and the third night. That third night I thought I could not bear it any longer. I would have to do something—if only I knew what to do! If it would ever get dark, quite dark, there might be something to be done. I had wild dreams of stealing out of the house and getting a ladder, and mounting up to try if I could not open that window, in the middle of the night—if perhaps I could get the baker's boy to help me; and then my mind got into a whirl, and it was as if I had done it; and I could almost see the boy put the ladder to the window, and hear him cry out that there was nothing there. Oh, how slow it was, the night! and how light it was, and everything so clear—no darkness to cover you, no shadow, whether on one side of the street or on the other side! I could not sleep, though I was forced to go to bed.

And in the deep midnight, when it is dark dark in every other place, I slipped very softly downstairs, though there was one board on the landing-place that creaked—and opened the door and stepped out. There was not a soul to be seen, up or down, from the Abbey to the West Port: and the trees stood like ghosts, and the silence was terrible, and everything as clear as day. You don't know what silence is till you find it in the light like that, not morning but night, no sunrising, no shadow, but everything as clear as the day.

It did not make any difference as the slow minutes went on: one o'clock, two o'clock. How strange it was to hear the clocks striking in that dead light when there was nobody to hear them! But it made no difference. The window was quite blank; even the marking of the panes seemed to have melted away. I stole up again after a long time, through the silent house, in the clear light, cold and trembling, with despair in my heart.

I am sure Aunt Mary must have watched and seen me coming back, for after a while I heard faint sounds in the house; and very early, when there had come a little sunshine into the air, she came to my bedside with a cup of tea in her hand; and she, too, was looking like a ghost. "Are you warm, honey — are you comfortable?" she said. "It doesn't matter," said I. I did not feel as if anything mattered; unless if one could get into the dark somewhere the soft, deep dark that would cover you over and hide you — but I could not tell from what. The dreadful thing was that there was nothing, nothing to look for, nothing to hide from — only the silence and the light.

That day my mother came and took me home. I had not heard she was coming; she arrived quite unexpectedly, and said she had no time to stay, but must start the same evening so as to be in London next day, papa having settled to go abroad. At first I had a wild thought I would not go. But how can a girl say I will not, when her mother has come for her, and there is no reason, no reason in the world, to resist, and no right! I had to go, whatever I might wish or any one might say. Aunt Mary's dear eyes were wet; she went about the house drying them quietly with her handkerchief, but she always said, "It is the best thing for you, honey — the best thing for you!" Oh, how I hated to hear it said that it was the best thing, as if anything mattered, one more than another! The old ladies were all there in the afternoon, Lady Carnbee looking at me from under her black lace, and the diamond lurking, sending out darts from under her finger. She patted me on the shoulder, and told me to be a good bairn. "And never lippen to what you see from the window," she said. "The eye is deceitful as well as the heart." She kept patting me on the shoulder, and I felt again as if that sharp wicked stone stung me. Was that what Aunt Mary meant when she said yon ring was the token? I thought afterwards I saw the mark on my shoulder. You will say why? How can I tell why? If I had known, I should have been contented, and it would not have mattered any more.

I never went back to St Rule's, and for years of my life I never again looked out of a window when any other window was in sight. You ask me did I ever see him again? I cannot tell: the imagination is a great deceiver, as Lady Carnbee said: and if he stayed there so long, only to punish the race that had wronged him, why should I ever have seen him again? for I had received my share. But who can tell what happens in a heart that often, often, and so long as that, comes back to do its errand? If it was he whom I have seen again, the anger is gone from him, and he means good and no longer harm to the house of the woman that loved him. I have seen his face looking at me from a crowd. There was one time when I came home a widow from India, very sad, with my little children: I am certain I saw him there among all the people coming to welcome their friends. There was nobody to welcome me, — for I was not expected: and very sad was I, without a face I knew: when all at once I saw him, and he waved his hand to me. My heart leaped up again: I had forgotten who he was, but only that it was a face I knew, and I landed almost cheerfully, thinking here was some one who would help me. But he had disappeared, as he did from the window, with that one wave of his hand.

And again I was reminded of it all when old Lady Carnbee died — an old, old woman — and it was found in her will that she had left me that diamond ring. I am afraid of it still. It is locked up in an old sandal-wood box in the lumber-room in the little old country-house which belongs to me, but where I never live. If any one would steal it, it would be a relief to my mind. Yet I never knew what Aunt Mary meant when she said, "Yon ring was the token," nor what it could have to do with that strange window in the old College Library of St Rule's.

John Davidson (1857-1909)

Thirty Bob A Week (1894)

I COULDN'T touch a stop and turn a screw,
   And set the blooming world a- work for me,
Like such as cut their teeth—I hope, like you—
   On the handle of a skeleton gold key;
I cut mine on a leek, which I eat it every week:
   I'm a clerk at thirty bob as you can see.

But I don't allow it's luck and all a toss;
   There's no such thing as being starred and crossed;
It's just the power of some to be a boss.
   And the bally power of others to be bossed:
I face the music, sir; you bet I ain't a cur;
   Strike me lucky if I don't believe I'm lost!

For like a mole I journey in the dark,
   A-travelling along the underground
From my Pillar'd Halls and broad Suburbean Park,
   To come the daily dull official round;
And home again at night with my pipe all alight,
   A-scheming how to count ten bob a pound.

And it's often very cold and very wet,
   And my missis stitches towels for a hunks;
And the Pillar'd Halls is half of it to let —
   Three rooms about the size of travelling trunks.
And we cough, my wife and I, to dislocate a sigh.
   When the noisy little kids are in their bunks.

But you never hear her do a growl or whine,
   For she's made of flint and roses, very odd;
And I've got to cut my meaning rather fine,
   Or I'd blubber, for I'm made of greens and sod:
So p'r'aps we are in Hell for all that I can tell,
   And lost and damn'd and served up hot to God.

I ain't blaspheming, Mr Silver-tongue;
   I'm saying things a bit beyond your art:
Of all the rummy starts you ever sprung,
   Thirty bob a week's the rummiest start!
With your science and your books and your theories about spooks.
   Did you ever hear of looking in your heart?

I didn't mean your pocket, Mr., no:
    I mean that having children and a wife.
With thirty bob on which to come and go,
    Isn't dancing to the tabor and the fife:
When it doesn't make you drink, by Heaven! it makes you think,
    And notice curious items about life.

I step into my heart and there I meet
    A god-almighty devil singing small,
Who would like to shout and whistle in the street.
    And squelch the passers flat against the wall;
If the whole world was a cake he had the power to take,
    He would take it, ask for more, and eat it all.

And I meet a sort of simpleton beside,
    The kind that life is always giving beans;
With thirty bob a week to keep a bride
    He fell in love and married in his teens:
At thirty bob he stuck; but he knows it isn't luck:
    He knows the seas are deeper than tureens.

And the god-almighty devil and the fool
    That meet me in the High Street on the strike,
When I walk about my heart a-gathering wool,
    Are my good and evil angels if you like.
And both of them together in every kind of weather
    Ride me like a double-seated bike.

That's rough a bit and needs its meaning curled.
    But I have a high old hot un in my mind—
A most engrugious notion of the world,
    That leaves your lightning 'rithmetic behind:
I give it at a glance when I say 'There ain't no chance,
    Nor nothing of the lucky-lottery kind.'

And it's this way that I make it out to be:
    No fathers, mothers, countries, climates—none;
Not Adam was responsible for me,
    Nor society, nor systems, nary one:
A little sleeping seed, I woke—I did, indeed—
    A million years before the blooming sun.

I woke because I thought the time had come;
    Beyond my will there was no other cause;
And everywhere I found myself at home,
    Because I chose to be the thing I was;
And in whatever shape of mollusc or of ape
    I always went according to the laws.

I was the love that chose my mother out;
   I joined two lives and from the union burst;
My weakness and my strength without a doubt
   Are mine alone for ever from the first:
It's just the very same with a difference in the name
   As 'Thy will be done.' You say it if you durst!

They say it daily up and down the land
   As easy as you take a drink, it's true;
But the difficultest go to understand,
   And the difficultest job a man can do.
Is to come it brave and meek with thirty bob a week,
   And feel that that's the proper thing for you.

It's a naked child against a hungry wolf;
   It's playing bowls upon a splitting wreck;
It's walking on a string across a gulf
   With millstones fore-and-aft about your neck;
But the thing is daily done by many and many a one;
   And we fall, face forward, fighting, on the deck.

Robert Louis Stevenson (1850-1894)

Thrawn Janet (1881)

The Reverend Murdoch Soulis was long minister of the moorland parish of Balweary, in the vale of Dule. A severe, bleak-faced old man, dreadful to his hearers, he dwelt in the last years of his life, without relative or servant or any human company, in the small and lonely manse under the Hanging Shaw. In spite of the iron composure of his features, his eye was wild, scared, and uncertain; and when he dwelt, in private admonitions, on the future of the impenitent, it seemed as if his eye pierced through the storms of time to the terrors of eternity. Many young persons, coming to prepare themselves against the season of the Holy Communion, were dreadfully affected by his talk. He had a sermon on 1st Peter, v. and 8th, "The devil as a roaring lion," on the Sunday after every seventeenth of August, and he was accustomed to surpass himself upon that text both by the appalling nature of the matter and the terror of his bearing in the pulpit. The children were frightened into fits, and the old looked more than usually oracular, and were, all that day, full of those hints that Hamlet deprecated. The manse itself, where it stood by the water of Dule among some thick trees, with the Shaw overhanging it on the one side, and on the other many cold, moorish hilltops rising towards the sky, had begun, at a very early period of Mr. Soulis's ministry, to be avoided in the dusk hours by all who valued themselves upon their prudence; and gudemen sitting at the clachan alehouse shook their heads together at the thought of passing late by that uncanny neighbourhood. There was one spot, to be more particular, which was regarded with especial awe. The manse stood between the high road and the water of Dule, with a gable to each; its back was towards the kirktown of Balweary, nearly half a mile away; in front of it, a bare garden, hedged with thorn, occupied the land between the river and the road. The house was two stories high, with two large rooms on each. It opened not directly on the garden, but on a causewayed path, or passage, giving on the road on the one hand, and closed on the other by the tall willows and elders that bordered on the stream. And it was this strip of causeway that enjoyed among the young parishioners of Balweary so infamous a reputation.

The minister walked there often after dark, sometimes groaning aloud in the instancy of his unspoken prayers; and when he was from home, and the manse door was locked, the more daring schoolboys ventured, with beating hearts, to "follow my leader" across that legendary spot.

This atmosphere of terror, surrounding, as it did, a man of God of spotless character and orthodoxy, was a common cause of wonder and object of inquiry among the few strangers who were led by chance or business into that unknown, outlying country. But many even of the people of the parish were ignorant of the strange events which had marked the first year of Mr. Soulis's ministrations; and among those who were better informed, some were naturally reticent and others shy of that particular topic. Now and again, only, one of the older folk would warm into courage over his third tumbler, and recount the cause of minister's strange looks and solitary life.

Fifty years syne, when Mr. Soulis cam' first into Balweary, he was still a young man—a callant, the folk said —fu' o' book learnin' and grand at the exposition, but, as was natural in sae young a man, wi' nae leevin' experience in religion. The younger sort were greatly taken wi' his gifts and his gab; but auld, concerned, serious men and women were moved even to prayer for the young man, whom they took to be a self-deceiver, and the parish tbat was like to be sae ill-supplied. It was before the days o' the moderates—weary fa' them; but ill things are like gude — they baith come bit by bit, a pickle at a time; and there were folk even then that said the Lord had left the college professors to their ain devices, an' the lads that went to study wi' them wad hae done mair and better sittin' in a peat-bog, like their forbears of the persecution, wi' a Bible under their oxter and a speerit o' prayer in their heart. There was nae doot, onyway, but that Mr. Soulis had been ower lang at the college. He was careful and troubled for mony thing besides the ae thing needful. He had a feck o' books wi' him — mair than had ever been seen before in that presbytery; and a sair wark the carrier had wi' them, for they were a' like to have smoored in the Deil's Hag between this and Kilmakerlie, They were books o' divinity, to be sure, or so they ca'd them; but the serious were o' opinion there was little service for sae mony, when the hail o' God's Word could gang in the neuk of a plaid. Then, he wad sit half the day and half the nicht forbye (which was scant decent) writing, nae less; and first, they were feared he wad read his sermons; and syne it proved he was writin' a book himsel', which was surely no fittin' for ane of his years an' sma' experience.

Onyway it behoved him to get an auld, decent wife to keep the manse for him an' see to his bit denners; and he was recommended to an auld limmer — Janet M'Clour, they ca'd her — and sae far left to himsel' as to be ower persuaded. There was mony advised him to the contrar, for Janet was mair than suspeckit by the best folk in Ba'weary. Lang or that, she had had a wean to a dragoon; she hadnae come forrit[1] for maybe thretty years; and bairns had seen her mumblin' to hersel' up on Key's Loan in the gloamin', whilk was an unco time an' place for a God-fearin' woman. Howsoever, it was the laird himsel' that had first tauld the minister o' Janet; and in thae days he wad have gane a far gate to pleesure the laird. When folk tauld him that Janet was sib to the deil, it was all superstition by his way of it; an' when they cast up the Bible to him an' the witch of Endor, he wad threep it doun their thrapples that thir days were a' gane by, and the deil was mercifully restrained.

Weel, when it got about the clachan that Janet M'Clour was to be servant at the manse, the folk were fair mad wi' her an' him thegether; and some o' the gudewives had nae better to dae than get round her door cheeks and chairge her wi' a' that was ken't again her, frae the sodger's bairn to John Tamson's twa kye. She was nae great speaker; folk usually let her gang her ain gate, an' she let them gang theirs, wi' neither Fair-gude-een nor Fair-gude-day; but when she buckled to, she had a tongue to deave the miller. Up she got, an' there wasnae an auld story in Ba'weary but she gart somebody loup for it that day; they cooldnae say ae thing but she could say twa to it; till, at the hinder end, the gudewives up and claught haud of her, and clawed the coats off her back, and pu'd her doun the clachan to the water o' Dule, to see if she were a witch or no, soum or droun. The carline skirled till ye could hear her at the Hangin' Shaw, and she focht like ten; there was many a gudewife bure the mark of her neist day an' mony a lang day after; and just in the hettest o' the collieshangie, wha suld come up (for his sins) but the new minister.

"Women," said he (and he had a grand voice), "I charge you in the Lord's name to let her go."

Janet ran to him — she was fair wud wi' terror — an' clang to him, an' prayed him, for Christ's sake, save her frae the cummers; an' they, for their pairt, tauld him a' that was ken't, and maybe mair.

"Woman," says he to Janet, "is this true?"

"As the Lord sees me," says she, "as the Lord made me, no a word o't. Forbye the bairn," says she, "I've been a decent woman a' my days,"

"Will you," says Mr. Soulis, "in the name of God, and before me, His unworthy minister, renounce the devil and his works?"

Weel, it wad appear that when he askit that, she gave a girn that fairly frichtit them that saw her, an' they could hear her teeth play dirl thegether in her chafts; but there was naething for it but the ae way or the ither; an' Janet lifted up her hand and renounced the deil before them a'.

"And now," says Mr. Soulis to the gudewives, "home with ye, one and all, and pray to God for His forgiveness."

And he gied Janet his arm, though she had little on her but a sark, and took her up the clachan to her ain door like a leddy of the land; an' her scrieghin' and laughin' as was a scandal to be heard.

There were many grave folk lang ower their prayers that nicht; but when the morn cam' there was sic a fear fell upon a' Ba'weary that the bairns hid theirsels, and e'en the men folk stood and keeckit frae their doors. For there was Janet comin' doun the clachan — her or her likeness, nane could tell — wi' her neck thrawn, and her heid on ae side, like a body that has been bangit, and a girn on her face like an unstreakit corp. By an' by they got used wi' it, and even speered at her to ken what was wrang; but frae that day forth she couldnae speak like a Christian woman, but slavered and played click with her teeth like a pair o' shears; and frae that day forth the name o' God cam' never on her lips. Whiles she wad try to say it, but it michtnae be. Them that kenned best said least; but they never gied that Thing the name o' Janet M'Clour; for the auld Janet, by their way o't, was in muckle hell that day. But the minister was neither to haud nor to bind; he preached aboot naething but the folk's cruelty that had gi'en her a stroke o' the palsy; he skelpt the bairns that meddled her; and he had her up to the manse that same nicht, and dwall'd there a' his lane wi' her under the Hangin' Shaw.

Weel, time gaed by; and the idler sort commenced to think mair lichtly o' that black business. The minister was weel thought o'; he was aye late at the writing, folk wad see his can'le doon by the Dule water after twal' at e'en; and he seemed aye pleased wi' himsel' and upsitten as at first, though a' body could see that he was dwining. As for Janet, she cam' an' she gaed; if she didnae speak muckle afore, it was reason she should speak less then; she meddled naebody; but she was an eldritch thing to see, an' nane wad hae mistrysted wi' her for Ba'weary glebe.

About the end o' July there cam' a spell o' weather, the like o't never was in that country side; it was lown an' het an' heartless; the herds couldnae win up the Black Hill, the bairns were ower weariet to play; an' yet it was gousty too, wi' claps o' het wund that rumm'led in the glens, and bits o' shooers that slockened naething. We aye thocht it but to thun'er on the morn; but the morn cam', an' the morn's morning, and it was aye the same uncanny weather, sair on folks and bestial. Of a' that were the waur, nane suffered like Mr. Soulis; he could neither sleep nor eat, he tauld his elders; an' when he wasnae writin' at his weary book, he wad be stravagin' ower a' the countrywide like a man possessed, when a' body else was blythe to keep caller ben the house.

Abune Hanging Shaw, in the bield o' the Black Hill, there's a bit enclosed grund wi' an iron yett; and it seems, in the auld days, that was tbe kirkyard o' Ba'weary, and consecrated by the Papists before the blessed licht shone upon the kingdom, it was a great howff o' Mr. Soulis's, onyway; there he would sit an' consider his sermons; and indeed it's a bieldy bit. Weel, as he cam' ower the wast end o' the Black Hill, ae day, he saw first twa, an' syne fower, an' syne seeven corbie craws fleein' round an' round abune the auld kirkyaird. They flew laigh and heavy, and squawked to ither as they gaed; and it was clear to Mr. Soulis that something had put them frae their ordinar. He wasnae easy fleyed, an' gaed straucht up to the wa's; an' what suld he find there but a man, or the appearance of a man, sittin' in the inside upon a grave.

He was of a great stature, an' black as hell, and his e'en were singular to see. Mr. Soulis had heard tell o' black men, mony's the time; but there was something unco aboot this black man that daunted him. Het as he was, he took a kind o' cauld grue in the marrow o' his banes; but up he spak for a' that; an' says he: "My friend, are you a stranger in this place?" The black man answered never a word; he got upon his feet, an' begude to hursle to the wa' on the far side; but he aye lookit at the minister; an' the minister stood an' lookit back; till a' in a meenute the black man was ower the wa' an' rinnin' for the bield o' the trees. Mr. Soulis, he hardly kenned why, ran after him; but he was sair forjaskit wi' his walk an' the het, unhalesome weather; and rin as he likit he got nae mair than a gliff o' the black man amang the birks, till he won doun to the foot o' the hill-side, an' there he saw him ance mair, gaun, hap, step, an' loup, ower Dule water to the manse.

Mr. Soulis wasnae weel pleased that this fearsome gangrel suld mak' sae free wi' Ba'weary manse; an' he ran the harder, an', wet shoon, over the burn, an' up the walk; but the deil a black man was there to see. He stepped out upon the road, but there was naebody there; he gaed a' ower the gairden, but na, nae black man. At the hinder end, and a bit feared as was but natural, he lifted the hasp and into the manse; and there was Janet M'Clour before his e'en, wi' her thrawn craig, and nane sae pleased to see him. And he aye minded sinsyne, when first he set his e'en upon her, he had the same cauld and deidly grue.

"Janet," says he, "have ye seen a black man?"

"A black man?" quo she. "Save us a'! Ye're no wise, minister. There's nae black man in a' Ba'weary."

But she didnae speak plain, ye maun understand; but yam-yammered, like a powney wi' the bit in its moo'.

"Weel," says he, "Janet, if there was nae black man, I have spoken with the Accuser of the Brethren."

And he sat down like ane wi' a fever, an' his teeth chittered in his heid.

"Hoots," says she, "think shame to yoursel', minister;" an' gied him a drap brandy that she keepit aye by her.

Syne Mr. Soulis gaed into his study amang a' his books. It's a lang, laigh, mirk chalmer, perishin' cauld in winter, an' no very dry even in the tap o' the simmer, for the manse stands near the burn. Sae doon he sat, and thocht of a' that had come an' gane since he was in Ba'weary, an' his hame, an' the days when he was a bairn an' ran daffin' on the braes; and that black man aye ran in his heid like the owercome of a sang. Aye the mair he thocht, the mair be thocht o' the black man. He tried the prayer, an' the words wouldnae come to him; an' he tried, they say, to write at his book, but he could nae mak' nae mair o' that. There was whiles he thocht the black man was at his oxter, an' the swat stood upon him cauld as well-water; and there was other whiles, when he cam' to himsel' like a christened bairn and minded naething.

The upshot was that he gaed to the window an' stood glowrin' at Dule water. Tbe trees are unco thick, an' the water lies deep an' black under the manse; an' there was Janet washin' the cla'es wi' her coats kilted. She had her back to the minister, an' he, for his pairt, hardly kenned what he was lookin' at. Syne she turned round, an' shawed her face; Mr. Soulis had the same cauld grue as twice that day afore, an' it was borne in upon him what folk said, that Janet was deid lang syne, an' this was a bogle in her clay-cauld flesh. He drew back a pickle and he scanned her narrowly. She was tramp-trampin' in the cla'es, croonin' to hersel'; and ah! Gude guide us, but it was a fearsome face. Whiles she sang louder; but there was nae man born o'woman that could tell the words o' her sang; an' whiles she lookit side-lang doun, but there was naething there for her to look at. There gaed a scunner through the flesh upon his banes; and that was Heeven's advertisement. But Mr. Soulis just blamed himsel', he said, to think sae ill of a puir, auld afflicted wife that hadnae a freend forbye himsel'; an' he put up a bit prayer for him and her, an' drank a little caller water — for his heart rose again the meat — an' gaed up to his naked bed in the gloaming.

That was a nicht that has never been forgotten in Ba'weary, the nicht o' the seeventeenth of August, seeventeen hun'er' an' twal'. It had been het afore, as I hae said, but that nicht it was hetter than ever. The sun gaed doon amang unco-lookin' clouds; it fell as mirk as the pit; no a star, no a breath o' wind; ye couldnae see your han' afore your face, and even the auld folk coost the covers frae their beds and lay pechin' for their breath. Wi' a' that he had upon his mind, it was gey and unlikely Mr Soulis wad get muckle sleep. He lay an' he tumbled; the gude, caller bed that he got into brunt his very banes; whiles he slept, an' whiles he waukened; whiles he heard the time o' nicht, and whiles a tyke yowlin' up the muir, as if somebody was deid; whiles he thocht he heard bogles claverin' in his lug, an' whiles he saw spunkies in the room. He behoved, he judged, to be sick; an' sick he was — little he jaloused the sickness.

At the hinder end, he got a clearness in his mind, sat up in his sark on the bed-side, and fell thinkin' ance mair o' the black man an' Janet. He couldnae weel tell how — maybe it was the cauld to his feet — but it cam' in upon him wi' a spate that there was some connection between thir twa, an' that either or baith o' them were bogles. And just at that moment, in Janet's room, which was neist to his, there cam' a stramp o' feet, if men were wars'lin', an' then a loud bang; an' then a wund gaed reishling round the fower quarters o' the house; an' then a' was aince mair as seelent as the grave.

Mr. Soulis was feared for neither man nor deevil. He got his tinderbox, an' lit a can'le, an' made three steps o't ower to Janet's door. It was on the hasp, an' he pushed it open, an' keeked bauldly in. It was a big room, big as the minister's ain, an' plenished wi' grand, auld, solid gear, for he had naething else. Here was a foer-poster bed wi' auld tapestry; and a braw cabinet of aik, that was fu' o' the minister's divinity books, an' put there to be out o' the gate; an' a wheen duds o' Janet's lyin' here an' there about the floor. But nae Janet could Mr. Soulis see; nor ony sign of a contention. In he gaed (an' there's few that wad ha'e followed him) an' lookit a' round, an' listened. But there was naethin' to be heard, neither inside the manse nor in a' Ba'weary parish, an' naethin' to be seen but the muckle shadows turnin' round the can'le. An' then a' at aince, the minister's heart played dunt an' stood stock-still; an' a cauld wund blew amang the hairs o' his heid. Whaten a weary sicht was that for the puir man's e'en! For there was Janet hangin' frae a nail beside the auld aik cabinet: her heid aye lay on her shoother, her e'en were steeked, the tongue projeckit frae her mouth, and her heels were twa feet clear abune the floor.

"God forgive us all!" thocht Mr. Soulis; "poor Janet's dead."

He cam' a step nearer to the corp; an' then his heart fair whammled in his inside. For by what cantrip it wad ill-beseem a man to judge, she was hingin' frae a single nail an' by a single wursted thread for darnin' hose.

It's an awfu' thing to be your lane at nicht wi' siccan prodigies o' darkness; but Mr. Soulis was strong in the Lord. He turned an' gaed his ways oot o' that room, and lockit the door ahint him; and step by step, doon the stairs, as heavy as leed; and set doon the can'le on the table at the stairfoot. He couldnae pray, he couldnae think, he was dreepin' wi' caul' swat, an' naethin' could he hear but the dunt-dunt-duntin' o' his ain heart. He micht maybe have stood there an hour, or maybe twa, he minded sae little; when a' o' a sudden, he heard a laigh, uncanny steer upstairs; a foot gaed to an' fro in the cha'mer whaur the corp wis hingin'; syne the door was opened, though he minded weel that he had lockit it; an' syne there was a step upon the landin', an' it seemed to him as if the corp was lookin' ower the rail and doon upon him whaur he stood.

He took up the can'le again (for he couldnae want the licht), and as saftly as ever he could gaed straucht oot o' the manse an' to the far end o' the causeway. It was aye pit-mirk; the flame o' the can'le, when he set it on the grund, brunt steedy and clear as in a room; naething moved, but the Dule water, seepin' and sabbin' doon the glen, an' yon unhaly footstep that cam' ploddin' doun the stairs inside the manse. He kenned the foot ower weel, for it was Janet's; and at ilka step that cam' a wee thing nearer, the cauld got deeper in his vitals. He commended his soul to Him that made an' keepit him; "and O Lord," said he, "give me strength this night to war against the powers of evil."

By this time the foot was comin' through the passage for the door; he could hear a hand skirt alang the wa', as if the fearsome thing was feelin' for its way. The saughs tossed an' maned thegether, a lang sigh cam' ower the hills, the flame o' the can'le was blawn aboot; an' there stood the corp of Thrawn Janet, wi' her grogram goon an' her black mutch, wi' the heid aye upon the shoother, an' the girn still upon the face o't — leevin', ye wad ha'e said — deid, as Mr. Soulis weel kenned — upon the threshold o' the manse.

It'a a strange thing that the saul of man should be that thirled into his perishable body; but the minister saw that, an' his heart didnae break.

She didnae stand there lang; she began to move again an' cam' slowly towards Mr. Soulis whaur he stood under the saughs. A' the life o' his body, a' the strength o' his speerit, were glowerin' frae his e'en. It seemed she was gaun to speak, but wanted words, an' made a sign wi' the left hand. There cam' a clap o' wund, like a cat's fuff; out gaed the can'le, the saughs skrieghed like folk; an' Mr. Soulis kenned that, live or die, this was the end o't.

"Witch, beldame, devil!" he cried, "I charge you, by the power of God, begone — if you be dead, to the grave — if you be damned, to hell."

An' at that moment, the Lord's ain hand out o' the Heeevens struck the Horror whaur it stood; the auld, deid, desecrated corp o' the witch-wife, sae lang keepit fae the grave and hursled round by deils, lowed up like a brunstane spunk and fell in ashes to the grund; the thunder followed peal on dirling peal, the rairing rain upon the back o' that; and Mr. Soulis louped through the garden hedge, and ran, wi' skelloch upon skelloch, for the clachan.

That same mornin', John Christie saw the black man pass the Muckle Cairn as it was chappin' six; before eight, he gaed by the change-house at Knockdow; an' no lang after, Sandy M'Lellan saw him gaun linkin' doon the braes frae Kilmakerlie. There's little doubt but it was him that dwelled sae lang in Janet's body; but he was awa' at last; and sinsyne the deil has never fashed us in Ba'weary.

But it was a sair dispensation for the minister; lang, lang he lay ravin' in his bed; and frae that hour to this, he was the man ye ken the day.

1 To come forrit — to offer oneself as a communicant.

with Fanny Van de Grift Stevenson

from **The Dynamiter**

ZERO'S TALE OF THE EXPLOSIVE BOMB **(1884)**[1]

I DINED by appointment with one of our most trusted agents, in a private chamber at St. James's Hall. You have seen the man: it was M'Guire, the most chivalrous of creatures, but not himself expert in our contrivances. Hence the necessity of our meeting; for I need not remind you what enormous issues depend upon the nice adjustment of the engine. I set our little petard for half an hour, the scene of action being hard by; and the better to avert miscarriage, employed a device, a recent invention of my own, by which the opening of the Gladstone bag in which the bomb was carried, should instantly determine the explosion. M'Guire was somewhat dashed by this arrangement, which was new to him: and pointed out, with excellent, clear good sense, that should he be arrested, it would probably involve him in the fall of our opponents. But I was not to be moved, made a strong appeal to his patriotism, gave him a good glass of whisky, and despatched him on his glorious errand.

Our objective was the effigy of Shakespeare in Leicester Square: a spot, I think, admirably chosen; not only for the sake of the dramatist, still very foolishly claimed as a glory by the English race, in spite of his disgusting political opinions; but from the fact that the seats in the immediate neighbourhood are often thronged by children, errand-boys, unfortunate young ladies of the poorer class and infirm old men—all classes making a direct appeal to public pity, and therefore suitable with our designs. As M'Guire drew near his heart was inflamed by the most noble sentiment of triumph. Never had he seen the garden so crowded; children, still stumbling in the impotence of youth, ran to and fro, shouting and playing, round the pedestal; an old, sick pensioner sat upon the nearest bench, a medal on his breast, a stick with which he walked (for he was disabled by wounds) reclining on his knee. Guilty England would thus be stabbed in the most delicate quarters; the moment had, indeed, been well selected; and M'Guire, with a radiant prevision of the event, drew merrily nearer. Suddenly his eye alighted on the burly form of a policeman, standing hard by the effigy in an attitude of watch. My bold companion paused; he looked about him closely; here and there, at different points of the enclosure, other men stood or loitered, affecting an abstraction, feigning to gaze upon the shrubs, feigning to talk, feigning to be weary and to rest upon the benches. M'Guire was no child in these affairs; he instantly divined one of the plots of the Machiavellian Gladstone.

A chief difficulty with which we have to deal, is a certain nervousness in the subaltern branches of the corps; as the hour of some design draws near, these chicken-souled conspirators appear to suffer some revulsion of intent; and frequently despatch to the authorities, not indeed specific denunciations, but vague anonymous warnings. But for this purely accidental circumstance, England had long ago been an historical expression. On the receipt of such a letter, the Govemment lay a trap for their adversaries, and surround the threatened spot with hirelings. My blood sometimes boils in my veins, when I consider the case of those who sell themselves for money in such a cause. True, thanks to the generosity of our supporters, we patriots receive a very comfortable stipend; I myself, of course, touch a salary which puts me quite beyond the reach of any peddling, mercenary thoughts; M'Guire, again, ere he joined our ranks, was on the brink of starving, and now, thank God! receives a decent income. That is as it should be; the patriot must not be diverted from his task by any base consideration; and the distinction between our position and that of the police is too obvious to be stated.

Plainly, however, our Leicester Square design had been divulged; the Government had craftily filled the place with minions; even the pensioner was not improbably a hireling in disguise; and our emissary, without other aid or protection than the simple apparatus in his bag, found himself confronted by force; brutal force; that strong hand which was a character of the ages of oppression. Should he venture to deposit the machine, it was almost certain that he would be observed and arrested; a cry would arise; and there was just a fear that the police might not be present in sufficient force, to protect him from the savagery of the mob. The scheme must be delayed. He stood with his bag on his arm, pretending to survey the front of the Alhambra, when there flashed into his mind a thought to appal the bravest. The machine was set; at the appointed hour, it must explode; and how, in the interval, was he to be rid of it?

Put yourself, I beseech you, into the body of that patriot. There he was, friendless and helpless; a man in the very flower of life, for he is not yet forty; with long years of happiness before him; and now condemned, in one moment to a cruel and revolting death by dynamite! The square, he said, went round him like a thaumatrope; he saw the Alhambra leap into the air like a balloon; and reeled against the railing. It is probable he fainted.

When he came to himself, a constable had him by the arm.

'My God!' he cried.

'You seem to be unwell, sir,' said the hireling.

'I feel better now,' cried poor M'Guire: and with uneven steps, for the pavement of the square seemed to lurch and reel under his footing, he fled from the scene of this disaster. Fled? Alas, from what was he fleeing? Did he not carry that from which he fled, along with him? and had he the wings of the eagle, had he the swiftness of the ocean winds, could he have been rapt into the uttermost quarters of the earth, how should he escape the ruin that he carried? We have heard of living men who have been fettered to the dead; the grievance, soberly considered, is no more than sentimental; the case is but a flea-bite to that of him who should be linked, like poor M'Guire, to an explosive bomb.

A thought struck him in Green Street, like a dart through his liver: suppose it were the hour already. He stopped as though he had been shot, and plucked his watch out. There, was a howling in his ears, as loud as a winter tempest; his sight was now obscured as if by a cloud, now, as by a lightning flash, would show him the very dust upon the street. But so brief were these intervals of vision, and so violently did the watch vibrate in his hands, that it was impossible to distinguish the numbers on the dial. He covered his eyes for a few seconds; and in that space, it seemed to him that he had fallen to be a man of ninety. When he looked again, the watch-plate had grown legible: he had twenty minutes. Twenty minutes, and no plan!

Green Street, at that time, was very empty; and he now observed a little girl of about six drawing near to him and, as she came, kicking in front of her, as children will, a piece of wood. She sang, too; and something in her accent recalling him to the past, produced a sudden clearness in his mind. Here was a God-sent opportunity!

'My dear,' said he, 'would you like a present of a pretty bag?'

The child cried aloud with joy and put out her hands to take it. She had looked first at the bag, like a true child; but most unfortunately, before she had yet received the fatal gift, her eyes fell directly on M'Guire; and no sooner had she seen the poor gentleman's face, than she screamed out and leaped backward, as though she had seen the devil. Almost at the same moment, a woman appeared upon the threshold of a neighbouring shop, and called upon the child in anger. 'Come here, colleen,' she said, 'and don't be plaguing the poor old gentleman!' With that she re-entered the house, and the child followed her, sobbing aloud.

With the loss of this hope M'Guire's reason swooned within him. When next he awoke to consciousness, he was standing before St. Martin's-in-the-Fields, wavering like a drunken man; the passers-by regarding him with eyes in which he read, as in a glass, an image of the terror and horror that dwelt within his own.

'I am afraid you are very ill, sir,' observed a woman, stopping and gazing hard in his face. 'Can I do anything to help you?'

'Ill?' said M'Guire. 'O God!' And then, recovering some shadow of his self-command, 'Chronic, madam,' said he: 'a long course of the dumb ague. But since you are so compassionate—an errand that I lack the strength to carry out,' he gasped – 'this bag to Portman Square. O compassionate woman, as you hope to be saved, as you are a mother, in the name of your babes that wait to welcome you at home, O take this bag to Portman Square! I have a mother, too,' he added, with a broken voice. 'Number 19, Portman Square.' .

I suppose he had expressed himself with too much energy of voice; for the woman was plainly taken with a certain fear of him. 'Poor gentleman!' said she. 'If I were you, I would go home.' And she left him standing there in his distress.

'Home! 'thought M'Guire, 'what a derision!' What home was there for him, the victim of philanthropy? He thought of his old mother, of his happy youth; of the hideous, rending pang of the explosion; of the possibility that he might not be killed, that he might be cruelly mangled, crippled for life, condemned to life-long pains, blinded perhaps, and almost surely deafened. Ah, you spoke lightly of the dynamiter's peril; but even waiving death, have you realised what it is for a fine, brave young man of forty, to be smitten suddenly with deafness, cut off from all the music of life, and from the voice of friendship, and love? How little do we realise the sufferings of others! Even your brutal Government, in the heyday of its lust for cruelty, though it scruples not to hound the patriot with spies, to pack the corrupt jury, to bribe the hangman, and to erect the infamous gallows, would hesitate to inflict so horrible a doom: not, I am well aware, from virtue, not from philanthropy, but with the fear before it of the withering scorn of the good.

But I wander from M'Guire. From this dread glance into the past and future, his thoughts returned at a bound upon the present. How had he wandered there? and how long—O heavens! how long had he been about it? He pulled out his watch; and found that but three minutes had elapsed. It seemed too bright a thing to be believed. He glanced at the church clock; and sure enough, it marked an hour four minutes faster than the watch.

Of all that he endured, M'Guire declares that pang was the most desolate. Till then, he had had one friend, one counsellor, in whom he plenarily trusted; by whose advertisement, he numbered the minutes that remained to him of life; on whose sure testimony, he could tell when the time was come to risk the last adventure, to cast the bag away from him, and take to flight. And now in what was he to place reliance? His watch was slow; it might be losing time; if so, in what degree? What limit could he set to its derangement? and how much was it possible for a watch to lose in thirty minutes? Five? ten? fifteen? It might be so; already, it seemed years since he had left St. James's Hall on this so promising enterprise; at any moment, then, the blow was to be looked for.

In the face of this new distress, the wild disorder of his pulses settled down; and a broken weariness succeeded, as though he had lived for centuries and for centuries been dead. The buildings and the people in the street became incredibly small, and far-away, and bright; London sounded in his ears stilly, like a whisper; and the rattle of the cab that nearly charged him down, was like a sound from Africa. Meanwhile, he was conscious of a strange abstraction from himself; and heard and felt his footfalls on the ground, as those of a very old, small, debile and tragically fortuned man, whom he sincerely pitied.

As he was thus moving forward past the National Gallery, in a medium, it seemed, of greater rarity and quiet than ordinary air, there slipped into his mind the recollection of a certain entry in Whitcomb Street hard by, where he might perhaps lay down his tragic cargo unremarked. Thither, then, he bent his steps, seeming, as he went, to float above the pavement; and there, in the mouth of the entry, he found a man in a sleeved waistcoat, gravely chewing a straw, He passed him by, and twice patrolled the entry, scouting for the barest chance; but the man had faced about and continued to observe him curiously.

Another hope was gone. M'Guire reissued from the entry, still followed by the wondering eyes of the man in the sleeved waistcoat. He once more consulted his watch: there were but fourteen minutes left to him. At that, it seemed as if a sudden, genial heat were spread about his brain; for a second or two, he saw the world as red as blood; and thereafter entered into a complete possession of himself, with an incredible cheerfulness of spirits, prompting him to sing and chuckle as he walked. And yet this mirth seemed to belong to things external; and within, like a black and leaden-heavy kernel, he was conscious of the weight upon his soul.

> I care for nobody, no, not I,
> And nobody cares for me,

he sang, and laughed at the appropriate burthen, so that the passengers stared upon him on the street. And still the warmth seemed to increase and to become more genial. What was life? he considered, and what he, M'Guire? What even Erin, our green Erin? All seemed so incalculably little that he smiled as he looked down upon it. He would have given years, had he possessed them, for a glass of spirits; but time failed, and he must deny himself this last indulgence.

At the corner of the Haymarket, he very jauntily hailed a hansom cab; jumped in; bade the fellow drive him to a part of the Embankment, which he named; and as soon as the vehicle was in motion, concealed the bag as completely as he could under the vantage of the apron, and once more drew out his watch. So he rode for five interminable minutes his heart in his mouth at every jolt, scarce able to possess his terrors, yet fearing to wake the attention of the driver by too obvious a change of plan, and willing, if possible, to leave him time to forget the Gladstone bag.

At length, at the head of some stairs on the Embankment, he hailed; the cab was stopped; and he alighted — with how glad a heart! He thrust his hand into his pocket. All was now over; he had saved his life; nor that alone, but he had engineered a striking act of dynamite; for what could be more pictorial, what more effective, than the explosion of a hansom cab, as it sped rapidly along the streets of London. He felt in one pocket; then in another. The most crushing seizure of despair descended on his soul; and struck into abject dumbness, he stared upon the driver. He had not one penny.

'Hillo,' said the driver, 'don't seem well.'

'Lost my money,' said M'Guire, in tones so faint and strange that they surprised his hearing.

The man looked through the trap. 'I dessay,' said he: 'you've left your bag.'

M'Guire half unconsciously fetched it out; and looking on that black continent at arm's length, withered inwardly and felt his features sharpen as with mortal sickness.

'This is not mine,' said he. 'Your last fare must have left it. You had better take it to the station.'

'Now look here,' returned the cabman: 'are you off your chump? or am I? '

'Well, then, I'll tell you what,' exclaimed M'Guire: 'you take it for your fare! '

'Oh, I dessay,' replied the driver. 'Anything else? What's in your bag? Open it, and let me see.'

'No, no,' returned M'Guire. 'O no, not that. It's a surprise; it's prepared expressly: a surprise for honest cabmen.'

'No, you don't,' said the man, alighting from his perch, and coming very close to the unhappy patriot. 'You're either going to pay my fare, or get in again and drive to the office.'

It was at this supreme hour of his distress, that M'Guire spied the stout figure of one Godall, a tobacconist of Rupert Street, drawing near along the Embankment. The man was not unknown to him; he had bought of his wares, and heard him quoted for the soul of liberality; and such was now the nearness of his peril, that even at such a straw of hope, he clutched with gratitude.

'Thank God!' he cried. 'Here comes a friend of mine. I'll borrow.' And he dashed to meet the tradesman. 'Sir,' said he, 'Mr. Godall, I have dealt with you—you doubtless know my face—calamities for which I cannot blame myself have overwhelmed me. O sir, for the love of innocence, for the sake of the bonds of humanity, and as you hope for mercy at the throne of grace, lend me two-and-six!'

'I do not recognise your face,' replied Mr. Godall; 'but I remember the cut of your beard, which I have the misfortune to dislike. Here, sir, is a sovereign; which I very willingly advance to you, on the single condition that you shave your chin.'

M'Guire grasped the coin without a word; cast it to the cabman, calling out to him to keep the change; bounded down the steps, flung the bag far forth into the river, and fell headlong after it. He was plucked from a watery grave, it is believed, by the hands of Mr. Godall. Even as he was being hoisted dripping to the shore, a dull and choked explosion shook the solid masonry of the Embankment, and far out in the river a momentary fountain rose and disappeared.

1 The Arabian author, with that quaint particularity of touch which our translation usually praetermits, here registers a some what interesting detail. Zero pronounced the word 'boom'; and the reader, if but for the nonce, will possibly consent to follow him.

To S. C. (1889, publ. 1895)

I HEARD the pulse of the besieging sea
Throb far away all night. I heard the wind
Fly crying and convulse tumultuous palms.
I rose and strolled. The isle was all bright sand,
And flailing fans and shadows of the palm;
The heaven all moon and wind and the blind vault
The keenest planet slain, for Venus slept.
   The king, my neighbour, with his host of wives,
Slept in the precinct of the palisade;
Where single, in the wind, under the moon,
Among the slumbering cabins, blazed a fire,
Sole street-lamp and the only sentinel.
   To other lands and nights my fancy turned —
To London first, and chiefly to your house,
The many-pillared and the well-beloved.
There yearning fancy lighted; there again
In the upper room I lay, and heard far off
The unsleeping city murmur like a shell;
The muffled tramp of the Museum guard
Once more went by me; I beheld again
Lamps vainly brighten the dispeopled street;
Again I longed for the returning morn,
The awaking traffic, the bestirring birds,
The consentaneous trill of tiny song
That weaves round monumental cornices
A passing charm of beauty. Most of all,
For your light foot I wearied, and your knock
That was the glad réveillé of my day.
   Lo, now, when to your task in the great house
At morning through the portico you pass,
One moment glance, where by the pillared wall
Far-voyaging island gods, begrimed with smoke,
Sit now unworshipped, the rude monument
Of faiths forgot and races undivined:
Sit now disconsolate, remembering well
The priest, the victim, and the songful crowd,
The blaze of the blue noon, and that huge voice.
Incessant, of the breakers on the shore.
As far as these from their ancestral shrine,
So far, so foreign, your divided friends
Wander, estranged in body, not in mind.

Apemama.

1 Sidney Colvin

"Fiona MacLeod"/William Sharp (1855-1905)

The Sin-Eater (1895)

SIN.
Taste this bread, this substance: tell me
Is it bread or flesh?
             [The Senses approach.]

THE SMELL.
Its smell
Is the smell of bread.

SIN.
Touch, come. Why tremble?
Say what's this thou touchest?

THE TOUCH.
Bread.

SIN.
Sight, declare what thou discernest
In this object.

THE SIGHT.
Bread alone.

                                    CALDERON,
                        Los Encantos de la Culpa.

A WET wind out of the south mazed and mooned through the sea-mist that hung over the Ross. In all the bays and creeks was a continuous weary lapping of water. There was no other sound anywhere.

Thus was it at daybreak: it was thus at noon: thus was it now in the darkening of the day. A confused thrusting and falling of sounds through the silence betokened the hour of the setting. Curlews wailed in the mist: on the seething limpet-covered rocks the skuas and terns screamed, or uttered hoarse, rasping cries. Ever and again the prolonged note of the oyster-catcher shrilled against the air, as an echo flying blindly along a blank wall of cliff. Out of weedy places, wherein the tide sobbed with long, gurgling moans, came at intervals the barking of a seal.

Inland, by the hamlet of Contullich, there is a reedy tarn called the Loch-a-chaoruinn.[1] By the shores of this mournful water a man moved. It was a slow, weary walk that of the man Neil Ross. He had come from Duninch, thirty miles to the eastward, and had not rested foot, nor eaten, nor had word of man or woman, since his going west an hour after dawn.

At the bend of the loch nearest the clachan he came upon an old woman carrying peat. To his reiterated question as to where he was, and if the tarn were Feur-Lochan above Fionnaphort that is on the strait of Iona on the west side of the Ross of Mull, she did not at first make any answer. The rain trickled down her withered brown face, over which the thin grey locks hung limply. It was only in the deep-set eyes that the flame of life still glimmered, though that dimly.

The man had used the English when first he spoke, but as though mechanically. Supposing that he had not been understood, he repeated his question in the Gaelic.

After a minute's silence the old woman answered him in the native tongue, but only to put a question in return.

"I am thinking it is a long time since you have been in Iona?"

The man stirred uneasily.

"And why is that, mother?" he asked, in a weak voice hoarse with damp and fatigue; "how is it you will be knowing that I have been in Iona at all?"

"Because I knew your kith and kin there, Neil Ross."

"I have not been hearing that name, mother, for many a long year. And as for the old face o' you, it is unbeknown to me."

"I was at the naming of you, for all that. Well do I remember the day that Silis Macallum gave you birth; and I was at the house on the croft of Ballyrona when Murtagh Ross—that was your father—laughed. It was an ill laughing that."

"I am knowing it. The curse of God on him!"

"Tis not the first, nor the last, though the grass is on his head three years agone now."

"You that know who I am will be knowing that I have no kith or kin now on Iona?"

"Ay; they are all under grey stone or running wave. Donald your brother, and Murtagh your next brother, and little Silis, and your mother Silis herself, and your two brothers of your father, Angus and Ian Macallum, and your father Murtagh Ross, and his lawful childless wife, Dionaid, and his sister Anna—one and all, they lie beneath the green wave or in the brown mould. It is said there is a curse upon all who live at Ballyrona. The owl builds now in the rafters, and it is the big sea-rat that runs across the fireless hearth."

"It is there I am going."

"The foolishness is on you, Neil Ross."

"Now it is that I am knowing who you are. It is old Sheen Macarthur I am speaking to."

"*Tha mise* ... it is I."

"And you will be alone now, too, I am thinking. Sheen?"

"I am alone. God took my three boys at the one fishing ten years ago; and before there was moonrise in the blackness of my heart my man went. It was after the drowning of Anndra that my croft was taken from me. Then I crossed the Sound, and shared with my widow sister Elsie McVurie: till *she* went: and then the two cows had to go: and I had no rent: and was old."

In the silence that followed, the rain dribbled from the sodden bracken and dripping loneroid. Big tears rolled slowly down the deep lines on the face of Sheen. Once there was a sob in her throat, but she put her shaking hand to it, and it was still.

Neil Ross shifted from foot to foot. The ooze in that marshy place squelched with each restless movement he made. Beyond them a plover wheeled, a blurred splatch in the mist, crying its mournful cry over and over and over.

It was a pitiful thing to hear: ah, bitter loneliness, bitter patience of poor old women. That he knew well. But he was too weary, and his heart was nigh full of its own burthen. The words could not come to his lips. But at last he spoke.

"Tha mo chridhe goirt," he said, with tears in his voice, as he put his hand on her bent shoulder; "my heart is sore."

She put up her old face against his.

"'S tha e ruidhinn mo chridhe," she whispered; "it is touching my heart you are."

After that they walked on slowly through the dripping mist, each dumb and brooding deep.

"Where will you be staying this night?" asked Sheen suddenly, when they had traversed a wide boggy stretch of land; adding, as by an afterthought—"Ah, it is asking you were if the tarn there were Feur-Lochan. No; it is Loch-a-chaoruinn, and the clachan that is near is Contullich."

"Which way?"

"Yonder: to the right."

"And you are not going there?"

"No. I am going to the steading of Andrew Blair. Maybe you are for knowing it? It is called le-Baile-na-Chlais-nambuidheag."[2]

"I do not remember. But it is remembering a Blair I am. He was Adam, the son of Adam, the son of Robert. He and my father did many an ill deed together."

"Ay, to the stones be it said. Sure, now, there was, even till this weary day, no man or woman who had a good word for Adam Blair."

"And why that . . . why till this day?"

"It is not yet the third hour since he went into the silence."

Neil Ross uttered a sound like a stifled curse. For a time he trudged wearily on.

"Then I am too late," he said at last, but as though speaking to himself. "I had hoped to see him face to face again, and curse him between the eyes. It was he who made Murtagh Ross break his troth to my mother, and marry that other woman, barren at that, God be praised And they say ill of him, do they?"

"Ay, it is evil that is upon him. This crime and that, God knows; and the shadow of murder on his brow and in his eyes. Well, well, 'tis ill to be speaking of a man in corpse, and that near by. 'Tis Himself only that knows, Neil Ross."

"Maybe ay and maybe no. But where is it that I can be sleeping this night. Sheen Macarthur?"

"They will not be taking a stranger at the farm this night of the nights,

I am thinking. There is no place else for seven miles yet, when there is the clachan, before you will be coming to Fionnaphort. There is the warm byre, Neil, my man; or, if you can bide by my peats, you may rest, and welcome, though there is no bed for you, and no food either save some of the porridge that is over."

"And that will do well enough for me, Sheen; and Himself bless you for it."

And so it was.

After old Sheen Macarthur had given the wayfarer food—poor food at that, but welcome to one nigh starved, and for the heartsome way it was given, and because of the thanks to God that was upon it before even spoon was lifted—she told him a lie. It was the good lie of tender love.

"Sure now, after all, Neil, my man," she said, "it is sleeping at the farm I ought to be, for Maisie Macdonald, the wise woman, will be sitting by the corpse, and there will be none to keep her company. It is there I must be going; and if I am weary, there is a good bed for me just beyond the deadboard, which I am not minding at all. So, if it is tired you are sitting by the peats, lie down on my bed there, and have the sleep; and God be with you."

With that she went, and soundlessly, for Neil Ross was already asleep, where he sat on an upturned *claar*, with his elbows on his knees, and his flame-lit face in his hands.

The rain had ceased; but the mist still hung over the land, though in thin veils now, and these slowly drifting seaward. Sheen stepped wearily along the stony path that led from her bothy to the farm-house. She stood still once, the fear upon her, for she saw three or four blurred yellow gleams moving beyond her, eastward, along the dyke. She knew what they were—the corpse-lights that on the night of death go between the bier and the place of burial. More than once she had seen them before the last hour, and by that token had known the end to be near. Good Catholic that she was, she crossed herself, and took heart. Then, muttering

>   *Crois nan naoi aingeal leam*
>   *'O mhullach mo chinn*
>   *Gu craican mo bhonn*

>   (The cross of the nine angels be about me,
>   From the top of my head
>   To the soles of my feet),

she went on her way fearlessly.

When she came to the White House, she entered by the milk-shed that was between the byre and the kitchen. At the end of it was a paved place, with washing-tubs. At one of these stood a girl that served in the house,—an ignorant lass called Jessie McFall, out of Oban. She was ignorant, indeed, not to know that to wash clothes with a newly dead body near by was an ill thing to do. Was it not a matter for the knowing that the corpse could hear, and might rise up in the night and clothe itself in a clean white shroud?

She was still speaking to the lassie when Maisie Macdonald, the deid-watcher, opened the door of the room behind the kitchen to see who it was that was come. The two old women nodded silently. It was not till Sheen was in the closed room, midway in which something covered with a sheet lay on a board, that any word was spoken.

"Duit sith mòr, Beann Macdonald."

"And deep peace to you, too. Sheen; and to him that is there."

"Och, ochone, mise 'n diugh; 'tis a dark hour this."

"Ay; it is bad. Will you have been hearing or seeing anything?"

"Well, as for that, I am thinking I saw lights moving betwixt here and the green place over there."

"The corpse-lights?"

"Well, it is calling them that they are."

"I *thought* they would be out. And I have been hearing the noise of the planks—the cracking of the boards, you know, that will be used for the coffin to-morrow."

A long silence followed. The old women had seated themselves by the corpse, their cloaks over their heads. The room was fire-less, and was lit only by a tall wax death-candle, kept against the hour of the going.

At last Sheen began swaying slowly to and fro, crooning low the while. "I would not be for doing that, Sheen Macarthur," said the deid-watcher in a low voice, but meaningly; adding, after a moment's pause, "*The mice have all left the house.*"

Sheen sat upright, a look half of terror half of awe in her eyes.

"God save the sinful soul that is hiding," she whispered.

Well she knew what Maisie meant. If the soul of the dead be a lost soul it knows its doom. The house of death is the house of sanctuary; but before the dawn that follows the death-night the soul must go forth, whosoever or whatsoever wait for it in the homeless, shelterless plains of air around and beyond. If it be well with the soul, it need have no fear: if it be not ill with the soul, it may fare forth with surety; but if it be ill with the soul, ill will the going be. Thus is it that the spirit of an evil man cannot stay, and yet dare not go; and so it strives to hide itself in secret places anywhere, in dark channels and blind walls; and the wise creatures that live near man smell the terror, and flee. Maisie repeated the saying of Sheen; then, after a silence, added—

"Adam Blair will not lie in his grave for a year and a day because of the sins that are upon him; and it is knowing that, they are, here. He will be the Watcher of the Dead for a year and a day."

"Ay, sure, there will be dark prints in the dawn-dew over yonder."

Once more the old women relapsed into silence. Through the night there was a sighing sound. It was not the sea, which was too far off to be heard save in a day of storm. The wind it was, that was dragging itself across the sodden moors like a wounded thing, moaning and sighing.

Out of sheer weariness. Sheen twice rocked forward from her stool, heavy with sleep. At last Maisie led her over to the niche-bed opposite, and laid her down there, and waited till the deep furrows in the face relaxed somewhat, and the thin breath laboured slow across the fallen jaw.

"Poor old woman," she muttered, heedless of her own grey hairs and greyer years; "a bitter, bad thing it is to be old, old and weary. 'Tis the sorrow, that. God keep the pain of it!"

As for herself, she did not sleep at all that night, but sat between the living and the dead, with her plaid shrouding her. Once, when Sheen gave a low, terrified scream in her sleep, she rose, and in a loud voice cried, "*Sheeach-ad! Away with you!*" And with that she lifted the shroud from the dead man, and took the pennies off the eyelids, and lifted each lid; then, staring into these filmed wells, muttered an ancient incantation that would compel the soul of Adam Blair to leave the spirit of Sheen alone, and return to the cold corpse that was its coffin till the wood was ready.

The dawn came at last. Sheen slept, and Adam Blair slept a deeper sleep, and Maisie stared out of her wan, weary eyes against the red and stormy flares of light that came into the sky.

When, an hour after sunrise, Sheen Macarthur reached her bothy, she found Neil Ross, heavy with slumber, upon her bed. The fire was not out, though no flame or spark was visible; but she stooped and blew at the heart of the peats till the redness came, and once it came it grew. Having done this, she kneeled and said a rune of the morning, and after that a prayer, and then a prayer for the poor man Neil. She could pray no more because of the tears. She rose and put the meal and water into the pot for the porridge to be ready against his awaking. One of the hens that was there came and pecked at her ragged skirt. "Poor beastie," she said. "Sure, that will just be the way I am pulling at the white robe of the Mother o' God. 'Tis a bit meal for you, cluckie, and for me a healing hand upon my tears. O, och, ochone, the tears, the tears!"

It was not till the third hour after sunrise of that bleak day in the winter of the winters, that Neil Ross stirred and arose. He ate in silence. Once he said that he smelt the snow coming out of the north. Sheen said no word at all.

After the porridge, he took his pipe, but there was no tobacco. All that Sheen had was the pipeful she kept against the gloom of the Sabbath. It was her one solace in the long weary week. She gave him this, and held a burning peat to his mouth, and hungered over the thin, rank smoke that curled upward.

It was within half-an-hour of noon that, after an absence, she returned.

"Not between you and me, Neil Ross," she began abruptly, "but just for the asking, and what is beyond. Is it any money you are having upon you?"

"No."

"Nothing?"

"Nothing."

"Then how will you be getting across to Iona? It is seven long miles to Fionnaphort, and bitter cold at that, and you will be needing food, and then the ferry, the ferry across the Sound, you know."

"Ay, I know."

"What would you do for a silver piece, Neil, my man?"

"You have none to give me. Sheen Macarthur; and, if you had, it would not be taking it I would."

"Would you kiss a dead man for a crown-piece—a crown-piece of five good shillings?"

Neil Ross stared. Then he sprang to his feet.

"It is Adam Blair you are meaning, woman! God curse him in death now that he is no longer in life!"

Then, shaking and trembling, he sat down again, and brooded against the dull red glow of the peats.

But, when he rose, in the last quarter before noon, his face was white.

"The dead are dead. Sheen Macarthur They can know or do nothing. I will do it. It is willed. Yes, I am going up to the house there. And now I am going from here. God Himself has my thanks to you, and my blessing too. They will come back to you. It is not forgetting you I will be. Good-bye."

"Good-bye, Neil, son of the woman that was my friend. A south wind to you! Go up by the farm. In the front of the house you will see what you will be seeing. Maisie Macdonald will be there. She will tell you what's for the telling. There is no harm in it, sure: sure, the dead are dead. It is praying for you I will be, Neil Ross. Peace to you!"

"And to you, Sheen."

And with that the man went.

When Neil Ross reached the byres of the farm in the wide hollow, he saw two figures standing as though awaiting him, but separate, and unseen of the other. In front of the house was a man he knew to be Andrew Blair; behind the milk-shed was a woman he guessed to be Maisie Macdonald.

It was the woman he came upon first.

"Are you the friend of Sheen Macarthur?" she asked in a whisper, as she beckoned him to the doorway.

"I am."

"I am knowing no names or anything. And no one here will know you, I am thinking. So do the thing and begone."

"There is no harm to it?"

"None."

"It will be a thing often done, is it not?"

"Ay, sure."

"And the evil does not abide?"

"No. The . . . the . . . person . . . the person takes them away, and . . ."

"*Them?*"

"For sure, man! Them . . . the sins of the corpse. He takes them away; and are you for thinking God would let the innocent suffer for the guilty? No ... the person ... the Sin-Eater, you know, ... takes them away on himself, and one by one the air of heaven washes them away till he, the Sin-Eater, is clean and whole as before."

"But if it is a man you hate . . . if it is a corpse that is the corpse of one who has been a curse and a foe . . . if . . ."

"*Sst!* Be still now with your foolishness. It is only an idle saying, I am thinking. Do it, and take the money and go. It will be hell enough for Adam Blair, miser as he was, if he is for knowing that five good shillings of his money are to go to a passing tramp because of an old, ancient silly tale."

Neil Ross laughed low at that. It was for pleasure to him.

"Hush wi' ye! Andrew Blair is waiting round there. Say that I have sent you round, as I have neither bite nor bit to give."

Turning on his heel, Neil walked slowly round to the front of the house. A tall man was there, gaunt and brown, with hairless face and lank brown hair, but with eyes cold and grey as the sea.

"Good day to you, an' good faring. Will you be passing this way to anywhere?"

"Health to you. I am a stranger here. It is on my way to Iona I am. But I have the hunger upon me. There is not a brown bit in my pocket. I asked at the door there, near the byres. The woman told me she could give me nothing—not a penny even, worse luck,—nor, for that, a drink of warm milk. 'Tis a sore land this."

"You have the Gaelic of the Isles. Is it from Iona you are?"

"It is from the Isles of the West I come."

"From Tiree? . . . from Coll?"

"No."

"From the Long Island . . . or from Uist . . . or maybe from Benbecula?"

"No."

"Oh well, sure it is no matter to me. But may I be asking your name?"

"Macallum."

"Do you know there is a death here, Macallum?"

"If I didn't, I would know it now, because of what lies yonder."

Mechanically Andrew Blair looked round. As he knew, a rough bier was there, that was made of a dead-board laid upon three milking-stools. Beside it was a *claar*, a small tub to hold potatoes. On the bier was a corpse, covered with a canvas sheeting that looked like a sail.

"He was a worthy man, my father," began the son of the dead man, slowly; "but he had his faults, like all of us. I might even be saying that he had his sins, to the Stones be it said. You will be knowing, Macallum, what is thought among the folk . . . that a stranger, passing by, may take away the sins of the dead, and that, too, without any hurt whatever . . . any hurt whatever."

"Ay, sure."

"And you will be knowing what is done?"

"Ay."

"With the bread . . . and the water . . .?"

"Ay."

"It is a small thing to do. It is a Christian thing. I would be doing it myself, and that gladly, but the . . . the . . . passer-by who . . ."

"It is talking of the Sin-Eater you are?"

"Yes, yes, for sure. The Sin-Eater as he is called—and a good Christian act it is, for all that the ministers and the priests make a frowning at it—the Sin-Eater must be a stranger. He must be a stranger, and should know nothing of the dead man—above all, bear him no grudge."

At that Neil Ross's eyes lightened for a moment.

"And why that?"

"Who knows? I have heard this, and I have heard that. If the Sin-Eater was hating the dead man he could take the sins and fling them into the sea, and they would be changed into demons of the air that would harry the flying soul till Judgment-Day."

"And how would that thing be done?"

The man spoke with flashing eyes and parted lips, the breath coming swift. Andrew Blair looked at him suspiciously; and hesitated, before, in a cold voice, he spoke again.

"That is all folly, I am thinking, Macallum. Maybe it is all folly, the whole of it. But, see here, I have no time to be talking with you. If you will take the bread and the water you shall have a good meal if you want it, and . . . and . . . yes, look you, my man, I will be giving you a shilling too, for luck."

"I will have no meal in this house, Anndra-mhic-Adam; nor will I do this thing unless you will be giving me two silver half-crowns. That is the sum I must have, or no other."

"Two half-crowns! Why, man, for one half-crown . . ."

"Then be eating the sins o' your father yourself, Andrew Blair! It is going I am."

"Stop, man! Stop, Macallum. See here: I will be giving you what you ask."

"So be it. Is the ... Are you ready?"

"Ay, come this way."

With that the two men turned and moved slowly towards the bier.

In the doorway of the house stood a man and two women; farther in, a woman; and at the window to the left, the serving-wench, Jessie McFall, and two men of the farm. Of those in the doorway, the man was Peter, the half-witted youngest brother of Andrew Blair; the taller and older woman was Catreen, the widow of Adam, the second brother; and the thin, slight woman, with staring eyes and drooping mouth, was Muireall, the wife of Andrew. The old woman behind these was Maisie Macdonald.

Andrew Blair stooped and took a saucer out of the *claar*. This he put upon the covered breast of the corpse. He stooped again, and brought forth a thick square piece of new-made bread. That also he placed upon the breast of the corpse. Then he stooped again, and with that he emptied a spoonful of salt alongside the bread.

"I must see the corpse," said Neil Ross simply.

"It is not needful, Macallum."

"I must be seeing the corpse, I tell you—and for that, too, the bread and the water should be on the naked breast."

"No, no, man; it . . ."

But here a voice, that of Maisie the wise woman, came upon them, saying that the man was right, and that the eating of the sins should be done in that way and no other.

With an ill grace the son of the dead man drew back the sheeting. Beneath it, the corpse was in a clean white shirt, a death-gown long ago prepared, that covered him from his neck to his feet, and left only the dusky yellowish face exposed.

While Andrew Blair unfastened the shirt and placed the saucer and the bread and the salt on the breast, the man beside him stood staring fixedly on the frozen features of the corpse. The new laird had to speak to him twice before he heard.

"I am ready. And you, now? What is it you are muttering over against the lips of the dead?"

"It is giving him a message I am. There is no harm in that, sure?"

"Keep to your own folk, Macallum. You are from the West you say, and we are from the North. There can be no messages between you and a Blair of Strathmore, no messages for *you* to be giving."

"He that lies here knows well the man to whom I am sending a message"—and at this response Andrew Blair scowled darkly. He would fain have sent the man about his business, but he feared he might get no other.

"It is thinking I am that you are not a Macallum at all. I know all of that name in Mull, Iona, Skye, and the near isles. What will the name of your naming be, and of your father, and of his place?"

Whether he really wanted an answer, or whether he sought only to divert the man from his procrastination, his question had a satisfactory result.

"Well, now, it's ready I am, Anndra-mhic-Adam."

With that, Andrew Blair stooped once more and from the *claar* brought a small jug of water. From this he filled the saucer.

"You know what to say and what to do, Macallum."

There was not one there who did not have a shortened breath because of the mystery that was now before them, and the fearfulness of it. Neil Ross drew himself up, erect, stiff, with white, drawn face. All who waited, save Andrew Blair, thought that the moving of his lips was because of the prayer that was slipping upon them, like the last lapsing of the ebb-tide. But Blair was watching him closely, and knew that it was no prayer which stole out against the blank air that was around the dead.

Slowly Neil Ross extended his right arm. He took a pinch of the salt and put it in the saucer, then took another pinch and sprinkled it upon the bread. His hand shook for a moment as he touched the saucer. But there was no shaking as he raised it towards his lips, or when he held it before him when he spoke.

"With this water that has salt in it, and has lain on thy corpse, O Adam mhic Anndra mhic Adam Mòr, I drink away all the evil that is upon thee . . ."

There was throbbing silence while he paused.

". . . And may it be upon me and not upon thee, if with this water it cannot flow away."

Thereupon, he raised the saucer and passed it thrice round the head of the corpse sun-ways; and, having done this, lifted it to his lips and drank as much as his mouth would hold. Thereafter he poured the remnant over his left hand, and let it trickle to the ground. Then he took the piece of bread. Thrice, too, he passed it round the head of the corpse sun-ways.

He turned and looked at the man by his side, then at the others, who watched him with beating hearts.

With a loud clear voice he took the sins.

"*Thoir dhomh do ciontachd, O Adam mhic Anndra mhic Adam Mòr!* Give me thy sins to take away from thee! Lo, now, as I stand here, I break this bread that has lain on thee in corpse, and I am eating it, I am, and in that eating I take upon me the sins of thee, O man that was alive and is now white with the stillness!"

Thereupon Neil Ross broke the bread and ate of it, and took upon himself the sins of Adam Blair that was dead. It was a bitter swallowing, that. The remainder of the bread he crumbled in his hand, and threw it on the ground, and trod upon it. Andrew Blair gave a sigh of relief. His cold eyes lightened with malice.

"Be off with you, now, Macallum. We are wanting no tramps at the farm here, and perhaps you had better not be trying to get work this side Iona; for it is known as the Sin-Eater you will be, and that won't be for the helping, I am thinking! There: there are the two half-crowns for you . . . and may they bring you no harm, you that are *Scapegoat* now!"

The Sin-Eater turned at that, and stared like a hill-bull. *Scapegoat!* Ay, that's what he was. Sin-Eater, *Scapegoat!* Was he not, too, another Judas, to have sold for silver that which was not for the selling? No, no, for sure Maisie Macdonald could tell him the rune that would serve for the easing of this burden. He would soon be quit of it.

Slowly he took the money, turned it over, and put it in his pocket.

"I am going, Andrew Blair," he said quietly, "I am going now. I will not say to him that is there in the silence, *A chuid do Pharas da!*[3] — nor will I say to you, *Gu'n gleidheadh Dia thu*,[4] — nor will I say to this dwelling that is the home of thee and thine, *Gu'n beannaicheadh Dia an tigh!*[5]"

Here there was a pause. All listened. Andrew Blair shifted uneasily, the furtive eyes of him going this way and that, like a ferret in the grass.

"But, Andrew Blair, I will say this: when you fare abroad, *Droch caoidh ort!*[6] and when you go upon the water, *Gaoth gun direadh ort!*[7] Ay, ay, Anndra-mhic-Adam, *Dia ad aghaidh 's ad aodann . . . agus has dunach ort! Dhonas 's dholas ort, agus leat-sa!*[8]"

The bitterness of these words was like snow in June upon all there. They stood amazed. None spoke. No one moved.

Neil Ross turned upon his heel, and, with a bright light in his eyes, walked away from the dead and the living. He went by the byres, whence he had come. Andrew Blair remained where he was, now glooming at the corpse, now biting his nails and staring at the damp sods at his feet.

When Neil reached the end of the milk-shed he saw Maisie Macdonald there, waiting.

"These were ill sayings of yours, Neil Ross," she said in a low voice, so that she might not be overheard from the house.

"So, it is knowing me you are."

"Sheen Macarthur told me."

"I have good cause."

"That is a true word. I know it."

"Tell me this thing. What is the rune that is said for the throwing into the sea of the sins of the dead? See here, Maisie Macdonald. There is no money of that man that I would carry a mile with me. Here it is. It is yours, if you will tell me that rune."

Maisie took the money hesitatingly. Then, stooping, she said slowly the few lines of the old, old rune.

"Will you be remembering that?"

"It is not forgetting it I will be, Maisie."

"Wait a moment. There is some warm milk here."

With that she went, and then, from within, beckoned to him to enter.

"There is no one here, Neil Ross. Drink the milk."

He drank; and while he did so she drew a leather pouch from some hidden place in her dress.

"And now I have this to give you."

She counted out ten pennies and two farthings.

"It is all the coppers I have. You are welcome to them. Take them, friend of my friend. They will give you the food you need, and the ferry across the Sound."

"I will do that, Maisie Macdonald, and thanks to you. It is not forgetting it I will be, nor you, good woman. And now, tell me, is it safe that I am? He called me a 'scapegoat'; he, Andrew Blair! Can evil touch me between this and the sea?"

"You must go to the place where the evil was done to you and yours—and that, I know, is on the west side of Iona. Go, and God preserve you. But here, too, is a sian that will be for the safety."

Thereupon, with swift mutterings she said this charm: an old, familiar Sian against Sudden Harm:—

"Sian a chuir Moire air Mac ort,
Sian ro' marbhadh, sian ro' lot ort,
Sian eadar a' chlioch 's a' ghlun,
Sian nan Tri ann an aon ort,
O mhullach do chinn gu bonn do chois ort:
Sian seachd eadar a h-aon ort,
Sian seachd eadar a dha ort,
Sian seachd eadar a tri ort,
Sian seachd eadar a ceithir ort,
Sian seachd eadar a coig ort
Sian seachd eadar a sia ort,
Sian seachd paidir nan seach paidir dol deiseil ri diugh narach ort,
    ga do ghleidheadh bho bheud 's bho mhi-thapadh!"

Scarcely had she finished before she heard heavy steps approaching.

"Away with you," she whispered, repeating in a loud, angry tone, "Away with you! *Seachad! Seachad!*"

And with that Neil Ross slipped from the milk-shed and crossed the yard, and was behind the byres before Andrew Blair, with sullen mien and swift, wild eyes, strode from the house.

It was with a grim smile on his face that Neil tramped down the wet heather till he reached the high road, and fared thence as through a marsh because of the rains there had been.

For the first mile he thought of the angry mind of the dead man, bitter at paying of the silver. For the second mile he thought of the evil that had been wrought for him and his. For the third mile he pondered over all that he had heard and done and taken upon him that day.

Then he sat down upon a broken granite heap by the way, and brooded deep till one hour went, and then another, and the third was upon him.

A man driving two calves came towards him out of the west. He did not hear or see. The man stopped: spoke again. Neil gave no answer. The drover shrugged his shoulders, hesitated, and walked slowly on, often looking back.

An hour later a shepherd came by the way he himself had tramped. He was a tall, gaunt man with a squint. The small, pale-blue eyes glittered out of a mass of red hair that almost covered his face. He stood still, opposite Neil, and leaned on his cromak.

"*Latha math leat,*" he said at last: "I wish you good day."

Neil glanced at him, but did not speak.

"What is your name, for I seem to know you?"

But Neil had already forgotten him. The shepherd took out his snuff-mull, helped him-self, and handed the mull to the lonely way-farer. Neil mechanically helped himself.

"*Am bheil thu 'dol do Fhionphort?*" tried the shepherd again: "Are you going to Fionnaphort?"

"*Tha mise 'dol a dh' I-challum-chille,*" Neil answered, in a low, weary voice, and as a man adream: "I am on my way to Iona."

"I am thinking I know now who you are. You are the man Macallum."

Neil looked, but did not speak. His eyes dreamed against what the other could not see or know. The shepherd called angrily to his dogs to keep the sheep from straying; then, with a resentful air, turned to his victim.

"You are a silent man for sure, you are. I'm hoping it is not the curse upon you already."

"What curse?"

"Ah, *that* has brought the wind against the mist! I was thinking so!"

"What curse?"

"You are the man that was the Sin-Eater over there?"

"Ay."

"The man Macallum?"

"Ay."

"Strange it is, but three days ago I saw you in Tobermory, and heard you give your name as Neil Ross to an Iona man that was there."

"Well?"

"Oh, sure, it is nothing to me. But they say the Sin-Eater should not be a man with a hidden lump in his pack." [9]

"Why?"

"For the dead know, and are content. There is no shaking off any sins, then — for that man."

"It is a lie."

"Maybe ay and maybe no."

"Well, have you more to be saying to me? I am obliged to you for your company, but it is not needing it I am, though no offence."

"Och, man, there's no offence between you and me. Sure, there's Iona in me, too; for the father of my father married a woman that was the granddaughter of Tomais Macdonald, who was a fisherman there. No, no; it is rather warning you I would be."

"And for what?"
"Well, well, just because of that laugh I heard about."
"What laugh?"
"The laugh of Adam Blair that is dead."

Neil Ross stared, his eyes large and wild. He leaned a little forward. No word came from him. The look that was on his face was the question.

"Yes: it was this way. Sure, the telling of it is just as I heard it. After you ate the sins of Adam Blair, the people there brought out the coffin. When they were putting him into it, he was as stiff as a sheep dead in the snow — and just like that, too, with his eyes wide open. Well, someone saw you trampling the heather down the slope that is in front of the house, and said, 'It is the Sin-Eater! With that, Andrew Blair sneered, and said —' Ay, 'tis the scapegoat he is! Then, after a while, he went on: 'The Sin-Eater they call him: ay, just so: and a bitter good bargain it is, too, if all's true that's thought true! And with that he laughed, and then his wife that was behind him laughed, and then . . ."

"Well, what then?"

"Well, 'tis Himself that hears and knows if it is true! But this is the thing I was told: — After that laughing there was a stillness and a dread. For all there saw that the corpse had turned its head and was looking after you as you went down the heather. Then, Neil Ross, if that be your true name, Adam Blair that was dead put up his white face against the sky, and laughed."

At this, Ross sprang to his feet with a gasping sob.

"It is a lie, that thing!" he cried, shaking his fist at the shepherd. "It is a lie!"

"It is no lie. And by the same token, Andrew Blair shrank back white and shaking, and his woman had the swoon upon her, and who knows but the corpse might have come to life again had it not been for Maisie Macdonald, the deid-watcher, who clapped a handful of salt on his eyes, and tilted the coffin so that the bottom of it slid forward, and so let the whole fall flat on the ground, with Adam Blair in it sideways, and as likely as not cursing and groaning, as his wont was, for the hurt both to his old bones and his old ancient dignity."

Ross glared at the man as though the madness was upon him. Fear and horror and fierce rage swung him now this way and now that.

"What will the name of you be, shepherd?" he stuttered huskily.

"It is Eachainn Gilleasbuig I am to ourselves; and the English of that for those who have no Gaelic is Hector Gillespie; and I am Eachainn mac Ian mac Alasdair of Strathsheean that is where Sutherland lies against Ross."

"Then take this thing — and that is, the curse of the Sin-Eater! And a bitter bad thing may it be upon you and yours."

And with that Neil the Sin-Eater flung his hand up into the air, and then leaped past the shepherd, and a minute later was running through the frightened sheep, with his head low, and a white foam on his lips, and his eyes red with blood as a seal's that has the death-wound on it.

On the third day of the seventh month from that day, Aulay Macneill, coming into Balliemore of Iona from the west side of the island, said to old

Ronald MacCormick, that was the father of his wife, that he had seen Neil Ross again, and that he was "absent" — for though he had spoken to him, Neil would not answer, but only gloomed at him from the wet weedy rock where he sat.

The going back of the man had loosed every tongue that was in Iona. When, too, it was known that he was wrought in some terrible way, if not actually mad, the islanders whispered that it was because of the sins of Adam Blair. Seldom or never now did they speak of him by his name, but simply as "The Sin-Eater." The thing was not so rare as to cause this strangeness, nor did many (and perhaps none did) think that the sins of the dead ever might or could abide with the living who had merely done a good Christian charitable thing. But there was a reason.

Not long after Neil Ross had come again to Iona, and had settled down in the ruined roofless house on the croft of Ballyrona, just like a fox or a wild-cat, as the saying was, he was given fishing-work to do by Aulay Macneill, who lived at Ard-an-teine, at the rocky north end of the *machar* or plain that is on the west Atlantic coast of the island.

One moonlit night, either the seventh or the ninth after the earthing of Adam Blair at his own place in the Ross, Aulay Macneill saw Neil Ross steal out of the shadow of Ballyrona and make for the sea. Macneill was there by the rocks, mending a lobster- creel. He had gone there because of the sadness. Well, when he saw the Sin-Eater, he watched.

Neil crept from rock to rock till he reached the last fang that churns the sea into yeast when the tide sucks the land just opposite.

Then he called out something that Aulay Macneill could not catch. With that he springs up, and throws his arms above him.

"Then," says Aulay when he tells the tale, "it was like a ghost he was. The moonshine was on his face like the curl o' a wave. White! there is no whiteness like that of the human face. It was whiter than the foam about the skerry it was; whiter than the moon shining; whiter than well, as white as the painted letters on the black boards of the fishing-cobles. There he stood, for all that the sea was about him, the slip-slop waves leapin' wild, and the tide making, too, at that. He was shaking like a sail two points off the wind. It was then that, all of a sudden, he called in a womany, screamin' voice —

"I am throwing the sins of Adam Blair into the midst of ye, white dogs o' the sea! Drown them, tear them, drag them away out into the black deeps! Ay, ay, ay, ye dancin' wild waves, this is the third time I am doing it, and now there is none left; no, not a sin, not a sin!

"'O-hi, O-ri, dark tide o' the sea,
I am giving the sins of a dead man to thee!
By the Stones, by the Wind, by the Fire, by the Tree,
From the dead man's sins set me free, set me free!
Adam mhic Anndra mhic Adam and me,
Set us free! Set us free!'

"Ay, sure, the Sin-Eater sang that over and over; and after the third singing he swung his arms and screamed —

"'And listen to me, black waters an' running tide.
That rune is the good rune told me by Maisie the wise.
And I am Neil the son of Silis Macallum
By the black-hearted evil man Murtagh Ross,
That was the friend of Adam mac Anndra, God against him!'
And with that he scrambled and fell into the sea. But, as I am Aulay mac Luais and no other, he was up in a moment, an' swimmin' like a seal, and then over the rocks again, an' away back to that lonely roofless place once more, laughing wild at times, an' muttering an' whispering."

It was this tale of Aulay Macneill's that stood between Neil Ross and the isle-folk. There was something behind all that, they whispered one to another.

So it was always the Sin-Eater he was called at last. None sought him. The few children who came upon him now and again fled at his approach, or at the very sight of him. Only Aulay Macneill saw him at times, and had word of him.

After a month had gone by, all knew that the Sin-Eater was wrought to madness because of this awful thing: the burden of Adam Blair's sins would not go from him! Night and day he could hear them laughing low, it was said.

But it was the quiet madness. He went to and fro like a shadow in the grass, and almost as soundless as that, and as voiceless. More and more the name of him grew as a terror. There were few folk on that wild west coast of Iona, and these few avoided him when the word ran that he had knowledge of strange things, and converse, too, with the secrets of the sea.

One day Aulay Macneill, in his boat, but dumb with amaze and terror for him, saw him at high tide swimming on a long rolling wave right into the hollow of the Spouting Cave. In the memory of man, no one had done this and escaped one of three things: a snatching away into oblivion, a strangled death, or madness. The islanders know that there swims into the cave, at full tide, a Mar-Tarbh, a dreadful creature of the sea that some call a kelpie; only it is not a kelpie, which is like a woman, but rather is a sea-bull, offspring of the cattle that are never seen. Ill indeed for any sheep or goat, ay, or even dog or child, if any happens to be leaning over the edge of the Spouting Cave when the Martarv roars: for, of a surety, it will fall in and straightway be devoured.

With awe and trembling Aulay listened for the screaming of the doomed man. It was full tide, and the sea-beast would be there.

The minutes passed, and no sign. Only the hollow booming of the sea, as it moved like a baffled blind giant round the cavern-bases: only the rush and spray of the water flung up the narrow shaft high into the windy air above the cliff it penetrates.

At last he saw what looked like a mass of seaweed swirled out on the surge. It was the Sin-Eater. With a leap, Aulay was at his oars. The boat swung through the sea. Just before Neil Ross was about to sink for the second time, he caught him and dragged him into the boat.

But then, as ever after, nothing was to be got out of the Sin-Eater save a single saying: *Tha e lamhan fuar: Tha e lamhan fuar!* — "It has a cold, cold hand!"

The telling of this and other tales left none free upon the island to look upon the "scapegoat" save as one accursed.

It was in the third month that a new phase of his madness came upon Neil Ross.

The horror of the sea and the passion for the sea came over him at the same happening. Oftentimes he would race along the shore, screaming wild names to it, now hot with hate and loathing, now as the pleading of a man with the woman of his love. And strange chants to it, too, were upon his lips. Old, old lines of forgotten runes were overheard by Aulay Macneill, and not Aulay only: lines wherein the ancient sea-name of the island, Ioua, that was given to it long before it was called Iona, or any other of the nine names that are said to belong to it, occurred again and again.

The flowing tide it was that wrought him thus. At the ebb he would wander across the weedy slabs or among the rocks: silent, and more like a lost duinshee than a man.

Then again after three months a change in his madness came. None knew what it was, though Aulay said that the man moaned and moaned because of the awful burden he bore. No drowning seas for the sins that could not be washed away, no grave for the live sins that would be quick till the day of the Judgment!

For weeks thereafter he disappeared. As to where he was, it is not for the knowing.

Then at last came that third day of the seventh month when, as I have said, Aulay Macneill told old Ronald MacCormick that he had seen the Sin-Eater again.

It was only a half-truth that he told, though. For, after he had seen Neil Ross upon the rock, he had followed him when he rose, and wandered back to the roofless place which he haunted now as of yore. Less wretched a shelter now it was, because of the summer that was come, though a cold, wet summer at that.

"Is that you, Neil Ross?" he had asked, as he peered into the shadows among the ruins of the house.

"That's not my name," said the Sin-Eater; and he seemed as strange then and there, as though he were a castaway from a foreign ship.

"And what will it be, then, you that are my friend, and sure knowing me as Aulay mac Luais — Aulay Macneill that never grudges you bit or sup?"

"*I am Judas!*"

"And at that word," says Aulay Macneill, when he tells the tale, "at that word the pulse in my heart was like a bat in a shut room. But after a bit I took up the talk.

"'Indeed,' I said; 'and I was not for knowing that. May I be so bold as to ask whose son, and of what place?'

"But all he said to me was, '*I am Judas!*'"

"Well, I said, to comfort him, 'Sure, it's not such a bad name in itself, though I am knowing some which have a more home-like sound.' But no, it was no good.

"'I am Judas. And because I sold the Son of God for five pieces of silver ...'

"But here I interrupted him and said,—'Sure, now, Neil—I mean, Judas— it was eight times five.' Yet the simpleness of his sorrow prevailed, and I listened with the wet in my eyes.

"'I am Judas. And because I sold the Son of God for five silver shillings. He laid upon me all the nameless black sins of the world. And that is why I am bearing them till the Day of Days.'"

And this was the end of the Sin-Eater; for I will not tell the long story of Aulay Macneill, that gets longer and longer every winter: but only the unchanging close of it.

I will tell it in the words of Aulay.

"A bitter, wild day it was, that day I saw him to see him no more. It was late. The sea was red with the flamin' light that burned up the air betwixt Iona and all that is west of West. I was on the shore, looking at the sea. The big green waves came in like the chariots in the Holy Book. Well, it was on the black shoulder of one of them, just short of the ton o' foam that swept above it, that I saw a spar surgin' by.

"'What is that?' I said to myself. And the reason of my wondering was this: I saw that a smaller spar was swung across it. And while I was watching that thing another great billow came in with a roar, and hurled the double spar back, and not so far from me but I might have gripped it. But who would have gripped that thing if he were for seeing what I saw?

"It is Himself knows that what I say is a true thing.

"On that spar was Neil Ross, the Sin-Eater. Naked he was as the day he was born. And he was lashed, too—ay, sure, he was lashed to it by ropes round and round his legs and his waist and his left arm. It was the Cross he was on. I saw that thing with the fear upon me. Ah, poor drifting wreck that he was! *Judas on the Cross*: It was his *eric*!

"But even as I watched, shaking in my limbs, I saw that there was life in him still. The lips were moving, and his right arm was ever for swinging this way and that. 'Twas like an oar, working him off a lee shore: ay, that was what I thought.

"Then, all at once, he caught sight of me. Well he knew me, poor man, that has his share of heaven now, I am thinking!

"He waved, and called, but the hearing could not be, because of a big surge o' water that came tumbling down upon him. In the stroke of an oar he was swept close by the rocks where I was standing. In that flounderin', seethin' whirlpool I saw the white face of him for a moment, an' as he went out on the re-surge like a hauled net, I heard these words fallin' against my ears,—

"'*An eirig m'anama* ... In ransom for my soul!'

"And with that I saw the double-spar turn over and slide down the back — sweep of a drowning big wave. Ay, sure, it went out to the deep sea swift enough then. It was in the big eddy that rushes between Skerry-Mor and Skerry-Beag. I did not see it again—no, not for the quarter of an hour, I am thinking. Then I saw just the whirling top of it rising out of the flying yeast of a great, black-blustering wave, that was rushing northward before the current that is called the Black-Eddy.

"With that you have the end of Neil Ross: ay, sure, him that was called the Sin-Eater. And that is a true thing; and may God save us the sorrow of sorrows.

"And that is all."

1. Contullich: i.e. Ceann-nan-tulaich, "the end of the hillocks." Loch-a-chaoruinn means the loch of the rowan-trees.
2. The farm in the hollow of the yellow flowers.
3. His share of heaven be his.
4. May God preserve you
5. God's blessing on this house.
6. May a fatal accident happen to you (lit. "bad moan on you")
7. May you drift to your drowning (lit. "wind without direction on you")
8. God against thee and in thy face . . . and may a death of woe be yours. . . . Evil and sorrow to thee and thine!
9. With a criminal secret, or an undiscovered crime.

Alice Clare MacDonell (1855-?)

The Weaving Of The Tartan (1896)

I saw an old dame weaving,
  Weaving, weaving —
I saw an old dame weaving
  A web of tartan fine.
'Sing high,' she said, 'sing low,' she said,
  'Wild torrent to the sea.
That saw my exiled bairnies torn
  In sorrow far frae me.
And warp well the long threads.
The bright threads, the strong threads;
Woof well the cross threads,
To make the colours shine.'

She wove in red for every deed
Of valour done for Scotia's need;
She wove in green, the laurel's sheen,
In memory of her glorious dead.

She spake of Alma's steep incline,
The desert march, the 'thin red line';
It fires the blood and stirs the heart,
Where'er a bairn of hers takes part.
"Tis for the gallant lads,' she said,
'Who wear the kilt and tartan plaid;
'Tis for the winsome lasses too,
Just like my dainty bells of blue.
So weave well the bright threads,
The red threads, the green threads;
Woof well the strong threads
That bind their hearts to mine.'

I saw an old dame sighing,
  Sighing, sighing —
I saw an old dame sighing
  Beside a lonely glen.
'Sing high,' she said, 'sing low,' she said,
  'Wild tempests to the sea,
The wailing of the pibroch's note
  That bade farewell to me.
And wae fa' the red deer,

The swift deer, the strong deer;
Wae fa' the cursèd deer
That take the place o' men.'

Where'er a noble deed is wrought,
Where'er the brightest realms of thought,
The artist's skill, the martial thrill,
Be sure to Scotia's land is wed.
She casts the glamour of her name
O'er Britain's throne and statesmen's fame,
From distant lands, 'neath foreign names,
Some brilliant son his birthright claims;
She has reared them amid tempests,
   And cradled them in snow,
To give the Scottish arms their strength,
   Their hearts a kindly glow.
So weave well the bright threads.
The red threads, the green threads —
Woof well the strong threads
That bind their hearts to thine.

Sources

Aytoun, W.S. "How We Got Up The Glenmutchkin Railway, And How We Got Out Of It." *Blackwood's Edinburgh Magazine* 360 (October1845): 453-466.
Baillie, Joanna. *A Collection of poems, chiefly. manuscript, and from living authors.* London: Longman, Hurst, Rees, Orme, and Brown, 1823.
Brown, George Douglas. *The House With the Green Shutters.* London: John Macqueen, 1901.
Brunton, Mary. *Discipline: a novel.* Edinburgh: Manners and Miller, 1814.
Campbell, Thomas. *Gertrude of Wyoming; a Pennsylvanian tale and other poems.* London: Longman, Hurst, Rees and Orme, 1809
Carlyle, Thomas. *Past and Present.* London: Chapman and Hall, 1843.
Chambers, Robert. *Vestiges of the Natural History of Creation.* London: Churchill, 1844.
Conan Doyle, Arthur. "The Man With the Twisted Lip." *Strand Magazine* 2.6 (December 1891):623-637.
Crockett, S.R. *Cleg Kelly, Arab of the City.* London: Smith, Elder, 1896.
Davidson, John. *Ballads and Songs.* London: John Lane, 1895.
Edinburgh Review, or Critical Journal 22 (January 1808): 285-289.
Edinburgh Review, or Critical Journal. 47 (November 1814): 1-30.
Ferrier, Susan. *Marriage. A Novel.* Edinburgh: Blackwood, 1818.
Galt, John. *The Provost.* Edinburgh: Blackwood, 1822.
Gordon, George, Lord Byron. "English Bards, and Scotch Reviewers: A Satire." London: Cawthorn, 1809.
Gordon, George, Lord Byron, "English Bards, and Scotch Reviewers; a satire." 2nd ed. London: Cawthorn, 1809.
Gordon, George, Lord Byron. *Hours of Idleness, a series of poems, original and translated.* London: Longman, Hurst, Rees, and Orme, 1807.
Grant, Anne. *Essays on the Superstitions of the Highlanders of Scotland: to which are added, translations from the Gaelic; and letters connected with those formerly published.* London: Longman, Hurst, Rees, Orme and Brown, 1811.
Hamilton, Elizabeth. *The Cottagers of Glenburnie; a tale for the farmer's inglenook.* 3rd ed. Edinburgh: Manners and Miller, 1808.
Hamilton, Janet. *Poems, Essays and Sketches.* Glasgow: Maclehose, 1870.
Hogg, James. *Songs, by the Ettrick Shepherd.* Edinburgh: Blackwood, 1831.
Hogg, James. "Strange Letter of a Lunatic." *Fraser's Magazine* 11 (December 1830): 526-532.
Irving, Edward, *Babylon and Infidelity Foredoomed.* Glasgow: Chalmers & Collins, 1826.
Johnston, Ellen. *Autobiography, Poems and Songs.* Glasgow: Love, 1867.
Johnstone, Christian Isobel. *The Edinburgh Tales, conducted by Mrs Johnstone.* Volume III. Edinburgh: Tait, 1846.
Lang, Andrew. *In The Wrong Paradise and other stories.* 2nd ed. London: Kegan Paul, Trench, 1886.
Macaulay, Thomas Babington. "Minute on Indian Education" in *Indian Musalmans*, ed. W.N. Lees. London: Williams and Norgate, 1871.
MacDonald, George. *Adela Cathcart.* London: Sampson Low, Marston, Searle, and Rivington, 1882.

MacDonald, Mary. "Child in the Manger," translated in *The Songs and Hymns of the Gael*, ed. L.MacBean. Stirling: Eneas Mackay, 1900.

MacDonell, Alice Clare. *Lays of The Heather: Poems*. London: Elliot Stock, 1896.

McGonagall, William. *Wm. McGonagall, poet: a choice selection …* Ed. Lowden Macartney. Glasgow: Burnside, n.d.

Maclaren, Ian. *Beside The Bonnie Brier Bush*. London: Hodder & Stoughton, 1894.

MacLeod, Fiona. *The Sin-Eater and other tales*. Edinburgh: The Lawnmarket, 1895.

McLevy, James. *Curiosities of Crimes in Edinburgh*. 2nd ed. Edinburgh: W. Kay, 1861.

Miller, Hugh. *My Schools and Schoolmasters or the story of my education*. Edinburgh, Constable, 1857.

"Noctes Ambrosianae. No XLVIII." *Blackwood's Magazine* 165 (April 1830): 659-667.

Oliphant, Caroline. *Life and Songs of the Baroness Nairne*, ed Charles Rogers. London: Charles Griffin, 1869.

Oliphant, Margaret. "The Library Window." *Blackwood's Edinburgh Magazine* 159 (January 1896): 1-30.

Pae, David. *Lucy, The Factory Girl; or, the secrets of the Tontine Close*. Edinburgh: Grant, 1860.

Porter, Jane. *The Scottish Chiefs; a Romance*. 5th ed. London: Longman, Hurst, Rees, Orme, Brown and Green, 1825.

Pringle, Thomas. *The Poetical Works*. London: Moxon, 1837/8.

Rodger, Alexander. *Stray Leaves from the Portfolios of Alisander the Seer, Andrew Whaup, and Humphrey Henkeckle*. Glasgow: Rattray, 1842.

Scott, Michael. *Tom Cringle's Log*. *Blackwood's Edinburgh Magazine* 204 (February 1833): 170-186.

Scott, Walter. "Thomas the Rhymer." In *Minstrelsy of the Scottish Border*, Volume II. Kelso: Ballantyne, for Cadell and Davies, and Constable, 1802.

Scott, Walter. "The Twa Corbies." In *Minstrelsy of the Scottish Border*, Volime I. Kelso: Ballantyne, for Cadell and Davies, and Constable, 1802.

Scott, Walter. *The Fortunes of Nigel*. Edinburgh: Constable, 1822.

Scott, Walter. "The Highland Widow." In *Chronicles of the Canongate*. Edinburgh: 1827.

Smith, Alexander. *City Poems*. Cambridge: Macmillan,1857.

Stevenson, Robert Louis, and Fanny Van de Grift Stevenson. *The Dynamiter*. London: Longman, Green, 1885.

Stevenson, Robert Louis. *Songs of Travel and Other Verse*. London: Chatto & Windus, 1896.

Stevenson, Robert Louis. "Thrawn Janet." *The Cornhill Magazine* 262. (October 1881): 436-443.

Tennant, William. *Anster Fair, poem in six cantos with other poems*. 2nd ed. Edinburgh: George Goldie, 1814.

Thom, William. *Rhymes and recollections of A Hand-Loom weaver*. 2nd ed. London: Smith, Elder, 1845.

Thomson, James ("B.V."). *The City of Dreadful Night and other poems*. London: Reeves and Turner, 1880.

Index of authors

Aytoun, W.E. (1813-1865)	219
Baillie, Joanna (1762-1851)	46
Blackwood's Magazine [John Wilson]	169
Brown, George Douglas (1869-1902)	313
Brunton, Mary (1778-1818)	29
Campbell, Thomas (1777-1844)	1
Carlyle, Thomas (1795-1881)	207
Chambers, Robert (1802-1871)	212
Crockett, S.R. (1860-1914)	306
Davidson, John (1857-1909)	370
Doyle, Arthur Conan (1859-1930)	324
Edinburgh Review [Henry Brougham]	131
Edinburgh Review [Francis Jeffrey]	135
Ferrier, Susan (1782-1854)	39
Galt, John (1779-1839)	182
Gordon, George, Lord Byron (1788-1824)	152
Grant, Anne (1755-1838)	22
Hamilton, Elizabeth (1756-1816)	9
Hamilton, Janet (1795-1873)	255
Hogg, James (1770-1835)	157
Irving, Edward (1792-1834)	203
Johnston, Ellen (1835-1873)	261
Johnstone, Christian Isobel (1781-1857)	238
Lang, Andrew (1844-1912)	291
Macaulay, Thomas Babington (1800-1859)	193
MacDonald, Mary (1789-1872)	272
MacDonald, George (1824-1905)	273
MacDonell, Alice Clare (1855-?)	406
McGonagall, William (1825-1902)	249
Maclaren, Ian (John Watson) (1850-1907)	300
MacLeod, Fiona MacLeod (William Sharp) (1855-1905)	387
McLevy, James	317
Miller, Hugh (1802-1856)	217
Oliphant, Caroline, Lady Nairne: 1766-1845	5
Oliphant, Margaret (1828-1897)	341
Pae, David (1828-1884)	262
Porter, Jane (1776-1850)	12
Pringle, Thomas (1789-1834)	191
Rodger, Alexander (1784-1846)	181
Scott, Michael (1789-1835)	185
Scott, Walter (1771-1832)	47
Smith, Alexander (1830-1867)	257
Stevenson, Fanny Van de Grift	380
Stevenson, Robert Louis (1850-1894)	373
Tennant, William (1784-1848)	24
Thom, William (1799-1848)	252
Thomson, James "B.V." (1834-1882)	281

CPSIA information can be obtained
at www.ICGtesting.com
Printed in the USA
LVOW13s1609090717

540717LV00004B/26/P

9 781849 210539